Isabella and the Sailor

Juan de la Cuesta
Hispanic Monographs

EDITOR

Tom Lathrop

ASSOCIATE EDITOR

Alexander R. Selimov
University of Delaware

EDITORIAL BOARD

Samuel G. Armistead
University of California, Davis

Alan Deyermond
Queen Mary and Westfield College of the University of London

Daniel Eisenberg
Regents College

John E. Keller
University of Kentucky

Steven D. Kirby
Eastern Michigan University

José A. Madrigal
Auburn University

Joel Rini
University of Virginia

Donna M. Rogers
Middlebury College

Noël Valis
Yale University

Ángel Valbuena Briones
University of Delaware

Amy Williamsen
University of Arizona

Isabella and the Sailor

by John E. Keller

Drawings by Hal Barnell

Juan de la Cuesta
Newark, Delaware

Copyright © 2000 by Juan de la Cuesta—Hispanic Monographs
270 Indian Road
Newark, Delaware 19711
(302) 453-8695
Fax: (302) 453-8601
www.JuandelaCuesta.com

Manufactured in the United States of America

ISBN: 0-936388-95-1

Author's Foreword

AMERICANS TRADITIONALLY have misunderstood Isabella. "She sold her jewels to outfit Columbus's ships," they will tell you (which she did not do at all), "and burned thousands of Jews in the fires of the Spanish Inquisition," also untrue.

To Spaniards she is Isabella the Great, another Joan of Arc, a concentration of all that made Spain the most powerful nation of her time and launched the discovery and colonization of the New World. She is for them a mighty force which welded a fragmented nation together, defeating the age-old Muslim enemy, and sweeping heresy from the land. Today she is only a step from sainthood.

Rarely does anyone think of the other Isabella, of the beautiful auburn-haired, blue-eyed little girl of five exiled by an inimical half-brother, Henry IV of Castile, to the drafty little castle of Arévalo with her insane mother and infant brother. Published chronicles and some still in the original manuscripts in which they were penned describe her as independent, even as a child, who at thirteen defied her king when he tried to force her to marry her aging uncle, the King of Portugal; those who explore in forgotten histories, legends and folktales her life of stress and strain, of persecution, of adventure and romance and love discover much that is unexpected. And those who search assiduously will find a child, a courageous and determined teen-aged lass and a young queen as independent, courageous and as human, too, as any of the great ladies of history. Not even Elizabeth Tudor, tucked away in shabby Hatfield House by Henry VIII; not Cleopatra forced to flee to the protection of a foreign invader to escape death at the hands of her own brother; not Catherine the Great whose disillusionment with her spouse failed to shatter her life; and not Christina of Norway, fleeing her country to escape the memory of a tragic romance, could equal all that Isabella, princess and queen, had to endure, rise above and emerge as mother of a new nation. She was not, then, the cold and haughty queen so many of us have come to dislike, even as we admire her abilities.

With Columbus it is somewhat the same. "He discovered America," we say, and there are many who call him a genocide, which he never was, and forget that without him we might be speaking French or Portuguese. What do we know of that enigmatic man? We know very little. In Spain his descendants have always held titles of nobility, and there has always been one of his line called Admiral. As in the case of Isabella titles often serve to smother the character and dull the brilliance of men like the Great Navigator. To this very day we do not know for certain who he was. Was he the son of a common wool dyer born in Genoa, as most historians insist? His highly educated son, Ferdinand, who wrote the Admiral's biography, never stated that he was Genoese but only that his parents were of respectable stock who lived in straightened circumstances in Lombardy due to the wars. How can it be that one of the world's greatest men, known across the face of the earth, concealed his origins so carefully and so successfully? Was he, as thousands today believe, the son of a noble Spaniard, a Catalonian, who had to change his name as he traveled from country to country, from Colom to Colombo to Coulon to Columbus and finally to the Spanish form of the name, to Colón? Was he the son of that Antoni Colom, who with his parents took part in the revolt against the King of Aragón?

Columbus was the same age as Isabella and Ferdinand, he was an adolescent when he went to sea, he experienced persecution, and if he was a teen-age exile from Catalonia who spent some years of his youth in Genoa, as he seems to have done, why must we insist that he must have been Genoese?

Truly behind Isabella and Columbus there is a human story with threads that twist and turn mysteriously and bind their lives together inextricably and undeniably. History tells us that they held each other in mutual respect. But to those who seek it reveals a great deal more; a closer view of these two enigmatic figures shows that they were very human and very much alive, not merely great characters, now shadowed by centuries, who once ruled or sailed the Sea of Darkness.

What was the unrevealable attraction between Isabella and her sailor without a past? Clues exist in old chronicles and manuscripts, in letters, and in other documents from that distant time. Even so, questions still emerge, and many of these have not been answered and may never be except in fiction.

Why did Spain's greatest queen have faith in a foreign adventurer recently rejected by her royal kinsmen in Portugal? Why did she refuse to let him accept subsidies freely offered by the wealthy Duke of Medina Sidonia and the Count of Medina Celi, forcing him to wait impatiently until she could ultimately be his patron? Why did she keep him on the royal payroll when he was destitute and was forced to leave his son dependent upon the charity of the monks of La Rábida? What motivated her to pity his poverty and to send him money for proper velvets and hose when he was summoned to an audience with her and Ferdinand? Why did she appoint new committees each time his enterprise was not approved, and what made her argue with the hostile Ferdinand on his behalf? And finally, why did she take Columbus's two sons, one of them illegitimate, into the royal household to be reared with her son while he was at sea and exploring the New World?

Was all this the fruit of Isabella's famous intuition? Did she, after having met Columbus and discussed the enterprise with him on that historic day in Cordova in 1486, decide in a flash of insight, that he was destined for future greatness? Would a practical and highly intelligent queen have acted so without more substantial and more personal reasons?

The events of this story of Isabella and the sailor do not distort the history of the period. The early meeting of the Princess Isabella and the young sailor are admittedly fictional; but historical or not, they definitely make more plausible the deep affection they had for one another. Before that day in Cordova an extended association simply had to have taken place to draw them together into such a mutual and touching sympathy. The queen's remarkable insight into human character is not enough to explain their very warm and even romantic relationship.

JEK

1

The Princess in the Tower

1

NEVER IN HER FIFTEEN YEARS had the Princess Isabella looked more beautiful. The moment she set foot in the tapestried audience chamber of the palace of Ocaña every eye came to rest upon her, and she was glad that she had taken time to slip into the new dress. Straight from the looms of Lyons, that dress, and there was not another one like it on the Spanish side of Pyrenees. She had made no mistake in this dress, for its deep blue laid the perfect background of contrast for her two russet braids and gave her wide-set eyes the exact indigo deepening needed.

At the far end of the long room she could see on the dais the person whom she hated most in all the world. Joanna, wife of her half-brother Henry IV, Joanna Queen of Spain and queen, too, of most of Spain's sorrows. That Joanna was angry would have been obvious to even the most casual observer, and Isabella's gaze was intent. She took note of the queen's back, stiff and unbending, saw the ugly thrust of the woman's chin. Was it the new dress that angered the queen so much? She did not care, but she could no more have laid it aside, once she had felt its shimmering, living silk, than refused the Holy Eucharist when the celebrant placed it in her mouth. The dress cried out to be worn. Still, if the queen had summoned, and had expected to see, the usually shabby Isabella, she would be disappointed and therefore unpleasant. Isabella wondered if she had acted wisely after all. A few months more of shabbiness could be endured patiently after a lifetime of it.

Standing her straightest and tallest, she started the long walk toward the dais where Joanna sat judge-like, accuser-like, and she wondered again about the dress. Was it cut too low? Were the cream lace, puffy sleeves too extreme? The bodice too tightly fitted? No matter now. It was too late to retreat.

Resolutely she kept her blue eyes from the Moorish palace guard, two long grim lines of them to left and right, as she paced between. These were King Henry's guards, his infidels, his pagans, in their blinding scarlet tunics, and taut white breeches like paint on muscular thighs and calves, and tendril-sprouting slippers and plume-crowned turbans. Holy Mother of Mercy, how she hated Moors!

And they were staring at her, these sun-browned, oily-bearded men. Refusing to see them, she could smell the spicy perfumes with which they drenched themselves, could feel the impact of their animal virility. Just below the dais stood Beltrán de la Cueva whom she had heard was with Henry in Andalusia. He must have made the journey with the king's courier. It seemed incredible that the queen's lover, the stud who had begotten his child on her in the name of the king, would dare flaunt his handsome face at court even in Henry's absence, but there he was. He met her gaze and winked. Better look at the Berbers than at Beltrán, and her eyes turned back to them.

"What crystal breasts!" one of the Moors muttered, and Isabella cursed herself for blushing. Yes, the neckline should have been a trifle higher, displaying less of her bosom and shoulders to these God-forgotten bravos of her half-brother.

Then she was at the dais, waiting gravely for Joanna to notice her. But the queen was reading, consciously ignoring Isabella, The royal seal dangled from the right corner of the parchment. An official communication, then, something from the absent king. And behind Isabella burned the hawk-eyes of the Moors.

Queen Joanna continued to read, fully aware of her standing there, but determined not to acknowledge it. Then suddenly she looked up, and as if startled, said, "Speak of the devil and he will run to lace your shoes; I was about to send for you again, Princess. You certainly took your time! But *you* are the Princess of Castile, and we should be happy to wait. We should consider it a pleasure and a privilege."

Isabella hated frivolous, irritable talkers who wasted words, but she smothered the sigh of resignation she ached to utter. No need to infuriate the already angry queen.

"Your forgiveness, Highness," she made herself reply with the calm dignity and gravity people had already come to associate with her. "I came as quickly as possible. I was not properly dressed for such an august assembly when your message came."

"And are you now?" asked Joanna spitefully, looking with surprise and grudging admiration at the way the blue silk clung to the tall slender body of her enemy.

Isabella knew that the queen's displeasure arose not so much from the dress' décolleté as from the way it became her. Actually, it was not as low-cut as Joanna's.

"Her Highness disapproves of the dress..." began Isabella.

"Never mind the dress," snapped the queen. "There are matters much more important to discuss."

Isabella tried to imagine what these things could be. Important indeed if Joanna passed on so rapidly to them, relinquishing such a fine opportunity for insulting her further. Something a good deal worse lay in store, no doubt, to judge from the greedy expression of anticipated pleasure so plainly stamped upon her flushed face.

"She is pleased about something," thought Isabella with apprehension. "When those sloe eyes gleam like that, someone is about to hear bad news."

"A letter has just come from the king," continued Joanna. "I am positive that it will arouse your interest, Princess." She pronounced Isabella's title as usual with a maddening inflection that made it an insult instead of an honor. "I took the liberty of breaking the seal, even though it was addressed to you. I was about to read it, but now that you are with us, perhaps you will be so kind as to read it to us."

Painfully Isabella swallowed the anger beginning to well up inside her. This was too much! Joanna had gone too far. What an unforgivable piece of bad taste! What a storybook sister-in-law! Something wild and dangerous deep inside her tensed and prepared to spring, but she remembered in time the lesson of five years of rebuff and clever reprisal. With no rights at court, no status, no authority—she was not in a position to open hostilities with the enemy. Joanna, she knew, was quite capable of having the dress torn from her body. She bit her tongue and waited. But her eyes did not falter. She stood straight in an attitude the whole court recognized, feet planted firmly, head drawn back with an unconscious hauteur, eyes fixedly upon the queen.

"How little Joanna knows me," she thought. "If shabbiness could have crushed me, I would have stopped fighting back long ago. It can't succeed, and it can't go on forever."

After all, she knew, most princesses eligible for marriage were much younger than she, and already she had heard an undercurrent of rumor about a proper husband for her. Once the time arrived for some important alliance to be made between Castile and a foreign power, they would remember that she was King John's daughter and the last female heir of the House of Trastámara, the last Spanish princess in whose veins flowed the blood of the Plantagenets. Yes, she could become a far greater queen than this beautiful and wicked creature on the dais. Rumor already had it that Louis XI hoped to wed his brother to some likely princess. And there were whispers of a match with one of the scions of that other branch of the Plantagenets in England. Possibilities were endless for a princess of Castile.

Isabella's eyes lingered proudly on the wonderful dress her friend Beatriz had given her. What a friend to have! A fine life hers would have been without Beatriz de Bobadilla! Not even Beatriz' marriage to young Andrés Cabrera had weakened the strong bond between them. She was always there, close and sympathetic, when Joanna seemed most cruel. The gift of the dress was but one further example of their friendship. Again she let her eyes wander to the soft cloth and knew that she would never forget the strange power that flows from dress to woman. Someday she would own others, many others just as fine, but not now. Not while she was a poor relative of the king who pocketed every *maravedí* of the revenues provided by her dead father.

"Are you going to keep us waiting all day while you moon and daydream? she heard Joanna ask, feigning a resignation she did not feel. "Read the letter, girl."

"Very well, Highness. Aloud?"

"Aloud? Of course, aloud. But, no. Let Don Francisco read it. His voice is stronger, and I want the court to hear every word. Read the king's message, Don Francisco," she said, beckoning with a hand that flaunted a ruby belonging rightfully to Isabella of Portugal, the princess's mother in forced retirement. "Play the herald as well as the courier."

Isabella wondered how the queen could hate her so. There must be more concealed behind that hate than jealousy or even the fear that Isabella might someday supplant Joanna's daughter. What else could it be?

Don Francisco was making his way toward the dais, and Isabella saw that he was more typically Moorish in appearance than the tall blond Berbers of the guard. He was new to her, and she supposed he had entered the royal service, as King Henry toured the cities of Andalusia. The king never failed to pick up a number of peculiar people from Moorish Spain.

As soon as she heard Don Francisco's surname she realized that he was either a Moor or a Mudéjar, a Mohammedan turned Christian, usually for gain. His name was Hasan. Henry couldn't even hire a courier who was not oriental.

As Don Francisco read in a voice that carried the length of the audience hall, her confessor, Alfonso de Coca, came and stood quietly beside her. At the same time she noticed that Beatriz and Andrés Cabrera had appeared at her other elbow. She was startled. Something in the deep concern of these friends made her uneasy. What did they know that she did not?

She made an effort to concentrate upon the king's message which was as usual long and flowery. At last the preamble came to a close and she could not believe what she was hearing. Don Francisco's deep voice boomed forth the core of the message, the part that really mattered, the part so carefully tucked away in a page of official verbosity.

"Therefore," he read, "we have betrothed our sister, the Princess Isabella, to one of our most staunch supporters and a grandee of our realm."

There it was, as cold and clear and sharp as an icicle. She had been betrothed without so much as a by-your-leave. She listened to catch the name of the man they would have her marry, but Don Francisco stopped reading suddenly and shot a quick, conspiratorial glance at Joanna. The queen smiled thinly. Isabella knew at once that this had all been rehearsed.

At last, after looking all around the hall, he held the parchment up again and began to read. "Prepare for the wedding," he read." The groom is on the way even now to Ocaña. He will arrive within the week."

"The marriage banns?" she wondered.

It was as though he had read her mind. "The banns have been posted."

"But the Church?"

"Holy Church has waived all its regulations and permits this unusual haste. All is arranged."

Isabella trembled with mingled emotions. First fear and then relief. She would be free of Joanna and her cruel court, but she might be just as much a prisoner if her husband-to-be proved to be like many of the Castilian nobility. A great deal depended upon the man Henry had chosen. And because she was very young and had read too many romances of chivalry, she arrived at the swift and pleasant conclusion that her half-brother had chosen for her a prince, a handsome, healthy prince not much her senior. Surely Henry would not again try to impose upon her as suitor another Alfonso of Portugal, middle-aged, fat, and Joanna's kinsman as well as her own. No one could have forgotten so soon what a terrible diplomatic debacle she had precipitated when at thirteen she had refused to accept that choice, but apparently every one had forgotten that startling event.

It was then that Don Francisco lowered his eyes to the parchment once more and something in his stance told her that he was about to read the name of her betrothed. She leaned forward eagerly to hear every syllable of his name. England? France? Burgundy? Aragón? She did not see that Joanna had leaned forward, too, and was staring with one hand on her voluptuous bosom. Don Francisco paused for effect. The entire court was on tiptoe. It was so quiet that Isabella heard the pigeons cooing high on the palace battlements.

Isabella's heart beat thunderously. Her hands felt cold and damp and she had to make an effort to keep her shoulders back and her head held high. She fought to hold back tears of fury which the people around her might take for tears of grief. In the next few seconds, she realized, Joanna and her husband, who was not even present, would try to decide her fate, her future, for the rest of her life. They would try to set the course of her country's future as well, and the results of their machinations she knew would be catastrophic. "I must not surrender," she told herself, "I shall not and I will not accept some monstrous choice of theirs."

Her eyes flew to the people around her, seeking support and finding only Beatriz's and Father de Coca's. She saw curiosity, amusement, fear, concern, but not the help she had counted upon. These people saw a girl of fifteen facing the combined strength of the most powerful people in Spain.

2

Then Don Francisco read the name of Pedro Girón. Isabella shuddered and turned pale. It couldn't be true! Stunned, incredulous, ill, she turned to Beatriz and found only tears. Father de Coca, with an impulsive movement reached out and took her hand in his. Andrés Cabrera had gone white.

After a while Isabella became aware that a hushed murmur was sweeping the assembly. Don Francisco was rolling up the parchment with apparent satisfaction. He rolled it with such vigor that she could hear the crackle distinctly. She looked at Joanna and found her aglow with triumph, her olive skin oddly radiant. On the faces of the courtiers she saw surprise indifference, and in a few cases, anger. Doña María de Benavente's eyes were filled with pity, Joanna's lady-in-waiting, Guiomar de Sandoval, was openly derisive.

"Well," asked the queen finally, with a smile too cruel to bear, "what do you think of that, Princess? You remember Pedro Girón, of course."

Isabella remembered him. He was Henry's man. He was a type she loathed. It wasn't that he was ugly, although he was that. It wasn't that there was something utterly sexual about his every movement, his every gesture. She had nothing against true masculinity, and indeed secretly admired virility. But Pedro Girón leered instead of looking, his body, even when he sat or reclined on a couch, seemed always ready for one thing. His reputation with women was disgraceful. Worse still, people whispered that he had gained King Henry's favor in the one way always certain to succeed. Her mind recoiled, as usual from the thought of that perversity. But she knew and believed that Pedro Girón was quite capable of even that. Yes, she remembered all about Pedro Girón. Her mother had warned her about him when she was still a child.

Joanna's voice cut into her thoughts. "I must say you show little enthusiasm, Princess. Pedro Girón is a great noble. His brother is no less than the Marquis of Villena, the king's most powerful supporter. He is wealthy, powerful. I see you are your usual ungrateful self. Don't you understand how fortunate you are, girl?"

Isabella's mind still rejected it. Not Pedro Girón. Not the lecher of lechers! Not the bi-sexual, the sodomite! The room swam and she staggered a little and had to lean against Father de Coca so hard that she threw him off balance, Don Francisco had sounded her death-knell, or so Joanna seemed to think to judge from her expression. Her lips curled wickedly.

"There is surely some error." It was the confessor confronting the queen, and everybody listened. "Pedro Girón," he announced quietly, "cannot wed the princess. He cannot marry anyone. Have you all forgotten? Girón is Grand Master of Alcántara and has taken the vows of celibacy demanded by that position." Father de Coca stood tall and straight and his shoulders looked like those of a man who has said all that needs to be said about a matter and stands waiting for his words to take effect.

Isabella felt the beginning of vast relief, but Joanna giggled and she noticed that a number of the courtiers were smiling. They all knew about Pedro Girón and the vow of celibacy. How could a priest as closely associated with the noble household as de Coca possibly be so naive? Didn't he know that Girón had more mistresses than the King of Granada had concubines, and that when he was on campaign and couldn't take them with him he found other means of feeding his inordinate lust? Had the priest forgotten the Moorish page boys?

Beatriz pressed her hand. "Don't worry, Isabella. We won't let it happen."

But Isabella did worry. It did no good for her to tell herself that no grand master of a military order like Alcántara had ever taken a wife while he held the office. Pedro Girón might defy Holy Church itself if the king promised to support him. The Church was after all a body of men, and men could be bought. Still, she had nothing but this last straw to grasp at and she grasped it frantically.

Joanna, however, quickly snatched it from her. "Didn't you know, Father de Coca," she asked, smiling cruelly, "that the king applied for and received a special dispensation from Rome? The Holy Father has permitted Don Pedro to resign from Alcántara so as to marry the princess. Indeed, he has already withdrawn, and although the revenues he loses are great, what the king offers will amply compensate him."

De Coca's confidence slipped from him like an old cloak and his shoulders were suddenly so tired that in the midst of her own defeat Isabella felt sorry for him. Then she looked up and saw on the dais above her Joanna, triumphant and mighty in her triumph. She wondered how any human being could be so beautiful and yet at the same time so evil. Tales of Satan's angels walking the earth crossed her mind. Joanna could be one of these, she supposed, nor would this be the first case of such a visitation in Spain. Devil or not, the day Joanna arrived with her train of Portuguese wantons, the Castilian court had lost what vestiges of morality it still clung to before her father, King John's, death.

The murmurs subsided and a silence fell that lasted for a long minute. Isabella realized that they were all waiting for her to speak. Every face was turned her way, every eye expectant.

She lifted her eyes again and stared into those of the queen, longing to bury strong fingers in that long black hair. Joanna's eyes shifted after a moment and she began a conversation with Don Francisco. It was then that Isabella found words. To her own surprise and amazement she heard her voice give them an answer.

"No!" she said calmly. "I will never marry Pedro Girón. He is an animal."

No one was prepared for this, not even from this unpredictable girl. Even Beatriz herself, who for several minutes had been aware of certain warning signals, looked surprised. A closer scrutiny of her friend showed Isabella's strong hands clenched at her sides, gathering handsful of heavy silk, wrinkling it. She saw the dress grow shorter, much shorter, as if some magic were at work.

Suddenly Isabella gathered the long skirts above her ankles and bolted like a deer straight for the winding stairway leading to Ocaña's tower. Beatriz took three steps involuntarily after her and then stopped. Others, she remembered in time, might borrow the idea and catch the fleeing girl. As it was, no one thought about stopping her, so quickly had she moved. Even the Moors stood open-mouthed at the vision of King Henry's sister dashing madly up the tower steps, decorum and dignity forgotten. They saw her race to the top, and the whole chamber stared in amazement as she stopped and cast down upon them such an intense look of fury and disdain that her face was silver-white and her eyes blue sparks.

Then above the hush rose the voice of Joanna. "She is going into the tower. After her! Guards, bring her back!"

As one man the sixty Berbers hurled themselves at the stair. Isabella saw them coming, and for a second hesitated as if to face them. Before they could reach her, however, she turned, darted through an archway and disappeared. Above the scuffle of feet on the steps came the slam of a heavy door. Beatriz leaned weakly against her husband. Isabella for the moment was out of danger.

3

On the same night when the Princess Isabella escaped into the tower of Ocaña's castle, another flight was in the making in the province of Segarra in Catalonia, in the manor house of the family Colom. This part of the Kingdom of Aragón had been in revolt some four years with enough success to alarm King John and his son, Prince Ferdinand. Already they had brought home from their Kingdom of Naples and Sicily substantial forces to be deployed in Segarra, and they felt that the time had come for even more desperate measures. All rebels and rebel sympathizers, they were determined, must be rooted out and put to the sword, unless surrender was abject, and unless enemy strongholds, as a part of surrender, would be razed to the ground.

During all four of the years of revolt the Coloms managed to avoid suspicion, for they had never been openly a part of the so-called Rebellion of the Generalitat, even though surreptitiously they helped the rebels, many of whom were their relatives. They relied on entities in the king's court, and one even in his own household, to allay any suspicion of complicity. It was a complete surprise, then, when events unfolded that evening as the Coloms sat down to supper as night was falling.

Young Juan Baptista Colom, aged fifteen, had never been so filled with mingled outrage and fury as when the blow fell. The last words of grace had just been spoken. Then, before any one could take a bite, the wild tattoo of a horses hooves rang out in the courtyard and the hoarse cries of the rider made everyone jump. Juan Baptista saw his father, Don Antoni Colom, leap to his feet and make for the door, calling to Juan Baptista and his brother Bartholomeu to follow. The rider, dusty, rank with sweat, and panting, plunged into the atrium crying, "Bar the doors! King John's troops are close behind." And so saying, he took a crumpled letter from his pouch and placed it in Don Antoni's hand. Juan Baptista saw his father break the seal and caught the panic his father felt as he read aloud. "It's from Uncle Bertrán, written two days ago in Barcelona."

The words of the letter fell on the family's ears like a clap of thunder, "My dear son, follow our plan. Flee on receipt of this message."

Juan Baptista and Bartolomeu exchanged quick glances and ran to carry out their prearranged parts in what had to be done in this very emergency, which no one ever thought would occur. As he ran, he saw his mother, Doña Magdalena, making for the servants' quarters.

"How long do we have?" Don Antoni asked the rider.

"Not long. Less than an hour, sir. When I left Tarroja, the king's men were mounting. Much less than an hour, I think. When your uncle, Don Bertrán, gave the message to me, he told me to ride to death as many horses as need be. But the king's men have not spared their own mounts."

"Run to the tower, man, and watch. I'll send someone to you with wine and cheese. Hurry!"

Just then Doña Magdalena returned from the kitchen with the five maidservants and the cook, all weeping and wringing their hands. Bartolomeu carried into the room his mother's jewel chest, and Juan Baptista led in the family's six men-at-arms, four lancers and two crossbowmen. Seconds later Don Antoni had opened the family strongbox and had taken out six sacks of gold coins.

"Don't forget the rations," he barked, and Doña Magdalena disappeared again with the cook in tow, soon to return with bags of cheese and dried beef and a hamper of wine bottles. The entire operation had taken less than ten minutes, and it was well that it had taken no longer. Down from the tower ran the rider.

"Sir, I can see them. The outriders will be at the door in minutes."

Juan Baptista looked at his mother and wondered at her composure. Any other woman, at the thought of leaving home and possessions, probably for the rest of her life, would have screamed and railed at her husband for his involvement in the revolt against the king. Doña Magdalena shed not a tear. She, like the rest of the family had drilled into her mind what she was now doing so efficiently. Their plan, she knew, simply had to work, for if it did not, all would be lost, including their lives, and losing them at the king's hands would not be a pleasant way to leave this world.

Don Antoni walked into the huge fireplace of the manor house's great hall, he turned a stone, and with a rumble an aperture appeared in the back of the fireplace. "Into the tunnel, all of you," he ordered, and even as he spoke, the thunder of fists on the outer doors rang with sickening thuds. Doña Magdalena shepherded the servants through the narrow opening. Next came the men-at-arms, and finally the father and his two sons. A third, Jaume, a child of ten, was away at a monastery school. Unfortunately, there was nothing they could do about him; but they knew that the abbot, his uncle by marriage into the Colom family, would see that he was sent to a place of safety.

Juan Baptista helped his father sweep ashes over their footprints, while Bartolomeu lighted a lamp from one of the candles on the table where their supper remained untouched. Then, as the outer doors crashed in under the blows of a ram, Don Antoni touched another stone, and the door of the tunnel slid into place.

"Not a sound," he whispered. "Quick! Follow me until we are far enough from the door not to be heard. What I have to say to all of you, I will say only once."

Some fifty yards into the tunnel, Don Antoni stopped. Still whispering, he addressed the servant women first. "At the end of this tunnel there is a wall between us and the outside world. As soon as the men knock it down, you women must make for the Church of Santa María de Tarroja. They are probably still at vespers. Mingle with the worshipers, and if you should be questioned by any of the king's officers, as I suspect may be the case, tell them exactly who and what you are—the wives and daughters of local farmers. Only you, María, who have been with us since my sons were born, should speak about our flight. Tell any one who inquires that you heard me say we would go to Lérida and stay there for the rest of the night." Then, opening his purse, he distributed coins to all the women, saying, "Here are your wages and a little more. We thank you for your service to us, and María, I wish we could take you with us, but you are too old to ride, if we get the horses I sent for two days ago."

To the men-at-arms he said, "We have ridden and fought together for many years. You know my affection for all of you. Tonight and for the next few days I must ask one last service from you. Escort us to Tarragona. Near that city is a harbor used only by a few merchants. There we must leave you, for we shall sail immediately and cannot take you with us. Here are your wages and as much more as I can spare. Once we are safe on board, all of you must ride hard for the mountains and the fortress of the rebels, where I know you will be welcome. Carry this letter. It will introduce you. Do not allow yourselves to fall into the hands of King John or that quicksilver son of his, Prince Ferdinand, since you know their reputation for cruelty. The prince is only fourteen, but he, in some ways, is more lethal than his sire. And remember this and mark it well; you all heard me say that our ship was bound for *France*."

Juan Baptista listened to all this and marveled at his father's aplomb, at his care in leaving no loose end dangling. "It pays to have a plan," he thought, "and it pays even better if men like my uncle Bertrán and my father make it."

"Husband," said Doña Magdalena, "do you have any real hope that the squire, Agusti, can bring enough horses for us and these men?"

Juan Baptista saw his father look long into her eyes, and it was a look of love and trust. "Wife," he replied, "Agusti is competent and faithful, even if he is only sixteen. We've all prayed to Our Lady, the Blessed Virgin of Montserrat, and we know that we are in her hands. What more can I say? We have done all that is humanly possible. She will do what she feels is best for *us*."

Suddenly Juan Baptista bumped his head on the roof of the tunnel which was sloping toward a blank wall. He was proud of his height and hoped to grow three inches more to match his father's six feet three. His mind raced as he stood and watched the men-at-arms dismantle the wall as quietly as they could. And, as he watched, the face of Prince Ferdinand flashed into his mind. What an enemy to have in an uncertain world! He would never forget their sole encounter, for it had left a mark upon his soul. How could anyone ever forget that face, those eyes, as intensely blue as his own, that familiar bright red hair, the exact shade of his, that dynamic personality? He remembered exactly how he had been riding alone, against his father's express command, since the king's troops were likely to be in the region. Just as he had rounded a grove of medlar trees, he came face to face with another rider, also alone, a rider who looked as young as he, but who bore himself with a manly grace that made him seem much older. Both had reined in their mounts and had come to a complete halt, not six yards from one another. And then, as he had looked closely at the youth who faced him, his mouth, he remembered, had fallen open with amazement. He felt as though he might be looking into a mirror. It was true that the stranger's eyes had to look up into his, making it plain that he was shorter by a head, but all the same they were like his own eyes, except for their mature and flintlike expression. He saw his opponent—for there was no doubt that they were opponents—brush back his hair with a motion which he knew that he himself made to get his hair out of his eyes. Then the youth spoke in a voice as self-assured and as commanding as his entire demeanor. This person's voice had long since taken on the depth of a grown man's. His own was likely to break into a childish squeak, especially when he was under stress or emotion. He was afraid to open his mouth.

"What are you staring at, Colom? You wonder how I know you? It behooves me to know all things. And take off your cap, you boor, now and whenever you're in the presence of majesty."

He remembered how his voice had indeed quavered, but how he had stood up to the unaccountable hate pouring out of those unusual eyes. "Majesty?" he had croaked, "What majesty?" But even as he spoke, he recalled with a shiver how he had snatched off his cap. He saw that the owner of those eyes wore garments of regal quality, and suddenly he knew with a terrible certainty that this was King John's son, Ferdinand, Prince of Aragón. What rashness, what courage, what rebelliousness against royal parental authority this prince displayed to ride alone in enemy territory! If he were captured, the entire fabric of the rebellion would be strengthened. And yet, the power, the compelling soul of this prince might even daunt a royal father.

Ferdinand replied. "What majesty? Come now, Colom, I see that you know perfectly what majesty confronts you, you rebel."

"My family are not rebels, Highness," Juan Baptista remembered saying, now hat in hand, as ordered, but not as awed as Ferdinand seemed to think he was. "As you must know, we hold a document from the king himself, penned by his half-brother, and all men know that that good man is a friend to the king as well as to my father's household."

"And I know why your 'Uncle Bertrán' long ago took your father under his wing, even if my royal father does not know. And when I tell him, matters will not go so well with you and all your rebellious family, including your 'uncle.'"

He pronounced the word "uncle" in a way that made it sound obscene. "And, Colom," he continued, "while he is not your *uncle*, he shares a common blood with you. You didn't know that, did you? Not many people do. But if one searches, one usually makes discoveries, Only a week ago I finally found out why that crafty old Bertrán long ago decided he had to persuade my father that you and your family are not supporters of the rebellion."

"If only I could capture him," Juan Baptista remembered thinking, "this war would end and Catalonia would be free from the House of Aragón. Four years, God knows, is already long enough." He recalled how he thought he had slyly concealed the tightening of his hand upon the shaft of his hunting spear and how the prince had instantly realized it.

"Don't even think it," he hissed. "If you attack me, I will, of course, kill you, if it pleased me, and I believe it would. But I disdain you, boy. Now get yourself down off that horse which I shall confiscate for our cause. A long walk home will quench your childish ambition to capture a prince. By rights I should let you feel my spear. By God, I think I shall!" And with those words, he had leveled the spear at him and spurred his horse into a charge.

Ferdinand had caught him off-guard. The lance glanced off his shield, which some blessed saint must have made him raise automatically, and he had suffered no more than a prick from its point as it glanced off the shield and scratched his leg. Quickly he had used his spear and had seen surprise and fury in Ferdinand's eyes, as he all but toppled from his saddle. Then, unexpectedly, with a cry of rage, the prince had ridden off, to wheel his mount and cry out. "We'll meet again, Colom, and when we do…"

It was only then that Juan Baptista realized the reason for the prince's sudden retreat. Ferdinand had seen lancers riding at full gallop toward him and correctly surmised that they had been sent out by Don Antoni to find his son.

Suddenly, Juan Baptista remembered how his father's men swarmed all around him, and their leader, old Ricart, who had taught him all he knew about weaponry, had berated him harshly. "My God, young man, you've nearly got yourself killed, you've assaulted a prince, and you've made an enemy I'm glad I haven't made! Wait until I tell all this to Don Antoni."

Juan Baptista had hardly listened, so impressed by the prince's presence that he could think of nothing else. "Why does he look so much like me, Ricart? Why does he hate me so?"

"You'd better ask your father the answer to your first question, for you certainly won't get one from me. The second I can answer well; he hates you because you came close to unseating him, and him a dubbed knight, as young as he is; he hates you because he knows you could have struck him again as he tried to keep his seat; yes, and he hates you because you're Don Bertrán's kinsman, and because that makes him and you...." Ricart had stopped in midspeech and turned away.

Juan Baptista was jolted from his reminisces by the voice of one of the men-at-arms. "Sir, the wall is down. Look you can see moonlight, and that red glare, I fear, is your burning house."

He heard his mother growl in anger. "Why must they burn it?"

"Because, my dear," his father said, "the king ordered it, or more probably his son. God spare us all when that whelp grows into a man and inherits the throne of Aragón!"

Just then, out of the night came the neigh of a horse, quickly stifled. "Agusti made it," said Don Antoni proudly. "We train our squires well. We do indeed!"

"And," added Doña Magdalena, "don't forget that we have had tonight the best of patronesses, and Juan Baptista believed her. Our Lady of Montserrat had made him her devotee, too, and he expected to pray to her all his life. It had been she, surely, who had caused his father to send Agusti for the horses.

Just then Agusti appeared at the head of a string of mounts, all saddled and bridled—four for the family, six for the men-at-arms, and two to carry the money bags, the jewel chest, the rations and blankets Agusti had thought to bring.

It was then that the rider who had brought the message asked, "What of me, sir? My horse is in the stables of your house."

"You'll ride one of the pack horses, man." said Don Antoni. "Did you think I'd leave you stranded here on foot?"

Moments later all were slowly riding along a footpath, hidden by trees from the king's troops busily looting the burning house. The maidservants and the old cook were disappearing in the direction of the nearby village. "It looks as though we may escape," said Don Antoni.

After they topped the crest of a low hill Don Antoni ordered everyone to ride at full gallop. "With care, good luck and the protection of Our Lady," he said, "we should reach Tarragona within three days."

And three days later they looked down from a bluff and saw the ships. "They're cousin Jeannot's," Don Antoni explained. "He'll take us where we'll have to go, where Uncle Bertrán planned for us to go.

Juan Baptista watched in surprise as he saw his always frugal father give a horse to each of the men-at-arms, and one to the messenger and the rest to Agusti. "All of you," he advised, "had best make for the border and the rebel army. Find my kinsman, Jean Baptiste Coulon. Tell him what has happened to us, and use this password; say to him WE COME AS A DOVE. When he hears that, he will know for certain that I sent you. Now, all of you, go with God and the blessing of Our Lady of Montserrat."

4

The slamming of the tower door left the audience chamber in complete silence for as long as it takes to hold a breath. Then the chamber burst into confusion. People milled about the queen until she, followed by her courtiers and ladies-in-waiting, made for the stairs. At her side strode the confessor, hardly able to keep abreast, but trying to calm her anger.

"Be gentle with her, Highness," he begged. "She is very young. Be gentle."

But Joanna was not listening. "Bitch! Bitch! Bitch!" she screamed, completely beside herself. "What good will this do her? Get axes. Break in the door. Drag her out!"

"Highness, Highness, be merciful!" pleaded the priest.

Beatriz and Andrés added their pleas. "She will come out," they said. "Be merciful."

Joanna was still shouting at the top of her voice. "She'll come out immediately. Instantly, or we'll break down the door." She shook with fury. Her black hair had lost its combs and it hung down around her face and shoulders in a long mane that poured over her out-thrust breasts. Her face, within that mane, was no longer olive. It shone like an altar cloth. De Coca had never seen anyone who looked at once so beautiful and yet so vicious. He stepped quickly behind a column and crossed himself with extreme care once from forehead to chin and once over the chest from shoulder to shoulder.

"*Madre de Dios!*" he whispered.

The space outside the door of the tower guard room quickly filled with people. Several Berbers had their shoulders against the heavy oak panels and were shoving mightily, but with no visible success. The door had been built to last. Excitement ran high and everybody wondered what would happen next. Nothing so thrilling had happened since the Archbishop of Toledo called Joanna an adulteress before half the court. When the tension was more than she could bear, Beatriz dropped to her knees and wept as though Isabella had already fallen into the hands of the Moors. Other ladies, overcome by emotion, used their handkerchiefs freely and their lips formed the name of Holy Mary.

Just then the queen appeared, at the head of the stairs, and quiet fell. Joanna walked straight to the door and the Berbers fell back quickly, falling over one another in their care not to let even her garments touch them. She *might* be a witch. People said so, and it never paid to take chances with the unknown and the evil. Joanna stood at the door waiting, tapping impatiently with a jewelled sandal. By and by the axes came, and the queen spoke.

"Open, Isabella. Come out! Now. If you don't, they'll break in and drag you out."

"In this room," replied a strange voice that was, and was not Isabella's, "there are three swords. The instant the door gives, I will fall upon the sharpest."

"And she will, Highness!" cried Beatriz, detecting no bravado in her friend's tone, no idle threat.

"I almost wish she would," said Joanna with a low, wolfish laugh that made Father de Coca cross himself again. "Leave her for the night," she went on. "Let us go down to dinner—and a very fine dinner we shall have. Tonight we dine on the venison sent by Abdullah el Zagral, Lord of Málaga. Yes, let our little princess remain in her tower in the company of bats and owls. She'll be happy enough to come out tomorrow and behave like a lady."

Isabella heard and sat down weakly on the rough bench, the room's only furniture. For the time she was safe, alone and had time to think and to pray. The door would hold. Outside the shuffle of feet grew fainter as the court descended the staircase, and she wondered if she dared look out and have the pleasure of letting them see her as they retreated. Her hand went to the bar and then she stopped. Better make certain. Pressing her ear to the door she caught the faint almost imperceptible whisper silk makes when it rubs rough wood. And through the panel came the unmistakable odor of a musky Moorish perfume. Joanna had stationed one of the guards on the other side of the door to catch her if she opened it.

After a while, when her heart stopped pounding, Isabella took stock of the contents of the room. The inventory required only a few seconds, for there was nothing but the bench, the sword-rack, and a small crock of stale water. The latter she set aside carefully, mindful of the hours she might have to spend there.

As the sun dropped below the rim of the far-off mountains, its last rays struck the turrets of the old palace, lighting them up in a weird afterglow that splashed from the stone and ran down to set the courtyard on fire. Far below ran Ocaña's outer walls, very ancient and in bad repair like everything else in Christian Spain. Beyond the fortifications she could still see the wheat fields and orchards and the endless gardens that made Ocaña the breadbasket of the country. Here and there lay the shadows of olive groves, rapidly disappearing in the gathering gloom. Then, as night closed down, only the golden color of the wheat reflected enough light to make the fields glow dully.

Isabella longed to fly like a swallow from the window of the tower, to sail far above the cobbled streets and green patios until she reached the Chapel of Our Lady of Remedies over against the walls of the great church, for sometimes the archbishop occupied a suite there and with him she could find sanctuary. Instead she had to look and wonder at the strangeness of life.

She stood up and began to pace the circular room with its rough stone walls and slab-paved floor, feeling like one of her half-brother's lionesses in its pit. In her hands she swung the sword which was old and rusty and very heavy, far too heavy for a woman, and yet she swung it and felt a defiant delight as its weight hurt her wrist.

Why should she, the princess of the realm, lock herself up in a lonely tower, chilly at night even in August, in a city her ancestors had wrested from the infidel? How was it that weak-minded Henry and his wicked Portuguese wife could control her destiny?

In Ocaña, a city she might someday rule, she was ringed about with God's tabernacles and Our Lady's chapels, but for all the good they did her the city might still be in Moorish hands as it was in the older times when its Muslim king, Aben Abed of Seville, gave it to his daughter Zoraida as her dowry. To look at the Berber guard and the many touches of Muslim life returned to it by Henry and Joanna, it might well still be the wedding gift of a Moorish princess and not a Christian city in the heart of Castile.

A soft knock at the door broke her revery. She heard the voice of Beatriz, muted and anxious, and with it the deep, hushed tones of the confessor.

"The queen offers you the opportunity of returning unmolested to your room," said de Coca. "I advise you earnestly, daughter, to come out. We must plan. There is still hope, for I have sent a message to the Archbishop of Toledo."

"Tell Joanna," replied Isabella, "that I refuse categorically to consider the wedding. Tell her that I said Pedro Girón is a parvenu, a second-generation Jewish convert, a baseborn person unfit to be the husband of the Princess of Castile. Tell her that death seems infinitely superior to life with a man like him."

"The queen already knows all this, Isabella," said Beatriz. "But you should come out. Staying locked up in there can't help. Won't you let me tell Joanna to call off the guards and let you walk freely to your room?"

"You know me better than that, Beatriz. Give her the message I've told you. Tell her I'll never marry Pedro Girón."

Beatriz, who did know Isabella better than anyone else, looked at the confessor and told him that they had failed. When the princess spoke with that stubborn finality, she would not change her mind.

"She won't come out, Father, unless the queen relents. We can try again tomorrow, but tonight I know it is useless to talk to her further."

Father de Coca said a final prayer, and then he and Beatriz went away.

Inside the now bleak room Isabella drew the rumpled dress around her shoulders and shivered, wishing it were wool and could pour actual warmth into its wearer instead of the power she had imagined it had given her earlier.

Ocaña lay cool and still under the crisp breeze blowing down from the airy snow-chain of the sierra. Isabella dragged the bench as far as possible from the window and lay down to try to sleep.

5

Dawn showing through the tower's window awakened Isabella but she could not open her eyes. They were two pockets filled with sand and sewed tightly shut. She lay quiet for a little while with the annoying light beating coldly against her closed eyelids. Then an insistent and irritating sound broke into her consciousness. She squinted through the merest slit and pulled the lids closed again. The prospect was not pleasant. A thin grey dawn with a patch of raw and colorless sky, drained of the last vestiges of the night's blackness and not yet touched by the first red glow of dawn, was all that was visible. An unpleasant sound increased its tempo, as she looked, until she identified it as a panicky, staccato drumming of knuckles on thick wood. Whoever was outside the door was rapidly losing control.

Drawn by the contagious urgency of the summons, Isabella hobbled stiffly to the door, aching and weary from the night on the bench. The new dress hung in a limp, rumpled mass of ugly wrinkles, and it saddened her to see it. From the cathedral she heard the bells thundering loud and clear in Sunday matins, and the tower trembled. She shook her head to drive out the residue of sound, but could not.

Beatriz stood in the corridor almost beside herself. She was the diametrical opposite of Isabella in times of stress. Dark, vivacious, talkative and ebullient, handsome though not beautiful like the princess, she bubbled over in every thought and mood. Where Isabella was cool and reserved, with feelings held in check by an inner calm, Beatriz by nature was nervous and volatile. Where Isabella glowed from within, Beatriz flashed like the glint of sunlight on the raw peaks of the sierras.

"Isabella!" she cried again and again, her voice rising suddenly to a scream. "Can you hear me?"

"Wait a minute," replied the princess, not quite awake. "I'll open the door."

"*Minime!*" came the sharp warning. "*Minime. Milites in porta stant!*"

So that was how it was. Soldiers at the door, and she and Beatriz must speak in Latin. Reason again to thank her mother's insistence that she and Beatriz learn the language of the Church. The Moorish guard understood Spanish as well as Arabic, but the language of the Ancients was beyond their comprehension.

"How is it that you can talk to me?" asked Isabella. "Didn't Joanna forbid it?"

"Not actually. And the guards, in the absence of orders to the contrary, see no harm in words. They know you can't escape while they're here, and the queen only told them to seize you if you opened the door. Besides, I think Joanna hopes your friends will persuade you to come out."

"Did you bring anything to eat?"

"I did, but they won't let me give it to you. They're finishing it off now, in fact, and wishing I had brought more."

"Can't you have Andrés arrange something. As High Steward of the King he can certainly order them to withdraw and let you pass me a little food."

"My husband commands the guard in Segovia, Isabella, not in Ocaña, which Henry gave Joanna as an outright gift. Even if he had control here, of course, the queen's order would transcend his. To countermand what she has already ordered would be treason. No. We cannot ask Andrés to do anything but I'll manage something. Just be ready when I give the word. I'll try again."

"Was it just yesterday, Beatriz? Have I been here only that short a time?"

"It was yesterday about the ninth hour, I believe. But it seems a week, at least. How can you bear it without water?"

"There was a jug about half full when I came in. If I'm careful and drink sparingly, I'll have enough to last today. But tell me, have you spoken to Joanna since last night?"

"You know how late she sleeps, Isabella. I wouldn't dare worry her this early, but I saw her before she retired and she was still growling. She hasn't changed her mind, I'm certain, and she won't change it. Either you do as she says, or you stay here and starve."

"Has any word come from the archbishop?"

"None yet, but there has hardly been time. However, the people in the city are demonstrating. They're wondering, too, how long you can hold out and there's betting in all the streets and plazas. If it's any comfort to you, the people hope you'll win, for in spite of all the king and Joanna have done to make them forget you, you enjoy a great popularity. How Joanna must hate that! And after she has tried so hard to make them respect that little girl of hers."

"Beatriz, people will never respect that child, poor little thing. Making me her godmother was another mistake, since it was known I didn't want to be. People know that she isn't Henry's daughter as well as we know it. Why, she even looks like Beltrán de la Cueva."

"That may be, Isabella, but it doesn't help you in your present difficulty. Pedro Girón is one day closer to Ocaña. What are you going to do when he arrives?"

"What I'm doing now. Praying. And there is always the sword."

"This is Beatriz, Isabella. You do not have to pretend with me. I know you and I know your faith. You wouldn't be a suicide. You're too good a Christian."

"Wouldn't I, Beatriz? You've been talking to the confessor. He's shocked at me, isn't he? Father de Coca forgets, but I remember a story he told us a long time ago at Arévalo. That story came from a collection of *exempla* gathered by the Archdeacon of Valderas for use in sermons. You and I were little girls then, not more than ten, but I recall the tale well enough, and I expect you recall it, too. It was the one about the Roman martyr, Euphrosina and how she escaped the lust of the Emperor Marcellus. What did Euphrosina do? She fell on her husband's sword while the emperor's soldiers waited in her atrium to take her to the palace. She preferred death to disgrace, and the moral of the tale was that self destruction transcends life with dishonor."

"Euphrosina was the wife of a Roman senator, Isabella, and what the Emperor Marcellus proposed was adultery. In your case it wouldn't be the same. The man involved would be your husband, and people will hardly consider that disgraceful."

"Pedro Girón's touch would be disgraceful. I've hated him from the day I first caught a glimpse of him. I was eight years old at the time. You know as well as I what he did, or tried to do to my poor mother. What an unmentionable proposition to make to a queen dowager! Have you forgotten what you and I, only little girls, heard him say to her as we listened from the alcove? From the way my mother wept we both knew it was something very bad, even though we were too innocent at the time to catch all the implications. Could I marry a man like that?"

For a moment Beatriz was silent. Then she said, "Isabella, I'm going to be cruel because I love you. Yes, I know about Pedro Girón's attempt and I heard what he suggested to your mother. It was a vile thing for the man to say, especially since he had been sent as the king's emissary, but your mother sent him slinking back to Henry and to Villena who had put the idea in his head in the first place. I admit that you have the best of reasons to hate Girón. But all that is a part of the past, and most people have forgotten all about it. You would do well, Isabella, to bury the past. There are worse men in Spain than Pedro Girón."

"I know of none, Beatriz. You needn't go on, for it is useless."

"I must go on. Suppose you had to marry a man like Joanna married."

Isabella had thought about that. Henry had proved no royal catch and might be to blame for most of Joanna's wickedness. He had let his country slip into near-anarchy, had not been able to prevent the civil war from flaring up, had allowed himself to sink into debauchery and degradation, and had ruined the national image abroad. Thousands of his subjects dubbed him "the

Impotent" and believed he had been unable to beget a child, and had permitted, perhaps hired Beltrán to beget one for him, and on his own wife, the queen herself. Then when he insisted on making the bastard heir to the crown, the nation split in two, leaving two powerful factions in control of the kingdom.

"Henry is pitiable," she said.

"But Pedro Girón is not like the king," said Beatriz. "He doesn't always take his pleasure with Moorish soldiers and boys. Nor is he as ugly as you insist. I'll admit he is overly hairy, but many women like that in a man and consider it a token of masculinity. And he's strong and a brave knight. Women find him attractive."

"I don't, and that is what matters, Beatriz. To me he is as ugly as a centipede, and I know his mind is uglier. He is cruel, coarse, vindictive, and the gleam that lights up his eyes when he looks at me, and even at little Alfonso, is ... revolting. My flesh crawls at the thought of those sweaty hands, of those thick lips—like raw liver. Pedro and I? Never! I'll find a way."

"Then you'd better hurry, for there's little time. If you're hoping Henry will change his mind, forget it. Even if he did, Joanna would countermand such an order, probably have the messenger who brought the message strangled. Your poor mother is shut up in Arévalo, or is it Madrigal this time? And if she were here, what could she do to help you? Did she ever, even once, thwart Henry? No, Isabella, with the Marquis of Villena, and Beltrán and Joanna determined to have Girón marry you, and with Henry as usual not his own man, you're as good as married to Girón already."

"Go away, Beatriz. You are cruel, as cruel as Joanna. I won't hear any more." Beatriz could hear her trying to stifle her sobs on the other side of the door.

Beatriz knew that she had gone too far, for Isabella rarely wept. Strange misgivings filled her and she wondered what had led her to say what she had. For a long time she knelt and then at last said, "I understand, Isabella. And you won't have to kill yourself for Pedro Girón. Leave him to me. I'll wait until the last minute. Then, if there is no other way, I have a dagger for Pedro Girón. If it means that much to you, never fear—I will use it."

6

On board their cousin's ship Don Antoni had much to tell his family. The thought that this might be the last chance to be together left him deeply moved. If only there had been time to send for little Jaume, but there hadn't been, so all they could do was believe that he would be safe in the little school in Pavia of Segarra. The less said the better about the child, and all of them, as though by agreement, left him out of their conversations. But that night, Don Antoni knew, he would have to discuss Jaume with Magdalena.

He went directly to the point a few hours after embarkation. "First of all," he told them, "our uncle Bertrán is not an uncle at all. He is my father and your grandsire, Juan Baptista and Bartolomeu. And he is King John's bastard half brother and Prince Ferdinand's uncle."

"But your parents, Antoni—Don Ferrán and Doña Clara," said Magdalena, stunned, "what of them? All of us thought they were your mother and father, and when they died, when Juan Baptista was a child and before Jaume was born, we all wept as though for family."

"They adopted me, took me in when Bertrán brought me here as a very young child, really an infant. But let me tell the whole story before you ask me more. Bertrán, when he was a page at the court of King John's father, fell in love with one of the old queen's ladies in waiting, a girl from Lombardy of noble stock. But Bertrán was illegitimate, and what is more important, he is the half-brother of the present king. Though he was a member of the royal family, her parents did not want their daughter to marry a bastard, so he and my mother threw discretion to the winds, and accidentally, of course, they became my parents. Her parents took her home, as soon as they found out, and there they married her off pregnant to a rich farmer. I suppose they dowered her well, and promised him God knows what to let the world believe that I was his child. Considering who her parents were, it is no wonder that the farmer agreed."

Doña Magdalena, still in shock, said that she supposed this accounted for Antoni's red hair, height, and blue eyes, as well as those of Juan Baptista's.

Juan Baptista took his mother's hand and she rested her head on his shoulder. "You never suspected, mother?"

"Never. But even if I had, I would have married Antoni. Ours was and has been a marriage of love, a rare thing in Catalonia. I was fortunate in this, far more so than the poor Lombard girl who bore your father and had to give up her lover and had to let Bertrán take him back to Barcelona."

Don Antoni took her other hand and then continued. "So this is our secret history. This is why Bertrán planned the escape which he feared we would some day have to make. He realized that once his half-brother John became king and learned that Bertrán had a son and three grandsons, all of us would be in danger."

Juan Baptista felt a chill run down his spine and congeal in his gut. "My God, father," he said, "this means Prince Ferdinand and I are cousins!"

"First cousins once removed, " said Magdalena, "but cousins all the same. Your father and he are first cousins. What an unlucky relationship!"

"Especially so, my dear, when Catalonia is in the middle of a rebellion. Think what would happen if the rebels had found out and tried to involve us. This is what Bertrán feared from the moment the rebellion began and why, when he learned that we were secret sympathizers of the king's enemies, he knew he had to plan an escape for us. This is why for years we practiced our escape from our house to avoid imprisonment or worse. What haunts me now is Bertrán's fate. Since the king's troops have attacked our house, I must assume that he knows our kinship with Bertrán. When Juan Baptista told me of his encounter with Prince Ferdinand and that he had threatened to tell his father, the king, I opened the tunnel which Bertrán had showed me long ago to make certain that we could use it. I examined the end of it, the part the wall covered, and I found that no one looking from the outside could possibly suspect that a hidden opening existed."

"Is there more to the plan, father?" asked Bartolomeu.

"Much more, son. All carefully worked out. I'll come to it a little later. I believe that Bertrán took every contingency into account. I know that we must follow his plan, even though we do not like parts of it. You will soon see what I mean."

Doña Magdalena shook her head. "I'm certain that Bertrán would never allow them to capture him, Antoni. He had an escape all his own. Once when you and I visited the capital, he took me into his study for a chat. I learned how well he knew King John and that being his half brother was nothing like security."

"Would the king torture his own half-brother to make him betray us, mother?"

"Look what he did to his son, Don Carlos, his *own son*. I'm certain Bertrán knew perfectly well what would happen to him, once the king learned our secret. That time in his study he said, 'Magdalena, we live in a wicked world. Therefore, we should always prepare for a quick exit from it. Your husband and I have made certain plans of which I'm sure he will acquaint you, but there is another method of escape, in case all else fails.' Then he handed me a small vial filled with a pale green liquid, and he said, 'This is the kind of exit I have in mind, my dear. Keep it, and although I pray you may never have to use it, you just might, since you live in Catalonia.' Yes, I believe that Bertrán, sensing danger, drank from his own vial and found his exit."

"Thank the Virgin of Montserrat!" said Bartolomeu fervently. "Just think, without Bertrán's plan and Our Lady enabling us to carry it out, we might, like Bertrán, be lying on a slab of stone with poison in our bellies."

For a long time no one spoke. The ship, under a strong wind, made good speed and with each mile they all knew they were nearer to safety. Even if they were pursued, they had a long head start and should reach their destination in Italy. And, of course, King John and Ferdinand must have been thrown off their trail by the stories that their ship had sailed for France.

Antoni continued his explanation and laid out the rest of the plan. "As you know, we're bound for Genoa, which is part of the realm of our enemies, for King John is also King of Genoa and Sicily. Naples seemed to Bertrán the safest refuge. And now I come to the part of the plan you will not like, and you, in particular, Magdalena. We can't stay together, and we'll have to change our names. Bertrán felt that we have to depend on kith and kin, since only family can be trusted. Your mother and I," he continued, turning to his sons, "shall travel immediately to Lombardy. Bertrán maintained correspondence with his Lombard sweetheart across many, many years. I carry a letter to her, and, even if she has passed away, she will have arranged shelter for us. Lombardy is vast and it's not under the sway of Aragón. Juan Baptista will stay with distant cousins in Genoa, and Bartolomeu with relatives in France."

For the first time in his life Juan Baptista saw his mother break down and sob. She looked as though she might faint, so he slipped his arm around her shoulders and held her close. "Antoni," she managed to say, "how can I ever forgive you? Do you mean to say that you plan to separate me from my boys. Hasn't the loss of little Jaume been enough? My God, Juan Baptista is not yet fifteen. How can a child look after himself in a god-forsaken city like Genoa, which they say is the cradle of criminals? He wouldn't last a week, even if you gave him money. And Bartolomeu, man though he is, must live with strangers in a foreign land? You go to Lombardy, Antoni. I'll stay with Juan Baptista, wherever you plan to leave him;"

"No wife, you will not. Did you really think I'd strand the boy and let him forage for himself? How could you think that of me? Bertrán arranged it all, and we will follow his plan here, as we have followed it with success so far. In Genoa the Coloms have poor relations, and their being poor will insure Juan Baptista's safety. Who would expect to find an heir to the House of Colom in the cottage of a woolmerchant and a dyer of wool? He'll live as the apprentice of a distant cousin whose name is Giacomo Colombo. Of course it's all to be temporary, but for a time, Juan Baptista will have a job and he can earn his bread. Remember, we are all but destitute. We have a little money and we have your jewels, but none of this will last. We have to consider every single opportunity. That is what Bertrán did when he drew up his plan. He even sent money to Giacomo to make certain that our son would be well cared for. And we can keep in touch, if we do so with care, and perhaps next spring, when they shear the sheep in Lombardy, Giacomo will bring him to make us a visit."

Magdalena, as if trying to grasp some hope from what to her appeared to be a terrible decision, tried to comfort Juan Baptista. "At least," she said, "Juan Baptista knows some Italian, which I certainly do not."

"I may know it better than you think, mother. I learned a good deal in our school in Pavia, and don't you recall the summer I went with Bartolomeu, that whole summer he was studying in Cousin Mossen's big school in Barcelona? If you had let me go there longer I'd have perfected all I learned with my brother."

"Father," interrupted Bartolomeu, "Juan Baptista took to education like a duck to water. He helped me study and he outdid me in philosophy, Latin, Catalan and Italian grammar, and even mathematics. Only in navigation did I surpass him, and he was good in that as well."

This last led Juan Baptista to return to a subject his father tired of hearing. "Oh father," he said, risking rebuke, "Why can't you apprentice me to Cousin Jeannot and let me sail with him on this very ship. Even the name, the *Montserrat*, would be propitious. You know how much I want to follow in Bartolomeu's steps, learn the sea, make maps, explore. Father, I beseech you! Let me go with Bartolomeu and Jeannot."

"Enough," snapped Antoni. "I am determined to follow Bertrán's plan, which so far, you'll all have to admit, has been perfection. By now King John and Ferdinand must know on which ship we sailed, so the *Montserrat* will not be safe for a long time in Aragonese waters. One of us sailing in Jeannot's ships will be enough. If Bartolomeu should be captured, you would be able to carry on our family line."

Bartolomeu was relieved that Bertrán's plan did not interfere with his career as a mapmaker and sailor. But he was not prepared for the details of Bertrán's plan for him.

"You," said Antoni, "are to sail from Genoa with Jeannot to Calais where he will introduce you to another cousin whose name is Guillaume Casanove Coulon. He's a wealthy man, important among navigators everywhere. And he's a corsair, too, secretly, as well as an admiral in the French Navy. Under Coulon you can strike many a blow at King John and that devil of a son of his."

"Now," said Magdalena, "I do hate Bertrán. His plan will turn one son into a tradesman, and not in a very good trade at that, and the other is to become a pirate."

"But a member of the Navy of France as well, mother," said Bartolomeu, already thrilled at the prospect of an exciting life in a foreign land under the backing of a powerful kinsman.

"There is one last lesson taught me by Bertrán," said Don Antoni, "and this is our password when we seek out other Coloms. You remember that I told it to you. It is 'I come as a dove.' I know you're aware that our name Colom means 'dove,' but sometimes people forget the meanings of proper names. When you tell a member of our far-flung family that you 'come as a dove,' you mean you come as a Colom. And there is another aspect of this family's name that we all have to remember when we travel in foreign lands. We change our name, but we do not change its meaning. In Italy our name is Colombo; if we use the Latin form, we are called Columbus; but Coulon in French does not mean 'dove,' so it must be a corruption of the Latin or Catalan form; and, of course, in Castile and León our name's Colón. But all of us have a dove on our coat-of-arms, and we all know that we form an extensive clan across most of the Mediterranean.

"And I should like to go back to Juan Baptista's mention of his studies in Pavia, in our little Catalonian Pavia of Segarra," continued Don Antoni. "When opportunity comes, state that you studied in Pavia, and people will think you mean at the great University of Pavia in Italy. Some of the world's great minds teach there in all fields of study. In Italy, indeed everywhere in Europe and in many parts of Asia and North Africa, the reputation of that university is highly respected. Any man who has studied there always can count upon the respect of educated people."

"So, Antoni," Magdalena interrupted, "what other surprises do you have for us? Today you have informed us that you are a bastard, you have taught your sons to practice the art of deception as to their education, that we shall depend upon your mother, who sinned with your father, if she still lives, or upon her friends; and now you make it plain that the family is practically a secret order. Your family makes far more of cousins than any people I know, except one. Are you soon to tell us that you and your sons have Hebrew blood?"

For the first time in the family's experience Don Antoni lost his self control, and, for the first time, too, they saw him slap his wife hard in the face. His voice broke. He looked apoplectic, and he could hardly breathe. He trembled and sweat appeared on his forehead. "Magdalena," he croaked at last, "I will swear that I did not hear that question. Never let me hear it again!" And insofar as Juan Baptista knew, no one ever did, for the topic was unmentionable.

7

Juan Baptista loathed Genoa, and he hated his cousin Giacomo, called the stingiest man in Italy, and his wife Carlotta, known as the meanest woman. He hated his new name and cringed when people called him by it—Giovanni Battista Colombo. What a parody of the good name that had been his! But Bertrán had decreed it so in his plan, which Giovanni now hated as much as he had come to hate the grandfather who had concocted it. Carlotta fed him little, she sold the clothes he had worn when he came to her house and all the ones he had in his valise. And his cousin Giacomo worked him all day at wool carding and made him stink of sheep. Only at night, when the last of the day's work had been finished and the supper dishes washed—by Giovanni Colombo, of course—could he leave the house and run to the harbor to meet three of the few friends he had made. All three, Pietro, Tomaso and Alfredo were sailors, only a few years older than he, and they owned a small sloop in which they ran contraband from Genoa to Corsica. He begged them to take him with them, and at first they demurred. Then one happy day they needed an extra hand and told him he could go. He couldn't believe his luck.

They departed one night after vespers, for *contrabandistas* worked after dark, and they had a second reason for departure by night. Giovanni had to wait until his work was done, the supper dishes washed, and his cousins in bed before he could leave the house.

"How long will the trip take?" he asked.

"All night and most of the next day to get there. And we'll plan that long to return. And we'll have to get home at night."

"If I'm gone that long, they'll beat me half to death," said Giovanni, wishing they could call him Juan Baptista and knowing they couldn't, "but it'll be worth it. God, how I need to get away from them and that house!"

The trip to Corsica was perfect over a calm sea and under a full moon. The three Italians sang and drank, when they weren't steering, and they told stories of escapades and of the girls they knew on the island. "We'll find one for you, Giovanni. You want one don't you?" And when he hesitated, their eyes grew large and they roared with laughter. "You're a virgin, ain't you, kid? My God, wait till Angelina gets her hand on you. Everybody knows how she loves to break in a virgin boy, especially one as pretty as Giovanni."

He recalled how he had squirmed in embarrassment, and then, how he had felt something rise between his legs the way it did when he dreamed and fantasized. Fearful and yet anxious, he could hardly wait until the early morning hours when the sloop slipped up a small tidal creek and ran ashore. Rough men helped to beach her and unload the cargo of Genoese red wine and Spanish daggers. Afterwards they hurried to a tavern, dark and tangy with the smell of fish, sweat and smoke, and there Pietro found his girl, Alfredo the woman who ran the tavern, and Tomaso a mulatto serving wench, so fat that Giovanni marveled that she could do what he knew Tomaso expected of her. He wormed his way into a corner near the fireplace and, now that the time had come, he wished he were home in bed, even in Giacomo's cold house. When he saw Pietro chuckling and pointing at him in his corner, he wanted to hide, but there was no place.

Suddenly he saw a tall woman was making her way between the tables toward him. "You're Giovanni, aren't you, the one they've told me so much about?" He stood up and saw that he towered over her. "I like a tall man," she said. "Come with Angelina, and she'll make you very happy."

And then he was going with her hand in hand. A new warmth ran up his arm from the hand she held and spread upward into his face and downward, too. In her bedroom she helped him remove his clothes, and even when she made him take off his *bragas*, he failed to feel the embarrassment and dread he had anticipated. Looking at him nude in the light of the lamp, she said what he would learn to hear in many bedrooms from many women. "Is that you?" she gasped as she touched him where no one had ever touched him before. "Are you really just fifteen? By all the saints, I'm glad I have you before you grow any more!"

Giovanni, guided by some ancient instinct, did what experienced men did when they were with Angelina. She didn't have to guide him. Somehow he knew, and knowing, was inordinately proud of himself.

"You'd be a god, Giovanni, if you weren't so skinny, but the part that counts needs no fattening up. I believe Pietro lied to me; If you're a virgin, so am I."

Five times that night Giovanni Battista Colombo pleasured Angelina, and she swore afterwards that in all her thirty years she had never been so satisfied. "He filled me to the brim," she told Pietro. "If you ever return to my tavern, don't come without that, that...."

***

Homeward bound they made him tell over and over all he'd done with Angelina. "Five times you say. You swear it?" And they assured him that they were pleased how hard he worked on board and how willing he was. "Lord, Giovanni, why don't you tell those cousins to go to hell and leave them? Your part of the pay for this trip is more than you'll get from being an apprentice for Giacomo in months."

Without a second's hesitation he accepted. To be at sea, to have become a man through a woman's machinations, to be making a little money, to have three friends as wonderful as these! Nothing could be finer except an able seaman's job on the *Montserrat*. Later he wondered why Our Lady prevented it, for he was certain she had.

Pietro was at the tiller and the others were asleep when Giovanni was jerked awake as wind struck the sail. Lightning flashed out of a sky that had only a little while before seemed moonlit and calm. Huge waves sprang up from nowhere. He found himself up to his ankles in cold water.

"What do we do?" he cried, trying to make himself heard over the wind.

"Grab a bucket and bail!" yelled Alfredo, who was already bailing. "For God's sake, one of you down the sail!"

Giovanni bailed with all his might, but the water kept rising. And then, before the sail could come down, an impossible wind struck and the sloop turned over.

In the waves, Giovanni struggled frantically. Someone, later he remembered, it was Alfredo, fat Alfredo with the ever-present garlic breath, who unfolded him in his arms and tried to mount him in the water. He struggled, but Alfredo, maddened, would not let go. He was pushing him under. Giovanni, strangling, fought valiantly, but realized his strength would soon be gone. And he began to pray to his patron, Our Lady of Montserrat. And as he prayed, as though guided by her, he realized what to do. He bit Alfredo's thumb. The fat arms loosened and he slipped free and with a frantic kick managed to shoot away into the next oncoming wave. When he emerged, he turned to look for him. He was gone and he never appeared again.

In the distance he heard the cries of Tomaso and Pietro and swam toward that sound. Three times waves caught up with him and pulled him under. The fourth drove him straight into the two young men. He felt the jolt of a body against his. Hands snatched at him, Pietro's hands he saw, then Tomaso's. A wave struck, and before it could wash it away he saw blood on Pietro's mouth and on Tomaso's forehead. Then they were pushing him under.

"Fight," said a voice in his head, "free yourself, swim away from them! They're doomed! You aren't! You have to live! You have too much to do to die here before you carry out your destiny!"

From a distance he heard their screams until they screamed no more, and then he treaded water until daylight came. And there, clearly revealed by the rising sun, he saw the outlines of the two spires of the Cathedral of Genoa. "If only it hadn't been dark," he moaned, "we'd have seen the shore and they wouldn't have been so scared that they drowned each other."

Fishermen headed out to sea found him still floating and treading water and turned back to take him to shore. For three days Carlotta had to nurse him, a task she did unwillingly. And all through his delirium, all through the pain of coughing and vomiting, one thought was in his mind. "Why did I live and the others die? Why were they so frightened that Pietro and Tomaso drowned each other and Alfredo tried to drown me?"

***

A month later, Giovanni experienced another evidence of what he was beginning to regard as divine protection for a purpose not yet clear to him. One afternoon when Giacomo was working him harder than usual, he rebelled, his back ramrod stiff. "I'm too tired, cousin," he said, "And the heat from the dye is making me sick. Let's wait until the cauldron cools and then I'll dye the skeins."

Giacomo was furious. "You'll dye them now, damn you, or you'll get no supper!" And to emphasize his point, he placed his hands against Giovanni's chest and shoved him toward the cauldron much too hard. Then, to his horror and Giovanni's, the boy stepped against the cauldron and fell backward into it. His scream brought Carlotta running from the kitchen. Together she and Giacomo pulled the moaning boy from the nearly-boiling liquid. He was dyed a deep purple and when they dried his body, they saw that he had been badly scalded.

"Damn you, Giacomo," cried his wife. "How will we explain this, if he dies, or even if he doesn't? I expect he'll have burn scars for life. His parents will take a terrible vengeance on us. That mother of his frightens me, and his father is a holy terror!"

"Get him to bed and I'll run for the doctor," shouted Giacomo.

The doctor, more of a quack than a professional, brought his assistant with him, his own ancient mother. She looked once at the half-conscious Giovanni, touched his burning skin, and shook her head. She applied olive oil mixed with pounded sweet basil, placed a sheepskin under him and propped sheets over him so that they didn't touch his body. "Pat the oil and basil on him, all over him, Carlotta, and do it every hour. Make him drink this laudanum for the pain. And force him to drink lots of water.

"Even at night?"

"Certainly at night, and all night, and every hour! You have a badly injured boy here. He may not live. And even if he does, I fear a terrible disfigurement."

For a whole week Giovanni lay as though dead. He felt nothing, and would only swallow water, laudanum, and a thin broth. Under the coating of oil and basil huge blisters formed and finally broke. At the end of the week he regained consciousness and kept calling upon his patroness, Our Lady of Montserrat. "He'd do better," said Carlotta caustically, "if he prayed to a good Italian Virgin."

"The Virgin is the Virgin, wherever She is," said Giacomo impatiently. "And from the way the blisters look, he'd better pray, for he looks like those souls we see in the paintings as they roast in hell."

When a month later, the dead skin flaked away, they were amazed to see clean, pink skin, with only an occasional spot likely to form a scar. The doctor raised his brows and his old mother shook her head. "This is the only time I've seen one live through what this lad suffered and come out practically unscathed."

"He prayed a lot," said Giacomo. "And so did Father Bertini."

Giovanni Battista Colombo listened and remembered what had happened at sea. He almost looked forward to a third assurance that he was destined for great things.

8

As usual when she began to fall asleep Isabella knew that she would dream, and she waited in anticipation no longer tinged with uneasiness. Father de Coca himself had assured her that all of the dreams she had repeated to him at confessional were messages sent her by God Himself. The last and most terrifying had been a nightmare which had left her weak. Perhaps as she lay down a second night on a hard bench in a chilly tower, the dream would be more pleasant. It flowed into her brain like a mist and filled it.

Ávila de los Caballeros, Ávila City of Knights, had always seemed to her to point a dark finger of stone at heaven. At the foot of the steep hill on which it stands flows the River Adaja, a trickle in the heat of summer, flanked by the *vega*, parched and dry. On that midday of June 1465 it loomed against the sun-washed sky like a beacon in gray granite behind its eighty-eight towers. Under its grim battlements even grimmer events were scheduled to unfold, and great crowds had assembled. Through the gates, hour after hour since dawn poured unbroken streams of humanity, moving slowly as if stunned at the news of what was to take place. From across the plain, almost hidden in clouds of ocher dust, came other multitudes wending their slow way in impatient lines along the roads to the city. All roads that morning led to Ávila, and Isabella knew that no one who attended would ever forget the famous impeachment play enacted in the center of the little plain under a burning Castilian sun with the long shadows of the great fortress lying cool and stark against the ground.

She and Don Diego de Bobadilla, father of her friend Beatriz, had ridden all night in order to arrive in time. Like thousands of other Spaniards they had felt compelled to witness what was to take place, and since what affected the king, indirectly concerned his half-sister, Isabella had insisted upon coming. Don Diego's spies had informed him that the League, which was in rebellion against the king, had been preparing a strange spectacle for weeks, and that although they could not learn the particulars, enough had leaked out to justify their report. The king was to be ridiculed publicly. Furthermore, they had it on the best authority that the young Prince Alfonso, Isabella's brother, would play an important and significant part in the day's events. The news that Alfonso would be there made Isabella very anxious to attend, since news of him was scant these days and that which reached her she found difficult to accept. They said that he had greatly matured, that he had become as wise an administrator as Villena himself, and that the League considered him a capable knight. All this seemed incredible to her, for she knew he was only a boy of eleven and she doubted that he could have changed so much in a few short months, since the League had spirited him away from the court, making of him more a prisoner than a leader.

Isabella remembered how relieved she had been to see him taken away. She had missed him terribly, for aside from Beatriz, Alfonso was the only human being at court she really loved; but she cheerfully suffered the pangs of separation, for in Ávila the boy was safe. There, under the tutelage of Alfonso Carrillo, Archbishop of Toledo, Primate of Spain, no spiritual harm could come to him. In the City of Knights there were no Moorish tutors instructed by Henry to corrupt the little boy, no Beltrán de la Cueva and his royal paramour, always hoping for some fatal accident which might remove the child from the succession. But the worst of all had been the dark presence of Pedro Girón, suggesting, posturing, and occasionally even exhibiting himself to the boy in some dark hall, and once even in Alfonso's own private bedroom. That time Isabella had heard the scuffle and had run to Alfonso in time to scare the man off.

She could hardly wait to see her brother, although she knew that it must be no more than a glimpse from a distance. It would not do for her to be recognized by people of the League. Don Diego had made it clear to her that for the present she should stay clear of any open association with the Archbishop of Toledo and her little brother. He pointed out that half the country's nobles supported the king, and that most of the clergy insisted, inasmuch as Henry was the Lord's anointed, that no one could lawfully supplant him, no matter how evil and inefficient he might be. Any revolt against Henry, she believed, was defiance of God Almighty, and she wondered if heaven would weigh Alfonso's part in all this to his discredit. Surely not, for the Prince was still a minor and not responsible for his part in the civil war. What puzzled her was the Archbishop's stance, for as Spain's Primate surely he should have supported Henry, but he was the staunchest of Henry's enemies. She agreed with Don Diego, however, as concerned avoiding direct contact with her brother, for she understood that she must remain unidentified with the League, that even though her sympathies were with the Archbishop and Alfonso, she must give the appearance of neutrality. There was the chance, Don Diego reminded her, that she herself might succeed to the throne, since Henry would not live forever, and who could say what Alfonso's part in the civil war would mean to his career? If both Henry and Alfonso died, a very possible contingency in days when poisoning was in fashion and plague was abroad, the succession might well be dropped in her lap whether she wanted it or not. The very thought of herself as a candidate for rule made her nervous. If she ruled, it would be at the dictate of duty, not because she desired a crown which had brought only grief to her father and mother and worse to Joanna and Henry. Still, if she saw a chance to prevent Joanna's bastard daughter from one day ruling, then she knew she would have to fight for the throne and the preservation of the country. That had been bred into her from the time she could comprehend what duty meant.

From the first day of the war the Spanish cities declared their preference. Valladolid declared for Henry and closed its mighty gates; Segovia was the king's also, as well as Madrid; but many great cities rejected him and his queen and supported the little Prince.

Henry had been panic-stricken at the cleavage made in the realm. He was afraid to leave the safety of city walls and did all he could to prevent Beltrán from venturing out, even when his duties demanded it. And when Beltrán was set upon by a group knights who attacked him in a body, Henry lost his head. Not even an attack upon his own person near Segovia had frightened him so much. He agreed to parley with his enemies and abjectly consented to whatever demands they made. No wonder Beltrán and Joanna were thrown into panic, for Henry at the League's insistence, removed Beltrán from his post as Grand Master of Calatrava. The fact that he made him Count of Ledesma almost immediately did not remove the alarm they felt. Henry then proclaimed that he was not the father of Joanna's daughter, he promised to disband his Moorish guard, to lead a more Christian life and to recognize his half-sister Isabella as his rightful heir. No wonder his advisers cursed him under their breaths. To sign all that away at the Concord of Medina del Campo had astounded them, one and all. Not even his remarks later that the Concord was only a scrap of paper and could be burned satisfied them. All that held them together was the knowledge that he had been anointed King of Castile by Holy Church.

Now, today, Isabella and all Spain would see the climax of his disgrace, if what the spies reported was true. She felt a strange uneasiness as she surveyed the rapidly filling plain, but was glad that Don Diego had brought her in time to find a place so close to the great stage she saw dominating the entire area from its earthen pyramid.

All round she recognized men she knew, some in disguise like herself, and realized that Henry's friends as well as his foes were in attendance. As she watched, the plain filled completely and the people spilled back all the way to the walls of Ávila and up into the rocks of the surrounding hills. She was certain that those on the fringes of the multitude could not possibly hear what the speakers would say from the platform, and again she congratulated herself for having such a vantage point. Not fifty feet away rose the pyramid. She would miss nothing.

As she surveyed the platform carefully, she gasped with astonishment. On a throne sat a figure she immediately recognized. It was the king! Yet how could it be? She knew perfectly well that Henry could not be there, for he was far away in Andalusia surrounded by his Moors whom he had reassembled almost before the ink had dried on the Concord of Medina del Campo.

"What does it mean, Don Diego?" she asked. "Who is that on the platform?"

"An effigy, Princess. A very life-like effigy,"

"I never saw anything so real, Don Diego. The robe is an exact replica of Henry's mourning cloak, the one sent him by the King of Granada. I know the patterns well, and there they are sewn into the velvet. And look what is around the neck. It's Henry's opal necklace, the piece he prizes most."

"The crown looks real, too," said Don Diego. "But it's impossible that there could be two pointed Gothic crowns like that, and yet I see one here before my eyes. If I didn't know that the authentic one was in the royal treasury in Segovia, I'd take an oath that it is here."

"What about the scepter and the sword?"

"From this distance, Princess, they look real, too, but as to what purpose they will serve I am as much in the dark as you. Anyway, we won't have long to wait, for something is beginning to happen."

She looked, shading her eyes against the intensity of the sun, and saw a line of heralds carrying the banners of Castile and León filing across the stage to form a brilliant wall of color behind the effigy. In the wind from the snow-capped ridges of the Guadarramas the banners rippled like things alive. She saw rank on rank of men-at-arms come to attention at the foot of the pyramid and heard a deep ominous roar from the multitude. A master hand had cast this drama. How crafty and clever to dress the men in the uniform of the Moorish Guard! Only the Archbishop of Toledo could have planned so well. She found herself adding her voice to the crowd's and realized that the people hated the Moors as much as she. Yes, the mind of the archbishop, who understood far better than King Henry the thinking of the Spanish people, had been the dramatist.

Even the choice of the plain before Ávila was a masterly touch. Gloomy even in dazzling sunshine, like no other panorama in Spain, with great piles of boulders tossed helter-skelter, as if giants in some bygone age had bombarded the city on its gray heights. A funeral setting for a royal demise.

People from all Spain had flocked to see this. She saw peasants from many provinces, easily identified by their distinctive costumes. Common people from Castile stood in groups everywhere, simple and sturdy, who were the nation's hidden wealth, its source of strength and greatness. Spanish knights and men from beyond the Pyrenees—Frenchmen, Burgundians, even Englishmen—waited avidly. Haughty contingents of Moors, emissaries from the Kingdom of Granada, and even from Barbary, made silent pools of color. Jews, less haughty, but equally proud, spoke to no one but missed nothing. Milling in that vast concourse she saw students from Salamanca and Paris, monks from nearby monasteries, wandering Dominican friars, soldiers, gypsies, jugglers, troubadours, public women, even an abbess and five of her nuns.

The drama was beginning. Down from the gates of Ávila wound a procession marching to doleful cadence among the Cyclopean boulders. Headed by a double line of monks chanting the soul-shaking, haunting diapason of the *Miserere mei*, the procession floated downward, imposing, dignified, the gorgeous vestments of the high clergy ablaze against the leaden escarpment rising toward the towers. These were the judges to sit at Henry's trial. The march was long, unending, and the Archbishop of Toledo had mounted to the top of the stairs leading to the platform and stood facing the effigy of the king when the stragglers passed out through the gates of the city.

High Mass began and Isabella stopped looking for Alfonso and allowed herself to be drawn into the vortex of pageantry unfolding before her. After the Archbishop had pronounced the *Missa est*, she rose to her feet with ten thousand others, her soul thrilling to the wild blast of a hundred silver trumpets. To the right and left she saw men-at-arms snap to attention as across the vast throng rang out the martial airs of the armies of the League. The exotic fragrance of incense exalted her, intense and pungently sweet as mountain herbs, and the deep-voiced priestly chant made her tremble. With thousands she fell to her knees again as a life-sized silver crucifix moved past her through the packed ranks.

Then swift as thought the music changed. Angels were singing now, a hundred choir boys raised their voices in the song of exultation that drifted clear and unbearably sweet into the heavens. Isabella and the men about her wept unabashed at the sheer divinity of it, knowing that of all the melodies of earth none is more beautiful than those sung by boys. All of a sudden she began to understand the reason behind the change in the song. This was all a part of the Impeachment Play.

Don Diego was clutching her arm in a grip that hurt. He was pointing and she saw in the distance a golden litter swaying between two lines of knights in full ceremonial armor. Majestically it moved down the corridor formed by lines of pikemen that extended from far back in the crowd to the very foot of the pyramid. Heralds carrying more banners of Castile and León marched on either side of the litter, and Isabella strained for a glimpse of her brother.

"Don't wave, Princess," whispered Don Diego, "You mustn't be seen by either party."

"I shan't, Don Diego, but it will be hard not to. He'll pass so close."

In jubilation the trumpets saluted the Prince. "Spain for Alfonso!" they screamed. "Spain is the League's."

Deafening waves of applause and acclamation rolled across the plain as Alfonso's cortège passed along the corridor of knights. Scores of censers turned the air to incense. Isabella trembled, lost utterly now in the spectacle, and her people trembled with her. She saw the Primate of Spain, the frightening Archbishop of Toledo, stride from the assembled prelates. Like the general of a victorious army he approached the throne where the effigy sat in gloomy splendor. To its right, facing it, sat the clergy, a pattern of dazzling color, and at the left the nobles, no less gorgeous in their robes of state.

Then a trumpet blared and the air was silver with swords uplifted, and lances sparkled in little stabs of gold in the twilight of dust curling around the base of the mound. Slowly Alfonso Carrillo raised his arms. Ten thousand people started as the trumpet screamed for silence. They heard the great prelate pronounce the benediction, thunder it, rather, and they knelt for the third time.

As Isabella rose, Don Diego leaned near her and whispered, "What a show! Look at the men bearing the Prince's litter. Great lords every one of them! There's Iñigo de Manrique, Count of Placencia. I see Don Álvaro de Zúñiga, too, and who is that with his back to us kissing the Archbishop's ring?"

"Rodrigo Pimental, Count of Benavente," replied Isabella. "I recognized his coat-of-arms before he turned. And look. Look! The new Grand Master of Alcántara!"

"Yes, and isn't that Pedro Puerto Carrero, Count of Medellín? Oh, they're all here, all the nobles of the League. Now they're mounting the stair."

Isabella watched the nobles find seats opposite the clergy. When all was still, a herald in crimson and gold stepped to the edge of the platform directly in front of the effigy. In his hand flapped a long document, officially covered with seals. Then his voice rose, unbelievably powerful in volume, strengthened by long years of practice, until it carried to the outermost limits of the *vega*.

"Hear, men of Castile, hear Grandees of Spain, hear nobles and commoners, and all the minions of Holy Church. King Henry, unworthy to wear the crown of his ancestors, can no longer wear it. God is pleased this day to remove him from authority through the ministers of the people of the realm. He is pleased to punish his many crimes.

"King Henry is unworthy," thundered on the herald, "to wear the crown he cannot call his own, for it is the pernicious Beltrán de la Cueva, Count of Ledesma, who rules Castile.

"He is unworthy of the scepter because he has betrayed his realm by naming a bastard, the child of Queen Joanna and Beltrán de la Cueva, his heir instead of his brother, Prince Alfonso."

Isabella's mind reeled. Every word of it was true and everyone in Castile knew it and gossiped about it. But today before the assembled subjects of the kingdom, before foreign diplomats, before infidel Moors and common folk from the mountains around Ávila, the royal house of Trastámara was dishonored publicly. Didn't Villena and the Archbishop realize that to cast filth on Henry was to cast it on Alfonso too?

There was more, and she forgot to think. Proclamation was abetted by symbolic dethronement. Don Diego's hand was hurting her arm again, but she scarcely noticed.

"Look well, Princess," he was saying, "for what you see today must never leave your memory. The Archbishop is going right up to the effigy."

Isabella saw the tall form striding purposefully to the figure of the king. Solemnly he lifted the Gothic crown from the russet wig made to look so much like Henry's hair. Then she saw what he was about to do and held her breath. He was going to hurl the crown down all the way to the base of the mound. Then he threw it, and she caught the flash of gold as it hurtled earthward to land in the dust. Symbolically Holy Church had removed the emblem of sovereignty from the Lord's anointed. Everyone saw it happen. Sacrilege? Blasphemy? And yet the Church had done this thing through its Archbishop. She wondered if ever before heaven had shattered one of Christendom's oldest traditions or if the Church had the right to countermand God's own choice of a monarch. She shivered and from the corner of her eye she saw thousands cross themselves and glance fearfully at the sky.

Next came the Count of Placencia, walking like a man in the grip of a great anger. Furiously he tore the sword of Justice from the effigy, and a streak of silver light arced its way down from the top of the pyramid into the dust. Every ignorant peasant in Spain understood this allegory.

The Count of Benavente was the third to approach the king, for now, even to Isabella, it was the king. From the royal hand he snatched the scepter and tossed it contemptuously over the edge of the platform. Isabella, the entire multitude, would not have been surprised to see the king rise from the throne and flee the stage.

When the scepter lay in the dust, the universal leveler, along with the other emblems of royal power, the final dishonor was perpetuated. It was Don Diego de Zúñiga who threw down the effigy of the king, his liege lord.

For a long moment no one moved. Then a sound, terrible, beast-like, inarticulate, horrible, struck her ears. The mob, now a monster, fell upon the pitiful figure of its king. It trampled, spat upon, tore, and finally burned the effigy until nothing remained of it but a heap of charred cloth and plaster. Isabella closed her eyes. Many people kept casting uneasy glances at heaven, but the sky stayed cloudless and God made no thunder. Serene, calm, God looked down and was indifferent to the degradation of the King of Castile. When she opened her eyes the last scrap of the effigy had vanished into the possession of souvenir hunters. Of the crown, the Sword of Justice, and the scepter, not a sign remained.

Again the trumpets, wild, triumphant. Alfonso made his entrance then. Isabella saw his knights lift him to their shoulders and carry him from the litter, just as the kings of the Visigoths had been carried long ago, to the throne atop the pyramid. She saw him kiss the Archbishop's ring, saw the stern old man embrace him, watched the great houses of Spain from Biscay to Gibraltar kneel and yield him fealty. How slender he looked, and yet how perfectly regal amid all that glitter of jewels and the flash of armor and miters up there half-hidden in the scarlet vestments and the clouds of incense! But he was still a child, still really a boy. She could see that well enough. She knew her brother. Alfonso was no ambitious prince, eager to wrest the throne from Henry's grasp, He was a pawn, and still the little brother she worshiped.

Don Diego and Isabella watched them lead him down from the stage to a beautiful white Arabian mare. They remembered how he loved horses, and in her mind's eyes she could see them wheedling him into his robes and his breastplate with the promise of a steed this fine. She and Don Diego did not follow him up into the city with the multitude to see his coronation. They had seen enough.

Chilled by the cold and stiff from the hardness of the bench, Isabella opened her eyes and wondered how she had returned from Ávila to the tower of Ocaña. Another day. What would it bring?

An hour later a strange thing happened. The palace servants looked up from their morning duties in amazement to see the queen pass across the audience chamber and mount the stairs to the tower. It was hours before her usual time of arising.

Clearly Isabella heard her voice in the corridor, heard her dismiss the Moors. Then her rap came and she called Isabella by name, a thing she rarely did.

"I am here, Joanna."

"Open the door and let me in, Princess. I must talk with you. The guards have gone."

"How do I know they have, Joanna? Some might have stayed. No. The door stays barred. Talk through it if you wish to speak to me. I shall hear you."

She heard the queen stifle a curse and knew how concerned she must be to exercise so much self control. Then she heard the click of Joanna's sandals as she walked to the head of the stairs to call sharply for a chair, heard her come back to the door. When the chair arrived, she must have sat down.

"Isabella, listen to me," said the queen, "even if it must be through the door. I want to help you and at the same time help myself. Pedro Girón will take you away from all of us you hate, far away to Andalusia or Extremadura. You'll be rid of us and I won't be forever at your throat. We might be at peace if we didn't have to look at one another day in and day out."

"That would be pleasant, Joanna, but I prefer even looking at you than at Pedro Girón."

"Isabella," continued the queen, swallowing her anger with great effort, "it wouldn't be so bad with Don Pedro. If you would go with him willingly there'd be no trouble. But let me warn you, don't go as a recalcitrant bride. Don't forget little Pilar González and what happened to her when they married her to that duke from Barcelona. She was in love with a page at this court, but her father needed the political connections the duke could supply. Remember? Would you want to be treated like that? Will you let them shut you up in some bedroom with Pedro Girón, thirsting to beat down pride and resistance? Some men are like that, Isabella, and Girón is one of them. I have heard an good authority..."

"Don't worry for me, Joanna. I have the sword."

"That's no way to escape," said Joanna who believed she heard the hint of uncertainty in Isabella's voice. "The stakes are too high. Let Girón believe you want to marry him, since marry him you must. That way it will be much easier. Before long there'll be a child, and after that he won't bother you much—maybe not even once a year, unless you appear unwilling. Remember he has his whores, his Moorish boys, your brother the king. If you could bear the first year, and even if you couldn't learn to love him, the world is full of beautiful young men and you could find one and be happy with him."

"You can't frighten me, Joanna, or at least you can't frighten me enough. You don't want me to die here, do you? It wouldn't do, would it?"

"Isabella," whispered the queen, "you go too far. You *are* hard! You don't realize how much I want to have you miles away from here. You make me uncomfortable, if you must have the truth. You're too good, too pious, and you don't fit. You never will. You belong in a convent. Why won't you listen? Can't you see my side of it? For God's sake marry Girón and leave us before it's too late. I know you can find happiness, but not here. You might even find It with Girón, if you set that stubborn mind of yours to it. Do as the rest of us have done: take a lover. Don't you know I've seen you slyly ogling the squires, especially young Gómez Manrique and that good-looking page from Burgos, the one with the shoulders and all the yellow hair?"

"Take a lover like you took one, Joanna?"

"Yes. And be proud to. Beltrán *is* my lover, and how glad I am that he is! I've never had even the smallest regret, not even a pinch of remorse. I can endure all the foul remarks, all the sly innuendos, all the hateful references to his lowly birth."

"In reply to your remarks about lovers, I say this: Joanna you are a whore, just as the *Couplets of Mingo Revulgo* say you are."

"Damn the *Couplets of Mingo Revulgo*! What are they but the filth some bastard ashamed to sign his name to has written. I wish I could get my hands on him. A whore, you say? Listen and I will tell you a story. It is one that no one has ever heard from my lips nor will again. I was about your age when the Castilian ambassador came to Lisbon and asked for my hand in marriage in the name of his master, Henry of Castile. Imagine how thrilled I was. I wanted to leave Portugal and see the world, and Castile sounded so romantic, high in the mountains, like another world. I was bored with Lisbon and with my brother and his court, even though he had been good to me. I was tired of hearing people gossip about me and call me wild. Actually I wasn't. All I did was keep a train of young ladies-in-waiting some didn't approve of. We played at having a court of love in the old troubadour way. There wasn't a speck of harm in it. Just pretty young nobles playing troubadour, singing sweet and inane love songs, and dancing to the lute. And my aunt was never far away. A proper woman, Aunt Beatriz, though understanding, nonetheless firm. She saw nothing wrong in love songs and low-cut gowns, for she could remember her own girlhood. She was careful, however, and was the perfect guardian for her brother's most valuable marriage pawn.

"The court was delighted with the match. I was jubilant. Little sixteen-year-old Joanna, not quite a woman, to be Queen of Castile! I could hardly wait to have a word alone with the ambassador, the lying dog! How could he have looked into my innocent little-girl eyes and told me what he did? The King of Castile, he told me, was a young man, athletic, blue-eyed, with the red hair of the Plantagenets. Another Richard the Lion-Hearted. A great hunter, and on the tournament field a champion, a Cid.

"I was enthralled. To be Queen of Castile and wed to a story-book king, not a soft, fat grub like my brother! I trembled with newly awakened love for this athlete, this Spanish Achilles, this demigod, and desire once born in me, leaped like a flame. I felt like Oriana awaiting the embrace of Amadís in that pretty novel, and I was happy.

"But not for long. My brother saw to that. Alfonso was always frank and honest. He wanted the marriage with Castile. Portugal needed allies. But he was fair and he held nothing back. Perhaps he considered it a kindness. I know he regarded it a necessity. It would never do to send me unsuspecting into the morass of the Castilian court. I have tried to keep the thought that he meant to be kind before me all these years.

"Well, that afternoon he told me in his bluff, brotherly way what he knew of Henry of Trastámara, Henry IV of Castile. I had heard, of course, about Henry's divorce from Queen Blanche of Navarre and of how he had packed her off to her brother. She was barren, Henry claimed, or something far worse, for common gossip had it that she had bewitched his manhood, thereby precluding carnal union. What a beastly woman, I thought when the news first came to Lisbon. But my brother set me straight, He told me shocking things, shocking even when padded by a brother's kindness and consideration. Henry, he said, was called THE IMPOTENT by his own subjects, and I could see that there was no doubt in Alfonso's mind that he was impotent. He told me that if I married Henry, that is when I married him, since marry him I must, there could be no romance, no love between us. He pointed out that although Henry insisted he was potent with other women than Blanche, he really wasn't. 'Henry will keep to his own shadowy sex life, sister,' he said, 'and you must make a life of your own. You will be Queen, wealthy, envied, even loved, as you are here in Lisbon.'

"That morning in my brother's study I grew up, Isabella. All at once the world took on a different sheen, hard, starkly clear in every detail. The haze of romance lifted, and I could see the sunlight glinting on the harbor. but the glint was tinsel; the ladies at court looked tawdry and painted; I smelled bad odors and thought ugly thoughts. In those days I had a large library, for I read a great deal. I haven't read a book since I left Portugal. Books? Lies! A waste of time! Romance, chivalry, love—these I renounced. I would be hard, but I would be the Queen of Castile, and I would live for Joanna and her pleasure. These are hard thoughts, Isabella, for a girl of sixteen to think."

"Joanna, you could have refused. You admit that King Alfonso offered you the choice."

"He offered no such choice. What you may have heard of a choice—and surely not from me—was lies. I knew he expected me to marry Henry and no one else. There was really no escape. So I made the journey. With me went my ladies. When we entered the border town where Henry and his train waited, I was actually anxious to see him and have the matter over. When I met him I wished I had been in less haste, for I felt what I knew you felt that day you met him for the first time. I saw the blue eyes and the russet Plantagenet hair. But for me, who was to marry him it was a thousand times more horrible than it was for you. A sister, even a half-sister never has to face what a bride must. How weak my brother's imagination had been. I wanted to vomit. I wanted to die and be carried back to Lisbon for burial. But life isn't like that, Isabella. I married Henry and went with him into the nuptial chamber. There he told me he was indisposed and he turned his face to the wall. He had, by the way, put a stop to that horrid custom of letting a delegation of priests and nobles sit just outside the curtained bed to hear the sounds accompanying consummation. So neither of us had to pretend, to groan or cry out as though penetration had taken place and orgasm had occurred. You cannot imagine the relief I felt at his indifference, for all day I had dreaded the moment when he might feel obliged to show me some attention.

"So our life together began. Henry was polite and kind to me, but to him I was a stick of wood, a piece of necessary palace furniture. A queen, he seemed to think, needed only a throne.

"But I was young and from a line of amorous women. I began to rebel, and as my body matured I began to look about for someone to relieve my frustrations. I even envied poor Blanche immured in some cell in Navarre. It must have been about then that I learned first-hand that it was true about the boys and the Moorish guards and what they meant to the king. Can you imagine how it is to hear, actually hear with your own ears what your husband and a band of Moorish studs are doing in the next bed chamber? Can you even conceive of my embarrassment and shame, yes, and fury, when people looked at me in pity and made small talk to distract my mind from the orgiastic bedlam? I was shocked, incredulous, sick… for a while. Then came acceptance. And by the time he discovered the first of the blond Berbers and sent to Barbary for dozens more, I found I could smile wryly at the whole affair. You can get accustomed to anything, if you have to."

Listening, Isabella agreed with the last statement. As a child she had gotten used to living in the run-down old castle of Arévalo, buried in the country where she wore cast-off clothing and ate the simplest fare. Later, when Henry decided to bring her to court at Segovia, she had adjusted to the insults and slights of Joanna, who had heaped them upon her with a large ladle from the first day. Yes, one can get accustomed to anything.

"Then I met Beltrán," she heard Joanna say with a lilt in her voice. "Henry brought him to court still smelling of the pig dung of his father's swine farm. I took one look at Beltrán and could not imagine him as one of Henry's boys, though he was young enough to be one. I ground my teeth when Henry found a wife for him, that little snit of a Mendoza girl, but that didn't keep him from falling in love with me and me with him. I knew with the insight only a woman who looks lovingly at a man can have that he was normal and that whatever it was that lay between him and Henry was due to necessity. What he permitted Henry to do, how he let himself be used, he had to do and so let be done. I am not wise enough to explain it, but I feel that Beltrán pities the king, even as he wrings all he can from him in the way of preferment. One cannot blame him for that in days when the surest path to success is the king's favor. Beltrán would never have been made Count of Lesdesma if he hadn't been what he has been to Henry. He is the embodiment of all Henry wants to be—virile, outgoing, popular, normal, handsome, loved by women and respected by his friends. It happens that way sometimes. Instead of hating the object of admiration the admirer loves him above self and in some peculiar way lives vicariously in him or through him. So Henry loves Beltrán—body and soul. When I fell in love with Beltrán, Henry knew I had. In fact, I now suspect he even helped it happen. Beltrán thinks so, too. Henry didn't tell Beltrán he could be my paramour, but he looked at Beltrán and said on numerous occasions, 'All I have is yours.'"

"Is it true, Joanna, that Henry was present when you and Beltrán begot la Beltraneja?"

Was there a sob in the queen's reply? Isabella almost believed there was.

"You are cruel, Isabella. Little Joanna is your own godchild, and you thus insult her?"

"I apologize, Joanna, for that. It was unbecoming of me. The fault is not the child's. Forgive me for saying it. Forgive, too, the filthy question I asked about her conception."

"I shall answer it, nevertheless," said Joanna defiantly. "Yes, Henry was present, actually right in the same bed. He sat glassy-eyed and forlornly saw Beltrán take my maidenhead, saw the hymeneal blood on the sheets, heard the cry of passionate agony I should have cried for him the night he and I got into that very bed to no purpose."

"So, at last you admit it, Joanna. Do you think I shall keep silent? I never promised to, you will recall."

"Tell what you will, Isabella. I'll deny it, of course, and in the long run the person who gossips about his own family is the loser."

"Forgive this, too, Joanna. I spoke out of the depths of my hatred. I'll never testify to what you have said today. And I'll believe that no matter how awful and beastly it all sounds, Beltrán is in Beltrán's own way kind to Henry. I suppose he is even fond of him, if one can be fond and yet have no respect."

"So it could be with you and Pedro Girón, Isabella. Fondness would come, even without respect, if Girón were the father of your children. And you could never be as unhappy with him as I have been with your poor half-brother, not as frantic, as tortured, as baffled. Marry Girón, Isabella, and if you can't love him, at least bear his sons and find some handsome knight who can make you happy. A woman is young but once. Seize the day!"

"Don't quote the pagans, Joanna. What would Henry say if he knew you talked about him so?"

"Henry?" laughed the queen wickedly. "Haven't you heard a word I have said? I tell you Henry knows it all, even my feelings about him. He doesn't blame me, just as he expects me not to blame him for his perversions. He's quite delighted with matters the way they are. He has all he expects from life, that is, of domestic life; he has an heir in my little Joanna, an heir in whom he can see the father who begot her; he has a pretty queen to grace his court; he has the perfect friend and lover in Beltrán de la Cueva in a kind of love sanctioned by the great Plato himself, if the Moors have interpreted him correctly; and, of course, as a surrogate to that irregular love, the even more irregular love he enjoys with the Moors. The only fly in the royal ointment is the controversy between Beltrán and Juan Pacheco. Henry needs the statecraft of Villena, since Beltrán cannot give him that, and Beltrán knows it. So, though they are at swords point, Beltrán and Pacheco lend one another an uneasy support. Hate, as well as love, can make strange bedfellows.

"But I have wandered. To you I admit that Beltrán is my lover. Why try to hide what you have seen with your own eyes? Castles aren't big enough to hide the comings and goings of people, not from the eyes of children like you and your nasty little brother. As to the matter of my child's paternity, that is a question no one can know but me. The Church—all but the horrible Archbishop of Toledo—says she's Henry's legal heir. People can think what they like, but they have no proof. Not a shred."

For a long time Isabella was quiet—so long, in fact, that the queen wondered if she had left the door. A sour smile rippled across her face. Then she heard a whisper and the smile became a snarl.

"Go away, Joanna," said Isabella. "I pity you. Honestly I do, and if I could help you, I would. But I will never marry Pedro Girón and I will not open the door."

"And I pity you, you little prude, you sniveling little nun! I hope Girón kills you! You deserve It. But I hope he does it slowly. And it will be very soon. Indeed, I expect him tomorrow. Just this morning a message came from Villarubia, an easy day's ride. He's resting there for the bout he expects to have with Castile's virgin princess."

10

The deaths of Tomaso, Pietro and Alfredo left Giovanni Battista friendless, except for an old sailor named Carlo, who sat all day and most of the night on a stone bench at the harbor. His wooden leg kept him confined to that area, for he could not negotiate the steep streets which wound their tortuous way to the higher parts of Genoa. Impatiently each evening he awaited Giovanni's arrival, for his greatest pleasure was in reminiscing and in telling the boy the stories he knew about exotic lands, sea battles, and his own amatory adventures. When Giovanni told him of his nearly fatal experience at sea and proudly mentioned the night with Angelina, the old man chortled loudly and slapped his wooden leg. "Started nearly as early as me," he laughed. "I had my first girl when I was twelve. We grew up quicker in them days."

From Carlo he learned that Arabs were even better mariners than Catalans, Portuguese and Italians, that they had sailed from the Red Sea to Cathay and even India and that some might have sailed to Asia around Africa. Old Carlo had another store of tales which he had heard read in coffee houses in the Levant, stories from *The Thousand Nights and a Night*. Soon Giovanni could quote the adventures of Sinbad the Sailor as well as Carlo could, and he shuddered deliciously at the thought of the Roc, that monster bird which fed on elephants, and he had nightmares about the Old Man of the Sea and about Sinbad's adventures in the Valley of Diamonds. What he learned from that bawdy classic about the intrigues and sexual adventures of harem women and their lovers stoked the fires of his ever-growing sexuality. Carlo had revived his own sexuality, living it vicariously in his protege. "You're driven, lad, and you'd best be careful. You have to pick and choose, and you must never bed a woman above you in station. That way is the road to dying a very unpleasant death."

When they spoke of Giovanni's urge to go to sea, their conversation took on an almost ritual quality, and repetition spiced it for them both.

"You don't think I'm too young, do you Carlo, too young to go to sea?"

"You're fifteen, ain't you? I was at sea when I was twelve. I was a deck hand. I carried water to the seamen, fetched their tools, emptied slops and helped the cook."

"I want more than that, Carlo. I want to be an able seaman. I can read three languages and speak two, I can use the astrolabe and the compass. I know rigging and I know ships, and I've sailed to Corsica. I'll be a captain some day, even an admiral."

"You nearly got yourself drowned," laughed Carlo. "No admiral would have."

"But that was on a sloop. I wouldn't be in danger on a ship like my cousin Jeannot's *Montserrat*. And Carlo, if I don't get away from Giacomo and Carlotta somehow, I won't want to live."

"Can't say as I blame you, Giovanni," said Carlo, wondering as always, why the boy grimaced in hatred of his name. "But forget them two, lad, and let's go see the ships that came to port today while you were carding wool."

Their evening stroll, always very slow, due to Carlo's leg, took them the length of Genoa's extensive harbor. "Some day," said Giovanni, "the *Montserrat* will come to port. Cousin Jeannot, I know, will take me with him. As a cousin, he'd have to, when he learned the rotten life I live here."

"Third cousins ain't very close, boy, but I always say that even diluted blood is thicker than water. Maybe Captain Jeannot *will* take you. Keep counting on it."

And then, wonder of wonders, they saw the *Montserrat*, carefully berthed and guarded by two sleepy sailors. "Cousin Jeannot's merchantman," cried Giovanni. "She's here at last!"

"Merchantman, you say, boy? Merchantman when it suits her, corsair when the captain feels the urge. Look at the lines of her."

The sailors told Giovanni the tavern where he could find their captain, and he left Carlo and ran madly up the twisting street to the better part of Genoa. As he expected, a man barred his way into the tavern. He grew frantic. In less than an hour Giacomo would lock him out, as they had once before, forcing him to sleep on the doorstep, a dangerous place to be at night in Genoa. He forgot he was a man. He remembered only that he was fifteen and an apprentice to people he hated and who were cruel to him. If he didn't speak to Jeannot, he would lose his last chance to get away from the drudgery of his life. Therefore he began to scream his cousin's name to beg him to come out, and he yelled in Catalan, which angered the doorman even more. He seized Giovanni and held him fast, and when the boy bit him, he cuffed him to the street and began to kick him. Suddenly the kicking stopped and Jeannot had him in his arms. "Who calls my name?" he asked. And then, "My God, its Juan Baptista! What is it, boy? Why are you bawling like a baby? I'm surprised at you! I thought you were a man. No more tears. I'm here. Now tell me all about it."

Juan Baptista poured out his heart and soul. And when he had begged Jeannot for the hundredth time to take him to sea, he said, "If you won't, by Our Lady, I'll drown myself and make an end of it!"

"None of that talk, my lad. You're talking sacrilege. Now shut up and listen to me. Have you written to your father to tell him how bad it is?"

"I couldn't, Jeannot. My father told me he would write and give me his address. He never did. And something else. I know my father paid good money to Giacomo for my keep. He thought I'd be fed the way I should be, and clothed, and treated like family. I'm a Colom, not a cheap Colombo. My father is a knight and my mother a noble lady. It's a disgrace to the whole family, even to you, a cousin, for one of us to be treated like the lowest peasant. Cousin Carlotta even sold my clothes, and makes me wear these rags you see."

Jeannot shook his head and for a long time sat in silence. The boy was right, he saw. He couldn't sail away and leave him to live in a way which Don Antoni and Magdalena had never dreamed he would. Why hadn't they written? Were they that terrified of the King of Aragón? Or had something happened to them? Could they have died? He had heard of plague in Lombardy. He made up his mind. He simply had to take the boy with him.

"This I promise, lad. The *Montserrat* sails two day from now at dawn. That would be on Monday. Go home now, say nothing of this to Giacomo or Carlotta, and I'll come for you on Sabbath night."

As it turned out, they would sail sooner, on the Sabbath itself, which would look unusual, but sometimes necessity overrules custom and propriety. On Saturday, just before vespers, three Aragonese galleons dropped anchor in the harbor. They flew not only the flag of Aragón. They flew the banner of Prince Ferdinand himself. As soon as Jeannot identified the ships and saw those banners, he turned pale under his tan. He barked orders to his crew to make ready to sail early the coming morning, yes on the Sabbath, as early as they could be ready. Then, cursing under his breath he ran all the way to Giacomo's house. Darkness had fallen and he saw no light. He knocked softly at the door and finally had to pound on it. At last a dim light appeared in an upper room, he heard a curse as Giacomo tripped over a piece of furniture. But at last the door opened a crack and Giacomo whispered, "Who's there?" Carlotta stood beside him, glaring as usual.

When he heard that it was Captain Jeannot, who had brought Juan Baptista to him months ago, he opened the door and invited him in. Jeannot made no bones about what he wanted. "Cousins, bring me the boy. I'm taking him with me tonight. He can't stay here. There is great danger."

Giacomo and soon Carlotta complained bitterly. "His father," said Giacomo and Carlotta simultaneously, "apprenticed him to us for three years and he has served only six months. We've only barely broken him in."

Jeannot wasn't listening. He saw Juan Baptista standing nearly naked behind them. "Go get your things," he said, "if they've left you enough to pack."

"He is staying," shrieked Carlotta. "Get out of this house, you pirate, or I'll scream for the night watch! You're not *my* cousin!"

"If you do it, woman, all of us are ruined. Listen to me, both of you. Prince Ferdinand, this boy's cousin and mortal enemy of the entire Colom family, arrived this evening with three galleons. He may be looking for Juan Baptista, and for his brother Bartolomeu and their parents. Do you want some one to tell him that you both are harboring the boy, who is being looked for everywhere in King John's realm, and therefore here in Genoa? Yes, I know Don Antoni didn't tell you all of this, but this was to protect you as well as Juan Baptista. Look at it this way, the two of you; yes, both of you as kinsmen, will be considered as accomplices of a fugitive from Aragonese justice. Now Carlotta, will you run screaming to the night watch? Go help the lad to pack his belongings, My God! Look at him standing there stark naked. Has he no nightshirt?"

Carlotta, for once in her life, was silent. Furious, but terrified, she left the room, soon to reappear with Juan Baptista, who carried a small and battered valise.

"I must write to my father and mother," said Juan Baptista.

Jeannot intervened. "Don't write anything, boy. And you, Giacomo, do the same. You can let them know what we've done tonight, when next you go to Lombardy for wool. When will you go?"

"I'll go next week," said Giacomo, obviously upset. "The sooner they know, the better. We want no more of their letters coming here."

"So letters have come for the boy," said Jeannot ominously. "Get them! And Giacomo, pay him his apprentice's wages for the work he's done. Hurry, for I grow impatient and must get the boy safely on board and hidden. I plan to sail tomorrow, yes, on the Sabbath, and if I were you, Giacomo, my dear distant cousin, I'd pack up this very night and go for a vacation with Carlotta until my ship has sailed and the hue and cry that is likely to follow that departure has ended. Why not close shop and start early tomorrow morning for an extended stay in some great city, where there are Colombos?"

***

As Jeannot and Juan Baptista made their way to the harbor, their minds were on their sailing the next morning. Had they realized that Prince Ferdinand had landed, brushed off the delegation of officials who had rushed to his ship the moment it had been identified, and had set up his headquarters in the palace his family maintained in the city, Jeannot and Juan Baptista would have been frantic and might have, in the interest of haste, made fatal mistakes. They would have surely been traumatized if they had known that, although Bertrán had used his vial of poison before King John's officers broke down his doors, he had not had time to destroy all of his papers. There were letters from Antoni which verified his parentage. But worst of all, he had written that Antoni and his family should sail to Genoa on Jeannot's *Montserrat* and leave their son with their cousin Giacomo, the woolmerchant.

Indeed, Jeannot almost made a fatal mistake. He was saved by a nightmare after he had boarded his ship the night before. In it he could see the Montserrat sailing peacefully past the three Aragonese galleons, when to his horror he saw one of the captains point to the flag fluttering from the *Montserrat's* mast, the flag of Aragón. Plainly the captain had been ordered by the prince to stop any ship under those colors. "Great God!" Jeannot cried out in his dream, "I forgot to raise the flag of France!"

In a cold sweat he got out of bed and ran to the deck, still dark in the last hours of night. Surely enough, there above him waved Aragón's banner. Jeannot lowered it immediately and replaced it by lilies of France.

When Prince Ferdinand's men arrived very early the next morning at Giacomo's house, they found it locked and empty. Neighbors reported seeing the Colombos leave at daylight. "I asked Carlotta where they were going," volunteered a neighbor's wife.

"And," barked the officer, "what did she tell you?"

"She told me they would travel to Rome to visit kinsmen. I hear there are more Colombos there than anywhere in Italy."

Ferdinand, on learning this, admitted defeat. "The trail grows cold," he muttered, "but it will warm again. I swear it by St. Ferdinand, my ancestor and patron saint."

11

A good many miles to the south that Sunday Pedro Girón with a dozen armed men, their lance points glittering in the chilly air of early dawn, reached a fork in the road. The great army of three thousand men, knights and foot, followed three miles behind him. No wonder Henry so willingly had betrothed him to the princess. With those three thousand, Henry might well defeat his enemies. The twelve who had not know their destination, since Pedro Girón was not a lord to confide or to be questioned, shivered and groaned under their breaths as they followed him into the branch that led to Ocaña. Pedro Girón shivered, too, and tossed his perfumed locks petulantly. Not even the king's letter, tucked safely inside his shirt and close to his heart, improved his ugly mood, although it had made his heart sing when he received it from the king's hand. Wryly he reflected that everything he had done or been forced to do had been worth it. Girón to marry the Princess of Castile! Marry her, not because Henry loved Girón and wanted to make him happy or loved his half-sister and thought of her contentment, but because he needed someone close to him—and surely Girón was as close as one could get—to remove the princess from the current of society, to get her off his hands, out of the way, so she could not marry some energetic and intelligent royal husband and attract followers of her own and his. To Girón the reason was not the thing; what counted was the fact.

Yes, reflected Girón, even playing the abominable role he had learned to play with Henry was worth the reward. The thought of the king made Girón's lips curl in derision. When his own brother, Juan Pacheco had told him that no other Spanish king in all the history of Spain bore the yoke of that disgrace, the label of homosexuality, he had laughed in disbelief, for how could a poor, warped, and downright odiferous creature attract partners for his lusts? Later he wondered less, once he had seen the queen and her lover, the far too handsome Beltrán de la Cueva. Henry had found Beltrán on the Cueva swine farm, where along with several handsome brothers, he made his odorific living. Henry had been hunting, the weather was hot for autumn, he and his retinue were thirsty and hungry. Juan Pacheco had staked out that very farm just because he knew that the king would meet and immediately desire Beltrán de la Cueva, the youngest and most handsome son of the pig farmer. Henry had never been so thrilled by a handsome youth. Beltrán at twenty, looked like a well turned seventeen. His lovely hair, as red as the princess's, Girón recalled, his wide-set blue eyes—unusually azure, they were—had captivated Henry on sight. He whisked the young man off to court, bought him the finest velvets and furs, made him his companion, and, if rumor was true, and Girón knew it was, persuaded Beltrán to become the queen's paramour. And little persuasion it had taken. What delighted the king the most was this: Beltrán had an eye for beautiful women and he was only too willing to bed Joanna, whose beauty was exceptional. Moreover, Beltrán, who knew exactly on which side his bread was buttered, did not permit his amour with the queen to stand in the way of his feigned amour with her husband. People wondered, often aloud, how so beautiful a young man could endure Henry's odor, for he almost never bathed, or how he could endure a kiss from a mouth filled with yellow, jagged teeth like the king's. Money, people surmised, could make strange bedfellows.

But Beltrán knew that power might make such a relationship even stronger. As soon as Joanna bore him a daughter—how he, Joanna and Henry lamented that it wasn't a son—Beltrán knew that his future was to be the brightest. The girl would, in all probability, supplant the Princess Isabella and make Beltrán someday the father of a queen. They named the little girl after her mother, using the Castilian spelling of Juana; but most of Henry's subjects nicknamed her cruelly, La Beltraneja, that is, 'Beltrán's get,' and she would carry that terrible sobriquet to her grave.

Girón's thoughts turned to more pleasant matters; the rape and domination of a royal princess, who would soon be his unwilling bride.

Just then, out of the corner of his eye he saw old Don Félix Quiroga, his private physician, falling in beside him. Damn the ancient quack! The old man's red-rimmed eyes and haggard face irritated him unreasonably. He scowled, but Don Félix had made up his mind to speak.

"Don Pedro," he began hesitantly, "the men are weary. We have all ridden far. Can we not halt and rest?"

Pedro Girón allowed his frown to deepen ominously, but the old man pretended not to see. He cleared his throat and continued. "We might spare ourselves, at least a little, Sir. The princess will be waiting in Ocaña when we arrive. No day has been set for the nuptials, and nothing can take place until you are there. And, Sir, though I know how it angers you when I mention it, you look most poorly. How do you feel?"

Slowly Pedro Girón turned his head and stared into the uneasy but resolute face of the physician. "So now you presume to advise me, do you?" he asked coldly. "Do you think that you, because you are my leech, can manage my life?"

"But your health... ?"

"Damn my health! I feel well enough. I have a cold and no more, and even you insist that fresh country air by day is good for colds."

He knew that the old man was thinking angrily that he should listen to medical advice. All doctors thought so. This one had been after him for hours to stop and rest and kept harping on a flush he claimed to see in his patron's face. Well the old fool and the grumbling lancers could all rest, and in beds, when they reached Ocaña, and no old dotard who had forgotten long years ago what it was to lie with a virgin, if he had ever lain with one, was going to delay him with a glum face and importunings about the state of his health.

When at last he called a halt and dismounted to bathe his hot face in a spring, the doctor dared to try again. Pedro Girón did not turn impatiently away this time when the old man touched his forehead and took his pulse. He was hot and he knew it without the doctor's confirmation. "The quack is right" he said insultingly. "I must be sick, for my head beats like a drum."

Don Félix was saying, "Sir, your face looks like a beet. You have a fever. You simply cannot ride on another mile. And you must take a draft. It is an elixir the king's own physician prescribes for him."

"What's in it?" grumbled Girón, not really to find out, but childishly to delay the dosing. "Does it taste like horse piss, like the last potion you poured into me? I can still taste it after all this time."

"Nay, Sir, it is tasty. A strong brew of Moorish coffee with a tincture of Indian hemp. The coffee drives off the pain, the hemp permits sleep and lowers tension."

"Bitter no doubt."

"With honey, no. It will taste good to you."

Girón scowled, but swallowed the elixir and even smacked his lips. Trust the Moors to produce a medicine both effective and tasty. Coffee he rather liked, for it tasted good and could revive a man half dead for sleep.

After a time Girón insisted that he felt quite well enough to ride. He mounted and rode on up the road, swaying in his saddle and talking in a voice too loud and in words unbecoming in a man of his rank. Even the lancers, rough men, sensed the impropriety. One doesn't speak of a virgin princess one plans to marry as though she were some whore to be used. Some of them, like the doctor, had seen her. They shook their heads. "Too bad," they thought, "for her. She deserves a better wedding night than this bastard will give her."

Don Félix knew they had another day and a night to travel. He wondered if it would do any good to slip an aphrodisiac into Girón's wine when they dismounted for dinner. He might not be too ill, might take to bed the Moorish boy he always traveled with. A bout with the lad might tire him enough to spare the Princess Isabella the worst of his bestialities. "Of course, I wouldn't dare," Don Félix said under his breath, "he has taken the fly often enough to know if I administered it. He would beat me half to death. The princess will have to fend for herself, poor lass. Girón has his mind set. Not even Juan de Valenzuela would distract him." At the thought of the prissy, mincing Juan, he flushed with anger. At Girón's suggestion Henry had made that catamite Prior of the Monastery of San Juan and had given strict orders that, even as prior, he could wear the female gowns he adored and drench himself with cinnamon and musk. Even after Girón had turned the transvestite over to Henry, Don Félix had seen him hold him on his lap and kiss him exactly as though he had been a woman. And what went on in the monastery after perfumed Juan arrived made a fascinating tale, if one's mind ran to such ordure.

Pedro drove his men unmercifully, in spite of a now raging fever. He would not stop. Ocaña and soft arms were waiting to cool his blood. And the king might change his mind.

Vesper bells sounded sweetly over the barren landscape. The lancers drooped in their saddles, and Don Félix looked like a corpse. The pain in Pedro Girón's head fled quite away so sharp was the new pain in his throat. "Too much dust," he rasped. He waved the doctor away before he could remind him how sick he seemed to be. 'We'll stop the night in Villarubia," he whispered. "We're almost there."

Don Félix agreed. "There's an inn of sorts, I recall. Yes, we'd best stop there and not try for Villa Real. Another five miles and you would fall from your horse."

Girón's skin felt dry and parched. The doctor, the lancers, the whole world shimmered before his eyes distorted and tinged with a reddish mist. His throat was killing him. He had never felt such pain. He would have screamed each time he swallowed, but for the fact that screaming hurt even more. When Don Félix had got him to bed and sent for a colleague, Pedro Girón was on the border of delirium.

By the time the physician arrived, Don Félix had closed the windows to shut out the noxious night air and had ordered a hot fire kindled in the fireplace. Don Pedro must sweat profusely. The air was hot and foul and almost unbreathable, but any good doctor knew that it was better than the treacherous vapors of evening.

The physicians conferred. Pedro Girón grew steadily worse. A quinsy undoubtedly, but one far more acute than any either had encountered. They never left his bedside, and all that their science had taught them they practiced. Pedro Girón could not rally.

Don Félix spoke at last. "A priest," he said. "We must send for the village priest." He went to the door, flung it open faced the frightened innkeeper and his wife as they hovered in the gloom. "Send for the priest immediately! My master is dying."

A terrible sound brought Don Félix back to the bedside. Pedro Girón was sitting up in bed, his face a twisted mask. Both hands clutched convulsively at his throat, tearing away his shirt, clawing at the flushed flesh.

The door swung open. The village priest was at the bedside. He started back at the sight of the thing in the bed. That hue! When human flesh turns blue, when a man looks like a corpse, the end draws near. He made ready to administer Extreme Unction. "Confess your sins, my Lord Pedro," he began, but Pedro Girón glared balefully and shook his head.

"Without confession, since he is conscious and could be confessed," the priest stated categorically, "I cannot offer him the blessed Sacrament, sirs. However, let me place it here on the table. Its very proximity has been known to work miracles."

Then what happened not one of the three would ever forget. From some hidden reserve of wickedness Girón drew enough strength to strike out and fling the Sacrament to the floor, hissing a stream of blasphemies. He croaked curses at God, His Son and the Blessed Virgin in terrible obscenities the simple priest had never heard. The poor old man sat down on the floor and wept for shame, but Pedro Girón laughed harshly at him. He laughed even as he lay gasping out his life. He looked so much like a man dying on the garrote that the three in unison, as if by solemn agreement, closed their eyes and crossed themselves.

Then a prodigy occurred. The hot eyes of the dying man opened, bulged. The eyes stared transfixed at the ceiling, or through it. The curses dribbled into a barely audible whimper. Obviously he stared at something, at some one.

"What is he staring at?" asked the priest, squinting nervously through bleary eyes at the soot-streaked beams. "Can you see anything, sirs?"

"No," said Don Felix. "Perhaps it's as well that we can't. But surely something is there, just beyond the vision of the quick, but well within sight of the dead or the dying."

Pedro Girón saw a red mist forming, like a cloud. swirling, curling above him. He looked up into it. He pushed at it, using both hands like a swimmer against a current of water. The mist thickened until It *was* red water. With both his hands he tried to part it. beyond the red water, looking down through it, a familiar face, the face of his bride to be, pale, drawn, haggard, yet strangely beautiful with a halo of hair the color of flame in sunlight. Girón knew with certainty that he was no longer in bed, but on the bottom of a red lake, staring up into light. It was perfectly clear to him that his ghostly princess, as close to death as he, was staring down at him through the turgid, thickening water that separated them. And whose were those pale hands, palms upward, questioning, weighing his life and Isabella's as though in a balance? He shrank from answering that awful question, for his soul told him as the souls of all sinners confronted by Her know full well. Those beautiful, yet terrible hands were about to decide his death or that of the princess he now hated more than he hated God. Writhing and tossing, to the priest's horror, he hissed "She is praying for my death!"

***

That same evening in Ocaña, Father de Coca heard that prayer through the door of the tower room where the princess lay, now close to death. It was a terrible prayer, not one he had ever expected to hear from Isabella. He crossed himself and knelt, as though somehow through his own prayers, he could excuse what his princess was calling upon God to do.

"Hear my vow." came the firm voice through the door. "In the Name of the Father, the Son and the Holy Spirit, I, Isabella of Castile, do swear that I shall pray both day and night to Holy Mary that God strike me dead or take the life of Pedro Girón. It is in Thy hands, Oh God. Pedro Girón or Isabella. I shall drink no water." And de Coca saw the pavement of the corridor grow wet as the water from the jug darkened it. "I shall taste no food. Take, Lord, the life of the one who pleases Thee least: Isabella or Pedro Girón!"

The bells of the cathedral sent peal after peal of thunder across the pale gray city and made a fitting backdrop for the fierce prayer.

"God of Battles," went on the voice, "if it be wicked to desire the death of a fellow mortal, forgive me. Take *my* life, if Thou takest not Girón's. Save my soul, my God, oh sweet Jesus, oh Holy Mother of Mercy! For if Pedro Girón lives and they take me to him alive from the tower, I shall surely kill him on the first night, and then myself!"

Father de Coca's face was paste. A stubborn girl, yes. But this! This was like Judith or Jael. He didn't know her. He could imagine her crouched to drive the tent peg deep into the temple of Sisera or severing the bearded neck of Holifernes, or, oh horror, plunging the knife into the breast of Pedro Girón!

And as he prayed, the news of Isabella's prayer reached Joanna. "If Isabella prays," she said, "so can I, and in addition I can and most certainly will here and now provide something more concrete and substantial. Heaven unstops its ear to those who pay the price. Let Isabella pray shut up in her tower. It will avail her little."

She recalled the old story about the woman who lived in adultery with her best friend's husband, and safely, too, for each day she said a Hail Mary to keep the Virgin from punishing her. Joanna of Castile could do better than a Hail Mary; she would match a hundred fine candles any time against a few paltry prayers. Let shabby Isabella and a whole tribe of sallow priests, living in itchy poverty, pray. Joanna was a woman and a queen, and so was Holy Mary. The Queen of Castile and the Queen of Heaven would come to terms. She might even throw in a new robe for Mary's image, in case the candles seemed too little. Relieved, she sent the gifts off by a delighted deacon and returned to her interrupted dinner. As far as Joanna was concerned, she and heaven had solved the problem.

As the queen made terms with Our Lady, the Archbishop of Toledo in Ávila learned of the princess's flight into the tower. He smiled a grim smile and knew that at last one of the Trastámaras would bring back the olden days when Gothic blood ran fierce and pure. This princess would one day make a great queen, he thought. What a pity that such fibre had to turn up in a woman!

In Segovia, in Ocaña, in Toledo, wherever the people heard of the vigil in the tower, they knelt in the streets and prayed. Heaven would listen to a princess like the young Isabella, they believed.

12

Will-power surged like a flood, caught fire in Isabella and her fevered brain cleared. She raised herself on her elbows, eased herself over until she lay prone, and still propped on her elbows, looking down now into the smooth slab on the floor. Like gray water was the stone, but the sun, just sending its light over the sill of the window was beginning to turn the gray to red.

The heat began to press down like a pillow. The air was fire. Water! The floor was water now, a gray-red lake of it, and she pressed her face into it. Her tongue lapped dryly against the cool surface. She could no longer utter the fierce prayer, but she could think it. "Pedro Girón or Isabella, Lord, Son of God, Lady who art Star of the Sea!"

The surface of the lake shimmered in a red mist, and crimson ripples stirred its surface. Suddenly the murk vanished and she could gaze into the depths. A familiar face floated below the surface, at present unrecognizable, but soon, she sensed, to be identified. The water cleared. She looked directly into the face and saw that its eyes were gazing directly up into her own. An evilly glaring face, twisted and ugly with pain, its hell-black eyes glaring up at her in full recognition, filled with surprise but nonetheless with unspeakable hate. The heavy, ebony hair, no longer curled, but matted with sweat and dust, dank against the white bed of the lake. The breath, fever foul even through the water, stentorian. Behind her and somehow above her music too sweet and strange to be of earth, made the air quiver. And beyond the upturned, hateful countenance two beautiful hands, palm upward, questioning. Not her own hands, but nevertheless the hands of a woman. The two hands asked: death or life for the owner of the face, for Pedro Girón, for now she knew it was he, or for Isabella? Before an answer could cone, the voice of Girón, frantic, fearful. "Death for her," he gasped, "not for me!" Then she heard her own voice. Clearly it enunciated the words, "Take, Oh Lord, the life of the one who pleases Thee least. Isabella or Pedro Girón." Then she saw what Pedro Girón was seeing. Clearly, distinctly she saw the pale hands close, clench, turn over, saw the left vanish and the right, index finger extended, point downward. Then, instantly, as though in confirmation of the finger, a voice she hardly could dare to identify said, "So be it."

The red water congealed into cold gray stone. The face of Pedro Girón grimaced and faded. The face of Isabella was all eyes, and the pallor of her flesh possessed the opaque color of candles just beneath the flame, an inner light, mystic, unearthly, touched from beyond.

***

But Beatriz and Andrés, Cabrera were of a more practical bent. They did not doubt the power of the Queen of Heaven to save a devotee, for they, like all Spaniards, knew of miracles which had occurred in their own lifetime. But no one could know when or if the Virgin would intervene. If she didn't soon in the case of Isabella, something else would have to be done. The important thing was to get Isabella out of the tower,

That Monday morning as they went to the grim door again, they found the halls lined with palace guards. A great muttering filled the entire building and all the way up the stairs stood lines of angry nobles. These, they knew, were the sympathizers of the princess, now alarmed by the duration of her imprisonment. Hands wandered to swords and eyes glared at the Moorish guards. And the Moors glared back, eager for an excuse to butcher these enemies, these Christian dogs.

Beatriz and Andrés waited and wondered if the queen would never arrive. They paced nervously back and forth, hand in hand, trying not to jostle Father de Coca who knelt before the door almost touching the Moorish guardsmen, who from time to time pressed brown ears to the panel to listen. Inside the room all was quiet.

Just then the queen appeared, unheard by anyone, and as was her custom, caught everyone off guard. It was this sort of thing that made the Moors uneasy when she was in residence. They swore that she could materialize out of thin air, out of the floor, from a pillar. They watched her, as without so much as a glance in their direction, she glided panther-like to the door. Quickly they drew back to let her pass.

"We shall surely break down the door today, Isabella, if you continue this idiocy."

From inside the barest crackle of speech. Isabella opened her mouth, but the words blew away. Even so, she had an answer. Out reached a little claw to rattle the sword. *That* was her answer. Joanna heard and interpreted correctly. With a strange look and then a shrug she strode away, never glancing back.

"She's worried," Beatriz told her husband. "She's wondering what the king will say if the princess dies. Isabella has placed her in a most uncomfortable predicament."

The Moors exchanged glances that spoke volumes. This princess they could understand. Her agony was reminiscent of what some of their mystics endured, or the holy hermits along the road to Mecca. Such was the steadfastness the Prophet praised. This Princess Isabella was a woman among women, a fit mate for a caliph, for an emperor. "Moorish blood flows here," they surmised erroneously. "Scratch a Spaniard and you find a Moor, though not always a good one. No doubt a redder stream flowed in the veins of this princess than in most of her people, a stream strengthened by some eastern strain. And they could admire her even if her blood was not blessed by Allah.

Stretched on the cool stone floor, Isabella pondered, "No one, except Beatriz, ever put my interests before his own. So I must do for myself, as always. And now here I lie like a tortoise on its back, whining to Our Lady, importuning our Lord and his Son to do for me. And yet, where else can I turn? With their help I can prevail."

Joanna, returning unexpectedly, tried again, and this time her voice revealed her fear.

"Open the door, Isabella. Girón is dead. "Truly he is," called Joanna. "The courier just arrived with the news. Open."

The first hint of fear in Joanna's voice roused her and she tried to speak, She could not. Quietly she lay on the floor and waited, not at all certain that this was not another dream. Let them break in if they wished to. She no longer wanted to stop them.

Outside she heard voices in hurried consultation. Then Beatriz said, "Be calm, Isabella. We must break in the door. If you hear and understand, if you agree, rattle the sword twice."

Isabella made a last effort and rattled it willingly, then heard axes bite into splintering panels. Blow after blow, the shiver of wood, the heavy impact. By and by a splinter dropped into the room and a shaft of light slipped through. A jagged slit appeared. It became a hole. A brown hand reached through to push the bar, sliding it slowly back. The hand could not reach far enough. More blows, the hand again. How slow it was! Then unbelievably the door flew open and Beatriz was kneeling at her side, Beatriz sobbing, pressing her head to her breast, screaming for water.

When the water arrived, Andrés took it from his wife and said, "No, Beatriz! Only a swallow. No more. Too much would kill her now!"

Isabella felt the cool wetness pass over her cracked lips and brittle tongue. She gulped madly at the elusive trickle. More, more, at any cost! But Andrés was firm. More later. Not now. Isabella looked up to see Joanna bending over her, eyes narrow in speculation, plainly apprehensive. Their eyes met and Joanna suddenly looked away. The Moors in the doorway, stared wide-eyed at this girl brought back from death by prayer. "Allah moves in strange ways," they whispered.

Somehow they raised her to her feet, for she insisted. "Let me stand. I will stand," she said.

The Princess in the Tower 59

Supported by Andrés and Beatriz, she stood and felt that she was floating bodiless above the pavement. She faced Joanna, the courtiers, the Moors, and tall Beltrán de la Cueva whose eyes fell abashed as she looked at him.

"Take her to my quarters," said Joanna. "She is weak and needs the best of care. Beatriz, find her woman, Margarita, and be quick! Isabella, how do you feel?"

"Wonderful, Joanna! Strong, sure, happy! I prayed to God and Our Lady and They listened!"

"Come along with us, Princess," said the queen. "Don Beltrán, help the Princess of Castile. Cabrera, send for a physician. This girl needs attention."

"Attention, Joanna? I have had the best attention. Step aside and let me go to my room. Or would you like to have me mention you in my prayers, as I mentioned Pedro Girón?"

Joanna stepped back, caught off guard, but it was naked hate that Isabella saw in her eyes, not fear. She wiped her hands on her skirt as if to rid them of something clinging there, and then before all those people she turned and hurried from the tower.

The last glimpse Isabella had of the room showed her Father de Coca, his face ecstatic, saying "God has wrought a miracle and we have all seen it."

2

The Woolmerchant

1

Isabella had gone to Ocaña a nobody, but she returned to Segovia the most important princess in Europe. People who usually snubbed her turned friendly and hospitable. Henry's supporters smiled at her. Beltrán looked at her in grudging admiration. Even Joanna was courteous, but her voice was controlled and brittle. Shadows gathered in smudges beneath her great black eyes and cruel little lines of bitterness hovered around-her full mouth and became permanent.

Isabella did not have to be told what it all meant. It was obvious. And it was thrilling and it raised her hopes. A letter had reached the queen from her husband, and a new world for Isabella dawned. Literally overnight the picture changed. She was too important to be wasted upon the likes of Pedro Girón or exposed to the kind of danger Joanna envisaged for her. Too much was at stake. Isabella's marriage must secure for Henry and his partisans an alliance strong enough to bring substantial support in arms, soldiers and money. Although Isabella shivered at the thought of what so much importance might mean, she breathed a new atmosphere and found it heady, especially when she caught the look of frustrated fury in the eyes of the queen.

One morning Father de Coca came to hear her confession, since Henry and Joanna feared that if she went to the cathedral someone from the League might pass her a message from a foreign power with a prince in the market for such an important bride. When she had confessed and was about to rise from her knees the old man laid a hand upon her arm and showed her a letter hidden in his sleeve. After making certain that no one could see it, he unrolled it and handed it to her without a word. A glance at the seals told her it came from the Archbishop of Toledo. His bold flourish was unmistakable. At the other end of the room she could see Joanna and Catalina. They were sitting in the embrasure of a window and had their heads together talking too animated a way to notice her. If they realized she was still on her knees, they must have thought she was more penitent than usual. But why did the confessor feel that he had to hide the letter?

After reading a few lines she understood. She shot a quick glance toward the queen. Then she heard the confessor whisper that he would keep his eye on Joanna so that she could read without interruption.

"I beseech you, Princess," wrote Alfonso Carrillo, Spain's primate, "and your brother joins me, not to agree to any of the plans the king suggests touching your marriage. We know here in Ávila what you had to endure in Ocaña's tower, for de Coca sent us the details. We are proud of you, Princess, and we are certain that God saved you from Pedro Girón for more than marriage to some prince of your half-brother's choosing.

"If you agree to marry the Frenchman, you will delight both the king and the queen and you will greatly sadden your brother and me. In France you would be far away from us all and Spain would soon forget you. Besides, if you marry one of King Louis's relatives, you will be in the camp of our enemies, for Louis plans to help Henry and Joanna against the League.

"If you consent to wed your uncle, Alfonso of Portugal, you bring his armies down on your friends like locusts, and Henry and Joanna will triumph. And you, as Alfonso's Queen, will spend your life in Lisbon bearing heirs to a fat old man, while the bastard daughter of Beltrán de la Cueva sits on the throne of your ancestors.

"We must not forget the rumored marriage with an English prince. Henry could use England's support and believes he could obtain it through such a marriage alliance. They are already mentioning the Duke of Gloucester, who is, I am told, a very fine young man. But England is even farther away than France. Off there in the northern sea, it is so far out of the orbit of Castile that you could never take a hand in your country's affairs if you married and went there to live. Spanish princesses have married English kings before and will again. And always they are lost to Spain.

"All of these marriages look favorable to Henry and Joanna, for any of them would remove you from Spain and clear the way for Joanna's child. Think long, therefore, before you agree to any of them. Delay as long as you can. And remember that with every day that passes your friends are working to make it possible for you to remain in Spain and perhaps some day to rule.

"I now come to the most important part of my message. I offer you in alternative to Henry's plans. Your kinsman, the Grand Admiral of Castile, who is with me here in Ávila, urges you to consider what I have to suggest. Touching your marriage, we have already made enquiries in a nearby kingdom and we know that the idea of its prince's marriage to you meets with approval there. Married to that prince, you would not please Joanna and the king, but you would make your people happy and you would bring them peace ultimately out of all this chaos.

As she watched the confessor roll up the letter with one hand and cross himself with the other, she saw Joanna and Catalina still talking. They had noticed nothing, and when de Coca left, his face calm and filled with satisfaction, they never noticed he had gone. The idea of the prince "from a nearby kingdom" fascinated her. The kingdom, of course, was Aragón, and the prince was Ferdinand. She knew that he was young, a little less than a year her junior. That made him only three years older than her brother Alfonso. She had hoped to find a husband a little older than this, one in his twenties or even in his thirties, a grown man and experienced in politics and in life, but she was willing to hear more about the Prince of Aragón. Some men mature earlier than others, she knew, and she hoped that Ferdinand was one of these. How strange that betrothal to him should so excite her. After all, for years she and he had been betrothed when they were children, really infants. When Villena, recognizing the danger of an alliance with Aragón, had persuaded the king to break the betrothal agreement, it had mattered little to her. But now, because it would be a forbidden betrothal and one secretly arranged, it was enticing.

She discussed the matter with Beatriz later that same day while the squires were exercising in one of the palace courtyards.

"I shan't marry anyone," Isabella said, "until I find a man I can love and respect. I know I can't expect them to let me choose the man I want, but by Our Lady, I vow to reject any suitor who is definitely unsuited or unattractive. I'll go even farther, Beatriz. The man I marry will be strong, healthy, and comely at least, if not handsome."

"Isabella, you sound like someone out of a novel of chivalry. You're as romantic as the women in *Amadís of Gaul*. It's the stuff of dreams—beautiful, but mighty impractical. May I go even farther, as a friend who knows her place, but must step out of it for the good of her friend? Very well. What I shall now say, I shall find hard to say, Isabella. Yet say it I must. I know of the penances Father de Coca imposes upon you and why he imposes them. I know you think of good-looking young men as much as *any* girl your age thinks of them..."

"Just as you thought of them, Beatriz, until you married Andrés."

"Quite right, Isabella. We all have fantasies until we marry, and some of us allow our fancies to continue after it. I used to have such fantasies and I have them now about my love for Andrés and my lovemaking with him. Andrés is loving, passionate, and I'm mad about him. I'm mad about his body, if you will forgive my saying so. No priest would approve, but I want you to know this."

"I commend you for telling the truth, Beatriz. But it's a truth I've known all along. Your eyes proclaim this truth when you look at Andrés. Once right here in Segovia I heard your voice proclaim it when you and he made love."

Beatriz blushed, then raised her chin and said, "I'm glad you heard. Yes, sometimes I cry out. I fantasize, but not about other men, thank God. I fantasize about Andrés and what I want us to do together, yet cannot ask him to do. Even in bed, and even when making love, even linked to his body by the strongest of all carnal ties, I just cannot reveal my innermost fantasies. Perhaps this is a sin, perhaps it is even bestial, but I can't confess it to any priest, even if I risk my immortal soul."

Isabella's face burned, but she smiled and said, "Thank you, Beatriz. I needed to hear those words. They make me feel less sinful, indeed not sinful at all. I've never confessed the details of my fantasies either. I can't. I won't. Not even to Father de Coca. But I can confess them to Almighty God, Who, I feel, placed in me the emotions the clergy consider unworthy."

"What of the devil, Isabella? The clergy say he is the author of carnal thoughts."

"The devil has nothing to do with my feelings. He may tamper with God's design in some people, but he shall not tamper with it in me. You know my needs, my cravings. You know, too, that I shall assuage them only once and that will be with the man I take as husband. With him I shan't be prudish, if I can help it, though I must confess that I wonder how I shall overcome my ignorance and succeed with all the inhibitions they have developed in me."

"Don't forget me and Andrés and our love, Isabella. A deep inner instinct warns me not to reveal to him, not even once, how sensuous my nature is. I fear his embarrassment, even his scorn. I believe that many men, most men, even the most passionate men, shrink from full intimacy, full reckless carnal knowledge with the mothers of their children."

"I hope I can be honest with my, husband, Beatriz. If I should be blessed enough by God to be mad about him, he'll know it from the outset. I'll find a way, delicate or forward, but I'll make him know. But back to my original thought, what I want and what I expect to have is a healthy and attractive husband."

"But what of age-old custom, Isabella? What of tradition and duty? Suppose, for the good of Castile, the husband chosen for you is not all you insist upon?"

Isabella scowled. "I'd reject him. You see, what I demand in a spouse makes sense, and you know how important making sense is to me."

"I do indeed, but does it make sense to ask for too much? Princesses are not like other people. They must place duty to the state over personal preference and above love and romance."

Isabella pointed and watched Beatriz's eyes follow her finger. "See that squire?" she asked. "The tall one with the green tunic and the very broad shoulders? Keep your eyes on him and I'll try to make you see what I mean. Those shoulders, that chest, even that profile. All that makes sense. And it's even patriotic to think of a man like that as a husband, Beatriz."

"Patriotic, Isabella? You'll have to explain that. Interesting and breathtaking, but hardly patriotic."

Isabella watched the squire beat his opponent down and clapped her hands. Then she said, "Yes, patriotic. Any princess could love a man like that. But how many princesses are allowed to? Look at all the royal marriages ending in unhappiness or adultery like Joanna's. Think of all the royal babies who are born ugly or imbeciles, or deformed, or feebleminded because people didn't think, didn't listen to their hearts. When I marry I want healthy children, not idiots, not grotesque beings like Henry, or wild pagan souls like Joanna. Therefore, the man I marry would have to be something like that squire down there. He'll be strong and sound in mind and body, capable of siring offspring of his own type. And I think it would be better, yes, and safer, if he were handsome, for if a woman is to be a happy wife and mother, she should be in love with her husband and admire him."

"The squire is handsome enough," mused Beatriz. "What is his name?"

"How should I know?" said Isabella, shaking her head impatiently. "I called him to your attention because he is an example of what I have been saying."

"You may be asking too much, Isabella. Even your inordinate determination may not manage as much as this."

"Wait and see," said Isabella, letting her eyes dwell again upon the handsome squire sweating away in the dazzling glare of the courtyard.

2

Joanna stood at an open archway gazing out across the incomparable landscape. She had been glad to leave Ocaña for Segovia, Henry's favorite city, and her own as well. Nothing compared with Segovia. She could see, if she leaned out from the massively graceful Tower of *Homenaje*, the gorge of the Clamores River, audible as it rushed along after a hard rain. A glance behind her revealed the royal throne room and beyond it the high-vaulted chamber roofed like a magician's cavern in endless plaster stalactites or some strange fruit. True opulence for once, but Henry preferred the slatternly old palace and his hunting lodge Belaén. The queen suddenly left the window and approached Catalina, a lady-in-waiting who listened attentively yet uneasily. She wondered, as she listened to Joanna's wild and incoherent voice, how a woman who had so much could be so unhappy. She decided she would not change places with the queen for all the wealth in Spain and for the love of Beltrán de la Cueva thrown in. Love needs peace and calm to thrive. Even wealth should go hand in hand with leisure and quiet. Love did not thrive in the sour air Joanna breathed. The queen's hateful words impinged upon her ears and frightened her. Would the woman never stop pacing back and forth like an angry leopardess? When at last Joanna stopped to catch her breath Catalina spoke,

"What you suggest," she said, "is a dangerous course. Suppose the king found out. Suppose someone told Beltrán. They wouldn't like it, Joanna, and I don't like it either. Isabella is no serving wench. The seduction of a princess, even at this court, is no small thing. Heads could roll."

"The King wants her out of the way as much as I." snapped the queen viciously. "I'm certain that he would be pleased to learn she had disgraced herself. And what better and more effective way to break that iron, prudish pride?"

Catalina thought for a moment. "But the nobles of the League? Alfonso, her brother, and the Archbishop of Toledo? Excommunication would be the least you could expect if it were traced to you, Joanna."

Catalina crossed herself. "I'm no angel, Joanna, and neither are you, but we both fear the Church, no matter how much we tell ourselves we don't. Let's think a little longer before we act."

"I have thought long enough, Catalina, and I see no other way." And she resumed her catlike pacing. Her beautiful hands were talons that opened and closed.

The two women looked at each other then, and each knew what was crossing the other's mind. The League would renew the war furiously, spurred on by the Archbishop. In the cathedral across the city the tolling of the bells reminded them of the power of the clergy in Spain and the rapid beating of their own hearts at the enormity of the offense the queen proposed made them catch their breaths.

Catalina looked pale as she said, "Do you remember the day little Alfonso ran into this very room with King John's sword, swearing he'd kill us all if we didn't stop trying to involve Isabella with the pages? I'll never forget it, for I was the one who stood at the sharp end of the weapon, feeling it jabbing me in the bosom. Alfonso couldn't have been a day over eight at the time. Now he's fourteen and has been in battle."

Joanna's full lip curled in scorn, "I remember all that," she replied impatiently, tossing her long hair over her shoulder. "The child is bold enough, but aren't all males? Henry excepted, of course. A child is a child, however, and battle or no battle, I'm not afraid of Alfonso."

Catalina couldn't raise her eyes, for just behind the queen she knew that a figure of the Virgin, carved in high relief in the arch of the doorway, looked down at them. She swallowed hard before she could reply. "But you're afraid of the Archbishop of Toledo," she whispered.

"Who would tell him? Do you think Isabella would open her pious little mouth? That's the beauty of it, Catalina. She'd be ashamed. Why she'd die before letting such a thing be known. But *we* would always know, and she would never forget that we knew. She'd live in a perpetual fear of the day we might decide to tell. I'm going to enjoy this, Catalina." Catalina's eyes grew round and she glanced hastily away from the queen's face, so feral that it repelled her. "I can understand why you want to place her under your thumb, Joanna. but why so much relish? Why the malice? The girl never did anything to hurt you, and if you'd let her alone, I think she'd be a good sort, Why do you hate her so? Do you ever remind yourself that she's little Joanna's godmother?"

"A fig for that," snapped the queen. "You know she had to be. They made her. I hate her for being herself. She's the only person at court I really hate. She's stiff-necked and cold. Yet she burns. I know she does. She makes me nervous. I'd sooner have a cat in the palace than that strange girl. But once we'd trapped her, she could be sent away. She'd be happy to marry anyone we suggested, I can't imagine why I never thought of this before."

The sun slanting through the window reminded them of the hour. It would soon be dark and Joanna's little court of ladies-in-waiting, a few young knights, and perhaps a troubadour or two would be gathering soon after the evening meal. Catalina was glad, for she hoped the activities they had planned earlier would distract Joanna and keep her from the plan she was obviously concocting. She was not prepared for what the queen said.

"We must find a man, a man for our princess."

"You called her cold not a moment ago. Do you think we could find a man who would interest her that much? Not once in all the years I've known her has she ever slipped, Not once. And that I cannot understand. A healthy girl, pretty enough, too, and yet she never looks at men. Why, by the time I was..."

The queen smirked. "Yes, Catalina. I know and so does everybody from here to Lisbon. You were barely twelve when they caught that page from the Algarve crawling out of your bed. Of my companions yours was the first maidenhead to tear. That's why my aunt packed you off to your parents, and that's where you'd be now if I hadn't sent for you once I landed here and assessed the situation. But between you and Isabella lies a world of difference. Isabella is cut from another cloth. She's a damned idealist. It wouldn't be holy for her to take a lover. No clandestine affairs for the virgin princess... unless we can breach her defenses."

"Well," said Catalina with finality, "it seems to me, Joanna, that you have answered the question and solved the problem. If Isabella won't look at a man that way, why go on? The plan of seduction fails before it gets under way. We have been basting before the roast is in the oven."

"Seduction," said Joanna, smiling archly, "Is not exactly what I have in mind. Seduction implies complacence after persuasion."

"Thanks for the lesson in lexicography, Joanna," said Catalina, safe behind the shield of familiarity and complicity.

But the queen was not listening. Her face had gone hard and graven with lines of thought. Her eyes passed once over the arch where the Virgin's image was, and she quickly moved them away. Then, defiantly, she lifted her chin. "Isabella would never be induced to surrender her chastity," she said musingly, as if she were alone. "But it could be taken from her by force or under the influence of drugs."

Catalina was aghast. "Rape, Joanna! *Dios mío!* Joanna, not even you would..."

Joanna's face was ugly. Her long eyes narrowed to two black slits. "Wouldn't I," she hissed, "wouldn't I, Catalina? Wait and see. There's no length to which I wouldn't go. And if rape fails, there's poison."

Catalina stopped up her ears until she could think. Then she said, "Joanna. Control yourself! Isabella isn't that important. Forget rape and murder. The King will marry her off! and that will be the end of it."

"No," said the queen. "It won't do. She might come back. Princesses have gone back to their countries after decades of exile. They have become queens. I cannot risk it. Stop to think for a moment. She might replace my own daughter. You'll see that I'm right. Isabella must be undone."

Catalina saw all too well. Spain hated Joanna with the hate reserved for foreigners who have usurped power. For years the League had fanned the flames of that hate into revolt against her and her paramour. People spat when they heard Joanna's name and cursed the sterile king when the child Joanna was mentioned. Thousands, either openly or in secret, supported Isabella, while others hoped that her brother Alfonso would eventually be the legitimate king. As long as a genuine member of the House of Trastámara lived in Spain, Joanna and her bastard must worry.

"This is the only way," she heard Joanna say. "The only way unless we consider poison. And what we do, we must do immediately."

"Who is desperate enough for such a deed, Joanna?" asked Catalina, her face a blend of fear and fascination, "Who would dare? People haven't forgotten about Isabella's prayers in the tower of Ocaña and what happened to Pedro Girón."

"Men die every day, Catalina," said the queen with a matter-of-fact air. "Girón could have died without Isabella's prayers, although I'll admit that at the time the whole affair was certainly impressive."

"You were impressed all right, Joanna. We all were. By the way, have you stopped sending candles to the shrines of Our Lady?"

The queen shot her a black look and Catalina glanced at the Madonna on the arch.

"I'm still sending them," Joanna admitted grudgingly. "It never hurts to play safe, you know. I fancy Our Lady can be very forgiving if properly reminded of a devotee's interest in serving her. But you asked who was desperate enough to seduce, to rape a princess if necessary. The palace knows of Isabella's chastity, but the people outside don't know how deep it goes. Besides, she isn't as cold as you think. Just yesterday I watched her while the squires were practicing in the courtyard. Isabella knows which pages have nicely turned calves and the kind of shoulders we all esteem. She's a woman underneath the penances, the cold baths and the *mea culpas*."

Catalina gathered courage to ask, "But who is desperate enough? You still haven't told me."

"Have you any suggestions, Catalina?"

"Young García Gómez might do. He's handsome as an Andalusian bull and he has the reputation."

Joanna shook her head. "But he's a duke's son and will be a duke one day in his own right. What if he betrayed us and persuaded her to marry him after it happened? He would be king-consort, if Isabella ever grabbed the crown."

"Then we need a nobody. Joanna, you are wise and wicked. I'm glad you're my friend and not my enemy. Yes, a nobody. That way marriage could never wipe out disgrace."

"Exactly. A nonentity. Someone Isabella could never marry under any circumstances. A man with no scruples, with no Christian scruples... do you follow me, Catalina?"

Catalina blanched and crossed herself three times, fixing her really frightened eyes unswervingly at last on the Madonna. "You mean a Moor?" she whispered, "Joanna, a Moor would be perfect, but would you go that far?"

"I would. And I have the particular Moor in mind already. Who is at court of that faith, handsome enough even for a princess of the blood? Who is rash enough and godless enough to seduce a Christian virgin? Who is given to hashish and beyond all redemption?"

"Fejjuan the Berber!" gasped Catalina, clapping a bejewelled hand to her mouth. She stood up quickly and slipped off her mantilla. Before Joanna could guess her purpose she had draped it over the Madonna and returned to her seat.

The queen pretended not to notice. Her lips, no longer seductive and full, were thin and hard. "Fejjuan the Berber, of course!" she said hoarsely. "Fetch him to me, Catalina. Have him wait out of sight tonight until the right moment. Then he will come in and sing for us... and for Isabella."

"The princess rarely attends your gatherings, Joanna."

"She will tonight at my express command. Yes, Catalina, tonight we can bring it off."

***

Soon after Isabella arrived perforce and irritated, Joanna began to bait her mercilessly. "Princess," she asked, "will you not tonight at least show some interest in a dancing partner or some young man to sing to you?

"Thank you, Your Highness," said Isabella coldly. Tonight I need no male companionship. In fact I never do."

"Now whom could we choose?" continued Joanna, pretending not to see the angry gleam in Isabella's eyes. "Whom would you suggest, Catalina? That young troubadour from Provence with all the long blond hair? Or Baron de Rosomithal's secretary? I've heard these Czechs are exceptional—even more passionate than Moors. Tell us about him, Catalina, for we all know how much he has seen of you."

Everyone giggled at this reference to Catalina's recent amour with the Czech and her priceless remark about his impossible Castilian making no difference in bed. They watched in great appreciation as she sighed like a gourmet savoring a delectable dish, rolling her eyes and rocking to and fro. And then they noticed that Isabella's face had gone from red to white, they nudged one another with delight and waited for the explosion.

"Catalina wouldn't agree to share him, I'm certain," said Joanna, looking thoughtfully from under her long eyelids, "Nor do I blame her. But I have a better idea. Princess, choose Fejjuan the Berber. He comes highly recommended. They say he hasn't overlooked the opportunity to climb into a hospitable bed from Granada to Pamplona, and that he always satisfies. A good many ladies here, I believe, could tell you about his capabilities and endowments."

"Just the man!" cried Catalina, clapping her hands until the rings jangled. "Highness, call Fejjuan and tell him we have a lady here who would like to have him... sing."

Isabella stood up and started blindly for the door, refusing to hear Joanna's voice reminding her that she did not have permission to withdraw. She felt the scald of tears on her cheeks and hoped no one had seen them, knowing all the while that everyone had. She heard the ladies' shrieks of mirth and Joanna's cruel little laugh as she made her way down the corridor toward her room, and the night air felt hot against her skin which had suddenly turned cold. Even after she had slammed her door she heard the sounds of mirth. Then came the melodious and powerful voice of the young Berber and the subtle notes of his instrument.

Tears of rage flowed on as she knelt before the image of the Holy Virgin, hoping to draw comfort from the serene face and soft blue eyes. On nights nearly as bad as this, great comfort had flowed from the face of this Gothic Mary fashioned by some hand beyond the northern mountains. She prayed that it would be so again.

The volume of the Berber's song increased. and she knew that Joanna had sent him to serenade her from the corridor. She tried not to hear the words, for like most Moorish songs she had heard at court, this one was uninhibited and pagan in its appeal to sensuality. Fejjuan sang in seductive tones and in Castilian which he knew very well. The words slipped like fingers through the heavy panels of the door and past her own fingers as she pressed them into her ears. He sang of a lush houri with moist doe-eyes and alabaster breasts; of sinuous grace and wanton, naked eagerness for love; of musk-anointed thighs and a navel likened to a goblet of myrrh, with the succulent aroma of Tibetan musk, and saliva smoother than curds and sweeter than honey. The physical impact of the words and the melody left her weak. Her mind teemed, as Fejjuan intended that it should, with unbeckoned, but nonetheless tantalizing images of the flesh.

At last the song ended, jut not until the houri had slaked her passion with a hard-mouthed young desert sheik with a nose like the beak of an eagle to match that other longer and unthinkable, yet inescapably well imagined sexual beak. She knelt shaking and sweating long moments after the last note had died. Then, drained and exhausted she crept into bed to sink at last into a sleep nagged by the foreboding that Fejjuan might be coming back to serenade her again.

3

The memory of Fejjuan's song kept Isabella awake for hours, but at last emotional shock and outrage lessened and she drifted into a tortured sleep. The moon, full and silver, thrust over the rim of the distant mountains and flooded her bedroom with a pearly luminosity. It flowed along the walls of the palace, seeping through the high windows and turning everything into an unearthly brilliant marble.

Down the corridor in that empty wing of the palace tiptoed Fejjuan the Berber. He came alone with the stealth of a man who does not want to be seen. Like a cheetah stalking its quarry, he understood the importance of silence. In his veins leaped the potent wine of Jérez de la Frontera, fired by the aphrodisiacal potions dropped surreptitiously into his cup by the queen's page. Fejjuan, lustfully drugged and drunk, wondered if his heart would break free and leap from his chest, and his oriental appreciation of the beauty of the night burned bright. He seemed to float across the floor, so silent were his footsteps, and this strange ability to float delighted him. He absorbed the loveliness of the gardens as their fragrance wafted into the corridor. He allowed the breeze to caress and sharpen his emotions. Everything, the night, the moon, the coolness of the breeze puffing gently down the corridor, blended as a catharsis to his feelings that were hot and agitated and arabesqued by the drug, the alcohol and his passion. As he moved through the moonlight, flashes of memory from the queen's boudoir burned in his soul like the golden threads of a tapestry. He remembered the ladies, especially Catalina and a certain Pilar, who had urged him to stay until the queen's frown silenced them. He would never forget the wasp-look in Joanna's eyes as she told him to leave on this particular mission. "The queen is a witch," he grunted, echoing what all his kind thought of the Queen of Castile.

Fejjuan paced carefully past the door of the princess's room, aware of the penalty of discovery. Queen Joanna had made that plain enough. She would not help him if he were taken. In fact, she would accuse him. He smiled an enigmatic eastern smile. Death was on his tread, but hashish and Jérez wine are stronger than death and the fear of death.

As he walked, the faded tapestries billowed like grayish cobwebs in the night wind and his feet feathered their way through the dust on the floor. He smiled derisively. You wouldn't walk in dust on the floors of the palaces of Málaga and Granada, but on thick carpets and polished tiles. Then a smile of another calibre, a thin and ruthless smile, flitted across his lips. Right under their royal noses he would do it! The queen had been right as always. Few people ever came down this passage. The dust was proof of that.

Certain that he was alone, he moved to the door and pressed his ear against it. Like most palace doors it was made of oak and probably had a thick oaken bar on the other side. This bar might defeat him, but not the lock with its great eye-like keyhole. The queen had provided the key. Silently he turned it and saw the door swing soundlessly inward. A moment later he stepped into the darkened room and closed the door behind him. For a full minute he leaned against the door, waiting until his eyes could accustom themselves to the unexpected brightness of the moonlight pouring through a large window. Half the room was silver, the other half ebony. The Gothic window, divided into two sections by a narrow pillar, cast a shadow upon the floor, the shadow of a cross. Fejjuan mouthed a silent incantation.

His eyes eagerly leaped across the room, found the bed only half-illuminated. Like all Christian beds he had seen it was high with heavy carved posts at the foot and the head. She had drawn back its thick curtains and had tied them to the bedposts to let in the breeze. Then his eyes descended upon the form of the sleeping girl. The background of the room blurred into silver mist and shadow. The focal point was the girl. Lying supine in the moonlight she seemed different and more desirable even than when she stood in the glow of candlelight. One almost supernaturally white arm hung gracefully over the side of the bed, and her hair billowing across the pillow was dull silver now instead of red-gold. Fejjuan's nostrils contracted and opened like the leopard he was. Already he was inhaling the aroma of her body, and his blood leaped to his brain.

Isabella turned uneasily in her sleep and woke to the full realization that something was wrong or dangerous. Her eyes opened only wide enough for her to see, for some instinct warned her not to open them enough for whoever or whatever it was in the room to discover that she was awake. Could she be dreaming? In the darkness and the ebony side of the room something moved. As her eyes penetrated the gloom more clearly she saw a man carefully removing his clothing. She watched him slip out of his long kaftan silently, like a snake from its skin. Then a faint click which she surmised was made by beads or jewels on his tunic as it dropped to the floor. She saw him freeze to immobility, his arms raised above his head, afraid to unwind the turban. The drama unfolded so weirdly, so silently, so purposefully that it had to be a nightmare.

She made herself lie still, hoping that the nightmare would run its course and end her terror. But then the man stepped naked into the bar of moonlight and she saw him stare down at his body and pass his hands over it in a gesture so voluptuous, so sensuous that she knew she was awake. The caress showed her that he loved his body more than he loved his life. He had a right to love it, she realized. He was beautiful as he stood there, slender and lithe, yet strong as a young lion, his skin pale gold and as smooth as a girl's.

Her eyes opened a little wider and she struggled to break the bonds of her fear and leap from the bed. She had never seen a man's body like this before. He was moving, gliding rather, toward the end of the bed and she could see the glitter of his eyes and the flicker of the moonlight on his wet lips. Every detail of his body stood out in relief. From the darkness below his navel, his manhood stood up, pointing directly at her. That, too was different from the tiny organ which she had seen sprouting from her little brother's lower abdomen. Were all men like this? Did they change so much as they matured? This organ was bare, uncovered by the sheath of skin she had seen on Alfonso when his nurse bathed him.

He must have been less than five feet from the bed when she opened her eyes completely. He stopped. He knew she was awake and that she recognized him. He deliberately stood in the light and arched his chest, his hands clasped behind his head, his belly pushed forward. But the vision he provided did not have the effect previous experience with women had led him to expect it would. Swift as a thought and before he could move to stop her, Isabella slid from the bed and stood facing him, their eyes almost on a level.

"She'll try to stab me," he said aloud in Arabic, as he caught the flash of steel in her right hand and lunged for it.

"Not so fast, little falcon!" he hissed. "I should have expected that, but your beauty lulled me."

His hands closed like vises around each of her wrists, holding her as helpless as if she were a child. How could she have failed to reach him with the dagger! She could have wept. She had lost her one opportunity. She did not struggle at first, but said calmly, "Let me go, Fejjuan, and then get out. Are you mad?"

"Mad with love, Princess. With passion! You are wise not to struggle, for it would do no good. No one would hear you over all the noise in the queen's apartments, and if anyone did and came here, what would he think? I will tell you. He would think that Fejjuan the Berber had won what no other man at court could have."

Isabella's mind worked feverishly. She knew he was right, that no one would hear her scream, for the sounds of revelry were too loud. Cautiously, speculatively, she strained against his arms. They were as strong as oak. She was completely helpless. If only she hadn't missed with the dagger! if only she could wrest her arms free and plunge it into his heart! But though she still clasped it, his hands gripped her wrists.

"Let me go, Fejjuan!" she commanded. "Go now and I will not report you."

"Let you go, jasmine flower? I did not come to let you go. I came for this!"

She could feel the moist heat of his body through the thin stuff of her gown and his hard, corded arms pressed her tightly against him. The aroma of his musky perfume and the sharp, male smell of his body overpowered her. She had to turn her head from right to left to breathe and escape his hungry, seeking lips. His long, hard organ burrowed maddeningly, inexorably, into her stomach. She pushed him back and they swayed apart for the moment, into the shadows and then into the moonlight. They made no sound, except that of heavy breathing and the light scuffle made by their bare feet on the floor. Then his arms tightened fiercely and she felt the rigidness of him again, felt her breasts flatten against his hard chest.

"Jasmine flower," she heard him pant in her ear, "don't fight. Be mine!" For a long moment Isabella slumped against him, gathering strength. Fejjuan took this as the beginning of surrender. He forced her back to look into her face. His eyes, almond and black, were the eyes of an animal. His mouth fell open, His wavy black hair fell down over his forehead. Straight into that handsome, feral face she stared. Miraculously she felt no flicker of fear. What she felt was blackest anger.

"Be not afraid," she heard him say gloatingly. "But do not forget either that you are the gazelle and I the leopard."

Then he began to bend her back toward the bed.

"Holy Mother of God." cried Isabella as she drew back her head and slammed her forehead as hard as she could against his mouth.

Fejjuan straightened up, still clutching both her wrists. The light from the window fell full upon his face. She marveled how it could change so completely. The last vestiges of beauty drained away. What she saw was the muzzle of an animal. the teeth fully bared, gleaming long and white and sharp, while from the corners of the mouth trickled two streams of blood. Fascinated, she watched it drip to his chest and run down in two black lines across the pectorals, the flat belly, to disappear into the mass of pubic hair. She could feel her forehead, cut by his teeth, was bleeding, too. "I'll have a scar," she thought. "So be it."

"Bitch" he shrilled through pain and blood. His grip tightened on her wrists until she had to grit her teeth to keep from crying out in pain. She saw that pain had driven lust away and left him frenzied. Madness gleamed in his eyes. He shook her brutally, flung her about the room, and the thing she saw glaring out of his eyes brought the first chill of terror to her heart. Then unexpectedly her right wrist slipped in his grasp and she struggled harder. Her wrist was slick with sweat and blood. She must free it from his grip. She stood still, now graven and quiet, breathing in gasps, the wine-scented breath of the man mingling with her own.

She lowered her eyes and saw that her arms, both of then, were red with his blood. With every ounce of strength she twisted her wrist and felt it slip free from his fingers. Then, before he could recover, she raised her hand and drove the dagger straight into his chest a little above the left nipple. Steel grated on bone, but the blade went deep and she heard him scream.

"You've killed me, you Christian bitch!" groaned Fejjuan.

Then he slumped to the floor on his knees, crawling slowly after her as she retreated in horror, drawing one foot after the other as she backed toward the door. At last he rolled over and lay still in a rapidly widening pool of blood. "Allah be merciful," she heard him whisper before he lost consciousness.

Isabella stepped over his body, careful not to get blood on her feet. The dagger had come out and lay to one side. She stooped and picked it up. Then she strode to the door, threw it open, and stepped into the corridor, her face set, her eyes ablaze. Down the dusty corridor she made her way toward the sounds of song and merriment coming from the queen's apartment. She did not knock. She pushed the door open violently. She burst in and marched straight across the room toward the low dais where Joanna sat with Catalina and two of her ladies. The dancers drew back and halted. Some invisible hand snuffed out the music like a candle.

She saw amazement and then consternation in Joanna's eyes. She heard Catalina scream at the sight of the bloody dagger. One lady closed her eyes and fainted. No one caught her as she crashed to the floor at the queen's feet.

Isabella halted directly in front of Joanna. Into the dark, hooded eyes she glared for a long moment. Victory was a wine she could feel running down her throat. Before anyone could move to stop her she tossed the dagger into the queen's lap.

"That Moorish carrion in my room," she said imperiously, "Have it removed." Then she turned and without another word walked out of Joanna's sight.

A few minutes later, as she trembled from reaction, she saw two of the Moorish guardsmen carrying the limp and sagging form of Fejjuan away. Drops of his blood fell to the dusty floor and rolled along, dust-covered, like small black pearls.

"He'll last until the king returns," she heard one of the guards say, "but not for long afterward. What madness could have brought him to this?"

"I thought Fejjuan too clever to try to rape with the praying witches," she heard the other whisper. "He won't try again, you can be sure, since the witch-queen will accuse him."

The wind ruffled the bed curtains, bringing the hint of dawn. Isabella waited until the rim of the sun appeared over the ridges behind the city. When the world was light she fastened a message to a pigeon's leg and tossed the bird into the cool morning air. Twice she saw it circle the turrets of the Alcázar before it shot away arrow-straight over the Roman aqueduct and off toward Ávila and the Archbishop.

4

An hour after Isabella's pigeon alighted in the dovecote in Ávila the Archbishop called Prince Alfonso for a conference. When the boy entered he saw the old man pacing, and since he knew him so well, he stood respectfully at the doorway and waited. When the Archbishop was ready to talk he would, and not before. As he watched, Alfonso had time to think. If anyone in Spain could bring about Isabella's rescue from Segovia, it was the Archbishop of Toledo. He felt so confident that he forgot to worry, until the memory of Joanna and Henry brought back the alarm he had felt when Isabella's message arrived.

He watched the Archbishop with even greater respect than usual, for fresh in his mind stirred his wild exhilaration as he had ridden beside him into battle at Olmedo. He would never forget the eyes of the enemy infantry as they saw the iron cleric bearing down upon them singing hymns and roaring curses. "God damn you traitors!" he had bellowed. "I curse you in His name."

Even here in his rooms, dressed in a simplicity bordering upon austerity, he emanated an awful power.

"The old man is an eagle," he thought. "I wish he would stop looking so fierce and tell me what he plans to do to save my sister."

The Archbishop showed no signs of ending his pacing, and at last the boy decided to risk rebuke. "We must rescue Isabella, Your Grace," he said. "We can't leave her in Segovia any longer."

The Archbishop agreed with a terse nod and resumed his pacing. After a while the prince tried again. "How can we reach her, Your Grace? Everyone knows Segovia is impregnable. Besides, if we attacked the city, who knows what Joanna will do?"

"Henry has always considered Segovia safe," said the Archbishop, deigning to speak at last. "But a city can be taken by ruse, as well as by onslaught. Remember Troy."

"Beltrán and Joanna would hardly be taken by a wooden horse," said Alfonso before he thought. He bit his tongue and shot an anxious glance at the old man. This was not the kind of thing one said to Alfonso Carrillo whose dislike for flippancy was well known. When he finally dared to meet the Archbishop's eyes, he caught the trace of a wintry smile that softened the hard, old face ever so little. Then the pacing began again. This time Alfonso waited silently and watched. He noted how the old man clasped his hands at his back as he strode back and forth, his head sunk low between his shoulders. He fancied he could hear the click of a steel beak and the rustle of iron feathers.

"As you know, lad," said the old man suddenly, "we've laid plans for taking Segovia. All that holds us back is the necessity of seeing if the king will actually send Joanna from the city to be placed under the charge of the Bishop of Seville. If the king in fact listened to his advisers and will indeed exile her to the South, believing that the nation wants her put aside, it might pay us to wait and let public opinion work for us. With Joanna out of the way, the danger to your sister diminishes. Henry wouldn't consent to have her harmed. But if the queen remains in Segovia, I fear we can't wait much longer. Isabella is in real danger as long as Joanna is queen and in the same city."

"Joanna will certainly strike again and if she feels she must leave, she may try before she goes. You do not know the woman."

"I know her, my son, far better than you. Nor have I forgotten what she tried to do to you through that Moorish tutor. But I must confess I was surprised at the role of Fejjuan the Berber. I never dreamed she'd go that far. She's utterly vicious, and with Girón dead she'll concoct some other threat against your sister."

"But what do you plan to do, Your Grace?"

"Move against Segovia tomorrow. I've informed our friends in the city to expect us. We have powerful allies there, you know. No man in Spain has endured more from the king or suffered as many insults as Bishop Juan Arias. His brother, the chanter, has fared no better, and together they control no small contingent of the populace. When our army moves up to the walls, we can count upon help from within. Beltrán de la Cueva will never be able to command all the defenses. Unless I am greatly mistaken we'll have the Princess Isabella with us here in Ávila tomorrow night."

"How, Your Grace?"

"At dawn our forces will move out of Ávila, marching along the road to Medina del Campo where Henry is encamped. When Beltrán's spies inform him of this, he'll think we plan to attack the king. He'll no doubt dispatch troops to rescue him, thereby weakening Segovia's defenses."

"You mean to attack Medina first, Your Grace?"

"Of course not, lad. We'll leave the road to Medina and swing back on Segovia. By noon we can be crossing the fords of the Clamores within the shadow of the Alcázar. They'll know our strategy by then, of course, but they'll have no time to prepare for our assault. Beltrán is in for a very unpleasant surprise."

5

By the time the Princess Isabella had escaped Fejjuan the Berber, Juan Baptista Colom had lived in Calais nearly a year. As she sailed the stormy seas of Castilian politics, he, in the *Montserrat*, sailed the actual stormy Ocean Sea to England, Scotland, even to Iceland, which men called Ultima Thule, and at last to France. His home was now Calais on the English Channel, and he had visited London on several sailings and had friends there, friends he would not forget in years to come.

Jeannot, who had secreted him out of Naples when Prince Ferdinand arrived there, looking for the fugitive Coloms, had touched port in many places far from Italy and Spain, fearful that he could no longer trade in waters under Aragón's control. The experience for Juan Baptista had been invaluable, since his cousin, who had taken a great fancy to him, trained him in the practical aspects a seaman, and later a navigator, needed and could not be found in books.

Many times he told Juan Baptista of their destination and their new life. "You'll meet another cousin there, my boy, Guillaume Christophe Casanove Coulon, who is a great man in those parts. He's an admiral in the French Navy, but he's also a merchant, and when the king needs his special services, he'll be, like me, a corsair. I'll ask him to give you shelter, train you, and make you a part of his enterprises. Cousin Coulon is as old fashioned and traditional as your father and me, so when you meet him, say right off, 'I come as a dove.' That's what I told him the first time I dropped anchor here."

In Calais surprises met them. The first was the presence of Bartolomeu Colom, who now used the name Columbus, which he said gave him the security of a Latin, rather than a vernacular name, one which seemed to lend him a respect he hadn't encountered before. "I could have become another Coulon," he laughed, "but Frenchies aren't too popular in Great Britain and Portugal. Colombo, far too Italian, where that race represents all that is shifty and grasping, just wouldn't do. And who, in England, even heard the name Colom." Bartolomeu then went on to say how glad he was that Juan Baptista had arrived when he had. "If you'd come just two weeks later, I'd have been en route to Lisbon, where Cousin Guillaume has found me a fine position with a mapmaker who has close ties with the king there. It's a rare chance and I look forward to it. And, when I'm settled, and if Cousin Guillaume agrees, you can come to work with me. So study hard here, as I did, and let them teach you all I know about cartography. They're famous for it."

An even greater surprise was the twelve year-old boy who threw himself into Juan Baptista's arms, shouting, "Brother, brother, it's me, it's Jaume!"

"Jeannot and I picked him up in Pavia of Segarra, where the priests were hiding him. He couldn't believe it was me. The poor little fellow thought his real family had deserted him. So here he is, safe and sound, and he lives, as you are going to, here in Calais with his new family. By Our Lady of Montserrat, it was a relief to get him out of Aragón. Prince Ferdinand must have known we were three brothers, so there was always the chance that one of his spies would have found our Jaume.

"But there is something I must tell you. Our cousins have suffered a tragedy and are in mourning. About a month ago their only son, Christophe, died in an accident at sea. So be prepared for what may look like a lack of cordiality and enthusiasm and attribute it to their sorrow. They'll come around, once the worst of their grief has abated."

When they entered the Coulon mansion, they saw every one dressed in black, but even so, when Guillaume heard Juan Baptista say, "I come as a dove," he immediately took him in his arms in a strong embrace. "I won't take you to my wife now," he said, "but this evening, after I've prepared her, you and she will meet, and, strange to say, young Juan Baptista, I think you are going to help me to cure her grief."

"In any way I can, cousin, but tell me how."

"Great God, young man, I wish some one had prepared *me* for the way you look. When you walked in, for a moment I thought you were our dead Christophe back from his grave!"

"I look that much like your son?"

"It's not so much as actual resemblance, although that is marked—your height, your complexion and eyes, your hair; it's something else—the way you walk, move your head, smile. I must prepare my wife for it, but I believe that, as shattering as it may be, it will help her in her grief."

Jeannot interrupted. "Your cousin Marie will need you, lad, and through her you can repay some of the debt you'll owe Guillaume for the opportunities you'll have from him—education, a home, and in time the chance to sail in his fleet."

Guillaume and Jeannot exchanged glances, before the older man said, "I know how glad you've been to have your old name back again and be free from the name Colombo. I don't blame you. But now, for several very good reasons, we believe you must give up Colom again. Wait! No immediate refusal. Listen to the why and the wherefore."

Bartolomeu, broke in, "Remember, brother, how our father urged us to follow Bertrán's master plan. I'm following it, as you've heard, for I traded Colom for Coulon, and now that I'm moving to Lisbon, I've decided to try our name in the language of the Ancients as Columbus. You'll soon get used to Coulon as a surname, but you may have a harder time adapting to a new set of given names. You'll have to give up Juan Baptista, brother, for those two names linked to Coulon would possibly provide a key to some of Ferdinand's searchers."

Jeannot, who saw Juan Baptista's mounting anger and knew how hot it could rage, interrupted again, "It's a fine set of names you're going to get, names you can take pride in. I'm going to let cousin Guillaume tell you."

The admiral laid his hand on Juan Baptista's arm. "I want you to be called after our dead son, Christophe, which is also one of my names. Just possibly in Aragón they'll think you are indeed my son, and this could bring a stronger degree of safety. A less practical and more personal reason for me, my boy, is this: I sense that if you become Christophe Coulon, my wife Marie will find comfort in it and in you. You can't replace our dead son, but you can help to fill our loss. If you'll pardon the unusual sentiment I'm entertaining for you already, you'll come to realize what the name Christophe can mean to you, in our home and in the world at large.

That night at dinner, Juan Baptista Colom, alias Giovanni Colombo, became Christophe Coulon. He shook his head and accepted it, for it sounded sweet on the tongue of the lady he would soon learn to call his mother. But he wondered if he would ever escape Bertrán's influence, which had followed him this far.

When Madame Marie raised her eyes to his and saw how tall he was, how red his hair, how blue his eyes, she could not speak at first. At last she said, "My boy!" And then, "Be welcome in your home."

As dinner progressed, the new Christophe, seated directly across from Madame Marie, saw her eyes widen from time to time and fill with tears, and he caught, too, an eagerness, a watchfulness, and a smile he could not fathom. Later Guillaume told him. "When she smiled, so did I. It was when we saw a gesture, an expression, and when we heard you laugh. Christophe, forgive our sentimentality, and please bring our new hope to fruition, and *be* our second son. We believe that God sent you here for this."

"God *and* St. Christopher," said Marie. "St. Christopher, who bore Our Lord upon his broad shoulders, like our own first Christophe, who carried our lives upon his, and like you, our new Christophe, who will do the same for us."

She then unclasped a silver chain she wore around her neck, at the end of which he saw, as she drew it from her bosom, a silver medallion about the width of a rose. It was, he was certain, a St. Christopher medal. "This belonged to my first Christophe," Marie whispered, stifling a sob. "Now it belongs to my second."

The new Christophe took the medallion and examined it attentively. He saw that it was very old and that it glowed as only ancient silver can. On it, the

Latin words, worn by the years and use, nevertheless leaped out at him: X*po fer-ens*, he read, X*po*, the abbreviation for 'Christ,' and 'ferens,' which meant 'bearing,' or 'carrying.'

"Christopher or Christophe," he mused. "A colorful variation. I like it and the time has come to add it to the collection of names given us by old Bertrán."

***

The new Christophe proved to be all that Jeannot had predicted. The maps he made were exceptional, and one on which he lavished hours of care, skill and affection he presented to Marie.

"It's worth a golden frame," she said, "but for now I shall not frame it. I want it where I can touch it, hold it, carry it about with me." And Guillaume told Christophe that she kept it rolled up and tied with a ribbon by her pillow when she slept.

6

It was in his first and only year in France that Christophe fell in love. Since Angelina many girls and women had known and wanted him. His great height, exotic coloring, his new and impressive musculature, and the confidence he had in dealing with women, as if he never dreamed one could tell him "NO," drew them to him and frequently into his bed or theirs. Since he had attained the six feet three of his father and Bartolomeu, women had to look up to him literally as well as figuratively. Instead of seventeen, he looked more like twenty or even a little older. And his tallness, his great physical strength and his bigness, made men view him with respect, sensing his quality.

The girl he fell in love with, who was well out of his reach socially, and would have been, even if he could have let it be known that he had noble blood, was Isabau, daughter of a count and countess. He had never met her, but even, he thought, as Dante had met Beatrice in passing her on the street and staring at her in church, he had come to know his Isabau. During services in the cathedral, their eyes met frequently and clung. Of course the countess soon noticed it and told the count. After that Isabau never looked his way, not even furtively, but when she thought his eyes might be on her, she blushed and hung her head.

"How can I meet her?" he wondered. "How speak to her and hold her hand? How kiss those lips? She wants to be with me. She would talk to me, if we could find a time and place, and, she might do more for her eyes tell me she would."

To himself Christophe said, "I'll ask Mother Marie to persuade the bishop to let me serve as acolyte so that I can carry the holy missal to each worshiper so that she can kiss it. He can't refuse Mother Marie, for she gives more to the diocese than any one." He believed the stratagem would serve his purpose perfectly.

On the first day of Advent, a Monday, Christophe, resplendent in red cassock and white surplice, extended the missal to the faithful. When he presented it to the kneeling countess, she glared at him, but kissed the volume and crossed herself with stiff piety. Then as he bent dutifully over Isabau, and as she kissed the missal, he whispered, the first fragment of his message: "Meet me…" On Tuesday he whispered, "at your garden gate." On Wednesday Isabau blushed and leaned forward too eagerly to hear him and he didn't dare to say a word. It was Thursday when he said, "…At midnight." Friday yielded, "of the Sabbath." And on Saturday, as her lips first touched the missal and then the tip of his finger, he managed to whisper as softly as a zephyr in the night the words, "I love you more than God!"

He could hardly believe he had done it, but the wink on Isabau's face as she raised it, just after her lips touched his finger, told him he had.

The eyelash moon was setting when she appeared wraith-like at the garden gate, where he had been waiting more than an hour. It was obvious that she was terrified. Her face looked as white as the petals of a regal lily, and she kept looking back over her shoulder toward the castle. A bird made a noise in the trees, and Isabau took three steps backward.

"Don't go," he begged. "Come back!"

She floated to the gate again and he seized her hand and held it. "I love you, Isabau. Give me the key."

"My father," she whispered, "if he finds us, he'll kill us both! This is madness! You'd better go!"

Suddenly she pressed the key into his hand. The iron gate creaked dangerously as it opened, and Christophe cursed under his breath as Isabau gasped in fear. He heard the lock click behind him as the gate swung shut. And then he took her in his arms and felt her breasts against the hardness of his chest. She trembled like a frightened dove, and her mouth was cold as he opened his over it. Then she relaxed and he felt her mouth grow warm and open under his instinctively. "Never kissed before," he thought, "but love has made her apt."

Suddenly her arms were around his neck, her hands fondling the thick hair at the nape of the neck. When he began to open her bodice, her hands flew to his and tried to stop him, but he persisted. When her hands fell away from his, he knew she didn't want him to stop.

"Slow!" he thought. "Gentle! She must want and enjoy this as much as I. And if we accomplish what I want this night, perhaps they'll let her marry me." But even as he thought it, he knew they wouldn't.

He tasted hot tears which fell on the breasts he was kissing. He lowered her to the grass, pulled down her shift and slipped out of his doublet and hose. Incredibly she opened her soul and her body to him. And then a cloud drifted across the waning moon. The same voice seemed to ring in his ears, that voice which had urged him on when he was drowning off the coast of Naples, that voice which gave him strength as he lay delirious after his scalding in the cauldron. Now the voice spoke prohibitively. What voice was it? Was it his own or the voice of his conscience? Were there really guardian angels who intervened or interfered in human lives? If so, he'd never forgive this particular angel. To have been so close to earthly heaven and to be torn away from it by something as elemental as unexpected and mortifying as detumescence!

For long moments there in the darkness she lay motionless in his arms. He did not try to hold her when she got to her feet, pulled on her shift and then her gown, and mutely left him on the ground naked and unfulfilled. At last, shaken, frightened too much to be embarrassed, he struggled into his clothes, picked up the key and opened the gate. Then he threw the key as hard as he could into the shrubbery and hurried home, wishing for the first time that some one not of this earth would stop controlling his life and actions.

**

If Isabau hadn't told her sister, who had told their mother, no trouble would have resulted, but Isabau had told her. The consequences turned out to be devastating.

The next night as he returned from a pressing task at the harbor, a premonition of danger made a shiver run down his spine. And then in the middle of a lonely square four shadows materialized, hooded and ominous. He caught the glint of steel in the pale light of the moon. The four separated and formed a ring around him. "This is for the Lady Isabau," one hissed, and another spoke aloud, "We're going to cut you so bad you'll never touch another lady."

Christophe knew fear, but under the fear arose that confidence, that knowledge that he was not going to die, not at the hands of an angry father's minions, not before he accomplished what he knew he had to accomplish, what heaven seemed to be saving him for. Drawing his own dagger, he ran at one assailant, who retreated, giving him a chance to dart into a doorway where he could hope to defend himself. "If I can get past them," he told himself, "I can outrun them easily." And then he acted. Whirling his cape, he caught one unaware and threw him to the ground, taking another with him. As he dashed for the middle of the street, a dagger's point caught him in the shoulder, just as his entered the attacker's chest. He heard a scream and muffled curses, but he was free and running, spurred on by pain and fear. His shoulder hurt and he could feel warm blood trickling down his arm.

At home Guillaume, as he watched Marie treat the wound, spoke as calmly as he could. "Christophe," he said, "I understand the way of a young man with a woman. Marie and I have heard about your whoring and the way you've chased every good looking woman you could. Yes, wife, when I was Christophe's age I did the same, but I never took it into my head to try to seduce the daughter of a count. My God, boy, of all the maids of France, you chose the one most likely to lead to ruin!"

"I didn't seduce her, cousin," said Christophe angrily.

"But you tried to," said Marie, still shocked at what had happened. "And trying, in the case of a nobleman's daughter is just as bad. Oh, my son, they'll hunt you down. You won't be able to leave the house and live. And the count, if his men can't catch you, may report this to the king. This entire household could suffer greatly."

Christophe grew alarmed at the thought, since he had never dreamed he could bring trouble on his cousins. "Send me away," he said. "I deserve no more of your goodness and kindness to me. I'll go tonight."

Guillaume, looked at Marie, and shook his head. "Young men," he growled, "young hotheads, young studs! Yes, you shall go away, but not skulking off into the night. The count's men would be certain to catch you, and now that you've wounded two and shamed two others, you wouldn't have a chance. I have a better plan. I hadn't thought to send you to sea so soon, but circumstances now demand it. You've seen how we're readying the fleet for action. Fortunately the king has just told me of an expedition he wants me to make for him. He has commanded me to sail and be ever-watchful for treasure ships on the way to Italy from England, ships bearing paintings, statuary, and other works of art to Lorenzo the Magnificent. We'll intercept those ships and Lorenzo will feel much less magnificent and we much richer."

Marie burst into tears. "Guillaume," she cried, "you'll be a corsair again, a pirate, and you'll turn our son into one as well. What has Lorenzo ever done to you?"

"I have nothing against Lorenzo, my dear, and neither has Christophe, but our king is eager to despoil him and to get his hands on what those ships are carrying. Danger will be minimal. Italians don't like to fight and they'll not risk their lives to save their ruler's valuables or his pride. There'll be three Italian ships and my fleet will number twenty vessels. They'll surrender the minute they see us bearing down up on them."

***

The fleet would sail three days later, while Christophe pined and paced in frustration in Guillaume's house, commanded not to show his face outside. News trickled in. The count had betrothed Isabau to an elderly duke in Picardy and the nuptials were moving to their end. Guillaume's informants reported that men known to be in the count's hire were prowling the streets near his home. It was plain they were trying to find out where Christophe was. On the night before the sailing a wain filled with wine casks left the house for the harbor under heavy guard. If the count's men suspected that hidden beneath the wine, which was packed in straw, their intended victim lay, they gave no sign. Soon Christophe and the wine were safely aboard Guillaume's flagship, and he was on his way to piracy.

But it was not Lorenzo's galleons that felt the power of Guillaume's fleet. His twenty vessels, long before they could reach the Straits of Gibraltar, came upon an even richer prize. What ships are these?" Christophe asked his cousin. "I count fifteen. Will we attack so many?"

"Of course," laughed Guillaume. "They're merchantmen and only two warships guard them. They fly the flag of Flanders, and Flemish ships usually carry very valuable cargoes."

"Will they surrender?"

"Of course they won't. They'll give us a fight you won't forget, but I wish we were not so close to Portugal. Somewhere on that coast line over there is the port of Lagos. If King Alfonso's war ships are in port, they'll probably prevent us from doing what we want to do."

"And with that in mind, you'll dare to seize the Flemish vessels?"

"In our line of work, Christophe, one takes his chances. I have no reports of Portugal's navy in these waters. I'm confident enough that her warships are patrolling the Spanish coast, for as usual, Portugal is plotting war against Castile, if war hasn't already started. Yes, we'll attack the Flemish fleet and take our chances with the Portuguese."

The battle was much more than Guillaume had bargained for. The Flemish vessels were well armed and their crews fearless. Guillaume's flagship engaged the larger warships He managed to outmaneuver her, but couldn't finish her off, due to the attack by the other. Suddenly the case was desperate. Both warships bore down upon him and the smaller unexpectedly rammed him. Suddenly Guillaume was not the attacker, he was the attacked. The flagship listed frighteningly. They were taking water.

The *Bechalla*—the larger Flemish warship—used her cannon effectively and Guillaume lost a mast. She listed more. Grapples from the *Bechalla* fastened themselves on her. Flemish marines were swarming over the side.

Christophe saw Guillaume go down under more men than he could count, saw him pulled to his feet and his arms bound. He followed them as they dragged him onto the *Bechalla* fighting his way madly. The Flemish fell back from his sword, but not for long. They cornered him at last on the deck. Ten marines were pushing him slowly to the rail. Guillaume, now subdued and bleeding, roared at him over the din of battle. "Overboard with you, Christophe. It's your only chance."

Then he was in the water and under it. The Flemish marines were firing at him. Just then, four of Guillaume's ships closed in and the *Bechalla* took the blow of a ram. He couldn't believe how quickly she went down. The undertow sucked him towards her, but he managed to pull away. Then, just as she slid beneath the water, there was a terrible explosion. Fire had reached her powder magazines. Men, sails, rigging, barrels, planks, spars fell into the sea in a fiery rain. Part of a mast struck him a glancing blow across the face and blackness covered his eyes.

As the smoke cleared he surfaced, half conscious and floundering without purpose at first. All about him he saw ships grappled together and men fighting to the death. Ships burned, the sea was dotted with men trying to survive. Dead men floated in the water. Through the haze of semi-consciousness he knew he must find Guillaume, and he clung to that thought. A spar washed into him, perhaps the one which had knocked him unconscious, and he threw his arms across it and held his face above water. He passed in and out of consciousness several times. Later he realized that he must have slept, hanging across the spar, for when he was able to see clearly and take stock of his situation, night had fallen. Of the two fleets he saw no sign, but in the distance he saw lights that did not move and he realized that not far away was the coast of Portugal. Then out of the night a ship appeared. Sharp eyes on board caught sight of him. Voices in a soft, yet sibilant tongues hailed him. "If he's Flemish, bring him in; if he's French, shoot him."

Christophe made ready to die, and yet that ever-present inner voice told him that he wouldn't. The Portuguese officer looking down at him gave another order. "Pull him in. Look at his red hair. He must be Flemish or Holland Dutch."

His inner voice rang out in his mind. "It's dark. By the time they lower a boat and get to you, you must shed your uniform. With it you're a member of the French Navy, without it you can be anyone."

And so when the boatmen pulled him out of the water, he wore only his shirt and hose. When the officer, once he was on board, spoke to him Portuguese, which he didn't speak, but which he found he could understand sufficiently, he replied in Italian and then in Catalan. And then blackness came down again and he knew no more for hours.

When he awoke again, he was lying on a stretcher and was being carried by two men obviously not sailors. They laid the stretcher on the floor of a lighted building and he saw that it was a chapel. A monk bent over him and asked his name. The monk spoke Italian and spoke it furtively, looking over his shoulder to make certain they were alone. "You're in the hospital of the Church of Saint Mary in Lagos. You're wounded in the head, but it's not serious. You'll be up and around in a day or so. Now tell me, what a man of my nation—yes, I'm Italian—was doing in the sea, nearly naked and near drowning. And what is that other language you speak so well?"

"What was the outcome of the naval battle, brother? Who won?"

"The Flemish lost half their fleet. The French a little less, or so it's said. Portuguese ships rescued the Flemish and drove off the French. I've heard they lost their admiral, that pirate Coulon."

"I left Naples more than a year ago," said Christophe prudently. "I joined the Flemish fleet when it anchored in Majorca en route home. What will the Portuguese do with me, brother?"

"You haven't told me your name, my son," said the priest.

"Mine is Mateo."

Christophe pretended to lose consciousness to give him time to think. It was time, certainly, to change his name again. He couldn't be Coulon in Portugal, not after the battle off Lagos so soon after Guillaume Coulon, the corsair and his son Christophe had violated Portuguese waters to attack a Flemish fleet. Brother Mateo thought he was Italian, although he supposed he might claim to be a Catalan since he had spoken that language, too, when he was picked out of the harbor. Then he recalled what Bartolomeu had told him the name he planned to take when he came to Portugal Barthomeus Columbus. He wondered where his brother was. Surely he must be in Lisbon, the center of navigation in the western world. Yes, that was the name he would take, the Latin origin of Colom, of 'dove.' He pretended to regain consciousness. "What were you asking me, brother, when I fainted? My name? It's Christopher, Christopher Columbus. Somewhere in Lisbon I think I have a brother named Barthomeus or Bartholomew. Have you heard of him?"

"Heard of him?" cried brother Mateo. "The saints be praised! I know the man. He comes often to my church. And you're his brother! He is the best known cartographer in Portugal. He knows the king and the prince and they respect him. He makes some of their best maps. How small the world is, my son, and how blessed you are by your patron saint. This is Thursday. On Saturday you'll be strong enough to take the boat to Lisbon to find your brother."

Juan Baptista, who could hardly remember his given name, alias Giovanni Colombo, alias Christophe Coulon, had taken a fresh new name and as Christopher Columbus he was going to Lisbon to meet his brother, another Columbus. "Bertrán must be smiling wherever he is," he thought.

7

When the men on the walls of Segovia saw the banners of the army of the League moving up the gorges of the two rivers, they were stunned. They saw detachments pouring over the plain and still others marching down the long road from the sierra. Segovia was surrounded. Only the swiftest couriers managed to outdistance the invading hosts to ride off toward Medina del Campo with the news.

Beltrán had been preparing feverishly from the moment he realized the presence of the army of the League, but he was not ready for the great host he saw deploying before his walls. Out across the plain he could identify the black armor of the Archbishop under his personal pennon and beside him the smaller figure of the Prince beneath the banner of Trastámara. "If only the old devil would ride a little closer," muttered Beltrán. "It would all be over before it begins if we could place a cross-bow quarrel in his gullet."

But the Archbishop valued his gullet too much and had too much respect for the Segovian crossbowmen to expose himself or Alfonso. Keeping well out of range, he dispatched a herald and demanded the person of the Princess Isabella. Beltrán, of course, refused, saying that she was the king's ward, left in his charge, and that she would by no means leave the safety of the city.

The Archbishop signaled attack by dipping his pennon, and the army poised itself. Beltrán could see no siege engines and wondered if the Archbishop had taken leave of his wits. Only a madman would send his men to certain destruction against walls that could not be breached. Then, since he knew Alfonso Carrillo's military genius, he grew uneasy. Putting himself in the cleric's place, he reached the conclusion that the besiegers expected help from inside Segovia. He cast an anxious glance down from the walls into the streets and found them empty. Every door and window visible was closed tight, and he knew that the inhabitants of the city were crouching in their cellars hoping that no granite catapult charges would strike their houses.

The trumpets of the League sounded silver-clear, and he saw the great Trastámara banner move toward the walls. The screech of the city's mangonels and the grating sound of the thousands of cross-bows being strung stung his ears and encouraged him. The Archbishop would receive a hot welcome if he moved much closer.

True Spaniard that he was, Beltrán shrank from the thought of butchering the fine horses he saw out on the plain, and he wished there were some way to save the many knights and footmen and to win them over to the king. But he was Spanish, too, in his determination to repel whatever attack might be made.

Suddenly the long line of knights broke into a gallop. Ocher clouds of dust exploded from one end of the line to the other. Like distant thunder came the rumble of hooves. The walls vibrated. Seconds later they were close enough for him to see that the cloud was shot through with the glint of hundreds of lance points. "Almost within range," he told his squire, as he watched the first mangonels let fly. He turned to his trumpeter. "Crossbows on the second blast," he said.

He could not remember later what happened during the next few seconds. Before the trumpet gave the signal to send the flight of devastating bolts into the advancing ranks of horses and men, the great bells in the cathedral set up a sudden tolling. Instantly the galloping ranks split like a stream of water against a boulder and flowed to right and left in two outward moving arcs paralleling the walls at first and then bending back into the *vega*. The trumpets sounded too late. The hail of cross-bow quarrels drove venomously at the retreating cavalry with only an occasional hit. The signal from the cathedral had saved the knights of the League.

While the quarrels were still in the air, the streets near the gates filled with armed citizens surging from houses and patios and even from churches and public buildings. Beltrán saw them cutting his men to pieces before they realized they were attacked. Scores died before he made himself heard over the confusion. He had hardly rallied his troops and driven the people away when a courier arrived from Andrés Cabrera. Citizens had taken the east gate and opened it. Already the League swarmed inside Segovia and fought its way along the streets behind the city's militia as it retreated toward the Alcázar.

Beltrán ordered a mass retreat toward the same fortress, and with a guard of ten knights hurried there as fast as he could make his way through the milling soldiery in the narrow streets. He planned to take the queen, their daughter, and the Princess Isabella with him into the Alcázar, Once there with the drawbridge lifted, Alfonso Carrillo and his forces could batter themselves to shreds against the sheer cliffs rising above the two ravines. Meanwhile, surely the king would be on the march from Medina del Campo.

Isabella was in the ladies' quarters of the palace when Beltrán burst in. She saw confusion erupt and spread like fire through dry wheat until the whole palace became a screaming shrieking mob of terrified women, running servants, and nervous Moorish guardsmen. Everyone pushed toward the corridors that led to the Alcázar.

"Bring the child!" she heard Joanna scream. "Bring the jewels! Leave the rest—they're fighting in the courtyard already."

Isabella saw Beltrán advancing toward her, his face ugly with blood and dust, and a deep cut over his right eye. She heard him barking commands which restored some semblance of order, and she realized that even as he moved to cut her off from the stairway, he kept his mind on the important business of evacuating the palace and reaching the safety of the Alcázar.

"Princess," she heard him call, but did not listen. She reached the door and then the stairway. On her way down she passed a few frightened servants, but Beltrán did not pursue. Only dimly now could she hear above her his stentorian bellow herding the women and servants into the escape corridor.

On she went until she came to the audience chamber, forgetful now of Beltrán and Joanna and the ladies, all of whom by then must have been running over the drawbridge and through the gate beneath the portcullis. From the courtyards came the sounds of fighting. Battles raged in every street leading to the palace. The fighting was near enough now for her to distinguish individual voices, hoarse and wild as the two forces clashed. The tread of marching feet and the hooves of war horses on stone grew deafening. Occasionally she heard a cry, terrible and high above the din. Then across the roofs of the city rang the piercing notes of the Archbishop's trumpets.

A sudden silence more terrible than the uproar. She leaned against the wall and her hands pressed hard into the cold stone. Again the clank of armor, the rattle of swords. Men marching down corridors. Whose men?

Straight and calm she waited just below the dais. Then they were in the room, falling back along the walls, exploring the alcoves, opening doors and thrusting their heads into halls and anterooms. They formed two mail-clad ranks from the outer door right up to where she stood beside the dais, and down that aisle of men she could see the Archbishop, tall and ominous in his black chain mail, the long robe with its white cross falling over his shoulders like a crimson cloud.

She could hardly breathe. The rank stink of leather and the sweat of men who have ridden long and fought hard stifled her.

Where was Alfonso? Her questing eyes found him—Alfonso in a silver cuirass and polished helmet looking more mature than she would have believed possible. As he hurried down between the soldiers she realized that his eyes were on a level with her own. It was more than stature, she saw, that made him seem grown up. A new, quiet grace, and a red down on upper lip and chin. A leanness of cheek had replaced the roundness she had known. In that face the fine bonework stood out, and the color of the skin spoke of long days spent in the sun. Her heart filled with pride. She gulped and refused to weep. Then she linked her arm in his, and together they walked out of the audience chamber of the old palace of Segovia, over the drawbridge and to freedom.

An hour later on the road to Ávila, Isabella realized for the first time in nearly ten years that she was free of the nagging fear of what Joanna might do to her or her brother. In Ávila she would begin a new life.

Alfonso, Isabella soon learned, had great plans. His ambition, unbridled for his fourteen years, startled her. Long before Segovia disappeared behind them he was telling her about what he would do when he was king. Castile was not enough, he said, and he would eventually have her sit beside him on the throne of all the Spains. As for Henry, Joanna and the Beltraneja they would all live in exile in some cold and inhospitable land.

Isabella was dubious. "Do you really believe, Alfonso, that you will rule all the Spains? Even Aragón? All is a great deal, and many people will never change sides or give up what they own."

"The Archbishop says they will. He says I rule half of Spain already."

"Has he told you that thousands of people think you have committed the sin of blasphemy by setting yourself up as king? People can never forget that Henry was coronated according to the oldest traditions."

"But he's unfit to rule," said Alfonso petulantly, looking again like the fourteen-year-old boy he was, "The Archbishop has said so a thousand times. They all tell me so, and they ought to know."

"I can't deny it," said Isabella. "Henry is one of the worst kings Spain has ever had, but you can't erase the fact that he was anointed with the sacred oil. That gave him heaven's blessing, God's approval."

"Ancient law tells us that tyrants can be overthrown," said Alfonso a trifle pompously, reflecting the very intonation of the Archbishop. "And Henry, is certainly a tyrant. He must be dethroned. *Sic semper tyrannis.*" Isabella wondered how the Archbishop had gained such complete control of the boy's mind. Alfonso seldom made a remark without reference to the old man's opinion. His every thought stemmed from the Archbishop's thinking. She was about to try again when she looked into his eyes and saw glowing there an enthusiasm so vivid for one so young that she waited to hear what he was about to say.

"You aren't the only one, Isabella, who's under the protection of heaven. The Archbishop had a sign from Our Lady who told him that I shall rule and Henry will die."

"What was the sign?"

"The Archbishop was not free to tell us, but he convinced me and everyone else that she spoke to him and gave him a message. And it really makes no difference whether we know the sign or not. We have the message. It came from

Our Lady, and that's enough for me. Besides, the soothsayers all predict Henry's death before mine."

"The Soothsayers! Alfonso! In one breath you speak of the Mother of God and in the next of the soothsayers?"

"King Saul went to the Witch of Endor, sister."

"And learned of his own downfall, brother."

"And our ancestor, King Sancho, called upon the powers of darkness."

"And learned from the spirit of his father, King Ferdinand, that he would die. You know, Alfonso, how I feel about soothsayers and all the people who deal with, or pretend to deal with the powers of darkness. It isn't that I fear the supernatural powers such people claim to have, for I doubt that they possess any of them. What I fear is the grasp they have upon the minds of men. People who will believe that a few birds flying in a certain direction foretell the future have too little faith in God. If you're going to let your life be shaped by ancient superstitions, or Moorish astrology, or the charms these Gypsies are bringing into the country, then you admit that you believe in powers other than God's and have already broken the first commandment."

Alfonso was not ready to put the soothsayers out of mind. He argued that they had foretold the outcome of the Battle of Olmedo.

"And what was the outcome? You claim victory, but so does Henry. All they predicted was that an eagle would fall. Was Henry that eagle or were you?"

She watched Alfonso's face take on its familiar little pout. "He's still a child," she thought, almost aloud, "in spite of all the fine words he utters to make people think he is the King of Castile." And yet, the more she thought about their conversation, the more she had to admit that he had matured. All his talk of foreign embassies and signs from heaven reflected at least an interest in affairs of state, no matter how naive that interest was. But, even so, he was no fit substitute for Henry and no foundation stone upon which to build a kingdom. He was not nearly old enough, and surely far from clever enough, to match wits with the experienced and ruthless minds using him as a figurehead around which to rally all the elements inimical to Henry.

She wished that in some way he could make his peace with the king and Joanna and end the civil war. People would soon forget that Alfonso had usurped the power and committed blasphemy. She decided to sound him out as to this before they arrived in Ávila and he had time to have his opinion further molded by the Archbishop and the nobles of the League.

"Henry will be overthrown only by God, Alfonso," she began, feeling her way carefully. "But who can say what His will is? If you could persuade Henry that you'd stop the war, provided he made you his legal heir on his death, then

I see two important results: you'd end this awful civil strife that is ruining Spain and our people, and you'd keep Joanna's daughter from ever ruling here."

"And how could I persuade him, Isabella?"

"By meeting him somewhere to discuss terms. I'd go with you, and Henry would listen, for he truly hates the war."

"We might fall into his hands again. Have you stopped to think what would become of us if that happened? We'd end up in same oubliette under the royal palace in Segovia and there we'd rot unless Joanna decided to end our suffering with a dose of poison. No, Isabella, I'll take my chances with the Lord, if I have offended Him. His punishment would be less to fear than the king's."

"I didn't mean that you should surrender in person, Alfonso. Prison would be the least we could expect, if we actually surrendered, and Joanna is quite capable of putting us out of the way once we were in her clutches. We would not allow ourselves to fall into Henry's hands. After the treaty we'd come back to Ávila. That would be part of the treaty. And Ávila is safe. The League would shelter us, even if, for a time we had no power and couldn't be used to further their plans.

"But if we stay here," she went on, "and make no peace, the war goes on and people suffer and die. Henry has very powerful allies abroad. Remember Portugal whose king is Joanna's brother. Louis of France may send troops any time. Why, Henry might even make a treaty with the Kingdom of Granada for levies."

"I have an embassy in Paris, too," said Alfonso, "although precious little good it seems to do me. The Archbishop says King Louis is waiting to see which side will win here. He'll help the winner, so as to ally himself with Castile against Aragón, and thus keep Spain forever at war within her borders."

"Will you promise me to think about making peace with Henry?"

"Not now," replied Alfonso. "The Archbishop wouldn't like it."

Suddenly he stood up in his stirrups and shaded his eyes. "There are the towers of Ávila," he said. "The palace is cool there, for the walls are thick. How nice it'll be to get in out of the sun. The Archbishop says the *vega* of Ávila is the hottest spot in July."

8

Politics makes the strangest bedfellows Christopher was to learn in the midst of his new happiness. Before it entered his present life, he believed he could never be happier. Bartolomew had welcomed him so lovingly, with such open and brotherly affection, that he soon forgot his parents, who might or might not be still alive in Lombardy, and even his adopted parents in Calais.

Sometimes he and Bartholomew talked about little Jaume still in that city, but they made no plans to send for him.

"Jaume never thawed out to me," said Bartholomew. "And I never felt that he was warm to you, once you had arrived and settled in. You were his favorite back home. What can have happened to him?"

"He told me frankly, brother. 'All of you,' he yelled at me when I tried to win him over, 'even my mother and father, deserted me when you left home. You should have sent for me. I'll never forgive any of you. And Bartholomew's bringing me here makes up for none of it.'"

"Well," said Bartholomew "at least he's safe in Marie's care, even if we think Guillaume is dead. She'll watch over him, and, if he'll let her, she'll mother him and he'll have a place in the world. He might, if he's bright at all, become her heir."

Christopher studied cartography with his brother and soon equaled him in skill and excellence. And when Prince João, well on the way to becoming Europe's most sea-minded monarch, would ask Bartholomew to bring his maps to the weekly councils of his navigators, sometimes Christopher was allowed to accompany him. The prince was cordial and even complimented his maps as well as Bartolomew's. And when his brother chortled that their future was assured and very bright, he agreed. Some day he knew he would sail the Ocean Sea, and not as an able seaman, but as the captain of his own ship.

He had not realized all that maps could mean, but Bartholomew was well aware of their importance. He had persuaded the prince to send him to England where he copied British maps of the northern Atlantic and where he had made friends by giving his own maps of more southern waters to the cartographers of the young Prince Henry, who quite possibly might one day be king. And when Bartholomew told Prince João that his brother had brought maps from France from the famous Admiral Coulon's archives, the prince had nodded appreciatively and even sometimes had invited Christopher to listen to the navigators.

Once, a letter arrived from Italy bringing back old memories and buried worries about their parents. A priest had written at Don Antoni's request, apparently, addressing the letter to Bartholomew "Your parents," it read, without setting down their names, "urge me to tell you to forget them and never try to communicate. Due to the wars in the part of Italy, where they now reside and of which you know, they are impoverished, but they are safe and are not in actual want. I must tell you that your father became involved in a certain rebellion here also, and must live in some obscurity. As for your less noble cousin Giacomo in the city where your second brother lived for some time, he too is well, but urges you not to write him. Pray to the Lord for your relatives, sir, and for their own good and for yours, never write to them again."

So the past must bury its past, they had agreed, and they turned their minds to the present and to the future, and both looked good. In Lisbon it was easy to forget, for no city in Europe seethed with more navigators, cartographers, geographers, and every kind of seaman. So Christopher was happy in that heady atmosphere and Bartholomew was proud of him.

**

One afternoon as he awaited Bartholomew in one of the beautiful parks for which Lisbon was famous, he saw two women coming toward him where he sat on his favorite bench. He stared in disbelief and leaped to his feet, bowing deeply as they came near. He had seen these two at the Portuguese court and would never forget them. One, tall lady, possessed of a feral but fading beauty, he recognized as the Queen of Castile who, he knew, was visiting her brother King Alfonso of Portugal. The other must be her daughter, he imagined, for she, he knew, had accompanied her mother. She was the young Princess Juana. He had heard her sad and lonely history. All Europe knew it. No wonder the child, for she was no more than a child in her early teens, looked so woebegone and pitiful. This was the daughter of Queen Joanna and of King Henry IV of Castile, that poor monarch who could not keep his realm intact. The child might not even be the king's, people whispered; many were certain she was the bastard daughter of the queen and the courtier, Don Beltrán de la Cueva, who, gossip said, was the lover also of the king. What a pitiful, shocking state of affairs! As he looked into the blue eyes of the princess, who might have been pretty, but for her stoic expression, he pitied her. What could such a person's life be with disgrace and calumny hanging over her like a cloud. They called her La Beltraneja, he recalled, and he knew what it meant.

He had thought they would drift on past him, but they stopped. At this he fell to his knees. "You may rise," he heard the queen say. "I would have a word with you. My daughter, the Princess of Castile, has seen your maps in the royal archives and has expressed an interest in them. She is smitten, as are my brother, my aunt, the Princess Beatriz, and half the court, with the lure of the sea and the route to Asia around the continent of Africa. Come here at this hour tomorrow and bring some of your newest maps with you. We shall inspect them and no doubt purchase a few."

"Highness," he murmured. "The maps are yours gratis. I would be honored to give them to the princess."

Again he dared look at the princess and saw in her poor, sad face, a spark of interest, but not enough to justify her mother's statement that she truly had set her heart on maps or the way around Africa to the Far East. The entire episode rang false, and it troubled him.

It troubled Bartholomew even more. In fact it frightened him. "Queen Joanna is a dangerous woman and very cruel. What can she want of you? She could have sent a messenger for your maps. I am concerned. But go, as of course you must, and Christopher, I wish I could stand there with you. Joanna is a crafty person. Say you'll do whatever she wants and mean it, for do it you must, no matter what it is."

The next day at the appointed hour Christopher seated himself on his bench, trying not to look too closely at the two chairs covered in red leather and embossed with golden nail heads, and trying even harder not to imagine what they meant. And the four soldiers in the royal guard, who stood in the distance to keep that part of the park private, did nothing to alleviate his anxiety. When two figures appeared in the park and made their slow way in his direction, he wished he was anywhere else, even back in Genoa. What in heaven or in hell had sent him the Queen of Spain and her brother, the King of Portugal?

When they had reached the chairs, which he now thought of as thrones, from his knees he watched them seat themselves, the deadly and beautiful Joanna and the vastly obese Alfonso. After a moment during which the king tried to make himself comfortable, Joanna spoke. "You may arise, young man, and seat yourself again. We have a great deal to say, so prepare yourself. I see that you have brought the maps. Leave them when we dismiss you and they shall be given to my daughter who will be expecting them."

Alfonso heaved himself more erect and spoke in a wheezy voice. He spoke in Catalan, and Christopher was so taken by surprise that he replied in that language. The queen laughed deep in her throat, but said nothing. "So," said Alfonso, "you are not Italian as we had heard."

The queen interrupted. "I thought so from the moment I saw you," she said. "What are you doing in Lisbon, young man? And why do you look so much like a certain person from Aragón? Are you a spy?"

"Highness," stammered Christopher. "I am no spy. I *am* a Catalan, or I *was* one, but I am no more. Please consider me a citizen of Portugal. And as for my resemblance to some person, I do not know what you mean."

"Young man," said Joanna with the cruel little laugh for which she was famous, "I forgive you this one lie, but never lie to me or to the king again."

Christopher fell again to his knees scraping his back on the bench. He felt more frightened than he had after his first encounter with angry royalty that day long ago when Prince Ferdinand had tried to spear him and had made his threat. He could hardly speak. "Highness," he croaked, "forgive me. I shall not lie again."

"Enough of this!" rasped the king. "We forgive the lie under the circumstances under which you told it. Return to your bench and listen, for it grows hot and I long for the coolness of my patio and its fountain."

As though anticipating Christopher's thought, the queen said, "We are here in the open because walls have ears even in that most private part of the palace. But continue, brother, for the heat increases."

"Why are you here, I repeat?" said the king. "And why *do* you look so much like the Prince of Aragón?"

"I am a Colom," replied Christopher. "My family and I were driven from Tarroja in Segarra of Aragón because King John thought we were part of the revolt against him."

"And were you?" asked Joanna.

"We were not, Highness, but we sympathized with the rebels, and that must have been enough for the king and his son."

"There must be more than that," mused the king. "And I suspect that it has to do with your fatal resemblance to King John's son."

Christopher opened his mouth and then shut it with a snap. How much could he dare tell these terrible people? And yet, how could he refuse to tell it all? Could any one be as bold as that? Besides, they had the means to elicit any information he refused to give.

The queen's voice cut him like a knife. "Don't daydream, young sir," she said, again with her cruel little laugh. "My royal brother has made a supposition, to wit, that your resemblance to Prince Ferdinand has much to do with the unhappy fate of the Coloms in Aragón. What have you to say?"

Christopher shivered. If only Bartholomew were here beside him! He would know what to say to this king and queen. "I look like Prince Ferdinand because my grandfather and his father were half-brothers, although my grandfather was a royal bastard. I believe that the prince and his father resented this."

"They certainly must have, Colom," said the king. "Why wouldn't they? Think what your family could have meant to the rebels, if they had known it and had exploited it!"

Joanna was counting something on her fingers. "This makes you, young sir, second cousin to the prince and great nephew of King John! It makes you even a cousin of Isabella, somehow, and, my God, of my little Juana! If I could unravel it, I think I'd learn that you are kith and kin of the king, my brother and of myself!"

Christopher groaned aloud, and the king shook his head and asked, "What have we stumbled into, sister? Do you think, after this unfortunate disclosure, that we can make use of this fellow's services? Do you think we can trust him with the mission you've concocted?"

"Perhaps we can trust him even more, brother. We have scores of kinsmen closer than this Colom, and all are too far removed to lay claim to royal descent. No, we have no need of concern in that respect. Rather we have a new and unforeseen advantage in this young man.

"You might explain," grumbled Alfonso. "When we summoned him here, our principal concern, insofar as he is to be involved, was to add more fuel to the fire we've lighted to destroy any possibility of a match between Ferdinand and Isabella. But I never understood just how this young man could play a significant role. What can he do for us?"

Joanna tossed her head impatiently. "Alfonso, when will you learn to keep abreast?"

Turning again to Christopher, the king said, "No wonder our royal relatives in Aragón tried to eradicate you and your family, and you have been wise, indeed, to change from Colom to Columbus. That was a very clever ruse."

Suddenly the king stood up and the queen also stood. "Return here tomorrow," she said. "And if you're thinking of flight, and I couldn't blame you if you did, remember your brother will be here in Lisbon and in our power."

9

All that afternoon and far into the night Bartholomew and Christopher conferred. Bartholomew saw his life, so carefully brought to the acme of success, about to end in disgrace or worse. What was the queen planning, he asked repeatedly? What could they do to avoid involvement and consequent danger? There were no answers, and toward dawn he said to Christopher. "Return tomorrow as ordered, brother. Find out what they want you to do and tell them you'll do it, which, of course, you must."

The next day, sitting on his bench and awaiting the inquisition he dreaded, Christopher tried not to look at the two red thrones before they were filled and afterward. The queen, as he had expected would be the case, did not delay in coming to the point. "You have seen the unhappiness of my daughter," she said. "She is miserable because, even if she is King Henry's daughter and my own, she fears that these wretched rebels, who call themselves the League, will deny all her claims and rights."

Christopher nodded his head and crossed himself. Why were they confiding all this to him, a foreigner of uncertain future? What could they possibly want of him? The mystery traumatized him and he must have turned so pale that the king noticed and had wine brought. Then, when they decided he had recovered enough to listen, the king continued his monologue. "Rarely, indeed virtually never, have my sister and I revealed our affairs as we are now revealing them to you. We do this because we believe it to be beneficial to us, and I may add, for you, because you possess a unique concentration of assets which can be beneficial to our cause. You, in one of the roles we want you to play, are a gentleman who speaks Catalan and is reasonably fluent in our Portuguese; in the other role, perhaps one much more difficult and requiring considerable deceptions and no small skill in histrionics—and in all this you will be trained—you will play the role of an Italian woolmerchant, recently come to Portugal to escape persecution in Italy for tax evasion. Your stay in Genoa with your kinsman makes you eminently well qualified for this role."

"The training," interrupted the queen, "will be learning to speak Castilian, of good quality, but colored with a heavy Italian accent. Your teacher will be no professor, mind you, but only a simple soldier who is a Spaniard, born and bred, who for years was in the Italian wars, and who decades ago defected to Portugal. He is a rascal and was one then, for he would be hanged if caught in Castile or León. He once stabbed a nobleman to death and robbed him. Our father hired him, for he is intelligent and helped Portugal a good deal against his hated native land. His Spanish will suffice nicely. We expect you to accomplish the facility we need in no less than two months. And it should not be difficult for a young man who already speaks Portuguese, Italian, Catalan and French, all related tongues descending from that venerable language still used by Mother Church."

The king spoke then. "How familiar are you, Colom, with the current political situation in Castile? You know, I suppose, that Henry IV, old King Juan's son by his first marriage, is trying to prevent his half-sister and half-brother, Isabella and Alfonso, from becoming his heirs. His own daughter and my dear sister's, the Princess Juana, whom you have met, should be his rightful heir. Scandalmongers and enemies of the king and Queen are in revolt under the banner of the League, headed by the hateful Archbishop of Toledo, who unfortunately is Spain's primate."

"It is our plan, nay, our duty," interrupted Joanna, "to right these wrongs. We must forestall our enemies' plots and plans and we must see to it that both Isabella and her brother Alfonso, who is about fifteen, are somehow removed from succession. We believe that we can rest assured that through royal marriage Isabella can be gotten out of Spain. We know, since we ourselves have had a part in the negotiations, that foreign delegations will soon visit Henry's court to propose marriage to their princess—one delegation from England and the other from France. Now this is all well and good; however, still a third would-be suitor is in the offing, and it is he, who, no matter what the cost may be, simply has to be stopped. No proposal of marriage has yet been made by either France or England, nor has Aragón publicly made a move in this direction. Yes, young sir, you may well show surprise, for the third and dangerous suitor is your old enemy, Prince Ferdinand himself. You can surely see what such an alliance, one between Castile and Aragón, could mean to their enemies, and Portugal would surely be their enemy. Those two kingdoms, united through the marriage of Prince Ferdinand to Princess Isabella would checkmate all King Louis's plans to help us by seizing lands in our peninsula, and it would cause great alarm here in Portugal. That marriage, even though it may be only in its planning stage, must at all cost be prevented!"

Christopher saw that Joanna had turned white in her fury and that her long fingers had turned into talons. He was glad that he was not her enemy, and even gladder that he was not destined for royal power.

Joanna continued. "We have tried and failed before," she said. "My royal brother, when that stubborn little wench of an Isabella was only thirteen, offered his hand to her in marriage. Think what that alliance would have done for Portugal! But can you believe it? She spurned him openly before the courtiers of Spain and the entire Portuguese entourage which had accompanied the king to offer marriage."

The king, noted Christopher, was turning purple at the memory. "And to think," he growled, "that I made the trip all that way, assured by Henry that Isabella would receive me favorably! It was unforgivable! Of course, Henry was stunned and furious, too, but with the Archbishop at the girl's side, egging her on, and with all his troops nearby, what could Henry do? So Isabella spurned the most advantageous marriage she could ever have had and gave up being Queen of Portugal."

Christopher pitied the Princess Isabella and wondered what fate was in store for Alfonso, her brother. Since he was male, he would be the first to threaten Juana's chances. How would they deal with him? She feared him more, since no royal marriage to a foreign princess would take him out of Spain. Joanna did not keep him in suspense, for Prince Alfonso was included in her plans as was, he realized, himself. "You are no doubt wondering what your service to us is to be, once you are trained as we have said you would be. When you reach the court of Henry, say that you are an emissary from the king, my brother, and that you are empowered by him to suggest an alliance between

Portugal and the rebels warring with Aragón. You will have the proper documents, which you will carry so well concealed that even an expert would not find them if you were searched. The documents will not be written on paper—they will be tattooed into your scalp. Yes, your hair will have to be shaved off in order to conceal the message, but if we shave it now, it will grow back in the two months you'll be preparing yourself. It is certain, I believe, that no one will think of looking for that document on an emissary's scalp. The ruse surprises you? I was delighted with it when a Moorish story teller related it in one of those wild tales from Araby. I never forgot it, and have used it several times with no one the wiser, except those who shave the heads for the message."

"Let me finish my part, Joanna," said the king. "Christopher will go, as I have said, as my emissary to King Henry. He will be believed when he speaks of an alliance between Henry and the Catalonian rebels, because a few years ago Henry actually had such an alliance and sent them assistance. It will seem perfectly plausible, since it had happened before. And Henry always is interested in damaging King John and Prince Ferdinand. Since Isabella is in Ávila and not under Henry's surveillance, she need never see you, Colom, in the guise of an emissary. So you can succeed in this particular role. To me this is the part of your involvement which is the most important—the part the queen has in store for young Alfonso, as far as I am concerned, is too dangerous for me, as king, to even think about, let alone take part in it."

Joanna grimaced, but did not contradict her brother. "Listen, young man," she hissed, "and it may be that both you and my brother, the king, will see that my plan having you pose as a woolmerchant from Italy, working in Spain because he cannot return to Italy due to a criminal record there is a very fine plan. Since the idea was mine from the outset, I will lay it out for you. I thought of it when I remembered what a paragon of charity, what a do-gooder Isabella is. As a poor woolmerchant, if you ask her help, you will receive it. The trouble with the plan is that I haven't been able to imagine how you can meet her, Christopher, but I'll think of something. And once you meet her and she agrees to help you, tell her you'd like to be a soldier and that you've heard her brother's bodyguard needs strong men. Tell her you've fought in the wars in Italy. Just look at you, Christopher. You have the reach of a formidable swordsman. Look at his chest and shoulders, brother, the muscles in his thighs and calves. The princess will be impressed, for she is always worrying about the size and strength of Alfonso's guard."

Christopher squirmed in embarrassment. The queen was looking at him, assessing him as though he were some fine piece of horse flesh. Her eyes took stock of all of him shamelessly. They studied even his loins where they bulged. "How can I escape these people?" he wondered. "The last thing either

Bartholomew and I want or need is political involvement, and yet, and yet, what a chance to strike at Ferdinand!" But he knew there was no escape for the present, so he did what his brother had told him, he said, "Highness, whatever you order I shall do."

"I hope," muttered Joanna, "that both plans succeed, and that we can manage between us, Christopher and I, to remove prince Alfonso permanently."

"Sister," thundered the king. "Hold your tongue. A few words more and you'll have told this young man so much that we'll have to execute him before we send him into Castile!"

That evening he told Bartholomew what he suspected, what he genuinely feared—the queen would want him to bring Alfonso down, and quite probably by assassination. "Bartholomew, that evil woman will stop at nothing. If she forces me to carry out some wild and murderous plan of hers, she'll deny complicity and even turn me over to the Spaniards of the League."

His brother shook his head. "God knows we have to think, to plan."

"Should I try to run away, brother?"

"No, for they'd send men to hunt you down, and, if you got safely across the border, they'd send a message to King Henry as well as to his enemies in the League to be on the lookout for you, a dangerous killer. All you can do is play along, at least for the time being, and who knows what changes will come about? They might even tell you they'd canceled the plans."

The next day a barber trimmed off his nape-length hair and shaved his head. The tattoo artist arrived a little later and inscribed the message in abbreviated form. He began his study with the crooked old soldier, who praised him from the first day for his linguistic facility. He realized how very astute Joanna was when she sent him to the foreman of one of the royal sheep farms to roughen his hands and give him the proper stink. From this he realized that she planned to have him carry out her own plan first. She provided lodgings for him in the foreman's own house, near one of royal lodges, and it was from that lodge that one morning she bade him farewell and give him her final instructions. He was to ride across the border and head for Ávila, where both Alfonso and Isabella lived safely behind the massive walls and the innumerable towers. She had him clothed in a very heavy and warm sheepskin jacket, lined with wool, with tough hose and high leather boots. All the articles of clothing were well worn, for they had been procured from shepherds after some search to find one as tall and well made as Christopher. She provided a strong old mule, since any kind of horse ridden by a peasant would have looked suspicious. "If you succeed in removing Alfonso," she whispered, looking around furtively to make certain no one could hear her, "you must then return swiftly, wash off the smell of sheep, dress as my brother's emissary, and make another foray into Spain."

And then, to his mounting horror, she handed him a silver vial. "If the prince employs you, as I believe he will, I know you'll find a time and place to speed him on his way to heaven."

There it was, as cold and sharp and hard as a stiletto. She wanted him to poison Prince Alfonso, and she was even providing the poison. His gorge rose and he was about to tell her he wouldn't. Perhaps she anticipated his reaction for she reminded him unequivocally and ominously. "In case you do not obey me, remember that your brother is here in Lisbon."

10

When Alfonso told Isabella he needed a vacation and rode off to Cardeñosa with some of the younger knights, Isabella realized how long she had been in Ávila. "It's June again," she reflected aloud, "and much has happened since Alfonso and I came here."

But of all that had taken place after her rescue from Segovia the most interesting event was Joanna's removal from court at the insistence of the nobles and of Cardinal Mendoza who had finally persuaded the king that his wife's wickedness actually hindered the course of the war. Who could help a king whose queen lived in open adultery with the king's favorite courtier? No doubt the cardinal had pointed out also that Joanna's daughter, a mere child, growing up amid all the immorality of the court, was a living affront to a decent people. Surely the one place for her was some respectable convent of which there were still a number in spite of the rapid decline of morale and morals in so many houses of religion. And so Joanna one morning rode off to live under the watchful eye of the Bishop of Seville who did not plan to incarcerate her, perhaps influenced by her arrogant stance and her fury. Even so, he planned to keep her out of the public eye, certainly in Spain.

Before she had to make the journey to Seville, he had allowed her one trip—she would go to visit her brother, Alfonso of Portugal and she would be able to take her daughter with her, but once in Seville, the bishop planned to keep her under house arrest and when she was permitted to go out to church, his guard would accompany her. Moreover, his own sister, a grim and pious woman, would have her under control both day and night.

Isabella smiled ruefully, as she said to the Archbishop, "Four sharp eyes are not enough to watch the queen, Your Grace. Argus of the thousand eyes himself, some of whose eyes never slept, couldn't keep track of Joanna. More will be heard of our gracious Joanna and soon."

Isabella missed Alfonso and worried about him. Plague was in the land, not widespread as yet, not yet epidemic, but nevertheless prevalent enough to cause alarm. Only a little more than a hundred years before that same Black Death had ravaged all Europe, and Spain had lost so many thousands that anything like a correct count had been impossible. Was it wise to let the boy live so far from the cool walls of Ávila behind which the plague had not struck? Fortunately Cardeñosa was within a day's ride and letters could be exchanged daily.

Saturday, five days exactly after Alfonso had ridden off, a courier with a message came, not to her, but to the Archbishop. She was present when he delivered it to the old man, and at his roar of rage she jumped as did every one within earshot.

"A lie!" he thundered. "The Prince cannot be dead! Speak man. Who sent you to me?"

"Don Pedro Mendoza," the man replied, somehow too promptly and unable to conceal a certain shiftiness as he spoke.

"Wait!" said the Archbishop. Beckoning a page with an imperious gesture, he sent him off on the run. The courier stood on one foot and then the other and looked furtively at the Archbishop's bodyguard flanking the door. Presently the page returned with a lady, Don Pedro Mendoza's daughter.

"When did you hear from your father, Lady Inés?" asked the Archbishop, casting a baleful glance at the now trembling courier.

"This morning, Your Grace. He wrote from an outpost on the road to Segovia. He will be here day after tomorrow, God willing."

"Thank you, Lady Inés, said the Archbishop. "Seize this man," he told the guard, "and lock him up until we hear the rest of this matter. No. Put him to the question diligently, sparing no pains to extract what we must know." Having issued the order he cast a sympathetic glance at Isabella. "Daughter, the Prince cannot be dead. As I had told you, he dispatched a letter to me as recently as yesterday and it arrived just after dark last night. He was not ill when he wrote the letter. He has with him the doctor I commanded him to take, and he is among his knights and friends. Moreover, Cardeñosa is strongly provisioned and garrisoned."

"And yet, Your Grace, perhaps something happened after the letter was dispatched. The courier may have left Cardeñosa after Alfonso's messenger. Something could have happened in the interim. In days of plague..."

"I've taken plague into consideration, Princess. Though it often strikes fast, it does give certain warning signals. No. It *must* be a false rumor, a deliberate lie. But why would someone concoct such a falsehood? It's this that alarms me. Did someone, well-intentioned or malicious, think that the prince was dead or want us to think so? Today I cannot leave Ávila, but tomorrow at dawn I leave for Cardeñosa. In the meantime, Princess, a courier will ride with a letter from me to your brother requesting an immediate reply."

There was nothing else to say or do, she saw. The Archbishop, a hard rider, would be at Alfonso's side the very next evening, and by then a courier would be in Ávila with her brother's reply. Perhaps the Archbishop would not have to go after all.

But by breakfast time the next morning no courier from Cardeñosa had arrived. Isabella, without breakfast, a meal she normally enjoyed, hurried to the courtyard from which she heard the old man's voice bellowing orders. In breastplate and chain mail, helmeted as though for battle, he strode purposefully toward a saddled warhorse, a huge beast bred for speed and endurance. "Give my letter to no one save the Bishop of Coria," he bellowed at a courier whose horse reared at the sound. "The package goes to the Grand Master of Santiago. You understand? Ride, then, man! Why are you waiting? And mind. Have them both send word to me by separate couriers."

When the rider was off in dust and clatter, Alfonso Carrillo turned to Isabella. He was at last making no effort to conceal his concern. His uneasiness left her perturbed as she watched him gallop off with a small escort of lancers. She wished she could have ridden with him, even if she did feel relief at his going. If the Primate of Spain would be in Cardeñosa with her brother, Alfonso could hardly be in danger.

All day she prayed and her ladies prayed with her. The day wore on. At eventide the courier arrived on schedule with a letter from Alfonso and in his own hand. He carried another from the Archbishop who had intercepted him as he rode, read his message and attached his own personal note to her. "I am well, Your Grace," Alfonso's letter read, "and had just arisen from siesta when your courier arrived in a lather from Ávila. I had a touch of fever and some stomach cramps yesterday, but it soon passed. How could anyone have reported me dead? I am confused." She studied the signature again. It was Alfonso's, replete with his personal flourish. His seal was clear in the wax.

Her first emotion was relief, but the matter of the fever and the gastric pains disturbed her. Either might be more serious than Alfonso believed. Her thoughts grew frantic and leaped to wild conclusions. Perhaps someone had given him poison and he had vomited it. Had some person who knew about the poison sent the report of his death before realizing that the murder had failed? That would explain the premature report quite clearly. She was certain that the Archbishop would reach the same conclusion. How glad she was that he by now must be in Cardeñosa! She could imagine him conducting a thorough investigation. What an inquisition must be in progress in the royal kitchens! She even pitied her brother's personal physician, removed no doubt from the boy's service, innocent or guilty. The Archbishop would take no chances.

Monday morning, as she embroidered with her ladies, a page appeared to tell her that a second message had come from Cardeñosa. "I hesitate, Highness, to bring the messenger into your presence," said the page. "He's a foreigner and no courier, but swears he has a message from His Highness, the Prince Alfonso. He wouldn't relinquish it, Highness, and will give it into no one's hands except your own. All he'll say is that the courier from Cardeñosa was hurt in an accident and enjoined him to place his message in your hands and no one else's."

"Fetch him," said Isabella. She was standing at the door when they brought him to her. Alfonso had certainly not sent this fellow. The young man wore a greasy doublet too small for him and he reeked of sheep and sweat. A peasant obviously, and yet his presence was not a peasant's. As to the message, she saw no sign of it. All he held was his cap, which he nervously passed from hand to hand. Assuming that the message came by word of mouth, she said, "What is it, man? What has happened? Speak."

He spoke with a heavy accent she could not place—she thought it was Italian—but his voice, deep and reassuring, made an impact upon her so strong that she wondered how it could do so, considering her state of mind. He looked straight into her eyes when he spoke. Obviously he was nervous, in a milieu so unfamiliar, but he maintained a singular calm, and his calm was contagious. Her legs, which felt weak, stopped trembling.

"*Principezza*," he said, "I'm a woolmerchant. This morning a little after dawn I was riding my mule toward Ávila when I heard a man on a horse coming up behind me at full gallop. I got the mule off the road to make room. As they went by I recognized the man as a royal courier. Not ten yards past me his horse stepped in a pothole and threw him. I got to him as soon as I could. He lay in the road, his leg broken, the bone sticking through the calf. The horse's foreleg was broken, too.

"He was moaning, *Principezza*. The horse screamed so loud that I couldn't hear what he was trying to tell me. I cut the horse's throat, since it couldn't be saved, and so I could hear what the courier wanted to tell me, 'You must take a message to her highness, the *Principezza* Isabella in Ávila!' he kept saying."

"With the help of some shepherds I got him to one of their huts not far from the road, and there he lies now with no doctor…"

"The message, man!" cried Isabella.

She saw him fumble in his jacket. He produced a parchment which he extended to her in fine, large hands that did not shake. She found it still limp and warm from the heat of his body and moist with his sweat. With fingers that shook she broke the seal and unrolled the message, reading with difficulty the twisted scrawl. "Come to me, sister," she read. "I am poisoned." Could this scrawl be Alfonso's? It might be, but it might be, too, that of a terrified scribe. It bore the date of June 4th—yesterday. Nothing rang true. A second message from Alfonso in an unreadable hand! A courier cut off in mid-career by an accident! Were the roads that bad? And now this woolmerchant, a foreigner, standing before her unafraid and sympathetic. Or was he? What was he? People of his class seldom if ever acted with the restraint he commanded. In the face of nobility they usually fell apart and stammered. Could he be an agent sent by Villena or Beltrán to lure her into the open? She looked again directly into the young man's eyes. He couldn't be much older than she. A man with eyes like that, frank, open, clear, filled with compassion could not be an enemy agent. His flaming red hair no enemy agent would have left undyed.

Aloud she said to no one in particular, "This letter, to have reached me today, Monday, must have left Cardeñosa yesterday evening. The courier with the broken leg rode all night. In the darkness he evidently missed the Archbishop on the road. The Archbishop by now must be in Cardeñosa, barring accident or a meeting with Henry's troops. Thank God for that!"

As her mind raced on she was glad for another reason. Had the Archbishop been in Ávila, she could never have done what she now planned to do. Turning to the woolmerchant, she said, "Will you ride with me to Cardeñosa? Take me first to the courier and then on to my brother?"

"Yes, *Principezza*. I will guide you."

"Then run to the stables and tell them to saddle horses. No, you, Íñigo, have them saddle the horses. Ask the captain to mount and equip a dozen lancers. Tell him I leave immediately for Cardeñosa."

The page ran. The Duchess of Benavente ranted in vain. Isabella waved aside every protest. Without even changing to riding clothes she hurried to the stables. The woolmerchant strode behind her, trying to shorten his strides to match her own. Out of the corner of her eye she saw his long shadow looming over her own. "He must be over six feet tall," she told herself.

Several miles on the road she realized how foolhardy she was and how furious the Archbishop would be when he saw her. What if the whole thing was a mistake or some trick hatched by Villena? A party as small as hers invited ambush. She looked behind at the ten lancers galloping almost at her horse's tail. Little chance she and they would have if a large body of unfriendly cavalry appeared. Farther behind still she saw the woolmerchant. He rode that spirited stallion as well as any knight, like no peasant should. It worried her, for anything odd at this time should be investigated. "I better let him catch up and ask him a few questions," she thought.

As she reined to wait for him, she studied him carefully for the first time, gaining more than she had from fleeting impressions. His face compelled respect and established confidence. Freckles, wide-set gray eyes, a generous mouth, and that close cropped fiery hair. His chin spoke for itself.

As he rode up, he called and pointed. "There's where the courier fell, Highness. The pothole's here. And here's the blood from the horse."

"The shepherd's hut?" she asked, flooded with relief that he had corroborated this much of his story. Now to question the courier, do what she could to make him comfortable, send to Ávila for a litter and a doctor. Startled shepherds appeared and then shrank back from her wild blue eyes. A crone beckoned diffidently and she stooped to enter a hovel. The courier, who recognized her, tried to struggle to his knees. Pain sent him back to the sheepskins spread on the bare floor as a bed.

"The shepherds set my leg, Highness," he said through tight lips in answer to her query.

"They shall be rewarded," she told him. She sent one of the lancers back to Ávila after a litter and a doctor. Now tell me what you can of the Prince."

The courier closed his eyes and swallowed. He asked for water and gulped it. Sweat stood out on his brow and upper lip. "Highness," he said at last, "the Prince is at death's door. The doctors say it is poison. But I'm not certain it is."

"What do you think, courier?"

"I don't know, Princess. But my family lives in Cardeñosa. They say the Prince has been hexed by the Minions of the Moon."

She brushed the suggestion aside. The Minions of the Moon, indeed! Old wives believed in such a coven of *brujos* and *brujas* who, they said, still practiced the cult of the pagan goddess Diana.

At dusk the gates of Cardeñosa, which opened before her captain could strike with his lance, closed behind her. She was expected. How? A narrow, winding street, lined with white houses from whose upper windows whiter faces peered eerily. Then the old mansion where Alfonso lodged rose out of the shadows. The captain laid a hand on her bridle. The woolmerchant slid neatly from his mount and bounded to help her down before the captain could reach her. Strong comforting arms caught her and lifted her down. Without those arms she would have stumbled.

A door yawned a few steps away and she walked toward it, still leaning on the arm she would not release. She caught a glimpse of a dark hallway. A frightened page she recognized as one of Alfonso's led her up a flight of stairs. Then another door around which clustered members of Alfonso's bodyguard, stiff and graven faced. The gleam of tears in masculine faces startled her. Suddenly the door opened and a pale face peered out. "Thank God! It's the princess!" said a voice that must be the Bishop of Coria's, but sounded like a man much older. She did not wait to greet him. She pushed quickly into the room, still clutching the arm of the woolmerchant. Two tapers barely lighted the bedchamber. A priest knelt at the foot of the bed. Over his shoulders floated a face so pale on its pillow that in the dim light she wasn't certain it was there. Above it, pale and lamp-like, drooped the face of the Archbishop of Toledo, his mouth turned down, his eyes soft and red. He looked so unspeakably sorrowful that she was afraid to look back at the figure on the bed.

"Is he dead?" she asked, torn between the hunger to know and the terror of hearing the worst.

"Not yet, daughter," replied the Archbishop. "He lives, but is sinking fast."

He came and took her hand, and her other hand tightened on the woolmerchant's arms, warmer and more reassuring and tender than the prelate's. Finally she tore her eyes from the old man's. She looked down at her brother. "Barely breathing," she muttered, "and his lips are blue."

"Speak to him, daughter," she heard the Archbishop say in a muffled voice. "Perhaps he'll hear you and respond. He doesn't respond to us."

Snatching her hand from the Archbishop's, she laid it on Alfonso's forehead and found it dry and icy. If he heard her voice, he made no sign.

"What is it?" she asked the doctor who had come to stand beside her.

"We don't know, Highness. The priest here says it's some sort of spell, and not poison at all, but who can hold with village superstitions, even from priests? Whatever it is, it is something I've never encountered before. The symptoms are strange. Then there's the mark." He lifted the flaccid arm and exposed the armpit. She saw amid the fine golden hair a tiny perfect black crescent, no larger than a splinter. To the question in her eyes the doctor replied, "We do not know its meaning or how it was put there. Could be Moorish, but I doubt it. The crescent is to them a sacred symbol. They wouldn't place it on an unbeliever. I'm not certain it has anything to do with the Prince's illness. But this I know. If the Prince has been poisoned, it's a poison I don't recognize. I know, too, Highness, that it's not plague, as some suspect. The glands under the arm aren't swollen and there's none of the black or bluish tinge characteristic of plague buboes."

"What medication has been given?" she heard herself ask.

"We purged him to remove the possible poison from his stomach, Highness. We were about to bleed him to remove any that might be in his blood when you arrived. With your permission we'll do so now."

She saw the instruments, the lancets and the long, sharp needles—like steel thorns. She made herself watch the doctors as they opened a vein in Alfonso's arm, feeling her fingers sink into the arm of the woolmerchant. The lancet sank deep into the dry, white flesh. No blood spurted forth. Instead a slow, half-coagulated oozing, not red as blood should be, but blackish. The doctors exchanged rapid, fearful glances.

"I've never seen anything like it," she heard one say.

"Could the priest be right, after all?" said the other, crossing himself. "Perhaps it is a spell. Maybe that sect back in the hills he talks about *is* responsible. But I hate to believe…"

Diana was a goddess of the moon and her diadem was a crescent. Isabella shuddered and turned to the woolmerchant. She could not, would not believe in the power of the Minions of the Moon. She would not admit into her soul the fear of the supernatural which is the most terrible fear of all. Let others keep coming back to the Minions of the Moon, to their devil-worship and the last surviving rites of an ancient pagan cult, old and well-rooted in Spain even before the Romans came. She turned back to the quiet figure on the bed, searching its face with frightened eyes, while out of the shadows rose the deep voice of the parish priest intoning the exorcism of evil spirits. The Archbishop did not utter a word of protest. Did Alfonso Carrillo, the most practical, worldly cleric in the land, also fear the powers of darkness? Perhaps not after all, for she heard him mutter, "It could be some new or unknown Moorish poison."

Blind rage flooded her grief. Always the Moors! Uncover a mystery, a perversion, any abomination whatever, and you find a Moor! She swore again that some day she would have a reckoning with the Moors.

When she looked at Alfonso again they were using the needles, but he did not respond, even when they plunged them deep into his calves, his thighs, and the soles of his feet.

"Beyond all sensation!" whispered the Archbishop. "Now is the time to pray for his soul." Turning to the people crowding around the bed, he cried in a piteous voice, "Penance, Grandees of Spain! Vows! Promises! Prayers! Beseech the Lord to spare the life of our king!" She had never seen him frantic before and it traumatized her. She listened, but so great was her dread that it killed all hope. She could barely look at the figure on the bed, but made herself. Not even the woolmerchant's muted pleas not to look reached her. As she watched, the form on the bed writhed feebly. Alfonso opened his mouth in a death-snarl, looking horribly like a dog impaled on a spear. His tongue flapped weakly back and forth and it was the color of slate. Ever so lightly came a sound like a rustle of a dry leaf scraped by the wind against stone.

She gave up. She slumped against the woolmerchant and let him lead her to the window. She could bear no more. Dimly the cries and lamentations of the people in the room penetrated the fog of her grief. She wondered vaguely why she didn't fling herself to the floor with the sobbing knights and pages, why she didn't scratch her face and beat her breasts and tear her clothing as they were doing. Even the Archbishop gave way and rent his cassock. Vaguely she realized her world was toppling. All Alfonso's interests and ambitions blasted, and she could do nothing. Isabella, the Prince's sister, felt detached. Why do people feel they must give vent to sorrow vociferously? Were sobs and incoherent shrieks purer signs of grief than her own more terrible silent suffering? Quiet, dry-eyed she stood with the woolmerchant and watched the madness boil up around her. She watched one of the knights tear off his doublet and his shirt, strip himself naked to the waist, exposing his hairy chest. He stumbled from the room and soon she heard his voice rising from the courtyard. She looked down. He was beating himself viciously across the back and shoulders with a heavy iron chain. The gashes dripped red in the torchlight. Soon others joined him. They took up chains and flailed one another unmercifully. Some fell unconscious to the pavement to lie in their spilt blood. The rest marched off singing hymns in the direction of the cathedral. She closed her eyes. Could Almighty God want men to flagellate the living flesh of their bodies to reveal their anguish?

In the middle of the room beside Alfonso's deathbed crouched a noble she knew, Don Diego Gómara. "Let the Prince live, Oh God," he babbled, and I'll renounce family, wife and estates to spend the rest of my life in a cloister!"

Another man she did not know swore to live on bread and water for six months, if heaven would spare Alfonso. And from behind the bed, where he lay prone on the floor, came the labored, choking sobs of the Archbishop of Toledo who had forgotten how to cry.

In the town bells tolled and weeping people lined the streets. The nobles, still wielding their chains and shouting their hymns like battle cries, staggered back. Seven times they circled the building where the Prince lay, through streets now packed with mourners, before they returned to the courtyard to kneel and pray.

"Come, *Principezza*," said the woolmerchant. "You can do no more."

The sympathy of his voice reached her across the clamorous demonstrations of grief. She let him guide her from the room and down the stairs, leaving behind the blackening body with the physicians fruitlessly and frantically massaging its arms and legs. A priest was lighting more candles at the foot of the bed, and the Archbishop was drawing a white cloth over the boy's face with its twisted mouth and staring eyes. Outside the darkness thickened. Alfonso of Trastámara, aged fifteen, was no more.

11

A soft morning breeze puffing through the window of the royal litter brought Isabella odors and aromas reminiscent of her childhood. The spicy tang of thyme and olive trees, the rich, dank smell of manure and animals wrinkled her nose as the first acrid hint of dust soon to rise in stifling clouds from the road impinged upon her senses. A swift glimpse of the dull grayness of dawn tightened her eyelids. She lay quiet, at peace, and yet vaguely troubled. What was the pungency permeating the litter, which now that she remembered, had permeated it during the night? Surely an earthy smell, a country odor, sharp, warm, animal, clinging, but not offensive. She drifted back again into the nether land of sleep, into the dark security provided by that spicy pepperiness, that homely smell, that earthiness. Soon, however, the birds began. A hoopoe called, a magpie chattered raucously, and from far above drifted down the song of skylark. Light expanded into day. Turning she looked point-blank into the sun tanned face of a man asleep. Her eyes, startled, widened quickly. She gathered herself to pull away, for she suddenly realized that the rhythmic movement under her head was the rising and filling of his chest as he breathed.

Isabella did not move, however, for several minutes. She waited until the pieces of the puzzle could fly together. She felt, rather than heard, deep in the body of the man the slow, regular beating of his heart. She breathed the acrid pungency of unwashed masculinity. Like raw wool, she thought, and strong enough to neutralize the odors of the countryside. As she watched he turned in his sleep. By stretching a little she could see his full profile. She studied his face for a long time. With his head thrown back in the careless abandonment of sleep, he displayed a corded brown neck in which a slow pulse beat. Red stubble peppered his cheeks, chin and upper lip. Luxuriant eyelashes matched the fiery shock of hair. Inside his open collar his chest arched in a virile way. More red hair, a pelt of it, that swept up to end in a rufous furze just below his Adam's apple.

She began to remember. His face assumed familiar tones. She thought it a sincere face, not handsome, for the nose was too large, but compelling, strong, and pleasing to look into. The chin, square to belligerency, balanced the length of long jaw and gave it proportion. Still half asleep and warm under the blanket, with his heartbeat reminding her of his proximity, she summoned back detail by detail the way this man had appeared in the doorway of the women's quarters in Ávila with a message. Then, swift as a swallow, the whole picture flew into focus; after the message, the wild ride to Cardeñosa with this woolmerchant; the dark tableau at the deathbed with the candles, the flagellants, the priest intoning the Exorcism; Alfonso dead at fifteen. Grief welled up in her throat at that until she could not swallow. At least she was able to weep.

She felt the woolmerchant's chest heave under her head and heard him sigh. She watched through tears as his eyes slitted, looked uncomprehendingly at her for a second, and then flew wide. He eased her head to the seat beside him. "Cry, *Principezza*" he said softly. "Tears are good medicine."

After that and for a long time Isabella's sobs mingled with the creaking of the litter and the muffled clip-clop of the horse's hooves on either side. As she wept, her hand found his and clutched it. "It was like this," she murmured, "back in Cardeñosa."

More memories. The scowl of disapproval on the Archbishop's face as she clung to the woolmerchant's hand during the whole nightmare at Cardeñosa. She had been clinging to that hand as the litter moved off into the night, leaving the group in the courtyard and the Archbishop explaining to the nobles why it was important for the woolmerchant to be with her, persuading the irate Bishop of Coria she must hold that unaristocratic hand.

"Let her have his company, my lords," he boomed. "Damn propriety, Bishop! If she needs the fellow, let her have him by her. Do you want her mind to snap and leave us with another insane woman like her mother?"

When she could cry no more, she dried her eyes and looked at the woolmerchant. "Where are we going?" she asked.

"To a place called Arévalo, *Principezza*. When you knew for certain that your brother lay dead, you kept saying, 'We must take him to Arévalo, we must take him to Arévalo and his mother." The Archbishop seemed to think so, too, and we were on the way and far along the road before the Bishop there caught up with us."

Isabella turned to look. The Bishop of Coria snored sound asleep on the other seat.

"What is Arévalo, *Principezza*?" she heard the woolmerchant say.

"A castle and a town. My mother has lived there for years and years and Alfonso and I grew up there. I was born only a few miles away in Madrigal de las Altas Torres. My brother should be laid to rest in Arévalo."

The Bishop stirred and cleared his throat. Half-awake, with his cap awry, he looked like any weary old man; but as soon as he set his beret straight and sat up, he became the Bishop of Coria. Looking at his stern visage, she was glad that she had the woolmerchant for a traveling companion. A good man, the Bishop but like so many of the higher clergy, too conscious of his importance and dignity to have much human warmth. When he fixed his wintry eyes on them, they were so much ice.

"I see you are awake, Princess," he said, without so much as a nod to her companion. "We're almost there, and they're expecting us. Hours ago I sent word to the Convent of St. Francis to make the crypt ready for the Prince's body."

"And my mother?" she asked. "Have you notified her, my Lord Bishop?"

The Bishop looked away. "Yes, Princess. She'll be at the convent when we arrive, no doubt." Shifting his eyes away again, he said, "She is well. Well in body, that is, but as you know, her mind..."

"I understand, my Lord. She hasn't improved in all the time Alfonso and I have been away?"

"You will see her soon, Princess, and then you can judge for yourself. I must caution you not to expect too much, however."

She closed her eyes and tried without success to remember her mother before her illness. Through the square frame of the litter's window she watched the familiar panorama unfold. Years had passed since she had come this way, and as they clopped along, long-forgotten ghosts of memory slipped out of the grain fields and walked beside the litter.

"Nothing has changed," she thought, for nothing broke the monotony of the landscape except the king's highway that drove arrow-straight across the golden fields of wheat, pierced the grey walls of Arévalo and emerged to continue with never a turn into the opposite horizon. In the distance the battlements of the old castle caught the first rays of the rising sun. But distances were deceptive in the clear, dry air of the Castilian plateau. It would be another hour, she knew, before they arrived.

As the horses plodded on through the dust-flecked morning, she turned to the woolmerchant and found him staring in fascination at the waving fields of wheat as they rolled away like the long billows of the Ocean Sea into eternity. His eyes were strange, she saw, and they reflected the oddness of the scene. There was indeed something peculiar, she told herself, in those fields, something that washed away all that was hateful and petty from the human mind and lured it into mystic speculation. She closed her eyes. Today she didn't want what the landscape offered. Not now. Not in a litter swaying toward a funeral. This was a panorama for nature-lovers and starry-eyed mystics whose souls longed to communicate with the invisible. Now she shrank from it and its powerful seduction. She wanted only the nearness of the woolmerchant and the comfort and understanding he emanated.

At last the horses came to a stop. They were at the moat. The sun, near zenith now turned the far-off hills into a line of quivering blue heat. She caught a metallic flash on water and wondered if the River Arévalo had changed as little as the castle which looked exactly as it had when she left it years before, reddish yellow, dingy and in poor repair.

For some minutes it appeared that they would have to pass the morning in the town, for no one stirred in the dark pile of the castle. Nothing moved except the ripple playing over the moat as the sunlight danced hypnotically across the stagnant water. The moat still stank of filth and garbage thrown into it and left to ferment. Lifting her eyes, she followed the stark walls as they swept up and up to break in mullioned battlement tawny against the turquoise of the day.

She began to tidy her hair as the drawbridge came crashing down and the litter passed over it. From the corner of her eye she saw that the woolmerchant was vigorously and uselessly brushing his fiery mane. Even the horses knew that they had ended the journey. They tossed their heads to protest at delay and snorted.

Isabella turned and saw the woolmerchant already on the ground ready to help her descend. Over his shoulder four priests with a stretcher stood waiting for Alfonso's litter to cross the bridge. They lowered their eyes courteously at sight of her who had lost her brother and wondered what she thought of these stark walls and sad battlements with their shadows and piping winds.

The funeral was a horror for Isabella. Her mother, far worse than she had been led to suspect, stared out of eyes like two empty windows that let her see nothing save that which moved. They followed the bier on its jerky way from the church. If she saw her daughter, she gave no sign. Isabella turned away at length and walked with the woolmerchant out of the chapel. To her mother the past was a blank, the present a void, the future shadow. It was better not to go near her.

People came and went. Alfonso's household arrived from Ávila and with it the Archbishop of Toledo who had stayed on at Cardeñosa to confer with the nobles of the League. He looked at her once with careful scrutiny and then plunged into the duties of the funeral. To Isabella the funeral banquet was the worst. Somehow she lived through it, trying to swallow a little of the food set before her, her mind vaguely pondering the barbaric quality of the meal. How macabre to serve dinner in the nave of a church from vessels set on the altar in lieu of sideboards! Who could have originated such a ritual and why had he not set a limit to the amount of food and wine guests could decently consume?

She missed the woolmerchant terribly, but understood why they had not allowed him to attend the banquet. Commoners could not sit at table with the royal family and the grandees.

When the hour came for her to leave Ávila, his presence caused a problem similar to the one it had when they had left Cardeñosa. She went to him and laid her hand on his arm. He placed his hand over hers. The Archbishop frowned and shook his head. "The peasant will not accompany you, Princess," he said, drawing his brows together most formidably, expecting immediate submission."

Isabella's eyes met his and did not fall. Her mouth and chin were firm. "The woolmerchant rides with me to Ávila, Your Grace. After we reach that city, he may leave me, but until then he stays in the litter."

The Archbishop, taken aback, brusquely turned away. "So be it," he muttered. "So be it."

But he was not satisfied. He summoned the woolmerchant to his rooms to question him. Afterwards, when the litter had departed, he rubbed his hands together and sighed with relief. Nothing to worry about in the peasant after all. The man was of a breed the Archbishop had forgotten existed. Trustworthy and honest, even religious, simple and free of political ambition, he was the perfect traveling companion for the Princess of Castile. What an unbelievably innocent soul! Even the old man's innate doubt of the possibility of true human decency cracked. Perhaps he should try to mold that uncorrupted spirit. But no, it would not be mete. The man must be used and then hurried away and out of the princess's life. He would have to go the moment they reached their destination. And the princess's escort would satisfy propriety, for the litter was open since the weather was warm. As for the princess, in Ávila she would rest. And where better and more safely than in the Convent of St. Anne? Later when she had recovered and had mourned a fitting time, she would realize who and what she was and the role she must play would be made quite clear. Isabella of Trastámara was now one of Europe's most important women. Only she could launch the final crusade against Henry and his waning power.

13

Somewhere along the way the bishop had left them with a warning to the woolmerchant to mind his manners in the company of royalty.

For hours the litter drifted across the plain and Isabella said nothing. She wanted only silence. Her companion understood and did not once break in upon her privacy. Though no third party rode with them, they did not speak. At last the sun came out and with it the return of the inevitable dust, once the dew had dried. Her eyes smarted and a fine grit set her teeth on edge. And yet she welcomed discomfort as a counter-irritant to grief. But comfort and discomfort were relative. Neither could prevent her mind from wandering, until wandering became a pleasure in itself. The sight of her mother at the funeral channeled her thoughts into streams wending back to Arévalo in the days of her childhood. Unbidden, unwanted, certainly unexpected, out of the vaults of the past rose up the specter of an autumn evening when she was six and Alfonso was a baby. It was all so clear and real that she gripped her fan until her knuckles shone whiter than the ivory handle.

She was back in the queen-dowager's apartment in the old castle of Arévalo. A fire leaped cheerfully in the great hearth, for the night was chilly. It made the entire room radiate warmth and peace. In his crib in the queen's bedroom Alfonso slept. Memory tightened her throat. How she had loved him as a baby! His two spaniels, Amadís and Oriana, lay inert, but with eyes open, staring into the fire. This was the most pleasant hour of the day.

With her studies over, she could sit and listen to the talk of the adults, and perhaps, if she was lucky, hear one of the wonderful stories told by Father Juan Pérez, the queen's young Franciscan chaplain, recently arrived at Arévalo.

She saw him cast a quizzical glance at her and then at Beatriz de Bobadilla, sitting at her mother's knee having her black hair combed. He was wondering, she knew, if the tale he planned to tell would be too shocking for such young girls. She pretended to doze, therefore, before the fire just as Beatriz pretended to farther back in the room.

Apparently they had disarmed him, for he decided the time was ripe and everyone came to attention. The queen craned forward in her chair, her strange, moody eyes avid for what the story might conjure up for her. The *dueñas* sat with their needlework in their laps, expectant, quiet. Even her old, windy tutor, brought out of retirement from Salamanca where he had been a professor, forgot his skepticism. He stood with his back to the fire warming his thin, blue-veined hands, his eyes on the priest's face.

Father Pérez folded his hands in his lap and began, "There was a miser living up near Oviedo," he said, "and he was as rich as the Caliph of Cordova in the olden time. He had so much money that he couldn't begin to spend it, but he clutched every *maravedí* until it squealed.

"Now rich as he was, flesh and blood are transitory, and at last he died. But when they read his will, there was great confusion. How they must have cried out against him! In his greed he had decreed that most of his wealth was to be buried with him. And although his wife railed and his children hired lawyers, they could not change what he had decided to do. The law is the law, you know, and a man has a right to make a will and expect to have it carried out."

The tutor unclasped his hands. "They were great fools if they didn't wait a little and then dig him up some fine night," he said practically.

Father Pérez lifted his hand for silence. "That's exactly what they did, Sir, but you are stealing my story. Just a week after the funeral the family, after dark one evening, went to the crypt and broke the seal of the family vault. They must have hesitated long before they pried off the coffin's lid. Later, as they told what happened, they claimed that they heard sounds as if some animal had gotten inside and was moving about. At last, however, they were certain no rat or other creature which might have gained access to their father's coffin could deter then and they lifted the lid."

"What did they see, Father?" asked the queen-dowager, her eyes wide and dark.

"Highness, they found the dead man lying in a pool of liquid fire, and at his side three black imps no larger than cats. They were pouring molten gold down the corpse's throat, and the corpse was writhing in a ghastly fashion.

"Needless to say, they ran screaming from the vault and never went back again, after the priests had sealed it. In Oviedo they talked of little else for months."

The three *dueñas* crossed themselves dutifully. Then Isabella saw her mother put down her embroidery with a sigh and turn to her rosary. The beads clicked swiftly, and everyone in the room moved his lips in unison, making the sign of the cross at the proper intervals. Amadís and Oriana might have been following the story, too, for they raised their muzzles and whimpered.

The last of the beads clicked and the queen, with the gesture of a nun, let the string fall to her side. She opened her mouth to dismiss the company, but before she could utter a word, a cry, a wail, a howl came out of the night with no warning whatsoever. Had hell opened its mouth just outside the casement and the dead returned to life, a more hideous sound could not have been made. As long as she lived Isabella would remember that cry. A voice, inhuman and otherworldly, wailed out a name which re-echoed against the upswept walls of the castle. "Don Álvaro! Don Álvaro! Don Álvaro-o-o," it went, and ended in an awful, hooting laugh of madness. It fell unexpectedly, like a clap of thunder on a cloudless day, and it left them mute and stricken. Then the tension broke, and the roomful of people lost its head.

Isabella saw her mother droop like a battered flower and slide slowly to the floor where she lay in a whimpering heap. Amadís and Oriana slank into Alfonso's bedroom. The oldest *dueña*, Margarita, forgot to cross herself and stared with terrified eyes at the dark window, as if expecting to see something black and hellish come winging its way out of the night. Father Pérez and the tutor went to peer cautiously out over the moat, but the night was a black curtain.

The *dueñas* lifted the queen from the floor and staggered with her sagging body to her room. All that long night Isabella lay wide-eyed and heard her mother's shrieks of terror and whimpers of despair. She recalled that it had been the turning point in the queen's life. Each evening after that, as the shadows fell, she would cast fearful glances at the window while the *dueñas* stuffed her ears with lambs' wool. Sometimes they had to bind her hands with soft woolen bandages to keep her long nails from her face. One never knew when the cry would come again, for whatever voiced it, at irregular intervals, repeated it. With each occurrence the queen sank deeper into insanity. In the litter Isabella still clutched the fan and a cold sweat beaded her forehead. The woolmerchant looked at her apprehensively. "What is it, *Principezza*? Are you ill?"

She started and answered, "Nothing. only an unhappy memory."

"Perhaps it would help to talk about it," he said.

She looked at his serious face, filled with genuine concern. "Perhaps it would, woolmerchant. Perhaps it'll help me out of my loneliness. I was re-living a period of my childhood when a strange voice frightened my poor mother almost to death. You saw her at Arévalo. You must have realized that she has no mind. An awful cry helped to drive her mad. You see, she thought that it was the soul of an old enemy whom she had done to death. As it turned out, it was the voice of a man sent by the Marquis of Villena to frighten her."

"Why would the Marquis do such a thing, *Principezza*?"

Isabella looked at him and envied his naivete. "Because he's Juan Pacheco, woolmerchant. He hated my mother, just as Henry hated her. She was Henry's stepmother and he never failed to make her feel unwanted. My father had hardly been buried when Henry bundled us off—my mother, Alfonso and me—to Arévalo. I was too young then to realize the power Pacheco had over Henry. But I sensed that Henry was not really cruel or hateful. Weak, yes, cowardly, yes, but not malicious, not diabolical like the marquis. Anyway, we lived at Arévalo just above squalor, for years and years. Sometimes I had really not enough to wear and might have been cold but for the Bobadillas. They also never let us go hungry. It was ages before Henry brought Alfonso and me to court, and only then because Villena persuaded him that we might be of some value in the making of royal marriages."

"And your mother?" asked the woolmerchant. "She stayed behind?"

Isabella's eyes clouded. "She stayed at Arévalo and went madder day by day. Horrible, isn't it? But I try not to think too much of that part of my life. Instead I remember my mother's love before her mind went. She was very good. She gave Alfonso and me a sound education, although the sacrifice must have been great. We studied Latin, history, geography, and sufficient rhetoric to prepare us for what some day we might have to face in the world. It was she who saw to it that we didn't arrive at Henry's court country bumpkins, the ignorant relatives he no doubt expected."

"*Principezza*, how do you know that the king, even at Villena's insistence, sent the man to frighten your mother?" he asked, still troubled by so inconceivable an idea.

"We learned one night, thanks to Don Diego de Bobadilla, Governor of Arévalo. He had been away when the cries first came. When he returned and saw how the queen had changed, I saw how shocked he was and how furious when he heard the cause. After all, my mother was in his charge, and he was appalled that a ward of his could have been so used.

"'How long, Father,' I heard him growl, 'have these cries been heard?' 'For nearly the whole time you were away, Excellency,' said Juan Pérez.

"'By Jesus' nails, man! And no one thought of sending to find out one fine night what made the sounds?'

"'No, Excellency,' said Father Pérez. 'Who in the castle would cross the moat after dark? Who in the town, for that matter?'

"Don Diego said little after that, woolmerchant. But I saw him send four of his crossbowmen to the far side of the moat with orders to hide in the reeds where the two rivers converge, and to seize anyone or anything that came that way after dark. Now these four men had heard the cries and the talk of the *dueñas* as to its cause. They, too, believed it was a soul in torment, and I could see how frightened they were at Don Diego's command. They asked for silver crucifixes and secreted on their persons some very unchristian amulets familiar to the region. Don Pedro saw all this, but said never a word. Something in his eyes, however, sent the men out into the night more willing to meet the ghost of Don Álvaro or Satan himself than the displeasure of the Governor of Arévalo."

"Who was this Don Álvaro, *Principezza*?" asked the woolmerchant, cursing himself for his duplicity, since he knew exactly who he was.

Isabella was surprised at his ignorance. "I thought even foreigners must know that story. It shook the entire kingdom. Don Álvaro de Luna was my father's favorite courtier, his very right hand. By the time I was born, Don Álvaro was more than the power behind the throne. He was the throne. They say that he held a terrible secret over my father's head. Once I heard ladies at court gossiping at the things he had made my father do or seduced him into doing. And—and this I can hardly mention—once I saw a medallion he had given my father. On one side was etched the royal seal, on the other the likeness of my father, of King John of Castile, committing an obscenity with a donkey. Don Álvaro was surely the most ambitious courtier Spain ever bred. Until the king married my mother no one dared oppose him or so much as question him. It was a great disgrace. Then my mother saw that same medallion. It confirmed, at least in her mind, all the gossip she had heard, although by then she had gained the king's love and had won him away from the obscenities Don Álvaro provided to titillate him in his old age. They say that the love of an old man for a beautiful young wife can work marvels. Certainly my mother's dark Portuguese beauty worked them. He forsook Don Álvaro, expelled the riff-raff he'd surrounded himself with and turned to my mother for affection, and I believe, the first real love he had ever experienced. My mother, though she feared Don Álvaro, was strong enough to oppose him. She realized that while he lived the king was in constant danger, and so were she and her children. She knew Don Álvaro had seduced her husband away from his first queen, Henry's mother, and might he not do so in her case if he exerted all his infernal powers? And so she set out to persuade the king to destroy Don Álvaro.

"My mother had her own weapons. I am afraid that she used her blandishments, her beauty, her youth and passion to capture and hold the will of King John. Somehow, unbelievably, cataclysmically she made King John condemn Don Álvaro to death, and his head rolled in Valladolid at her insistence. They say Don Álvaro couldn't believe it, even as he mounted the block. He kept looking about for his countless knights, but no one came.

The woolmerchant said nothing, but a glint in his eye told her that such things were repugnant to him.

Nervously she fanned herself and continued, wondering what he thought of a princess who could discuss the matters she had discussed, who even knew and comprehended such matters. "I was about to tell you what happened that night at the far side of the moat. Night falls early in the winter and it was quite dark as we sat in my mother's room waiting. We had begun to think that there would be no cry and that the soldiers were shivering in their icy breastplates for nothing. Perhaps ghosts did not like bad weather, we thought, as we watched the grey curtain of rain drift past the window. Then, with its usual suddenness came the cry. 'Don Álvaro! Don Álvaro! Don Ál...' it went, breaking off quite sharply in the middle of a word.

"We were transfixed. Down went the drawbridge with an awful crash. Don Diego vanished from the room without a word. When he returned, he strode straight to my mother. 'Highness,' he said tersely, 'my men have shot the ghost of Don Álvaro de Luna. They loosed their crossbows without trying to capture him, and after hearing the cry I cannot blame them. The ghost was a man, Highness, as I suspected from the first.' 'Who is he?' we all asked, except my mother, who only stared.

"Don Diego shook his head. 'Time for explanations later. Four crossbow quarrels in the gullet cut a man's life short. Father, he needs you. There may be time for confession, if you hurry.'

"No one saw me as I slipped from the room on tiptoe down the steps behind the governor and the chaplain. We went out into the courtyard. A fine rain still fell steadily. It clung to everything. Then I saw the ghost. The soldiers had flung him on his back on the bare flagstones and were standing around him speaking in whispers. When they caught sight of Don Diego, they stopped back and saluted.

"I heard the lowest of moans from the figure on the pavement and saw much blood. The four quarrels still projected from his neck and chest. His face looked green in the torchlight. I watched in horror as the chaplain knelt in the water at the fellow's side. 'My son,' he said, 'I am the chaplain of Arévalo.'

"'Father,' the man gasped in a voice almost too faint to catch. 'The Marquis of Villena and his brother sent me, on the king's orders. They paid me well...'"

"*Principezza*," said the woolmerchant, with complete sympathy and sincerity, "let us talk of other things."

She looked at him for a moment and swallowed. Then she continued.

"Then, woolmerchant, the man died. They buried him that same night in the crypt under the castle. Don Diego gave strict orders. No one, on pain of death, was to mention what had happened that night, and no one ever did. We all sensed how dangerous it would be if Villena ever suspected what had become of his minion. I think that it was then, really, that I realized what a terrible person the marquis was, and what a weakling the king, my half-brother."

"*Principezza*," said the woolmerchant after a pause, "Your childhood was as sad as mine. And now, I repeat, let's speak of other matters."

She nodded and turned quickly to the window of the litter. "That would be better. There are many things more pleasant than my childhood at Arévalo."

14

She felt much better after the long reminiscence. "It is as though I've made a confession," she told herself. "Anyway, I feel the way I do after one. Why did I tell this man all I have told him?" She realized suddenly how easy it was to talk to him and how kind his eyes were and how sympathetic. She would never forget how he had led her, guided her through the horrors of Cardeñosa and Arévalo. No one had ever brought himself as close, made himself as much a part of her, drawn her so to him. She blushed at her unbidden affection. Could grief for her brother fade so soon?

He saw that she was looking at him quizzically. "You are the most mannerly commoner I've ever met," she said. "you must tell me all about yourself."

Instantly fear clutched him. She mustn't suspect any more about his real social background. So he yawned and unconcernedly scratched beneath an arm. "He doesn't know," she thought with amusement, "that it is not polite to do that in a lady's presence." The fancy courtiers at Joanna's gatherings would have preferred death to a yawn like that and such scratching. Oddly enough she respected the woolmerchant for his uninhibitedness. She added up new attractions. The way his muscles heaved and pressed against the thin cloth of his shirt, when he moved, delighted something in her that she had suspected was there but had never felt so strongly. It was more stirring than watching the squires exercise. The squires she had watched from a distance, but the woolmerchant sat close to her, so close that the pungency of his maleness tickled her nose and not unpleasantly. A forbidden excitement made her heart beat faster. "How different he is from other men!" she said to herself. "He's like the old crusader heroes I used to worship as a child, like the Cid Ruy Díaz, like Cœur-de-Lion. The great English hero had had hair like this woolmerchant. She pictured him like Richard, in a crested helmet riding a white charger. What big hands! What a craggy brow! What clean young brawn! When suddenly his eyes met hers candidly, she flushed in spite of herself and lowered hers. But not for long. The carriage of his head as he turned it to look deep into her eyes held hers captive as did the well-shaped, columnar neck with its collar of coppery fur, the magnificent shoulders, the way he moved—like a young lion, like a stallion. His utter maleness drew her, lifted her eyes back to him and to his face and eyes. Suddenly one of his big, graceful hands came down and covered hers where they lay in her lap. The fan slipped to the floor. Fire ran from his hand into hers. The weight of his hand was crushing. How strange that one of her hands crept from under his and softly stroked the sun-tanned skin, letting her fingers riffle the golden hairs that grew profusely on his wrist.

When he uncrossed his legs, she knew he had to, and she looked again and saw that it was true. Something was leaping up inside her. Her heart? Or something deeper inside her body. His face was very close. His breath smelled clean. Words flowed through her mind. Joanna's words heard not long ago, "Take a lover, Isabella…" As his fingers tightened on hers, she wondered if she could. Had she come this far? Was she actually considering what she longed to do? Did she really have carnal instincts as bold as these she felt? Was this where fantasies squelched in cold showers had led her? Was Satan tempting her?

"I mustn't," she said aloud, to herself, not to him.

"Sometimes one has to," she heard him murmur as his lips touched her cheek and began to move toward her mouth. When they stopped an inch away from her lips, she knew he was waiting for her to turn her head and take his kiss.

What was holding her back? The curtains were drawn. No one could see. Why, they could undress and make love, and who would know? She couldn't believe her mind had strayed so far. Until now she considered him a friend, perhaps the best friend she had ever had, aside from Beatriz, but still no more than a friend. Now she saw him, yes, wanted him as a man, as a lover, as a mate! Why couldn't it be as it had been before his hand covered hers, before she let her fingers toy with those stiff little golden scimitars almost hiding the tan of his big wrist?

"What would happen," she asked herself, "if we could turn the litter aside into one of the bypaths and leave the escort behind? What if we could then unbridle the litter-horses and go into the fields on foot. How much happier life could be than the way it is. She smiled a pragmatic smile. It was the stuff of dreams. But could there be anything wrong in dreaming, if the dream never came true? Beatriz always understood about her dreams, for Beatriz had dreams too, only hers at last *had* come true in the arms of Andrés Cabrera, handsome, serious Andrés, who barely realized what a passionate treasure he possessed.

Suddenly, as his fingers pressed her harder, commandingly, the remembrance of his honest face, the kindness of it, the face people trusted instinctively, even people like the Archbishop of Toledo, who had allowed her to be alone so long with the owner of that face, yes the very memory of that chaste countenance fled and she saw a new face. The wide-set friendly eyes now glowed lambently with far more than friendship's fire. The lips, generous in humor, were slack with longing, then with hope and finally with expectation. They were the eyes of a man who had had a way with many, many women and the women had not been peasants.

The physical impact reached beyond her comprehension. Something arcane and primitive inside her, something held down, but all the same alive, reared its head. The vivid, clear-cut quality of her emotions made her hot, and she understood better than ever before what it meant to burn in the way the priests condemned carnal burning. She, who had always controlled her emotions, felt control slipping. The physical man, she knew, was leading her. And yet he was a friend, he had helped her, he was good and kind. Wasn't the pull of his soul as powerful as the pull of his flesh? She owed him much. How could she ever pay her debt?

She felt him trembling, felt the beating of his heart against her breast. It was then that she realized that before true spiritual love for a man could burgeon, before the love for his soul could, the love for body must be realized. How easy it would be. All alone in the litter, completely shut off from other people, an awareness, an intimacy, a summoning of flesh by flesh had invaded and could conquer. Each sensed complete reciprocation of body and soul.

He had drawn her very close. Her mind raced. His hard chest was crushing her bosom and her hand somehow had found a place behind his head. Something that once would have terrified her, but now fascinated her as he touched her thigh.

She caught her breath. "Holy Mary!" she said aloud. "This close, this dear, and I do not even know his name!"

Suddenly he was sitting in the far corner of the litter. He smiled, abashed, fearful, actually terrified. The moment had passed, both knew, and would not come again. She saw now the face of a commoner who had presumed too far and knew it. One word from her, she realized, could send him to the gallows. Quickly, she moved closer and laid her hand, now cool, on his, now icy. He kept his eyes lowered. His lips trembled. "I am sorry, *Principezza*," he whispered. "I deserve to die."

"Nonsense, woolmerchant," she said. "What we both let happen, we won't again, but I'm glad it happened, just this once."

"You are?" he asked, so amazed that he forgot to be afraid. "I can't believe it, *Principezza*."

"Believe it," she said quietly. "What happened, woolmerchant, told us something, made us feel something I'm glad we felt, even if we mustn't feel it again, or if we do, we must suppress it. What happened made us see that we are friends, and could be more, if life permitted it. But life won't. You have one way to go, I quite another. But as I wander my lonely road, I'll remember you and how close we are, and your friendship won't often desert me when I need comfort or when I'm lonely, as I shall have to be."

Again his hand covered hers, and she understood the effort it caused him, for he still trembled and his voice shook. He said nothing, but his eyes told her how well he understood. For a long moment his hand remained on hers. Then he quickly drew it away, for he felt, as he knew she did, a renewal of the fire that touch still kindled. "You said you didn't know my name, *Principezza*, and it's true you don't. It's Cristoforo, *Principezza*, Cristoforo Colombo."

"I shall call you Christopher," she said. "And it's a fine name. The name of a saint."

"It means Christ-bearer," he said ingenuously, as though a princess of the blood would not know. She didn't smile, for pride in the name lighted up his face.

"It has the same meaning in Spanish," she said. "But I can't place your accent, Christopher. Italian, isn't it?"

"Genoese," he lied with a touch of feigned pride. "Not Tuscan, the Italian of the educated, the Italian you'd have heard at court."

"You're a long way from home, Christopher. What brought you to Castile?"

His eyes darkened and fell. Evidently she had touched a tender spot. Let him keep his secrets. She had not meant to pry. To change the subject she said, "Some day you'll go back. How wonderful it must be to be free to come and go! I wish I could."

Christopher had never been as uncomfortable in his life, as guilty, as ashamed of himself. And yet, until it was safe, he had to maintain his Italian subterfuge. His life by now depended upon it, and he feared her faith in human kind did too. He had never felt this way about a woman. Her loneliness, so like his own in Genoa, her goodness, her virginity, her devotion to the divine Lady he had too often forgotten, all combined to touch his soul as it had never been touched before. How could he have believed all the lies about her that they had told him in Portugal? He had heard of her virtues, too, as had most people. And yet he had listened to Joanna's vituperations against her, had heard them call her an ambitious bitch, willing to sacrifice body and soul for royal power, eager to deny a poor maligned child, her own goddaughter Juana, her birthright. "This princess," he told himself, "is unique in human kind. She's a lot like me—passionate, human, essentially kind, but unlike me pure and a virgin. And she'll have to spend her lonely life married off to some man she cannot love. But she'll survive it for she has the same strength which has let me endure what life sends me. At this moment, then, I renounce my ties with Queen Joanna and King Alfonso."

A longing to dispense with guile and lying wracked him, but for the present he could not yield to it. But he could hope for the day when he could. He had to hope, because he now believed, with no shadow of a doubt, that he and she were in a way he could not fathom, inextricably linked in destiny. "After our Lady of Montserrat," he swore, "this is the woman most worthy of my devotion."

His eyes, suddenly serious, even stern, looked straight into hers. "You, *Principezza*, are bound by the greatness of your blood. You'll never be free to come and go. You've got to realize how important you have become since your brother died."

"Important, Christopher?"

"Yes, *Principezza*. Before we left Cardeñosa the Archbishop made it plain to me. You have only to look outside this litter at the size of your escort. There must be nearly a thousand knights riding around and behind us. Others keep joining the cavalcade. I doubt that Ávila can house them all. The Archbishop said you'd be Queen of Castile, and very soon."

"The Archbishop could be wrong," Isabella said firmly. "It is true that I'm the last of the direct line of the Trastámaras except King Henry, but I'm far from being Queen. Henry still lives. So, Christopher, I'm no more than a poor relative, the king's insignificant half-sister."

He was amazed at how quickly he had changed sides politically. He was about to persuade her, whom before, he would have ruined, not to give up the future he now knew must be hers.

He shook his big head in disagreement, but she went on. "I'm a non-entity, and that's all I want to be. What did a crown do for Alfonso? It got him a niche in the crypt of Arévalo before he was sixteen. What has it given Henry? A wanton for a wife and ten thousand enemies. Even Joanna. What did the crown bring her? A bastard daughter, a husband who's not a man, and very soon imprisonment and a life leading straight to perdition."

"The Archbishop believes that you'll change all this when you are queen."

"Listen to me, Christopher," she said, raising her hand, palm forward, in a gesture that commanded silence. "Listen and you'll understand a great deal more than you do. What I say to you now I haven't even mentioned to the Archbishop. But he'll hear it soon enough. I plan to enter the Convent of St. Anne when I step from this litter. I mean as a supplicant for the sisterhood. I've had all I want of kingdoms and crowns. Let Henry and Joanna, when he takes her back, as he will in time, rule Castile. Through the doors of St. Anne's I can enter a greater kingdom than any of this earth. Let them have Spain, I say. Spain drove my mother mad. Spain shamed my father. Spain killed my brother before his time. I want none of it. Spain won't destroy me as well."

She looked at him and was startled. Grim-faced, he was, and for the first time she saw white ridges of muscle play along the line of his jaw. Grimness became anger, anger rage. "You listen, *Principezza*," he dared to say, making her flinch before the intensity of his voice and eye. "It cannot be. You cannot, like a coward, like some helpless orphan or widow, run from trouble to a convent. You never have. You never shall!"

In his rage, his raw emotion, he dropped his Italian accent and was speaking his own native Catalan which she understood quite well. Neither so much as noticed it.

"But I have made up my mind, woolmerchant. How dare you question me? If you knew me better, you'd know I seldom change my mind. Do not presume to preach duty to me! Leave that to the Archbishop and the nobles of the League. I saw what was in their eyes before the crypt closed upon Alfonso. But I will disappoint them one and all. I renounce royal duty. When we reach Ávila, I'll become a nun of St. Anne and render my duty directly to God, Our Lady, and Her Son."

She saw his eyes soften a little. His jaw relaxed. He smiled, but still grimly. "Go to the nuns to rest, Princess, to mourn, but not for life. You have a destiny and so do I. Let us not ever let them lie fallow. Let us see that we do the things heaven wants us to."

"What does a woolmerchant know of destiny?" she asked.

His eyes were no longer soft. Suddenly they burned almost maniacally. They opened to their full capability and stared straight through her and into space. They so dominated his face that they erased the freckles and the laughter lines and the youthfulness. They captured her eyes and held them. She could not turn away, she could not argue, she could not speak. She found herself tumbling into those wild blue eyes, into their depths, which suddenly were bottomless. She had heard of possession, and at last she understood it. She crossed herself mechanically. "Destiny," he said in a low, committed voice that stammered as it slipped unnoticed back into his accented Spanish, "is like the law, like the hand of God. A man—and a woman—cannot run from destiny. It is always there. It runs after you, if you run away, and it drags you back. Like a rule of life, a guardian angel, like your breath, like the light in your soul. When you have a destiny, there's nothing to do but fulfill it. God wants it so."

Her surprise mounted as he continued. Here was a side of him she would never have suspected. It was so incongruous that she wanted to smile, but some instinct warned her not to. Christopher was completely serious, utterly absorbed in himself. What he was saying was not pompous and hollow sounding; to him it was sacred.

"How do you know about destiny, your own destiny and mine, Christopher?"

"People with a destiny always know they have it, Princess. I know mine. Signs, things, *portents*, matters difficult to explain, have made me see my destiny. I'm to be an instrument in the hand of God. Yes, I a woolmerchant, a peasant, you'd say, I shall be used by the Lord God to work His will. Let me tell you something about my life in Genoa, something no one else has heard or ever will hear. When I was fourteen, my parents sent me to live with a cousin who was a woolmerchant, one Giacomo Colombo. Sometimes I would slip away from his house, although he would beat me for it—you see, I was his apprentice—and I would go to the house of a wealthy boy named Sabatini, and like boys, we never allowed his social position to get in the way of our friendship. But his mother was ashamed to have me in the house, me, the apprentice of a common woolmerchant."

She saw his face darken at the memory. Apparently it was a bitter pill to swallow. No wonder he had left his native land and his Italian relatives. She admired him for his bitterness, his refusal to accept what he had been born to accept. He *was* much like her, she decided. Bitterness is superior to shame. It kept him proud.

"In the house of Sabatini's father lived an old man. He was the grandfather of my friend and he was very wise."

"His grandsire," she repeated, fascinated by the teller and the tale.

"That afternoon the grandsire read a story to Sabatini and me. It was the story of St. Christopher, my patron saint, and the old man's voice gave the name a new meaning. You recall how St. Christopher carried Our Lord across the stream and felt the weight of the world on his shoulders? That day in that house I felt its weight on mine. That day I recognized my destiny and how I must carry it out."

"But how could you, Christopher? Not many meet destiny as soon as that."

"I learned it as that day progressed, *Principezza*, but the story of St. Christopher, as read by the grandsire, was a small part of the whole—it was a beginning." He tossed his hair from his eyes and wiped his mouth with the back of his hand. "This dust is awful," he said.

Isabella nodded. "You were going to tell me about the rest of that day, Christopher," she reminded him.

"Yes, *Principezza*. As I was saying, I learned more later. A *buon intenditore poche paroli*. I heard some words that day, and I listened too well ever to forget them."

She watched his shoulders set and wondered what made his voice deepen and sound much older. "Words?" she asked. "What words?"

"There is a street in the mercantile district of Genoa," he said, "where the houses lean toward one another and almost meet above the pavement. Over one of the shops lives a great teacher. In the afternoon he talks with his disciples. In the heat of the day, when the traffic and the people are quiet, you can stand beneath the windows of that house and hear his voice." As he spoke, something like awe veiled his eyes. "That afternoon," he continued, "I heard him reading. He read in Latin…"

"You know Latin, woolmerchant? You amaze me more and more."

Christopher shook his head, frantically wondering how he could tell a lie good enough to convince this most intelligent princess. Of course he could read it, since he had studied it while at school in Pavia of Segara, and, of course under his tutors at home. But the princess must not know. After all, she was Prince Ferdinand's cousin. Therefore he said, "I've studied it only a little, but any Italian can piece a few words together and catch the drift of short passages. I didn't understand all that the great man read, but I heard and understood enough to make me want to understand it all."

"What did you hear, Christopher?"

"One of the disciples asked the master to put the words into Tuscan. I believe God inspired the pupil to make that request of the teacher, so that I could understand it. What he read branded my soul. He translated from Seneca, and this, too, shaped my destiny."

"I've read a little Seneca," said Isabella, "but I recall nothing that stirred me very deeply, except the essay on friendship."

His face glowed. Confidence struggled there with modesty. Shyness made him flush. She realized it might be the first time he had ever bared his soul.

"These are the words, *Principezza*, 'In the latter days of the world will come a time when the Ocean Sea will shed its chains, and a great land will be made visible, and a new pilot like that one named Tiphys who guided Jason, will discover a new world. Then Thule will no longer be the furthermost of lands.'"

The words rolled from his mouth, sonorous, reverent, eager, and Isabella knew instinctively how dear they were to him. They were as Holy Writ. "A new world," she mused aloud and hidden. "Did Seneca say that, Christopher?"

"Yes, *Principezza*. And his words sank into my boy's soul as water into sand. All the legends were true! Somewhere out in the Ocean Sea beyond the Gates of Hercules lies an unknown world. I believe that the world may be India or some eastern land, but to us seen from across the Ocean Sea, it is a new world. Not all of Asia is known, you realize, and very little even of Africa, which is closer. Yes, there *is* a new world and I intend to find it, God willing, and He *is* willing."

It was one of those statements, she thought, which reveal the little extra vision that makes the poet. She didn't smile at the mention of legends. Many were true, she believed, as did all intelligent people.

"St. Brendan discovered some such land," she said, "or so they say, although there are those who doubt. Also St. Amaro."

"They certainly did," Christopher said positively. "And there have been others. God must have guided them, as He will guide me. Think of it, *Principezza*. All that pathless water and no compasses in those early times! And yet sailors pushed their way past Syria and Asia to the furthermost boundaries of East Asia. Have you heard the names of the brothers Vivaldi, who left Genoa two hundred years ago? They had two galleys and they hoped to sail around Africa. They sailed away and they never came back."

"God must not have guided them," said Isabella.

"Perhaps not, *Principezza*, but perhaps they did not have the call. Perhaps it was not their destiny."

"How on earth did you ever hear of these lost Genoese navigators, Christopher? Two centuries is a long time, especially since they did not succeed. They hardly made history."

"Remember the old master whose words I heard under his window? I heard him tell his students about the Vivaldi brothers. He knows all there is about navigation and its history. He filled my mind with Marco Polo, who traveled by land and reached Asia by foot and horseback. His name is Toscanelli."

"I've never heard of him, Christopher."

"Some day you will. Some day maybe I'll study with him. it is one of my fondest dreams. Toscanelli believes the old legends. He knows they're more than the tales old salts tell along the quays of Genoa, more even than the lives of long dead saints. The Ancients said a world lay hidden out there in the Sea of Darkness, and Toscanelli trusts the Ancients. So what the sailors say may be true; what the Ancients say *is* true."

Isabella shared with Toscanelli and Christopher a respect for the Ancients, whose wisdom no one doubted, but like all landsmen she regarded the Sea of Darkness as a great, grey world of heaving solitude, a world of mystery and danger men could never penetrate.

"Do you think that man will ever find the new world, or the way to India, even if such a way exists? The Ocean Sea is an awful place. How does the maxim go? *Mare tenebrosum est periculosum?*"

"Dangerous, yes, *Principezza*, but I'm not afraid of it. Someday a man will sail out into it and find that land. This I know. You see, I am that man."

"How can you be certain, Christopher?"

"I know because I know," he growled, as his fist smashed into his hand, making her jump. "Aristotle, the wisest of all the Ancients wrote that the earth was round and that if one would sail past the Gates of Hercules and westward into the Ocean Sea, he'd finally get to India. Later a Roman named Strabo wrote that men had attempted the journey. Could Aristotle be in error, *Principezza*? Moreover, I've had signs."

"For one who can't read Latin, let alone Greek, my friend, you've accumulated much knowledge," she said gently.

"I owe it all to Toscanelli, *Principezza*. One day I climbed up to that window whence came his golden words, and his servants caught me. They dragged me into the house and led me to him and his students. At first the students laughed, when I told them why I'd climbed up to the window, but when Toscanelli had heard me out, he rebuked them. Later he took me aside and talked to me. After that, once a week, after his class, he let me come to his room and he told me much that I shall not forget. He taught me more of maps than I had learned before; he taught me a little Greek, and he made me see the need for Arabic, a mariner's language, if there ever was one. He told me I had a destiny and I believed him."

"Believe it, and you will, Christopher. But tell me more about your destiny. You say you'll sail the Ocean Sea to India or to a new world. Sailing takes more than inspiration and faith. How can a woolmerchant, a landsman, explore and travel?"

"I have not always been a woolmerchant, *Principezza*. I left Genoa as a seaman. I've sailed from one end of the Mediterranean to the other."

"But even a seaman can learn little of the science of navigation. To sail the Ocean Sea as the captain of a vessel requires much wisdom and experience. And there's the matter of money for ships and sailors' wages."

"All this will come in its own time," he said confidently. "God will provide, for He has fixed my destiny."

"Clearly you believe this. But you spoke of signs. What signs?"

The reverent look again. "There have been several. *Principezza*, the day I fell into a dye vat in my cousins' shop. The doctors told my cousins I wouldn't live. The skin of my whole body was scalded terribly. But here I am without a scar to show."

Isabella nodded politely. "It could have been a sign, Christopher, or the skill of a good doctor. Were there other signs?"

"There were three. One night I sailed in a little boat with some friends my own age out into the sea to Corsica. We hoped to sell some contraband there, but a storm caught us on the way home, and sank our boat. Four of us in the sea, all good swimmers, but the other three drowned."

"Luck or coincidence, perhaps," said Isabella, not yet convinced.

"I cannot believe that, *Principezza*. Then came the third sign—our sign." He blushed furiously, like a youth confessing his love for a maiden far above him socially. "Yes, the third sign concerns you, *Principezza*. It concerns us. Can you doubt that destiny brought us together for its own purpose? Why was I on the road when the courier's horse threw him and he broke his leg? Suppose I had been asleep in some shepherd's hut or had been traveling on a different road."

Isabella's eyes widened in surprise and she, too, blushed. "You believe our meeting and our friendship mean more than they would appear to mean?"

"I do. You are destined for greatness. You brother, who would some day have been king, has been removed by some destiny of his own. The present king is ailing and he has no heir, for no one believes that the girl his wife bore to Beltrán de la Cueva is more than a bastard who can never rule. You, *Principezza*, will some day be Spain's queen and you will always be my friend. And when my need is greatest—and surely there will be great need—you will be there to help me, if I should call upon you."

His words went to her heart and brought tears to her eyes. He had been, he was her friend, when he barely knew the circumstances about her life. He had risked the displeasure of important nobles and great clerics to stand beside her. Even now he might be in some danger, for who could know how those powerful people might act if they should think that he had been too close to her in her time of need. How easy it would be for them to decide to eliminate a mere peasant, a foreigner who might at some future time remind them of those hours he and she had been together. And he was correct in assuming that one friend would help another and that she would, indeed, help him, if she could.

"Christopher," she said, placing her hand on his, "I too, see our meeting and our friendship as destiny. You are making it seem very convincing and plausible."

A strange light flared in Christopher's eyes, which had darkened like the sea darkens on a cloudy day. "Destiny put me there on that road, *Principezza*, and we must believe, we do believe that your destiny is linked to mine. Something binds us together. Everything proves this. I was terrified at the thought of carrying the message to you in Ávila, for reasons I cannot today tell you, and yet, I went to you. Suppose the palace guards had thrown me out or locked me up. So much hangs on a string, the string of destiny!"

For a long time neither spoke. The bright glow remained in his eyes. Then he said, "So you see, it is all ordained, my destiny to sail the Ocean Sea, yours to rule this land. I shall reach the realm of the Great Khan, and if there is a new world, I know I shall find it where the Ancients said it was, *A chi vuole, non c'è cosa difficile.*"

"Which must mean 'nothing is difficult for him who has the will?'"

"Exactly."

"Then I believe it will come true, woolmerchant, just as you've dreamed it. You have faith, and faith, they say, moves mountains."

He didn't seem to hear, but sat as though exhausted, deflated by the intensity of his vision. A mystic veil covered his eyes. At last he shook his head, as though he had not heard what she said. "Have you not considered destiny's signs that you will someday rule?"

"What signs, Christopher?"

"*Principezza*, you know them as well as I. All Spain knows your portents," he said, beginning to count them off on his fingers. "It all began long before I came that day to Ávila. Everybody has heard of your vigil in the tower at Ocaña. Along with all Spain, I believe that Our Lady saved you from Pedro Girón. Why, they've composed ballads about it. The shepherds near Ávila were singing them while I was there. And people never tire of repeating that story in all the inns and taverns, *Principezza*."

She watched him count off on his second finger. "And what was your trip to Gibraltar and your refusal to let them marry you off to King Alfonso of Portugal, if not destiny?"

"How on earth did you learn of that?" she asked in surprise. "Is that a ballad too?"

"You've guessed it, *Principezza*. People don't forget so soon. Ballads carry more news than royal proclamations and live on and on."

"Do people say heaven had a hand in that, too?"

"Why wouldn't they? Don't you, if you look back on it and see how it went? How many thirteen-year-old girls could prevail over two kings, a queen, and advisers like the Marquis of Villena? I tell you it was God's hand saving you for a greater destiny than bearing sons in Portugal."

"I hadn't thought of it that way," she said. "But I still think that the convent..."

He laid his hand on her arm, respectfully, like an old friend would, and his eyes didn't flicker as he watched her eyes see and accept the gesture. "I've talked too much," he said awkwardly. "I apologize. But I know that all I've said is true. I feel it here, in my heart. I know, *Principezza*, that you have a destiny as well as I know that I have one. *Che l'uomo il suo destino fugge de raro.* And you will not flee yours. Heaven has destined you for greater affairs than a convent of nuns."

With a terse movement she snatched her arm from beneath his hand. "Why can't you stop?" she cried. "I don't want to rule. I want only the walls of the convent and peace. I want to escape from the life I'd have to lead as a queen."

"I have more arguments, *Principezza*; the first I'm embarrassed to mention, but God knows I must. Just now, when our bodies, or Satan, tempted us and we came near to succumbing, you said 'Holy Mary." We both know that when *you* call on her she always answers. She answered then and we… we … our sinful bodies, chilled by her immaculate purity, recoiled and disappointed satan."

"And the second, Christopher?"

He said nothing for a long time. Was he angry or hurt? Then he spoke quietly and to the point. "You said 'escape,' *Principezza*. That's the coward's way, not yours. God has all the nuns he needs to do His bidding. Let them pray. You must serve in other ways."

"But why not the convent? Castile is a land whose convents need cleansing, purifying. As a nun, and as royalty, I could do much."

His hand was on her arm again, and she did not shake it off. "It's very well to hear mass, *Principezza*, but it's also good to look after one's own house. Your house is Castile. The veil is not for you."

Suddenly the wind sprang up and whistled around the litter. His voice, she realized, had risen too. He almost shouted the last words. She felt their power. Something came out of him, entered her, and forced her to hear and believe. She smiled ruefully. "You're a difficult opponent, woolmerchant. I shan't forget what you have said."

His face grew suddenly sad. "Look," he said. "Ávila. We'll soon be saying goodbye."

Though much remained to be said, neither could break the silence of something too deep to put into words. Their eyes met, spellbound. He looked unutterably sad. When he spoke, his voice was low. "I'll never forget you, *Principezza*," he said, staring into her face as though to memorize every feature. She saw that he wanted to say a great deal more and felt he couldn't or didn't dare to.

"Nor I you, woolmerchant."

They didn't speak again until the coach stopped at the gates of the city and the Archbishop of Toledo climbed into the litter. With a curt nod of his head he dismissed Christopher. Isabella's lips tightened into a thin line. "A little longer, Your Grace. He has served us well."

Through the streets of Ávila they went, the Princess of Castile, the Primate of Spain, and Juan Baptista Colom, alias Cristoforo Colombo. Too soon for Isabella the litter came to a stop at the door of St. Anne's. All three climbed out and stood in uncomfortable silence. The Archbishop didn't exist for them and he knew it. They saw only one another. Each realized that there is no word for the instant recognition of oneness. Each wished for much that hadn't happened and quickly suppressed the wishes.

Just before the convent door closed, she looked at him once more and saw him brush back his hair. She leaned forward to catch his words. "Not the veil, *Principezza*," he whispered.

Then the door of St. Anna's closed behind her. She followed the Reverend Mother and the two old nuns down the whitewashed corridors to her new quarters. "Holy Mary," she exclaimed, to the discomfiture of the nun, "We have been speaking Catalan part of the time. I wonder why."

Juan Baptista stared at the closed door of the convent for a long time before he turned away to look for an inn. And as he walked the unfamiliar streets of Ávila, he prayed that none of his lies would ever do her harm, and he thanked Our Lady of Montserrat that his destiny had foiled all the dirty plans of Queen Joanna and her brother. Suppose he had become a member of Prince Alfonso's household in Cardeñosa when some one had poisoned him or hexed him. Almost certainly Joanna would have betrayed him, thereby putting an end to his destiny forever.

3

Ferdinand and the Suitors

1

THE ARCHBISHOP SENT WORD that he would visit her at four the next afternoon and that certain gentlemen would accompany him. She was to appear promptly and be prepared for momentous tidings. The delegation that arrived at the hour stated and so splendidly that the nuns were thrown into confusion. Even the Reverend Mother, a duke's daughter and a lady who rarely grew flustered, was beside herself. Robes of state, jewels worn on only the most formal occasions, retinues of pages and squires moving in stately procession along the sunlit street, flashed and postured and glittered and emanated aromatic perfumes as they passed into the well-kept patio, brilliant with potted plants. From an upper window Isabella watched and wondered. She saw the Archbishop, robed in scarlet like a cardinal, disappear into the building in which she stood unseen. Four canons followed him, and two pages held up his trailing robe. No less than four notaries and four lawyers, two of whom she recognized as among Ávila's greatest, walked solemnly behind him. Then followed the nobles of the League, their ceremonial uniforms catching the light and reflecting their sheens of azure and gold.

The whitewashed walls of the refectory, the only room spacious enough to contain so large a group, and the pealing of the bells in the campanile offered a strange contrast to the worldly splendor of the visitation. By the time they had disposed themselves to receive her, Isabella had descended the stairs and had reached the doors. Pages solemnly opened them, two heralds announced her on silver trumpets, while a third intoned her name, her titles and her parentage. An unaccustomed fluttering of excitement, an anticipation of what she did not know, and a deep response to the coming challenge made her go pale and flush in succession. It had been like this, she remembered, that day so long ago when she had rejected the King of Portugal at Gibraltar. She felt the same loneliness, the sane emptiness, and yet there was a difference. Perhaps it was that she was older, wiser, and more cognizant of the fabric of her world. If only Father de Coca were here! If only the strong hand of the woolmerchant supported her arm! She watched in silence as she paced with what dignity she could muster through the assembled nobles to meet the Archbishop, who stood on the dais to greet her. His face was as grim as the faces of the nobles, the lawyers, the canons and even the pages. Behind the grimness lurked a universal curiosity, an interest, a hankering to know what she would say and do. No one, no, no teen-aged girl at least, had ever received more attention than this. She thrilled with a new and haughty exhilaration that embarrassed her. She had never felt so proud before. When the Archbishop addressed her as Highness, although it was a title properly reserved for kings and queens, she closed her eyes and blushed furiously. And as the grandees turned their expectant eyes toward her, defiance and pride flamed in her cheeks.

The Archbishop unrolled a parchment, thick with official seals and almost black with signatures, no doubt inscribed there by some of the most important men in Spain. She heard the Archbishop once again list the long line of Henry's crimes, and saw his eyes gleam with a frenzied and terrible indignation, more wrathful than righteous. He mentioned blasphemy, railed at abnormalities and oriental perversions, almost choked when he brought forth the accusations of churches turned into mosques and convents into houses of prostitution, since fresh in his mind was the scandal about St. Peter's in his own episcopal see. Lack of breath, not lack of invective, made him pause.

Drawing a long breath, he thundered, as loudly and as indignantly as before, "All these stains on the fair escutcheon of Castile must be cleansed away. Our departed King Alfonso had already undertaken this task, when the Heavenly Father called him to His bosom, thereby delegating it to others, or better said, to one other. Nobles of the League, to whom did God remand this responsibility? Who alone of all the souls in Spain has He chosen to carry out His will?"

Rehearsed, she knew immediately, the grandees thundered their response, "He has given this trust to King John's daughter, to the Princess Isabella!"

She listened, thinking of all that had to be done, all that she truly wanted to do, all that she alone might do. In spite of her resolve, the challenge caught her and held her in its grip. The convent and all it offered receded like a fog swept away in the wind. The voices of the confessor and the woolmerchant filled her ears, "The veil is not for you." Heady inspiration indeed! To go down in history as the scourge of evil! To be regarded as the champion of purity! To be, perhaps, a saint! She knew that the nobles were staring at a new Isabella, at a queen in the making. Their eyes confirmed it, their sudden smiles of approval as her eyes met theirs. "They think I look magnificent," she told herself, "regal, puissante," and as she thought it she tried to make herself measure up to these yeasty adjectives. They must see her as she now saw herself tall, stately, statuesque, queenly. A beam of sunlight falling through the window and athwart her head, transformed her hair into a crown of light. Tossing her head slightly, she accepted their approval with joy.

The voice of Alfonso Carrillo rolled on. "You, Isabella of Castile, are Castile's last hope. Accept the crown we offer and lead the hosts of light against the minions of darkness. Lead the armies of the League, which are the forces of Almighty God, against the Babylon of Madrid and the salacious paganism of Segovia. Dethrone Henry, our fatherland's most heinous ruler. Exile the Portuguese harlot, Joanna, and send her limping on her bad ankle with her two bastard offspring to her brother in Lisbon. Restore the House of Trastámara to its past splendor, to its greatness in the family of nations. And lastly, arm your people for a new crusade, the crusade against the cesspool of Granada!"

She was almost ready to speak, to accept, to welcome the crown she knew would be placed upon her head that very afternoon symbolically in anticipation of a proper coronation. In her mind's eye all that she had ever dreamed of accomplishing—and there was much, she realized with surprise—ran together in a brilliant tapestry, a mosaic of glorious deeds. She conjured up the vision of Henry, his mantle pulled over his head, galloping off into oblivion; Joanna, supported by the tall and handsome Beltrán de la Cueva and the beautiful young stallion, Pedro of Castile, still coltish in his newfound potency, limping madly for the Portuguese border, wading frantically into the river at Badiloz; Catalina de Sandoval, banished into limbo; a vengeful angel with a cloud of flaming hair, an angel named Isabella, hard on her lecherous heels; streams of frightened Moors pouring from the gates of Málaga and Granada, madly seeking the sea and ships for Barbary. Hordes of Jews anxious for conversion to the True Faith.

Then out of the din of battle and wails of Henry's Armageddon, out of the trumpeting of angelic hosts a sharp voice pierced her to the heart. A woman's voice, melodious in its sharpness, imperial and imperious, a voice she had heard before on the day Pedro Girón sank beneath the red lake while she prayed him dead in the Tower of Ocaña. "It cannot be!" said the voice. "The king still lives, and he is God's anointed."

Something in her face communicated itself to the Archbishop and the waiting nobles. The Archbishop took a step forward. "Are you ill, Princess? Will you take a little wine?"

She raised her hand, palm outward in a gesture for silence. At last she was ready. She watched the assemblage, as a strange tension spread across the faces of the men staring at her out of eyes suddenly stricken by they knew not what. Every eye sought her face and then looked away. When she spoke her voice was deep and rich as a fall harvest, mature, and as imperious as had been the voice which said, "It cannot be." As etiquette prescribed she spoke in the third person. Scribes copied furiously. Grandees committed her words to memory, so as to be able to repeat them to their friends and relatives.

"Isabella of Castile is deeply honored and grateful, oh grandees of Castile," she heard her new voice say. "She is grateful for the goodwill and affection with which you have come to serve her. Some day she hopes it will lie within her power to repay you. Your motives are honorable, but your plans do not please Our Lord. What, save serious evils, partisan factions, discord and war can come to those who seek after novelties and changes in the sovereign state? Would it not be better, in order to avoid these things, to accept some of the present evils? Neither nature nor the law permits two rulers. Fruit that matures early and out of season does not last."

The Archbishop was stunned. He looked like a man who has been without warning or reason struck in the face by a lackey. She could not look at his outraged and shocked countenance. "I have made a terrible enemy," she said to herself. "I doubt that he'll ever forgive me." Then she fixed her eyes on the assemblage, which had begun to shift and mutter, and she continued, changing for effect, into the first person.

"I should like for the life of the present king to be long and his majesty more enduring. Before I can become queen, Henry must pass away. Restore the kingdom, then, to him and you will restore peace to the land. I shall consider this the best service you can render me, and this will bear more timely and wholesome fruit than that which you are attempting to harvest."

She stopped, wondering whence the words had come to her. The images she had employed were not her own, not the kinds of things she was wont to say. The phraseology was foreign to her, contrived, inserted into her mouth by whom or what she did not know, yet by whom, she all too clearly suspected. She shivered and crossed herself. The silence in the refectory was deadly. Every eye swung from her to the Archbishop, from whose purple countenance the blood had receded, leaving it white behind the dark shadow made by the beard beneath his shaven skin.

"But the iniquities, the immorality, the bastard!" he whispered hoarsely, all dignity aside.

She looked at him levelly and said, "Your Grace, gentlemen, inform the king that his sister will not lead a rebel army against him. Tell him she wants only his love and goodwill and that she would be his legal heir if he would renounce for once and all the daughter of Joanna and Beltrán de la Cueva."

Her countenance, more regal than any they had seen in the memory of the oldest grandee, brooked no uproar, no protest. "They don't like it," she told herself, "but they respect me for it. Some day they'll see how right I am. Then they'll be proud to follow a queen who wouldn't imperil her soul with rebellion against established authority and tradition. A deed once committed *is* committed and cannot be undone."

She watched them bow themselves out, whispering and shooting reproving glances at the Archbishop, who alone of all the delegation, dared glare at her and mutter. When the door finally closed behind the last of them, she sat down, drained. She had settled it. The die was cast.

A door burst open and Father de Coca rushed to her. His face, livid with excitement, was also slack with relief. "What did you say to His Grace, Princess?" he queried. "I never saw him so furious. What did he mean when he muttered, 'That chit of a girl to defy me, Alfonso Carrillo, Spain's Primate!' Did you defy him, daughter?"

"I refused the crown, if that is defiance. Should I have turned rebel?"

His expression hovered between conviction and doubt. "But the iniquity, the ruination of the country, which I am certain the Archbishop reminded you about?"

"Through the King of Spain God condones these things, Father. For His own purpose, of course. Perhaps as divine retribution for our sins. I will not head a revolt while Henry lives and is able to rule. I will not commit blasphemy."

"I knew you wouldn't, Princess," he said in awe. "Will you forgive me for urging you to refuse the Archbishop and then for wondering how you dared to do it?"

"Forgive *me*, rather, old friend. And hear a confession. I wanted the crown with an intensity that was sheer covetousness, pure greed."

"But you resisted. Why, when you had it in your hand, and only an old priest and a woolmerchant, perhaps, would not approve?"

"I remembered my brother's death mask in Cardeñosa. I knew then that I could not defy heaven, as Alfonso defied it. I owe heaven too much, Father. And even today I felt that heaven supported me in my refusal. You see, I heard a voice, Her voice, I'm certain. I had to obey it."

2

A few days later the Archbishop returned. One glance told her his mood had changed. He passed over amenities with his accustomed terse nod and plunged headlong into the good news he said he brought. "Since you refused the crown, Princess, we have asked the king to receive you as his heir, an idea, by the way, with which he and his advisers have toyed for some time. Wait until you hear what he did shortly after my letter reached him. When you hear, you'll not believe, so bizarre it is, but daughter, it is true. We have made great strides."

She waited, smiling inwardly at the way he had adopted her decision and made it his own. "What is the news from Henry?" she asked, careful not to sound too eager. "Will he recognize me as his heir?"

"By public proclamation he has already recognized you as his only and legal heir. Do you realize even partially, what this means? He has admitted to all Spain, to all Europe, to the world, that the bastard is the fruit of Joanna's and Beltrán's adultery. Let him revoke this proclamation, as almost certainly he will in time. No one will forget he made it. Publicly he brands his wife for what she is and thereby destroys the future of the Beltraneja."

"I hate to hear people call the poor child by that name. She's only a little girl, and it is not her fault."

"You are too kind, daughter. All of Spain calls her Beltraneja."

"Will I have to go and meet Henry, Your Grace?" knowing his answer before he gave it. "I don't trust him, and try as I may, I don't like him and never shall. And how can I forget that he made this same proclamation at the Concord of Medina del Campo not long ago and quickly reversed himself, no doubt harried into it by Joanna and Villena. What could I find to say to him and he to me?"

"Nevertheless, go you must and bestow upon his lips the kiss of peace."

Rebellion boiled up inside her. She would do no such thing! But then she saw the Archbishop's face and knew that he was right. It would be a nightmare. She had not seen Henry for years. She hardly knew him, had hardly known him when she had lived in the palace. Always retiring, always shrinking from public functions, always following Moors and followed by them, always leaning on pretty boys or robust studs like Beltrán de la Cueva. In all her life she had actually spoken to Henry only a few times. When they met, how could she broach the state of the realm? How remind him that the country was in need of a strong hand, how refer to his weakness, his self-effacement, his peculiar friends and his trashy acquaintances? Surely he knew how matters stood, so why remind him? He had seen the ravages of the civil war, he surely understood that the aristocracy had one motivation, greed. He had contributed to the demoralization of the clergy. He had countenanced the devastation of the towns by the barons, the battles between aristocrats and the free municipalities. He had made the appointments of criminals and dishonest officials. How could she, a young girl, make him see that the nobility and the clergy should pay taxes, when the most venerable of the Spanish legal documents, the very fabric of the juridical system, the famous *Seven Divisions of Law*, assembled by her famous ancestor

Alfonso the Wise, had exempted both nobility and clergy? From that time henceforward the clergy excused themselves from contributing to the maintenance of the roads, the upkeep of bridges and all other works of general utility. How could she bring up the decline of agriculture, the ever-present Jewish and Moorish questions, the immorality of the court, the monasteries and convents, the general depression of the country?

The roads were lined with people as she and her retinue passed, bound for the rendezvous. She saw bareheaded farmers and villagers stare at her in awe and heard them shout, "Long live the princess!" Companies of knights saluted and roared, "Castile for Isabella!" And once, in a packed village street, hardly wide enough to permit the litter to pass, she heard a voice she swore she recognized call out to her and say, "God will reward you, *Principezza*, for ending the war. You shall have the throne because you will not seize it!"

She could not stop the litter to look for him, but she knew he was there, and her heart was light for the first time on that journey, as light and warm as the wisps of wooly clouds hanging above the sierra.

How could she regret her decision, her defiance of the Archbishop and the League? She had been right. She knew what the confessor would say if he were with her. He would say, "It was the hand of God, daughter." But the woolmerchant would say, if she could speak to him, and not in a crowd, "Destiny." She smiled and saw him again, as he had been with her in that other litter, clenching his big fists, his wide mouth set in his simple, plain face, in lines she liked to remember. "Destiny is like a law, like the hand of God. You don't escape it."

3

When he had seen the convent doors close upon his *Principezza*, Christopher hadn't known where to go or what to do. He had not forgotten his earlier thoughts after Prince Alfonso had been done to death, whether by poison or some supernatural spell; that he simply could not return to Lisbon. His surmises of an earlier date would, he feared, come true. Joanna could not afford to let him live, whether or not she believed he had managed to poison Alfonso. He worried about his brother, also, for Joanna would surely realize that Bartholomew would have been in his confidence.

The thought of playing his other role, that of an emissary to rebels in Catalonia, simply daunted him. He simply couldn't attempt it. Joanna and her brother, through spies at Henry's court, might even have set a trap for him, not because they didn't want him to succeed, but because they thought he had carried out their plan to murder Prince Alfonso. They would want him out of the way so that he could not implicate them.

He still had most of the money Joanna and her brother had given him, and he lived on it until it had all been spent. Then, to earn a living, he put to use the hated profession he had learned in Naples; he became a woolmerchant. He bought a mule to replace the one he had ridden to the meeting with Isabella and he was wearing his woolmerchant's clothing. For months he wandered the highways of Castile, worked his way up into León, where he saw the marvelous cathedral; he accompanied a group of pilgrims all the way across the north to Santiago de Compostela, which contained the shrine of St. James, Jesus' beloved apostle. In the shrine he felt the divine impact of the saint's presence and kissed the Romanesque column on which was carved the saint's likeness; he climbed the steps so that he could embrace a wooden statue of St. James from behind, so old from the ages and the constant pressure of human bodies eager for his blessing, that he was certain a new likeness would have to replace it soon. He watched the multitude, all sure in their faith that James would save their land from Henry's Moors, just as he had saved it in older times, when on his white charger, he had ridden down from heaven in his silver armor to deliver them; he had heard of this shrine and how from time immemorial countless thousands, possibly millions of pilgrims had paid their respects to the apostle, some from as far away as Palestine and Ethiopia. It was from Compostela, where many spoke the Galician dialect of Portuguese because Portugal was so close, that one night he crossed the border at Tuy and made his way south toward Lisbon. He must make contact with Bartholomew somehow. He moved rapidly and was so preoccupied that he overlooked much that later he wished he had seen. From all that long and arduous journey only one city stood out in his memory, Porto, birthplace of the famous port wine he had come to savor.

He stopped in the village of Estoril, as near to Lisbon as he dared to go, and with almost his last coin sent a coded message to Bartholomew. The very next day his brother was pounding on his door.

"Where in God's name have you been, Juan Baptista? Why didn't you write me sooner?"

"There was no time to, and if I could have written, I would not have dared to, brother. I feared your mail would be intercepted. I even thought that the queen or her brother might have imprisoned you or worse."

"I was never approached," said Bartholomew. "Queen Joanna was forced to go to Seville at her husband's orders. As for the King of Portugal, he is afflicted with what I believe is senility. They say his mind wanders. They say on some days he plans to invade Spain again; on others he vows to make a long excursion to France to enlist the aid of Louis against both Castile and Aragón; but for the most part he sits in his patio and eats. The last time he got out of his coach to enter the cathedral, it took two strong lackeys to hold him up, so fat is he.

You're safe, Chris, the fat king has certainly forgotten you, and, if Joanna remembers, she has lost all interest, since she is beset with unbelievable problems. Prince João is really Portugal's ruler, although he humors Alfonso, his father, and this prince is our friend."

It seemed stranger to Christopher to be back in the royal office of the mapmakers, to speak to the prince and show him new maps, to feel a part of something vital and ongoing. He was allowed to work in the royal archives where he unearthed from the dust of the ages maps which no one bothered to look at because the documents which were attached to them were in Arabic. Such ancient maps were regarded as obsolete curiosities by the archivists. Two of these maps, buried under others on a dusty shelf, he studied with mounting interest. "I could simply steal them," he told Bartholomew, "but it might be dangerous. Some one might miss them, though insofar as I can tell, no one ever consults them, and I can't find them in the libraries catalogues."

"For God's sake, don't steal them, Christopher. Sooner or later they would be missed during some inventory. Yes, the prince does occasionally demand inventories and he even runs his eye over them. A hundred to one, he knows those maps are there. He really doesn't need an archivist. What are the maps, brother? Why do you want them so much?"

"When I've copied them and you can study them as I have, I think you'll know. But don't go to look at them. Another interested person poking about in that part of the royal archives might very well arouse suspicion."

"Even copying maps from the royal archives, Christopher, is very risky business. Be very, very careful."

He had been careful, but at times anxiety nagged him, for one day, after he had replaced the maps which he had smuggled home to copy, he found them closer to the top of the stack than he had placed them. No inventory had been taken. He could not imagine why any one would go through that dusty stack, but some one had.

Another anxiety nagged him, too, one he would never share with any one, not even with his brother. He could not get the *Principezza* out of his mind. Unbidden, she kept coming into his thoughts. He would awaken at night and think he smelled her perfume or the scent of her hair as her head rested on his chest in the litter. He longed for her company and realized that he had never confided so much of his thoughts and ambitions to any other person as to her. And—and this sometimes alarmed and troubled him most—he often dreamed of her as a woman whom he could kiss and love. That way, he knew, lay madness and frustration beyond the power of healing. But even when he made love to other women and many accepted him—she would float into his mind at the most inconvenient and embarrassing moment. He found that he was comparing and contrasting her with his paramours, always to their detriment. And slowly, perhaps due to her ever-present essence, her incomparable charm, perhaps to the stress of work and the gnawing of ambition which he barely managed to hold in check, he took less and less interest in assuaging his heretofore driving sexual urges.

When Bartholomew brought up marriage, he fended off his suggestions. He wanted to confess his thoughts, his mad and presumptuous fantasies to his priest, but the words were locked in his soul. No one had a right to know, no one, not even his brother, could or should ever know or even suspect his feelings about his *Principezza*. He realized his folly and he knew he would never see her again, but all the same he could not rid his mind of her. That one last time when he had called encouragement to her in the crowded streets, would probably be his last word to her, and yet something told him they would have to meet again. And that it would even be devastating to meet her, for how could she, involved in the center of her country's political upheavals, amid proposals of marriage from the sons of great rulers, recall, or if she recalled, their romantic little interlude in the litter, ever admit it? He knew he should cast her from his mind, but he found it impossible. Sometimes in the night, in his dreams at first, but with ever growing frequency when he was awake, he would speak to her, explain his problems, ask her opinions, and the answers he put into her mouth soothed and encouraged him. It was the day he heard of her betrothal to his one-time nemesis, Ferdinand, that he fully realized how necessary it had become for him to expel her from his thoughts. The news left him at first bereft and unbelieving. This was the last thing he had wanted for her. Not Ferdinand, arch-plotter, who had haunted his nightmares, who had ruined his family, who had pursued him heartlessly! Not Ferdinand, as handsome as a Greek god, beautiful in his regal robes and puissant in his armor, not the man who was and would be all he could never hope to be to his *Principezza*! Not Ferdinand who, to his mounting rage and horror, was suddenly the focal point of the most terrible and the most foolish jealousy he had felt in all his life! He wanted to murder him! He wanted to calumniate him to his *Principezza*. He wanted him dead and buried!

Then, in the midst of his rending passion of hate for the Prince of Aragón, a new and foolish rage assailed him, an unreasonable rage at the lady whom he had created as his soul-mate, at the sensible and courageous Princess Isabella who he felt, somehow was about to betray him. How could she of all the princesses in Europe, have chosen that hateful rival?

Bartholomew could not reach him in the mists of his fury. He could only keep his eye on him and one night bring him home drunk for the first time.

Bartholomew knew that something had to be done. Be believed that his brother needed the one thing that might cure him of his malady, his impossible love for a princess far beyond his reach. "It's time you thought of marriage Chris. The way women look at you, decent women I mean, not to mention the usual harlots and daughters of riffraff of the harbor. I believe we could find a good match for you and that this would give us one further claim to Portuguese citizenship. Our new name, Columbus. Is already respected. Have you seen any one who interests you?"

Christopher hadn't. The whores and harbor women had sufficed, but his secret love for his *Principezza* still burned. He tried not to imagine her in the arms of the Prince of Aragón, but disgusting images would rush unbidden into his mind, and he would reach for the wine bottle. He found himself listening to Bartholomew. He was getting older. He was lonely. Perhaps, now that the object of his foolish dreams and longings had irretrievably been removed, he had better think of a wife and offspring.

Bartholomew made inquiries and, to his surprise, met with negative responses. He talked to Father Basilio and received an unwelcome reply. "Sir Bartholomew, the families I spoke to about your brother, hesitate to have him call upon their daughters because they say he is a foreigner. If you will allow me to seek a candidate at some lower level of the social ladder, I may have more success."

Bartholomew understood, and so did Christopher, but both were angry. They found it hard to think of what they regarded as 'marrying down,' and they resented it. When one is born of a noble mother and father, with even the blood of kings in his veins, and the former respect of his own community, one will not face willingly the mingling of his blood with inferiors.

"I'm an aristocrat," stormed Christopher , "and by Our Lady, I want a wife with a decent lineage."

Father Basilio understood perfectly. "Let us take another path. Since it is a matter of lineage, perhaps Christopher would compromise, accepting a young lady from a fine family fallen on bad times. I mean a lady with no dowry."

Bartholomew looked at Christopher for agreement. "I would accept that," he said, "given other advantages—a decent appearance, good manners, and a spotless reputation."

"Across the city," said Father Basilio, "there is a convent school for girls of good, and some of noble family, who are too poor to attend the more prestigious seminaries for young ladies. Such a school is run by nuns of my order out of the Convent of All Souls. There are poor young women of all ages, some, I expect, too old to attract a suitor. One or two are in their mid and late twenties. Your brother Christopher would go to the Church of All Souls with my blessing. I conduct vesper services there every evening and I know all the girls, from the smallest maid of seven to the older ones."

Christopher went, expecting little from the daughters of impoverished aristocrats, but he realized that one never knew what one would find without investigating. His Catalonian practicality had taught him that.

4

Father Basilio suggested that Christopher stand by the column nearest the choir stall. He liked the little chapel immediately and didn't wonder at the saying that if a poor girl wanted to find a husband, she should hear vespers in All Souls. The floor was scrubbed clean enough to eat off of, the walls had once been elegant, for they were of a pink Italian marble, much chipped and cracked, and the choir stall was decorated by simple but handsome carvings by men who knew their trade.

Soon the choir entered and took places on little seats which would fold back when they stood up. There were sixteen girls in white surplices over green cassocks, and they ranged from very young to their early twenties. A tallish pale young woman with enormous black eyes shepherded them in and then took her place among them. Running his eyes over that choir, Christopher saw two rather pretty teen-aged girls, one as dark as a Moor, the other fair. He was deeply impressed by the entire choir. They had been well trained, he thought, and their voices were sweet and high. All looked as innocent as angels, even the oldest one who watched over the young possessively. "My *Principezza* looked as innocent as these," he muttered to himself. "How innocent will she be, once she has married that ruthless stallion?" His mind raced on, set on a course he had not intended it to take. "Or can he corrupt that innocence, that frankness, that tenderness? Oh, *Principezza*, how I would like to shore up my sinful life under your influence! How I need to talk to you about my destiny!"

The third night of vespers, a blonde teen-aged girl who, he had noticed, from time to time shot a glance at him, dared to smile. Instantly the shepherd of the flock leaned close and whispered something, and the girl lowered her eyes sulkily. And then, as though seeking the object of her ward's attraction, the black eyes searched him out half-hidden by his column. Stern and peremptory those looked into his, and then they changed. He had never seen eyes like hers, so moist, so doelike. He had read of eyes which a poet called 'two black suns,' and these eyes were such suns. The stern look changed instantly to surprise and to abject and open need. He had never had a girl look in just that way at him before. He felt a current, as though a ray of light ran from her eyes to his and from his to hers. He smiled, and she blushed so deeply that her pale skin was suffused, and then she lowered her head to stare at her missal. No one seemed to have noticed, and when the next hymn began, she lifted her face and kept it fixed unswervingly upon the huge hymnal at the far side of the nave where every other eye in the choir was turned.

Christopher went home that evening wondering how he could have failed to notice her beauty. Now she stood out like a beacon among the simpering children in her charge. Something about her reminded him of his *Principezza*, not in her physical appearance, for two women could hardly look less alike. Whereas the princess was fair and blue-eyed, this young woman had hair as dark as ebony and her eyes, yes, her eyes *were* two black suns, as black and shiny as those huge figs he had tasted in a village whose name had slipped his mind. What he saw in her that he had seen in Isabella was the same innocence, trust, melancholy, courage, and a hopelessness which she struggled against with determination. The princess had had at least the chance of future prosperity, if she could overcome the forces which opposed her, but this young woman, he believed, knew she had no future at all, and yet hoped for one.

"That young woman," Father Basilio told him, "is Felipa Perestrello whose father was a well-known but impoverished soldier and a nobleman. She is the poorest at the convent. She lives with her widowed mother and earns enough to feed them by teaching the younger girls in the convent school and by directing the choir. Frail, as you have seen, but dauntless and devoted to her work."

"She has a certain charm," said Christopher. "I sympathize with her."

"She does have charm, her education is broad, and young men have looked at her; but all have turned away when they learned of the lack of dowry, and, now that she is twenty-five, no one looks at her any more. But the saddest part of her life is this—she has a brother out in the islands who is master of a shipyard. He is in a position to send her more than the pittance she and her mother receive from him. Sons are often ungrateful."

Each evening Christopher watched Felipa at vespers, and when she felt his eyes upon her, she began to look back at him fleetingly, and occasionally she smiled, ever so slightly. He felt encouraged to be the object of such innocent observation. He decided not to send Father Basilio to talk for him to her mother. That could come later, since such was the custom in Portugal. He preferred a stratagem of his own, one which could tell him whether or not the smiles and the peculiar little glances meant real interest or some mere passing whim, some instinct that would make a girl look at a young man. He didn't even consult Bartholomew, but he devised a plan.

"Will she respond?" he asked himself. He sensed she would, but he had to know. "Will her mother think I am good enough for her? Probably not, but poverty is a strong governor of human thought. I make enough money, I have the respect of the community. Father Basilio approves of me, though he might not if he knew my record of lustfulness."

So, choosing a night when the moon was bright, he stood just around the corner at which she had to turn onto her own street as she made her way home each night. He would walk around the corner just as she did and they would collide. It worked like a charm.

"A thousand pardons, lady," he said. "I have made you drop your basket and things have spilled from it. Let me pick them up for you."

She knelt quickly, trying, he thought correctly, to pick up the crusts of bread and the two apples that had spilled onto the pavement before he could. She thanked him and tried to hurry on, but he stopped her gently. "I've seen you so often in the choir," he said, and, "pardon me again, you have seen me. I feel I know you. Allow me to walk you home, for it has gotten dark and we are not far from the worst section of the harbor. Give me the basket and let me carry it for you."

He saw that she was brimming with gratitude and sensed that she hadn't had this much attention from a man in a long, long time. But when they reached her door, she grew flustered and quickly told him goodbye and closed the door.

The next evening her mother was among the worshipers at vesper service, and she waited until her daughter had finished her work and walked her home, with Felipa not looking for a second in his direction. He had his answer, or part of it—he must now seek help from the priest and possibly even from his brother, if the mother proved too difficult.

Later, after he had gained permission to call and sit in the scantily furnished family parlor, and after they were accustomed to one another, she told him much. She never tried to conceal her poverty, her lack of suitors, her belief that some day some proper man would seek her out. Her eyes told him a great deal more, for they were adoring eyes, eyes which looked at him with such open and frank admiration, which glowed when she spoke to him, which opened her timid, yet friendly soul to him, and which made it clear that if, through some miracle, he deigned to propose to her, she would accept him and so would her mother. And when one day he brought her roses, not the wild ones you could gather along the hedgerows, but those sold in markets, bound with silver ribbons, two tears stole from her eyes and down her cheeks. When he kissed them away, she leaned against him and with utter inexperience lifted her mouth and received his lips ingenuously yet eager. He hadn't kissed a girl like this since Isabau, and she, though innocent, had read enough to know which way the wind was blowing when he kissed her. Felipa, he knew with tenderness and with concern, would have to be taught the entire course of love and ultimately of passion.

On their wedding night in her own room, for he had agreed to share their home, she let him hold her and feel against his chest her breasts and the beating of her heart. Apparently, probably at the last minute, her mother must have imparted some basic knowledge to her, for she let him help her out of her gown and into bed. She, at his request, helped him undress, but she turned her eyes away and would not look at his nakedness in the half-lit room. He had never been so gentle, so patient, so willing to wait. He realized how terrified she was, and he admired her modest urge to withdraw from him and understood her fear of failing to please the one man she had ever loved. He never dreamed the night would progress and end as it did, with her as virgin at dawn as she had been at dusk. But the look of thanksgiving in her eyes and the promise of better nights to come were among the most precious rewards he had ever had from a woman. So would he have made love to his *Principezza* on their first night, if she had willed it so. He was never sorry that he had waited, for when, after a week of trying patience on his part, not to speak of certain aches and pains, on the seventh night she came to him in eagerness, and even the pain he caused her against his will she endured in a strange new happiness which made pain turn into ecstasy.

As her love making grew more intimate and experienced, she surprised him with her ardor and alarmed him with its effects upon her. She grew even thinner, she coughed a good deal, and her mother complained at the way she took so much time to carry out her household tasks, for she no longer taught in the convent, but stayed home to keep house for her husband. The district's doctor first, and then a well-known physician, suggested richer food, and with grim shakes of their heads, less activity in bed. When Christopher agreed and told Felipa why, she was obdurate in her refusal to deny them their greatest pleasure. So she ate the richer food and concealed her weakness. But when she became pregnant, even she had to admit her limitations, and Christopher, frightened at her health, slept in another bed to remove temptation from them both.

Almost ten months after Felipa conceived, she gave birth to their first and only child, a healthy little boy whom they named Diego. Felipa wept when the doctor explained that if she suckled the child, the strain would be too great for her. She must have a wet-nurse, and so Diego flourished on the copious bounty of the neighborhood carpenter's wife who had enough to feed Diego and her own son.

One night Felipa came into his bed and he could not resist her. He hoped that everything could be as it had been after their first week of marriage. Unfortunately Felipa quickly conceived again, and this time the results were frightening. She carried the child only two months and then aborted. For weeks she lay in bed, barely conscious and obviously in pain. The nuns came, fearing the worst, and with them Father Basilio. The doctor visited Felipa twice a day. Her reaction to being bled was so traumatic that he never tried that cure again.

Slowly Felipa regained her health, or some semblance of it; but when she told him she felt well enough to have him back in bed with her, the doctor, on hearing this from Christopher, warned him against it. "If you sleep with your wife, my friend, inevitably you and she will start another baby. I do not believe that she could survive another pregnancy. You must deny yourself, as difficult as this will be. And, sir, you and I are men of the world, and we know that there are palliatives to assuage the needs we feel in cases such as this."

A few months later, still weak and sleeping alone, she received a letter from her brother. He suggested that Felipa bring her husband to his shipyard in Mallorca, a place surely, Christopher thought, named after some relative, since the harbor was named Porto Colom. It seemed the best of omens, for things were going sour for Christopher in Lisbon. Moreover, the physicians thought that climate in the islands would be beneficial to Felipa's health. And so they went, and for a time Christopher felt that his destiny, which had been at a standstill, would be strengthened, since his duties centered around ships and the sea.

5

As they neared Guisando, the Archbishop grew uneasy. "The king may be planning a trap," he said. So saying, he sent a large body of cavalry to reconnoiter. But the spies returned with little to report: the king was waiting at the Inn with a token guard. It appeared to be safe to meet him with their small group.

The next afternoon after siesta she dressed in her best blue gown and threw a costly mantilla of Holland lace across her shoulders. Her hair rippled like flame, for Margarita had brushed it until her scalp burned. The little coronet made her feel queenly as she trotted her mare out into the field where Henry's pavilion stood surrounded by the gaudy uniforms of four Moorish pikesmen. She had only a moment to glance at the strange stone beasts which gave the place its name. Not bulls, these grotesque, formless sculptures. They might as well have been called lions or bears, or even horses. She smiled. They were bulls to her people. And they were as old as time.

As she reined the mare toward the pavilion, her excitement communicated itself to the animal, which pawed and reared, just as they reached the space before the entrance. Henry didn't move, but she could see him smile. He liked the horse, at least. No sign of Beltrán or any of her other enemies, but they might be watching from inside the pavilion or from the nearby inn.

Henry got to his feet, stumbling over his cloak, and took a few steps to meet her, teetering as usual on his high heels. She looked more closely and found his large face greatly changed, aged and grey. Smudges of dark shadow lay under the ox-like, watery eyes. His lower lip hung even more lax than she had remembered, and she clearly saw his huge, horse-like, yellow teeth. Somehow they had gotten his hair washed, and it was a fine mane of russet blond, not far removed in color from her own. His face and clothes, were clean for once, and even his big splay-fingered paws looked presentable. They had drenched him with musky scent and had placed rings on his fingers, on Henry who thought rings got in the way when he was hunting.

Gracefully, trying not to let him see how his appearance shocked her, she dismounted and walked toward him. A page from her retinue took the reins of her mare, holding the animal where she could mount it if there were need. When she was as close as she could bear to go, she knelt and reached for his hand, for she knew she had to kiss it. But Henry chose to be magnanimous. He drew her to her feet and pulled her into a hearty *abrazo*. She stiffened and did not shudder, steeling herself against his touch. She forced herself to return his hug, refusing to look into his fishy eyes which she realized were not fixed on her at all, but on something over her shoulder. Their expression revolted her. Out of the corner of her eye she saw to her left, and a few paces behind her, the figure of the page still holding her mare. The light in Henry's eyes shone for the page.

"Poor, God-forsaken soul!" she thought. "Even here with the world watching and assessing his every move, he is helpless against his itch!" To divert him, she lifted her face to his and said, "Sire, I crave the kiss of peace."

The eager eyes lost their light, and he bent and kissed her on the lips. She was thankful that they had made him chew cinnamon and cloves. His breath, which she had remembered and dreaded, blew scented upon her as his lips touched hers and quickly recoiled from her touch.

She stepped back then and one of the lawyers began to read the terms of the treaty. Stealing a glance at the Archbishop, she found his eyes dark, and his brow creased in a scowl, for he, too, had noted the handsomeness of the page. Not so much as another glance did he cast at Henry, and even when the Bishop of Coria nudged him and whispered, "Your Grace, it is time to administer the oath," he fixed his eyes on a point in the air above the king's head! He took the large hands in his own because tradition demanded it, and he gave the oath with the expression of one forced to handle carrion. His face above the king's, for Henry had to kneel, was stone.

Isabella and all those present heard Henry swear that she was now his legal heir, that his wife Joanna, Queen of Castile, was an adulteress and the mother of a bastard child begotten upon her in sin by Beltrán de la Cueva. As she listened, Isabella's flesh crawled in humiliation. But Henry himself felt no shame, not a shred of It. It meant less than nothing to him to degrade the name of Trastámara. Suddenly she realized that people were looking at the earth in embarrassment. Even Henry's retainers and servants looked hangdog and crestfallen.

Then the oaths were taken, and she and Henry left the village and passed the Bulls of Guisando for the last time. She wished she were a thousand miles away as she saw him simper at the soldiers and lean down from his horse to pat the page on the head as he passed him. Still, it had been worth all the mortification and embarrassment. The people had seen her and the king together, as brother and sister, and in apparent affection. Graphic illustrations of love, sights the people could see and understand, were necessary. In less than a week, she knew, every hamlet would hear how King Henry had met his sister, the Princess Isabella, and had given her the kiss of peace.

Once, however, a serious breach almost occurred. Henry wanted her to ride at once with him to Madrid. The Archbishop and the nobles of the League, however, insisted that she return to Ávila with them. She thought frantically of a way out of an embarrassing situation quite capable of becoming dangerous. Then it came to her.

"Let me go to Ocaña, Sire. Your Grace? From there I can keep in close touch with Madrid as well as Ávila." Henry had been holding court at Ocaña, she knew, but stayed there as little as possible. He had never felt at home there, and Villena's enthusiasm for the little town was lost on him. Better far for Henry either Seville, Segovia, or Madrid. She remembered that Seville had lured him at the time she had fled into Ocaña's tower. And yet, nominally, if not actually, Ocaña was the court, even if the king gave it a wide berth. By choosing Ocaña, even if it had belonged to Joanna as part of her dowry, even if it reminded her of Joanna and Beltrán and the little Beltraneja, it reminded Henry of those matters, too, and therefore repelled him. She knew he would not live in a city that reminded him of his failures, his impotency, his unhappiness. And besides, she knew that Ocaña would be safe for her. The Archbishop often occupied a fortress castle in Yepes only seven miles away. Any treachery that she failed to uncover, the Archbishop would surely see.

Strangely even Villena agreed, fearful, yet confident that she could be contained, where she was, so long as it was a place under the king's influence, which meant Villena's. Henry was delighted. Her presence had always embarrassed him and would have done so in Madrid if he had to see her every day.

She shot a quick glance at the Archbishop and found him studying her with deep speculation. Ever so slightly he nodded his head, and the glint in his eye was of approval, mingled with puzzlement. The nod said that Ocaña had been the best of all possible choices, with Ávila ruled out, of course, which he opted for. The puzzlement arose from his inability to fathom her, to him, newfound sagacity. "He still regards me as a child," she said to herself. "He may never realize that I do have a mind of my own and am not just a stubborn adolescent full of willfulness."

6

In Ocaña she was happy for the first time in years, no, in all her life until then, in fact. She had money at last, not much, but enough to insure respectability and the first measure of independence she could recall. She had a little court all her own with ladies-in-waiting, pages, servants and her own chaplain. She could command people and did. Obedience to her every word was a balm to a sore long smarting. She sent a trusted messenger, one supplied by Beatriz, to the shepherds' hamlet to inquire after the woolmerchant, but the messenger returned with the news that Christopher had long since left the region, They knew nothing about his whereabouts.

Her mind turned to the suitors she knew would soon be at her door. She could pick and choose among them. Henry had promised not to force any unwelcome match upon her. Without Beltrán to urge him on, perhaps Villena couldn't manipulate him too much; but, on the other hand, reason told her that he could and would. He always had, even from afar. The sky, even so, seemed brighter, the air cleaner, the future, not only less grim, but even shot through with gleams of light.

The first of the suitors was represented by no less than a cardinal from France sent by King Louis himself. The absent suitor was none other than the Duke of Guyenne, the king's own brother, since Louis had no issue. The Archbishop didn't like it and told her so. She could hear his ringing voice thundering, even as she waited for the Cardinal to appear. "Daughter, reject the French always. Deceit and intrigue were born in Paris and nurtured in France. Marry a Frenchman, and off he'll pack you to one of those frilly castles while Castile flounders in the grasp of Villena."

"And yet, Your Grace, would I not be free, also, of the intrigues of the League, the threats, even the dangers hatched by the followers of the poor Beltraneja, and above all of Villena's focused hatred?"

Without consulting the Archbishop, she granted the Cardinal an audience and watched his wise old eyes, cold and wintry with life's disillusionments, take stock of her and approve. But his *sang-froid* and his calculated approbation froze into barely concealed alarm when she asked him for a description of the Duke. Too courtly and diplomatic to register visible surprise, he barely allowed himself to blink before he collected his Gallic acumen and made reply. "He's thinking," she told herself almost aloud, "that though my question is inelegant and gauche, it may be owed to my tender age and the barbaric background I've grown up in. It'll horrify him even more when I ask to see a likeness of the Duke, as most certainly I shall."

When she made the request, he winced almost imperceptibly, just as she had thought he would, but went on quite undaunted. "The Princess shall gaze upon that fair portrait this very day, nay this very hour." And turning to a page, he sent him off to his quarters to fetch it. "In the meantime, Princess, let me assure you that the Duke of Guyenne is a very remarkable young man, like no other in all the Kingdom of France."

Something in the way he said it aroused suspicion. The words, she knew, meant nothing. In fact, their very emptiness, or perhaps the very enigmatic quality behind them, proved it. Not a hint of detail, not the mention of a single physical characteristic. She didn't like it at all. She would wait, chatting amicably with the sly old fox, until the page returned with the likeness. Then, when the Cardinal presented it to her with the flourish of triumph she anticipated, and which she could already detect in the nascent glint of purest duplicity and satisfaction she caught in his eye, she would give him her reply. The Cardinal's look seemed to say, "Well, my dear young thing, resist, if you can, this divinity I hold out to you."

The portrait, a miniature painted with care and by an artist of considerable talent, was in her hands. "If this is the way he looks," she whispered to Beatriz, "no angel in heaven is more beautiful, more manly, more perfect!" But to herself she said, "What a head! What classic features! What grace! Not even the woolmerchant had better shoulders and arms! Not even Beltrán's thighs and calves are better sculptured! A man like this one in the portrait would father fine sons and beautiful daughters. But I wonder."

Her eyes returned to the likeness. The Duke wore a hunting costume. The artist had not stinted when he drew attention to what bulged beneath his chamois trousers. "He's too good to be true, even allowing for artistic exaggeration," she said to Beatriz, still whispering.

Facing the Cardinal again, she said politely, "My Lord, you must give me leave to think, to study at leisure the divine likeness you have so graciously provided." She hoped it would give her time to carry out a plan; she feared it wouldn't, for France was proud, and Louis too wise to be deceived. She watched the Cardinal bow himself out, his back stiff, the wrinkled parchment of his face stiffer. She could imagine the effect upon Villena, and therefore of course, on Henry.

Not a week later Henry's emissaries brought another name—Alfonso of Portugal again. In this she saw Joanna's hand and knew with near despair that the queen still plotted to remove her by the simple expedient of burying her in Lisbon, leaving the way free for the Beltraneja. The matter of Portugal troubled her deeply. To reject King Alfonso a second time would render any future friendship with that monarch out of the question. She longed for Beatriz who had returned to Segovia. She pined for the strength of the woolmerchant. She had to content herself with the cold comfort offered by the Archbishop who swept into Ocaña shortly after the arrival of Henry's emissaries, and small comfort it was.

"The League, daughter, will regard it as an act of bad faith on your part, even of hostility, if you accede to the king's desire, which is Villena's, as you well know. The League, yes, and I myself, favor an alliance through marriage, with Aragón. Let us secretly restore the long ago broken betrothal between you and Prince Ferdinand who is, I hear now a fine young man, already his father's right hand. He's only a little younger than the Duke and is young enough to be the grandson of Alfonso of Portugal. And remember, Princess. You cannot wait much longer. King Louis will not be kept dangling, nor will the Portuguese.

In the midst of it all Beatriz arrived from Segovia, which Andrés now commanded. When they were alone, she asked to see the Duke's likeness again. "Isabella, it may be authentic. I saw another, painted by a different artist, I would say, and depicting the Duke in robes of state and on a golden throne. Would two different artists falsify his appearance?"

"Two artists, Beatriz, can lie as well as one, especially if they paint for the King of France. The picture you saw in Segovia, the one I expect Henry has seen, may deceive him, and even you, but I must be certain. There can be no turning back, once the banns are published. You see, my friend, I remember another time, the time they took me to meet my uncle, Alfonso of Portugal at Gibraltar when I was thirteen. You were there, so you, too, remember. I had a picture of a dashing, hardly middle-aged king, a knight in armor on a white stallion. The face under the upturned visor was handsome, dark, virile. His eyes flashed, his lips were made for kisses and laughter. Instead, I met an oldish monarch—fat, tired, with a pot belly and the breath of old age. I shan't be duped for a second time by the painting of a pretty face and a spurious virility."

"But would the King of France stoop to this? Would he dare deceive the sister of an ally? Why, it would scandalize all Europe'"

"Would it, Beatriz? And wouldn't the Spider King attempt such duplicity? He would revel in it. And Europe would laugh instead of being scandalized. The King of France devises treaties with twisted clauses, scraps agreements he can't pervert, hires assassins to murder his enemies, even when they are kinsmen; and adds the image of a new saint to his cap each time he plans some new atrocity. Louis gag at faking a likeness? Some instinct warns me. Something stinks in the French proposal."

"What, then, Isabella? You can hardly go to Paris to look the young man over."

Isabella smiled. "I can do the next best thing. I've sent someone to look him over for me."

"Who on earth, Isabella? Whom can you depend upon to bring back a trustworthy report?"

"Whom but the confessor, Beatriz? As a priest he can go anywhere, cross any national border. He can ascertain what I must know."

"But the French and Portuguese embassies? How can you keep them here cooling their heels while you wait? There'll be trouble, I heard this morning, as I rode through the streets, that fights have broken out between French and Portuguese retainers."

"Father de Coca'll be back in Ocaña quite soon, I think. I sent him off the very day the Cardinal handed me the portrait."

"I might have known. And did you send someone to Aragón to observe Prince Ferdinand?"

"What do you think, Beatriz? Of course I did. Father de Coca will return from Paris by way of Barcelona. I must have all the facts in hand when I decide. It pays to be thorough."

Beatriz glanced away. "Isabella, what of the forbidden degree of consanguinity? Ferdinand is your first cousin."

"The Church waived that prohibition when our fathers betrothed us as infants. Rome, the Archbishop assures me, will concur again."

"I wonder, Isabella. That other time a different Holy Father occupied St. Peter's throne. Pope Sixtus may not concur. They say in Segovia that he regards Henry as Spain's rightful ruler and will not oppose him in his choice of a husband for you. And Henry will never agree to an alliance between you and the House of Aragón. Villena would not let him. I would not count on Rome, if I were you."

Beatriz was correct, Isabella knew, but the Archbishop was the primate of Spain and he vowed to secure the Pope's approval, even if it meant a trip to the Vatican to visit Sixtus. Moreover, if the clergy of Aragón added their insistence, as they surely would, the Pope would of a certainty grant the waiver. In spite of Beatriz' doubts, she refused to be uneasy. Soon the confessor would return with the needed report about the suitors. And if the Prince of Aragón proved acceptable, she believed she would consent to an alliance with him through marriage. France was, after all, another world, Aragón was a part of Spain. Yes, she favored Aragón over France, unless the confessor found that the Duke of Guyenne was a paragon and Ferdinand unsuited. But until she knew of a certainty, she must fend off the Cardinal, the Ambassador from Portugal, and the Archbishop of Toledo.

7

When Alfonso de Coca entered her room, Isabella took him directly to a chair and asked Beatriz to join them. They were to hear at last, and it was a good thing. The French demanded an answer, the Cardinal of Arras could not be put off.

"What of the Duke of Guyenne, Father? What of Prince Ferdinand?"

"I was able to see both of the young men, Princess. The duke came to Mass once when I was first acolyte to the celebrant in Notre Dame. Prince Ferdinand, who has the reputation of being very religious, attended services four times while I was in Barcelona."

Isabella tried to look as though she considered this of even greater importance than she did. "I'm happy to hear of their piety," she said, hoping that de Coca did not see how eager she was to hear about the physical appearance of the two men.

The confessor feigned great weariness and looked about for a more comfortable seat. After he had moved to a deeper chair, he sighed wearily and returned to the subject, although not from the direction she had hoped. "I was amazed to see the changes in France, Princess," he said. "I hadn't visited Paris in years, not since King Louis ascended the throne. Now in the time of King Charles..."

"Father, tell me about the changes later," said Isabella steadying her voice and refusing to notice that Beatriz was smiling behind her fan. "I want to hear about the Prince of Aragón and the Duke of Guyenne, not about the changes in France."

De Coca pretended he was hurt, though she knew he wasn't, for he was merely teasing her. When she handed him the small portrait of the duke, he looked and rubbed his eyes in disbelief. "This is not the likeness of the Duke of

Guyenne," he said at last. "The Duke of Guyenne, King Louis's' brother," went on the confessor unperturbed, and pretending not to notice how she bit her lip, "is not like this at all. He has a large, bulbous head that wobbles like King Louis', and his legs are bandy. One day two stout pages had to help him as they brought him to the communion rail. And, Princess, the poor young man drools incessantly."

"Was he inebriated, Father?" asked Beatriz.

"No, Lady Beatriz. He has some affliction in the legs. But there's more to it than that. I was able to observe him at very close range, Princess, as for the celebrant's assistant, I placed the wafer on his tongue. His eyes are large, even larger than King Henry's, and they're pale and rheumy. They drip continuously, alas, and he had to dabble at his cheeks many times before he left the church. The Duke is unsound, and even defective."

"That settles the French marriage," said Isabella vehemently. "This poor duke may have a name and a high position at the French court, but what kind of children would he father?"

"Now all you have to do is settle with the Cardinal of Arras," said Beatriz dryly. "And I don't envy you that duty, Isabella."

The confessor looked worried. "Is the Cardinal in Ocaña, Princess?"

"He arrived just after you departed, Father. What do you know of him?"

"The Cardinal is a stern man, linked by blood to all the great houses of France, even to the king's. It's most unfortunate you must offend him. They say he is implacable in his anger. Think well before you send him on his way."

"I have no means of sending him away, Father, although no doubt he'll leave of his own accord when he hears my decision. The Cardinal doesn't worry me; it's Henry and Villena. When they learn that I've refused the French marriage, who can predict what they'll do? And if I reject King Alfonso of Portugal for the second time, I don't even want to think of the consequences. Father, you must make it plain to the Archbishop of Toledo that my fate may rest in his hands. Make him realize that he may have to come to my assistance again, if the king, in his anger, decides to punish me."

Beatriz watched Isabella's face and sensed her disappointment. "Father," she asked, "what can you tell us of the Prince of Aragón? Surely he's not as ill-favored as the duke."

"About your cousin Ferdinand, Princess, I can give you better word. I saw him not only in church, but on the jousting field. You may have forgotten it, but I come from a noble house and my father was a well-known knight…"

"Yes, Father," said Isabella, foreseeing another digression and trying to head it off. "Everyone knows the renown of the House of de Coca and the exploits of your noble sire. Now, you were saying that you saw Prince Ferdinand on the jousting-field..."

"That I did, Princess. It was a sight to remember. He recalled to my mind the days at my father's castle when my two older brothers were training as squires. In those days I used to haunt the stables whenever I could escape my tutors. Horses, and knights, and fine armor—those were the things I dreamed about as a lad, but they gave me to the Church. My memories took me to the jousting field in Barcelona, in case you're wondering."

"I understand," said Isabella, afraid to say more for fear he might stray off into a new digression.

"While in Barcelona, then, I allowed myself to be persuaded by a priest I know there to attend a joust. It was there that I saw Prince Ferdinand in action. What a superb horseman! With sword and buckler and with lance he excels them all. I've seen few grown men with stronger backs and shoulders, and he's only seventeen. What will he be like when he gains his maturity? He wears the heaviest armor as though it's his own skin!"

Isabella's color was high in her cheeks as she listened. The confessor continued. "Prince Ferdinand is most informal, Princess. Many Castilian nobles would go so far as to consider him ungentlemanly. He's on familiar terms with everyone, even grooms and stable hands, and in Barcelona everyone worships him. That afternoon on the jousting field, the prince tilted so much he scarcely had time to dress for a parade he was to lead. When he realized how late it was, he did something no Castilian aristocrat would have dreamed of doing. He sent for his festive robes. Then, off came his clothes until he was mother-nude, if you will pardon the expression, Princess, and he bathed right in the stable while one groom scrubbed him with a stiff brush and another poured cold water over his body."

"Is he handsome, Father?" asked Beatriz.

"He has the muscles of a young Hercules, Lady Beatriz. Handsome? He's very comely, yes. He has clear skin with ruddy tinges and his eyes are very blue. They are eyes that attract and command, and they dance. He loves life. But when he's not laughing, his face is grave and sagacious. His hair is rather chestnut than russet, and has gotten a little thin at the temples. It makes his forelock noticeable and reveals his brow. If I were a young lady, Princess, I'd be forced to say that Prince Ferdinand is fine enough for any princess or any queen."

"And his life and habits, Father?" asked Isabella

"I haven't spoken sufficiently of his prowess on the field," said the confessor, very obviously attempting to change the subject.

"Father," said Isabella, "I must know it all. What are you trying to conceal?"

"I believe I know," said Beatriz. "It's the scandal. Isn't there an illegitimate child, Father?"

"Yes, Lady Beatriz," replied the confessor, lowering his eyes and crossing himself. "It's the prince's only flaw. He's of an amorous vein. Only seventeen and the father of a bastard! *O tempores, mores,* as Cicero said."

Isabella was disappointed. She realized she had been nurturing a preconceived idea of the Prince of Aragón. She had painted him in colors too clear and too pure. But seventeen-year-old princes simply weren't virgins, and conduct of this kind was openly condoned everywhere. Was there a royal court in Europe without its bastards? She knew of none. And what could she expect of a young man, obviously the toast of his father's court, with good-looking women probably falling all over him.

Beatriz finally said, "Prince Ferdinand is very young. You aren't betrothed to him, and you may never be. If you were, there would be cause for anger and disillusionment. As it is, you must regard the whole matter as perfectly natural in a prince, in any healthy young man, Don't let it discourage any considerations you have as to betrothal. And, if you'll pardon me, Father, for being indelicate, the very existence of the bastard child proves the prince is fertile. There's always the chance, you know, that a man isn't."

Isabella knew Beatriz was right, but wished she hadn't been so specific before the priest, who was rubbing his chin and looking fixedly out the window.

"Who was the woman?" Isabella asked.

"One of the queen's ladies-in-waiting, and unmarried, Princess, if you're thinking of adultery."

Isabella's eyes flashed. "I won't let it make any difference, although I'm very sorry it happened. Bastard children create so many problems, as we know well here in Castile. But if he'll undertake penance and set matters right with the Church, I shan't pursue it again."

Father de Coca revealed that the archbishop had authorized him to talk to the Aragonese about betrothal and that the Aragonese were interested. "While I was there, Princess, King John assembled his privy council. All agreed that this marriage has much to offer both nations; it would provide Aragón with Castilian soldiers to fight off the French invasion; and Castile would gain a strong ally against the Portuguese."

"What does the prince think of the idea? What was his personal reaction?" asked Isabella.

"Prince Ferdinand regards it with enthusiasm. He'll work for this marriage. Of this you can be certain."

"You spoke to him about it, Father?"

"Privately, Princess. The prince is very inquisitive. He asked many questions."

"What sort of questions, Father? About the affairs of Castile? About money? Things like that?"

"He left things like that, as you call then, to his father's advisers. By this, however, I don't mean to imply lack of interest on his part. For a man so young, I regard Prince Ferdinand as very businesslike in every Aragonese sense of the word. But his questions were of a more personal nature. Our conversation reminded me of the very questions you were asking me to find answers to, for you, in Paris and Barcelona."

Isabella's heart beat faster. "What were the questions, Father?"

"He wanted to know what you look like—the color of your eyes, your hair, your state of health. In short, Princess, the young man is romantic, and the idea of a beautiful bride-to-be, living in the shadow of danger from a cruel half-brother, has stirred his blood."

"I've known, of course," said Isabella, "that negotiations with the court of King John have been progressing, but how far have they gone and how much has the Archbishop of Toledo withheld from me? Father, what is your opinion? How soon can we inform the Aragonese that I want to marry Prince Ferdinand?"

Beatriz interrupted. "So you *are* willing, Isabella. Father, your powers of description are great, and the archbishop should be grateful to you. But, Isabella, you must be careful. The king must not suspect what you have in mind, what apparently you are already planning to do. Henry is Henry, and when he learns that you've rejected the French marriage, who knows what his reaction will be?"

"Lady Beatriz is correct in this," said de Coca, his face a study in concern. "You must never forget the seriousness of these negotiations with the Aragonese. Statecraft is a new field for you, Princess, one that you'll not fully understand at first. Be most careful, for King Henry and his counselors will try to make everything you do appear as treason."

"I'm glad I'm not a princess," said Beatriz. "I do not envy the role you'll have to play, Isabella."

Fall had come early that year to Valladolid. At night cold winds swept across the flat grain lands and howled over the granite walls and towers. In the day, however, when the sun was out, the weather was warm enough for light clothing and long hours out-of-doors. Here King John, Isabella's father, had made his residence, bringing to the old city pomp and luxury and the most splendid court Spain had seen in decades. Here had died Don Álvaro de Luna at the insistence of Isabella's mother. And from Valladolid King Henry had driven the queen with her two small children. Now, years later Isabella was back. The ways of God are strange, she thought. She had departed the city at Henry's order, and now she returned a refugee from his persecution.

Isabella worried. She was safe enough behind the high walls, and the archbishop assured her that the city would remain loyal to her, But her safety didn't concern her. The trouble lay in her isolation. Her marriage seemed even more remote than before, for between her and Ferdinand Henry had thrown a line of troops, effectively sealing the border to all but the most daring and highly trained emissaries. Ferdinand must certainly not attempt to reach her, risking his life and their eventual happiness. Nor for the present was there a way for her to escape into Aragón.

It would be a long time before she understood all that had happened to bring her to Valladolid. First had come Henry's letter stating that King Alfonso of Portugal was en route to Ocaña to ask for her hand. "Receive him well, sister," Henry had written. "Accept the great honor he wishes to do us, and you'll reign as Queen of Portugal."

Reign in Portugal, indeed! Not while Joanna was Alfonso's sister. She might live in Lisbon, but little power would come her way. The best she could expect was a life of bearing children to the fat king, while she drifted into oblivion, insofar as concerned Castile.

Henry should have consulted her. Now with Alfonso on the road, it was too late and there was little she could do but wait and think of the wording of her rejection—that and the explanations she would be forced to offer Henry. And the archbishop was of little help. "Daughter, you must avoid this Portuguese alliance," he said, leaving the entire burden of refusal to her. "Do as you did the other time," he advised. "Tell King Alfonso you must await the approval of the Grandees."

King Alfonso arrived in Ocaña with the Bishop of Lisbon and a retinue so splendid that she knew at once Henry had promised him she would agree. Panic seized her when he came to meet her down the long aisle of Castilian and Portuguese knights. The pleased look in his tired eyes told her how difficult it was going to be.

"He looks much older than the other time," she said to herself. "But I can see what people mean when they say he was handsome in his day. Buried under the burden of all that fat I can see the traces of a vanished charm. When a man holds himself like this, he knows that he has been attractive, and the knowledge sustains him."

After that, pure nightmare. Alfonso's eyes, blank with disbelief, then full of hurt and embarrassment, finally dull with an anger so terrible that he had broken down and wept. She had felt great pity for him, for she understood what it meant for a great king to be rebuffed for a second time before his own nobles and those of a foreign power. Suddenly he had drawn himself to his full height, and she realized that he was a tall man. His obesity had made her overlook it. Then out of the audience hall he stalked, followed by his white-faced retinue and the stricken Bishop of Lisbon.

"He will never forgive me," she thought. "Not this time. Holy Mother of God! What will this day mean to Spain?"

Events moved swiftly after that. Some day historians would write it all in their books, she supposed. Maybe then she would be able to comprehend the rapidity of what took place.

Henry arrived from Madrid too late to intercept Alfonso of Portugal in his angry withdrawal from Castile. Isabella had never seen him so furious. Even his ennui dissolved as he stormed into Ocaña with the Marquis of Villena, threatening her with imprisonment and a husband far worse than Pedro Girón if she dared defy him again. "Take the next one, Isabella," he cried. "Take him, or by the bones of St. Ferdinand you will regret it!"

Isabella stood firm on her rights. "You swore at the Bulls of Guisando, Henry, that you'd force no unwelcome marriage on me. Will you forswear yourself?"

"She is in fact, within her rights, Sire," said the archbishop. And Henry had been forced to agree.

"You'll find the next suitor satisfactory, even to you," he growled. But something in his eyes told her that if she refused again his threats of imprisonment would not be empty.

Worse still, he refused to leave Ocaña. He lingered on, and by day led his nobles out of the city on hunting excursions. At night he talked with the French envoys, and Isabella knew that very soon the next suitor of whom he spoke would be brought to her attention. She wasn't surprised, then, to find herself one afternoon sitting on the dais flanked by the king and the archbishop with the hall full of French nobles and again the frightening presence of the Cardinal of Arras.

The audience could not have been more harrowing. Beside her Henry sat, his eyes a living threat when he looked at her and deferential when he looked at the cardinal. The cardinal stood and glowered at her as if accusing her—, and his challenging gaze offended her. But worse than either of these was the Archbishop of Toledo who feared neither Henry nor the Cardinal of Arras. Every line of his grim countenance radiated hostility, and his nose wrinkled, as if he found the very air the French breathed polluted. Tension was so taut that it fairly hummed.

The cardinal tendered the request in the name of King Louis. She felt Henry's eyes upon her from the right and those of the archbishop from the left. At the foot of the dais stood the cardinal, his wrinkled face as hard and uncompromising as flint. As she started to speak, no one breathed.

"Castile is honored," she said, "by the King of France. Convey to him, Your Eminence, our gratitude again and our regret that we cannot answer until the Great Council of the Grandees of Spain can meet to decide the matter."

She got no further. Suddenly Henry staggered to his feet, clutched his throat, and toppled headlong from the dais before anyone could catch him. He lay white and twitching at the feet of the cardinal for long seconds before anyone moved. In the ensuing confusion Isabella left the room and hurried to her quarters. The French had their answer. There was nothing she could do but wait until Henry recovered. What he would do then no one dared think.

Henry moved swiftly. From his bed he bade farewell to His Eminence, who had little to say before departing for Paris with his entire retinue. They left gifts for Henry and even for her, she learned, but etiquette demanded this. And as they rode through the streets of Ocaña, the citizens lined the way jeering and filling the air with a new song.

> Flowers of Aragón
> Are in Castile.
> The banner of Aragón!
> The banner of Aragón!

The message was clear enough. The French would understand. Spaniards wanted no French duke for its princess. Popular feeling was all for Ferdinand.

Henry dispatched soldiers to arrest Isabella even as the French were riding through the gates. The palace swarmed with his men, and Isabella realized she had lost. Through the window she could see a heavily guarded coach rolling toward the palace. In it she would ride to Madrid, perhaps for the last time, and once there, disappear from the world, soon to be forgotten. She squared her shoulders and waited for the knock at the door. When she left, no one could say she went downcast.

She saw Henry step from the coach. Instantly he was surrounded. Citizens and soldiers jammed the street from side to side but they were not Henry's. The archbishop and the League, foreseeing events to come, had roused the city. Henry's troops were outnumbered by the lancers sent by the nobles who had rallied to the archbishop's call. Soon word came that her supporters were barricading the central plaza, and that citizens had closed the gates. The King of Castile, trapped in his own realm, would not take her off to prison in his capital.

> Flowers of Aragón
> Are in Castile.
> The banner of Aragón!
> The banner of Aragón!

The streets rang with it. Children ran everywhere waving miniature Aragonese banners. She found herself shouting also with the great crowd that hemmed in the king's coach.

When the archbishop came to say that Henry asked for an audience, she hardly realized the significance of his words. And not until long after his coach rolled away through the chanting citizens of Ocaña did she realize how deep the rift between them was. With white and tear-stained face Henry of Trastámara had sobbed and said, "God will punish you, sister, if you break your promise. For God's sake and mine go no further with the Aragonese marriage. I beg you, sister." He had humbled himself to her, to his little sister! He had ridden out of a city, once his own, under the ridicule of its populace. But back in Madrid he would not forget and would certainly not forgive.

At the archbishop's insistence she had gone to her birthplace, Madrigal de las Altas Torres. Her presence in Ocaña could bring harm to the people who had risen in her defense. In Madrigal, out of public life, Henry might leave her alone. Perhaps he would believe her when she wrote to tell him of her decision to stay with her mother, now in the care of nuns in the great house in Madrigal, once one of the family's homes. He might even trust her when she promised to go no further with the betrothal.

But no word of any kind came from Madrid, and slowly she allowed herself to believe that Henry had decided to overlook what had happened.

No punishment descended on the city, and the king kept his troops well beyond the borders of the territory occupied by the League. Then one day a prodigy occurred—an Aragonese cavalcade appeared at the gates of Madrigal. No one knew how they had eluded the cordon of Castilian troops, but there they were and they asked for an audience with the princess.

The archbishop crowed with jubilation. "We're moving, daughter," he said. "Prince Ferdinand has not forgotten us."

"I don't know what to say, Your Grace. On holy relics I swore to Henry I would do nothing new with regard to the matter of Aragón and Ferdinand."

The archbishop looked triumphant. "Daughter," he said at last, "I heard the oath you swore. You promised the king that you would not take any new steps in the matter. You had already taken the important steps. Long ago you and I informed the court of King John that you would accept a proposal of marriage from Prince Ferdinand, and the Aragonese made it plain to us that the proposal would be forthcoming. Tacitly we and they agreed, did we not? Each party expects the other to abide by that agreement."

"But Henry didn't know this, Your Grace."

"Then he should employ better spies, Princess."

"That may be so," she said. "But I feel in some way we're being not quite honest."

"Let it be a lesson in diplomacy, daughter. But if you still feel guilty, let me remind you—the oath you swore at Guisando hung upon the king's oath not to force you into unwanted betrothals. Did he not bring pressure twice—once with Alfonso of Portugal and a second time on behalf of the Duke of Guyenne? And didn't he even attempt to arrest you and carry you off to prison? Any court, lay or ecclesiastical, would find you absolved of your promise."

She received the Aragonese and learned they came direct from Ferdinand himself. Much had happened, they told her: King John had gone blind with cataracts; his wife had died; the French stirred up new revolt in Catalonia. Ferdinand vowed he hadn't forgotten her. He swore that he considered her his betrothed. And, as a token of his love, he wrote that he was sending her a gift. When she laid down the letter, the Aragonese ambassador handed her a flat ebony chest.

She opened it and gasped. "Holy Virgin! How can anything be so lovely!"

"This is the famous necklace of Balas rubies, Princess," said one of the emissaries. "It belonged to the Prince's mother and is one of the greatest treasures of Aragón."

"And the prince wanted you to have it," said another. "He hoped it would help you to realize how much he loves you."

Before they left, Ferdinand's representatives presented also a chest containing 20,000 gold florins. The necklace was the gift of their prince in the name of the love he bore her; the florins he sent because he and his people understood that King Henry had revoked her revenues. Ferdinand could not bear to think of her in want, the Aragonese said. It was a daring gift, for if taken wrongly, the betrothal might suffer. Castilian pride was proverbial. But Isabella understood the sentiment behind both gifts and received them graciously.

Even when the Bishop of Burgos, in whose diocese was Madrigal, sent a report to Henry of the visit from Aragón and Henry protested, she refused to see in the gifts anything but a blessing. And when the archbishop's lancers snatched her out of Madrigal Just before Henry's troops could reach the town, she had her faith confirmed. The gifts settled the uncertain course of her life. There could be no more fencing and shadow boxing with her brother. The blame lay at his door. From Valladolid she could defy him forever, if need be, and from the safety of its mighty walls she could turn her attention seriously to her marriage with Ferdinand of Aragón. It might take a long time, for Henry's troops still patrolled the border, but sooner or later a way would open.

Isabella's hands shook as she rolled up the archbishop's letter. Even the prospect of reading the one that had arrived from Beatriz was insufficient to rouse her from her mood of gloom. Now that the old man had given her the news, at least four Castilians had it in their possession, and where four people know a secret, others soon manage to learn it. In Aragón still others knew. Ferdinand, madly romantically, heroically, planned to cross the border and visit her in Valladolid. It was all in the archbishop's message, and apparently it was already too late to prevent Ferdinand's departure from Barcelona. She gripped the parchment until it complained, and wondered how long before Henry took steps to intercept him.

At first she bitterly berated the archbishop for agreeing with her betrothed, for letting him begin such a journey. She called him ambitious, self-centered, so determined to dethrone Henry that nothing mattered, not even the safety of an ally. But on reflection, she had to admit that the old man acted out of loyalty to his people and his faith. As he explained in his letter, the time was as good for penetration of Henry's lines as it would ever be. An unexpected uprising in Andalusia would keep Henry occupied and deplete his troops along the border of Aragón enough to give Ferdinand the chance he needed.

Though Isabella worried, even fear and anxiety couldn't smother her fierce pride. Ferdinand wanted to see her so much that he would risk capture to do so! She loved him for it. "Mother of God, protect him," she prayed, "and forgive him this wonderful, foolish courage."

The archbishop's letter brought other news. Henry had been persuaded to revoke the treaty of the Bulls of Guisando. Worse still, again he publicly proclaimed the bastard his heir and had betrothed the child to Villena's son. A stab of real fear made her shiver at the archbishop's words. "If Villena is not stopped, daughter, they will establish a new dynasty in Castile and the House of Trastámara will sink into oblivion."

The apparent haste with which the Aragonese entered the negotiations for the betrothal surprised her. She understood Ferdinand's interest and eagerness, but the council of the nobles ordinarily debated long and slowly made decisions. Yet Ferdinand was young and romantic, and so was she. Each believed the courtship would be the most romantic in history. Like the knights in the fairy tales and the novels of chivalry he would challenge the ogre, defeat him in combat, and carry off the fair princess as his bride. But the nobles of Aragón were cut from a different cloth, and romance and fairy tales never entered their calculations. The archbishop pointed out their reasons—the betrothal looked like good business. With their prince wed to a princess of Castile, border tariffs would cease to exist; great expense in the maintenance of patrols would end; Castilian levies could be expected to assist Aragón in her wars with the French; Portugal would be weakened. "Show an Aragonese a way to make money," ran the proverb, "and he'll be your friend." The archbishop understood so well, and explained it all so clearly, that she had to struggle to keep uppermost in her mind that the gift of the necklace and the 20,000 florins had been anything but a kind of investment which Aragón expected to recoup after she and Ferdinand were wed.

"Aragón will support us, Princess," the old man wrote. "Those shrewd men have not committed themselves to the extent of the necklace, which I am told on the best authority is worth no less than 40,000 florins, plus the additional 20,000 in cash, out of love for Prince Ferdinand and his happiness in marriage. They play for keeps, daughter, and we must take full advantage of the assistance heaven is sending us."

All this was true, she realized, but she was too sensible to let it dampen the feelings she had for the prince. He was still the knight on the white charger poised to ride across the mountains and rescue her from the wicked king. But she clenched her hands and wished there were something she could do. For the present, wrote the archbishop, they could not even dispatch troops to meet the prince after he crossed the border. Any troop movement whatever would alert Henry's patrols and draw attention to the prince. "Wait, Princess," wrote the archbishop, "and pray that my emissary to the court of King John will guide your betrothed safely over the mountains and past your brother's border guards."

She turned at last to Beatriz' message and grew cold again.

"Isabella," she read, "you must manage to prevent Prince Ferdinand's entry into Castile, at least for the present. Henry knows already that some such plan is afoot and has taken steps to prevent it. A spy Andrés and I have placed in the king's household has reported this, and we have every reason to believe it's true. I can chance writing you this now, for the spy has returned to Segovia where Henry and Villena cannot reach her.

"The woman of whom I speak has long lived in Henry's household. She was one of those he kept with him, hoping that people would believe they were his mistresses. You'll recall he started this shortly after people began to doubt he'd fathered Joanna's child. There have been several of these women, but this one stayed with him longer than any other. She even slept in his tent while he has been campaigning in the south, but everyone saw through the ruse."

Isabella felt a pang of pity for the king. She wondered how many women had sponged off his generosity, giving him nothing but a spurious reputation for promiscuity, while they gossiped about his impotency and relationships with the Moorish guards.

"So you see, Isabella, why the archbishop must get word to his spies in Barcelona and warn them not to let Prince Ferdinand attempt anything at present. Later, when the excitement dies down and Henry thinks you've given up your plans with Aragón, an opportunity will present itself."

"Beatriz knows me better than that," said Isabella aloud. "Opportunities don't present themselves—people make them."

9

Palencia and Cárdenas exchanged glances and shrugged while they waited in the little antechamber that adjoined the prince's sleeping quarters. At least they would see him without all those people fussing about. No dance was about to begin, and from the way things looked, they would be the first business of his day.

"He's not at all what the archbishop led us to expect," said Palencia. "I expected a man who would sit down and talk, not a handsome lad rushing off to dances and bullfights."

"We did arrive unexpectedly," said Cárdenas. "What little I saw last night I liked. God, but he's mature! I can't believe he's only seventeen."

"Physically mature," said Palencia. "Well, we'll soon know more about him. And I'm so glad I managed get here at all that anything would please me. I tell you, Cárdenas, that was the worst journey I ever made. Henry's troops were just behind me all the way. The worst was when they rode into that fortress not fifteen minutes after I had ridden away. And when I think what would have happened if the fortress's commander had suspected what I was up to... well, I don't have to think about it. I'm here."

Cárdenas didn't reply. He was thinking of the dangerous return to Castile. And with the prince along it would be sheer peril. He frowned grimly. The prospect of escorting a spoiled young man across mountains like those he'd crossed and through dangers that might change the course of European history held no allure for him. The responsibility was much too great.

The door opened and a servant beckoned. Beyond the door they found Ferdinand pacing unconcernedly in front of a window, stretching and filling his chest with the crisp autumn breeze. Cárdenas looked at Palencia as if to say, "No Castilian gentleman would be this informal," but Palencia was not listening. He was studying the prince and arriving at the conclusion that pleased him. The archbishop, if anything, had been modest in his assessment. Even dressed in bragas that covered only his belly and upper thighs he looked like a prince. Cárdenas couldn't be blamed for wondering how he could be seventeen. Most men in the full prime of their maturity never attained muscular development like his. In the sunlight pouring through the window, Prince Ferdinand looked like the statue of a gladiator he had once seen in Rome. He was filled with honest admiration and envy.

"Have you breakfasted?" the young man asked. "I can have something brought in."

They had already eaten, and looked askance at the remains of what must have been a very hearty meal. The prince was still munching, but he quickly finished and picked up a map. He tossed back his rumpled hair and waved then to a seat on a long bench. "Here," he said, as he spread the map across their knees, "is the way I think we must go. Here runs the highway into Castile."

They watched the strong tanned fingers lay out the route and realized that the prince had sketched in the likely positions of Castilian troops and the line of the Mendoza castles and fortresses strung along the entire frontier. The two Castilians exchanged glances of relief, apparently the prince had a good concept of the terrain and realized the danger after all.

"We won't take the highway, of course," continued Ferdinand in a surprisingly deep and vibrant voice. "We'll follow a back route something like the one you followed coming in, my friends. I know part of that territory, for I've hunted over it, but I don't know it all. We'll need guides."

"You've drawn a line of arrows along the main highway, Prince. What do they mean?" asked Cárdenas.

"Along the main highway we'll send two hundred knights in full panoply. They'll guard a large pack train and several royal litters. Henry's scouts will think I'm proceeding toward his borders with a cortège. They'll be certain of it, for a friend of mine will go with that cortège. He'll wear my armor and carry my banner."

Cárdenas smiled. "You want Henry's men to think that you're hoping to talk your way into Castile. And while they wait for parley, we'll be across the mountains. It's a good stratagem, Prince Ferdinand."

Ferdinand nodded. "I want you both to take a mule train and head for the mountains. Wait for me at Verdejo near Gómara. It's a little hill town, but I've found it to be clean, and you can rest there in the inn until I arrive. Henry's troops won't be looking for you there. They'll have their eyes on me, or whom they think is me, on the border road."

"How long, Prince?" asked Palencia.

"Let's see. Three days. I must go to Barcelona to see my father. He's blind, you know and I've got to see him before he undergoes an operation a Jewish physician wants to perform on his cataracts. I promise to meet you in Verdejo three days from today."

Palencia didn't remain in Verdejo with Cárdenas, but hastened on to Burgo de Osma to prepare for the prince's arrival. Cárdenas, left behind with a guide named Villaroel, waited impatiently in Verdejo. As the evening of the third day drew on he became more and more apprehensive. Where was the prince? The thousand things that could have happened to him plagued his imagination. Henry's spies could have learned of the plan. They might have ambushed him. And since Cárdenas had lived at court and knew the king and Villena well, he had a very clear idea of what would become of Ferdinand if he fell into their hands. There would be an accident, and blind King John would receive a regretful report from the King of Castile to the effect that his son had died in the mountains. Cárdenas sweated and kept his eye on the road.

The mountains fell away like an army of green tents above which scudded thin white clouds before a chilly wind. Higher in the cordillera he knew snow would be falling, and this added to his already plentiful supply of worries. If enough fell, the entire project might have to wait.

At last, far down the valley, he caught sight of a mule train, so far away it looked like a rosary of many-colored ants. It grew larger, but only gradually, for the trail wound and twisted, making only slow progress toward the village. When finally it disappeared behind the mountain on which the village perched, he gnawed his knuckles and stood at the gate of the inn yard to see the men as they entered.

There was no sign of Ferdinand. A quick count showed him twenty rough characters in the drab costume of Aragonese mountaineers. Almost frantic, Cárdenas went to the villainous looking leader of the train and asked for news of other travelers on the mountain trail. The man had seen none, he said.

Cárdenas was at a loss. He turned and found Villaroel, his lieutenant, at his elbow.

Villaroel looked at the line of mules and shrugged. "He'll be here today," he said and started back for the inn. Then, over his shoulder, he called back through the gathering shadows, "He'll come, my lord. He said he would."

Cárdenas wished he were as certain. It was almost night, and if these men hadn't seen another party, how could Ferdinand reach Verdejo before dark? He cast his eyes down the ranks of the little cavalcade of mules as it filed toward the stables, and suddenly his mouth fell open and his eyes popped. Peering from under a rugged mountain cap, and doubled up with laughter, he saw Ferdinand of Aragón looking as seedy and ragged as any of his companions. He slouched along beside his mule in such a good imitation of the gait of the muleteers that Cárdenas gasped.

"You made it!" he cried, forgetful that it was the Prince of Aragón he was pounding on the back and hugging. "I wouldn't have recognized you in a thousand years. The disguise is perfect!"

"It has to be, Cárdenas. Tomorrow we'll pass straight through Henry's lines. That'll be the test. And by St. Peter I hope the Castilians still believe I am in the cortège on the highway. It must be under the eyes of his observation posts by now. Where's Palencia?"

"In Burgo de Osma, Prince. From there he can safely send to the archbishop for troops to meet you somewhere near the border, secretly, of course."

Just then Villaroel burst from the door of the inn and sprinted toward them across the yard. "Troops on the road above the town," he warned. "I saw them from the window. They're Castilians for sure, my lords!"

Let's run for it," cried Cárdenas.

"We couldn't get to the bend of the road," said Ferdinand calmly. "No. We've got to stay and chance It. We'll test the disguise tonight."

Villaroel scratched his head and wondered if Cárdenas could stand the strain. The prince was right, of course, for on mules or on foot they could never escape cavalry.

When the troopers trotted their mounts into the yard, they found the mule train bedding down for the night. Cooking fires lapped at dry logs and the aroma of food, mule dung, and smoke cast a haze over the little plateau in front of the inn. A gypsy strummed a guitar tunelessly, and Cárdenas, white-faced under a two days growth of beard, tried hard to look like a merchant waiting beside the fire for his supper. By sheer will he kept his eyes from searching out the prince, who he hoped, would have the good sense to stay out of the firelight. When three officers dismounted by his own fire, he leaped to his feet like any merchant would in the presence of his betters. Hat in hand and eyes on the ground he waited.

"You came through Gómara?" one of the officers snapped.

"Yes Sir," replied Cárdenas, eyes still lowered.

"Did you meet any mounted men, any knights or gentlemen along the road?"

"Not today, Sir. But yesterday where the road turns back toward Saragossa we saw a party riding hard for the border."

The officer turned to his superior. "You hear that, Captain López? It might have been the prince. He's got to be somewhere in this area, and the party this fellow saw was headed toward Castile."

"Perhaps," said López. "But we can't be certain. Ferdinand is a goddamned fox. Think how long he kept us watching that cortège on the highway. Hell, we'd be there yet but for the spy who finally told us the prince wasn't there at all!" Then turning to Cárdenas, he said, "We'll sup with you, merchant, unless you can recommend the inn."

"They have no kitchen, Captain, nor any decent food. Seems the innkeeper's wife has gone somewhere. But we'll be honored to have you share our supper." Cárdenas wondered if he had lied convincingly enough.

The captain nodded. "Our thanks, merchant. We've ridden hard all day and carry few supplies."

Casting a furtive glance around the yard, Cárdenas in horror saw Ferdinand a few steps behind the officers stirring something in a large skillet balanced over three stones.

"Holy Mary!" thought Cárdenas. "What's he up to?"

Then the prince staggered toward them clutching the skillet with a rag and sloshing its contents along the ground as he walked. He wore his ragged cap perched on the back of his head and he held his tongue between his teeth, screwing his face into a grimace. As he banged the skillet down beside the fire, Cárdenas cursed under his breath. "This is what comes of dealing with minors," he thought.

Gradually his hopes rose, however, for the prince looked so seedy and stupid that the officers hardly noticed him. He spread a blanket for them and then handed each a wooden bowl and spoon, pretending not to notice their scowls at the way he held the bowls out with his dirty thumb inside. When he served the stew, he slopped it clumsily on the captain's doublet, chattering puerilely in a terrible mountain dialect almost beyond Cárdenas' comprehension. As the gravy stained the doublet, the captain cursed him roundly and he cringed and slunk out of reach of his boot with a startled cry.

Cold sweat trickled from Cárdenas' armpits and moistened his leather jacket. Never, not even in the thick of battle, had he known tension like this, and he made a vow to reprimand the prince, if they were lucky enough to get out of this alive.

An hour later the troopers departed for Gómara, a hearty supper under their belts, but cursing all the same their luck at having to ride in the dark. Ferdinand, hat awry, looking like a bumpkin charmed by the fine horses and uniforms, waved them out of camp as Cárdenas collapsed on his blanket. Ferdinand walked to the fire and stood warming his hands over the glowing coals. Then he stretched out on the ground in his blanket and instantly fell asleep.

The next morning they awakened to find three hundred lancers surrounding the camp. Their leader was Don Gómez Manrique, one of Isabella's strongest henchmen. Palencia's messenger from Burgo de Osma had gotten through to Valladolid. That day they moved more boldly, and before night the Count of Treviño joined them with two hundred additional men dispatched by the Archbishop of Toledo. Five hundred strong they could chance an encounter with any detachment Henry might have in the mountains.

As they rode out of Gómara twenty dazed mule drivers stared in awe. They would tell their children and their children's children of the time they crossed the mountains with the Prince of Aragón in their midst as one of them. They would say that he was a man of the people, not a perfumed courtier.

Toward midnight under a pale, cold moon, the van of Ferdinand's cavalcade trotted wearily out of the hills and beneath the walls of Burgo de Osma. They could hardly sit their mounts and knew that for miles back in the darkness their fellows were leading other tired horses, wondering how they had ridden so far in so short a time. They watched the prince leap to the ground and run toward the gates, and they shook their heads. What energy? What vigor!

Then Cárdenas saw something that Ferdinand failed to notice. On the wall above him a machine moved on oiled hinges, and a ton of stone swung out into the blackness. Cárdenas shouted, the stone plummeted earthward, and the Prince of Aragón flung himself aside, turning over and over on the ground.

Forgetful of their weariness, the men leaped from their mounts and ran across the frozen turf. As they reached him, he sat up and shook the snow out of his hair. "Close call!" he shouted. "St. Peter of Osma stood by me tonight'"

Suddenly they heard Palencia's voice out of the darkness above them. "Cárdenas, Villaroel, is it you?"

Ferdinand grimaced. "Tell the man who dropped the stone he has a good eye, Palencia. It scraped my shoulder! And tell him he'll hang for it!

He laughed then, but Cárdenas and Palencia didn't. Watching the surgeon apprehensively as he treated the already darkening bruise. Two inches more, no even one, and the Princess of Castile would not be getting a husband.

The next morning they moved to Dueñas, through light snow and sleet. The city received them joyfully.

10

Ferdinand waited and rested in Dueñas two full days, until Palencia returned from Valladolid. "Tonight's the night, Prince Ferdinand," he said, his eyes sparkling. "We'll start right after the banquet."

"For Valladolid? Why must we banquet here?"

"For two good reasons. In the first place it isn't safe to go in daylight. We may be in error, but we believe not all of Henry's forces are still searching the mountains or laying siege to Burgo de Osma. We have good reason to suspect that Villena may have large forces not far from here. So far we've been mighty lucky. Let's not chance losing all we've gained through impatience. The princess will be in Valladolid when we arrive."

"You said two reasons."

"All the knights in and around Dueñas are in the city, and many from as far away as Valladolid. You mustn't disappoint all these men, Prince Ferdinand. They have a right to meet their future king, and this is the time to strengthen your rapport with them."

"I know," said Ferdinand with a sigh. "I must attend the banquet, but by Our Lady, I've had about all the waiting I can take."

Palencia smiled. "The princess will have her hands full with this young firebrand," he told Cárdenas. "Talk about young stallions champing at the bit! It's a good thing we ride right after the ceremonies tonight!"

Somehow Ferdinand got through the banquet and the speeches, but his mind wasn't on the Castilian nobles and what they had to say. He was thinking of the importance of the step he had taken, a step from which there was no turning back. What if Isabella was not all that de Coca and the archbishop said she was? Suppose they had lied, and when he met her, she would turn out fat and pop-eyed, or too lean?

His fears pursued him long after the guests departed, while some accompanied him as he rode with Palencia and the lancers toward Valladolid. As the leafless vineyards and empty grain fields whirled across his vision, he didn't see them. He could think only of what was waiting for him in a city he didn't even know. Ferdinand had experienced disillusionments before, but the idea of an ugly princess, who would later make an ugly wife, daunted him as nothing had before. Not long ago in Saragossa, before the Castilians had come with their proposal of betrothal, he recalled vividly how he had burned to bed a certain dark-haired lady-in-waiting whom he had never seen except at a distance. She was an Aphrodite, his friends kept telling him, a firm-fleshed white flame with hair that poured like black smoke across her pillow. He hadn't been able to sleep until they had arranged an assignation in her father's summer place beside the sea. God, how fair she seemed in the moonlight of her garden! And in the cold light of dawn how plain and stout! Then came the report of Isabella's beauty. After that he could think of no other woman. And now he was riding to meet her with a lump in his stomach and cold fear of what he might find. Beautiful as an angel, or ugly as a toad, he'd have to marry her. Aragón depended on that marriage. And, as he rode, he crossed himself and prayed to his patron saint, to let her be at least no worse than homely. "St. Peter," he whispered, "help me in this!"

By and by he noticed they had left the fields behind and were riding toward the fortifications of a great city. Valladolid loomed larger than he had imagined it would. Behind its walls rose lofty towers of churches, which seemed to move while he and his companions and their horses sat still.

"That's St. Mary the Ancient," he heard Palencia say in a low voice. "To the left, St. Paul's. Both are very old. Beyond, where the wall dips, is the College of the Holy Cross, and that's the University on the little rise. Valladolid is one of Castile's greatest cities, and was, as you've probably heard, King John's favorite residence. The Princess Isabella lived here as an infant, and here Don Álvaro de Luna lost his head."

Ferdinand listened attentively, conscious only of the blank, staring walls rising out of the plain. Even as he smoldered in romantic fancies, he observed carefully, as he had been trained to do. This would be his realm some day. He must not fail to assess its worth.

He wondered why they were avoiding the gates and kept following the walls, keeping to the shadows. At last they stopped. Against the sky he could see the roof of a large building topping the walls above him. A church, he wondered, a palace, a barracks? Then Palencia was standing at his stirrup. It was time to dismount. In the darkness they stumbled over stones and clinging weeds and headed straight toward the bare wall. He caught no sound but the whistle of the wind and the whispered conversation of Palencia and the lancers. He waited impatiently while his guides found what they were searching for. Twice a poignard hilt struck masonry, and then a door, so small it seemed a window, opened silently in the wall itself. He had seen doors like this. They were as thick as they were high, and when braced from inside, were as strong as the walls they pierced. He stooped and crawled behind Palencia into a stygian tunnel. Behind him one of the lancers cursed softly as he bumped his head. The passage was low, narrow, damp and very cold, and seemingly endless.

"This leads to the house of Juan de Vivero," whispered Palencia. "He's an important nobleman. The princess is staying in this house. You'll meet them very soon."

Then they were out of the tunnel and walking down the corridor of a fine house. In the shadows he caught glimpses of tapestries and rugs and armor hanging on the walls.

Then they came to a door, heavy oak and studded with fine brass. Palencia knocked, and the door opened soundlessly. Light, and warmth, and color struck his eyes like a fist. He had the impression of fine hangings and a fire lapping logs in a great hearth, and then caught the dull flicker of flame on polished walnut and soft damask. But the focal point of his gaze was the woman gazing into the fire with her back to the door.

Then a distinguished elderly gentleman with a well-trained grey beard hurried to greet him, crying, "It is he! It is he!"

At this the woman turned. The light of two tall silver candelabra behind Ferdinand fell full upon her face and hair. He drew a long breath and expelled it slowly. How given to understatement Castilians were in describing women! Isabella was not simply beautiful. She was divine!

No one moved, held spellbound by the thing that flowed almost tangibly between the man and woman as they looked into each others' faces. Isabella wore blue, and in the candlelight, with the fire behind her, she seemed to be clothed in water, colored by the deepest summer sky, water that rippled as she breathed. Then he saw the necklace. The rubies burned against her flesh like fire. The largest, the pendant, resting just at the cleavage of her breasts, shone like a ripe plum, dull but alive.

Isabella's heart beat wildly. She rose to her feet slowly. Even in his drab leather lancer's jacket he was a god, she thought. His hair was red in the firelight, his eyes wide-set and blue. His shoulders loomed broad and impressive. "Holy Mother of God!" she whispered. "He looks like the woolmerchant!" She saw quickly that he was not as tall, and that his hair was russet like her own, not the living flame that was Christopher's.

Still, the resemblance was undeniable and therefore disconcerting!

Seeing in Ferdinand traces of Christopher gave her a sense of foreboding. It was like suddenly and unexpectedly confronting an old friend. It finally broke the ice, but it continued to raise vague feelings of alarm. The prince's features were perfect, where Christopher's were not. He looked like a prince, poised, polished in even his lancer's uniform, and aristocratic to his fingertips. He was not casually put together, especially not in his face, as was the woolmerchant.

His square, strong chin didn't come jutting out craggily like Christopher's. But the touch of his hand was just as strong, though it was smooth, and his nails were buffed. The pungent leather of the jacket, which he must have been wearing since he left Barcelona, brought Christopher to mind, until beneath it she caught the scent of the civet nobles like to use.

"The perfect knight, and the perfect gentleman, the perfect prince," she thought, as he bent to kiss her hand. "Heaven has been kind in bringing us together."

After a while Juan de Vivero led the other guests away, leaving Isabella, Ferdinand and the Archbishop of Toledo alone. The old man said little, and after a time his head nodded. Finally his chin dropped to his chest, and from his regular breathing they judged he was asleep.

Isabella's tongue clove in the roof of her mouth. She cursed her silence. Weeks she had practiced exactly what she planned to say at this moment, and the words refused to come. What must he think of a tongue-tied, dull girl like her, a dunce?

She need not have worried. Ferdinand took her silence for becoming modesty and was relieved to find a woman who would never be a noisy, garrulous person like his mother. It was a woman's place to let her husband do the talking—and the ruling of the realm, he thought. Just enough chatter, and no more, was what he wanted in a woman. Better a mute than a chatterbox.

"I hope you will come to depend on me, Princess," he told her, "for I am strong. And how fortunate that both of us are young. My father was old when he sired me, and it was my mother who often had to guide the ship of state when he was ailing. It was not mete, of course, and I shall not impose upon your patience in that way."

Isabella nodded. "Your mother's statecraft is well known," she said. "She did what she had to do. But even though you are capable and strong, I'll bear my share of the burden."

Ferdinand smiled indulgently. "Spoken like a Princess of Castile," he said. "Of course you'll help and do your part, but you must understand how much I want to protect and relieve you of the full and tedious aspects of ruling. Your duties should revolve around the children I hope God will bless us with."

"Yes," said Isabella, blushing and dropping her eyes for the first time. How direct and unabashed he was! She wondered if he could blush.

Suddenly his arm slid around her waist and she felt his clean breath on her cheek. As his lips sought hers, she turned her head, but his lips merely possessed the cheek she turned and then dropped softly to her neck. She wanted to respond. She couldn't. She pushed him gently away, still looking at the floor, and didn't see him smile slyly and even more indulgently.

Just then a flame found an untouched portion of a log and leaped high. The archbishop's eyes opened, and he yawned out loud. He straightened his cap which had slid to one side, revealing the whiteness of his tonsured scalp. "I must have dozed off," he apologized. "Highness, Princess, I hope you'll forgive a tired old man."

"Tired old fox!" she heard the prince whisper, "The old rascal was probably pretending the whole time."

At this the door opened and John de Vivero appeared with his guests. Isabella realized that it was time to say goodnight. She was glad, for she needed to return to her room and to think about this prince and his ambition and passion. The feel of his lips on her hand where he had kissed it just before departing still burned, and the power she had felt in his arm as it encircled her waist still made her wince with pleasure. It would be easy, she realized, to lean on an arm like that, actually and figuratively, and what woman could resist such leaning. She stood for a long time looking out into the night and her heart pounded. Life with the Prince of Aragón would never be dull, and unless she were determined, it might engulf her in its uninhibited, onward rush. Even now, she admitted, she had drifted under the sway of his dynamic personality, had thrilled to his presence, and trembled at what he let her see blazing in his eyes. What more could any woman, even a princess, long for, she asked herself. But, as she turned back toward her bed, she wished he had the tenderness and understanding of the woolmerchant.

11

Ferdinand rode back to Dueñas at full gallop. The rocky road was velvet, the sharp autumn wind a zephyr, and the pounding of his heart the thunder of all thunders. The taste of Isabella's skin, petal-like and cool, still clung to his lips. And he knew with certainty that she had liked his looks. Approval, admiration, perhaps even more, looked out at him from her eyes, not that this surprised him. He would have been the first to admit quite frankly that it would have surprised him had she reacted in any other way. No woman ever had.

He considerately thanked his patron saint and vowed to light a hundred candles in the parish church at Dueñas on the following morning. The vision of those hundred lighted candles, tall ones, not the shorter kind, pleased him as much, he suspected, as they would please the saint. One hundred candles represented no small sum, if the candles were made of beeswax.

The girl kept floating back into his mind as she turned to him and into the light from the candelabra. He couldn't forget her. God, how straight and tall she was and well made! He remembered how her breasts rose and fell as she breathed—like the wild Valencian oranges behind the tight bodice. It had been hard not to reach out and cup them both. His nostrils contracted still savoring her delicate perfume, and the feel of her hand in his was as real, even now, as what still surged in his loins and made his riding difficult.

Isabella, quiet in her bed with the curtains drawn against the chill, felt even deeper stirrings, since they were new to her. Life, which had walked slowly in the first sixteen years of her life, was suddenly breaking into a run. The speed with which betrothal and marriage were bearing down on her made her tremble. For weeks she had longed for Ferdinand's arrival, had dreamed of seeing him face to face, had planned the life they could lead in Valladolid or Dueñas. Now, with the betrothal two days off, she felt unprepared, uneasy.

The archbishop had pooh-poohed her suggestion of being engaged at least a month so that she and Ferdinand could grow better acquainted. "There isn't time, daughter," he said. "The king still doesn't realize the Prince is in Castile. The day they give him the news, he'll bend every effort toward preventing the marriage. You and Prince Ferdinand must wed and bed before he knows it."

Isabella had not retreated. "I wish I could risk it, Your Grace. Most girls have a year's engagement. They talk to their betrothed, even alone with only a grating between. They come to know each other in this way."

"But you already know Prince Ferdinand, daughter. You spent a whole evening with him and you have read his letters."

"Is that enough, Your Grace?" asked Isabella, remembering how quickly the woolmerchant had put her at ease.

The old man's face softened as much as it could. "Princess," he said, "If I had married and had a daughter of my own, I couldn't love her more than I love you. What I say to you now, I'd say to that daughter I never had. This marriage must take place, and it must take place this week. By then, if not before, Henry will know our plans and will move to stop us. You are the most sensible young woman I have known in a long life. You will not truly insist, therefore, upon this bit of feminine nonsense girls and their families indulge in, will you?"

"But I feel so strange, Your Grace. So uneasy."

"All maidens feel so, I'm told," said the archbishop. "That's the way of the world. The burden falls upon the husband to dispel such feelings on the part of the bride. Prince Ferdinand is a fine young man of great experience. He'll guide you safely and pleasantly, I imagine, along this unfamiliar path. You'll see, daughter, and you'll love him as deeply as your mother loved King John."

He went on to remind her of her duty to Castile, that Henry might die at any time, since he wasn't well, that the bastard would have no rival to the throne unless she and Ferdinand founded a new line to compete with her. Long before he had finished, Isabella had relinquished the hope of a longer engagement. The archbishop was right, of course, so she would offer no further objections. But her acquiescence didn't prevent her from wishing that she and Ferdinand could go riding over summer roads where birds sang and flowers bloomed. If they could have that, she felt, it would be much easier to follow him into the nuptial chamber. Something tender, something nearly like what she felt for the woolmerchant might be theirs, if they had time to let it burgeon.

The two days passed rapidly. Suddenly it was the eighteenth of October. The betrothal procession from Dueñas, with Ferdinand at its head, entered the city at ten o'clock in the morning. It moved slowly along packed streets. Most people had never seen Isabella, and almost none had caught even a glimpse of Ferdinand. Thousands waved Aragonese banners and chanted "The Flowers of Aragón" as the column made its way toward the Vivero mansion where Isabella waited.

She stood on the steps and watched him approach. He looked like a militant angel in his betrothal robes. At his right rode the Archbishop of Toledo, and at his left the Grand Admiral of Castile, his grandsire and her great-uncle. Behind came the knights and lords of Dueñas and Valladolid, and after them the men-at-arms.

Ferdinand rode bareheaded, looking more like a young Gabriel than a mortal man. As the sun spun his chestnut hair into a halo of bronze, again she thought of Christopher.

"I must try not to see the woolmerchant in him," she thought. "He wouldn't like it. Besides, it isn't proper. Ferdinand will be my husband, not the woolmerchant."

As he drew closer she saw that the resemblance was much less marked. Ferdinand's face, in all its features, was perfection—the woolmerchant's had been carved by a rougher hand.

A page brought her horse, and she mounted and rode beside him toward the chapel where the betrothal vows would be said and the marriage contract heard by the assembled witnesses. By the time they reached the plaza, they could hardly make their way through the mass of humanity. Inside, hundreds waited in expectation, craning to see the Princess of Castile and her prince from across the mountains.

The archbishop raised aloft a parchment for all to see, and a low gasp swept like wind through the church and out into the street to silence the multitude. It was a papal bull, the one granted by Pius II when Ferdinand was three. It bore his signature, and the great papal seal dangled free for all to see. This piece of parchment, signed by a man long in his tomb, made it possible for her to marry Ferdinand in spite of the fact that they were within the prohibited degree of consanguinity. It carried all the authority of the living pope who sympathized with Henry and would not give his blessing to the marriage. She trembled at sight of this document which meant so much to her future, and she saw that the faces of the people were grave. It was as precious as scripture itself. To hear the words of this pope, of God's vicar on earth, was strangely moving, for it was as if he spoke from across the void that separates heaven from earth. Duly and with deep reverence she crossed herself, and listened; out of the past unbidden came the voice of the woolmerchant. "Destiny is like the hand of God."

As they read the marriage contract she watched Ferdinand's face. He had pored over that contract many times, she knew, but as the words were read she saw pleasure and triumph give way to seriousness. There were parts of the contract she knew he didn't like and had tried to change. The discordant note sounded, even in this time of joy, and she was sorry. Why must affairs of state intrude? Beatriz would say it was one additional penalty for being a princess.

12

She reflected on her marriage and again she felt queasy as she often did, and usually earlier than this each morning. She wished fervently she hadn't eaten so much breakfast. But after she had taken a few drops of lemon juice, she felt well enough to get up, but not enough to leave her bedroom. Since she couldn't ever be truly idle, she took up her diary and began to catch up on what had passed since the last entry. She could hardly believe how the days had sped. Why, she hadn't set down a sentence about her wedding night. So she began.

He was gentle, and understanding, tender and considerate! she wrote, and oh, how wise and knowing. What a sure guide he was for a virgin embarking on the sea of matrimony! The woolmerchant himself couldn't have been more considerate. Ferdinand, I believe, would have let the night pass without deflowering me if I had asked him to, not that he would have liked it, of course, for he burned hot. Without his wisdom, his kindness and his help the foul, barbaric, and age-old custom, we faced would have been unbearable. All this because he's inherently good, innately wise, so instinctively perceptive, and so uninhibitively sensuous that he swept me along in his passionate wake. The entire trauma of a wedding night, which is so often either horrible or disappointing, under Ferdinand's supervision resulted in a dream of carnal bliss. Without him my abysmal ignorance and inexperience would have shattered all chance of a happy marriage. I'm firmly convinced, despite what others say, that a good start in bed makes for a successful journey through a married couple's life.

I recalled that I'd heard how Henry had defied tradition and refused to have three witnesses sit just beyond the curtains where he and Joanna lay their first night. He did so because he feared, not because he *knew* he was impotent and could not deflower his bride. The witnesses the archbishop himself and two other men, one an ecclesiastic, the other a kinsman, had acquiesced, for all three knew perfectly well that it would be a waste of time to sit all night in a chilly bedroom when the groom was impotent.

Ferdinand didn't seem to mind, and even winked at me before we climbed into our nuptial bed. But I am getting ahead of my account. He truly didn't care, and perhaps even thought it a novelty to take a woman and let other people attest that he had taken her. He wanted no chronicler writing what they wrote about my half-brother. I can never forget the ugly words, "The young queen arose the next morning," wrote Palencia, the historian, "as untouched as the day she came into the world."

I was close to shock at the thought of those three old men, ears cocked, eyes bright with macabre fascination, who would wait to hear me scream as my hymeneal blood flooded out upon the sheets which, I shudder to say, were to be displayed from the window of the palace the coming morning. Barbaric? Too barbaric, and Moorish to boot! I'm certain, for the Moors still have the practice. Someday someone must put a stop to it. Why, even harlots have the right to privacy when they lie with clients. I wondered if even a worldly man like Ferdinand with such an audience could truly function normally as he should. I recalled how I had gotten nowhere with the archbishop. "Daughter," he scolded in his matter-of-fact and scornful fashion, "why are you so embarrassed? One would think you weren't a virgin and feared discovery. Shame on you! Defloration and insemination, God provided means of procreation, are as normal as eating or sleeping. Your groom is clean and healthy and as handsome as any man has a right to be. Not many brides expect or get as much. You're healthy, too, and I hear quite smitten with carnal fantasies, if that can be such a gift. I'm your oldest friend, my girl, and de Coca loves you like the daughter he could never have. Then there's your uncle, the Grand Admiral. He's family. After all, he's Ferdinand's grandsire and your own great uncle. He loves you well, both of you young people. I doubt that any bride anywhere went to bed with her groom and with as kindly and benevolent an audience at her bedding. After all, Princess, the curtains are heavy, we are all old men, so we'll drop off."

"No one had to listen to Henry," I muttered.

"True. But there was no need. The world knew, as did I and the other two witnesses, what he would do. He turned his face to the wall, and these ears of mine heard him, as he excused himself in his clumsy way. He never laid a finger on her. So we were glad to escape a long night's vigil, hearing nothing except perhaps a bride's frustrated sobs."

And so they forced me to face what others had. It was part of my destiny, as Christopher would say. Foolishly I thought of him as I awaited Ferdinand and wished Christopher could have lead me to Ferdinand and held my hand.

The ladies-in-waiting, some old hands at bedding brides, clucked and shook their heads as they undressed and bathed me. My mind fluttered like a dove in a net. I longed for it to be over, even as I longed to have it begin. I did love Ferdinand. I did lust for his embrace, even though I dreaded it. And yet, as the moment drew closer all my resolves, all my hungers, all my determination to succeed, dried up and flew away. I had no real conception of what defloration actually involved.

Why hadn't I learned better what I needed so much to know? Why hadn't my mother been willing to answer my carefully couched, timid questions? Instead of answers I got only disapproving frowns. "It's hardly mete, daughter," she snapped evasively, shaking her weary head, "for a princess of the blood to talk like a slut and expect her mother to reply in kind."

I then turned to Beatriz, practically newly wed, with no better luck. "If you and Ferdinand are compatible, Isabella, as Andrés and I were from the moment we got in bed, you'll know what to do. It's instinctive. No one can tell another how to act. And, as you know, there's no instruction book or manual, no royal etiquette."

"Thank you, Beatriz," I told her coldly. "Perhaps God and Our Lady will show me what you couldn't or what you wouldn't."

No one in all Castile and Aragón, no one on earth could possibly imagine where I had obtained the little that I knew as I let the ladies make me ready. From an ancient crone named Chata, who carried out chamber pots and garbage, came my basic knowledge. It was in the garden of Juan de Vivero's mansion where I had fled to be alone and pray to Our Lady to stand by me in my hour of need. Chuckling and clucking, old Chata sidled up to me where I sat sniffling on a stone bench. She patted my shoulder.

Chata and I went back a long way together. She'd known me as a child back in Arévalo, and had ended up here in Valladolid when they uprooted my servants, or my mother's, and brought them to staff my new household. She sat odorously down beside me. In the old days she'd brought me sweets, when she could sneak them from the kitchen. And when I first bled, it was Chata who told me not to worry. "You're a woman now, my girl," she'd said. "That's what the blood means, you know."

Our Lady surely sent old Chata to me that terrible afternoon when inadequacy haunted me and ignorance crushed my soul. Chata gave me important insights. What she said was in no way ladylike, and not attractive, but it was common sense and it reassured me vastly. Uncouth, even obscene it was, but all the same I could grasp it. My mother would have died if she, in her dim world of emptiness, could have heard our conversation.

"Oh, Chata, what'll I do tonight. I'm as innocent as a nun!"

"Ain't ya watched the rams and ewes, *querida?*" she smirked.

I had perforce. Who could avoid them in the rutting season in Castile, where sheep outnumbered men? Yes, I'd seen the rams, bleating frantically, running desperately after the ewes in heat, snuffling the air as if each breath could be their last. The thought of Ferdinand like that appalled me. I hoped he wouldn't look like that uncovered.

So I replied to Chata, "I've seen the sheep."

"Well, then," laughed the old woman, shooing some flies away which were drawn by her awful odor, "so now ye know. A man's not much different from a ram. When your young man beds you, deary, he'll do just what the rams do to the ewes. The ewes bleat a lot and turn and twist, but all the same they want it. So ye'll like It. Ye'll see."

I was so desperate for knowledge that I cast propriety aside and royal pride as well. This crone, this poor dirty old peasant whose life had been one long bad odor, had to tell me now what my mother never would. So I blushed, swallowed my pride, and blurted out, 'But, Chata, I don't know where. Is it—and I couldn't say the word—in front or in the other place?"

Chata was stunned at first and then uproarious in her mirth. But suddenly her old face cracked and tears ran down her rheumy old cheeks, leaving runnels through the dirt. "They've not been fair with ye, honey," she sobbed. "It ain't proper neither! Why, ye know less about your parts than a statue in the church. And you eighteen!"

I admitted it, weeping all the while. "What am I going to do?" I bawled.

Chata looked me straight in the eye, every line of her old face heavy with responsibility. She crossed herself and looked over her shoulder to see if we were overheard. She grew suddenly formal. It was now "Lady Isabella" and "Princess," and "Your Highness." No more '*querida*.' and yet she spoke with warmth, understanding and real sympathy.

"Lady Isabella, poor little lamb, when the prince is ready, he'll do what the ram does to the ewe and in the proper place and he'll make you happy."

"Oh," was all I could reply.

"Ain't your mother never even told you *that?*" she asked, incredulous.

I said she hadn't, that no one had.

Chata eased herself closer on the bench and put her arm around my shoulder. How she stank, for she never washed and she kept spilling nasty things on her clothes, and, like so many old women she smelled of urine. But I didn't care. I snuggled close against her withered breast. What a comfort it was to have her take my hand in horny claws and pat it!

"Lady Isabella, I'll do what I kin to help, though ye've waited long. Prince Ferdinand's a fine young fellow, the prettiest'un I ever seen. Not 'pretty' pretty, mind you, but 'manly' pretty. All man, Prince Ferdinand. Ain't you noticed his crotch?"

My face burned. I knew it was unseemly to hear talk like that. I'd been taught never to talk to rough persons, but this coming night was my wedding night, and as old Chata said, I was as knowledgeable as a statue.

"I've noticed," I stammered, ashamed of the admission, yet stubbornly proud that I had noticed and that there was something worthy of notice.

"What am I doing here talking like this," I asked myself. "And how can I confess all this to Father de Coca? It would make him faint dead away!" But I knew I had to hear the rest. Tonight might make or break my marriage. What I could learn in the next few minutes might be the beginning of heaven or hell. It could make me love Ferdinand even more or it could make me loathe him. Every instinct of modesty and propriety, of dignity, screamed at me to run from the cackling old hag as from the plague, yet every instinct of preservation urged me to stay and hear her out.

For the first time since I had wept over Alfonso, while the litter swayed along the road to Arévalo with the woolmerchant's shoulder rubbing mine, I let myself go and wept, and wept, hard and bitterly, unrelentingly, in pure and maudlin self pity.

I heard Chata running on, carried away with the role of instructress of a princess. "The prince is a gentleman, Lady Isabella, and he loves ye dearly. Anybody, even old Chata, can see that clear as the nose on yer face. He wants ye, too. I mean in bed. He knows ye can be a good queen and all that, but he wants ye to be good in bed with him. I can tell. His flesh yearns for yourn."

"You're certain, Chata?"

"Dead certain, sweeting. I'd bet my soul on it. But he's a man, and a young one, hot-blooded and horny. So if he burns too fast and tries to hurry, just kiss him on the mouth and say, 'be gentle, love,' and he will because he's gentry. And honey, don't look scairt, whatever ye do, and don't pull away. Please God, don't shet your eyes, no matter what he tries to do. Not even when he pulls off your gown and then his own. A man that pretty knows he is and wants his bride to see him."

"You mean, he'll be immodest?"

Chata laughed uproariously again and slapped her thigh. "They's all immodest, child. My old Mingo, afore he passed, would parade his undressed self around the house and make me look at him, not that I didn't want to. Even after his hair and fur turned gray and grizzled Mingo was a man and good to look at."

I couldn't ask her for more specifics, so I let her ramble on. She dissertated volubly. "One last thing. Don't never say no to him, no matter what. And if you truly want to hook him well and good, gaff him with the barb of the hook. I mean where he touches you, you touch him there. Do that and he'll crave you night and day and make you a very happy bride. Listen to old Chata, and ye'll see."

I couldn't eat a bite of the nuptial dinner. My heart beat too fast, my stomach churned in warning. But I was no longer terrified. Bedding was to be a challenge. All married women had to face it, even Joanna. If she faced it, so could I. And, I had to admit it to myself, I wanted, even though I shrank from the thought, to go to bed naked and with a naked man, if that man were Ferdinand.

I *will* enjoy it I told myself, and to reinforce my vow I summoned up the hottest of my fantasies. It was just then that the expected knock came at the door. "Are you ready, Princess?" asked the dueña. "It is the prince. He's waiting in the corridor. Are you all right?"

It was like a drama. The ladies posturing, bowing out, curtseying to me and then to Ferdinand as they passed him in the doorway. The younger ladies giggling, slanting their eyes at him. The old straight-laced and straight-faced. The archbishop, the confessor, and the Grand Admiral entering as though by cue. Father de Coca's white-seamed, elegant face, distasteful. And I, the heroine of it all, trying not to cower.

The archbishop yawned impatiently, anxious to have it over so he could go to bed. The admiral speculative, observant, expectant. What happens here, his shrewd old eyes told me, will be the making or the breaking of two nations. I tried to smile at him, and couldn't until he winked. The old man loved us both. He wanted more than consummation; he wanted happiness for his favorite niece and grandson.

Then Ferdinand, resplendent in a night robe of azure with golden arabesques and a collar of fine miniver, with ermine at the openings of the long sleeves, stepped unabashedly into the bedchamber. His kiss of peace was real and serious. His eyes ablaze with what I hoped was love yet knew was also lust. The scent of spikenard and civet noblemen all affected filled my nostrils like an aphrodisiac. I nearly swooned with desire and also fear. Would I be good enough?

The ladies disappeared. The three witnesses took their seats in the three armchairs provided. Ferdinand took my hand in his. How large it was, how firm and masculine, nearly as large as Christopher's, I thought. In dignified cadence he led me to the bed, a great four-poster, curtained heavily in wine-colored velvet. Thick enough, I hoped, to deaden sound. The bed, I had heard, had come from Aragón, a gift of his father.

"Did it really come all the way from Barcelona?" I asked, rather than stand dumb and silent.

"It did," he replied pleasantly, without so much as a quaver in his voice. "I was conceived and born in it."

At his words an eagerness pent up for years washed over me. In this very bed my uncle, King John, had taken Johanna Henríquez, and, as the Bible puts it, had gone in unto her. Tonight this tall young god would go in unto me.

With what courtliness he took my hand and helped me to mount the four steps to the dim arch made by the curtains held open by silken ties! I wondered if I could crawl into that bed, and maintain my dignity. Suddenly I giggled, low in my throat, and I heard Ferdinand stifle a giggle of his own. The air cleared. My hand squeezed his and received his squeeze in return. Then I was in bed. The tough, leather straps that served as a foundation gave ever so little and silently, I thanked the Lord. I lay on my back, fearless, though my heart thundered.

I saw my husband roll gracefully—everything he ever did was pure grace— into the bed beside me, a feat few men accomplish. "It's stuffy here," he whispered. "Wait until I let in some air. Not on the public side, my dear, but on the one that opens on the window. Not three feet beyond the curtains I saw the window, which once he'd opened it, let in fresh, wintry air. No one could see us, but we could see the snow in the fields and hear the sheep bells in the sheepcotes. The cold air cleared my brain. In the bedroom beyond the closed curtain it made the archbishop sneeze. I heard Father de Coca murmur, "*Salud, Your Grace!*"

Bright moonlight flooded through the window, for the skies were cloudless. I watched as Ferdinand, propped on an elbow, looked down at me. "I love you," he said simply. "And I you," I replied. His breath was sweet with cloves and Málaga wine.

After a long stare into my eyes, while I felt my blood pound and rise to stain my neck and flush my face, he said in a calm and matter-of-fact voice that I admired, "We must undress, you know. Will you let me help you?"

How straightforward, how polite, how sweet he was! In such a mood he was too much like my Christopher. I nodded and tried to smile. I would learn later how he hated intercourse entangled in gowns and nightcaps. I sensed how he liked the feel of his hairy chest against smooth breasts, his hirsute legs entwined in smooth ones like my own. I wondered how many women he had bedded, and then I didn't want to know. He would bed no more, not after this night. I would see to that. He wouldn't want to. I sat up and lifted my arms to help him pull the gown over my head. Up it went over my shoulders—featly, easily, with grace and efficiency. Had he had that much practice? I wondered. Then marvel of marvels, Chata's voice impinged upon my memory... Don't shut your eyes. I stared down at my nakedness, a thing I had been taught never to do, for it was sinful. The heat of his stare popped beads of perspiration on my brow and upper lip.

"Now help me," he quipped familiarly. I helped him, drawing the rich silk over his head, not featly, as he had done it for me, for I rumpled his hair. I helped him put it in order and we both laughed. Beyond the curtain three chairs squeaked as the three old watchers leaned forward and cocked their ears.

Try as I would I would not look away from what I very much wanted to see, I stared in amazement relief and excitement at my first completely nude male body not counting Fejjuan the Berber's. My mother had grimaced, I recalled, every time she had to look at my brother's tiny parts. "Men are so hideous undressed," she used to say, turning up her nose and drawing in her lips in squeamishness until they didn't show. I wondered, as I stared fixedly at Ferdinand's beautiful masculinity, how she could have felt so. I suddenly understood what the Scripture meant when it said Adam was made in God's own image, for Ferdinand was godlike in his beauty.

Suddenly his mouth swooped down and he kissed me full on the mouth. It was my very first such kiss and it startled me. But more and better followed. I felt his tongue on my lips and then as it hammered at my clenched teeth, I opened my mouth to protest, and that hot red tongue went purposefully into it. I was appalled. I didn't know what to do, so surprised was I, but, as though by instinct I found myself doing what Ferdinand was doing. I gave him my tongue and I felt him start and grow tense.

"I can't believe you haven't been kissed before," he stated evenly. "Who was the man?"

"There's been no man. I swear It. I'm following your lead, my dear, and I plan to continue to follow it," And this I did, no matter what my husband did. I thought it a good Idea, but I soon learned how foolish my thought had been. He failed to realize that I was only following his teaching. To my horror, I learned that he thought I was experienced in the art of making love.

"God, what an eager virgin," gasped Ferdinand, after one of my attempts to copy his passionate foreplay. "I've known whores who were less expert."

No one who writes in a diary, and very definitely no princess of Castile, could pen all that transpired on her wedding night, but I knew I would never forget a moment of It. But perhaps I can reveal a little more. I remember after reaching the peak of sensation Ferdinand let out a long, low cry, a little like the howl of a wolf, kissing me while he uttered It. My own cry must have rung out as loudly as his, for we heard the scraping of chairs and muttered words of concern.

"All is well," I managed to call out. "Withdraw, my lords, for what you waited for is accomplished."

Later, comparing notes with Beatriz, who had compared notes with other brides, I realized what I jewel I had in Ferdinand. Surely no one, not even Christopher, could perform like him. The Prince of Aragón was unbelievable. No wonder he had had so many women in Catalonia, indeed, in most of his father's extensive kingdom.

My experience with sex is still limited to my husband, but even so, I know beyond all shadow of doubt that I am the most privileged of women in having not only the perfect spouse but also the most perfect and adept of lovers. Ferdinand was passionate that nuptial night. He was lewd, I suspect, but he was understanding and he was gentle. Moreover, he was completely uninhibited, and he by his own special magic, taught me to be as unrestrained as he. I found it not unusual, as I look back upon it, for I now believe that lying underneath my prim and proper upbringing something primitive and untrammeled lived. I cannot resist a few more lines about the delights we shared, lest in the course of the years I forget them. But first I must set down what might well have turned out to be a horror and the end of our marital bliss. It came about like this.

Ferdinand, propped up on one elbow early the next morning was looking down into my face as I awoke. "My love," he said suddenly, "never let a priest at confession or some woman tell you that what we've done in bed is wrong. It isn't unnatural to savor carnal love. And you and I must continue to savor it, nor should we be afraid of overindulgence. Our bodies will tell us when they've had enough and make us rest. Until they tell us so, if they ever do, you must go on like this with me. You are the most sensuous woman I've ever met, and you have amazed and shocked me with your experience. I can forgive you this, and indeed, I do forgive you. You couldn't know that someday we'd be man and wife, so how could you have saved yourself for me. Last night you betrayed yourself, Isabella, for you took to our bedding like a duck to water."

I sat up with a start and looked into his face. Did I detect a shade of disillusionment? "But you are the first," I said. I lifted the sheet to prove It. "Virgins bleed, experienced women don't," I cried.

"Don't get upset, my love," he chortled, with a wry little laugh I did not like. "The patching of maidenheads is an old, old art, and I believe you've practiced it."

I couldn't believe he could talk to me like that. I wriggled out of the bed and into my dressing gown, heedless of the spectacle I presented. And then I wept as I had never wept before.

He was at my side in an instant. "I told you it didn't matter," he said.

"It matters to me," I shrieked at him. "We're married, Ferdinand, and I love you, but you have left scars on my soul which may never heal. I *was* a virgin and you should know it. Like a duck to water, indeed!"

"It was a bad reference," he said. He even blushed. His apology seemed sincere. I forgave him, fool that I was, and I would always forgive him, no matter what he did or said. I loved him and I still love him more than a woman should love a man.

"I'm beginning to believe, Isabella, that I am the only man, and that belief means much to me. I think pride would make me believe what you tell me, even if it were not true. I'm even ready to believe that you'd never kissed before.'

"You are the only man and there will never be another. Can't you see how you guided me in love, taught me, helped me to follow your lead? Can you imagine what it is for a princess, or any proper young lady, to burn throughout her adolescence? I did penance after confessions. I took cold baths. I exercised, I prayed, but the fire burned bright. I've wanted what you gave me tonight as long as I can remember. But you are the only man. I've looked at others, admired their physiques and handsome faces, and once a young man nearly kissed me, and his body, in a litter, set mine on fire. But the kiss didn't materialize, and he knew as well as I that what almost happened really never could have."

The minute the words were out of my mouth I knew I had made a terrible mistake. His eyes flew open, then narrowed ominously. "So there *was* another," he snarled, and again I saw that in anger, or hurt, or in remorse, the cloak of gracefulness could slip from his shoulders. He sat up in bed and thrust me from him.

I put my hand on his wrist, but he shook it off. "None of your wiles," he grated. "Just tell me who he is."

I made another mistake. I carefully explained. I told it all to him from the time Christopher appeared in his dirty sheep clothes to bring me the message from my brother, through the horrors at St. Pedro de Cardeña, the ride in the coach to Arévalo, and finally to Ávila and the Convent of St. Anne. I left nothing out, not the way I found my head on Christopher's shoulder, not the conversation and the confidences, not the matter of destiny—Christopher's and my own, and how he believed our destinies were somehow intertwined. I stressed what I owed Christopher, indeed, what he, Ferdinand owed him, for I tried to convince him that without that steadying presence, without that understanding and assistance at a most critical time, I might have collapsed and might not have given him, Ferdinand, what he received so joyfully the night just past, what he was ready, and just as hungrily, to take from me that morning.

He heard me out, his face lost a little of its belligerency, a bit of its hardness. His lips took on a little pout not unbecoming to his handsome face. His hand at last crept out and covered mine. "You swear on the name of Holy Mary,

Isabella, that nothing beyond what you've told me occurred with that peasant? Nothing whatever?"

I swore and told a lie. I suddenly realized I couldn't tell him that in my own way I truly loved the woolmerchant, that I could have gone off into the hot wheat fields and could have lain with him, that is, my body could have, had I not been forbidden by my sense of duty, my breeding, and by the presence of the Blessed Virgin on whom I'd called. "Nothing further happened, Ferdinand," I swore. "Christopher was a friend in need and nothing more." I would have to confess the lie, I knew, but not soon. For I knew I could never push Christopher completely out of mind. He was too firmly ensconced there. I needed him. I'd forgotten how often my mind kept coming back to him in times of stress. Sometimes when I talked to myself, I talked to him and even constructed conversations, taking his part and then my own. But I hadn't let myself love his flesh, and I had loved Ferdinand's and would always love it. I no longer wanted Christopher in bed or on a field of ripening wheat, as I had that sunny afternoon. Not for all his great hands, his hard, male body and his strong, rich pungent aroma of masculinity. Having lain with my husband, having seen what a naked man displays, I had tasted all the joy I needed — and yet, even now I might possibly slip into pleasant fantasies — against my will, of course, in which Christopher might still play a role. I shook my head to rid it of already encroaching images of the tall woolmerchant, taller by some inches than Ferdinand. He couldn't come between me and my husband and my lover, sitting there so sternly beside me with his eyes as cold and as hard as marble.

Ferdinand, certainly the sharpest man I'd ever met or probably ever would, missed little. His face relaxed and assumed a kind of tolerance that enraged me. I'd seen it often enough in the eyes of men; in the archbishop's, when he found me trying, or innocent, or stupid in his opinion; Henry and Beltrán looking at me in that selfsame way; the look said, "Oh, she's only a woman and can't help herself."

I pressed down my rising resentment. This was not time to raise a row. I had Ferdinand on the run, as it were, and I must not jeopardize all I'd gained. Already he more than half believed my innocence and trusted my virginity. Why wouldn't he want to believe it? Any husband would. His pride, his royal pride, could hardly let him accept a wife who was damaged goods no matter how she thrilled him under sheets. He was more than half convinced because he had to be. As to Christopher, I felt I had nothing to fear. Pride again was my strongest ally. No prince of Aragón, Ferdinand least of the long list, could possibly consider a Genoese peasant his rival. To Ferdinand, Christopher could never be more than an animal, which like some sympathetic dog, had comforted a silly, grieving, teen-age adolescent when she needed sympathy. Grudgingly he might be led to feel obligated to Christopher or to a dog.

He drew me close and I learned for the first time how wonderful a healthy male can smell after a night in bed with his beloved and before he bathes. I inhaled him shamelessly and burrowed my face into the beautiful fur on his pectorals. When we were like this I could forgive him anything and knew I always would.

I shan't write here of our lovemaking that morning or of how he roared and ordered the archbishop away from our bedroom door. Let it suffice to say that we learned much more about each other and we came out at last with most of the guidelines of our sexual life starkly delineated. I knew the depths of his jealousy, I learned he could be rough, offensive and even vulgar in speech, when he was angry; I knew his pettiness, his unreasonableness; but I knew his common sense and how it would never let him follow his emotions beyond wise limits. Ferdinand is deep and devious, he's not the best of Christians; he has a pagan's heart as well as the body of a pagan god. I knew, too, that possibly the only chink in his adamantine armor is his pride. I vowed not to wield this knowledge or turn pride against him if we ever disagreed, but all the same I carefully stored away in a dark, safe place this very dangerous knowledge, this weapon, that could pierce his armor, just in case I ever had to take it out and plunge it into him.

14

I had known how clean Ferdinand was, for in all my being in his company before we married, I never smelled unpleasant body odors, not even the odor of stale perspiration except the night he rode into Valladolid and met me in Juan Vivero's house. And even then I liked his smell. Some men smell good, even when they perspire. The woolmerchant had, and likewise the Prince of Aragón. But I'd never imagined how often he liked to bathe. He called for tubs that morning, one for me and one for him, and ordered hot water and bathing oils. He sent his valet away and I my maid, and we bathed each other, another new and delectable experience. His hands on my oily body, the massage he gave me, the slickness of his hide beneath my hands, led us straight into still to me another unusual sensory experience—the sexual act in warm, oily water in a room moist with steam and redolent of perfumed oil and clean human bodies, male and female.

"Hasn't your body, Ferdinand, even whispered that it's time to rest?" I gasped as I stepped out of the water and onto the thick oriental rug.

"No more than a faint whisper," he chuckled, "but I suppose we must get dressed and let them know how we've survived. They'll be whispering all over the palace and indeed out in the city, too. By now they've all seen the sheets they asked you to toss into the corridor two hours ago."

"I know," I blushed. "I'll blush for days," I said, "and whenever some citizen looks at me and smiles. Did we truly have to let them display those bloodied sheets?"

"Custom, my dear, custom. Would you have disappointed so many of your subjects?"

We were eating the healthy meal they'd brought us after we'd dressed, when he laid his big hand on mine again and I felt the old fire shoot up my arm and to my heart. I thought he was about to suggest the bed again, but he, catching my thought, laughed and shook his head and said expansively, "Not now, *querida*, though you know I could. No, I have a little gift for you, a morning-after-the-first-night present. You deserve much more, but this, though it's a poor thing, it's mine."

He drew out of his sleeve a small package and solemnly handed it to me across the table. My fingers shook with eagerness as I opened it. When I removed the wrapping I saw a small flat box, wrought in carved ivory. I caught his approval as I studied the carvings and didn't simply rush to see what was inside, though I knew that it had to be a jewel. Ferdinand is a sybarite and a critic, too, of fine art. The box was different from any I had seen. The carving strange, exotic. I could see animals and people in visualized events. The carvings told a story, or many stories.

Ferdinand, pleased at my perceptiveness, said, "Hindu work, my love. Narratives. I'll bet you can't decipher what is happening."

"I'll bet I can," I replied, and prayed I could. Something about the figures touched a familiar chord, I saw a yoke of oxen and a man driving them. In another panel, really in the same one, for two events were pictured in each, the action separated by the bole of a tree, I saw one bullock lying mired in mud and the driver leading away the other. Next appeared a lion surrounded by his court, with a jackal prominently displayed talking to the king of beasts. Suddenly I recognized the story. I sighed with relief. I would impress my husband now with my literary accomplishments.

"This is the story of the Lion and the Bull, my love. It comes from the *Book of Calila and Digna*, translated out of Arabic at the behest of our ancestor, Alfonso the Wise. I can even tell when the book was finished; in 1251, just before Alfonso received the scepter of Castile and León."

In delight Ferdinand leaned across the table and kissed me. It was I, of course, who spilled my wine, not the graceful Ferdinand.

"You're wonderful," he said and meant it. "How proud of you I'll be when you grace my father's table in Barcelona and Valencia. How did you know that book? I know the story of the Lion and the Bull, but I never knew from where it came, except that it was Arabic."

"I have a copy, one of the few extant, I suppose. It's back in Madrigal. Some day we'll read it together."

"The story of the Lion and the Bull makes lots of sense," mused Ferdinand. "*Calila and Digna* is surely an oriental wisdom-book. One who rules can do much worse than read the wisdom of the Ancient East."

Suddenly the story of the Lion and Bull reminded me of a story I had searched for unconsciously and had to tell him. And what better opportunity than now, with stories, wisdom-stories in their mind, so I took his hand and said, "I know a good such story, for I've read it only recently, I want you to hear it. It's as relevant as any in *Calila and Digna* I think you will agree." I didn't wait, but launched right into it.

"In Venice, I'm told, lived a beautiful maiden named Camilla, courted by a fine young nobleman, just like you. He sought her hand, and, since her father had died some years before, he asked it of her lady mother. He got it, too, and they were married and he took her home to bed. There he made love to his virgin bride, and found her as apt in bed as he, and he had been sexually active for several years. Like you, my love he sported with his bride and thanked his stars, like you, that he'd found one who knew how to please him. She gave him the best loving he had ever had and, like you, he arrived at the conclusion she was adept from practice. And, because she delighted him so much, he told her he forgave her. But, as time passed, he felt the first twinges of resentment. The more she improvised to pleasure him, the more he wondered whom she'd lain with before she married her. One of his friends, or was it in truth one of his enemies, persuaded him that people were laughing at him behind his back. At last he began to leave his wife alone.

"She grew pale and wan, for she was hot blooded and needed her husband's amorous attentions. He watched her and had her watched, hoping to catch her out, but she never strayed. Then his friends influenced him to put her aside, to get an annulment and marry again. The fool decided to follow their advice.

"He led her weeping to her lady mother, his face dark with pent-up self-righteousness and hurt. Grim-faced, he told her mother she had sold him damaged goods. 'Take her back,' he growled, 'and good riddance!'

Domina Genoveva, for such was the mother's name, studied his grieving face and laid her hand upon his arm. 'Do you mean you feel this way because she pleased you on your wedding night, because she was warm and loving, and knew what she must do?'

"'Yes,' he snapped. 'Why, Domina, she took to it like a duck to water!'

"'Riccardo,' said Domina Genoveva, 'if I could prove you wrong, would you take my daughter back, this very day, and save her from a life of everlasting sorrow and yourself from one of doubt? I know you still love Camilla. She was truly all you desired until you let your evil mind harbor doubts about her virtue. Be your decent self again. Can you face the chance that you've been foolish, that you can ruin two lives?'

"'I'm listening, Domina Genoveva,' he said grimly. 'I am a gentleman and fair and honest. Say what you can, for I do love Camilla, or I did love her until I realized what she'd done to me.'

"'Riccardo,' said the mother, 'some women are born with the art of love implanted in them. I was so born myself, and my husband at first delighted in my art and then deplored it, for like you, he came to doubt. My husband, shortly after Camilla was born, left us for the wars and died in Flanders. He never knew how innocent I was, and, if he hadn't died, I believe he might have repudiated me. Don't be like that, Riccardo. Listen and listen well. I have the proof that some women are born expert in the game of Venus, and are, even as virgins, able to give their husbands on their wedding nights all that the most trained courtesans can give.'

"'I'm listening,' repeated Riccardo glumly. 'I hope you can convince me, for it's true your daughter is a paragon in Venus's art and that I can't forget her.'

"'Come,' she said, and taking him by the hand, she led him to the barnyard and to the poultry house. He followed, shaking his head in wonderment. She stopped at a nest on which sat a large white duck, her feathers ruffled, her voice a long complaint at the humans disturbing her. The mother lifted the duck from the nest and revealed a dozen fuzzy ducklings, some still damp from their recent hatching. She handed the duck to Riccardo, and picking up the ducklings placed them one by one in her apron. 'Come with me, Riccardo,' she ordered, and he followed her with the angry duck struggling in his grasp."

I glanced at Ferdinand and found him looking at me quizzically. Already the light was beginning to break. He was that quick, that intelligent, but I continued the story to its end. "Domina Genoveva walked to the edge of the moat, and before Riccardo could suspect what she was about to do, she opened her apron and spilled the ducklings down into the green water of the moat. The duck herself went wild, and Riccardo loosed her. Off she fluttered, sailed across the water, landed with a splash and called her brood, The ducklings, one and all, even the two or three not yet dry from the moisture of the egg, paddled serenely toward her.

"Domina Genoveva turned to Ricardo. 'Did you say,' she asked him, smiling, 'like a duck to water?'

Ricardo understood. He rushed back to Camilla and bussed her soundly. Then, hand in hand they ran to their horses. Together they thundered home, heads high, their marriage saved."

Ferdinand smiled, and opened his arms and I flew into them. "Yes," he chuckled, "I, too, said like a duck to water, my love, didn't I? And I was right. You did take to it like the proverbial duck. You've made your point. When all is said and done, there's nothing like a fable to prove one. No wonder the Church depends so much on its *exempla*, and seldom leaves one out of a sermon, however serious."

I went straight to him and placed my hands on his broad shoulders. I stood on tiptoe and kissed him on the cheek, and smiled as his arms came up and pulled my head up to his lips, "Never doubt me again," I said in a voice that I kept soft but nevertheless instilled with firmness. "not ever, Ferdinand!"

He laughed and promised, and I believe he meant it. "Maybe it's best we quarreled," he said. "We've reached a perfect understanding, one few people ever find. I know you now, my love, as no man has ever known a bride of hours. And I learned a thing I never suspected, with all my experience. Instinct can be everything. Like a duck to water, indeed you were. I'll never forget my wedding night and how my virgin bride kept up with me."

4

The Crucible

1

THE YOUNG COUPLE SETTLED down to a year of mingled bliss and unhappiness. Isabella's pregnancy drew her and Ferdinand together as nothing had before, not even their passion. But not even this could dispel her distrust of him and his impatience with her.

Anyone who had lived in Dueñas that first year would have known what occasioned her first distrust, and not her last, of Ferdinand. But the only person with whom she could share her feelings was Beatriz de Bobadilla Cabrera. Thank God the princess had that friend!

When Henry's letter came it left her shocked, incredulous and desolate. For the first time since their wedding night she insisted on sleeping alone. It was their first quarrel and it was serious. Ferdinand left for Barcelona in a huff, not saying when he would return. He told her angrily that he found it inconceivable that she refused to see what he had done had been for her good as well as his, for Castile's good as well as Aragón's. And why, he asked, should she take it out on him, when as a matter of fact it had been his father and the Archbishop of Toledo who had concocted the idea and carried it out? He was no more, actually, than a pawn in their master game. She would not soon forget his ranting as he paced furiously up and down the room, slamming his fist into his palm, shooting hurt and angry glances her way, cursing, as only an Aragonese can curse. She had had to cover her ears.

Plainly and succinctly, he had witnessed and helped to perpetrate a serious forgery. When they had married, they had done so with the sanction of a pope, a dead pope, yes, but all the same he had issued and signed the bull that dissolved the prohibited degree of consanguinity. Cousins couldn't marry, not first cousins, unless the Church consented. Pope Pius II had released them from the prohibition. Isabella remembered his great seal dangling from the bull, and had seen his purposeful signature herself. No one had told her the new pope had to sign. But under Henry's insisting he had cancelled the former bull and would not issue one of his own. When King John and the Archbishop of Toledo learned this they had a new bull penned and the new pope's name forged and placed upon it.

"It means," she had shouted at her husband, "that you aren't my husband and that the child will be a bastard! Doesn't *that* move you even a little? But the worst of all, you lied to me, you tricked me, Ferdinand."

"For your own good," he said. "If you're too foolish to watch out for yourself, someone has to watch out for you. Who better than the man you were to marry?"

"I repeat," she had said, "doesn't the legitimacy of the child mean anything to you?"

"Not a jot," Ferdinand had yelled back at her. "Princes have defied popes before and gotten by with it. Do you think this pope is going to do this to us in the face of my father's anger? He wouldn't dare. Henry, yes, has gotten to him and we have not, but mark my words my father will. And don't forget, Miss High-and-Mighty, that Aragón rules the Kingdom of Naples and Sicily, right in the pope's back yard. We'll get the bull we need, never fear."

"But until we get it, Ferdinand, and even after we get it, we have been living unwed all this time. Do you swear it will come before the child arrives?"

"How do I know?" he had snapped. "I hope so, but if not, all will be well. And suppose your damned half-brother, that drooling catamite of Moors and the dregs of Castile, *has* sent you a nasty letter? Do you actually care, Princess? Words don't kill, or even wound, unless we let them. Surely the words of a king who hates you and whom you hate should bounce right off you like water off a duck's back."

"I don't hate Henry," she objected. "I pity him."

"Tell that to your confessor, my love, not to me who knows you. But since you're in such a mood, I think it better if I leave you to work your way out of it. I'm off to Barcelona, maybe to Valencia, where I have many friends. Rest well, Isabella, keep well, and when the child is near, let me know and I'll ride like the wind. For now, goodbye."

And with that he had left her to her tears, and she had shed a number with the realization that the cruelest cut of all to bear is being duped by a husband who is also a lover.

Fortunately, in the midst of her unhappiness Beatriz arrived from Segovia, and with her friend to discuss her troubles, Isabella at last overcame, outwardly at least, the sorrow that gnawed her from within.

They talked of the baby coming in the spring, and Beatriz, recalling old discussions about love and ideal husbands, smiled and said, "Is he as wonderful as you boasted, Isabella?"

Isabella pretended not to hear. "What does Andrés hear from Henry?" she asked. "Does he show any signs of relenting? Will he ever forgive us for getting married against his wishes?"

Beatriz observed the change of subject, but decided to overlook it. "The king never forgives, Isabella. You should know that. However, for reasons Andrés and I can't fathom, he hints of reconciliation. That terrible letter he sent you was meant to break your spirit and tempt you into making peace at his price. He did send it, didn't he?"

"Indeed he did," said Isabella, "and when you return to Segovia, you may tell Andrés to assure him it hurt me as deeply as he hoped it would."

"I'm so sorry, Isabella. Andrés begged him not to dispatch it, but Henry was determined."

"I would have heard the news by now, anyway, Beatriz. Henry only brought it to my attention a little sooner, which was just as well. The hurt has lessened, and I can even talk about it now. The letter is in that chest beside you. Hand it to me and I will let you hear in the king's own works."

"I didn't mean to imply that I wanted you to read it, Isabella. If you would rather not…"

"No, let me read it. Then we can talk at length and that will help." She ran her eye down the parchment. "Here is the part that hurts. 'You certainly surprised me, Princess, although Villena says it's just what we should have expected of you. Have you no shame, you hussy? Live in sin with the Prince of Aragón like a common harlot, would you? Did you believe that your secret would remain undiscovered? Vain delusion! Nothing remains hidden for long. You might have known that a man with a nose for scenting out wickedness like the Cardinal of Arras would ferret out the forgery of the papal bull. Now the world knows that you aren't legally married to your prince. What a hypocrite to marry under a forged bull! Couldn't you wait even a few months for your lover? What has become of your vaunted piety and your renowned propriety?'"

Beatriz was furious. "Wordy, as usual, and how malicious! I'll bet Villena was dictating."

"Probably, Beatriz. And they haven't wasted any time in spreading the news. Did you know that heralds have read proclamations in every major city under Henry's control? That preachers announced it to their flocks even in the villages?"

"I knew, Isabella. But the people aren't believing it. Don't doubt what I'm telling you, for I've seen Segovia's reaction, and it's a well known fact that the people aren't taking the bait. When preachers announce it, congregations are glum and sullen. Sometimes there's vociferous denial. Andrés says the people will never believe it, that it would take a sign from heaven to convince them. If they think you're like the rest of the Trastámaras, what hope is left for a better world when Henry dies? So they cling to their faith in you."

Isabella's eyes returned to the letter. "If only it weren't true, Beatriz. But it is, Ferdinand couldn't deny it. Oh, he explained the way the forgery came about, and I admit I understand why he thought he had to do it. But he lied, Beatriz! He let me think the bull was authentic when he knew perfectly well it wasn't. And the Archbishop of Toledo lied. King John of Aragón lied. Now I don't know whom to trust."

"How did he explain it, Isabella?" asked Beatriz, furious at the people who had hurt her friend.

"They said they did it perforce. Ferdinand admitted he didn't dare tell me before the wedding because he knew I wouldn't marry him. I'd have insisted on waiting, and it would have endangered everything, I'll admit."

Beatriz's lips curled. "I can hear them, Isabella. 'We haven't a moment to lose,' I expect they told you. 'Henry will attack Valladolid the day he knows Ferdinand is here!'" And then they told you you owed it to your people. And of course you wanted to be married to him and have him near you."

"They said all that, Beatriz, in their famous explanation. And Ferdinand? Persuasive? You wouldn't believe how much. He couldn't chance losing me, he said; he loved me too much to let me ruin my life over a piece of paper. And that part he meant, Beatriz. I cling to that when there's nothing else to cling to. And, naturally, I forgave him and we're as much in love as ever, but oh, how I wish he hadn't lied to me!"

"Did he actually tell you the second bull was authentic?"

"Not in so many words. But he and the archbishop had the document, it was displayed before all the people at the betrothal. They asked me to read it, and I read it. They didn't have to tell me. I saw. I read. I believed. Everyone did. The pope's signature was there as clear as day."

Beatriz shook her head. "Ferdinand is a strange mixture," she said at last. "Piety and the new ethics. The end justifies the means. A convenient philosophy, isn't it?"

"Most convenient," replied Isabella dryly. "And very successful. Look at Louis of France. Duplicity personified, and yet he keeps adding a new saint's image to his cap every time he steals another province. And if the reports are true, he lives frugally, gives alms to the poor, builds churches and prays devoutly, even as he cheats."

"And France has become a great power," said Beatriz. "The old order changeth, as the saying goes."

"Yes, Beatriz. Everything passes, they say also, and everything must change. Since I cannot change my husband, I shall not try. But I do not have to follow the new morality."

Suddenly Beatriz asked an unexpected question "What really made you forgive him, Isabella?"

Isabella answered straight from her heart. "Why did I forgive him, Beatriz? Because I love his flesh." And, she thought to herself, I would love him more if he were more chaste and like the woolmerchant.

"What now, Isabella? What can be done now that the fat is in the fire?"

"Oh, they've rectified matters. The archbishop and my husband are much too clever to let anything as dangerous as a forged papal bull lie around to incriminate them. Even before the betrothal, the archbishop dispatched an envoy to the Holy See with a full report of Castile's depravity under Henry and Villena. The Holy Father was shocked and alarmed to hear such things from Spain's primate. The archbishop left nothing unsaid, apparently—Joanna's adultery, the birth of her bastard daughter, the degradation of Holy Church, the ascendancy of Islam, and even Henry's perversions. The Holy Father's legate arrived quite soon thereafter in Valladolid. He is a great noble named Rodrigo Borgia—a name that is Spanish and was Borja before the Italians changed it. He brought another bull declaring that the marriage was perfectly legal. My reputation is saved, and in the League's dominions the heralds have read the proclamation and copies of the bull have been distributed. Soon all Spain will know that Henry lied, and people will believe that he was lying from the start, even this one time when he wasn't, when what he said was true."

"Henry has cried wolf so many times, Isabella. He deserves not to be believed."

"What is happening to the world, Beatriz?" said Isabella, pressing her fingers to her temples. "What can one believe when the primate of the Spanish Church, the most powerful ecclesiastic in all Spain, teeters on the thin edge of the truth, and allows a lie to hide behind the implication of veracity, and then as a last resort forges a papal bull?"

"Isabella, the world is moving away from honesty and forthrightness. Great thinkers worry, shake their heads, and say the times are almost at a nadir."

"Ferdinand says so, too, Beatriz. He believes no one can afford to be trusting and naive, that frankness is passé. He likes to quote a Muslim proverb apropos to this. 'Dupe the world or be its dupe.'"

"You needn't worry about Prince Ferdinand's being duped, Isabella," said Beatriz, carried away by the subject which was evidently one close to her heart.

"He has learned better than most men to walk on the thin edge of truth. He is an apt student of this new art, and already people are beginning to call him a fox. They even liken his diplomacy to King Louis's."

"Ferdinand," said Isabella, "is a mixture of the old and new, Beatriz. All you've said about him is true, and yet no one is more pious. He is never absent from Mass, you know, and his faith in Our Lady goes as deep as my own."

"He couldn't have been reared in Spain and be otherwise," commented Beatriz with the slightest hint of sarcasm. "Is it true—that he wears an undershirt made in part from the chasuble woven by the Holy Virgin for a bishop many years ago?"

"You remember which bishop, Beatriz, and it was an archbishop named Ildefonso. No one was to wear it save him. But when he died, Siagra, his successor, insisted on wearing it at Mass. The chasuble contracted on his neck, beheading him as effectively as a sword. Ferdinand swears it gives him invulnerability in battle. Silver threads, the finest I have ever seen, run all through the silk, and they never tarnish. Furthermore, its warp and woof is unknown to me, and I know a bit about such matters."

By the time Ferdinand returned from Aragón Isabella had pushed the matter of the bull into the recesses of her mind. She thought mainly of the child. "We should name him John, if God sends a son," she said. "John, after your father and after mine. But if He sends a daughter, I'd like to call her Isabella after my mother."

Ferdinand laughed. "We can hardly name her Juana for mine. Henry's Joanna ended all chance of that. But there'll be no problem, Isabella. Our child will be a boy." And he looked so confident that she wondered if he had had a premonition.

Having none herself, Isabella could only wait. And when the daughter arrived, she was secretly glad. Through this little being she would live vicariously the childhood she never had. No shabby cast-off dresses for this Isabella of Castile! No loneliness! No fear of a wicked step-sister, no loathing for a brother like Henry of Trastámara.

When Ferdinand came quietly to her bedside, he took her hand and smiled in his most tender way, reminding her of Christopher. But his eyes were bleak as he saw the baby. They only lighted up when she reminded him they would have many children and the next would be a boy. Not all men would let their disappointment show. She knew one who wouldn't.

The first time they made love after the birth of Isabella they were as uninhibited as before. She forgot the forgery completely, the lie, the duplicity. Only his body mattered. And when he was summoned again to Aragón—the French were on the border making trouble as usual—it was like the nail parting from the flesh. It frightened her. Should her body care that much for his? Should she think more of the loss of passion while he was gone than of how their souls had learned to blend?

Handsome as a young god she saw him ride away at the head of his lancers, blowing kisses to her while the men smiled and saluted. And his words of parting came back, warmed by the light in his eyes.

"Yea, between the bitter and the sweet standeth my heart."
The gall of parting, and the honey of the kisses."

She smiled fondly yet sadly. These lines, penned centuries ago by a Toledan Jew, should sound unbecoming on the lips of a Christian prince, but they didn't. Their poignancy, their rightness, lingered after he had gone and she kept repeating them. Some day, beyond the shadow of any doubt, she knew the bitter and the sweet of their two lives would flow together. She feared that time, but until it darkened their days—the poetry of Yejudah Halevi would keep her from that shadow. But other events and an invitation to make a visit to the home of a friend also helped to make her forget her doubts.

"It'll do me good," thought Isabella, when she received the invitation from Doña Mercedes de Guzmán. "I feel so useless here. Ferdinand away helping my people, as well as his, in the war with the French, and here I sit like a cabbage, doing nothing. Yes, the trip will do me good, and in Doña Mercedes' house I'll surely pick up some useful news about Segovia and Madrid. A pregnant woman can be of some use, if she has the mind to be."

When she told the archbishop, he frowned and offered objections. "You're carrying a child, Princess, who may one day be King of Aragón and Castile. That should be enough for a woman to be doing for her country. Moreover, the prince would not approve."

"But what harm could it possibly do, Your Grace? The road from here to Aranda is in good repair, the Convent of the Holy Child is exactly halfway along the way, and I can spend the night there and break what otherwise might be a tiring journey. Even the weather is right, for everyone believes that winter won't come for several weeks."

The archbishop weakened. She did look pale, and since the embarrassing matter of the forged bull had come to her attention, he knew that she had not been herself. If he dispatched a company of his lancers to escort her to Aranda and Doña Mercedes' mansion, what harm could come from the trip? "Very well, then," he said. "Go, but be careful, daughter. And travel by litter all the way, mind you. Don't even consider riding a horse."

"I won't ride, Your Grace," she said. She was not likely to, after the two doctors had expressed the opinion that a longer interval should have passed before a second pregnancy. Even Urraca, the famous midwife sent by King John to assist at the birth of her daughter, had shaken her head and clucked. Urraca, who had delivered Ferdinand himself, spoke with the familiarity only Spanish servants know how to exercise.

"Too soon," she croaked. "Much, much too soon. A field should lie fallow for a time, you know. But now that you have planted your garden again, we must all care for it."

Isabella looked up at the stark Castilian mountains and drew strength from them. It would be good to leave the flat lands of Valladolid behind. She loved the highlands and their crisp winds. The raw starkness of rock-ribbed slopes and the jagged peaks etched white against the cobalt sky, already the harbinger of coming snows, had shaped the soul of Spain and she felt most at home when in their shadow.

The journey renewed her spirits and quickened her blood. The litter moved smoothly on the long poles supported by four ambling mules. Beside her sat Margarita, her *dueña*, chattering like a magpie, filled with the excitement of the trip. Isabella could feel her color returning. Everything was perfect.

She liked the deep male voices of the lancers and the peals of hearty laughter. Occasionally the roar of a cataract, swollen by snows already deep in the mountains that floated like white clouds in the cobalt air, mingling its thunder with the sullen roar of the wind in the pine forests. The horses tossed their manes and strained at their bits. Even the mules pricked up their long ears and brayed enthusiastically.

Isabella had never visited the Convent of the Holy Child. How strange to be spending a night again in a house of nuns! The woolmerchant inexorably flashed into her mind for the first time in months, as she looked down into the valley where the convent nestled. Soon her litter swung to a halt before its gates and she forgot him. She raised her eyes to the mountains and saw enough to make anyone forget anyone. Above the tiled roofs of the hamlet that clustered around the yellow convent walls thrust the towers of the chapel and the village church. Above these loomed, grey and impressive, the battlements of a ruined castle. And over it all rose incredible pinnacles of snow-capped sierra with long rows of dark pines marching around their slopes and foothills.

The sun, just disappearing behind the distant ranges, dyed the snow fields above a shimmering silver, and pearl, and rose. The mountains, the snow, and the sky transformed themselves with incredible rapidity into a world of weird pastels, lavender, ice blue, and the cold iridescence of polished steel. It was a fairy world but perilous and lethal.

She found the convent buzzing, since the archbishop had dispatched a courier to advise the Reverend Mother of her arrival. Nuns flitted like grey swallows along dimly lit halls and the refectory glowed with an array of candles only lighted for special occasions. It would never do, she realized at once, to insist on dinner in her room with Margarita. The sisters would be crushed.

Isabella enjoyed her dinner, realizing how hungry the mountain air had made her. She ate a second dish of trout and realized that she hadn't enjoyed food since the day Ferdinand had ridden off. If only some miracle could be wrought to have him there to spend the night! As it was, the dinner, the chat with the Reverend Mother, and the pleasant hours dozing before the fire in her room, munching Margarita's roasted chestnuts and sipping the convent's famous yellow wine, lulled her even as they restored her enthusiasm and sharpened her zest for life. The child stirred vigorously. Surely a boy, with a kick like that.

Only a bed of coals glowed. Margarita moved softly on her couch when a light knock sounded at the door. What could they want at this hour?

A sister carrying a lamp stood shivering in the windy corridor. "A lady seeks an audience, Princess. She arrived at the gate a few minutes ago and was so insistent that the Reverend Mother felt that we had better notify you."

Isabella frowned. Only a few people knew she was here. Perhaps this was a message from Doña Mercedes, although it was odd that a woman would bring it and after dark. "Who is the lady?" she asked the nun.

"She would give her name only to the Reverend Mother, Princess, but I heard her say she knew you well."

"Who could it be but Beatriz?" she asked herself aloud. "But why would she arrive at night mysteriously?" Slipping into a robe, she followed the sister drifting down the corridor like a silent spirit, her lamp barely lighting the way.

Margarita still slept. The almost imperceptible scrape of her own sandals made the only sound in the stillness.

The nun opened a door and stepped aside. Isabella saw the dancing light of a log fire. "The Reverend Mother had it lit, Princess, as soon as the lady said she must see you. The loquatory is far too cold otherwise on nights like this."

She only sensed the closing of the door behind her. All her attention focused on the woman gliding out of the shadows. Suddenly she shivered, and not from cold. She sensed that something was very wrong. Why hadn't she brought Margarita with her? Now, alone with her visitor, it was too late.

The tall woman, without speaking, threw back her hood. Isabella drew back in shock. "Joanna!" she gasped, looking into the expression on that still beautiful face and finding it feral in its ferocity, its pure animal hate. How old she looked and she walked with a definite limp.

"Surprised, Princess?" same Joanna's throaty laugh. "Whom did you expect? Who else would ride twenty miles across these hellish mountains on a night threatening snow to pay her respects to you?"

"You came because you knew I was here, Joanna? How did you know?"

"I keep in touch, my dear. I know what's been going on in Dueñas and Valladolid," said the queen mysteriously. "Yesterday my agents told me you had started toward Aranda and would stay the night here. I rode as soon as I heard the good news."

"But why, Joanna? And where were you staying to have arrived so soon?"

"One question at a time, Princess," purred Joanna. "Nearby is one of the houses of Pedro of Castile. But, can't you truly imagine how delighted I was to hear you would pass this way? If you hadn't made the stop, I believe I should have chanced the meeting in Valladolid itself. You see, I bring tidings you'll want to hear."

"Did Pedro come with you?" asked Isabella, startled at the thought of a possible attempt to take her from the convent by force.

Joanna smiled and limped to a chair near the fire. "Sit down Princess. No, Pedro is far away. Don't be afraid. I came with only four of his servitors, and you have five times as many. You are quite safe tonight."

"I'm not afraid, Joanna. Only cautious. Now, if it isn't too much to ask, why this visit?"

The queen stretched like a cat and smiled, as if marshalling her forces for a leap. When she was comfortable, she began to speak.

"The king, they say, is ill. Too much hashish, no doubt. Too many Moorish pages, too much carousing in the taverns. I haven't seen him, mind you, since he packed me off to Seville, but I know his every move, as well as yours and that Prince's you dote on so inordinately."

"But why aren't you in Seville? We've heard you've been under house arrest since the day you got there."

"You haven't heard I escaped my guardian, if you chose to dignify an aged female Argus in whose charge your kind half-brother left me?"

"I've heard rumors about your story, Joanna. That you got pregnant by that lad Pedro, the bishop's nephew. That you managed to outwit your guards and let yourself down from a palace window by a rope and that you broke your ankle…"

"And that I," said Joanna, taking the tale from Isabella's mouth, "managed to hobble bravely across fields and forests to shelter with the Mendozas. God damn Henry and the rest of you! Only in your god-forsaken land could a queen experience such things!"

"What ails Henry really, Joanna?"

"He's more than ill, my dear, he's quite mad at last, not just demented. He hasn't had a clean shirt on his back in months and months, and of course he hasn't bathed. All he does is lounge in taverns and ride up to those lodges in the mountains. God only knows what goes on up there. Orgies, they say, perversion, even devil worship. And you can smell him coming the length of a drill field. At least, I'm out of that!"

"The king is a strange person," said Isabella non-comittally. "Pray God he recovers."

"You may try, Princess, but you can't fool me with your pious concern. You can't wait to hear he's dead, can you? You think the way will then be clear for your ascendancy. How terribly you want the crown!"

Isabella had heard enough. Joanna was the same. She had no intention of prolonging a needlessly unpleasant interview. "Thank you, Joanna, for your concern in bearing me these tidings. Now, if you'll excuse me, I'll say goodnight. It's been a long, long day and, as you can see, I need more rest than usual."

"Wait," cried the queen, and her eyes flashed with the well-remembered malice Isabella wished she could forget. "Wait, for I have news about your husband."

Isabella, who had opened the door to the corridor, closed it again, but not before whispering to the frightened nun who waited to escort her back to her room. "Run for the captain of my lancers," she said.

She was glad she had given the order, for as she turned back into the room again, she saw Joanna arranging the folds of her cloak over something that flashed momentarily in the firelight.

"I'm waiting to hear the news about my husband," said Isabella, hoping the nun would find the captain quickly.

"Your precious Ferdinand is a very remarkable man, my dear. What timing, what finesse in the matter of the two bulls! He's already as sly as the Archbishop of Toledo. Think of it, the authentic bull already in his hands before you learned from Henry's letter about the forgery!"

"That's past history, Joanna. Ferdinand and I have reached an understanding about that bull... Do you even know the name of the papal legate who brought it?"

"Of course. Of course. Roderick Borgia. Do you think for a moment Villena's spies in Rome are dolts?"

Isabella heard no hastening feet. She moved away from the queen and stood beside the fireplace. The long poker wasn't two feet from her hand. Joanna alarmed her. She sat forward in her chair, one hand knotted into a fist, the other concealed in the folds of her skirt. Naked hate glared out of her white, heart-shaped face with its prominent cheekbones and frame of dark hair. Her lips had begun to twitch.

"And now, my dear," said Joanna expansively, "we come to the part I like the most. This news about dear Ferdinand should bowl you over quite."

"She's about to loose the barb," thought Isabella. "What can she have dreamed up now?"

Joanna didn't keep her waiting. "Hadn't you heard, dear Isabella, that your wonderful husband has planted the seed of another bastard in Aragón? I see you hadn't, Princess. How glad I am to be the one to bring the happy news?"

Isabella wasn't prepared for this. Her hands clenched behind her back, but she didn't speak. What could she say? What left her truly speechless was that she could believe it. Holy Mary, how could a single statement, a few stark words, bring her world toppling down around her? Al the doubts she had felt after the forgery, doubts she kept smothering with love and faith, now solidified in all their ugliness. In horror she realized she could believe anything. She swayed and leaned heavily against the mantle. At last she made herself say, "It's a lie, Joanna. I know it is." But alas indeed, she knew she wasn't sure.

Joanna caught the sadness in her voice and interpreted it correctly. A smile of evil wreathed her full, red lips. "I see you understand," she gloated. "Once a man's lied to you, he'll lie again, and Ferdinand is like the rest."

"He wouldn't lie again, Joanna. He's too responsible. We have too much." But she had to force herself to say the words. Memory of the bull loomed large.

Joanna tossed her long hair over her shoulder and leaped from her chair like a leopard. The dagger gleamed in her hand. She thrust her face in Isabella's. The reek of wine and something bittersweet was palpable. Her eyes probed deeply as she whispered, "This is the ultimate in betrayal, isn't it, my dear? The one deceit beyond your bearing." And then her face, no longer beautiful, but ugly with pure physical gratification, moved closer. Isabella could feel droplets of moisture on her lips. Joanna cupped her long white fingers around one upthrust breast. She emanated such an animal gloating joy that Isabella stretched out her hand to grasp the poker. Joanna's eyes were starting from their sockets and veins stood out an her temples and on her neck.

"You know it's true," she screamed. "He's as lusty as a bull, isn't he, and as polygamous? You'll never tame him. Whatever made you think you could? For every seed he sows in you, he'll sow a dozen in his mistresses. Ferdinand is too much man for you, my little bride of Christ."

Down the corridor came the sound of running feet. Joanna heard them. Up flashed the dagger. Isabella tried to use the poker, but Joanna wrested it from her grasp. She raised the blade and advanced rapidly. The door burst open and Isabella fled past the captain who disarmed the frenzied queen. She was screaming still and the officer was cursing her for slashing his cheek, when Isabella slammed the door of her cell and leaned against it. But even then, since the officer had to drag the queen past her door, Isabella heard Joanna's final message. "Ask him about María Méndez. Ask him about his visit to Valencia."

Isabella knew she would ask those questions when she saw Ferdinand. Wearily she undressed and went to bed. And before she fell asleep another face, as well as Ferdinand's, rose up before her eye, a face of friendship and comfort—the woolmerchant's.

2

When Isabella reached Aranda, Lady Mercedes took her straight to her room. The meeting with Joanna, she knew, as soon as Isabella had told her, was enough to drain the strength of anyone, let alone a pregnant woman. "Did the queen know you were on the way here, Princess?" she asked in deep concern. "I'm afraid she did. She *knew* I'd be at the convent, too, She came there to talk to me. Yes, she knew I was on the way here. God grant she won't make trouble for you!"

Lady Mercedes was a realist. She shook her head. "The queen is a terrible woman. The worst I have met in a long life of terrible people. I do wish she hadn't found you at the convent. And I fear she'll turn up here, but don't worry about it tonight. Our doors are strong and we have your lancers and my retainers. Go to bed. There'll be time enough to worry tomorrow."

Isabella went to bed, but before she went she talked to the captain of her lancers. "At dawn," she told him, "send a courier to the archbishop, No, send one tonight. He'll be rewarded to make up for such a trip."

She was more concerned when on the morning of her third day at Aranda still no word had come from Valladolid. Obviously the messenger had not reached the archbishop. Otherwise, the lancers she had requested would have arrived. She knew that if she had no word by another morning, she would have to set out for home, regardless of the risk.

That same afternoon she received an unexpected visit which changed her plans. A servant came to say that a peasant woman and two men were asking to speak to her. Looking through a carved screen, one of the many heritages of Moorish civilization, she and her hostess studied the woman and her companions. The men looked like soldiers, even in their peasant garments, and the woman was tall and more slender than most country women. As they watched she thrust back her hood and Isabella's jaw dropped. Beatriz de Bobadilla!

"You can't stay here another hour, Isabella," said Beatriz by way of greeting. "The king's troops are on the way. They must not find you here in Aranda."

Lady Mercedes moved swiftly. She sent to the kitchens and had food prepared. "You can't ride on empty stomachs!" she said. As they ate in the mansion's dining hall with her lancers at a long table across the room, Isabella learned the facts. Henry had been in the midst of a plan to invite her to Segovia for a new peace treaty. In fact, his letter had been received by the archbishop. She must have missed it only by hours. Another letter came from Joanna, warning the king and Villena that Isabella had ventured from the safety of the city and was in Aranda. Joanna swore, Beatriz said, that she had spoken to Isabella at the Convent of the Holy Child and believed she must have reached Lady Mercedes' house. At this Henry had set out to capture her before she could go back to Valladolid. All this Beatriz and Andrés learned the day Andrés persuaded the Segovians to cast off Henry's yoke and offer allegiance to Ferdinand and Isabella."

"But when did this rebellion against Henry occur, Beatriz?"

Beatriz thought a moment. "Let's see," she said, "Andrés seized power on Tuesday. He imprisoned Henry's agents."

"The very day I reached the convent of the Holy Child, and the night I saw Joanna."

"Let me see," said Beatriz. "Joanna sent her messenger that same night. So Henry by Thursday knew you were here. That's why on Thursday evening, just before the gates were closed, his courier came from Madrid with a letter for Henry's regent in Segovia—Andrés, that is."

"But you said Andrés had taken over the city."

"Henry and Villena couldn't have known it before he dispatched the letter to Andrés. Anyway, the letter told us you were to be arrested, so I disguised myself, set out, and here I am."

Isabella's eyes filled with tears. "Then you must have left Segovia last night, Beatriz, to have reached Aranda this afternoon. You had to ride all night and half a day! You must be dead. No wonder you look so tired!"

"It was the only way, Isabella. A courier would have been stopped, since Henry's forces may be anywhere."

Lady Mercedes shook her head apprehensively. "Beatriz, it wouldn't do to start for Valladolid, for they'd be watching that way. You must try for Segovia. Following the old mountain highway with luck and Our Lady's help, you should get there before dark tomorrow. You'll travel light, of course. Just enough food for twenty-four hours, and blankets when it's time to rest. It'll be a long, cold journey, I'm afraid."

"How far is the first inn?" asked Isabella.

"There's one on the highway just over the first mountain," said Lady Mercedes. "You could put up there."

"Too dangerous," said Beatriz, "No, the way I came is best. It has no inns and the king's troops won't be looking for horsemen or people on foot on that trail." Suddenly she stopped speaking and turned pale. "Holy Mother of God!" she cried. "I had forgotten about the baby. Isabella, you can't ride a horse!"

"Oh, yes I can. I must. The child is months away."

"I won't have it, Princess," interrupted Lady Mercedes. "We'll barricade the house and try to reach the archbishop again."

But Isabella prevailed. From the first everyone knew that there was no other way. In less than an hour they were departing. The two women rode in silence, pretending not to know the guides Lady Mercedes provided, fearing snow would fall and soon.

In Aranda Lady Mercedes waited grimly for the arrival of Henry's cavalry. She had carried out every possible detail in her preparation to delay them, if they could be delayed. She had a fine dinner cooking, and the best candelabra and plate gleamed in the dining hall. If they would only stay to dine and spend the night!

When finally the sound of hooves and the jingle of spurs filled her courtyard, the snow had begun to fall. Great feathery flakes as large as rose petals drifted down silently. By the time she received the officers in her parlor the air was so thick that the sierra vanished behind the white wall. She could see no farther than the gates of the mansion.

When the servant who admitted the officers had taken her to them, they were pacing nervously before the fire, their coats unbuttoned, warming their chilled hands. Lady Mercedes allowed herself to look surprised at their question. "The Princess Isabella is no longer here, gentlemen. She departed for Valladolid this morning. By which road? By the lower road, of course, so as to avoid the passes which will soon be blocked with snow. It's nearly twice as far that way, but there are comforts that make up for the distance. I thank our Blessed Lady that she left long enough ahead of the storm to reach the first inn. The Black Bull tavern is a good house. She'll be comfortable there even if she should be snowed in for a week."

The officers exchanged glances of relief, and when Lady Mercedes made her next move, their tired faces lighted up. "You and your men," she said, "simply cannot venture on the roads tonight. You must do us, sirs, the honor of having dinner and of staying the night. We have rooms for you both in the mansion, and your men will find accommodations at the inn with a little crowding."

"We should be delighted," said the older officer quickly. "But tell me, how far is the Black Bull tavern? We could send a courier there in the early morning with the king's letter to the princess."

"Quite so, quite so," agreed Lady Mercedes. "And there's no real hurry, captain. It's a good day's journey by litter, but a mounted messenger should reach it in a fraction of that time, unless the snow drifts too deeply on the road, which in these mountains it often does. In any case, the princess will be there when the courier arrives, in fact, until you and your lancers reach the inn. She is pregnant, you know, and will travel no farther until the weather breaks."

When Lady Mercedes excused herself after dinner, begging the officers to sit before her fire as long as they wished, and supplying them with mulled wine and sweetmeats, she didn't go directly to her room. She went out into the patio and into the chapel. Her feet sank into snow above her boots. Ten Hail Marys made her feel better, and she knew the tracks of the princess's party were now so covered that no one could possibly follow them. But she remembered that snow could be a danger as well as a concealment. Suppose it blocked the passes and the princess was forced to spend the night in the open. She crossed herself and knelt until her feet were numb on the chapel's icy floor. "Surely Our Lady has not brought her this far only to let her freeze to death," she said.

***

Isabella and Beatriz urged their mounts along behind the men as they broke a path through the deeper drifts the wind was piling up along the narrow trail. It was too late to turn back, they thought, so they forged on. Twice they had to dismount and stand shivering in the meager shelter of a pine tree or bluff while the guide and the lancers cleared the trail.

"Thank God Lady Mercedes thought of the shovels! It's a lesson to remember," Isabella told herself. "Even little things count. Study the difficulties and obstacles, and then equip yourself to overcome them."

She looked at Beatriz and found her face pinched and her eyes wide with worry, "Are you all right, Isabella? We shouldn't have started when it looked so much like snow."

"We had to, Beatriz, and it's too late to go back now. At least Henry's men can't follow me here. And if worst comes to worst, we can stop, build a fire, and spend the night. We do have blankets."

"Yes," said Beatriz, shivering, but not from cold. She knew what would happen if they had to stay out all night in a storm such as this, and she knew that Isabella knew. Segovia and the entire region of the mountains is a white hell in the dead of winter.

Suddenly snow stopped falling. It was as though a white curtain had lifted from before their eyes. On every side they saw, under the light of the moon which now spilled from behind the clouds, a world of mountains tossing like a glittering frozen sea. From somewhere a wind sprang up and the air turned to liquid ice.

"It must be close," the guide said.

"What's he talking about, Beatriz?" asked Isabella through chattering teeth.

"A cave, Princess," interrupted the captain. 'When we find it, we'll have you where it's warm and safe."

"Is it large enough for us all and the horses?"

"It's really some sort of grotto, not a real cave, Princess. But it's deep enough to shelter us all. The horses, too. The important thing is to get out of this wind, and it's big enough for that."

"Thank God!" shouted one of the men. "I think I've located it. Yes, here it is and half stopped-up with snow."

They looked where the soldier pointed. The guide was already digging furiously, pushing aside the low-lying branches of a pine.

Inside and free of the tearing wind, Isabella thought the air felt warm, but their condensed breath and the steaming of the horses denied it. She began to feel drowsy, but she wolfed down the hot stew the captain brought her, then stretched out on the blankets with Beatriz at her side and fell asleep.

The next morning, with grim faces, they left the grotto to continue their flight. It was noon when they made a turn in the trail and saw far below the flatlands, and in the distance, so small that it seemed a city of ants, the outline of Segovia. Two lancers urged their horses through the deep snow, ordered by the captain to break through and notify Andrés Cabrera of the princess's approach.

It was dark again when Andrés met them with a litter, fresh horses and more hot food, and it was midnight when they passed over the moat and into the Alcázar. The two rivers far below were silver ribbons of ice, but the Clamores murmured in its channel. As the portcullis thundered down behind them,

Isabella wondered at the strangeness of life. Here she was again in Henry's favorite city and Joanna's one-time stronghold, but now it was hers, and therefore the sharpest thorn in Henry's side. The confessor would have an explanation, she knew, one she could easily accept. "Our Lady again," he would certainly say. Ferdinand would say, "Your incredible luck." But the woolmerchant would call it destiny.

3

"Only Our Lady is my surest refuge," mused Isabella as she contemplated the debacle brought on by their invitation to Henry to visit them. "But," she added, "the devil and bad luck so often ruin our plans." Henry had accepted their invitation with alacrity. He had seemed childishly anxious to put the past behind and to work toward peaceful solutions to their many differences. He had laughed and joked, had delighted in the madrigal singers, and since every even mildly handsome page had been kept out of sight, he had settled down to feasting and the usual enjoyments of a morally proper Spanish court.

The day Henry departed for Madrid sick and angry, something happened that made Isabella make a dangerous decision. It centered around poison, actually a possible attempt at poisoning Henry. Isabella didn't believe anyone had made such an attempt, but Henry swore they had. It happened at a banquet she and Ferdinand had given in his honor. The king had, as usual, stuffed himself with too rich food. He had grown ill, quite ill, and had been carried from the banquet hall vomiting. In an hour the court buzzed with gossip, for his retinue vowed he had been poisoned. No one suspected Isabella, not even her enemies, but in Ferdinand's case gossip took a different turn.

"It'll die down," said Ferdinand shrugging. "After all, the best physicians in the city disclaim any trace of poison. Even swine, when they overeat, can lose their dinners."

Isabella looked at him directly. "You asked me an embarrassing and insulting question once," she said carefully. "Now it's my turn to ask you one. Do you know anything about this alleged poisoning, Ferdinand?"

He looked at her balefully, unforgivingly, and her heart sank. She had touched on deep emotions—pride, outrage, hurt. "What do you think?" he said in a voice so low she hardly caught his words. "Do you dare think what your words hint?"

"I think nothing, Ferdinand. You're my husband and I love you more than life, but I have to ask. Others are asking already, many others."

He drew himself to his full height. His eyes blazed in a way she hadn't seen them blaze before. "To reply to an insult is a disgrace," he said, and then he turned upon his heel and stalked from the room. Grace was no part of his departure, for he was furious.

Their encounter made her next decision even more difficult. He was in no mood, she knew, to be asked about the bastard, if one was on the way, as malicious rumor said. Joanna swore he had gone to Valencia and had impregnated María Méndez. But Ferdinand, without being asked about his travels, had mentioned how he missed his usual journey to Valencia, especially since the weather in Barcelona had been bad during all his stay there. At first she had not put two and two together, but one night as she read her diary and came to the episode with Joanna in the convent, his pique at missing Valencia, exploded in her mind like a firecracker. Had he or hadn't he gone? Should she believe Joanna or her husband? Naturally, she believed Ferdinand. He might lie about a forged bull, which he believed had been forged for her own good as well as his; but he would not lie about another woman, because there could be no other woman. The memory of the past night's passion, even after his rage at being questioned about Henry's illness, proved that beyond any shadow of doubt. No man who deceived his wife could perform as Ferdinand performed, in a fashion so abandoned, so intimate, so fierce and also tender.

Why, then, did a tiny flicker of doubt, which she refused to recognize as doubt, keep dancing in the darkest corner of her mind? She dismissed it again and again, but it kept coming back. Then she remembered his eyes, open, deep and clear, innocent eyes as they blazed with love. No one, no human soul, could look with eyes like that and be deceptive, unfaithful. "I love you more than God," he told her, for which she had rebuked him.

They made love again that night, and his radiant charm, his sweetness in the midst of his violence, again erased suspicion from her mind. She would not think of Valencia. She was too much in love.

Then Beatriz came on another visit. She had heard from a friend in Valencia that Ferdinand had been there. The friend had seen him in church at Michaelmas. The friend was certain there could be no doubt in her mind, for she knew Ferdinand well. Still Isabella made herself dismiss the thoughts that crouched in dark corners and tried to leap out at her. Ferdinand wouldn't betray her, couldn't. Not with eyes like his when they made love.

A green Valencian scarf set in motion a plan for which she hated herself, a scarf and Ferdinand's eyes, this time focused a little too attentively on one of her ladies-in-waiting. The girl was Anna Marila Torra, a Valencian, and the daughter of a count. Isabella had seen him look at pretty women before, and had joined in light banter with him and lighter accusations. He had always laughed and said, "Pretty, yes, my love, but she's not your match in the open, so why should she be in the dark?"

Anna Maria stood at a window, gazing out over the rooftops of the city. She made a lovely picture silhouetted against the light. One dusky arm supported her as she suddenly leaned out and gazed downward, the other rested on her quite substantial hip. Beneath the low-cut bodice of her emerald gown her bosom rose high, firm, seductive, and her dark hair caught the setting sun and seemed to absorb the light. "She'll be fat and sloppy in five years," Isabella said to herself, and was ashamed.

From where she stood she could watch her husband without his knowing he was being watched. Ferdinand *was* watching Anna María fixedly. She thought the glance was more a stare and too unswerving, too speculative, too downright interested. She walked slowly to the window and chatted a moment with Anna María, contrasting the girl's dark coloring and flashing almond eyes with her own Gothic fairness. If Anna María didn't have Moorish blood, and not far back, her eyes, and skin, and hair gave every impression of it. Valencia, she reflected, had been held by Moors for centuries, and many of the best families bore the traces. She remained with Anna María long enough to give her husband ample time to make his own comparisons. Then she continued on across the room, glanced at Ferdinand with feigned surprise, for which she hated herself, and went directly to him. "I didn't expect to see you sheltering yourself in such a private spot," she said. "You're usually in the thick of things."

"I was reading," he said, "but let me tell you that you made a lovely picture there at the window, Isabella. The way the sunlight caught your hair, it made a halo! And wear green more often, dear. I like green, and it brings out new lights in your eyes. At this moment they're almost green themselves. Red hair and green silk are a delightful combination."

She didn't comment that Anna María's gown was a deeper green than hers, and neither did Ferdinand. At that moment he took her hand and drew her down on the divan beside him. As usual the touch of his flesh aroused her. He looked so much like a husband, proud of his wife's good looks and deeply in love with her, that she wavered and almost let the moment pass. She even had to look away, and her glance fell upon the volume lying open in his lap. One strong brown finger, manly with silky hairs, marked the line he had been reading.

"What's the book?" she asked casually.

"Nothing you'd like, my love. Just something I happened on in the library. It's Villasandino's poems, and you know he wrote rather erotically for your taste. I was looking for a hot passage to read to you tonight in bed just before we..." His voice trailed off and he smiled maddeningly at the flush that crept up from her bosom and suffused her face. He loved to tease her by references to personal matters, just out of earshot of others, but with people near enough to embarrass her. She never failed to look alarmed.

She took the book from his hands, careful not to lose the place, and read aloud:

> He who loves a maiden fair
> Must be readily forgiven
> Though she have a Moorish air.
> Once I saw a lovely rose
> Locked in secret, guarded well,
> Planted in a garden close
> Of the race of Ishmael.
>
> Old Mohammed, clever wight,
> Ordered maids should look like this:
> Cleanly wrought, breasts crystal-white,
> Alabaster-clear and bright.
> What was under her chemise
> (Surely what I say is right)
> Must have had that very air.
>
> Hapless sinner that I am,
> I would leave my soul unshriven
> Just to have such dainty ware.
> He who loves a maiden fair
> Must be readily forgiven
> Though she have a Moorish air.

"Strange," she remarked with no special feeling, "how men like this sort of thing. Rather sticky, I'd say, and not the best verse, either."

Ferdinand smiled and held out his hand for the book, but she held it back. "It's written by a man, Isabella, and for men. Naturally women don't enjoy it. If they did, there'd be something strange about them."

"Perhaps, but if you want love poetry why not read Macías or Iñigo de Mendoza?" Then she let her eyes go to the window again, consciously following his there. "The scarf Anna María is wearing came from Valencia," she said. "If I'd known you were going there, I'd have asked you to bring me one like it. Valencian silk is the finest."

It was said, and no one could have said it more guilelessly. She truly hated herself now, but she had to know. She was conscious that he had turned and was looking at her quizically. Their eyes met, and she thought she saw for the fraction of a second the barest flicker of suspicion. If it had been there, it vanished. It was exactly as though he had said to himself, "She's too innocent to wonder even, let alone suspect. She'll believe anything I tell her."

"I thought I mentioned I had missed my yearly vacation in Valencia," said Ferdinand. "I did. I can remember exactly when I told you."

"So you did," said Isabella. "It was while we were talking to those Germans who had come from there. I'd forgotten."

To cover her near confusion, she leafed through the volume indifferently, clucking a little at some of the titles. "When you think about it, I'd like a scarf like Anna María's," she said.

Ferdinand looked straight into her eyes. "The Torra girl does look attractive in the one she's wearing. Did you happen to ask her from what merchant she bought it? I'll order one for you immediately."

She almost gave up her plan, but again the flicker, this time of sly satisfaction in his eyes. Leisurely he stood up and cast a last glance at the window. Anna María was no longer there. "I think I'll have a ride before dinner," he said. "Don't read too much Villasandina or tonight I won't be able to contain you." Isabella wanted to stamp her foot. She had gotten nowhere really. He had said twice that he hadn't been to Valencia. Beatriz's friend and Joanna reported that he had. She decided to believe what she wanted to, what she had to. Ferdinand was telling her the truth. And yet, and yet... It was then she did stamp her foot. Why wasn't he as simple to read as the woolmerchant?

4

The news rocked Segovia and threw Spain into a ferment. Henry of Trastámara was dead. Neither faction was prepared. Ferdinand was off patrolling the frontier where the French had started another war of skirmishes. The Archbishop of Toledo had returned to his see. She found she would have to act with only her own judgment to guide her.

In less than an hour after the message reached her she had dispatched a courier to Ferdinand and another to the archbishop. "Henry is dead," she wrote, "and I shall be in Madrid by the time you receive this message. Come to me immediately, You know the need for haste."

The funeral cortège which departed from Segovia moved like no cortège ever seen in Spain. It did not move out of the city in stately cadence, draped in funereal trappings, banners trimmed with black, the members of the king's family following sedately in litters. It hurtled down the road at a full gallop, for every member of the cortège was on horseback. Isabella rode at its head on a black mare. She wore simple riding habit, as did the men and women who accompanied her. No one dared inquire about the need for so much haste. Nor did

Beatriz, who half suspected, enlighten them. Isabella's face and determined eyes discouraged questions.

No one in Madrid expected them, and the men-at-arms on the walls hesitated before they opened the gates. She found her brother's body lying in state. Frightened courtiers paced about, officers saluted, and no one knew what more to do. Beltrán de la Cueva was there, and for a moment Isabella thought he looked relieved to see her. He touched her arm, wanting to say something, but she brushed past him and understood why he coughed and withdrew.

When she reached the bier and stood looking down into the face of the dead king, Isabella said nothing, but her lips curled. Even in death the Moorish touch was there! They had embalmed him after the Eastern fashion. His sallow cheeks glowed with exaggerated color, his shaggy hair and beard, dark with henna, glistened with fragrant oil, and his flabby lips, so carefully painted, looked almost alive in an awful fetching smile. "He never looked like this alive," she mused, "but in spite of all they've done, he looks abominable. Thank God his eyes are closed! The fishlike stare is absent."

When the cardinal told her how Henry had died, she shook her head. The cardinal's eyes were sad, angry and confused. "He wouldn't tell us, Princess, who was to be his heir. I begged him to, for the sake of the realm and of his soul's, but he would say nothing to help us."

"He gave no indication at all, Your Eminence?"

"When I knelt to plead with him, Princess, he looked at me with uncertainty and turned his face to the wall. 'Let it be on their heads,' he murmured. He would say no more."

The next day Isabella's banners went draped in black beside the king's. Behind them the royal litter carrying the coffin, and after that Isabella on the black mare. The cortège, Isabella's last tribute to her half-brother, moved impressively along silent streets lined with people. No one wept except a few mountaineers with whom Henry had hunted. How could anyone weep for a king like Henry of Trastámara? And Isabella, who understood perfectly the people's mood, silently thanked them for their consideration. At least they didn't cheer. Had she not been there, she suspected, they would have cheered and danced.

After the funeral events moved with breathless speed. No sooner had she returned from the service, than she issued orders. "Conduct the king's body for interment to the city he loved best, to Segovia," she said. "Tomorrow I shall be coronated in the cathedral there. Make the arrangements, for there is not a moment to lose."

"Why tomorrow, Isabella?" Beatriz asked. "You certainly won't go through a coronation without your husband. And he can't arrive that soon."

The archbishop, who had come just in time for the funeral, answered for her. "We cannot wait, Lady Beatriz. A week, nay even a day's delay might undo us. The princess must mount the throne before Henry's followers can gather their wits and try to prevent it. For this reason we cannot even wait for the arrival of the Prince of Aragón."

"It frightens me," said Beatriz. "Suppose Villena arrives while a coronation is in progress?"

"Villena is dead, Lady Beatriz," said the cardinal. "He died strangely, like his brother Pedro Girón. An ailment in the throat. And men say..." he glanced hastily at Isabella and looked away.

"And men say that I was at my prayers again, Your Grace?" she asked.

"Yes, Princess, they do. They say, too, that from the moment the king received the news of Villena's death, he too, sickened. It is this fear of you that now keeps Henry's nobles silent."

The archbishop rubbed his hands together in ill-concealed delight and opened his lips to speak. Isabella snatched the words from his mouth. "And so, while they're in hiding and undecided, we must strike. Yes, the coronation will take place tomorrow, Beatriz. It is imperative."

"But what of Ferdinand?" insisted Beatriz, fearful of what he, if so slighted, might do. "What will you say to him, Isabella? How will you salve his pride?"

Isabella smiled a peculiar smile. "I'll tell him that it was expedient, Beatriz. Can Ferdinand object to expediency?"

Hundreds of carpenters worked all night in the central plaza of Segovia. A tall pavilion rose in the center of the square. Rich awnings covered it, but they had been drawn back to let the people see all that happened. Isabella wanted as many people as possible to witness her coronation. Above her, as if suspended in the morning sunlight like a purple cloud, hung the canopy. She sat like an empress, like Cleopatra in all her glory, beneath it.

"She looks like a queen already," thought Beatriz. "And how well she knows her subjects! She's certainly providing a spectacle today. I didn't dream she had so many jewels."

Fifes and kettledrums made the air vibrate. The multitude roared "Castile! Castile for King Ferdinand and Queen Isabella, proprietress of these kingdoms!"

Everyone saw her anointed with the sacred oil from the ancient Visigothic crisma; everyone saw the archbishop place upon her head the ancient crown of Castile and León; everyone saw her descend from the throne, mount a white stallion, housed in the richest trappings set with jewels. At her side marched the grandees of Spain, and before her, as escort, that same Gutierre de Cárdenas who had ridden with Ferdinand when he crossed the mountains and penetrated Henry's lines to meet her in Valladolid.

Cárdenas marched proudly, carrying before him a huge naked sword. He held it like a cross, poignard upright, glittering with rubies in the sunlight. This was the symbol of Castilian power, the mighty, the ancient sword carried in coronation before the kings of Castile for generations the sword of justice. As it passed, Beatriz crossed herself. No queen had ever presumed to so much. The significance of it shocked, yet pleased the people. Isabella was the first queen in history to order it carried before her in a coronation. In so doing she proclaimed herself alone as ruler of Castile.

The ceremony progressed to its climax. Great nobles, even the majority of Henry's supporters, came and knelt at her feet to offer fealty. Before the sun set couriers galloped along every highway with the news that Castile had lost a king and gained a queen. Isabella could imagine what the news would precipitate. Joanna and young Pedro of Castile would make a dash for Portugal, taking the poor little bastard with them; nobles who held titles and estates unlawfully under Henry would fortify their castles and defy the new queen; the thousands of robber barons, grown fat on pillage and tolls, would hole up in their aeries in the hills and refuse her homage; and the kings of Portugal and France would wonder if the time was ripe for invasion before she could consolidate her realm.

On the ride back to Madrid, however, hope rose. In her retinue rode most of the very nobles who had supported Henry. As she traversed the road, others fell into the cavalcade and sued for peace. Among the former enemies rode Beltrán de la Cueva, no longer an enemy but her sworn vassal. She wondered what he was thinking, riding along and chatting so amiably with people who had hated him and always would. How strange, how hypocritical that he could ride so calmly, knowing how many of these people loathed him and would like to see him stripped of his honors and even dead. What would Joanna say if she could see him, not that she loved him now. Beltrán still boasted, Isabella's friends told her, of how he had turned her away when she came limping on a broken ankle after her escape from the palace of the Bishop of Seville. "Let old spindly-legs seek aid somewhere else. I'm done with her!" he had chortled to his companions that sad night for Joanna.

Beatriz seemed to read her thoughts. "Joanna wouldn't like this, would she? Today you have her throne, her realm, her subjects, and the man she loved the most, and he's at your beck and call."

"I know," said Isabella. "And knowing is sweet. I know also that the handsome Beltrán has had his day, even if he hasn't realized it. He won't get away unscathed, I promise you."

"Enjoy yourself while you can, Isabella."

"You mean till Ferdinand arrives and demands an accounting?"

"Don't you think he has the right?"

"No doubt he does, Beatriz, and he shall have it. I'll await him in *my* Segovia and I believe he'll see *my* expediency and accept it for what it is."

6

Ferdinand arrived in Segovia and did not smile. In the audience chamber he found his wife hearing cases. He managed to keep his face stiff and carefully composed like a man who has thought long as to how he will act and what he will say. When they were alone he stood and stared at her for a long time balefully. At last, almost too calmly he spoke. "You might have warned me, Isabella. I had the news from the archbishop two days after your coronation."

"Strange," said Isabella, her composure shaken. "I sent two couriers to you on the day we left for Madrid. That was four whole days before the coronation. I shall certainly inquire about their failure to reach you, although I'm beginning to suspect why they didn't."

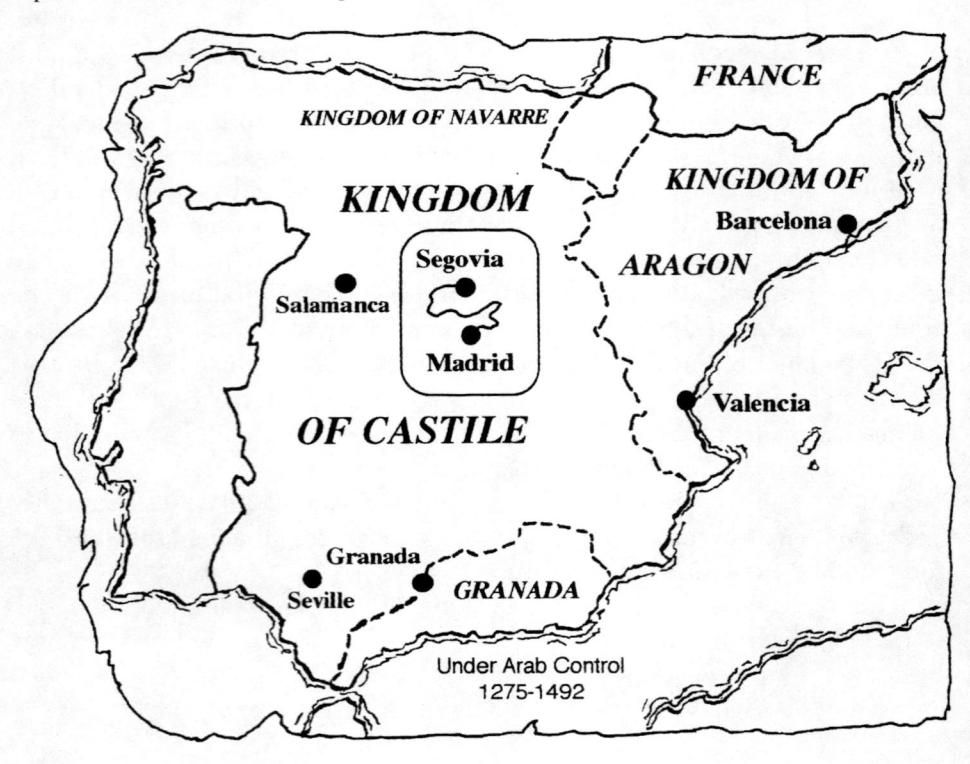

She suspected her own nobles and she didn't like it. They, as well as the archbishop, hadn't wanted Ferdinand crowned beside her. They preferred that Spain see her crowned as queen alone. Later she could welcome her husband to rule beside her. It was the last time, she swore, that anyone would interfere with her life. The time had come to show them all their place, even the Archbishop of Toledo.

It proved once more that in some circles they still considered Ferdinand a foreigner. It gave her cause for thought. He had a right to believe she had purposely prevented his coming to Madrid, so as to be crowned without him. It hadn't been that way at all, of course, and she would swear it, but Ferdinand would be hard to convince. It's what he would have done in her shoes, she knew.

Ferdinand looked grim and gave no hint that he had accepted the explanation. "No couriers reached me," he snapped. "But that is nothing as compared with what you did in Madrid. To have the sword carried before you without me beside you! What are you trying to do, Isabella? Have I no rights in Castile?"

"You have the rights you agreed upon at the betrothal. You can hardly have forgotten the text of that agreement."

"But I thought..."

"Did you, Ferdinand? Did you believe, even for a moment, that I'd forget? You married the Princess of Castile, but you did so under the agreement that you would have no authority in Castile over hers."

"Aren't we equal, then?"

"Not here, Ferdinand. You are not a Castilian. I think that my people love you, but not enough to receive you as their ruler. I am Castile and León; you are still Aragón. Even so, if you had come to Madrid, we would have been crowned together."

"Then why didn't you wait?"

"There was no time, and I am sure you can imagine why."

Ferdinand's frown deepened. "But how do you think I feel, Isabella? What will *my* people think when they hear? What will my father and the nobles of Aragón say?"

It did little good when she pointed out that King John and the Great Council of Aragón had read and signed the wedding contract. It enraged him even more when she told him that she had made certain changes and additions which she believed would please him.

"I suppose you have already framed the terms," he said, trying not to smile. "Isabella, you are a queen. You'll be invincible in spite of your forthrightness. Open your desk and read me the new terms which I will like so much."

As she unrolled the parchment and read she watched his face from time to time and was glad to see the lines of displeasure fade. He actually admired her grudgingly. "In all privileges, writs, laws, and on all the coinage," she read, "the name of Ferdinand goes first, followed by that of his wife; but all castles and fortresses shall be held in the name of the queen. and the treasurers and accountants will swear in her name in administering the monies of the land; the appointments of bishops will be made by both king and queen; when Ferdinand and Isabella are together, they will administer the law together, and when they are apart, each will administer it where each is, whether in Castile or in Aragón."

He took the parchment and ran his eyes quickly over it, "It is better than it was," he admitted sheepishly.

Isabella was disappointed. The terms were so much more favorable to him than the former pact that she had expected more warmth in his response. "We need no written document between us, Ferdinand. I had this one drawn to satisfy the grandees who have been loyal to me. In time you'll have greater equality in Castile, perhaps even complete equality. But not now."

Ferdinand understood. Her people feared that if he shared the power equally with her, Aragonese would be swarming into lucrative posts. Understandable, his expression said, but his disappointment showed nevertheless. He couldn't keep it from his eyes, and the scowl turned to petulance.

Isabella tried again. "Tell me this, Ferdinand. If it were changed around, what would the nobles of Aragón say if you made me your equal in Aragón, allowing me to bring my people into their country and garrison their forts?'

"I can see all that, Isabella, but..."

"Isn't there something you haven't thought of?" she asked. "We have one child, a daughter. Suppose the child on the way should die and there should be no others. Suppose this daughter married a foreign prince. Would you want him to rule Castile as well as Aragón after you and I had died? I can see you wouldn't. And yet this is exactly what you are asking *me* and *my* people to agree to. Think of it in connection with your own daughter. Spain's rule—and I mean Aragón's as well as Castile's—would pass into the hands of our daughter's foreign husband and his people. You see? What we do will set a precedent."

When she had finished, Ferdinand sat forward, head resting on palms, elbows set belligerently on the table. It was very difficult for him to accept the fact that his wife had thought of things he hadn't. He didn't know her at all, he suddenly realized. She was a person of depths he had never dreamed of. How had he so misunderstood her, so underestimated her? In her he saw a little of his own mother—the same sweep of unopposable determination; the same ability to act on the spur of the moment and wisely in emergencies; the same ruthlessness when it came to the defense of the family. But in Isabella there was more. Could it be her fear of God and a piety deeper than any he had encountered? How wise he had been not to tell her about the second illegitimate baby. The thought of her reaction sent a cold chill up his spine.

Suddenly she laid a hand on his arm. "There's one other point," she said, and something in the way she said it and the hurt in her eyes brought his attention into abrupt and careful focus. His eyes fell before hers as she said, "You see, I know about the woman and the child in Valencia."

He raised his eyes at last, and in them instead of contrition she expected, she saw rage and embarrassment. "How long have you known?" he hissed.

"Joanna told me that night in the Convent of the Holy Child."

"Then you knew the day you asked about the green silk scarf," he said, and his face was white. "You let me lie to you!"

"You didn't have to lie. I would have understood, or at least, I would have known how to forgive."

He shook his head in defeat. "You may suppose you would have, Isabella, but not you! You'll never understand!"

"Not completely, I suppose. I hate deceit, But I would have reached an understanding with myself."

Ferdinand was silent, and she knew he was collecting his thoughts. Finally he said, "Isabella, I love you very much. I love you as I have never loved before, and I shall always love you most."

"Then why...?"

"Why others? I don't know. Honestly, I don't. They mean nothing really. Remember, when you think of them, that it's you I love."

"And I love you Ferdinand. Therefore, I shan't ever pry again. This I promise. But if in the years to come when you must do this thing again, keep it from me as you've tried to keep this time. Some things are better when not known."

He felt relief flowing through him. She didn't know about the latest bastard. Maybe now she'd never know. At least she wouldn't be trying to find out.

She laid a hand on his arm, and felt the usual carnal thrill. She smiled and kissed him. And Ferdinand slapped his thigh with his gloves and laughed. Her smile, like his laugh were the intimate and tender things they shared, the hot love that couldn't be infringed upon when they were touching or very near one another. Later, as that night they made love; she remembered Yehuda Halevi and smiled wryly. "Yea, between the bitter and the sweet standeth my heart. The gall of parting, and the honey of the kisses."

5

Destiny

1

As Isabella went to mass one morning a hermit called out to her. "The Crescent still flies in Granada. How long, Highness?"

"First things first, my friend," she replied. "I haven't forgotten Granada, and the time will come, But not now.'

She understood the hermit's feeling. Granada had to fall. As long as the Moorish kingdom lasted, the Muslim world had an open gateway into the heart of Christendom. Through that gateway hordes of Berbers, led by Arab chieftains, had once swept the length of Spain to the Pyrenees, and had crossed the mountains into France. For centuries afterward her people had warred against them, slowly pushing them back, until at last Islam held only a small kingdom between the mountains and the sea. No Spanish king had been able to take Granada. There, secure, they had laid the foundations of an impenetrable state, small but powerful, forced to pay tribute to the Christian kings of Spain, yet resentful and restive. Presently they were defiant. Men in power in Muslim Spain still dreamed of the day when Islam would preach a holy war and once again make the Iberian Peninsula a center of Mohammedan life. Constantinople had fallen to Islam not long before, when Isabella was three. She still recalled tales of Saracen atrocities. People remembered the East and shivered.

"First things first," she told herself. "Granada must wait until Ferdinand and I can consolidate the realms we hold. I shan't forget the Moors, but they will have to wait." When she allowed herself to dream of the crusade, she would see herself riding in full armor at the head of a great Christian host against that last stronghold of the infidel. "Not now," she thought, "but the day will dawn when Crescent and Cross face one another, and for a moment the naked body of Fejjuan the Berber arose before her, reeking of wine and hashish. Then the vision of Alfonso, gasping out his life in a dark room in Cardeñosa with a black crescent in his armpit. After that Henry and his abominations with Moors. She crossed herself and cursed Islam, wishing she could have a crusade preached tomorrow.

Then reality returned. The imminent need was peace and order at home. Sections of the country still refused to recognize her authority. The robber barons, fattened on brigandage, still pillaged outlying towns and made the roads unsafe. Ancient and evil laws still existed. She had refused at first to believe that some of the nobles still honored the *jus primæ noctis*. This law, which was truly no law, but an ancient custom, made law by force; this law of the first night, gave any lord the right to possess a peon girl on her wedding night before her husband possessed her. But the peasants were rising against it. That village of Fuenteovejuna had killed its lord for his rape of vassal women, and she and Ferdinand had judged the entire village guiltless. But as long as lords like that lustful Comendador still ruled, and bandits were at large, the Moorish question would have to wait.

Interminable feuds raged between the nobles and battles involving thousands of men were fought. In the cities new and more terrible pogroms against the Jews kept occurring, turning entire cities into armed camps. The state of the royal treasury appalled her. Henry had virtually depleted it. People still preferred barter as the safest means of trade, distrusting the coinage of the realm. Even the reliable coins she and Ferdinand issued were suspect, and the people continued to barter. No wonder the French and Germans sneered, and called Spain a land of barbarians.

Worse still, the clergy had reached such a nadir that people were avoiding priests in the street like they avoided black cats. Thousands of priests and lesser clergy were still illiterate and so corrupt that many people would not confess. Priests, everyone knew, kept concubines after all she and Ferdinand had tried to do to stop it. Gossip about convents and monasteries still rivaled the most pornographic novels. Not for nothing did sculptors carve beneath the seats of choirs the obscene little scenes that caused so much laughter.

True or not, the scandal about the Bishop of Seville and Queen Joanna persisted. The high clergy was wealthy beyond reason. Some still owned tracts of land as extensive as the richest nobles. The Archbishop of Toledo kept a zoological garden and fed meat to the lions and leopards while Spaniards lived on vegetables and olive oil. People still talked of one banquet given by another archbishop at which trays laden with jewelry were passed, and the ladies present were allowed to choose necklaces and bracelets worth a fortune.

The immorality of the court polluted the lower levels of society and corrupted the populace. People no longer batted an eye at the mention of royal adultery or Moorish perversions. They smirked and shrugged or kept silent.

And over all this weakness and corruption hovered again the threat of war with Portugal. King Alfonso was raising a great army. Isabella's spies informed her that Joanna and her daughter were in Lisbon and the king Alfonso had betrothed himself to Joanna's child, his own niece. Married to the child, he could lay claim to Castile, for Joanna, and her supporters swore that Henry had, at the very last, named her his daughter and rightful heir.

Isabella and Ferdinand did what they had to do. They summoned the grandees to Segovia for urgent meetings and borrowed so much money that both were dazed.

One afternoon, dejected at the seeming hopelessness of their prospects, they returned to their quarters to rest. There they found Father de Coca. When he suggested prayer, Ferdinand shook his head. "Let's plan, Father. Let's pray later." And even Isabella was glad to say a short prayer and return to the many problems that faced them.

The confessor rose from his knees and dusted his cassock. His luminous eyes gazed first at Isabella and then at Ferdinand, and when he spoke they realized that he agreed. The time had come for talk and plans.

"Never forget, Highness," he said, looking at Isabella, "what strength lies in Spain and her people. This land and its people will become a nation of consequence in the world. Portugal will not stand in the way forever."

Isabella sighed. "I wish I could be as certain as you seem to be, Father. Look at what we face. Nobles rotten and corrupt, feuding among themselves and wasting their substance and strength, when every ounce of both is needed. I wouldn't repeat it outside this room, Father, but to you and my husband I must say that I am discouraged. All I have to go on is faith."

"Not all the nobles are evil, Highness. What of the Manriques? The Cabreras? All the others who have not fallen into evil ways?"

Isabella and Ferdinand nodded, but continued to look dejected.

"And the people," continued de Coca, warming to his subject, "In the people lies the hope of the nation. Have you thought of this people and how strangely strong it is? No other race is like ours. What other has lived for nearly a thousand years under a state of alert for fear of infidel invasion? Picture what this means. Think of it! Eight centuries of wondering if the Cross would win or lose! Eight centuries in a state of arms! Yes, Spain is unique, my children." He glanced hopefully at their faces and continued. "I have seen the French and the English, yes, and the Burgundians and Italians. They rally to the battle cry, but they are never prepared. Their kings maintain mercenary armies, of course, but in times of peace these armies are reduced and sometimes even disbanded. Kings are fearful of large armies in times of peace."

Ferdinand laughed derisively. "Where are the Spanish armies, Father? Do you think Spain is prepared to fight?"

"Yes, my son, I think so. Go to the castle of any noble in this land. What do you see? Men in arms, weapons, and the best horses in the world. Even in peace, Highness. Our people learned something from all the dark centuries of warfare and occupation. Why, I'll venture to say that there isn't a single gentleman, even among the commoners, who doesn't have a warhorse and a few retainers. At the first trumpet call an army would materialize."

"It takes a farmer to keep a soldier," said Isabella. "And the plight of the farmer is grave."

"You should have said it takes two farmers to keep one man in arms," interrupted Ferdinand. "Neither of you has lived and traveled with an army, I have. If you don't fill the soldiers' bellies they ravage the land, and they don't care a *maravedí* whether it's friend or enemy they pillage."

Father de Coca raised his hand. "And yet, here in Castile the plight of the laborer and the farmer is not as serious as elsewhere. We have lived through a terrible civil war and now face invasion from Portugal, and yet not many have starved nor are many likely to. In even the worst times we produce foodstuffs, for the land is good and the climate favorable. Starvation rarely has affected Spain."

Isabella had heard almost as much as she cared to. "Father, you yourself have complained that the people barter and spurn the coin of the kingdom. What of that?"

"That is my point, Highness. They have the wherewithal to barter. That is not starvation. We grow the necessities. We can continue to do without the luxuries."

"Pride goeth before a fall," said Ferdinand dryly.

"That is true, my son. But my pride in the people of Castile is justified. You said a moment ago that every soldier needed one or more farmers to support him. We have those farmers. Spaniards have always respected their soil and the men who worked it. It is almost a cult as strong as the old pagan love of the Earth-Mother. Everyone knows the value of agriculture and the rural life. Our poets, from the time of the Romans, have glorified it. No one scorns the farmer, and the farmer knows this. And the Spaniard of today loves the land just as the Roman Spaniards loved it and as the Moorish Spaniards love it now. This love is the strength of Spain and is as valuable to us as our natural resources themselves."

They had to agree, but there was more than the problem of supplies. Could she and Ferdinand cope with the people? Henry had certainly failed. The people were headstrong and egocentric. Would the people believe in them?

The confessor read their thoughts. "The Spaniard is a difficult quantity to measure, whether Castilian, Navarese or Aragonese," he said. "Just as each individual differs from his neighbor, so Spain differs from other countries. I have traveled in Italy. There man has planned his life around the cultural and practical—economics, trade, the accumulation of material wealth, science, art. Diplomacy is stronger than integrity or valor. Religion is *pro forma* in Italy, at least in the higher strata of society. Italians strive for what is new and improved. If they have any national spirit, I haven't seen it. They pay lip service to patriotism and the Holy Faith as long as these are profitable.

Ferdinand nodded in agreement. After all he ruled the Kingdoms of Naples and Sicily. The confessor continued. "We hear much, too, of the French and the rise of a strong central power among them. How well their monarch catches the drift of things out there in the world beyond our mountains! With Paris as a hub he has, by deceit and lies, brought France to heel. Like the Italians, from whom he learned a great deal, King Louis has seized control by the new mercurial diplomacy. Like them, too, he builds upon what he considers safe, sound, materialistic, and this in spite of his vaunted prayers to holy images."

Ferdinand did not smile when he said, "The world has changed, Father. The Italians and the French are ahead of us."

"But one can hardly admire them," said de Coca.

"Whether we admire them or not," said Ferdinand, "we must admit they are forging ahead. The whole world is in a state of flux, and the old values of our ancestors are dying. Reason will triumph over faith, although I like to believe that faith and reason can live side by side."

Isabella watched the confessor's face. He could hardly contain himself. "Spain will not change easily, my children," he cried. "Consider your people for a moment. What a strange amalgamation of emotion and common sense! The Spaniard cannot now, nor has he ever in his history, been able to see himself as a member of national collectivity. The world revolves around him. The earth is his satellite and he is the center of his world. He can no more conceive of his place in the scheme of a central state than he can understand the mysteries of the Trinity. He refuses to conform to rules, but bows before tradition which he fails to recognize as the most exacting of masters. He will fight, he will kill, he will die to escape regimentation of any sort. From region to region he differs radically, nay from village to village in the same region, and even from neighborhood to neighborhood, and from street to street."

Ferdinand didn't understand. "Aren't you arguing in circles, Father? First you tell us the nation is strong, and then that its people are so egocentric that no one can rule them. How can a nation be strong if its people rebel against centralization?"

"You and the queen represent the one star Spaniards will follow. They believe that God Almighty pitied Spain under Henry's rule and removed him. They believe that He placed you here to lead them to dominion, power and security. You will notice that I said 'lead them.' They revel in a great leader and will follow him anywhere. Spanish political emotion is violent and terrible, and also poignant. How they despised King John and hated Henry! And how they love you both! This is the Spanish way—strong hates and strong loves. You must profit by this and you must lead. To understand them will be difficult, if not impossible; to guide and control them will demand divine assistance."

"I hope we can lead them against the Portuguese," said Isabella.

"You will, daughter. They have faith in you and your husband. The history of Spain has been a long and tragic series of illusions and disillusions; but always the illusions, or better said, the dreams, the faith, have carried the nation forward. Have you ever thought of this as a kind of sickness? I have. I like to fancy that all Spaniards are ill with a very peculiar and strictly Spanish malady. Like epilepsy it can impair thought and vision, but, as in the case of epilepsy, it often goes hand in hand with wisdom."

"I'm not clear as to what you mean by a sickness, Father," said the king.

"The sickness of Spain, or of every man and woman in Spain, is the need for action," said the confessor. "Without action, without an inner and imperative drive, stagnation occurs and Spaniards vegetate. They don't turn to concentration or philosophy. They vegetate. But give Spain a problem requiring action, heroic, mighty, epic action to survive or improve herself, and she is at her best. History proves this repeatedly and conclusively. Without this refusal to submit, to act in the face of no matter how great opposition, without this intense something inside us that makes us glow, we should long since have become a part of Africa.

"When the Moors defeated the forces of King Roderick, they thought to see Spain collapse like a mined wall. They destroyed the kingdom of the Visigoths, our ancestors, and made Spain an oriental caliphate. They occupied the entire peninsula, except that thin line in ancient Asturias. Europe beyond the Pyrenees trembled. The Crescent flew from the French border to Gibraltar. And then something happened. We call it the Reconquest."

"But," said Isabella, "there was divine intervention in the Reconquest. God sent St. James to save us."

"Of course he did, daughter. But there was something more than divine assistance in our Reconquest. St. James did appear on a white horse. Thousands saw him bearing the banners of our Faith against the infidel hosts. Without heaven's help our people might have succumbed. But they had the saint, he inspired them, he showed them that God and His Son remembered them. St. James was the leader who had come to show them the way, the chance. Once they understood, they rose to a man and fought their way southward. They carried on a crusade for all those long dark centuries. They had the stimulus which is the panacea for the ancient Spanish sickness of which I spoke. Spain must have a stimulus, and if very soon she does not receive a new stimulus, she'll vegetate again as during the past two reigns. The Spaniard must be up and doing.

"I recall a passage from Pérez de Guzmán's *Generations and Likenesses* that is apropos," said Isabella. "You must remember it, too, Father. 'Castile is better for winning something new than for keeping what she has; for often she herself destroys the very thing she has in her possession.'"

Isabella looked at her husband and wondered if he understood the Castilian mind, so different from the Aragonese. "I see exactly what you mean, Father," she went on. "Do you, Ferdinand? No? Then let me explain it by my own experience. When I was a little girl I used to play in the sand along the River Arevillo with Beatriz and my brother Alfonso. It would take us all day sometimes to build a great castle, and our minds seethed with plans. Here we would place a barbican; there the soldiers would man the drawbridge and the portcullis; in the courtyard would walk fine ladies and gentlemen; battles would rage along the walls. I can see Beatriz now, beside herself, and Alfonso so excited that he stammered. Then when the last crenel had been outlined and the last embrasure in the tower made with the poke of a finger, we would stand back and survey our handiwork. We never played war games and peopled the fortresses with dolls. The fun was in the building, not in the finished product."

"Exactly," cried de Coca, clapping his hands. "You've described the Castilians perfectly, even the Aragonese, I suspect. The fun *is* in the building. The Spaniard must be a building. This is the secret of his success. You and the king, daughter, must provide a castle to build, a castle of state. Better still, provide a crusade. Granada still stands as Islam's last bulwark in the West."

Isabella's eyes glowed. "Someday, Father. For the present we face the rebel nobles and the Portuguese, if they invade Castile. But I shan't forget the Moors. You know my reasons for remembering them."

"I do, daughter. Defeat the nobles first. Then summon the people to holy war. Under its impetus you can build a great nation on the ruins left by the last half century of misrule. The people will follow you. Their faith in you both will sustain them."

"Have they a faith?" asked Ferdinand, oblivious to his wife's sudden optimism. "Look at the court, or what Henry left of it."

"Yes," said Isabella sadly. "And add to that the convents and what we know of then. I wonder, too, if there's enough faith in anything to sustain our people."

"All Spaniards have a faith," said de Coca proudly. "Sometimes it isn't the kind of faith that guides to good conduct, although Holy Church has tried to guide, God knows. Spaniards go to church, they believe in the dogma with blind faith, they fear hell and long for heaven, they are Christians, but alas they are Spaniards, too. The Spaniard's faith is a faith of 'me,' of the individual. He isn't a part of his faith; it is a part of him. He breathes it in like air and makes it an integral part of his body. Take, for example, the religious ecstasy seen in processions during Holy Week. The men chosen to represent the Savior feel they *are* the Savior. I have talked to them. They insist upon the scourge, the crown of thorns, the sponge soaked in vinegar, the insult of being spat upon. They beg for even greater torments. Not long ago in Toledo I heard the confession of one who persuaded his friends to nail him to a cross. The man died, daughter, from the shock and the cruel wounds of the nails. Faith like that is more than blind; it is all-consuming, frightening, terrible, and yet wonderful. You, as rulers, must channel this fierce faith into more Christian streams."

Isabella's eyes darkened. Then she said, "And yet my people are touched by the fatalism of the East."

"Another aspect of the many-faceted Spanish character," said the confessor. "Without the explosive stimulus of faith, the Spaniard might indeed drift completely into fatalism. The Moors in eight hundred years have left us that unfortunate heritage. Who among us has not quoted those lines that seem so suited to a thousand daily problems:

> Would you escape from all worry?
> Then let the ball roll on;
> For whatever comes from God's hand
> Will return to it anon.

"What a revelatory quatrain, Highness! Even God is linked with fatality in the minds of the people."

For several moments the confessor sat quite still allowing his thoughts to wander far. At last he leaned forward and placed his right hand on Isabella's arm and his left on Ferdinand's. "My children," he said, "you have in Spain a motly aggregation of ideals, illusions, superstitions, pride of race, suspicion of foreigners, and fear of change. But never forget courage and faith, and the will to conquer. With God's help and your own wisdom and energy you can make this land come into its own."

"Castilians," reflected Isabella, "are as stubborn as iron mules and much harder to convince." She wondered what luck she would have in recruiting in Soria, a town as Castilian as the granite peaks of the Sierra de Mondayo towering seven thousand feet into the cold air. If it was no better than in the last town, King Alfonso and his Portuguese army might invade the country with little if any opposition. Her recruiting was yielding meager fruit so far.

Soria and its people were the hub of the valleys of the Duero and the Ebro, but they were cut off by mountains from the rest of Castile and had little interest in any but their own isolated universe.

Her retainers could give her no sensible counsel, but one and all they warned her not to penetrate into the fastnesses of the Sierra de Mondayo. Of course, nothing could dissuade her and so it was that she found herself descending into the valley in which she could see Soria In the distance. She was beginning to wonder if this visit would be as futile and the last. How could she persuade them to fight the Portuguese?

The moment she entered the city, its frenzied excitement impinged upon her. Lines of people on foot and on horseback moved out of the gates and took the road into the sierra. She hailed a priest. "Where is everyone going, Father?"

"To San Pedro Manrique for the fire-walking," he said. She saw his eyes go wide and knew that he had heard of her presence in the district. He had just realized who she was.

"Have the nobles gone there, too, Father?"

"By tomorrow, Highness, there'll be scarcely a soul in Soria. Yes, the nobles have gone, and if you hope to speak to them before they return next week, you'll have to journey to San Pedro."

"How far is it, Father?"

"Nearly thirty miles from here at the very border of Navarre. And the road is poor. Better wait until they return, Highness. But if you must go on, you'll find the great men and their families at the castle of Don Agapito Manrique which stands on a mountain above the village. There they'll stay until after the fire-walking."

"What is fire-walking, Father?"

The priest seemed reluctant to speak. "They walk upon a bed of incandescent coals. I have seen them do it, although I do not approve. They stink of the old gods of these mountains, even of witchcraft. I take a serious view of such rituals, although I know that many priests laugh them off. That's why I never go, Highness."

"What does the bishop of the district say?" asked Isabella.

"Like the others, His Grace sees no harm in it. But I hate it because it is unchristian. All of these things—maypoles in the village square, the bonfires they build and leap through on St. John's Eve, bathing in the fields on the dawn of Midsummer's Day, and the gathering of medicinal herbs wet with magic dew. I say they stink of witchcraft, and if the people who play at these things knew what they meant in the olden times, they'd abjure them. Why, I know an old beldam up on Mount Urbion who vows that in her grandsire's time it was not Our Lord and His Holy Mother men honored, but Diana and the old gods, some of whom predate the Romans who once held Spain."

Isabella saw in the priest a garrulous country bigot, but she had to admit there was some virtue in what he was saying. People easily move from what appears to be no more than childish superstition into more dangerous practices. There was more and more devil-worship reported in remote areas. The simple priest understood this danger better than his sophisticated bishop,

"Tell me about the fire-walking, Father," she repeated. "I may decide to travel to San Pedro Manrique to see this spectacle."

The priest warmed to his subject, although he still feigned reluctance. "They bring in oak logs from the slopes of the sierra, Highness. Oak logs, mind you. None other will do. I see you're wondering why this is, and I'll inform you. Oak was sacred to a pagan deity, to Jupiter. Then they pile the wood into a mound of logs as tall as a man. Inside they heap brush and faggots, and when it's set on fire, the flames shoot high into the air and the heat is terrific. It burns for hours, and when the fire subsides, it leaves a heap of fiery ash and charcoal. Men beat this with boughs and rake it into a bed outlined in stone and prepared to receive it, The bed is seven or eight feet long and a yard wide, and the ash is six inches deep, It glows like the sun and emits blue and white tongues of flame. I've stood as far as twenty paces away and have had to protect my face from the heat. The men who rake the coals have singed hair and scorched eyebrows."

"Do you expect me to believe, Father, that anyone can walk over an expanse of hot ash like that? What's the trick behind it?"

"Highness, I've witnessed it many times—that is, before I gave up going. The villagers swear they have Our Lady's help and protection, that only the people of San Pedro can walk the fiery way, and that outlanders who try are always burned and not only do the people hereabouts walk the fiery way, sometimes they even carry others on their shoulders. Oh, it's all very strange and terrifying. And it's as old as time. No one can remember when there were no fire-walkers there on St. John's Eve. People come from all over the region. And that's why you see the population of Soria is now en route to the sierra."

Isabella decided that she would have to go to San Pedro Manrique. A week's wait was out of the question. Besides, if all the important men were at Don

Agapito's castle, it would save much time and expense if she could find them together. Ferdinand, recruiting to the west, would certainly expect her to go, and go she would.

As she and her retinue neared the village that evening Isabella heard the piercing scream of an instrument unfamiliar to her, even as the wild melody of mountain bagpipes and the hoarse little drums of the region made her ears ring. It was not difficult to imagine a night a thousand years ago and people of the highlands assembling to do honor to ancient earth gods. The priest's words returned, and she crossed herself. A strange custom; perhaps a dangerous custom.

Don Agapito's household was amazed and startled when the Queen of Spain materialized out of the shadows and asked for shelter. Her presence in the two valleys had been the subject of much discussion, but no one expected her to penetrate so far into the mountains to recruit on the very perimeter of her domain. She must be desperate to come so far. Don Agapito sensed how tired she was. He wondered what she was thinking of festivities at a time when war threatened the realm at any time. Her lancers seemed even more weary.

He listened gravely to what she told him of the danger from Portugal. He hadn't heard, he told her, that King Alfonso had gone so far as to amass troops at the border. The matter *was* serious. But when he learned she had come to ask for men in Soria and San Pedro at the height of the feast of St. John's Day, he tried to dissuade her.

"Wait at least until tomorrow, Highness;" he begged, at a loss as to how to act with a queen who was a girl. "Tomorrow is St. John's Day. The ceremonies will be over then and the men will have had time to sleep and clear their minds. Don't speak tonight. This is a strange celebration, Highness, one not likely to please you. Some of the more orthodox of the clergy object to it, even if the bishop considers it harmless. 'Let men beget sons on St. John's Eve, so long as they beget them on their wives,' he says. 'What harm is there in that?' Yes, leave the people to their rites tonight, Highness. Better still, return to Segovia and wait until I, with the knights of the area, can come to you there for a parley. I expect we can recruit a good many soldiers, and in any case you can count upon me and my castle's garrison."

"How many men do you have, Don Agapito?"

"One hundred," replied Don Agapito proudly. "One hundred of the finest in Spain."

Isabella looked straight into his eyes. "We had counted upon a thousand from this area, Don Agapito."

"A thousand! Holy Mary! We couldn't raise a thousand, Highness. What of the harvests, the land, the herds?"

"If I don't raise the necessary levies," said Isabella firmly, "the land will long lie fallow and there will be no herds. The Portuguese will drive them off. On paper King Alfonso has already apportioned all Castile and León to his nobility. Your own castle and all your holdings will belong to a Portuguese count whose name has slipped my mind. You're not in a position. Don Agapito, to think of lands and herds. You face invasion."

Don Agapito paled. The mention of his land already assigned to a Portuguese nobleman hit the mark. He excused himself and held a hasty consultation with his neighbors from castles scattered across the mountains. After a while she saw them coming toward her across the room. On every face she saw alarm and anger. Her retainers looked frightened.

"Highness," said Don Agapito, who acted as spokesman, "my friends agree with me that you should speak to the people tonight in the public square. You'll have an opportunity to be heard by important nobles, as well as by the elders of the villages whose influence counts heavily in these mountains."

He looked cooperative, but the others looked askance. "They think I'm too young to rule," she almost said out loud. "I see it in their faces."

Isabella smiled. Let the personal holdings of men be placed in jeopardy and they would seize their swords. Ferdinand would be proud of her when he heard her stratagem. She had paid a spy very well indeed to secure the report about the apportionment. It was proving to be money well spent.

Don Agapito continued. "You have our sympathy, Highness. And the nobility and the people have heard that you are saintly. But do not expect too much. King Henry had evil rumors circulated, and these rumors went even beyond San Pedro. And there's more. Mountaineers are free men and independent. They may refuse to help."

Isabella thanked them graciously, but her mind shifted elsewhere. A sudden idea was forming. She needed to talk to someone who could tell her more about the fire-walking. Perhaps she could turn it to advantage. She sent for Father Pinedo, Don Agapito's chaplain, and asked him to tell her everything he knew about the ceremony. "Do the fire-walkers treat their feet in some way to harden them? Do you, as an educated man, see anything supernatural in the act? Any spell? Any chance that people are made to think they see what they do not?"

The priest was straightforward and intelligent. "No, Highness," he said. "The feet of the *mondidas*, the chosen virgins who walk in the fiery ash, are at soft as your own. And the men who follow them no different from other men. You asked about artificial protection. There is no manner of curing the skin to protect it from intense heat, I believe."

"Before we go any farther, Father, why do they call the virgins *mondidas*? What does it mean? It's a word I've never-before heard."

"It's an ancient word, Highness. The people say it means 'the pure ones.'"

"How do you think these people endure the heat? Surely you, who have lived here all these years, must have some explanation."

"The people believe that Our Lady turns the heat back into the ashes. This may, indeed, be true, but sometimes people get badly burned. Sometimes she fails to protect them from the fiery way. I have confessed some who died from their burns, so I know whereof I speak."

"I thought so," said Isabella. "Now mind. I have the greatest faith in Our Lady, for I have seen her at her work. But I doubt she would bestow divine protection on people trying to prove they can walk through fire in what to me seems little better than a stunt. It's too much like a game, Father, too much like a vulgar show. The Virgin would have no part in such a thing. If these *mondidas* walk the fiery way unscathed, it's something they accomplish without Our Lady's help."

"What do you think it is Highness? Witchcraft?"

"I don't believe in witchcraft," snapped Isabella. "Witchcraft is against everything in heaven, and God wouldn't tolerate it. There's some logical explanation of this fire-walking. I'm certain of it."

"Highness," said Father Pinedo, "there's one element we have not discussed, in fact have barely mentioned. Others walk the fiery way, after the *mondidas* finish. Boys, men, even married women, and once, I hesitate to mention it, I saw a harlot come off the fiery way unburned."

"Are those who got burned from San Pedro, Father?"

"Rarely, Highness. And when one is, the people hereabouts say it's lack of faith. But never has a person not of San Pedro walked the fiery way and not been burned."

Just then Don Agapito appeared at the door. The time had come. She would have to ride down into that semi-pagan village to address the people in the midst of their festival. As she descended the mountainside, she realized that the sounds of merriment had ceased. It was as though some great hand had snuffed it out.

She saw a plaza packed with people, and felt the stares of others from windows and even rooftops. What must they be thinking of this foreign queen riding her great white charger, her riding cape drawn around her to keep out the chill, her coronet set firmly on her head? "How young and small I must look," she whispered, "and yet in these faces I see something reminiscent of approval." She realized that the glowing effulgence of the fiery way threw her every feature into relief and set her hair aflame. Looking down at her hands, she saw they glowed golden in the weird glare, and that the horse was no longer white, but golden, too. She wondered what symbolic message might take root in the popular mind.

She sat in silence while Don Agapito addressed the people, turning his eyes from time to time on an old man dressed in a long black cape and wearing a broad-brimmed, high-crowned hat. She saw that the old man leaned upon a staff as tall as himself. He would be the mayor. She examined him more closely. Every line of that leathery old face was as hard as stone, but the eyes were intelligent, clear and frank. Here was a man who knew his world and its people. He was one of the old Castilians, clever, shrewd, just, ready to judge. As the mayor of a free Castilian town, he knew his power. He was a man to respect And she respected him.

Don Agapito told the people how their queen had come to them to recruit troops to defend the country against the armies of the Portuguese who were ready to invade the land. Her spies, he pointed out, reported great movements of men along the border. Other spies in Lisbon sent word that King Alfonso was soon to strike. He told them how the King of Portugal had recently betrothed himself to the bastard daughter of Queen Joanna and Beltrán de la Cueva, and Isabella saw the people cross themselves and spit. Evidently Joanna and Beltrán were no favorites here. When they heard that King Alfonso had allotted their lands and castles to his nobles, the knights scowled and shook their fists and the people muttered. But when Don Agapito told them that the queen would speak to them, they grew silent and waited, judge-like. If there was an ounce of enthusiasm in these people now, she could not feel it.

She hardly remembered what she said, but whatever it was, it aroused little response. In stony silence they stood, and every eye kept slipping from her to the face of the old mayor who stood never saying a word, waiting. She finished by assuring them that they would be paid for their service in the national armies, and that she and the king would not forget their help when the war was won. She never suggested that it might be lost. At last she finished.

Don Agapito said, "Men of Soria and San Pedro, you have heard the Queen of Castile. You know our peril. What is your answer?"

The mayor stepped forward and tapped his staff on the flagstones for silence. He reminded Don Agapito in a deep and well-modulated voice, that the region was protected amply by its mountains, that to a man his people would die to protect their homes, but that he doubted the wisdom of leaving territory they knew to fight on foreign soil.

"You would be fighting in Castile, Mayor," said Isabella, speaking directly to the old man whose eyes did not waver. "It would not be foreign soil."

"It is the same, Highness, to my people. Soria with the Duero Valley and the surrounding mountains is native land to them. Castile beyond the area is foreign."

"How like my Spaniards," thought Isabella. "How like them to consider their own region as their country, and the nation itself foreign." She doubted if she could ever explain the difference, and discouragement tugged at her heart. The child stirred in her womb. He must be as dead tired as she. To make them give up this fierce regionalism and see from a national viewpoint would be as difficult as trying to persuade a country priest that a local miracle had never occurred.

She heard the mayor's voice again. "Can you explain to us, Highness, for we are a very simple people, how it is that King Henry's daughter is called queen by some? How can two queens rule in the same land? Will there be two Spains, each with its own queen?"

"This old man is clever," she thought. "Very clever." The whole affair had taken an unexpected turn. She had taken it for granted that they would at least consider her right to the crown. And yet she could forgive then. They were what the old man in his cleverness was using as a kind of foil, they were simple people. They had called Henry king, and now saw his sister come to claim the throne, while his alleged daughter still claimed it. She needed to prove that she was the queen rightfully and that God Almighty was on her side. And however she proved it, she must be convincing graphic, and easily understood. She had no time to plan, she knew. No one was going to help her. She was entirely on her own. Could she sway these villagers, these rustic knights and nobles? If their own lord, Don Agapito, had failed, what could she, a stranger, do?

She heard Don Agapito try again. He said, "The queen is God's choice. Did not King Henry name her his legal heir and the Beltraneja a bastard?"

"We heard the report, my lord," said the mayor. "It was proclaimed in Soria's plaza, but who can be certain of paternity? A little later the king sent another proclamation. It revoked the first and called the child Juana his daughter. Again I ask, who can be certain of paternity? No one, my lord, except God and sometimes the child's mother. And if the mother has been lax in her morals, even she may not know, leaving only God with the certain knowledge."

"The old man is quicker than Don Agapito," thought Isabella. "And now he's had his say and can retreat behind his years and his position."

"How do we know that you are God's choice, Highness?" she heard him ask. "You tell us so, but so did King Henry tell us when he proclaimed the girl you call his bastard. What proof do *you* offer?"

She turned to the old man and for a long time their eyes met and held. Neither turned away and neither flinched. Over the mayor's shoulder Isabella could see the glow of the fiery way. She realized that it was almost midnight and the time for the *mondidas* to tread the glowing ash. In a few more minutes it would be too late, for already she could hear people in the crowd muttering. They were tired of listening to her. The fiery way seemed to grow even brighter and to engulf the entire plaza. All of a sudden she knew what she had to do to win the Duero Valley and its men. Our Lady might be guiding her. She prayed she was.

"You ask for proof, Mayor," she said calmly, evenly. "Would you consider it unequivocal proof that I am Our Lord's choice if He gave me the power to walk barefoot on the fiery way with the chosen virgins?"

"That would be a test, Highness," said the old man, obviously moved and alarmed at the same time. "But we could never permit it. Suppose you were burned? And, Highness, you would most certainly be burned, and then what of us and of the village of San Pedro Manrique? The king would come at us like an angry bull, and where'd we be then? No, Highness, you mustn't even think of it!"

"But suppose I made a contract," said Isabella, following up her unexpected suggestion. "Suppose I swore that I did this of my own free will, that I alone would be responsible. Then the king, and no one else, could blame you and the village."

"It would be folly," cried, the mayor, shaking his head and displaying at last some loss of composure. "It's well known that none but the inhabitants of San Pedro can walk the fiery way unharmed. Only the villagers have Our Lady's protection and walk unhurt among the embers. You'd suffer terrible burns. Think! That we could not have, Highness."

"The man is right, Highness," cried the chaplain, plucking at her robe. "This is pure madness."

The Captain of her lancers, who had been stunned at the suggestion, finally realized the seriousness of what the queen was proposing. He added his objection. "Highness," he complained, "I beg you to reconsider!"

"I'm thinking," she said. "If the girls of San Pedro can walk those embers, protected by Our Lady, then so can I."

"What do you hope to gain by this, Highness?" she heard Don Agapito ask.

"Yes, Highness, what?" asked the village priest, unable to fathom this beautiful lady from the outside world.

"I must convince them that I am queen and that Our Lady stands beside me, Don Agapito. Our Lady would protect no imposter. So if I can show them this, they will follow me, and the Duero Valley will send its men."

"If you could do it, Highness," said Don Agapito, "it would certainly convince them, for it would be a miracle. But for all our sakes, please don't try. Listen to your captain, to your retainers."

"It's useless to try to dissuade me," said Isabella, thrusting out her chin. "If Our Lady protects the *mondidas*, she will certainly protect me."

"Highness," said the mayor, most truly concerned for the village, if this rash woman came to harm, "it cannot be. It cannot be!"

"Mayor," replied Isabella, her face now waxen even in the glow of the ash, "Our Lady has helped me in greater straits. Have you heard of Pedro Girón?"

"We have, Highness," replied the old man, crossing himself, his eyes darting here and there as if looking for a way out of the dilemma.

Suddenly he crossed himself again and called the village lawyer. "Don Gonzalo," he said, "prepare the contract for Her Highness. She must take full responsibility. If she burns, it's Our Lady's will, not the fault of the village of San Pedro Manrique."

She refused to listen to the priest. When the contract was thrust under her nose, she signed it and added her flourish to make it binding. As she glanced up from the parchment, she caught sight of the procession of the *mondidas* entering the plaza followed by a line of young men and girls from the village as well as people from Soria and some of the neighboring towns. The tumult almost deafened her and she shook her head to clear it. Again the music of the bagpipes and more of the notes on the instrument she had not been able to place when she heard it the first time. She saw now what they were playing. Three very old men stood near the fiery way and played on odd flute-like pipes with three holes, over which their fingers darted like wrinkled snakes, boneless and limber.

The fire glowed white-hot, a bluish haze shimmering over it. The first *mondida* arrived. Above her head soared her headdress made of a large basket without handles covered with lace and bound with rose-colored ribbons. In the basket she saw loaves of bread covered with roses and green leaves, and out of it all sprouted five forked sticks like antlers, their bark removed and dyed with saffron. Straight and sure, barefoot, the *mondida* made her way toward the fiery path. Isabella slipped off her own shoes, and had to smile at the white face of the chaplain crossing himself and repeating the Psalter. "Mother of God," she heard him say. "Protect her Highness."

At the fiery way, the *mondida* stopped only for a second to adjust the heavy headdress with its load of bread. Then, resolutely and without a quiver, she was on the embers. Isabella scrutinized her closely. The *mondida's* steps were even and firm, she saw, and neither rapid nor hesitant. She pressed the soles of her feet flat against the coals, so that their full surface made contact before she lifted her foot.

And then it was over, and the *mondida* was walking serenely across the plaza toward a seat prepared for her. She didn't limp, and, except for a light dusting of ash, her feet looked as white as they had before she stepped onto the fiery way.

The second virgin was already on the glowing embers, and the third was moving into position. Isabella watched the third walker with unwavering concentration. She saw that for a second, just after the girl's feet lifted from the embers, dark footprints showed outlined clearly against the glow.

After the last *mondida* had taken her seat, other walkers came. A young man approached with a companion. They slipped off their sandals. She gasped. What were they about to do? She could hardly believe it. The young man, stalwart, but lean as a willow, stooped and allowed his companion to mount his shoulders. Then, with the same sureness displayed by each of the *mondidas* and the same steady tread, he walked the fiery way. The crowd roared. Others walked, until five men, each with another on his shoulders, had crossed the embers with no apparent hurt.

Then a man from Soria stepped forward, unbuckling his sandals and squaring his shoulders.

"Let me try it, mayor," she heard him say. "If Pedro Alva and the others can do it, so can I. The *mondidas* may be pure, but Pedro Alva and the others, they didn't come here from hearing Mass. I know, for I have been with them. Let me try the fiery way."

"The way is open, Soriano," replied the mayor. "But remember, the fire is hot, and you do it of your own free will."

All watched as the man took his first step. Isabella wanted to cry out and tell him to set his foot down firmly, not to hesitate, not to tread lightly. Then the foot touched the embers, and with a howl the man rolled sideways to avoid falling into the coals. A moment later he sat holding a blistered foot while the village doctor applied goose grease. She had seen the man no more than touch his foot to the embers and receive a burn. Was there anything in the belief that only the people of San Pedro Manrique could walk unharmed? No matter. She could not retreat now. Too much was at stake. And besides, she had Our Lady.

With a prayer she went to the spot where each person had stood before he began the walk. The silence of the plaza weighed down upon her shoulders like a pall. The chaplain no longer begged her to give up. She could see him kneeling in the dust. Then Don Agapito and the mayor fell to their knees, and soon not a soul was standing. She heard herself call for one of the heavy baskets and felt them tie it to her head. She balanced it to get its feel. She felt as though she were standing far off watching herself. She stood erect, calm, her face a study of pure faith and determination. At her breast hung a silver crucifix with one pearl in its center. She felt her hair move in the rising heat as if it were alive.

Don Agapito had gotten off his knees and was about to speak.

"If you want to have me fail, Don Agapito, talk to me. But if you want to see me walk the fiery way unharmed, be silent."

Don Agapito bit his tongue. The whole town was on its feet again, watching. She forced her lips to move. "Holy Mary, Mother of God, be with me,"

She spoke again, for they must hear her next words. "If I am not God's choice let me burn; but if I am, spare me."

This was what they had to see to understand: the act of faith.

Without moving her head, she spoke to the mayor. "Mayor," she said, "catch my cape, lest it trail in the fire and burn."

She heard the sound of withdrawn breath as she stepped out of it. The sound came from the women who noticed first. Then the men saw and a second gasp followed the first. The queen was great with child! She would walk the fiery way with child. She carried a double burden like the men. No pregnant woman had walked the way before.

She realized the mayor had opened his mouth to call her back, and she heard him close it with a snap, as she took the first step.

Holding herself almost rigid, statue-like, she felt her bare foot press against the intense warmth of the bed of ash and embers. She felt no pain. The heat retreated from her foot as she pressed against the fiery way. Five times her feet made contact with the embers, and on the sixth step she felt the cool stone of the plaza. It was over.

For a long moment she permitted herself the luxury of standing relaxed. Then she turned slowly and faced the mayor and found his face a study of astonishment and vast relief. Proudly she waited.

The mayor found his voice. "We've seen tonight a miracle never witnessed before, Highness. An outlander and you not burned! A pregnant woman, and unscathed! You called upon Our Lady and trod the fiery way unburned! You asked our Lord to save you if you were his choice and to burn you if you were not. You have no burns. You are God's choice, and the men of the Duero Valley will march with you to fight the Portuguese."

As she passed the village priest, wrapped again in her cape, her shoes again on her feet, she saw him bow low before her and cross himself.

"Our Lady heard again," he said.

"Yes," she whispered, "but only insofar as she gave me the courage to attempt it, Father. We will talk of this later when you came to my room."

She heard the captain swear under his breath and thank God that King Ferdinand would not have him executed.

Later she said, "Most phenomena have a scientific explanation, Father, and walking on the fiery way is no exception. Sometimes, rarely, heaven will set aside a natural law. We've all seen this occur. We call it a miracle. But if one examines most miracles reported, he discovers that many are not miracles at all. This is true in the case of the miracle you thought you witnessed tonight."

"I don't understand, Highness."

"Did you notice the imprint of the *mondidas*' feet in the ash, Father?"

"Yes, Highness, and I saw the same imprint of yours. For a moment I could see the black outline of your feet. Then, the second you lifted your foot, the incandescence returned and the print vanished."

"You said 'returned,' Father. That's exactly what happened. The heat withdrew for a second and then returned. I could feel it withdraw, and before it returned, I raised my foot."

"But what made the heat withdraw?"

"My weight. I believe my feet snuffed out the heat for a second or two, or somehow drove it back. In that second I could feel the heat lessen, for it was pressed back for that brief second. The black imprint against the glow was the charcoal."

"And the man from Soria," said the priest. "I watched him, too. He barely set his foot to the surface of the ash. He left no imprint, snuffed out no heat, and his foot got burned. Can this truly be the secret of the fiery way?"

"It is, Father, or so I believe. It makes sense. Do you really believe that God, beset with all the evils of mankind, and Our Lady, would trouble themselves over the feet of a few peasants who wished to show their bravado? I doubt they would."

"You explain away a very pretty miracle," said the confessor wryly. "I'm disillusioned. I should have preferred to remain in ignorance. It seems a pity, Highness. In fact, I shan't allow you to convince me. I believe that heaven has again put its hand into your affairs."

"We shall never be certain," said Isabella. "But you have my explanation, for whatever it is worth. No matter what, I've won the people of the Ebro Valley over. This in itself is miraculous."

2

After Soria Isabella went to Toledo and lost count of the days and weeks, but she knew her recruiting had been successful. The promised levies poured in, and even towns she hadn't visited sent men. News of the queen's miraculous walking of the fiery way spread rapidly. If King Alfonso waited a little longer, Castile might throw into the field an army that could hold him back.

Ferdinand also had success. He wrote, a week after she had walked the fiery way, almost jealously, she thought. "We heard what you did, Isabella, in San Pedro Manrique. From this distance it all seems very strange. Heaven never fails you, does it? Sometimes I wonder why we trouble to raise an army. Maybe if you would retire into some tower, Our Lady would win our war with Portugal for us, or rather for you. When we meet again, you must tell me how you worked the miracles."

Isabella smiled sadly. She could feel his disappointment. Her recruits outnumbered his. Men were like that, a woman should not outdo them. Well, it would be a while before she outdid him again; for the child was too close for that. She smiled as she thought of him riding from town to town, cajoling as only he could cajole, pointing out the apportionment of Spanish estates to Portuguese nobles, even entering the lists against rebel nobles who rebuffed his calls for levies. She prayed he could bring in more recruits than she had.

She picked up his last letter and read his own account in the bold, slanting hand. "I had to joust with a man yesterday," he wrote. "He was the biggest fellow I ever crossed lances with, and the horse he rode was an elephant. If he unhorsed me, he'd provide no soldiers, but If I defeated him he'd send one thousand lancers. He went down like a tower, Isabella, and when he regained his feet, he gave me an additional four hundred men. Not as wonderful as your miracle, but effective, you'll have to admit."

The child stirred vigorously, and she thanked God she could rest and await his arrival. In this one act, the bearing of his children, she could excel her husband and not be criticized.

Her eyes went back to his letter, the saddest he had ever written or would ever write. In it she read the depth of human disillusionment and hurt, and fury. The archbishop of Toledo, Alfonso Carrillo, her friend, her mentor, her protector, as well as Ferdinand's, had defected to the enemy! How could they believe it, accept it, cope with it? Why? Holy Mary, why? She could hardly read Ferdinand's words, for obviously his hand had trembled as he penned the message.

"The old reprobate has betrayed us," he wrote, "and defected to the Portuguese! Infamous and treacherous are words too soft to describe that wicked old man. And the excuse he gave—dear God, you won't believe it! That you and I pay too much heed these days to Cardinal Mendoza!"

Indeed she found it difficult to believe, and yet she knew Ferdinand's care when he wrote a report. He always validated or blasted rumors he had heard, always looked into everything before he accepted it as truth. The reason was insufficient to him as it was to her. Senility, surely, or illness, perhaps even worse. Too many years. Too much hardship. Too much fighting in the field and in the Church. If only she could speak with him!

The courier who had brought the message requested permission to speak. "Highness, the king feels that you should leave Toledo this very day, indeed this very hour. The city isn't strong enough to withstand the Portuguese army if it lays siege. And we believe Afonso is even now on the march against you. Therefore the king commands you to leave immediately. Above all you must not fall into their hands. Go to Ávila, Highness. Your husband did not write your destination, lest this message fall in enemy hands. And, Highness, I know the Portuguese are only a day's ride away."

She heard his voice trail off into silence, but clearly he had more to say. His eyes fell and he wet his lips with his tongue. "What is it, man?" she asked crisply.

The courier took his courage in both hands and blurted out, "Highness, the king commands you to travel by litter. It is his word. You are not to ride a horse."

Suddenly she felt sorry for the fellow. He was Ferdinand's man and had said what he had been told to say. He feared her, but he feared the king much more. Her face softened in understanding. "Go with God, courier," she said. "You have delivered your message."

Ferdinand had been wise in his choice of Ávila. If the League had held out all those months against the united armies of Henry and Villena, then from behind Ávila's walls she could keep the Portuguese at bay for months as well. To Ávila she could go.

Looking up she saw the courier was still standing before her pale-faced and nervous. "Is there something else?" she asked.

"Yes, Highness. The king ordered me to escort you to Ávila and sent with me the necessary cavalry."

This time she did not smile. She had her own lancers, and what her husband was doing seemed highhanded. She was now more determined than ever. Isabella of Castile would not leave the narrow streets of Toledo in a slow-moving litter like some old woman, like a captive even.

"Very well," she told the courier. "We shall go immediately. Assemble the escort in the courtyard."

Hurrying to her rooms, she began to put on riding clothes, at the sight of which Margarita protested violently. "You can't ride, Highness. The doctor forbade it. I forbid it."

"I must," said Isabella, adjusting her collar. "Say no more about it. I command you."

Just then the midwife appeared, and when she saw her mistress, tall and stately in spite of her pregnancy and undoubtedly about to ride, she was even more vehement. Clinging to Isabella's arm she wailed, "Travel by litter, Highness."

Isabella shook her off. By the time she reached the courtyard the courier was there with a litter and the four mules to carry it. His men were lashing it to the long poles while two of the dueñas, their arms full of pillows, were on their way to convert it into a traveling bed.

Isabella walked past the litter, and calling a page sent him on the run to the stables for her favorite bay. The captain of the escort, aghast, protested. His face flushed deep plum-colored and he said, "I won't permit it, Highness. The king expressly commanded me to see that you took the litter. I cannot be responsible if you ride. He'd have my head!"

"The responsibility is mine, Captain," she said, and something in her voice ended his protest.

As she swung into the saddle, which the captain noted with horror was a regulation cavalry saddle and not the sidesaddle women should always use, Isabella saw the confessor, walking in the stiff-legged way of one who wishes to hurry but deliberately refrains from doing so to preserve his dignity. His face was white and sweat stood in beads upon his forehead and tonsured pate by the time he reached her stirrup.

"The child, daughter," he panted. "Think of the child, if not of yourself."

"Pray for the child, as I shall pray, Father," she said. "There is no time for the litter. Listen. The Portuguese crossed the border yesterday at Badajoz. They pushed on to Plasencia and were in Arévalo without meeting opposition. All Galicia and Estremadura will be in their hands before the week is out. This very city is in imminent danger of siege. I will not chance capture. Too much rests on my shoulders. I must go today, now, and no litter can carry me as fast as I must travel."

She didn't look back as she spurred out of the courtyard, but she knew that the confessor was by then kneeling on the flagstones. She could hear Margarita and the *dueñas* wailing. She knew they crossed themselves. It didn't matter. She was on the way to Ávila.

Toward noon the woolen blanket of heat left her clothing wet and heavy; she felt light-headed. Two brazen suns, one in the low-hanging washed-out sky, the other a few feet to her left, where the captain's helmet bobbed, blinded her. The captain rode close, wanting to take no chances. "Ride beside Her Highness," the confessor had warned. "Do not let her fall."

It was well that he had. Suddenly came the first of a series of stabbing pains. "Not the child!" she commanded. "It's not due for months." But when the second gust of agony made her drop the reins and fall forward to clasp the neck of the horse, she knew the worst. The child was on the way. When a woman has suffered the pains of labor, she cannot mistake them.

The dust had suddenly caught up with her in a thick swirling yellow cloud that made her cough. She could barely see. After that she remembered little. The captain stopped her horse—that much she recalled. He put his arm around her to keep her from falling. She was aware of that. But she didn't know how she came to lie on the ground with a canopy of riding capes protecting her from the sun. She heard a woman screaming, shrill high, terrible, but she didn't recognize her own voice. When the pain became unbearable she fainted and heard no more.

After a while, as from a distance, came the muted voices of men, and through a fog of agony. She saw the captain's grim face bending over her, a face shiny with sweat and dust-blotched in smudgy patches. He was trying to smile with dismal failure.

She struggled to get up, struck by a horrible fear. "Don't let me die here," she heard a cracked voice say. "The Portuguese must not find me like this."

"Rest easy, Highness," said the captain, laying a heavy hand on each of her shoulders to hold her down. "You must not move. I've sent my men for help."

The fear in his eyes drove her own fear away. Then the pain returned, deeper this time, unbearable. "Go away a little," she told him. "Leave me alone for a while. But don't go far."

He understood. He wrung his big hands in helpless inadequacy. If only a peasant woman would come along to help the queen have the baby she was about to have! When he could think no more, he knelt in the dust of the road and prayed. And all around him knelt his men.

Isabella felt the child emerge as their voices reached the words, *"Ad te suspiramus, gementes et flentes, in hoc lacrymarum valle."* Comfort flowed from the deep male tones, and her lips moved silently in unison. *"Eia ergo advocata nostra, illos tuos misericordes oculus ad nos convertet"*

Then it was over. The sun stood at zenith, and from far above the blanket of heat drifted the far-off, fervent, and compelling closing of the prayer. *"O clemens, o pia, o dulce Virgo Maria!"*

As the men rose from their knees in awe to watch, Isabella stumbled from the shelter of the capes and toward the horses. In her arms she carried something tiny and pathetic wrapped in her jacket. She asked for her traveling chest, and when they brought it, had them empty its contents on the ground. They watched in awe as tenderly she deposited the bundle in the chest and laid her cheek against the wooden top. The expression on her haggard face was so poignant and beautiful in its sorrow that it made them forget the blood and sweat that stained her skin. They crossed themselves then, and more than one wiped his eyes with the back of his hand.

They were not surprised when they heard her say, "On to Ávila!" And although the captain argued, they all knew that she would have her way.

"Highness, Highness!" he groaned. "Let me send to the city for a litter. I cannot possibly let you ride. Not now!"

Isabella turned to him slowly like a person too weary to argue, but determined to have her way. "Will you help me on the horse, Captain, or must I mount by myself?"

After that he said no more. He mounted his horse and over her protestations ordered her handed up to him, and she rode that way with his arm around her. Far ahead rode two of his men at full gallop in the direction of Ávila.

Fifteen miles from the city they met the litter. They transferred her to it, and in it she entered the one-time capital, of her dead brother Alfonso and the League.

She was able to read Ferdinand's letter when it arrived two days later. She smiled at his authoritativeness, grateful at last to be told what she must do. "Don't stir from Ávila! Later, when completely recovered and when the doctors gave their permission, you may travel *by litter* to Valladolid." He wrote of the invasion, and she was relieved to learn that King Alfonso seemed content to remain in Arévalo while his troops ravaged the region and disrupted commerce and travel between the cities of Castile and León. June slipped into July and still the Portuguese feasted in Arévalo and pillaged. Men said that King Alfonso was again in the clutches of the passive phase of his well-known malady. Until his humors returned to normal, he would rest and eat and grow fatter. But once his apathy left him, he would lead his hosts against Castile.

Isabella thanked God for this military respite, knowing that Ferdinand was feverishly whipping his levies into the semblance of an army. As the news of the rape of Arévalo spread across Spain, recruits poured in and volunteers sprang up from nowhere in regions where they had failed to recruit a soul. Still more materialized when word spread that King Alfonso was hiring Moorish African mercenaries. Mention of Moorish soldiers on Spanish soil raised the ghosts of ancient fears and made even peace-loving men take arms.

By late August she was back in the saddle scouring the mountains for supplies Ferdinand had to have to feed, clothe, and arm the host he had assembled before Valladolid. Eight thousand cavalry and thirty-eight thousand men-at-arms, counting footmen, engineers, and other units, consumed an unbelievable quantity.

Battles were frequent, and endless skirmishes took place, so often that she couldn't remember where they occurred. Even the chroniclers found it impossible to record them all and contented themselves with pitched battles and diplomacy, and, of course with Afonso's remarkable offer to fight Ferdinand in single combat. They were careful to set down why Ferdinand refused, pointing out that Afonso's request that Isabella and the bastard be sent as hostages to the castle of a neutral noble was unacceptable. Ferdinand was too clever to fall for a trick like that. He had everything to lose if the neutral noble handed his wife over to the Portuguese, and Alfonso would lose little, if the bastard fell into Spanish hands.

Months later, after a hopeless confusion of attacks and retreats, of sieges and surrenders, she and Ferdinand thought they saw a turning point in the war. In their retreat from Zamora, the Portuguese suffered a severe defeat, and only the fact that they held Toro saved then from annihilation. King Alfonso, weary of war and already beginning to feel the inroads of depression, returned to Lisbon. But in Castile he left Toro heavily fortified and strongly garrisoned-until such time as he returned.

Castile celebrated the retreat of the Portuguese armies with fiestas and solemn religious ceremonies. Pilgrimages regained their vogue and churches filled with people thanking heaven for deliverance. But Isabella didn't celebrate. Until the last Spanish town was freed of Portuguese domination, and the last Portuguese soldier had quit Spanish soil, she would not rest. She placed Toro under siege immediately, and during the ensuing breathing spell prepared for the invasion she knew would come, once cool weather stirred the apathetic blood of the King of Portugal. But worse news than his recovery came. Afonso had traveled personally all the way to the court of Louis XI to ask for arms and money. The war was far from ended; Spain had won only a temporary reprieve.

3

The Portuguese army moved steadily up to relieve the garrison in Toro. The men marched glumly and for the most part in silence. What was there to talk about? The war was not popular in Portugal where even Alfonso's son talked of peace and the proper emphasis on trade and exploration. People said that Afonso himself had sickened of fighting in Spain and had actually gone to the court of Louis XI for a rest, and not for the mercenaries he promised he would get.

Near the end of the column, where the dust was thickest and the complaints most vociferous, marched two young men who differed from the general run of the soldiers. They talked volubly, as new friends will, heedless of the scowls of the older men or the supercilious glances of the younger ones. They stared about them curiously at the hills through the shimmering heat waves that hovered above the plains. The Portuguese they spoke was fluent enough, but their accent was foreign. The officer who rode nearby and who was suspicious, could not place it. He thought that the tall red-haired fellow would make a good soldier. He had the long arms a swordsman needed and the shoulders to carry the weight of armor. More pertinent to the matter was the skill in swordsmanship he had displayed in training. But he was far too eager to reach the front lines, and so was the shorter man. Soldiers traditionally hated battles. This pair would bear watching, careful watching. He shook his head In puzzlement and tried without success to comb a little of the sand from his beard. If barracks gossip was true, the tall one was an Italian sailor out of funds and willing to do a hitch in King Afonso's army. The little bow-legged fellow was a sailor, too, and a jailbird who had skipped across the border to escape the queen's justice. He shook his head again. Their stories must be true. Wouldn't good liars have better stories than theirs? He edged close enough to hear their conversation. Innocent enough. He spurred his horse and rode off toward the front of the column where the dust was thinner.

It seemed incredible to Christopher to find himself stepping back in time, taking up the oldest deception of all, his hated Italian pseudonym. But there seemed no other way, given the destination he had chosen and the purpose of this journey. If he appeared before the *Principezza* with a different name, what, but negative, would be the result. How well his Italian had returned to him! His companion and most recent friend, Paolo Sabatini, heard it and believed he was a compatriot. They spoke Portuguese only when an officer was near.

"We're lucky, Colombo," he said as they marched. "We needed a job, and here we are in King Afonso's army with good pay, good food, and good weather. Not a bad assignment at all."

"I could stand less heat and a cool ocean breeze," said Colombo.

"Is it always this hot in August here? And this dry?"

"Always in August, but you'll get used to it. You'd better, for there won't be a change for weeks. Colombo…"

Colombo smiled a wide-mouthed smile. "Can't we drop Colombo and use our given names? Mine's Cristoforo. We're friends, so let's use first names." Even as he said it Juan Baptista hated himself for his double dishonesty—to the *Principezza*, as soon as they met, if they could meet, and to Sabatini. He had thought that when he went ashore in Lagos and spoke Italian until he found Bartholomew, that he was done once and for all with that language. And here he was using it again, because it was easier for his new Italian friend than Portuguese or Spanish. Everything circles back, he mused; Juan Baptista Colom, to Giovanni Colombo, to Christopher Coulon, to Christopher Columbus and now back to Colombo.

Sabatini's voice reached him in his musings. "My name's Paolo. Where are you from in Italy? I can't place Your accent. I'm from Rome, or was originally.'

"From a little town near Genoa, above Chiari in the Valley of Fontanabuona," he lied, remembering that this was the place Bartholomew had thought up early in their subterfuge."

Paolo rolled his eyes suggestively. "I had a girl in Chiari once," he said. "It's no more than twenty miles from Genoa, and I used to ride to see her on an old mule I rented. They sell fine wool there."

"That they do," said Cristoforo. "My family left the place, however, and moved to Genoa in '55 when I was just a child. My people are weavers and wooldyers."

"Lisbon's a long way from Genoa, Cristoforo. What's a sailor like you, with the sea all over your face, doing here?"

Christopher looked at his new friend and smiled. "No stranger than for you to be in the Portuguese army. The sea's written all over you, too. But for me it isn't really strange at all. Ever since I could walk to the harbor I wanted to sail. I used to run off from carding wool in my father's shop to listen to the sailors and fishermen. When I was old enough to go to sea, I asked my father's permission, and he refused it. So I ran away, too, Paolo. You know the Genoese saying, *Bisogna voltare la vela seconde il vento?*"

"That means, 'As the wind blows so must you set the sail.'" I heard it a lot when I was in Italian waters. Have you been back to see your family since you left?"

Cristoforo avoided shaky ground. He hardened his heart against truth and cursed the fate that made him have to lie. But this time he could tell the truth. "I never got along with my Genoese family," he said. "They didn't treat we well. They used me like a servant. I never speak of them."

Paolo discretely changed the subject. "You've been in Spain before. I once heard you speak Castilian while we were in training in Lisbon."

"I can get along in Spanish, but I do better with Portuguese. Yes, I was in Spain back in '68, when I was eighteen. It was smack in the middle of the civil war between King Henry and his half brother, Prince Alfonso, What a wonderful experience I had! I'm certain no poor Italian sailor ever had one like it. Paolo, you won't believe me, but I met the Princess Isabella over near Ávila. She was eighteen, too, or thereabouts. I even saw her escape from Segovia. As she rode away I called to her, but I doubt that she heard my voice."

"Go on, Chris. Sailors are all liars. They never meet princesses except in their winecups. But tell me more, it'll help us pass the time."

Cristoforo's eyes were so sincere and his freckled face so serious, that Paolo wanted to hear more. Something in friendship, hearty, and generous and honest, made him say, "Would you like to tell me about it?"

"It's true, Paolo. By St. Ferdinand, it is! A courier fell off his horse and broke his leg. He begged me to take his message to the princess in Ávila. I took it, and it turned out to be from her brother Alfonso. He'd been poisoned."

Paolo interrupted. "Prince Alfonso died about then. Everybody said it was poison, but it wasn't proved. There was a good deal of the plague that year."

"It was poison all right, Paolo. The message said so, and the prince himself had signed it. Besides, I saw him die, and I'm certain it was."

Paolo thought rapidly. "Then you must have gone to Cardeñosa. That's where they say he died."

"Yes, that's the place. The princess read the note, she turned and looked at me. I'll never forget her eyes, pained and scared, so young and yet so brave. She didn't take time to change her clothes, but ran to the stables, after asking me to go with her. You see, I knew where the courier lay with his broken leg. I'd never ridden a horse. How fast she rode! I was sore for a week. The princess rode like a man, astride, and she rode like the wind."

Paolo looked thoroughly impressed. "So you rode with Isabella of Castile. You spoke to her and she to you. A rare honor, Chris, for a poor sailor."

"I know it. And she treated me like a gentleman. Me as ragged as a beggar and stinking of sheep. I'll never forget how she said, 'We're all sons and daughters of Adam' and how she made me believe it."

"I've heard she's like that," said Paolo. "And she's decent and good. Nothing like that whore Joanna. Beautiful, too. I saw her last year riding with King Ferdinand and their little girl. People in Castile worship them."

"Worship her, at least, Paolo. Worship Ferdinand? Of that I'm not so sure. They say she made a good match. I pray she did. But unless he's changed a lot, I feel sorry for her. Ferdinand is a tough character—ruthless cruel, false-hearted, and vengeful. Yes, I've heard that he's brave and wise, and I agree to this. Do you believe she's happy with him?'

"Must a queen be happy?" said Paolo surprised. "I never thought much about happiness in royal families. I suppose she's as happy as a woman can be in an arranged marriage, now that the war's over. She and her husband have had hard years, but it looks as though they're near the end of bad times. And in this war we're in, I think they have the Portuguese on the run, in spite of Toro. All old Alfonso is doing in holding that city is saving his pride. We won't see much fighting, Chris. That's why King Ferdinand has gone back to fight the French, leaving the queen to fight the Portuguese."

"He left her to wage this war alone?"

"Had to—but don't worry about the queen. She'll manage. Without her the king would never have won Zamora, and he knows it. He's a great captain and as brave as any knight in the world, but he knows how much he owes his wife. Without her supply lines, her police force to guard the rear, her constant recruiting and collecting money, the Portuguese might have won. By now all Spain knows just what a queen Isabella is. They say the rebel nobles are sweating right this minute at the thought of what'll happen to them when she runs the Portuguese out of Toro."

Cristoforo tried not to let Paolo see how interested he was. No one had a right to know. It wouldn't even be safe, for anyone to know. He was sure he would see her again, but this time it would not be a coincidence. This time it would be deliberate, because he, her woolmerchant, would find the way to see her. His face, naturally open and easy to read, grew tense as unfamiliar lines marked it. As innocently as possible he said "Tell me more, Paolo. Twice during the years since I met her," he lied, "I was in Barcelona and I had a little news. But not much. What happened after she got back to Ávila in '68? The last glimpse I caught of her she was going into the Convent of St. Anne there."

"By Jesus' nails!" Paolo said, "people here talk of little else than Isabella and what she's doing for Spain. And the funny thing is that people—peasants, sailors, everybody—, *care* to know what she's doing. That's unusual, my friend. The man in the street gave Henry as wide a berth as he could. But you wanted facts. Let's see. You've heard, I expect, how shabbily King Henry treated her. Tried to lock her up at Madrid, but she gave him the slip and escaped from Ocaña and into Valladolid. All that's history now."

"I heard that much in Barcelona," said Christopher. "They're already making ballads about it. Later I heard she'd married Ferdinand of Aragón and had a daughter. After that I lost track."

"Well," said Paolo "they lived here and there—in Dueñas and Valladolid and other places. When old Henry died, Ferdinand was on the French border and Isabella got herself coronated without him. They say he didn't like it, but he got over it and they were reconciled. Then he was off to fight the French again. You asked if the queen is happy. That kind of life wouldn't be happiness for me. I'd rather be a sailor."

Cristoforo lowered his eyes, and Paolo thought he saw him blush, and grew suspicious. "Is she happy with the king as a husband and a man?" Paolo did not laugh. Could this simple Italian sailor be a spy? He banished the thought before it crystalized. "That's a strange question," he replied. "But it's one that's being asked a lot. Did you know he has fathered his second bastard?"

"His second!" cried Cristoforo scandalized and angry. "I hadn't heard about the first!"

"It isn't the first that troubles people," said Paolo. "The first was born before he ever saw Isabella. But the second came after Isabella married him."

Cristoforo's freckles stood out on his white face. He clenched his fists but said nothing. Paolo went on. "Don't be too hard on him, Cristoforo. If I were a king and looked like Ferdinand, and all the women rolled their eyes at me, I believe I'd do the same. The king is a man of flesh and blood like the rest of us."

"God take him!" Cristoforo said hotly, his face still white. "How could he dally when he has a wife like Isabella? She's beautiful, Paolo, the most beautiful woman I ever saw."

"They say she's cold," said Paolo. "If it's true, who can blame the king?"

Cristoforo's eyes blazed. "A lie," he grated. "I rode in a litter with her for two days and nights, I talked to her. She's as warm as sunlight. And sweet. I wish I... No matter what I wish. But I say the king's a fool not to stay at home and cultivate his garden. The sweetest fruit isn't always on the other side of the wall."

Paolo glanced about uneasily, hoping no ears had heard. "That almost brings us up to date," he said. "The war was bad, but it's about over. Old Alfonso hasn't married the bastard yet, wily old fox. No need to marry and consummate a sacrament of Holy Church if people won't believe the bride's legitimate. Besides, the girl's his niece, Joanna's daughter. Wouldn't that be incest?"

"How long have they been at war?"

"Since the spring of '75, so it's been a year and a few months," answered Paolo.

Cristoforo assessed what he had heard. Castile was poor, Isabella was fighting a war with Portugal while her husband fought off the French, and the rebel nobles plotted against them both. The country must be bad off.

"It could be worse," said Paolo, reading his thoughts. "Old Henry died. Villena choked to death like his brother Pedro Girón, some say prayed to death like his brother. Joanna's out of the picture, for the time, and maybe forever. Isabella's worst enemies are gone or weakened."

"Isabella will win in the end." Paolo saw his friend's eyes, wide now with awe and, could it possibly be with love? He turned away, embarrassed and uneasy. What kind of a fellow had he made his friend?

"Destiny," said Cristoforo. "It's like the hand of God."

4

The army bivouacked behind a ridge above the Valley of the Duero and the walled city of Toro. in the twilight they could not see clearly, but Paolo said you could stand on that ridge in the daytime and see the cathedral and the castle of the Marquis of Santa Cruz and the bridges spanning the Duero.

The silence was almost total, deathlike. Not even a frog croaked, but in the gathering darkness they could feel the presence of the mountains and, if they strained, could catch the murmur of the Portuguese encampment behind them, bedding down for the night. From across the river, narrow at this time of year, but still swift in stretches, came the very slight whisper of the sleeping city. Men who guarded walls all day and people who had to support them went to bed early and no one danced or sang. Looking back from the ridge, they could see the Portuguese campfires no longer twinkling, but glowing like spent fireflies across the hillside where the tents stood invisible in the vanishing light of day.

After the last of the afterglow faded, Paolo looked about cautiously. They were alone, and certainly no one missed them in the Portuguese encampment. "I'm going to try to reach the other side," he said in a hoarse whisper. "That's why I came here, Chris."

"That's why I came too. I'm going over with you."

Paolo put his hands on his friend's shoulder. There was no need for words. Each understood. Each knew they might be taken for spies by the Spaniards. Then Paolo remembered what Chris had said about the queen and wondered if he entertained some harebrained plan of seeing her. "You don't hope to speak to the queen, I hope, Christopher. You could get us killed, you know."

"I won't make any trouble, Paolo, but I didn't come this far to give up now. When the proper time comes I'll see her. I must."

Paolo decided to rely on his friend's good sense. "Very well," he said, "but don't be disappointed if she doesn't remember you. And even if she does, how can she say so? Queens and sailors can't be friends, Chris."

In the darkness they descended from the ridge, and cutting behind a little knoll, scrambled down to the water's edge. They went on hands and knees, once on level ground. Moments seemed hours. Why didn't it get dark? Why did some ghostly light cling like phosphorescent liquid to stones, and sand, and driftwood?

At last they felt they could make their try. They could hear the Duero murmuring in its banks and could see the dull surface of the water sparkle in the light of the rising moon. "We're below the last sentry, I'm certain," said Paolo, so we can swim and nobody'll see us. Once on the other tide, we'll surrender to the first Spaniard we meet. The thing is not to get an arrow in us while we're swimming. And Chris, let me do the talking. With your accent, they might let us have an arrow before we got a chance to explain."

Cristoforo thought fast. The time had come. Should he really go? If he went, he might spoil all his chances of returning to Lisbon, and Lisbon was the one place on earth where he could learn what he needed, if he planned to sail the Ocean Sea. If they found him a deserter, he'd end up behind prison bars or lose his head, and if he crossed the Duero with Paolo the Portuguese, once they found him out, would see him as a traitor. Then he remembered why he was standing on the river bank. He followed Paolo into the Duero and let the tepid water close over him.

The Duero in August was so narrow that moments later they were in the shallows on the Castilian bank. Both men shook off the water, but were grateful for the coolness of their wet clothes in the still, hot night. Suddenly strong hands grasped his arms. He saw Paolo similarly held. Oddly, the clipped Castilian tones gave him the impression of coming home, even as he felt rough hands searching him for weapons.

The queen kept an orderly camp, he noticed, as they were led through it. The streets were straight and well-swept and the tents in good alignment. Up ahead he could see the huge pavilion which the queen no doubt occupied. Above it fluttered the banner of Trastámara, and the Castle and the Lion were clear in the torchlight. His heart beat faster at the thought of seeing Isabella again, but the pavilion was dark. If she was there, she was asleep. They wouldn't meet until it was light, if even then. But would a queen, even when morning came, deign to remember a foreign nobody she hadn't seen in seven years? Cold, uneasy thoughts assailed him. Should he have crossed the Duero after all?

At dawn an officer questioned them carefully and Paolo did the talking, which apparently suited the officer, for after a word with Cristoforo, whose intonation seemed to confuse him, he turned to Paolo, whose many stays in Castile had given him virtually perfect Spanish. He and the officer talked at length, and what he said apparently satisfied him and he offered them places in the queen's army and assigned them to a sector on the front. He smiled gleefully at what Paolo told him of the Portuguese encampment and swore he would put that information to the best of use. The queen would commend him for the capture of the two deserters and would want him to keep an eye on them, as he most surely planned to do.

Soon they learned from the soldiers that the queen's headquarters were in Tordesillas and that she seldom visited this outpost. The day before they had expected her for an inspection, but for some reason she hadn't arrived. Trouble in Segovia, they guessed, and when later a courier arrived on a lathered horse with a message, they knew it. They saw many knights in armor and three companies of lancers depart for the rear minutes after the courier's arrival. He was glad he was in the platoon of infantry ordered to line up before the pavilion. When he learned that the queen had sent for troops, he nodded knowingly. Destiny at work again no doubt. He was going to Segovia where she must be. Only *destino* could have placed him and Paolo in this platoon which would march to where she was. He couldn't know, of course, that the captain had purposely included them in the ranks.

With the platoon marched a chaplain on the way to visit the queen, since he hadn't found her in the camp. It was from him Cristoforo learned why she needed such reinforcements.

"It's but one more example of the queen's courage," said the chaplain. "How like her to ride defenseless into an enemy stronghold and restore order there."

Cristoforo didn't understand and neither did Paolo. "I thought Segovia was the queen's," he said.

"It is, or was," said the priest. "You see, the trouble lies with the bishop. He's never liked the queen's commander, Andrés Cabrera. The bishop and a man named Alonso Maldonado, whom Cabrera discharged from the post of *alcalde* of the city, incited the people against Cabrera and seized the Alcázar. They killed Don Pedro Bobadilla, Lady Beatriz's father, and tried to seize the queen's daughter, the little Princess Isabella. But Andrés Cabrera's steward managed to escape into a strong tower with the child and there he and his men barricaded themselves and are holding out. Luckily they got off a dispatch to the queen in Tordesillas. Of course, Isabella..."

"Rode straight to Segovia," interrupted Cristoforo.

"Yes," said the priest, looking slightly disgruntled. "To receive the news and to leap on a horse was all one for her. Most women ponder, hesitate, and don't know where to turn, but not the queen. She has the mind of a man, I believe, and she acted immediately.

"By the time she reached Segovia, the gates were shut and locked. Inside she could hear the uproar and fighting in the streets. The bishop sent a man to warn her off, saying that she could not enter through the Gate of St. John, which the Cabrera faction held, and that if she did so, the populace would turn upon her, so great was their hatred for the Cabreras. He told her he would personally receive her at another gate. Moreover, he advised, that if Lady Beatriz was in her retinue, she might as well turn around and ride back to Tordesillas."

"But what made the Segovians turn against her, their favorite citizen, their ruler who had saved them from King Henry and Villena?" asked Paolo.

The priest smiled. "I wish I could answer every question as easily as this," he said. "The Segovians never liked Cabrera while he held the city in Henry's name, and they like him less today. They claim he and his wife are Jews, you know. The truth is, they were, three generations back, but that helps little. You know how Christians regard converts, whether from Judaism or Islam."

Paolo added, "And yet King Henry made Segovia the beautiful place it is. The parks, the gardens, the streets. I've heard that the queen has continued its improvements."

"No matter," said the priest. "The bishop and his faction so hate the Cabreras that when the queen continued Andrés in his post, they spurred the citizens to revolt."

"What did the queen do when she found the gate closed and heard from the bishop?" asked Paolo.

Cristoforo interrupted, before the chaplain could open his mouth. "She entered through the gate held by the bishop and no one dared stop her as she rode through the streets. What do you think she did? Turned tail and went back to Tordesillas to parley? Not Isabella of Trastámara. Am I correct, Father?"

"You are, soldier, but how did you know? I thought only the officers and the queen's chaplain had that information."

Instantly he wished he had bitten his tongue. He saw that several of the soldiers had heard him and were looking askance. "Please go on with your story, Father," he said. "I shan't interrupt again."

The chaplain, crushed for fear his story had been preempted, took courage again and continued. "The queen rode straight up to the walls," he said. "Then she pulled back her visor to let them see her face. 'Tell the knights and citizens of Segovia,' she cried, 'that I am the Queen of Castile and that this city is mine, for my father the king bequeathed it to me. I need obey no laws nor fulfil any conditions when I care to enter it. I will enter by whatever gate I choose, and with me will ride the Count of Benavente and the rest of my retinue. Tell then to come before me, all the leaders, and be ready to obey what I decree. Tell them that all fighting and looting must cease through the entire city. At once! Otherwise I shall not be responsible for what occurs!'"

"And they opened the gate?" asked Paolo.

"They opened it, my son, and the queen rode in with her small retinue. The Count of Benavente was at her right and the Lady Beatriz at her left. No one dared hinder them for they say the queen's eyes were a shield between them and the mob. The crowd fell back before those awful blue eyes, so like ice when the sun glances from it on a clear winter day. The queen can be a lioness you know, when provoked by injustice or insubordination. She can be merciless! Many trembled that day in Segovia."

They both listened eagerly, as the priest explained how the bishop and Maldonado accelerated their attack on the tower, hoping to take it and the little princess before her mother could arrive and stop them. The Count of Benavente, considered to be the bravest knight in Spain, begged the queen not to go farther into the city, and Lady Beatriz added her pleas, but Isabella would not listen. Commanding them to wait, she rode into a small courtyard near the gate and sent a herald to acquaint the mob of her presence there and her desire to speak to their leaders. In seconds the street was black with men with drawn swords and daggers, even with clubs and hatchets and kitchen knives. Scores crowded into that courtyard to look at this queen who dared alone their displeasure. One look was enough. Sitting on her horse, tall and silver in her armor, she faced them. She made the sign of the cross and raised her face to heaven. She prayed, for her lips moved and those closest to her heard her call an Holy Mary. But her mailed hand held the Sword of Justice and her eyes, when she cast them at the mob, were bleak."

"I can imagine how she looked," said Cristoforo. "Tall and in silver mail—like an avenging angel. And I can imagine what she told them. I'll wager they were cheering her in minutes."

The priest looked sharply at him and said, "Were you perchance there? That's exactly what took place. The queen spoke calmly but with firmness. Surrounded completely and at the mercy of a hundred blades. Someone, anyone, could have stabbed her and vanished without a trace, without being recognized. And some had bows and could have pierced her from afar. The queen knew this, of course, but she expected nothing but submission. We all watched in fascination, and I must tell you that every mother's son of that mob kept looking up at the sky. They all had heard, of course, of Pedro Girón and they believed without a doubt that Isabella had prayed him into his grave. They believe, also, that she had done the same for Villena, his brother. I can tell you it served to cool their anger.

"Then the queen spoke. 'Justice,' she said, in that clear, compelling voice of hers, 'will be carried out against the offenders, but it will be tempered with mercy in the case of those who surrender now. And remember this, citizens. War rages not a day's journey from Segovia, so what you are doing here today is worse than revolt. It's high treason, and punishable by death.'"

"It was then that heaven in one of its equivocal moods must have inspired her. What she did was at once defiant and wryly humorous. 'You shall have a governor whom I trust and respect, one who will rule you well and honorably, whose acceptance by you will please me as much, whose rejection will not.' They all knew whom she meant, their enemy Andrés. But they knew they'd have to swallow him, or else.

"Then, just as you have said, soldier, they all cheered at the top of their voices. Only a true leader can quell a Spanish mob, or only a very beautiful woman. The queen is both.

"Maldonado fled. In half an hour the walls and fortresses were secured and in her hands. When the queen rode through streets, which hours before resounded with cries for her blood, she heard only cheers and praises. She heard vows of loyalty, too, and remorseful voices begging her forgiveness. Yes, mobs are like that, fickle as weathercocks, one minute bold, the next sniveling.

"And when she had the child in her arms and rode those once noisy but suddenly chastened streets, some said she looked like a lioness with her cub; but others who were more perceptive, likened her to the Madonna and her Child.

"I don't know how things are in Segovia," continued the chaplain, "but I believe by the time we get there all will be well in hand and all pockets of possible resistance rooted out. The queen's justice never fails, high and low, rich and poor, if men sin, she makes them pay. She plays no favorites, but she can be moved to pity. If only they hadn't threatened her daughter! To forgive that will be hard indeed…"

As evening fell they could see the walls of Segovia rising out of the plain, the great Roman aqueduct striding off toward the mountains, and the Alcázar grim on its perch above the two rivers. They all knelt at vespers and the chaplain prayed. Before he left them he walked to the side of the road and called to Cristoforo.

"What's your name, soldier?" he asked, struck by the young man's red hair and foreign accent.

"Colombo, Father."

"Colombo, Colombo… not Cristoforo Colombo?"

Christopher's face opened in surprise. "How did you know, Father?"

"You're the man who helped the queen a long time ago near Ávila. I'm her confessor, Alfonso de Coca. She told me you were a man to remember."

Christopher's heart leaped. This old priest might help him meet the queen again. Boldly he said, "Father, I've come a long way to see the queen. Can you help me?"

The chaplain's face creased with a smile. "Have no misgivings, Christopher. You will see the queen, and soon. You have my word."

5

The moon stood high over the Alcázar when de Coca appeared at the house where Cristoforo and Paolo were billeted. "The queen is working late as usual," he said. "When I told her you were here, however, she sent me after you at once. You're to come, too, Paolo. There are some questions she thinks you can answer best."

In the Alcázar they followed him down shadowy corridors and finally stopped at an open door where two soldiers stood at attention. Inside sat the queen, her head bent over a table. She was writing a letter. Apparently she meant to finish before she talked to anyone, and Cristoforo and Paolo took advantage of the opportunity.

"She's even more beautiful than I remembered," whispered Cristoforo, moved by the clear profile etched against the dark arch of the window. Then he turned to whisper to de Coca, but the confessor had vanished.

Just then Isabella signed the letter and affixed her seal. Only then did she look up. Recognition and pleasure colored her voice. "As I live," she said, "it *is* the woolmerchant!"

After that only their eyes spoke until Paolo, shifting uneasily from one foot to the other, coughed. Instantly the queen lowered her eyes. Had she blushed? She was sure she had. But when she looked at Paolo, her face was the face of a queen. She questioned him about the Portuguese army on the ridge behind the Duero and listened attentively to his reply. Obviously she made mental notes, and twice she took up her quill and made notations. And when she had heard all he could tell her, she took his hand and said, "Thank you, my friend. Now go with the guard who'll take you to Commander Cabrera, who must hear all you've told me and maybe more as you remember it."

As Paolo departed, he cast one glance back and saw two heads, one fiery red, the other pale russet, glowing in the lamplight. What could the two have in common? he asked himself. That they could talk at all was a miracle — a queen and a common soldier! He was rapidly revising his ideas about life.

"It can be romantic," he said to himself, "More romantic than fairy tales or Moorish adventure stories."

***

When they were alone, Isabella sat staring at the friend she knew as Christopher for a long while before she spoke. At length she said, "Seven years, woolmerchant! Can you believe it's seven years since we said goodbye that day at the Convent of St. Anne?"

It was as though they had parted only yesterday. They might as well still be swaying along in the litter, the ocher dust swirling around them and hot sun of August turning the road into a ribbon of fire. He remembered the perfume of her hair as her head rested on his shoulder. She wore the same scent, and as he breathed it in his heart began to pound so violently he knew she must hear it. He had to shake his head to clear it of a vision suddenly too familiar, too personal to be conjured up. Did she, too recall that moment when they almost kissed, when they had thought the wildest, maddest thoughts?

"The hour is late," he heard her say. "But I hope you're not too tired to talk. There's much to be done, and I have so little time, that when a chance like this comes for a few stolen moments, I seize it with both hands."

His eyes told her how willing he was, and she continued. "What on earth were you doing in King Alfonso's army, Christopher? And how is it this time you enter Castile from Portugal?"

"I was washed ashore there, *Principezza*. I had no choice." Then he realized she had a new title and blushed. "I mean Highness," he corrected himself.

"*Principezza* will do nicely, woolmerchant. But what were you doing in Portuguese waters in the first place?" He hand gestured to the chair beside her. "Sit down," she said. "I'm getting a crick in my neck from looking at you. Sit and tell me about your ducking in the Atlantic and how you changed from woolmerchant to sailor and then to soldier in the army of my enemies."

Christopher knew he had to lie and lying now was far worse than to Paolo. How could he do otherwise? Now she was married to his most mortal and dangerous foe, to Ferdinand, now even more powerful than when he had been a prince. To Ferdinand who would never forget their enmity, who would, if given the opportunity, arrest him and throw him into prison, if he didn't have him executed outright. Of course, he reflected, he had known all the way to see her that he would have to lie to her. And so, with his story long since concocted, he launched into the telling of it.

"The important part of my story began off Lagos some months ago. I was a seaman on one of five ships sent by Genoa with a cargo of Chian mastic, and bound for England, Portugal and Flanders."

Her eyes were round with interest. So far he had told enough of the truth, in case she made an investigation. Rather than say that he was a corsair on his cousin's flagship, he told the story as though from the side of the vanquished rather than of the victor. "I was aboard the *Bechalla*, a Flemish vessel in the pay of Genoa. Just as we sighted the Cape of St. Vincent and knew we were at the entrance of the Lisbon Roads, a large fleet flying French colors attacked us. It was the famous Guillaume Casanova Coulon, and because France was at war with Burgundy and the *Bechalla* flew the Flemish flag, he considered us fair prey. We fought all day, and three of our ships went down, among them the *Bechalla*." Again it was all true, at least historically speaking. Their ship had attacked the *Bechalla*. The *Montserrat* had grappled with the *Bechalla* which had already been rammed and was sinking. He, Christopher, had leaped from the *Montserrat* onto the Flemish vessel. And as she went down, he had been thrown into the sea.

He saw concern in her eyes and heard it in her voice when she asked, "Did you have far to swim, Christopher? Were you injured?"

"I went overboard when I saw the ship was sinking. Luckily I found a sweep floating free. I managed to paddle it to shore which wasn't far away. I wasn't wounded badly." And he showed her the scar, which made his lies seem plausible. "During the entire battle, *Principezza*, we had seen the shore not six miles across the water. I made it to shore safely enough, but all I had to show from my voyage from Genoa was my scar."

He wanted to push his chair closer, but did not dare.

Isabella looked at it a moment and then away. "I suppose you found the Portuguese hospitable enough. They must be quite accustomed to harboring shipwrecked sailors."

"Yes, they were kind. The parish priest took me to his own house, and when I'd rested, sent me on to Lisbon with a letter to a priest there who put me in touch with the Genoese colony."

"That still doesn't answer the question. Why did you join the Portuguese army?" The question was unexpected.

He lowered his eyes. "I needed money, *Principezza*. I met Paolo and he wanted to join... I wanted to come back to Castile."

"Why, woolmerchant?" asked Isabella with her accustomed frankness. "Why did you want to come back to Castile?"

"Because it's your war, *Principezza*, and I wanted to see you," he blurted out, and this time his eyes didn't falter.

She smiled at his forthrightness and liked him for having kept it across the years. This was the kind of an answer she liked — truthful and to the point. She saw how the years had matured him and thought she could catch the glint of a few silver hairs in his fiery mane; but mature or not, the light in his eyes when he looked at her hadn't changed. His feelings for her floated close to the surface, dangerously close. Hopeless, adoring, sensitive he was, and he couldn't hide what he felt.

"He must top Ferdinand by half a head," she thought, "but Ferdinand's more graceful and poised." She looked at him again and could not imagine his long muscular legs gliding in the mazy dances of the court or his big hands plucking a lute. She did not try. In his own way, with his own blunt grace, he was as attractive as the king in his.

"I'm glad you wanted to see me, Christopher. I've wanted to see you often, to thank you for all you did for me. Who knows how deep an effect your words had? 'Destiny is like the law, like the hand of God...' I you see, I remember."

He flushed with pleasure and sat forward in his chair, his voice rich with feeling. "'It is there always, like a rule of life, like a guardian angel.' I said that, too, *Principezza*, and it all came true. Seven years, and you astonish the world."

"We're retracing an earlier conversation, woolmerchant. To keep the pattern I should ask you about *your* destiny. I hope you haven't lost faith in it."

"I haven't, *Principezza*. The little I saw in Lisbon, even in Lagos, makes me believe that destiny placed me on the *Bechalla* and washed me on a sweep to Lagos harbor. Portugal's the land of voyagers, and Lisbon the capital of world exploration. You have no idea what those men are doing."

"My mother was a Portuguese princess," said Isabella. "I have an aunt, another princess, in Lisbon. King Afonso is a relative. Even Joanna brought me into contact with the Portuguese, for with her came many people from that court. Yes, I have an idea and you are quite right, Christopher. Of all nations, Portugal breeds the greatest seamen. They're the most nautical-minded people in the western world, and now that the Turks control the route to the East through Constantinople, the Ocean Sea must become their highway to discovery."

Both knew that only the Portuguese were enlarging the borders of the known world. It was they who discovered and populated the Azores, certain that if St. Brendan in the sixth century could sail the Ocean Sea and find new land, they could do as well. Her aunt had told her of two islands discovered by Portuguese sailors, far beyond the line where land was supposed to lie. What might they discover beyond those two islands, Caryo and Flores? For a man who dreamed of sailing the Ocean Sea, Portugal was the place to go.

He saw her stifle a yawn and noticed the violet shadows beneath her eyes. "I must get a little sleep," she said. "You'll have to excuse me, Christopher. I have much to do before tomorrow. Portuguese troops still hold Toro, you know, and until I have Toro back again I can't rest completely. And Our Lady knows how much I need to rest. This isn't farewell, however. I'll talk to you again before you leave."

Back in his quarters, he said, "I've dreamed it all! But no, I did sit and talk with her. I smelled her perfume and breathed the sweetness of her skin. I felt the old warmth and so did she. I know she did! My heart pounded so loud I think she heard it, and I *knew* hers pounded, too. He smiled wryly in memory of such an off-handed manner she had told him she had to rest, without embarrassment, like a close friend would tell another. And he would see her again before he left. Yes, she had said before he left, so she knew he had to go just as he should know it. What had he expected her to say? What more could the Queen of Spain say to a woolmerchant? And yet, how gracefully she had handled the situation, how honestly, how like a perfect friend! "Truth and a rose have thorns," he told himself. "A romantic boy of eighteen years saw only the rose; the man of twenty-five must surely see the thorns. And when he saw her again, he could make the request which had brought him to her.

6

Toro surrendered on the nineteenth of September, and joyful Isabella rode into the city with her victorious army while the people cheered and thronged the churches. Christopher marched in the procession, but not with the Spanish soldiery. At the queen's suggestion he marched in his Portuguese uniform with the prisoners to be exchanged so as to avoid suspicion. If he planned to return to Lisbon, it would not do to go there suspected of desertion. He smiled ruefully, and admitted her plan was excellent. But would it prevent his seeing her one more time before he left? It wouldn't, he knew, for she had made a promise.

Then one day the longed for summons came. He squared his shoulders and followed the page. They went up and up and he realized they would soon be on the battlements; she must be there surveying her conquest, or perhaps she'd gone up there to be alone with him. The page stopped and opened a door. He saw her then standing in the sunlight gazing intently out across the countryside already turned gold beneath the autumn sun. A certain intensity in her face revealed how deeply she was moved. By what she had won or because she knew he would soon be with her? How dared he ask himself, but dare he did.

He came up behind her softly and looked over her shoulder. Still she didn't see him. The view over the edge of the battlements was as stirring as any he had seen in Spain. No wonder Spaniards had fought so hard for this fertile land of fields and orchards and vineyards. But the expression on the queen's face had told him she would have struggled equally hard for the barest, starkest mountain in Old Castile.

Without turning she said, "Was it beyond that ridge, my friend, that you bivouacked with King Afonso's army?"

He was just behind her now, and the wind brought him the aroma of her perfume. He whispered to keep his voice steady. "Yes, *Principezza*. Over there to the left of that knob-shaped little rise. Didn't his army ever strengthen the garrison in Toro?"

"No," she answered. "They retreated the day after you and Paolo reached our lines. Afonso never made contact with the Toro garrison."

Suddenly he felt he could not return with the Portuguese army to Lisbon. She would not be there. In Castile, though he might never talk to her, he could sometimes catch a glimpse of her riding her horse, waving to her people, and perhaps just once, at least, she would catch his eye and wave at him.

Isabella's mind harbored similar thoughts. "What would he think, what would he do," she asked herself, "if I asked him to stay? He would stay, to please me, but that would end his destiny." She couldn't think of him at court, trying to learn the flowery etiquette of the nobility, forcing his great limbs into courtly garb, enduring the sneers she knew would follow him because he was a commoner. "I'll never let that happen to him," she vowed. "It would be like clipping the wings of an eagle and chaining him to a perch." She shook her head. Slowly, unconsciously, she stripped the petals from a rose she had been sniffing. What would the confessor say when she admitted these wild thoughts? Christopher had to go, of course, and the sooner the better for them both. But why must she keep comparing him with Ferdinand, why take such deep satisfaction in the belief that he would never betray her with another woman? Why did it matter? Why not free him, drive him out of her mind? Why not hope he'd find a decent girl of his own class to have sons by?

She collected her flying thoughts with difficulty. The last petal drifted to the pavement. She could now speak with a steady voice. "Christopher," she said, "this may be our last farewell. I hate goodbyes. They remind me of funerals. So

I shan't say goodbye, but rather go with God until we meet again, as I pray God we shall some day.

"And Christopher, in Lisbon I see a productive life for you. Go there, learn navigation, learn all you must. And remember, if you ever fall on hard times and need my help, you must not fail to ask me for it."

He wondered what she would do if he suddenly stepped close and put his arms around her. He wanted to so badly that the naked carnality of it frightened him. "My God," he told himself, "I'm getting an erection! Suppose she felt it? By St. Ferdinand I'd rather die than have her know." That way lay madness and ruin. And yet, if she turned and said "Stay. Give up the Ocean Sea," he would stay and live on whatever crumbs fell from her table. Then something in the cast of her head told him she wouldn't change her mind. Now was the time to ask the favor, but he couldn't ask it.

"You are right, *Principezza*," he said. "So it must be. I'll say go with God to *you*, and pray we'll meet again."

Isabella tried to look into his eyes and for the first time failed. "My God," she burst out. "My God, woolmerchant, you've made me weep!"

He saw her fingers fumbling at a purse hanging at her waist. Her hands shook. Then she placed the whole purse in his hands. He felt the heaviness and heard the clink of gold. "I'm rich," he told himself, feeling no resentment in the gift, for he sensed the spirit in which she gave it.

"It's gold," she told him. "Take it for now, for he gives twice who gives quickly. You'll need money in Lisbon, and what chance would I have to send you more, once you're there? Buy with it what you need, Christopher, and never forget your dream of the Ocean Sea."

"But it's so much, *Principezza*," he faltered, afraid to look at her face and ashamed of his elation. He hadn't even had to ask!

Isabella, calm now that the gift was given, took time to advise him. "Be practical, woolmerchant," she said, "but indulge yourself a little, at least from time to time. And need I say it? Never, never mention this gift, or any other that may come from me to you. The sheep that bleats loses a mouthful. Oh, I could suggest a hundred uses for the money in Portugal, but it is yours with no strings attached. You'll spend it wisely—on your destiny.

Down in the courtyard the exchange prisoners were forming ranks. Their moment was running out. "Advise me, *Principezza*," he said, hoping to prolong the moment.

"If I were a man going to Lisbon to learn navigation," said Isabella, swallowing and looking again over the parapet, "I'd study Latin, Spanish and Portuguese until I could write and speak them all, and well. These three are the important tongues for navigation, in the Ocean Sea. Arabic might be, if one sails far enough to the east.

He hung his head, ashamed to lie again, but ready to, due to his need for safety. "I read a little Italian," he said.

"You needn't blush," she said kindly. "Not many men are educated, and few in Spain and Portugal can read and write even their native tongue. Fewer know Latin. Even the clergy—yes, many priests can't read. What a disgrace! God's minister unable to read the Holy Scripture!"

"I'll learn, *Principezza*," he said, his long jaw taking on determination. "I've heard some great scholars are commoners and have risen high. By St. Ferdinand, I'll learn if they did!"

He was right, she knew. There was an increasing aristocracy of the mind. Anyone who had intelligence to enter a university could become such an aristocrat. In fact, even the determined few who wanted to learn and had no money, might sometimes get ahead. Christopher could learn. But who would teach him manners, give him the polish he'd need? There were no schools of manners. And no one could learn courtly ways at home, unless he came from aristocratic stock. But there were books. She had known commoners who learned their manners from books like *Amadís of Gaul* and the *Trojan Chronicle*. And Don Álvaro de Luna, her mother's arch enemy, had written a book with an imposing and useful title—*The Book of Illustrious Women*. There were, of course, books on illustrious men. How important manners had become! No one, noble or commoner, succeeded these days without polish. Courtiers all knew this and read assiduously, emulating the well-mannered heroes of romantic fiction. The old virtues of courage, determination and physical strength were yielding to the courtly graces. People no longer immortalized the rough and ready Cid—they preferred the knights like Amadís and Lancelot.

"Christopher," she said, "after the sciences and the languages you must learn other things. Read *Amadís of Gaul* and the novels of chivalry. Read them with care in Portuguese or in Spanish. And as you read, remember that all Portuguese and Spanish gentlemen, nobles as well as middle class, value these books for the lessons in manners they present. They swear by these novels, particularly by *Amadís* as the greatest sources of courtly ways, and chivalric morality, for Amadís was the model knight and perfect gentleman, even more polished than King Arthur's best. I know many knights who carry *Amadís* with them wherever they go, even on campaign, and when they're in doubt, they consult it. The king himself is one such knight. My uncle the King of Portugal is another. Follow the ways of *Amadís* and you won't stray far from the path of virtue, courage and good manners."

He understood what lay behind her words. Suddenly he knelt at her feet, thrilling at the touch of her fingers on his shoulder. He felt the fingers tremble. He lowered his head. She must not see how red he was. "She's telling me I'm the boor I've made her think I am. And there's no way to let her know that I'm a gentleman, born and reared, no way to let her know that I'm related to her husband. My God! he is her cousin and I am his. Sweet Jesus, this queen and I share the heritage of blood, though distant! The books? *Amadís*, of course, I know, and also the *Trojan Chronicle*. And, when I can, I'll read the others because she wants me to."

A trumpet sounded in the courtyard. She drew him to his feet, hesitated a second, and then clasped both his hands between her own. Symbolically she had made him her vassal in the ancient way. She doubted he so much as suspected it, and was surprised when he said, "I owe you fealty, Queen."

For a long minute she held his hands in hers, looking deep into his eyes. He read her hopeless message, just as she read his. Then she was gone. Dazed, he made his way to the barracks to pick up his few belongings. Later, as he moved through the packed and narrow lanes, he didn't hear the derisive shouts of the populace nor feel the offal they hurled at the Portuguese captives on their way to freedom. He hardly knew it when they were marched out of the city gates. Only once he looked back hoping to catch a glimpse of blue gown and golden hair up on the battlements. If she was there, he couldn't see her. The distance was too great. Then the army topped the ridge and moved down into the plain on the other side. Toro became the past to him, the happy past. To Paolo he confided not a word about the money she had endowed him with, for he regarded it as an endowment, but with Paolo he shared one thought, "She is still my friend and she will help me If I ask again."

6

The Last Crusade

1

THREE YEARS HAD PASSED since Isabella said goodbye to her dearest friend in Toro. During those years she had little time to think of him, but she made time. When she despaired, when Ferdinand strayed, as now he often did, always carefully, always slyly, she let her mind go back to the woolmerchant. But now even Christopher faded from her mind. Afonso of Portugal had invaded her realm again. This time, since he must have known he couldn't win a war with Spain, he could only have been moved by pride and stubbornness or have been put up to it, nagged into it by Joanna. Isabella wanted no war with kinsmen. She had all she wanted with the upstart nobles and enemies across the Pyrenees. Perhaps this time she could win with brains and not with men and material. She wrote, therefore, to her Aunt Beatriz, who was the king's sister-in-law and a princess in her own right.

The princess replied immediately, confirming what Isabella suspected: no one in Portugal wanted war, not even the king; he had ordered his army into Spain to save face, also because he was too stubborn to give up his plans for the Beltraneja, poor little bastard of Beltrán, now in adolescence; and lastly because Joanna, his sister, never let him rest. But he would deplete his own and Castile's treasuries unless he could be mollified.

"Could you arrange, Isabella," wrote Aunt Beatriz, "to meet me near the border—in Spain, of course, and come prepared to make a treaty? You have the power and Afonso will give me the same power. He'll be relieved if you and I can work out something and stop this foolish war. His son, João, is even more anxious than he. Portugal has too much at stake in other spheres to waste its substance on useless hostilities.

Isabella smiled as she read. She knew of her aunt's own speculations in mercantile fleets. War could only hamper her interests and scuttle her income.

The meeting took place at Alcántara. To a casual observer it appeared to amount to no more than informal chats between two noblewoman who strolled rather aimlessly through the palace gardens and sat under the great oak trees, sipping cool drinks and picking at figs and sweetmeats.

In Lisbon, King Afonso grew restive and asked his son, "What can they be doing, João? They've been at it for days. By now they should have arrived at some conclusions." He went so far as to send couriers, but all the reply he got was that matters were making progress. Then one day good news came. The ladies had come to terms. They surprised each other at the ease with which it came about.

"You know," laughed Aunt Beatriz, "we should have done this the other times. No one is the loser. The boundary remains unchanged. And what Afonso wants, as to marriage ties with Spain, is really no concession on your part, niece."

"Well," said Isabella, "he wants me to betroth my Isabella to his grandson. I think that idea excellent. It's time the two countries were linked again in marriage. After Joanna and Henry, it's time, indeed. I do wish however, you hadn't insisted Isabella live in Portugal, but I suppose there's wisdom in it."

Aunt Beatriz laid a hand on Isabella's wrist. "It *is* necessary, Isabella. Your daughter, if she's to rule Portugal some day, must mature into a Portuguese princess. But she'll grow up in my house under my special care, and I promise you she won't forget her roots."

"It does make sense," mused Isabella sadly, "and what are a princess's desires when this kind of sense is made? With you beside her, and growing to maturity in Lisbon, she'll learn what's expected of her, and she'll meet and grow up close to the prince she'll marry one day."

"That settles it, then," said Aunt Beatriz. "Once the two families make the betrothal official, what hostilities can remain between them?"

"And the Beltraneja, Aunt Beatriz? That's what worries me the most."

Aunt Beatriz's face grew stern. "João leaned hard on his father, Isabella, and so did I," she said. "I told him that you'd never consent to the betrothal so long as he left that girl under the influence of her sluttish mother. I told him you'd have to be certain, not merely assured, that Joanna wouldn't devil him again into making war on Spain and, above all would not trouble your daughter."

"You made a compromise I don't much like," said Isabella, "and Ferdinand may be quite angry. Perhaps the Beltraneja will choose the proper option."

"Well," said Beatriz solemnly, "the girl has choices and that's more than most girls get in her position. She can be betrothed to your infant son Juan or she can go into a convent as a novice. I think she'll opt for the latter. Juan's age will persuade her. After all you only baptized him a year ago. Better far, she'll think to be a nun, a rich nun, in the Convent of Santa Clara in Coimbra. Her mother will insist, I'm certain. Can you even dream Joanna would let her flesh and blood be united to yours through royal marriage? I can't."

"That's the one hard nut to swallow. Our blood mixed with Joanna's and Beltrán's! Holy Mary! You simply *must* persuade Joanna and young Juana to choose the convent of Santa Clara!"

"I'm confident I can, Isabella. Poor little Juana, whom you Spaniards insist on slurring as the Beltraneja, is tired to death of being pulled and tugged. She can't go on living on dashed hopes and endure her mother's ravings. When I tell her she can take the veil, which by the way, she's thought about, I feel she'll take it as soon as she finishes her novitiate."

Isabella's eyes were moist. "Poor little god-daughter!" she said. "I've never hated her, you know. She was such a pretty baby. She had to be, no doubt, bred by two people as beautiful as Joanna and Beltrán. If she chooses Santa Clara in preference to little Juan, she'll make a wise decision. And, Aunt Beatriz, convent life can be appealing. I once considered it myself when I wasn't much older than Joanna's daughter. And two of Ferdinand's sisters long since entered convents to keep from being wed to God knows whom. I knew one of them when I was a child in Madrigal before my father died."

"I didn't know you ever thought that way, Isabella. What made you change your mind?"

"Aunt Beatriz, you wouldn't believe it if I told you, so I won't."

2

Aunt Beatriz yawned, and her head nodded. "Shall we go in and rest a bit?" asked Isabella.

The older woman shook her head. "I'm not sleepy." she apologized. "It's that heavy dinner we had. Let's stroll again and chat of other things than diplomacy, planned marriages, and forcing a child into a convent."

The fountain rose like a white plume and the air was mellow and warm in the high-walled garden. Birds sang, bees hummed in flowers, and suddenly war and ruling and planning faded. Aunt Beatriz was prattling of court life in Lisbon and of recent scandals.

"I'm not really interested," Isabella told herself, wishing she could tell Aunt Beatriz so. "But I must listen, for sometimes gossip affects statecraft and changes history." But she suddenly pricked up her ears when Aunt Beatriz mentioned the Perestrello family. Once, long ago when she had been a child, she had met a Perestrello woman and her daughter in Lisbon. She told Aunt Beatriz so.

"I'm glad you remember the mother and the daughter, Isabella. It always helps when one gossips about people other people know. You really won't believe how unconventional the daughter's marriage was. The court talked of it for weeks. All this was several years ago, but I haven't seen you in a long time and I like to bring people up to date "

"I'm beginning to remember the daughter, Aunt Beatriz. Wasn't her name Filipa? And her mother was Dona Isabel, I think."

"Correct on both counts, niece. You've got an excellent memory. Yes, Felipa's the one. A quiet little thing. But she grew up into a rather good-looking young lady, although afflicted with a certain lack of lustre. But for that dullness she'd have been a great favorite at court, in spite of her poverty. As you may recall, she belongs to one of Portugal's first families. Her grandfather was Don Gil Ayres Moniz who distinguished himself at Ceuta when he fought in the army of King Henry the Navigator. Lately the family has fallen on hard times, leaving Felipa and her mother to depend entirely on Felipa's brother who holds a captaincy in Madeira."

Isabella's mind wandered drowsily. Suddenly her aunt's words jerked her to attention. "We were all amazed when we learned Felipa had married a Genoese parvenu."

"A Genoese, Aunt Beatriz? Do you recall his name?"

"Oh yes, I remember it, even though he had it Latinized. I don't blame him, for Columbus is a heap more civilized than what it was in Genoese. So the change made sense. Why wouldn't he change it, when everyone in Lisbon is clamoring for the expulsion of the Genoese colony? They make trouble, you know, wherever they light, more trouble even than the Jews, if the truth were known. Columbus is not Italian, it's Latin."

Isabella kept her voice steady. "What's his name in Italian?" she managed to ask.

"Oh, I forget."

"Was it Colombo, Aunt Beatriz?"

"That's it, Isabella. But how did you know? Has someone told this already?"

Isabella shook her head. "I met a man named Colombo once. This husband of Felipa might be the man I knew."

The princess doubted it, and continued her account, relieved that no one had told the story to her niece. "We all wondered how the Perestrellos could allow the match." she said, wagging her head in disapproval. "Then the facts came out. It was the need of money. Felipa's mother turned out to be as poor as a church mouse, and her son either couldn't or wouldn't send money for his sister's dowry. So no one courted her, and her chances were as nil as they could get."

"How in the world did Felipa meet the Genoese, Aunt Beatriz?"

"In the usual place. Where did Dante meet Beatrice? In church, of course. The Genoese and his brothers were cartographers and made their maps in a studio in the district near All Saints' Convent where Felipa and her mother lived. The convent's chapel served that neighborhood as a church, and Columbus, who at least, is pious, took communion there and saw her. We have proverbs in Lisbon, 'If you want to find a wife, hear mass at All Saints.'

"I suppose he fell in love with her placidly pretty face. Possibly she smiled at him. She was twenty-five, you know, and must have been desperate. Before long Lady Isabel allowed him to come calling. She even left them alone at the grating. From there it was but a step to the parlor and betrothal."

Isabella tried not to look too intent. "Have you seen the Genoese, Aunt Beatriz?" she asked.

"He was pointed out to me in church, niece. Not at all what I thought a Genoese would look like. Not short, and dark, and oily. Rather handsome in a rough-and-ready way, tall, with hair like a torch and manly shoulders. I could see why Felipa was attracted to him well enough. Big, husky, powerful. But I'd have chosen someone for her less virile and energetic. He'll be too much for her, mark my words. And, Isabella, I felt as though I'd seen the man before, but how could I have? Probably he looks like someone I know, but I can't think who it is. It tantalizes me, I can tell you. Sometimes I can almost put my finger on it, and then it slips away."

Isabella knew exactly whom Aunt Beatriz was groping for. So far as she knew, no one else had identified the same features, the same wide-set eyes, even the same hair coloring and texture of skin. Of course, she herself had better cause to note the resemblance. It had never ceased to haunt her, and, sometimes when Ferdinand made love to her, it wasn't too difficult for the other face to drift across his own and mask its less attractive features. She quickly changed the subject, steering her aunt along another line of thought.

"How long have they been married?" she asked.

"Several years, Felipa became pregnant, naturally, and is said to be very, very happy. She said she didn't care whether or not Lisbon society accepted them. She always was a wallflower, so maybe it's just as well. I'd say society made her nervous. Anyway, they soon moved out to Madeira where the Genoese worked for her brother. The Perestrellos have a mercantile firm there, and even a fleet of ships in Mallorca. In the colonies, family matters mean less, I'm sure. I hope they found their place. I haven't thought or heard about them for a long time."

All the way back to Segovia Isabella thought about the woolmerchant and his marriage. She reconsidered the resemblance and wondered if it was true, as she had heard, that people who look alike, even when they are not related act alike. Was Christopher in bed with Felipa like Ferdinand with her? If so, Felipa could have done much worse. Ferdinand was an ardent lover and extremely talented. His amorous skills made up for many other faults. Christopher's marriage, however, sounded to her like a marriage of convenience, "He's more practical than I had supposed," she told herself. "I wonder how his Spanish and Portuguese have progressed. With a Portuguese wife, who speaks Castilian fluently, he may be very fluent himself by now. And, trading in the islands, living in a nautical world, sailing for her kinsmen, could surely prepare him for his destiny in the Ocean Sea. So he was married. She wished him well, and somehow a little of his lustre faded. Thinking of him married and making love to another woman saddened her. She had suspected that a man as vigorous as he, of course, had women in his life, but somehow women like that seemed not to get in the way of her feelings for him. But a wife was something else, and she realized why it was. She had taken comfort in fantasizing about him single, and faithful to her memory, and always there mentally, if she needed him, or he needed her. Now he had a wife, and it seemed she was a woman who would lean upon him hard. She feared she, Isabella, couldn't lean upon him now, not with Felipa leaning. But she would miss the woolmerchant more than she cared to admit. "And so," she told herself, "a piece of the fabric of my life is worn away. He's now out of the sphere of my world definitely, in his Ocean Sea, with a pretty wife and child to come home to, he'll find his destiny without me, and I will never know it."

3

On the twenty-second of April 1486 Isabella was thirty-five years old, and it chanced that one of the chroniclers met her strolling through the palace gardens. He wondered how a woman barely up from childbirth could look so youthful and lovely. He planned to say so in his history and when he wrote it, he described her thus.

"She is fair and blond," he wrote, "with eyes midway between blue and green. Her glance is pleasant and frank, her features carefully fashioned, and her entire face beautiful and happy with a gaiety that is decent and contained." He went on to explain that all this beauty was the reward of a life well-spent and of excellent habits, overlooking the fact that those excellent habits included riding over snow-covered hills in icy armor or through the fiery dust of summer to relieve some city or punish a rebel noble. He meant to convey the idea to posterity that she didn't indulge in alcohol, or in the coffee introduced by the Moors, and didn't spend her nights in orgiastic festivals like Joanna's. And since the classics were gaining great vogue, he likened her to a sturdy Penelope, and Joanna to a Circe. "Few women," he wrote, "look as fair and lovely and pure at the age of thirty-five as Isabella of Spain." He would have enjoyed continuing this pleasant excursus, and would have written more in the same vein had there been time; but the queen made history so rapidly he found it difficult to keep up with her in his writings. He hadn't yet recorded all the important events since the war with Portugal, and here she was about to plunge into what might well prove to be the most cataclysmic campaign of her career—the war with the Kingdom of Granada.

Isabella soon forgot the chronicler and his approving glance, never suspecting how she had troubled him. Her mind was on Brother Antonio Marchena's letter which arrived that morning from La Rábida. The woolmerchant was coming to Cordova. "He must speak with you, Highness," Brother Antonio wrote. She felt her face grow hot and didn't care. Ten years since that day in Toro when he had marched off to Lisbon with her purse of gold pieces in his grateful possession! And she hadn't succeeded in forgetting him, married or not.

Ten years! Holy Mother of Mercy how those years had flown! How much has come to pass! They hung on the wall of her memory like some dark tapestry, a blurred panorama shot through here and there with gleams of light. These gleams, she thought were rather like gold threads in a real tapestry. They served to focus her memory on outstanding happenings. Above all they marshaled a series of faces out of the past, faces that recorded events for her better than the most lucid chronicles. The woolmerchant's face in her mind, burning beside Felipa's ice; Joanna, banished to insignificance, with a gap-toothed smile and lips which could still leer at any man who looked in her direction; bright, terrible hate glaring from under the visor of a rebel noble who stood in chains and watched her soldiers turn his stronghold into smoldering rubble, the last of forty-six such holocausts; the bird-torn, parchment-like mask of a dead brigand hanging from a medlar. tree, swinging gently in a summer breeze, with clouds of green flies wheeling after it, back and forth, endlessly; Ferdinand's countenance aglow with pride and ownership as Aragón accepted him as king and her as queen when his father died; the soul-shaking, naked fear on the face of a renegade writhing in a mantle of flame on the *quemadero* erected in Seville by the Holy Inquisition; the lines of weeping, defrocked nuns leaving their convents to make atonement for their profligate lives; four hundred defrocked priests, abjuring their faith in the face of reform, fleeing to Morocco to accept Islam; Beltrán de la Cueva stripped of the greater part of his vast fortune, smiling ruefully at her and saying, as he knelt before her, "What will be will be, Highness;" the haughty, cruel king of Granada, described by her envoy who went to demand payment of the tribute, "Tell the Queen of Castile and her king that steel, not gold, is what we coin in Granada!"

She passed her hand over her face like a person sweeping away cobwebs. All those long years! And now the woolmerchant is coming out of the past again, out of the long but never dead past, to see her. She wished she had succeeded in erasing him from her mind, married or not, but he was always there, his wide-set eyes staring out of the darkness, the sound of his laughter and of the more serious quality of his voice ringing in her ears. For a little while he might make her forget all the grimness and horror of these years. He was coming soon. His letter said so, and even if she knew it could only be a few moments of forgetfulness, it would do her good. She could set aside a little joy for her coming to Cordova with her husband. After Christopher had come and gone, of course, they could return to their plan for the conquest of Granada, last stronghold of Islam in the peninsula. But she could for a day or so stop interviewing knights from all those foreign lands who had come to offer their swords, for a price, of course, to help them extinguish the light of Moorish power. She was tired of halls filled with ambitious soldiers of fortune, her own and from abroad, all eager to loot rich Moorish cities like Málaga, Vélez-Málaga and Granada itself. Yes, she could slip away also from priests and bishops, athirst to convert the thousands of infidels or drive them into the sea.

The other letter from La Rábida also still rested inside her gown. She couldn't lay it aside or show it yet to Ferdinand, though she realized she must do so and soon. Fondly she remembered Brother Antonio Marchena from that same distant past. He was a man to be heeded, when he wrote. Even Ferdinand would receive Columbus at Brother Marchena's request. The priest was far more than a successful administrator of the Franciscan sub-province of Seville, more than a former chaplain and father confessor of the present Queen of Spain. She would never forget his kindness when she had been a disinherited waif at Arévalo. And now, he knew better than any man in Spain the importance of what had been done and was being done in exploration and discovery. Even kings listened when he spoke out of the great fund of his wisdom. Yes, Ferdinand would hear Columbus out, at the request of Antonio de Marchena, but he wouldn't let anything distract him from his one, growing ambition the conquest of Granada and the wealth it would tumble into his pockets. To him the Ocean Sea and its exploration might someday be an interesting hobby, one practiced at present by his cousins in Portugal, but no more than that. Ferdinand saw little but Granada, and beyond Granada the strengthening of his borders against the French, with possibly future conquests of certain Italian duchies.

She unrolled Brother Marchena's letter and ran her eyes over it, smiling proudly from time to time. "Columbus is a man of imagination. And courage," wrote Brother Antonio, "with a zeal tempered with common sense and broad experience. He knows every cove and harbor in the Mediterranean; moreover, he is one of the few continentals to have sailed to Thule. Modestly I tell you, Highness, that I have studied mathematics and the latest treatises in navigation and geography. Humbly I report that Columbus surpasses me. This I find remarkable in a man not yet forty."

She read on, nodding in approval. Christopher had done well. He now read and wrote Latin, Spanish and Portuguese and had a reasonable familiarity with Arabic. He produced excellent maps, and he and his brothers had been successful in their sale. He had bought—piece by piece, she suspected—some of the best navigational instruments available. He was ready, in short, to meet his destiny at last.

His letter had a great deal more to relate. "A friend of mine, a widely traveled man," she read, "is canon of the Cathedral of Lisbon. His name is Fernão Martins. Once while in Italy he met a Florentine physician, one Paolo del Pozzo Toscanelli, a man so well-known and so scholarly that he exchanges letters with no less a personage than King João of Portugal. One of those letters told of a shorter route to the Spice Islands and Cathay. If what he wrote is true, which I strongly suspect is so, then this route is much, much shorter than the one the Portuguese hope to open up by sailing around the continent of Africa. Toscanelli sent a copy of this map to Lisbon with the route well marked all the way to the realms of the Great Khan. This route showed the location of many islands, among them the famous Antillia. But enough of Toscanelli. I now come to the reason that led me to this lengthy digression, Highness; Columbus has read Toscanelli's letter to King João and owns a copy of his map. Who can say how he came into possession of these? And, Highness, who cares, in spite of the scandal it aroused in Lisbon? The point is he has that map, and no doubt has long since sent copies of it out of Portugal to be on the safe side, in case his possessions should be searched in Lisbon. I have never asked him about the map, and if I had, I doubt that he would have confided in me, for it is his greatest secret. So even if the map, or the illegal copying of it and other maps must have lost him his place in Portugal and has sent him scuttling for safety across your border, he knows what few men know. Also, Highness, Columbus has written to Toscanelli and has had replies, for Toscanelli, although he is in his eighties, remembers a Genoese lad who dreamed his own dreams."

Isabella frowned again at the mention of the map. The Portuguese royal archives were not open to the public. If Columbus owned copies of important documents belonging to those archives, the less said about them the better. No wonder he had gotten into trouble.

She turned again to the letter. "Columbus is an unconventional fellow, Highness. He differs radically from the experts and even with Ptolemy, and though the Portuguese now doubt that Ptolemy was always correct, they still respect him and won't put him down for the sake of agreeing with a stranger like Columbus. Not even Toscanelli's similar beliefs have swayed King João and his nautical counselors."

Isabella knew how quickly Ferdinand would seize on this unfavorable information, and since it was in Brother Marchena's letter, there was no way she could keep it from him. Had she dreamed Ferdinand had known Columbus, she would have felt the bite of panic.

Brother Marchena's letter continued, "So even in Lisbon, where new ideas are heard and often adopted, Columbus's theories are considered dubious. King João's scholars call him a fool, another glib Italian full of lies and fantasies, even another Marco Polo, they call him, and therefore among the greatest liars of all time. King João dismissed him summarily and dashed his hopes of royal support in Portugal for his enterprise."

Isabella sat down on a stone bench and allowed the letter to slide to the floor. At least Christopher hadn't given up his dream. Now, even disillusioned by Portugal, he was setting out to talk to other rulers. If he had convinced Brother Antonio of his cause, others would have to listen. Her mind roved again through the content of Christopher's letter which moved her most. Apparently his life had been successful and even happy. Then bad luck had come. Felipa, after bearing him a son in Madeira, had sickened. Believing she couldn't improve in the islands, he had brought her back to Lisbon, as it turned out, to die, not to recover. They had buried her in the church at Carmo, and the funeral had beggared him, for he was proud and had given her a fine one. After that, troubles multiplied. King João, who at last had agreed to listen to him, who even promised a small fleet of caravels, refused when his committee of scientists vetoed the enterprise. Columbus, desperate, had threatened to go elsewhere for support, and King João, angered, refused to see him again, and in pique commissioned two Portuguese navigators to undertake the very enterprise he had set his heart upon. The fact that Fernão Dulmo and João Estreito failed to sail across the Ocean Sea to Cathay, and even King João's willingness to talk to him again in spite of his threats, were not enough to keep him in Portugal. Facing debtor's prison and in flight from Portuguese agents of the law, for the suspected theft of maps, he made for Spain with his son. There he had to leave the child at the Monastery of La Rábida in the care of the monks. It is a great pity, she thought, that men of talent, and faith, and dreams are to be subject to poverty and the sorrows it brings.

She carefully put the letters away. No need for Ferdinand to see them now. But she must see the woolmerchant soon and privately. If he was coming to her to gain the support he failed to find in Portugal, she must sound him out and find out what he needed. But what terrible timing, she thought, to seek her help when every *maravedí* was planned for the war against the Moors. Even so, she resolved not to let him leave Cordova with blasted hopes.

4

The Cathedral of Cordova, once the largest mosque in the world after that of Damascus, was a vast and shadowy place of subdued light and moving shadows. It looked to Isabella like a forest of marble columns with hardly two alike, since all had been carted to Cordova by the Moors from churches they had pillaged across the world. Their number was infinite and unbelievable. The tiny chapel she had selected for her private meeting with the woolmerchant was remote. They would not be interrupted. Beatriz had spoken to the dean who had promised complete privacy, raising his brows as he did so, but quite properly refraining from comment. Like most of his countrymen he believed that impropriety turned into courtly etiquette when the queen committed the impropriety.

At the entrance of the chapel she could see Beatriz waiting. Suddenly her heart leaped, for faint, but unmistakable came the sound of a man's footsteps somewhere out in the forest of stone. What would he look like, how would he talk, would he still smell of sweat and leather as he had the time she had sent him off from Toro with a purse full of gold? Then his tall form materialized and he came striding boldly toward her out of the gloom.

"He hasn't changed," she whispered to herself. Then on closer inspection, she changed her mind. He was heavier, as a mature man should be, but he was not meaty. His hair still flamed, as the lamp hanging from the vaulted ceiling, touched it with light, but silver, now in abundance streaked its fire. He was all but white at the temples. His eyes looked older, more piercing, and somehow not as frank and open. His skin so deep a copper that its color exaggerated the whites of his eyes and his teeth. And, even matured, he resembled Ferdinand—too much for comfort. He wore a decent doublet of good material and tailoring, and his hose and boots were proper. He could appear like this before anyone and be respected.

Before she could speak, he was kneeling at her feet, and for a long time, even after she commanded him to rise, he knelt with his face on a level with her own. Little crowsfeet radiated out from his eyes and testified how many years had passed and how the sun had taken its toll. Around his mouth, still too big and still capable of laughter, she saw lines carved by sadness and disappointment. Injustice and frustration had graven deep channels on both his face and his heart, she knew. His face said so, and she believed what it told her of his soul. But what surprised her most was a new reserve she didn't like, a kind of patient courtesy.

The time had come to speak. Why couldn't she say some of the warm and friendly words she had planned to say? Unaccountably, she wanted to plunge straight into the matter of his enterprise, something she had scheduled for the following afternoon. "I called you, my friend, because I thought we should talk before you face the king," she said.

"I had hoped you would, *Principezza*," he replied with a new, quiet charm. "It was gracious of you. I hardly expected so much."

She couldn't keep her eyes from his face, nor could he from hers. Their eyes spoke what their lips never could. Neither said anything personal, and both felt the new strangeness of it, for in all the years they had known one another they had been at ease. She made herself speak, say what she should, not what her heart wanted to say. "Brother Antonio has written a great deal about you, Christopher. And you have told me in your letter of your bereavement. I met Felipa once. Did you know that?"

"So now she knows," he thought, "and yet her eyes tell me that it has not changed her feelings for me entirely, perhaps not even greatly. What change there is may be for the best."

"She told me, *Principezza*. We spoke of you often. She thought it strange that I, a commoner, had known you better than she, a noblewoman had. She remembered you kindly from the visit you made to Lisbon so long go."

He stopped and sadness dampened his eyes. She longed to brush a lock of his hair from his forehead but joined her hands instead. "I know your sorrow is fresh," she said. "May Our Lady soon assuage it. I know, too, that you have a son. Have you brought him with you to Cordova, or is he still with the monks at La Rábida?"

"Still with them, *Principezza*. Diego wanted so to come, but I couldn't have him on my hands. When I brought him ashore at Palos, I didn't know what I'd do with him. He's too young to take about with me. The only people I know in the area are Diego's aunt and uncle in Huelva. But they're poor and had never seen the lad. I was too embarrassed to seek them out. Then I learned that the monastery up on the hill belonged to Franciscans and that they had a school for boys. Trusting in their proverbial hospitality, I dared ask them to keep Diego for me until I could make other arrangements. Then, when Brother Antonio met us at the gate, I knew my prayers were answered. The brethren have taken the best care of my son."

He lowered his head, "He's praying," she thought. Then he looked up with the movement that fondly reminded her of a lion, and continued, "Brother Antonio is a remarkable man, *Principezza*. He has read everything! He's formed amazing opinions! I believe most firmly that my destiny sent me to his door."

Isabella was pleased to hear him speak of destiny. This was more like the old woolmerchant on the road to Ávila.

"Brother Antonio writes me you have formed a few opinions yourself," she said. Then, seeing him about to speak, she hastened on. "Christopher, why didn't you come to me at first? Why did you go to the Duke of Medina Sidonia and the Count of Medina-Celi?"

She saw frankness as she had known it before, when he looked at her. "*Principezza*," he said, "I can never forget hearing you say first things come first. Brother Antonio explained your concern with the war against the Moors. He believed King Ferdinand wouldn't even hear any plan not connected with the war. And the duke and count showed such active interest from the first. In fact, the duke was ready to let me have the needed ships when that unfortunate incident occurred for which you and the king banished him from Seville."

Isabella burned at the memory. "He had a common brawl with the Duke of Cádiz right in the streets of Seville, and not far from where the king and I were lodged! We never tolerate brawling between the nobles. Nothing shows less respect for majesty. Yes, we banished him along with his adversary. I'll wager they'll ponder long the next time their sword hands itch! We'd warned them twice to give up feuding, but it's a waste of time to speak with the deaf or with Andalusian nobles!"

"After the brawl that ended in banishment of my would-be backers," Christopher said grimly, "Brother Antonio suggested I appeal to the Count of Medina-Celi. I did and was elated, for he owned ships and actually promised me four caravels... four! I actually saw them, walked on their decks in his shipyard at Puerto Santa María. And then you, *Principezza*," he said, looking at her reproachfully, "sent word to him to revoke his offer and withdraw his support! I didn't know what to do then, but the count allowed me to stay on at his yards and work in his offices. I was ready to give up in Spain and try some other country when Brother Antonio informed me he had persuaded you to talk to me. It seemed to be the only thing to de since I knew we were good friends. And here I am to ask you what I'm to do."

"I can't tell you my motives, Christopher, not yet, at least. Later I hope you'll understand. For the present believe me when I say I'm doing all I can. I know the Count of Medina-Celi better by far than you. And, if you must drag it out of me, I wanted no one else concerned with our double destiny. I want to be your sponsor.'"

"That makes sense," he said, "but how long must I wait? I've been a patient man, *Principezza*, but even my patience is running low."

She looked at him askance. Never had he displayed such an attitude to her. The years had been long, too long. "Think," she said a little sternly. "Twice already events have brought us together for our mutual advantage. I believe those meetings were providential. I feel we mustn't let strangers, even well-intentioned ones, intrude into our common destiny."

He looked like a man who has had his first premonition of death. "But the king," he began. "Will he listen? Will he allow you to be my patron, provide my ships, give me the power and money I need to sail the Ocean Sea for Spain?"

"He'll listen, woolmerchant, but he won't help you at present. We have no funds to spend on exploration. We're dedicated entirely to the war. It's our crusade, Spain's last crusade, against the infidel. Granada must fall before you have your fleet."

She stopped when she saw the look of bleak disappointment clouding his eyes, the confusion in his face, and the sudden grimace of hurt and disillusionment. Two very deep lines drew his mouth at the corners, making him look much older. She could think of nothing to say but "First things first," and she knew she said it lamely.

He closed his eyes and listened bleakly. When he opened them they were baleful and fierce with rage, rage at her, she knew, and she shrank back in surprise.

"You really don't understand, do you Christopher?" she asked at last. "You don't because you've decided you don't want to. Christopher, Christopher, I can't tell you how sorry I am, or how necessary what I am doing is for both of us."

"But," he growled, "but for you I might even now be outfitting the caravels of the Count of Medina-Celi. Again I ask. Why did you forbid him to finance me? The reasons you've given are not sufficient."

She could hardly believe her ears. Could this be her woolmerchant, this man who dared to question the Queen of Spain? Anger, fierce and hot, because it grew from hurt, boiled up in her. She had to grip the arms of her chair to keep from uttering words she could never recall, words which would end everything good that existed between them. God, how stubborn, how uncompromising, how rude he was! She made herself go on. She explained the importance of Granada and tried to make him see how its people led lives in utter contradiction to all that all good Christians regarded as right and proper. Spaniards, especially young men who went there on business or as members of her frequent embassies, breathed the pestilential air and often were corrupted hopelessly. Strange perversions, exotic excitements, intemperance in drugs like hashish, polygamy, even sodomy, existed there and were condoned. Some said even were deliberately propagated.

He raised his eyes and stared into hers still unseeingly. "The Moors are as God made them, *Principezza*. Must you try to change them?"

She chose to ignore the irresponsible remark, attributing it to his dismay. She stumbled on, realizing how futile it was to explain to a man too hurt and furious to listen, but on she went. "I cannot rest, therefore," she said, speaking too quickly, "not while Granada stands in open defiance of us, refuses to pay the yearly tribute which has been paid for two hundred years, and I will not endure the present persecutions of our holy faith. That evil, opulent city must fall before we can begin to undertake your enterprise, no, *our* enterprise. Bear with me, Christopher. Wait!"

He said nothing for a long time. Then he blurted out, "*Principezza*, I've waited too long. Granada is strong and may never fall. Your people have been trying to bring it down past memory. I've tried to make you understand. I see you can't, or worse still, you won't. Must I crawl back to Portugal and try to untangle the mess I made of my life there, or must I try France? I need your answer and I feel I must demand it."

"Demand it!" she said involuntarily. "You dare demand of me, your queen and sovereign, of me, your friend?"

The look on his face stopped her flow of words. It had broadened startlingly. Muscles rippled along the line of long jaw rounding it, stealing away its angles. His chin seemed to vanish in his pouting lips. His head, with its thatch of hair seemed like an angry round red sun. But his eyes were granite, not kind or worshipful.

"What more can I say?" she asked. Then she reached out to take his hands in hers again. He deliberately withdrew them from her reach. "Oh, Christopher, woolmerchant!" she cried in real alarm. "What's becoming of us and of our friendship? Think, man! Arrows don't hurt as much when you see them coming. That's why we had this meeting. I called you so I could point out the arrows before they struck. The king will certainly reject your proposition, but I shall not. Trust me. Keep hope in your mind. More propitious times will come. I swear they will."

She had to lean forward and strain to catch his words. She had never dreamed he could become so enmeshed in the throes of feeling. Again his eyes clashed with hers in anger, and stirred anger in hers likewise. She watched his great fists, like hammers of tension, knot and clench and open and close. "I shall try to understand," he was saying, "though it is hard. But the matter of the Count of Medina-Celi... Oh God, why couldn't you have let him be?"

"Stubborn," she thought. "As stubborn and proud and determined as an iron mule." "Someday you'll learn," she snapped at him, "that when the air is frosty, a late mulberry's better than a flowering almond."

He rose slowly to his full height, towering far above her. Every line of his big body radiated resentment. "Am I still to meet the king?" he asked.

"Of course you are, Christopher. Didn't I say you would? Tomorrow at the sixth hour, and be prompt. My husband will listen, I promise you. And who knows, maybe he can convince you where I can't."

When she had dismissed him as politely as she could, when he strode away, his spine a ramrod, his gait as haughty as a king's, she sat drained and desolate. Could the friendship be revived out of ashes such as these? Had she killed his dream and deprived herself of a surrogate lover? "Holy Mary," she said aloud. "Did I think that thought? Is this what I've been living with all these years? I won't admit it, even to myself. If Christopher rejects my offer, then reject he must. He will have one more chance. And I can live without him in my mind but only with God's help.

5

"To speak without thinking is like shooting without taking aim," Isabella told herself. "But to keep silent when it's time to speak is far, far worse. Watching her husband and the woolmerchant face to face for the first time, she realized how unwise she had been not to prepare them for the fatal resemblance. Now that it was too late, she could do no more than regret her reticence, watch in fascination, and wonder what thoughts were passing through their minds. Something portentous it seemed!

"I should have told Ferdinand, at least" she berated herself silently. "Of course, he's furious and confused. If only I hadn't told him about that ride with Christopher in the litter! He is thinking about that, I suspect but even so, he knows me better than any one else in the world, and he trusts me and only me."

Then she focused her thoughts on the woolmerchant. He, too must be nonplussed and probably more than curious. Could he, in his strange new perceptiveness be daring enough to think that she sometimes imagined he was with her when she was with her husband? Banish the thought! He could hardly bear to tread on ground so dangerous.

As to Ferdinand's anger, there was no question of its presence. He was scrutinizing the woolmerchant with his most enigmatic look, the one that revealed nothing but hinted much, the one that made her wish he didn't have it.

Christopher returned his gaze with hostility, and this, too, infuriated her husband. Then Christopher turned his eyes to meet her own. His expression made her drop her eyes to her belt and study its buckle with remarkable concentration. In spite of herself she blushed when she caught a knowing look, in its way more enigmatic and speculative than Ferdinand's. He, too, noted the resemblance. He was thinking what she hoped he wouldn't. She was certain of it. But there was something else. She sensed that this confrontation between her husband and her friend was to be cataclysmic. It was as though two opponents, who knew one another very well and hated everything they knew had unexpectedly been brought face to face. Surprise, first on Christopher's face and then on Ferdinand's blossomed, and then suddenly vanished as though by mutual consent. But a hatred, as though smoldering across many years, now burst into flame. She could almost hear the flames crackle. How could such feelings surface and yet be held under such cold-blooded control. How could two men who had never seen one another feel such obvious antipathy? Could they have met? How could they have when one was a king and the other a peasant? And yet she and this same peasant had met and become friends. The interview went wretchedly. Ferdinand listened politely, but coldly, out of deference to Brother Antonio's excellent reputation, not because he felt the least compulsion to interest himself in a foreign dreamer's hare-brained schemes or because his wife was taking a singularly mysterious interest in them. He was still sweating with the anger engendered by Christopher's unfortunate remark to the effect that he hoped the king had taken time to read his proposal carefully. Ferdinand, she knew, prided himself on never discussing any matter he hadn't studied with meticulous care and suspicion. The look he bestowed on Christopher was surely the most baleful he could summon without damaging his vaunted diplomacy in public.

He caught her off guard as well as Christopher by assuming one of his rarer stances. He made himself appear insultingly patronizing, the way fathers sometimes are when explaining a simple matter to a stupid offspring. In measured, polite, but coolly clipped accents he reminded them both, but especially Christopher, who as a proclaimed foreigner could not be expected to understand Spain's internal problems, that the country was at war with Islam. Granada had to fall. He even quoted Cato, substituting Granada for Carthage, "Granada *delenda est*," he intoned, implying that the Genoese, of all people, should understand what the threat of Islam means. Had Christopher, he asked, forgotten the seizure of Otranto almost yesterday and the fleet that Spain sent to the city's relief? If Islam dared attack continental Europe itself, even Italy, where no Moors lived, how much more terrible the threat to Spain where uncounted thousands of the infidel had dwelt for generations? He let himself be carried away with martial zeal and repeated a metaphor that Isabella had been hearing for several months. "Granada is exactly what its name means. It's a great, ripe pomegranate, filled with the seeds of discord. I intend to squeeze it seed by seed, Moor by Moor, until I hold in my hand the shrunken husk. Only then will Christendom rest secure!"

While he spoke Isabella saw Christopher stand stock still with shoulders very squared and stiff, head lowered like a dutiful petitioner. Then a slow wave of red swept from his neckline to disappear into the roots of his hair. She prepared herself for a terrible explosion.

Ferdinand was in his element and she hated it. There he was, savoring the weight of his own rhetoric, making each word a sledgehammer's blow, "The sovereigns," he said, drifting into the third person, "would find it impossible now and under the present circumstances, to consider anything that might distract their attention or channel away a single *maravedí* from their purpose. You must accept our reasons," he added. "And convey them correctly to Brother Antonio de Marchena when next you see him. Indeed, we shall ourselves dispatch a letter. "The sovereigns regret," he went on with most regal formality, "that they must arrive at this decision, but for the time the navigator must consider it final and unalterable. In months to come, however," he went on to say, by way of conclusion, "and once the war is won, the sovereigns might quite possibly listen again to the petition of the navigator."

The explosion never came. Something, not resignation, settled over Christopher. He shot an appealing look at her and in it she again saw naked fear. It shocked her, for she had never seen him afraid of anything. How could this fear smother what she had expected to see—sodden, angry disappointment despair, and then the return of confidence in a destiny, a blind faith that not even Ferdinand's rejection could dispel? The fear in Christopher's face, for now it suffused his entire countenance, was contagious. She found that she was trembling and something told her that only she could hope to dispel that fear and that the task would be one of her most trying.

Isabella looked at her husband, who looked as though at any second he would summon his guards. When her eyes returned to Christopher, she was pleased to see how well he had profited by her advice to read and learn the manners of Amadís. His shoulders didn't slump, as would a lesser man's, as would any one who was not of noble blood, but he lowered his eyes to conceal their anger, their terrible hatred and their fear. No longer did he appear as the impetuous youth she had loved so much and dreamed of who had opened his heart to her on the road to Ávila, even though he knew she was a princess. The man of forty, who had dared glare at her and question her motives only yesterday, had changed into a courtier, who was masking his feelings, because he realized it behooved him to, and, she kept thinking, because he is truly scared to death. Before Ferdinand of Aragón and co-ruler with Isabella of Castile, he was forcing himself, as any other frightened courtier would do, to conceal the disillusionment that comes at an age when one realizes he has made too many wrong decisions and must make no more. She sensed a nearly frantic desire to get out of that chamber and even to take to his heels. She could not approve of these changes, but she instinctively knew that they were motivated by something deep in his past and in Ferdinand's.

Ferdinand later referred only once, and then succinctly, to his resemblance to Columbus. "You might at least have warned me, Isabella. It took me quite off guard to gaze into that face so like my own and yet so different. It was damnably disconcerting, like looking into a distorted mirror."

She made herself look at him innocently and wondered if his duplicity was rubbing off on her. "There is, now that you mention it, some slight resemblance," she said, 'But the man's hair is so much redder and much more coarse, and he lacks your grace and breeding. Your aristocracy contrasts so with his peasantry..."

"Thank you," said her husband dryly, "but let me tell you this; there is more nobility of blood, but not in character, in this Columbus than you might suspect, my dear."

"I don't understand," she said. "I first knew him as a peasant, but we all know that with the proper training a peasant may emerge as a polished gentleman. I'll admit that today I saw something of such a metamorphosis. And Ferdinand, I saw something else, or sensed it. There was fear, the kind of fear that royalty can inspire, especially the grim royalty you displayed to him. Why was the man so fearful? Why did you and he look at one another like ancient foes? Have you known this man in the past?"

His face assumed that furtive, careful expression which she had learned to know meant, "I'll have to ponder this before I give an answer. This is not the time to discuss it," he said, "but the time will come, and of this I assure you.

To divert him she asked, "Whom shall he appoint to the committee?"

Ferdinand raised his brows infuriatingly, as only he could. "We, my dear? What committee? I hadn't heard there was to be one or what it was to treat. "

"I thought we might have qualified, learned men look into Columbus' enterprise," she said.

"Since you say a committee must be appointed, I'll leave it in your hands. This is Castile, not Aragón, so you appoint whomever you wish, and let's be done with this accursed would-be Genoese."

The second he pronounced the words 'would-be,' she saw he was furious at himself for failing to hide something he didn't care to discuss. It disturbed her, for rarely did her husband unintentionally reveal his feelings. "What did you mean," she asked "by 'would-be' Genoese? Why do you suspect that he may not be one?"

He actually smirked at her pityingly, condescendingly. "All in due time, my dear. All in due time." And he would say no more.

She knew him well enough not to insist. In due time he would give her the answer, and she was afraid she wouldn't like to hear it. Perhaps she could learn that answer from the woolmerchant, if or when she could find him, since she wanted to tell him about the committee. That should serve to bring him back to his destiny.

She was glad Ferdinand left her free to appoint the committee to examine the woolmerchant's enterprise. She wouldn't weigh it in his favor, but she would try to appoint men with clear and scientific minds and no preconceived antipathies. She named as chairman Father Diego de Deza, principal of St. Stephen's College at the University of Salamanca. His reputation as a mathematician would impress even Ferdinand, and Christopher would have to acknowledge how great her interest was. She resolved to give up the services of her present confessor, Brother Hernando de Talavera, and place him on the committee, balancing him with no less than Cardinal Mendoza himself. Christopher could never say she didn't have the enterprise at heart.

Ferdinand's refusal to touch the procedure freed her from discussing with him a pension for Christopher while he waited the results of the committee's deliberations. Nevertheless she broached the matter to him, because she knew his skill with figures and respected his concepts of matters commercial. His reply infuriated her.

"Do as you will, Highness," he had said tartly. "You are the Queen of Castile, and I'll abide by your decisions. As for me, I'll have no part in providing bed and board for this, useless fly-by-night. Pension him if you must. But turn him over to Don Alfonso de Quintanilla, your own comptroller. I trust that man, for he knows what makes the world go round and respects its hardness and its jingle. But do, please, Isabella, accept one word of counsel from your Aragonese husband; keep the 'Genoese' away from the professors. His manners, his very air, his crust—for that is what he has—will militate against him. Among such august scholars he'd be worse than the proverbial bull in the china shop. He's a rebel against what we, or at least what I, hold dear. And nothing will ever change him!"

Ferdinand's advice, even though couched in enigma, even though with references which seemed incongruous about rebelliousness proved sound. Columbus, at her suggestion, wrote up his plans and submitted them to the committee, along with his maps and calculations. Then he waited while the ecclesiastics pondered everything. Wisely, she thought, she had not scheduled the meetings at the University of Salamanca, but to give the matter a less formidable air, in the Dominican Monastery of St. Steven, in which she had reserved Columbus' lodgings. The professors had had to come to him, as it were. The ecclesiastics worked slowly and thoroughly, determined to live up to the queen's expectations, and never to fail to take into consideration the burden of religion. After all, religion and learning were identical disciplines. The Inquisition was ever-present in people's minds, especially in those of the clergy. Every opinion had to be researched assiduously to see if could be considered heretical. Opinions which were regarded as dangerous to the faith were rejected and often the minds which produced such opinions were burned away along with the bodies which housed them. Isabella had no idea how prejudiced the committee was against her woolmerchant. He was in some of their minds a young delinquent and a foreigner. At best he seemed an adventurer and a man who wanted to deceive the Spanish people with untenable theories. At least two who were not aristocrats were heard to whisper that they resented his ambitious plan.

Christopher soon sensed and then learned for certain that his greatest sin in their eyes was this: they considered him presumptuous in maintaining the discoveries he had made concerning navigation and geography were reserved for him and not for all those myriad sailors who had been sailing the seas since biblical times and all the great philosophers such as Aristotle and Seneca. Perhaps of equal wickedness was his statement that there could exist a part of the earth fictitiously knows as the Antipodes, where all was upside down, including people. Worse still, St. Augustine had made it clear that there could be no inhabited lands on the other tide of the globe, since Adam's descendants could not possibly have crossed so much water. Some of Christopher's theories actually contradicted the Bible, which insisted that all people had descended from Adam.

These ecclesiastical deliberations had taken place without the presence of Columbus, but at last the time came when they must question him face to face. Isabella nervously awaited the results. What she heard upset her. Christopher and the committee to a man had clashed violently. What Father Diego reported disheartened her. "The navigator," he told her, "was unreasonable and irascible. The progress of the deliberations has slowed down appreciably, Highness."

When she told Father Diego she wanted to attend the next meeting, he demurred. "Wait a little longer, Highness, if you please. The navigator is insisting that the Ocean Sea is narrower than it can possibly be. Until we hear him out and convince him of his error, Brother Hernando and I feel…"

"Who spoke of Brother Hernando?" asked a deep voice from the doorway.

"Come in, confessor," said Isabella, startled by his unexpected arrival. "Father Diego was just telling me you disagree with Columbus's calculations. Do, please, nevertheless hear him out, even if his statements about the Ocean Sea discompose you. Brother Antonio has great faith in him, you know, and so do I."

Hernando Talavera bowed his head. With his long sleeves rippling in the morning breeze, he reminded her of an old and very scrawny raven.

"We shall hear him out, Highness. But I must tell you this in all frankness: the man is headstrong—worse still, he bases his reasoning on erroneous ideas already fixed firmly in his stubborn mind. Moreover, he is rigorous to a fault, Highness, and he alarms—I might say, frightens—the good professors accustomed to the calm of the cloister and the respect of students. If they were not divines I fear he would be so carried away as to lay hands on some of them. Fortunately, the fellow respects the cloth, which is a credit to him, and is content with turning red and pounding the table with his fists. One would think he was noble, so confident is he."

Isabella concealed a smile at these references to the woolmerchant's fixed ideas and violent gestures. She had fixed ideas herself. When she knew she was right, nothing could change her mind. Christopher knew he was right, believed firmly in himself, and would not, could not understand why the grim old men at the university could not follow his reasoning.

Talavera hadn't finished. "We suspect his accuracy also, Highness, and this is serious. The man has had little formal schooling. He makes mistakes. And alas, he places too much credence in Ser Marco Polo, the greatest liar of them all. Marco Polo contradicts Ptolemy! So does the Genoese."

Having voiced so dreadful a statement, Brother Talavera stopped to observe its effect upon the queen. When she didn't react, he was dumbfounded. Had her mind wandered to some other subject? "I was saying, Highness, that he dared to contradict no less an authority than Ptolemy. Can you even imagine what it means to belittle Ptolemy in the halls of the University of Salamanca? The professors will never get over it."

Isabella parried. "But what of Toscanelli, the great physicist and geographer? He, too, refutes Ptolemy."

Brother Talavera swallowed before he could continue. "Toscanelli is like Marco Polo and your hardheaded Genoese. The committee considers Ptolemy far superior to any Italian alive today. Did Ptolemy ever mention this island of Cipangu harped on so much by Columbus and his compatriots? Never! Did any of the Ancients? Not one.

"Then there is the matter of the distance from Spain to Cathay. Every professor on the committee, as well as several in retirement, believed that one would have to sail ten thousand nautical miles into the Ocean Sea to reach Cathay, if indeed it could be reached by water. Columbus insists, and stubbornly, Highness, that the distance is no more than twenty-four hundred miles. It cannot be so close. Even Toscanelli places it at five thousand! The committee is angry. How, they ask, can this Genoese juggler of figures stand before them and presume to argue with his betters? They would have rejected his entire enterprise long ago but for your interest in it."

Isabella sighed. "You and the professors must be patient, Brother Hernando. Columbus has great faith, and faith moves mountains. Perhaps he isn't entirely wrong."

"Highness, we are patient!" cried the confessor, unable to overcome his emotions. "We explain it to him over and over, carefully, slowly, as one would explain to a little child. We point out that even if he *could* sail with perfect winds, if there were no delays of any kind, and if his ship could average four knots all the way, it would still require fourteen long weeks to arrive in Asia, if, of course, the journey could be made at all. And you will not believe me, Highness, when I tell you his answer. He says he is right because he knows he is! The man cannot bear the thought of failure, for failure is more intolerable to him than the annihilation of his immortal soul. And, Highness, the fellow does not know his station"

"I admire his faith, Brother Hernando. Let's pray he justifies it."

"Children have faith, Highness, and in them it is commendable. But the faith of the Genoese smacks of immaturity."

Isabella looked at the confessor until his eyes fell before hers. "A pity," she said, "that more people are not so immature. The world would be a better place." She felt sorry for the woolmerchant hemmed in at the University by all those gowns and beards, but by Holy Mary they would hear him out. Meanwhile, he would continue on the payroll of Castile.

She was not surprised when the committee made its report. It was what she had expected. The professors, resting on the firm foundations of an ancient and venerable tradition, reported the enterprise unfeasible, and therefore unworthy of royal support. In short, they sent a flat rejection.

"I shan't reject the enterprise," she told her husband, whose smile of triumph faded on his lips. "Another committee shall study it while we renew the war."

6

After the committee rejected his enterprise Christopher dropped from official view and appeared only to collect his pension. Isabella, too busy with the war to inquire, asked Beatriz de Bobadilla to keep an eye on his comings and goings. Beatriz, who had grown to like the woolmerchant, as Isabella still insisted an calling him, made detailed inquiries. She learned he had taken up arms and was training in a recruitment center on the outskirts of Cordova. Isabella was touched, but Ferdinand rolled his eyes and opined that Columbus hoped to get more out of service than the satisfaction of a patriot. Isabella turned away to conceal her anger. At last she said, "He'll run great risk as a common soldier. But heaven won't let him die. Not after it has let him come this far and dream so boldly."

Beatriz continued her inquiries. It would do no harm to keep an eye on him as long as she could, for once he was off to war, she realized, it would be too difficult. Also she was the overseer of his pension in that it was she who stood behind the treasurer and saw that he dispensed the money promptly each month. She thought a great deal about the Genoese, as her husband still called him. Ever since Isabella told her years ago about his solicitude in the litter, his consolation at the funeral, and above all, about his insistence that she follow her destiny, even as he planned to follow his, she had allowed considerable affection for him to fill her heart. Moreover, she saw depths in him that no one besides the queen seemed to see. The man possessed some rare quality, she was certain, and one deep look into his enthusiastic dreamer-eyes told her he was indeed destined to go far. Christopher Columbus was no ordinary mortal. It surprised her that others failed to see it too. So it was not difficult for Beatriz also to become a guardian angel. And once she made her mind up she never faltered. Christopher would never know all she did for him, nor, even, would Isabella. She managed at last to make her husband see at least part of what she saw, and thereby won Christopher a supporter he was certain one day to need. It was Beatriz, too, who first got wind of his affair with Beatriz de Harana, a matter she thought it best to keep from Isabella. It would hurt her, she knew, and might jeopardize the very outcome of the enterprise. Smaller matters than a queen's hurt had changed the course of history. No need to disillusion Isabella when she needed all the illusions she could hold onto. No need either to jeopardize Columbus's chances. "Isabella," she told Andrés, "wouldn't revoke the pension of someone she didn't know, but she knows Columbus well, and as I've often told you, my love, she feels for him. Hurt and disillusionment might make even Isabella petty."

Andrés, in his manlike, straightforward, no-nonsense way came directly to the point he wished to make. He could, Beatriz knew, not comprehend a platonic friendship between a beautiful queen, whose husband strayed and grieved her with his bastards, and a well-knit man like Christopher. "Are you dead certain, Beatriz," he asked "that nothing happened in that litter?"

Beatriz's eyes blazed. "Andrés, you know the queen. You know it couldn't have! For part of the ride they had priestly chaperons and at no time were the people in her escort out of sight."

"I suppose not," he admitted. "When I look at her, as lovely as she is, I see only a puissante queen with an eye not for men, but for wars and ecclesiastical reforms. Yet you tell me she burns like any other healthy woman, and you, of all people, know her best. I trust your judgment, Beatriz. But never forget that if you're wrong and she ever slips, the repercussions will shake the world. And Isabella was a healthy, teen-aged virgin, and Christopher was a lad also teen-aged when they traveled all those miles together in the litter. Today she is a woman experienced in love."

Beatriz leaned over and kissed him. "Andrés, my love, be certain that I am correct. Isabella inexplicably cares for Christopher, may even in her saddest hours of disillusionment with the king, wish she could exchange his royal arms for the rough ones of the woolmerchant; but the wish will never get beyond just that, a secret wish, if it really is a wish. I'm not really certain what she feels for him. He's such a physical person, so big, hearty, warm, and I'm certain, sensuous. He radiates something no woman can resist. He ensorcells them, I tell you, and I've not seen one who could look at him and maintain her aplomb. I'm moved myself, Andrés, for when I look at Christopher, see his eyes when he speaks about his destiny, feel the emanation of the boundless energy that burns inside him, I feel what any woman of flesh and blood must sense—power, sympathy and an animal magnetism. If I didn't have you, my dear, and I mean in bed, I could do worse than dream of Christopher."

"God!" laughed Andrés. "You women! You're all alike when it comes to that! I'd best look out when the Genoese is in the neighborhood. But as for me, I can't see in him what women must. Big, yes, strong and handsome in a craggy sort of way, but still a peasant and therefore unacceptable." Beatriz squeezed her husband's hand.

"Of course you don't," she laughed, "and if you did, I would begin to have bad thoughts about you. Christopher is a man, all man, and so are you. So there's your explanation. Also Andrés, I don't believe he is a peasant."

Andrés scratched his head. "And yet, with all that magnetism and animality which obviously the queen hasn't failed to notice and be attracted by, you're certain she'll never step beyond the bounds, especially if he has noble blood."

"I'm certain, Andrés. I know I can't explain it. Even I have doubted and feared. I've seen his eyes when he looks at her and doesn't realize I am there. It was like that the day he visited her in the Cathedral of Cordova. I met him as he left her and I saw his eyes. He told me goodbye and even bent to kiss my hand, but he hardly realized I was there. Those eyes of his, as large as the eyes of a stag, glowed with a light I'd never seen before in the eyes of a man. Oh, I recognized love, perhaps even desire, I'll go so far as to say, definitely desire. His eyes burned, Andrés, with a light I've seen in paintings of St. Anthony under his direst temptation—a combination of earthly love and spiritual devotion, with the latter washing out the former in what I can best explain as a kind of holy passion. Christopher worships the queen with the kind of love a true devotee lavishes on his special saint. And yet he worships her, too, with the hot and hopeless devotion of a knight in some chivalric novel who longs to possess his idol carnally, yet never can and knows it. It's a stricken, burning, guilty, yet contained passion, a kind of holy sublimation that, as I've said, reminds me most of poor St. Anthony facing all the temptations of the flesh in the Egyptian desert. No peasant could feel that kind of emotion."

Andrés pondered, forgetting the game of chess they had been playing. "How fortunate it is that they're never long together," he said. "The fellow makes me uneasy, and the more you talk about his passion, the more my flesh creeps. I pray the king never suspects."

"It is fortunate, Andrés, for Isabella, I'm sure, loves Christopher in a way a red-blooded woman loves a man, and there's no doubt in my mind that she knows the way he feels about her and senses that he knows her feelings, too. I've seen her eyes, too, when she looks at him and thinks no one is watching… It's the strongest, the most touching and poignant passion I have encountered. It makes me believe that those men who penned those tales about Amadís and King Arthur's knights wrote fact after all and not pure fiction. Christopher, in the throes of his very human love for Isabella suffers as deeply as ever did Sir Gawain or Lancelot, and she languishes as passionately as ever did Guinevere for Lancelot. My heart bleeds for them because of the hopelessness of it. If Isabella were any other queen, I'd turn my head and hope she could find a little happiness with Christopher, but she is Isabella and cannot, will not let herself steal a little happiness, when its discovery would wreck her world. She wouldn't sin with him, even if no one could ever know, because she is too good to do it. I tell you, Andrés, some day Isabella will be made a saint."

"You're not the first to say so," said Andrés. "And if she manages to quench what she feels for the Genoese and never once treads on shaky ground, she'll deserve to be. The temptation of the flesh is the strongest of all temptations, I think. But Beatriz, we were talking about the pension and whether or not the queen would revoke it if she found out the Genoese was having an affair with another woman."

"We were, weren't we, Andrés? I let myself go off a very different tangent. I must look more closely into the matter. The more I know, the better I'll be prepared to step in and shield her, and him, once she learns the news."

The very next day, unable to contain her curiosity any longer, Beatriz decided she must see the Harana woman. The place to go, she thought, would be the parish church where the Haranas worshiped, and there she went at vespers one cool autumn afternoon. It was the night before Christopher would march off to war, so she felt certain they would attend services. She entered the church early and found a shadowy vantage point. Christopher entered first, taller by far than any other man. His red hair, a fiery halo, seemed to Beatriz de Bobadilla rather the nimbus of a pagan deity than of a pious Christian bent on the preservation of his soul. His eyes kept sweeping the congregation, which that evening was large, since many Cordovans were leaving for the war in the morning, and their families had come to worship with them, possibly for the last time.

Suddenly Christopher's eyes came to a halt and focused on a dark corner. Beatriz's eyes followed his and beheld his mistress. The Harana woman surprised her. All that Isabella was this Cordovan Beatriz was not. Her hair, so black it didn't catch a ray of light, made her face float in the gloom as though disembodied. Even the dark blue hood that covered her head blended into the darkness. High cheekbones, with dusky shadows underneath, contributed a quality magnified by huge doe-eyes as black as pools of jet.

Beatriz managed to leave the church before Columbus or his Beatriz. She stationed herself facing the door and across the plaza in such a way that she would be able to see them clearly as they rounded the building and came into the light of the setting sun. Columbus emerged first, his face intent, and his eyes were the eyes of a hunter. She had never seen his face cast in its present mold. The other times she had seen him, his intentness had been of a different brand. It had been the gaze of an ambitious man as he marched out of Toro, shackled and pretending to be a prisoner being returned to the Portuguese army; and when he had come striding toward the chapel in the cathedral, his great tallness dwarfed by the soaring columns, his eyes had shone with uneasiness and embarrassment, but also with the light of confidence and devotion for a woman he loved and knew he could not have. But the gleam in his eyes as he strode purposefully across the plaza alone and vanished through an arch that opened into one of the four streets that debauched into the square, was as she had at first thought, the eyes of a hunter. Christopher was hunting for sexual gratification, for a mate, even, and the mate was Beatriz de Harana, who followed him some fifty paces behind, almost running so as not to let him outdistance her too far.

Beatriz de Harana still perplexed her. She had studied her face carefully as the light of the setting sun fell full upon her. Again the contrast to Isabella was striking. She was all women, this Cordovan Beatriz, but she was far too tall, taller even than the tall queen. She had let her hood slip back, and her long mane of ebony hair fell down her back and around her olive face.

"This woman isn't beautiful at all," said Beatriz to herself. "Her shoulders are too wide, her bosom far too prominent to be in style, and I'm glad my hands and feet are not so large. Yet, even so, I see quite well what attracts the woolmerchant and must attract other men. Not a man in the plaza isn't staring as she goes by."

Beatriz de Harana went straight across the square and vanished through the arch where Christopher had disappeared only seconds earlier. Beatriz de Bobadilla longed to follow her, but knew it was out of the question and would be fruitless anyway. "I didn't need to, really," she told Andrés that night. "I could see they loved each other and were off to bed."

If she could have followed, she would have seen them walk furtively, the man a hundred paces ahead of the woman. She would have seen him stop before two heavy oaken doors where he waited nervously until Beatriz came up to him. She reached into the folds of her skirt and pulled out a set of keys, inserted one into the keyhole and pushed the door open. It swung open on well-oiled hinges and let them enter after one first careful look to see if anyone had seen them. Inside they kissed passionately before she tugged free from his arms, blew on some ashes in a firepan, the kind mariners use on ships to preserve the fire they need, and lighting a taper, led him to the ladder that went down to the wine cellar. There even the ancient, unchanging coolness of the ages did not cool their lust.

It was their last time together before he went off to war. They had used this place before, at least a score of times, and it had a special meaning. Here Christopher had perfected all he wanted to teach her after their first intercourse near the river. Here, titillated with anxiety that their moans might awaken Rodrigo and Diego Harana, her kinsmen, they had squirmed and bucked in ecstasy and quickly learned what each held in store for the other. Even that her kinsmen trusted her seemed to add a piquancy, for Beatriz had one of the keys to the wine cellar and locked up every night and opened every morning, but Diego and Rodrigo each had keys as well.

That night their love was violent, each sensing it might be their last. He held her so close she could scarcely breathe, and the sheer might of his physical greatness, his unquenchable hunger, the hard, pounding impact of his body against hers, left her in despair when she thought of his leaving. When they could do no more, they lay in each other's arms while she waited for him to drift into sleep, a habit, she had noticed, that never failed. It amazed her how quickly that body, one minute alert and a raging inferno of human energy, could slide into deepest slumber in a matter of seconds. She loved those moments of silence and sweetness when she could pillow his head on her shoulder and inhale the peppery aroma of his passion's sweat. She could gauge the depth of his passion and reminisce about how many times he had reached a climax and had she. From what women told her about their lovers around the neighborhood fountain, she gathered most men, if they were strong and young enough, could perform the act of joy as many as three or even four times a night. Christopher had no limit she could recognize, and she firmly believed the only reason he called a halt was that he thought she might wear out. He could go on and on and on, indefinitely. Beatriz, no gentle maiden when he took her, but a full-blown woman ripe for the plucking, knew she would languish, perhaps even pine away without this brawny, potent creature who could drive out everything in her mind but her own need for satiation. She kissed his ear, and since he had thrown one of his arms back and lay with his head resting on it, she was able to stare at the vigorousness of his maleness.

What would this body of hers, stoked like a furnace with his body's heat, do when he was gone? How could she live without her body's boundless feeding on his? Idly she wondered if he had got her with child. She hoped he had, for that would be another part of him to savor. And God would not let him die, He would send him back like a blazing torch which only her body could quench and restore to peace.

Since Beatriz never fell asleep while Christopher was with her, no matter how released by the stress and strain of love-making. She willed sleep away. She couldn't go to sleep and miss a minute of his nearness, for they were confined to only once a week—Thursday from late afternoon to midnight—when Diego and Rodrigo dined out with others, hooked by the lure of navigation. Their one long session in the wine cellar never satisfied them. How nice it would be if they could be together every night and every afternoon for siesta!

An hour later, Beatriz felt her lover stir and knew the time had come for him to leave. "It's time to go," he sighed.

Reluctantly she felt him leave her arms. "God, how I'll miss you," she moaned. "What'll I do when I can't have what we've had this evening?"

"You'll manage, as I plan to manage," lied Christopher. "You'll keep faith with me and do without until I'm back again. And then, Beatriz, let's seriously consider getting married.

She disengaged his hands, kissed him softly on the lips and said, "We'll see. But no plans now." She wondered, as she said it, why she never leapt at this chance so often offered. Clearly she loved him and she knew he loved her in his own passionate way. Their flesh was one flesh, their souls one soul. Why did she hesitate? Why put this offer in abeyance? What warning was it she felt when she thought of marrying him? Did he feel he had to marry her? That could not be it, for he knew perfectly well that he didn't have to. Was he at last freed of the memory of poor dead Felipa? And what of the peculiar sentiment he hinted he felt for the queen? If Isabella cared for him, as he thought she did, would she frown upon such a marriage. "After all, the queen would know that Christopher's mistress was not of noble blood, whereas Felipa's had been noble. Finally, she came to realize that her reasons for not marrying him were both selfless and selfish; selfless because she knew that if she married him, it would damage his career, for she could never appear with him as his wife in the salons of the palace; selfish, because she wanted to protect herself from the insults and slights she would inevitably encounter if she tried to move among her social betters.

7

Vélez-Málaga fell after a long siege, and Ferdinand moved immediately against Málaga, where the siege made no headway at all. Málaga seemed impregnable. When his at last frantic letters reached Isabella, she smiled proudly, for his words proved how much he needed her. Not often did he ask her help in matters military. "Come to Málaga, Isabella. The men call daily for you. They can't forget the war against Portugal and your handling of it while I fended off the French. I need you, too, and I love you very much."

When a few days later she descended from the mountains and onto the Vega of Málaga, beholding for the first time the breathtaking panorama, she swore a solemn oath that this land would some day belong to Christian Spain. This endless sea of rolling green hills, with the city tossing like a white ship on its bosom, deserved more than occupation by infidels. What a contrast to arid Castile! Behind the formidable line of its citadel bulged the impossible curve of the Mediterranean. Málaga the Beautiful was no misnomer. Where the hills swept up suddenly from white beaches stood the great fortress of the Gibrálfaro, once the site of a Roman lighthouse. It rose unbelievably high and grim behind hexagonal battlements. Those mighty walls, she knew, were double, since there was a second line which paralleled the ones she saw. And inside that double line of defense lay moats, and finally minefields and hidden traps. Málaga might withstand an endless siege. And while the city held out they could not move against Granada.

To divide the forces would be to court disaster. Both Granada and Málaga sheltered large hordes of fierce Gómeres. Their very name made her shudder. Hired to defend their softer brethren, the Gómeres from Africa were the outcasts of Islam whose delight was murder and the foulest torture, whom even Muslims shunned in times of peace. Isabella had seen the results of their brutality—eyeless, footless castrates, too pitiful to gaze upon. As she rode toward Málaga, she tried to picture it as Ferdinand had described it. Its ruler, el Zagrel, before he retreated behind its walls, had put the torch to everything. Not a farmhouse remained, not a village in all the *vega*. The lush plain had been, as Ferdinand advanced, one huge black column of smoke. In the charred remains, the Spanish soldiers found nothing remotely usable. Even the trees lay on the ground, cut off by feverish slaves as the Moorish gentry deserted their homes and farms. Livestock which couldn't be taken into the city were slaughtered and their putrifying bodies jammed into wells.

She entered Ferdinand's encampment in the midst of an artillery barrage and stopped to watch the granite missiles go whistling through the air far overhead. She could follow their trajectory clearly and see sudden puffs of dust when they struck the fortifications. Balls of stone like these, she knew, could batter houses, block streets, crush people. Fired repeatedly, they ground away relentlessly, and the strongest walls would crumble, yet the walls of Málaga seemed intact.

Suddenly she saw several large barrels trailing smoke go hurtling above and straight into the city. She shuddered, trying not to visualize the horror she knew was taking place at the bases of the columns of greasy smoke that rose from where each barrel exploded. Pitch and Greek fire burn long and furiously.

A young officer approached and saluted. The noise drowned out his words. The air shook with the thunder of the streaming missiles, the wicked strum of mangonels, and the creaking of countless crossbows being wound, followed by the whir of the quarels as they sped up toward the defenders on the ramparts.

At her side the chaplain pointed and crossed himself. Looking up and in the direction he indicated, she felt her mouth open in consternation. Were human beings flying into the city to attack its inhabitants? Amazement turned to horror. Could Spaniards resort to this? Could Ferdinand countenance it? She too made the sign of the cross when she understood. The human bodies flying above her, were the corpses of the Moorish slain, flung into Granada by Ferdinand's catapults. Each seemed to drift slowly, turning head over heels with dangling arms and legs and genitals, for all were nude. If Ferdinand's artillery was casting dead bodies into Málaga, the situation must be desperate indeed.

Armies fought like this when they wanted to spread plague into a beleaguered city. Everyone knew that decaying flesh carries the seeds of that corruption. But plague could be a two-edged sword. She nodded to a priest whose eyes were blinded with fear. She hoped his prayers would help others than himself.

At the top of a small rise near the pavilion where the Trastámara banner snapped in the stiff breeze from the sea, she could obtain a full view of the harbor. Ship after ship, all Christian by the crosses on their masts, also bombarded Málaga. Could any stronghold, even with walls like these, withstand such punishment for long? Apparently Málaga could, for the city had been absorbing this hellish catapulting for weeks and gave no sign of yielding.

Ferdinand, advised of her arrival, came galloping from the front where he had been directing the assault. Out of his face, black with dust and smoke and streaked with sweat, his eyes glared wildly under his open visor. Though he stank, before all who cared to watch, she took him in her arms. Theirs was no formal embrace; it was a kiss of passion engendered by the violence they had seen and by long separation. Then he led her into the pavilion.

"Only the good God knows how happy I am to see you, Isabella! Or how I need you! Now help me out of this armor and let me bathe. Then come to bed."

And while men died on both sides, while the bombardment continued unabated, while bugles snarled and drove men forward or pulled them back, while horses neighed or screamed in the agony of death, Ferdinand, stubble-faced and barely clean took his wife to bed and thrilled her with the urgency of his passion. She hadn't known how the violence of war could stimulate the sexual urge.

Afterwards Isabella bathed and dressed carefully for the inspection of her troops. Whatever ostentation and pomp she could muster, she mustered. And when she emerged from the pavilion, the startled sentinels who had stood outside and straight-faced, trying not to listen to their monarchs' passion, gasped when they saw her. Isabella took note and blushed in embarrassment for what she had let them hear, but flushed with pride at the worship in their eyes. Spaniards love spectacle, and she in her new armor provided that. No one who saw her that day, as she inspected her troops, would ever forget her. She had made certain of that.

Silver armor sheathed her limbs, and she carried her helmet in the crook of her left arm, leaving her long hair free to ripple like flame in the lively breeze whipping in from the water. "God, how beautiful!" an officer said aloud. Gratefully she heard and pretended not to. When she caught another whisper, "She wears her mail like an angel of the Lord," she walked a little taller, her head thrown back. This kind of pride, she reflected, even heaven condones, for it leads to heaven's goals. But she hadn't prepared herself sufficiently for the full impact of the army's adoration. As she strode, her armor clanking, between two long ranks of Castilian lancers, tears overflowed and ran down her cheeks. Suddenly, contrary to tradition, both ranks went to their knees as she passed through. The expressions on their hard-bitten faces made her repress a sob. She was a woman, their eyes said, but their sex-starved faces reflected nothing but pious devotion and respect, as though they were gazing on a beautiful saint of God. No woman had done what she was doing since the Maid of Orléans, not many years before, marched out against the English hosts in France.

Ferdinand was delighted. "You can't imagine, Isabella," he gloated, "How morale has tightened." Then he said something she never expected to hear from his lips. He remembered words she had all but forgotten. "Recall, my love," he said, "what old de Coca told us before he died, 'Spaniards revel in a great leader and will follow him anywhere. He could have been describing you."

She touched his mailed fist lightly. "I'm happy you recalled that for me," she whispered, "but even happier that you, a man among men, the general of a great host, could feel you needed a woman to help you win the war."

"A general must utilize all weapons when he fights a war like this," he said, almost spoiling his earlier praise, but she refused to let it, and smiled her sweetest smile.

"Yes," he went on, "he must use even his wife's beauty and her boundless courage, if she has these attributes, and St. Peter knows you have."

"Whatever I've done to raise morale," she said, "will pale to insignificance tomorrow when the army sees what I have brought from Cordova. Even you will be surprised, husband."

"More cannon?" asked Ferdinand hopefully.

"Not cannon, Ferdinand, but something which in the long run will mean more to this army than the best artillery in Europe. Wait and see."

On the next day strangely burdened mule trains labored into the Spanish encampment. They were too heavily loaded to keep up with Isabella as she had descended into the Vega of Málaga. "What on earth?" asked Ferdinand in disappointment.

"The Queen of Castile," said her chaplain, "is more than a saint of God, Sire, Who must be watching over us. She is an angel of the Lord."

Then, slowly six enormous tents, dwarfing even the largest pavilion, rose above the dusty streets, their function gradually becoming evident. Men cheered and priests led them in prayers of thanksgiving. A deep new consciousness of their queen's unselfishness, of her motherliness touched the army to the quick. But Ferdinand's reaction disappointed her. "Where, for God's sake," he cried, "did you find the money? We need more cannon, and you bring a portable hospital!"

Even when he had carefully inspected the six great tents, assessed their equipment, spoken with the corps of physicians and surgeons, and counted the number of male nurses, he still clung to his original thought, "Mother of God," he moaned, "how will we pay? With more weapons, wouldn't Granada have succumbed much sooner, Isabella?"

Her face hardened in displeasure. "It's a fine thing to hear mass," she said quietly, "but it's also good to look after one's own house."

"But the expense...?"

"Damn the expense, Ferdinand! The cost in money will be paid in morale. Think what it'll produce even in personal valor. A soldier who knows he won't die of a festering wound, as they so often do after a battle, will fight harder and retreat more slowly. Once our men know that at the very edge of the battlefield doctors and nurses wait, they'll fight like demons. Wait, and you'll see. And back home, think of the effect upon their families! Think how mothers and fathers will be relieved to know that sickness and disease won't decimate the troops. Why, you well know wars have been lost because of illness."

"How much did we spend, Isabella? I have the right to know."

"*We* spent nothing, Ferdinand. Not a *maravedí* came from the funds of Aragón, I spent a great deal, but it's all Castilian money. I asked for funds for this enterprise of mercy and it showered down on me like rain. It came out of hiding, Ferdinand, money we never suspected people were hoarding. Remember this: materialists think with their eyes. Idealists with their souls. Be for one day an idealist, my dear, and you'll see what idealism can accomplish in a materialistic world."

He scratched his head. Maybe his wife was right. It was beginning to dawn on him that she usually was.

8

Christopher's patrol of twelve made its way stealthily across the dark *vega*. It was blackest night. Like all patrols they went well-armed and fully cognizant of danger, but he didn't care. If his men suspected, they didn't show it. He still bristled with anger whenever he thought of the king's refusal and the committee's rejection. Even Isabella's pension seemed meager. And with the enterprise delayed and now in the hands of another stodgy committee, why should he cool his heels in the corridors of Salamanca? He needed action. His body craved it even more than his soul. Better a good helmet and breastplate and the chance to strike a few blows for God and the Cross, than restless waiting. And, he muttered under his breath, "No one had better tell me I've lived off the queen's bounty and rendered no service in return. I'm good enough for anybody's bounty even the Queen of Spain's. And It's time that this Colom lived up to all my father taught me of honor and knighthood."

It was much too dark, he felt, for a foray, but the officer had ordered it. They sloshed through irrigation ditches, fell over heaps of earth and the burned-out ruins of farm houses, and once he tripped over the body of a rotting horse. The Moors they sought, supposedly smuggling supplies into Málaga, did not appear, but visions of what had happened to other Spanish patrols flashed across his mind and his men's with grim reality, and made them glad the reconnoitering was fruitless.

Suddenly all twelve heard the unmistakable sound of steel scraping stone, and a muted command in Arabic. The twelve flattened themselves in the mud, at Christopher's whispered command. The sound, to their dismay, came from behind, over terrain they had patrolled. They were cut off from the camp! It was then that raw fear gripped him hard, fear he mustn't show his men. Even the enterprise faded from his mind. God must have nodded, he thought, when He let them choose him for this damned patrol. What a waste if he should die! Suddenly fear faded. He couldn't die. God depended on him to carry out His plan.

Hastily he consulted the men, and in whispers they agreed they must push ahead and try to circle around the Moors behind them. He pondered and then led them sweating, and now more angry than frightened. He was glad he had Pedro García in his patrol, for Pedro was a giant and beyond the fear of God or man. Pedro stood at his shoulder, and whispered, "What now?" Suddenly they emerged from the sugar cane, and there rose the walls of Málaga. As they went closer, hoping to skirt along the base, torches suddenly burst into light far above and flashed on the metal of his breastplate. He stopped, scooped up mud, and smeared it across the polished metal, and ordered the men to do the same, hoping it wasn't too late. He stumbled into a ditch and cursed silently as he slid into water to his hips. García pulled him out as though he had weighed nothing. All around tepid slime soaked them and they heard the earth sucking greedily, like a great reptile breathing its rotten breath into their faces. Visions rose in his mind of the crocodiles he had seen in swamps like that in some of Portugal's African possessions, even though he knew none lived in Spain. The rank stink of rotting grass and weeds made him gag, but worse was the heavy stench of male sweat turned rank with terror. He wrinkled his nose and moved away from Pedro García who stank the loudest. Probably he smelled as bad, and knew the man behind him was wrinkling his nose, too.

Frogs ceased their croaking as the patrol progressed. "By St. Ferdinand," he cursed, "the Moors can mark our passage by the silence of the frogs!"

He called a whispered halt, and the men gathered around him, kneeling in the mud, their faces white, their breath coming in muffled gasps. In the silence they listened and heard nothing. Then an owl hooted, a fish jumped in deep water, and here and there frogs began again their courtship or challenges. Mosquitoes hummed wickedly and he hungered to slap them, but did not dare. Neither did his men. The sound of a slap on wet flesh would tell the listening Moors exactly where they were.

As he gave the command to proceed, a feeling he had come to respect from previous experiences warned him something was about to happen. The muscles of his belly tightened. "Down, men," he ordered. They waited. Nothing happened.

"What's up?" asked García.

"I don't know. Keep quiet! Let's wait. I thought I heard something." He gripped his sword. Waiting became torture. He raised his head and peered into the darkness, half illuminated at the base of the wall by the torches above. Nothing! Then, out of the night, something came flying toward him. He ducked, but too late. It struck him in the forehead and flung him back into the water. From a great distance, and before he lost consciousness, he thought he heard the wild yapping cry Moorish soldiers scream in the heat of combat. Then he lay full length in the mud, his legs up to his thighs under water.

9

He regained consciousness flat on his back on a dank stone floor. It was inky dark, and the dark and the chill in the stone told him he was somewhere far underground. Deep breathing and snores informed him he wasn't alone, Reaching out a hand, he touched a hairy leg, and a voice said, "Who are you?" García's voice. He would have known the heavy Catalonian accent anywhere. García, powerful, stocky, blond like so many northern Spaniards, was a prisoner too.

"We must be under Málaga." said Christopher.

"Far under, Chris. I'm glad you've come around. You've been out for hours and hours, maybe all day. The stone got you in the head and came close to killing you. You've been bleeding like a stuck pig. I couldn't make it stop. I thought you were dead in the water, but a Moor looked you over and I heard him say, '"The redhead's alive. Bring him with the others.'" We're ten now, Chris. Torra caught an arrow in the gullet, poor guy, and they used their swords on López. Torra was a fine lad, clean and strong and good. I'll miss him much."

When after what seemed months later his head stopped pounding and he could feel the gash had stopped bleeding, his mind revolted against what the prisoners had to bear—the narrow, cramped cell with the ceiling so low you butted your head if you sat upright, the putrid food, the lack of water for bathing and the cruelty of the Moorish captors. Even worse, the stench of the open trench they had to use as a latrine.

"How long do you think we've been here, Pedro? when I feel my beard, it makes me think it's weeks, not days."

"I'd say close to two weeks. I've been scratching on the wall with my finger nail when they bring food. They must bring it only once a day. I count thirteen marks."

The food came just then, and they scrambled to get their share, for the amount was growing more meager every day. There was only a little watery rice smelling of urine. They had seen their Moorish guards piss in their drinking water and laugh in their faces.

After the pittance of rice, the usual—men relieving themselves in the open trenches that served as latrines, one in each corner of the dungeon—Christopher wondered how long they could survive treated in this way, and he suddenly realized that he did not really care. Only the dream of destiny was sustaining him and even the thought of that was losing its power to make him want to live.

A little later guards came with whips. They drove Christopher and Pedro into a line with many comrades. The guards were almost as gaunt as their captives, for food was very scarce. García had been right, Christopher reflected. Their time had come at last. Would it be the ramparts where they might last a while, or would it be the castrator's knife, followed by life as eunuchs guarding some eastern harem?

Other lines of prisoners joined their own. A priest, as naked as all the others, and displaying more embarrassment then the soldiers, paced along bravely among his comrades. "It's all in God's hands now," he said.

"Small comfort," whispered Pedro. "God has forgotten us."

They entered a courtyard where they saw the upswept walls towering high above. Moorish bowmen lined the battlements, shaking their fists and screaming maledictions. One of the guards enlightened them. He spoke Castilian as well as they and he had no Moorish look. "He's a renegade," said Pedro under his breath. "They're worse than Moors!" He spat on the ground carefully lest the renegade see him.

The renegade saw, however, and lashed Pedro across the shoulders. "It's the goddamned red-haired witch you call your queen," he hissed, adding an even harder lash for emphasis. "Every day she rides all the whole circuit of our walls in her silver mail on her white horse. But one day she'll ride too close and that will be that for her."

Christopher dared to ask the renegade a question. "Why do you call the Queen of Spain a witch?" The query got him a lash and a blob of spittle in his eye. "Because she *is* one," snapped the renegade, spitting again and wiping his mouth. "Only a witch could do what she does and get away with it. But we have exorcists and spell-workers and by Allah's goodness they will bring her down eventually—and let us eat like men."

"By St. Ferdinand," said Christopher, "I wish I could see her, if only once!"

"Perhaps you will," said the guard grimly "before you die on the ramparts." The priest's voice broke in. "Pray with me, brothers," he called, and the men's deep voices took up the prayer and then sang a Hail Mary. "Holy Mother, Star of the Sea, do not forsake us," they chanted, bearing the furious lashes as best they could.

When the door opened for them, they caught the smell of wood smoke and pitch and excrement, and from farther on one wild and terrible cry rang in their ears.

Then it was that García balked. Standing like the mountain of muscle he was, his head flung back, lips in a feral snarl, his face pasty, he raised his great hand and hit the renegade with all his might in the side of the head. The man went down like a felled ox and lay motionless. For a moment confusion reigned. Then two guards forced García to the floor and sat on him, while one ran for a physician. The doctor took one look at García's fist and the renegade's skull and shook his head. "The guard is dead," he said indifferently. "Remove the body." Then he turned on his heel and went back through the door, which now Christopher and García regarded as the door to hell. "The guard's last words rang in their ears, "'Lord Malik does not want them marred, so spare your whips.'"

The guards glared wickedly and fingered the handles of their whips, but they knew Lord Malik's fury and none lashed them again.

Beyond the gate they found still another passage lined with naked captives, who looked at them with dull and frightened eyes.

At last their segment of the line halted before a pair of slender gates, studded with brass, made of the thickest oak. No one would get past those gates without a battering ram, or out of them, once inside. Suddenly silently on oiled hinges the panels swung slowly open, and Christopher, who was tall enough to see above the men in front of him, wished that he hadn't. Involuntarily he leaned back against García, while the man in front of him shrank back on him. He breathed deeply, but softly, as though deliberately trying not to upset the equilibrium of the moment. "Thank God we're not the first!" he croaked.

The guard who pushed him roughly forward said, "Your turn'll come, Christian dog, and it'll be worse, for the knives will be dull by then."

The spacious courtyard glowed with infernal light. Everyone, guards and prisoners and officiating surgeons, were as red as devils from another world. The enclosure looked more like hell than any picture Christopher had seen, even in Tuscany, where scenes of inferno followed the descriptions of Dante in *The Divine Comedy*. No preacher, however fanatic, could have summoned into the minds of a congregation a scene more hellish.

In the center of the courtyard a fire burned red. A huge cauldron of molten pitch seethed audibly and made the air acrid. It burned, Christopher's throat and he coughed. Two enormous gaunt black men, mother-nude, with shaven heads and torsoes gleaming silver with sweat stood waiting. Between them, and completely dwarfed by their towering presences, crouched an ancient Moor, his white beard tucked into his belt, his garments blood spattered. His eyes darted from the prisoners to the low bench where glinted a cluster of crescent-shaped, sickle-blades no longer than a human hand.

At sight of this nightmare García sank to the pavement and clasped Christopher around the calves, his eyes madly alert and narrowed to dark pinpoints of wild speculation. The guards came quickly and dragged him to his feet, forcing him to walk. Christopher caught him, and together they shuffled forward in a line that became ever shorter. All in the world that mattered was not to be the first, and finally not to be the next.

The column of prisoners snaked slowly around the courtyard in a long curve, hiding nothing of what went on near the fire and the cauldron. "Don't look!" whispered Christopher as his own eyes clung in awful fascination upon the abomination near the fire. Every few seconds the two giant blacks leaped forward like leopards to seize the next man in the line. Each then extended a long ebony leg that quickly pinned one of the prisoner's legs in a vise-like grip, while vast black arms held him motionless. Then, with the alacrity of a spider, the old Moor darted forward, took hold of the victim's scrotum, and with the little curved knife made a deft slash. When the man screamed, the other prisoners leaned back and moaned. García, after each scream, went to his knees and had to be lifted up by Christopher. The old Moor smiled thinly, held up the severed scrotum, then flung it atop a heap of similar horrors.

Christopher, since he couldn't close his eyes, stopped thinking consciously, but the screams curdled his soul. He couldn't cover his ears, else García would slump to the pavement again. Suddenly he tried to swallow, but like so many others, vomited, fouling his feet, García's and the legs and buttocks of the man in front of him. No one seemed to mind. Slowly he realized he and García were second and third in line. The man ahead was already in the black men's clutches. He saw in every detail all that happened not six feet in front of him. He watched as the old Moor, brushing aside his bloody forelock, applied the blade and stepped back with his trophy. How strange a pair of testicles looked separated from their owner's body, dangling obscenely and dripping blood in the withered brown hand of an ancient infidel! The assistant then plunged a long ladle into the cauldron, scooped up liquid pitch, and swinging it like a censer, cupped it to the dripping wound where scrotum and testicles had hung. Dimly, through eyes that streamed and through his vomit, he calmly watched the two blacks drag the drooping unconscious man, purposefully across the stones, toward one of the walls to drop him against it unconscious. Then from a shadow nearby stepped another demon with a glowing iron, but the victim didn't scream when it branded his shoulder, sending up a little puff of smoke and steam. "I'm sure he's dead," he heard himself say aloud in a voice that he did not recognize as his own.

García was babbling. He talked of his boyhood and begged his father not to beat him. "I won't do it again," he sobbed. "Uncle José made me, father! I didn't do it willingly!"

Suddenly Christopher stumbled and knelt beside the now kneeling García. "Mother of God," he moaned, "let me not feel!"

But conscious clung to him like an itch, and his senses were quickened; he saw and heard and smelled it all. Groans and screams made the air throb; he gagged on the reek of mingled sweat, blood and filth, for some of the captives' bowels had loosened and they soiled the floor, mingling ordure with vomit.

Inexplicably, as though detached by some devil's chemistry in his blood, he found he could view whatever happened with eerie equanimity. Perhaps, he thought, when a man has seen too many others gelded, has heard too many screams of despair and agony, and seen too many groveling or motionless shadows in the long line by a wall, even when he knows his time is coming, he let's his mind grow dull and escape from his body entirely. "If you're among the lucky ones, this is what happens," he thought. Only dimly he realized it was García's turn. And after that his own. He couldn't believe he had shoved García unprotesting in front of him. Only later would he recall and feel a useless remorse.

García's turn! "Oh God!" he moaned, as his mind cleared and he faced what nothing could save him from. García's quaking shoulders, cold with the sweat of deepest fear, pressed against his chest. The big man looked not at the approaching blacks. His eyes looked over his shoulder and sought the eyes of his friend which could do no more than vainly sympathize.

As the black hands seized García, Christopher looked into his soul for his own salvation and suddenly found it. At the bottom of his being he found the courage for what he had to do. "There is a way," said his soul, "if only you can make it work. Call on your destiny."

The rough stones of the pavement rasped his bleeding knees as he forced himself to crawl relentlessly toward the cauldron and the fire. The two guards were dragging García forward, just ahead of him, and dull eyes focused on that tragic trio. García had begun to yell in a deep, thunderous bellow. The walls resounded with it. Christopher had heard an Andalusian yearling bull bellow like that as they smashed its testicles on an anvil. García leaped and threw himself about in the grip of the blacks so that even their great strength barely held him. All three whirled in a mad saraband, back and forth before the fire, twice almost overturning the cauldron and once, actually turning over the table with the knives. The old Moor kept looking apprehensively at García's biceps and flailing fists. One of the blacks had a broken nose and the other's mouth streamed blood.

"Don't damage his looks," cried the old Moor, dashing close and then away as García aimed a kick in his direction. "Lord Malik wants his eunuchs handsome."

Christopher's guardian angel, who gave directions to his battered soul, made him see the runnels of blood trickling from the settling mound of severed testicles. The blood slithered along like two scarlet serpents until it found a hollow in the stone and made a pool. Swift as a thought, he dipped some up and smeared it over his belly, thighs and crotch, and as he did it, he uttered to himself a mad little laugh. "They are not looking," he said to himself in that strange voice he now possessed. "Just a little more and I'll be safe!"

Next came the molten pitch. His eyes darted to the cauldron. It sent up thin smoke. The attendant with the ladle had left the fire and stood beside the old Moor, as if to protect him from García's lurchings. The blacks at last got their legs around García's and stretched him back across their thighs, exposing his genitals. At this the old Moor scuttled forward with his blade. The firelight fell full upon his face, terrible to behold, his eyes aglow with sadistic blood lust, his hands and beard, and even his turban red.

Then out of the depths of some secret reserve of strength García twisted free and fell to his knees. The blacks were on him in an instant. He rolled neatly onto his back, and with one of his ham-like fists caught the nearest black full in the mouth and sent him tolling straight into the cauldron which toppled with a dull crash spewing out its viscous, searing contents.

The old Moor screamed a high thin scream, like a woman, and leaped nimbly out of reach of the pitch. Then the second black struck García with a chopping bow to the neck, and the battle ended.

Christopher moved quickly, from the moment García struggled free. While the battle raged he scooped up from the puddle of pitch two handfuls that burned his palms and fingers and made him bite his lips. Flinching from the heat, he plastered his loins, his belly and his thighs. Only sheer will and the power that now ruled him utterly forced him to continue, for at that precise moment the old Moor seized García scrotum and made the fatal slash. García's cry froze him in mid-motion, but while the mad howl mounted to its peak and sank to a moan, he quickly reached the wall and flung himself down beside the most recent of the castrated prisoners. The man lay dead still and made no sound. There he lay supine, his legs crossed over his pitch smeared crotch, his hands cupping his genitals as though to protect what had been left of them. Many of the pitiful castrates were doing that, he saw. Then, moaning and crying like some of the others, calling out to God and the Virgin to let him die, he waited to learn if his ruse had succeeded or failed.

When García's unconscious body crashed down beside him, he closed his eyes, but he kept up his weeping and his groans, and his hands never left his pitch-smeared genitals which hurt from the burns as much as they would have from the knife. He hoped García was dead, and free from pain. What had been removed had meant so much to García that he wouldn't care to face life without it, regardless of his philosophizing. When he was certain the blacks had gone, he carefully slitted his eyes and snatched a glance at his friend. He dared to feel his pulse, for back at the cauldron the blacks held another struggling figure, and the old Moor again harvested with his bloody sickle. García was alive, for his pulse beat weakly. Soft little whimpers ruse from his throat. Christopher crossed himself and swore. "Let me live long enough, my God, to get even," he begged, "Let me tell the Queen of Spain that she was right and that Moor and Christian cannot live side by side. God take them! God take them all!" he wept.

11

Weeks drifted by in the courtyard as a slow starvation gradually rendered the survivors oblivious to pain. The priest died first, for he had given his pittance of food to his comrades.

García lived, but for five terrible days Christopher feared infection would carry him off. And all the while the terrible, relentless sun converted the courtyard into an oven. Their skin darkened to deep mahogany. Rapidly his flesh shrank away until he felt light enough to float to the water trough. On its murky surface he saw a face so peaked and drawn he hardly recognized it. Wild whites of eyes, startling against the darkly baked walnut hue of his hide, stared back at him. "I'm a death's head," he muttered through parched lips. "I'm an old man! My hair's as white as snow! I look like St. Mary the Egyptian after her forty years in the desert!"

But it had been only weeks, not years, as the scratches on the wall proved. "No more scratches," he said one day. "I'm too weak to make them, and I don't care." Later he talked to himself again, a habit now firmly fixed, for there was no one else to talk to, except García, who merely stared at him out of blank eyes and never made a sound. "The guard must be too weak also, or even dead," he told himself. "They haven't come today. Why should they? And as for destiny, he said after a long pause, "I think my destiny has left me."

Men drifted away, squirming like reptiles when they could not find a shady crevice to protect them from the sun. When one died, then Beelzebub, Lord of Flies, sent his iridescent minions to make the air hideous with greedy buzzings. The shrunken corpses clothed in their green and cobalt robes of flies, swelled up and sometimes heaved turgidly with a vast burden of maggots, and Christopher wondered idly how those pitiful heaps had once been living men.

Beyond the walls now only dead silence, interrupted occasionally by the crash of a granite cannonball. After such crashes he sometimes caught, but only faintly, the pitiful cries of those trapped in the rubble of their homes. When he heard such cries he smiled, for he knew that they were Moors.

On Sunday, the nineteenth of August of 1487, only the flies stirred in the courtyard. Not even the din and uproar of the entering Spanish army impinged upon the prisoners. García was dead. Only Christopher clung to life and barely breathed. He never realized that Málaga was starved into surrender. He lay at death's door and missed the keening lamentation of the Moorish citizenry, dragging itself out into the *vega* to be despoiled. The roar of drums and the deep thunder of thousands on thousands of marching feet fell oh deaf ears. He failed to see the banners of Trastámara, Santiago, and Calatrava leap from the topmost turret of the Alcabaza alongside the silver life-sized cross of the Apostle James. Even when the knights of Calatrava broke down the gate and stamped into the courtyard looking for possible survivors, he was past the knowing or the caring.

"Phew!" cursed a soldier, holding his nose. "Nothing here but the dead. Let's move on."

"The orders were to examine every body for signs of life, soldier," said his immediate superior. "So let's get on with it. Hello! That one's breathing. See, old white-head there just moved his arm. Bring water. Not too much! Want to kill the old bastard? I hope you haven't let the others gulp that much. Water'll kill 'em as surely as a sword when they're in a fix like this."

They placed him then on a stretcher and forced hunger-weakened Moors to carry him to one of the hospitals the queen was preparing in the city's mosques. Out of other courtyards came a few more prisoners. And from dungeons far beneath the ground crept still more human skeletons, not burned deep bronze like Christopher, but pale and waxen, like termites never exposed to light. These clapped hands to eyes and cried out as the bright glare seared their eyeballs.

The sovereigns passed through the city, but could not stay. They crossed themselves, prayed in the largest mosque, turned Christian church, and retreated with horror to the clean air of the *vega* where they could breathe. "God keep Granada from this!" said Isabella.

"Yes," said Ferdinand. "I plan to get some good out of it, and I won't, if we find it like we've found it here."

12

Once Christopher awoke to the pealing in of Christian bells and saw flashing the sun above the rooftops the huge silver cross. "I must be dead or dreaming," he muttered to no one in particular. And then he dozed again, as his body gathered strength. Many days later he learned of the surrender of the city and licked his lips with glee. It was no more than the Moors deserved, harsh as the terms had been. As he saw it, the time had come and passed for clemency. Ferdinand had condemned whole segments of the Malagans to slavery. No one would call *him* soft or say his tender-hearted wife had influenced him to mercy when no mercy was deserved. One third of the Malagans he dispatched to North Africa in exchange for Christian captives; another third, the property of the crown, he sold as slaves and used the money to defray part of the expenses of the siege; the rest he distributed to his nobles and the sovereigns of friendly powers. One hundred of the best and strongest warriors he sent to the Holy Father to become papal guards, once they had accepted conversion, of course. The Queen of Naples, his aunt, received fifty of the most beautiful and noble Moorish virgins. The Queen of Portugal, his daughter and Isabella's, got thirty more. Only one Malagan noble, Ali Dardoux, he spared so as to teach Islam a needed lesson. "This one man's efforts to persuade the Malagans to yield deserves some rich reward," said Ferdinand. "Now let this be a warning to Granada."

When the news of the dispersal of the Malagan population reached the East, Islam seethed with rage. Sufis preached holy war, and the West prepared and waited, but no war came.

Still on legs that only let him shuffle like a tired old man, and supported by a staff, Christopher made his way each day from the hospital through the principal streets of Málaga to the great square before the Alcabaza. On one such outing he witnessed an *auto de fe* conducted by the Holy Inquisition, since Málaga swarmed with Christians turned Muslim and converted Jews who had slipped back into their fathers' faith. One *auto* was all he could stomach and he returned to his hospital room and waited for his strength to return.

**

October came before he felt equal to riding a mule to Cordova. He felt weak still and had to rest whenever he came on a village along the way. Each night he went to bed at dusk and took long death-like siestas, feeling the strength slowly flow into his skinny frame.

In Cordova at last, he was too weak to walk and had to be carried to the Harana's. His lower lip trembled with emotion, with longing for a soft lap to hold his head while he poured out his troubles and the agony of his imprisonment. He wanted Beatriz to take him in her arms, to bathe him, bring his meals to him in bed, and tuck him in at night. He wanted to see his friends, of course, both old and new, but later, and above all he wanted to find out if the queen's pension had kept coming in his absence.

"Is it really you, Don Christopher?" asked Rodrigo Harana, who answered his knock, looking incredulously, even suspiciously at the silver hair and swarthy skin of the tall skeletal figure being carried to his door. "Can war change a man so much in so short a time?" he whispered.

Christopher winced. He had grown accustomed to his emaciation and his ravaged face, and they hadn't shocked people who didn't know him in Málaga or along the way to Cordova. Apparently he looked worse than he thought, to judge by Rodrigo's shocked appraisal. Gaunt and bony, with the hair of a very old man, and with eyes truly haunted by horrors no one could imagine, he supposed he did barely resemble the robust seaman who had marched off in the king's army. And what would Beatriz say when she first clapped eyes on him? He dreaded facing her now and prayed she was off at the market or down under the bridge washing clothes. He needed time to bathe and comb his hair. And he knew he smelled as bad as he looked and Rodrigo's barely concealed sniff corroborated it.

Rodrigo continued to hold the door open. "Come in. Come in, old friend," he said in exaggerated politeness. "Let me take your bag and help you to a bed." And when they were in the room formerly occupied by him, he continued his litany of comfort. "Stretch out here, sir. The bed is comfortable. Take a little wine and go to sleep till supper time. And, sir, since the room is vacant and you need friendly care, why not stay here? The rent is very little…"

"Beatriz?" Christopher managed to gasp as the softness of the bed began to drain away his consciousness.

Rodrigo lowered his eyes and kept them on the floor. "She went to Cádiz to her aunt," he said, Christopher thought a little pointedly, "right after you went off with the army."

Suddenly Christopher went cold. Rodrigo knew about him and Beatriz. Knew all this time and yet was still his friend. Warmth flowed back into him. If the Haranas, for no doubt Diego knew it too, wanted his friendship, even in the face of his liaison with their kinswoman, they were friends indeed. The idea that they might be opportunists didn't occur to him at the time. That thought came later.

It bolstered his ego to have two men he liked and respected tolerate their kinswoman's immorality because she had been immoral with so important a man as himself. He must be more notable than he'd thought. That modesty of his had been becoming in a man without a certain future, but if it mattered so much in Spain, he must shake off his unpretentiousness and assume his proper place. So he looked boldly into Rodrigo's face, as soon as he raised his head, and dared to wink. Rodrigo didn't so much as blush. He laid a hand familiarly, a bit too familiarly, Christopher thought, on one of his gaunt arms and said, "We understand, Christopher."

Christopher was stunned. Where was Spanish honor? Where propriety and pride of family? Rodrigo and Diego plummeted from his high esteem to something that soon would make him condescending.

"When'll she be home?" he asked conspiratorially.

"When you send for her, Don Christopher. She thought she'd best be out of town and her aunt, my sister, agreed to take her in till her time had come, but God willed otherwise. Perhaps it's just as well. The child was born dead."

Christopher pressed Rodrigo's hand just short of contemptuously. "I can't have her see me like I am," he laughed, "I look like death. Let me put on a little weight and get my vigor back, then we'll send for her."

Rodrigo didn't bat an eye at the conspiratorial "we."

"You decide, my friend," he said. "And now sleep until I call you to supper. We eat well here, even without our Beatriz. We'll fatten you up again and give you back your strength."

And so he stayed on with Diego and Rodrigo Harana and in a different atmosphere. The always addressed him now as Don Christopher or Señor Columbus. He enjoyed it, felt a heady power at their obsequiousness. It puffed up his vanity which, as the days flowed by, was but one of the changes in his personality. "Let them acknowledge my importance," he gloated. "It's time someone did. God knows how precious little I've had since I left Portugal."

In a month nature did wonders. His ribs fleshed out, and the hard muscles of his chest began to bulge again with their old seductiveness. The way the silver wings of hair spread their tendrils close against the dark walnut of the skin of his chest intrigued him. Still more he wondered at his pubic hair which retained all its fiery red, as did his underarms. Only the hair on his chest echoed the whiteness of his head. He rubbed the skin all over his body with good olive oil each night before he went to bed, regardless of the sheets, and the harsh dryness faded, leaving his skin as smooth and dark as well-tanned leather. Beatriz would still find him attractive. He could hardly wait to take her. He wondered if she would still be as wild for him, and decided of course she would. She had always thought him something special, a man with attributes just short of godlike. Yes, she would be as passionate in spite of his altered appearance. Then a new unworthy thought sprouted and burgeoned in his mind. At first it shamed him, but gradually he grew used to it and accepted its right to be there. Beatriz would do well to please him. Her brothers knew it already, and soon she would know it too. He wouldn't be hasty again, and like some callow youth with his first love, offer marriage. Not Christopher Columbus, friend of the Queen of Spain. He couldn't really marry into a family where the men turned their heads when a roomer slept with their kinswoman. Beatriz was a wench, and he ached to bed her, imagining he would take her fiercely, as hungrily as he had on their last night before he had left for the war. It would be the way she wanted it and so he asked Rodrigo to send for her in a month, and Rodrigo with eyes abject, said that he would. Familiarity does breed contempt, thought Christopher.

He had thought of tinting his hair, for he had loved its fire. Now he changed his mind. He had red hair where it counted with his mistress. A mane of white hair gave a man distinction and dignity and didn't make him look old, not if his body and face were young. He did look great, he told himself. His mirror confirmed it every day, and he looked in it often to make sure that the ghost who had been carried out of the courtyard in Málaga had been laid to rest. He was glad he hadn't tinted it, after he overheard the Duke of Medina-Celi tell Rodrigo that white hair was to his advantage. "Our Columbus had a too youthful look, Rodrigo. It wasn't becoming to a man of his age, and I fear it had no little part in the opinion of the professors who rejected his enterprise. Dotards like those up at Salamanca resent a youthful face, you know. Columbus's white locks will help to soothe their rancor when next he faces them."

And so he made ready for Beatriz's return and planned how it would be. She would catch no hint of embarrassment about his changed appearance, and very definitely he would not babble again about a marriage he no longer wanted or thought he owed her.

Meanwhile, he waited and felt his vigor increase and he picked up the queen's pension and occasionally a letter from the Cabreras, always in Beatriz de Bobadilla's hand, not Andrés's. Life was good for a pensioner of the queen. He bought new clothes, and wore jewelry, and used perfume. People looked up when they saw him, and some stood when he entered a room. It never occurred to him that most of these folk were poor and impressionable and that at court a page boy would scarcely rise for him. But he was far from court, which was wherever the sovereigns happened to lodge, no matter how small the town they lodged in. His only concern was a nagging little dread that Isabella and Ferdinand had put him away on ice. But because Málaga was far behind, because he was the center of his small social world in the Esbarraya tavern, and because his mistress—for now he considered Beatriz just that—would soon return to warm his bed, he allowed his life to drift.

How would it be, he wondered the first night of her return, with Rodrigo and Diego possibly listening from their darkened rooms? It would certainly add a special zest to have them there, and , instead of remorse at such unworthy thoughts, all he felt was an overweening vanity for what he had become.

One afternoon he joined the now rather large group of men who frequented his favorite tavern. The wine was excellent, for Diego had chosen a keg of his father's very best. And Leonardo, the owner, had sent his boy for sweets. The men were hanging on Christopher's words. "The sovereigns," he said knowledgeably, "are still in Barcelona, planning the war against the Moors. They'll be there long, I warrant, for Granada will be a harder nut to crack than Málaga. Moreover, between the sovereigns stands Baza, no small fortress in itself."

"You're right in that," said Leonardo. "I've traded in both cities. Granada's the greatest Moorish stronghold of them all. It sits on a high eminence and behind a ring of mountains that may well make it impregnable. I hear they've been provisioning it for months, have strengthened all its fortifications and are waiting disdainfully for the sovereigns to appear."

Christopher hated to hear it. It meant he would have to wait and wait, and of all things waiting upset him most. "You know," he said unexpectedly, "I should go to Barcelona to speak to the sovereigns, especially my patroness, the queen. Granada may take a year and more. By St. Ferdinand, as Leonardo said, it may be impregnable! I can't wait out my life here. If I'm not careful, someone else will steal my enterprise."

The assemblage nodded in unison, but Juan Pérez, once the queen's chaplain, urged caution. "Don Christopher," he said, "wait. The sovereigns are busy with their new war. Wait until they return to Castile. Don't disturb them now. I know the queen, possibly better than you do. Don't try to hurry her. It would not be mete."

So he waited, restless, for word from Isabella, but resigned for the time, to wait. Beatriz de Bobadilla Cabrera's encouraging letters meanwhile helped considerably.

More and more important men began to visit the Esbarraya shop, and most came to hear Christopher, the only person in Cordova pensioned by the queen. He was in his element at last. He bought still more new clothes, was able to invite the right people to dine in decent inns, and be invited. He learned to preen himself just to the correct degree and not in an obtrusive manner. His very stance seemed to convey to his audiences that he had a right to accept their full attention and that they would all profit by listening to him. He could now drop names that made ears prick up, and never hesitated to drop such names. And he somehow managed to make it plain that his pension kept coming in and that his friendship with the royal family never dimmed. Since Ferdinand had apparently decided to take no steps against him, he concluded that the queen had made it clear that he was to be left alone. He dreamed of announcing his nobility, but wondered if he ever could. And best of all he basked in the esteem of these important men who recognized true worth when they saw it in a man, in a fellow like himself, of course. Everyone listened when he spoke, and when he mentioned his voyages out of Madeira along the coast of Africa or his journey to Thule or Iceland, in the very waters where St. Brandon made his famous discoveries, a great hush fell. and heads nodded as if to say "Here is a man who knows of what he speaks, who will go far. No wonder the Queen of Spain herself recognizes his great potential!" Best of all, not once did he encounter the damnable raising of eyebrows he couldn't bear at court, nor did anyone who ever came to Leonardo's shop, look down his nose and sneer. He could breathe there and hold his head higher than the best of them. It was all very heady, and whenever the duke appeared and clapped him on the back and took him aside to talk of his own sponsorship, if ever the queen decided not to help him, his heart swelled so with pride, yes, even with vainglory, that it left him speechless, which for Christopher in those days was unusual.

The assemblage represented a wide variety of learned investigations—astronomy, cartography, medicine, and navigation. Shipbuilders dropped in, and men who studied the myths that explorers brought back and assessed their verity. But always most important and most frightening to his mind were the reports of Portuguese exploration, for he knew, as did all the others, that the king of Portugal had more foresight as to the potential of exploration than any man in Europe. What happened in the world of sailing would very likely happen to the Portuguese. And he, who had lived in Lisbon as a cartographer, who met many of the great captains, knew all too well what they might accomplish. If only the damned Moorish war hadn't intervened, he might even then be far out in the Ocean Sea or sailing along the very coast of Cathay!

He never left Leonardo's shop without gleaning some fascinating and valuable piece of information or bit of useful knowledge. He learned chapters of history and maritime law, he pored over maps of the known and the unknown oceans. He learned words from many languages and even a few in Chinese, brought to the shop by one of his own countrymen whose great-grandfather had known the famous traveler Marco Polo. Yes, when he reached Cathay, he would at least know how to say more than "hello" to the emperor.

Leonardo's shop was better than a university. The hum of life, the thrill of being somebody, helped him forget Beatriz, except in his bed at night when wild fancies kept him awake and in a state of sexual excitement. In bed he would realize that his strong body, rested and celibate for months, needed her terribly. He thought of the prostitutes he saw and wondered why he didn't seek one out, and had his answer in the face of the *Principezza*, which always materialized when his mind drifted in that direction. Strangely, she didn't appear when he dreamed of taking Beatriz. At first he believed it meant she didn't disapprove, because he planned to marry her, but some sixth sense told him it wasn't that. He finally interpreted it as her displeasure at the thought of such a marriage and wondered if she had some noblewoman in mind for him. In broad daylight, of course, he realized the wildness of that fantasy. The nearest he had gotten to nobility had been Felipa, and she had been a special case. His own nobility, his Colom nobility, of course, must remain as always hidden, buried, forgotten.

Sometimes unbidden came the face of his son Diego, off at La Rábida with the monks and, he would squirm in guilt and self-condemnation. How long could he leave the lad there, even if now he could send his keep each month to Father Antonio de Marchena? He had a responsibility to Diego, and from Father Antonio's veiled hints he gathered his son needed a father's companionship. "In due time," he would tell himself, or, "When I can get away."

13

One morning, after a virtually sleepless night, when desire wracked him, he spoke to Rodrigo and Diego, "It's time to send for Beatriz," he said in a matter-of-fact way. "No need to wait a full month."

The kinsmen exchanged quick, pleased glances. He saw the approval and, felt like the King of Granada must when his ministers procured for him a special concubine. He mentally smacked his lips, but he wondered inexplicably what the *Principezza* would think if she knew he had no intention now of making Beatriz his wife. The very fact that Beatriz's own uncle and first cousin could allow her to come to the bed of a boarder, because they thought he was highly placed enough to help them, made it beyond the pale that he could ever marry Beatriz de Harana. People at court would ferret out the whole affair in all its sordid circumstances, he reflected, and they would give her, and him because of her, a very cold reception. Could she even begin to keep up with the haughty ladies of Segovia or Barcelona? With Beatriz Cabrera? He shuddered at the thought. And with the Queen of Spain? He shuddered even more. Why, there wasn't a noble female in the two kingdoms who would even stoop to spit on her. A man can rise on his own merits in life, but not a woman. Marriage with Beatriz was out of the question, as far as he was concerned. In his newfound self-esteem he wondered how he could ever have been indiscreet enough to offer marriage in the first place. He supposed it was the flesh. "She is, of course," he muttered under his breath, when he remembered the tie between them, "the very best I ever had in bed, even if I did have to teach her all she knows."

Could he give her up, he asked himself, give up those lush curves, those breasts like cool, smooth melons? That wonderful secret part that had its own special ways of maddening him? Give her up and break her heart when she found she could not enjoy him for the rest of her life? It would be a cruelty to them both. Why shouldn't he just drift with the current, take his pleasure and give her hers, be lovers as hot as at the hottest. Suddenly he realized her kinsmen had figured out the answer long ago. She would be his mistress. He would clothe her well, buy her the jewels she wanted, and take her with him here and there. but not to court. "Thank God," he exulted to himself, "that she didn't take me up on my proposals!" Suppose she had. Well, he would propose no more and give her no chance to hook him now. "I'll take what I can get and she can too," he chuckled.

One day a letter came from Cádiz. "Expect me before Christmas," she wrote. "I can't wait to see all of you and especially Chris. Tell him I can't come now because Aunt Gloria's daughter will have her child this month."

So it was done, and Beatriz would soon be on the way. That night at supper, when they had cleared the table and the serving wench had gone, he wondered aloud in Rodrigo's and Diego's company why Beatriz hadn't married.

Diego answered, "I think she's cold," he said, or, correcting himself, "I used to think so, before…"

"Before I came?" asked Christopher candidly.

"Well, yes, if you must make me say it. We'd always hoped she'd marry, but though men came around and one or two even got as far as serenades at the grating, she always turned them down. Then we hoped you'd marry her, Don Christopher, but she even refused to marry you, although she didn't refuse you otherwise. Oh yes, father and I knew this almost from the first. We aren't deaf, and sound carries from the wine cellar. We don't harbor guilt, my friend, for the blame is Beatriz's. It's why you're still our friend. It's not as though you used her and told her she wasn't good enough. The fault is hers."

Rodrigo broke in, nervously, relieved to have it in the open. "I'm glad it's you, Don Christopher, and it's made me, her guardian, if one can think of her as having one, feel much better, as though I'd tried to do the best for her and only failed because she's obdurate. Why, if she wouldn't marry you before you went to Málaga, with your child already stirring in her womb, she'll never marry anyone."

"Was the child—you said it didn't live—a boy or a girl?"

"A boy, but he came almost too soon to tell."

He took the hand of each in his condescending way feeling like a feudal lord being magnanimous to the family of a virgin bride he had taken before the groom by the law of the first night. "You're fine men," he said, not really meaning it, "and I respect you for your tolerance. I think, even so, that Beatriz is wiser than any of us. She knows what she wants, and we must humor her. And more important, she knows what she can do, what she can manage or handle in the world, and is wise enough not to go too far. I say let her have her way."

"Oh, we agree, Don Christopher. What Beatriz does is in God's hands."

Afterwards he felt better. "It's all out in the open, now," he said to himself, as he whistled a merry little tune before he went to bed that night. "They know I know and I know they do. And, since they're practical Spaniards, they realize that there are advantages to all concerned. But if they think I'll ask her again, they're greatly mistaken. Through Beatriz or because of her they'll do well, and I shan't forget their tolerance, even though I rather scorn it."

The night before they expected her, his thoughts ran riot. Erratically they leaped from Beatriz and her charms to poor Felipa and the *Principezza*—Felipa, pretty, little aging Felipa with her pale white-violet beauty, pure sweet and colorless. So fragile she had made him feel a brute when he took her maidenhead and heard her stifled cry. How unlike the flower that Beatriz was, a flaming, spicy, passion flower, all vivid and filled with tendrils and heady aromas, and with more warm, honeyed sweetness inside her than a passion fruit is crammed with honeyed pulp and seeds. And then there was the Queen of Spain, who always managed to insinuate herself into his fancies when he thought of other women. What sort of blossom did she evoke in his mind? A flower out of reach, of course, like those great, golden lilies he as a youth had so enviously longed to pluck in the palazzos of Genoa, safe in their lush gardens behind their grillwork of iron. Felipa, he mused, had remained unattainable, even after he had attained her flesh; the queen was utterly out of reach, as distant as a star; but he had attained Beatriz in all her special, torrid splendor and he would have her again, and always in her special place.

That morning he stared into his mirror and stared with care. Looking in it daily when he shaved, which he did assiduously and never skipping a day, told him little. But looking with deliberate, close attention, told him much. "I'm still a rather handsome fellow," he said aloud. "When you know you are, I've always told myself, why not admit it. Yes, I'm good-looking and I know why women still turn in the street to look at me. I'm barely past forty. My eyes are still deep blue and the whites are clear with none of the brown splotches so many fellows have. And I haven't lost teeth, and they gleam against the bronze of my face in a way that lets the world see they're clean and that my breath is good. What if my nose and chin are oversized? A big nose tells a woman how well-hung I am; and a chin like mine means courage and strength and determination to get what I go after. Women have eyes for a chin like mine. They recognize the nobility I cannot reveal."

And then she was home. She ran into the *zaguán* with never a thought that Rodrigo and Diego would see her kiss her lover. He kissed her soundly and open-mouthed. Only then did she turn to greet her kinsmen with staid kisses on their cheeks. Christopher thought they stood a little stiffly, but that was to be expected. Later they would grow accustomed to caresses and blatant signs of love.

That night in the patio under a golden moon her flesh was cool as he slipped the bracelet over her hand and clasped it on her wrist. She looked at it long, and her eyes grew moist. It was good, red coral and had cost him dearly. She lifted her face, though she didn't have to lift it far, for she was tall and he was already bending to receive her mouth. The months they had been apart vanished like thistle-down in a strong breeze and they were again as they had been the last night before he left for Málaga. The only difference was that they were in the patio, for anyone who cared to look, and not in the private, secret, forbidden world of the old wine cellar.

His big hands slid familiarly over her breasts. She opened her blouse quickly and when his hands grasped her, she put her hands on his and made his move rhythmically under hers. He could feel the hardness of her nipples. Her tongue was a flame burning in the roof of his mouth. Her body burned against his, and time stood still. And she didn't ask, she told him to meet her in the wine cellar after midnight.

"Let's not go there," he said. "Let's sleep in my room or yours, and let's go now!"

"Not so fast, my stallion," she laughed in her deep throaty tone. "There's a light in Rodrigo's room, and Diego's still out tomcatting. Go back to your room and wait till twelve."

"But why?" he asked petulantly. "They both know what we've done and what we're going to keep on doing. We have their consent. Why lie on a thin blanket on a moist cold floor? Let's try the bed."

"This first night, Chris, I simply can't. I'm a woman and I'm not a whore. I know they know, but even so, tonight, our first together after all this time, I want it as private as it used to be. Now go, for you've waited this long and can wait another hour."

He hadn't liked it, but back he had stamped to his room. As he lay tumescent in his bed, the door half open so he could hear when she left her room to tiptoe to the cellar, the *Principezza* again flew into his mind, though he thought he had closed her out. Was she, tonight, like him, lying in the darkness waiting for her horny king? What do they do together, he wondered? Was she like Felipa and too many Latin wives, cool and collected and sensible between the sheets? Or did she become an animal like his Beatriz? Could Isabella actually feel a prurient, primitive hunger for her royal mate? He suspected she did and that the lusty Ferdinand therefore fathered so fewer royal offspring. And what about himself and the Queen of Spain? Had he really caught a glimpse of something she felt for him through a chink in the amor of her propriety? Would she have yielded to him, given the perfect and secure opportunity? He shook his head, rolling it back and forth on the pillow impatiently to rid his brain of such rotten thoughts. To think of the Queen of Spain like that was as bad as thinking it of the Queen of Heaven. He loved the *Principezza*, he admitted it in his secret heart. He loved her soul and that was the test of the truest love of all. He needed a pure love, and he knew he would never find one except in her. Oh hell, he loved her body too, but he knew with no shadow of doubt that he could never bring his body to touch hers sexually, not even if she took him to some secret and romantic spot for consummation. There are fleshly loves one cannot consummate, that one's afraid to, that the hand of God forbids. "The *Principezza* is a saint," he groaned in hopelessness, "And I am a man who cannot take a saint."

She kept him waiting two full hours with his mind on fire. The feel of her lips under his, her tongue, her pile of thick and lustrous hair, heavy and redolent of her favorite sachet, was aphrodisiacal. Strangely balmy for December, the air flowed through his open window carrying the far-off melody of *villancicos* and the scent of flowers still blooming in neighborhood balconies. The monks in the cathedral, once a mosque, were practicing compline not far from the old tower where the muezzins once called the faithful to prayer. From across the plaza on which the house faced, someone began a *villancico*, soft, plaintive, sensual. The moon had frozen the whole world into a breathless peace.

Then he heard the door of her room open. In a bound he was in the hall beside her, leading her down the stairs. The cellar door creaked, as they opened it, and again when it closed behind them. They didn't notice.

The next night and the next she made him meet her in the cellar, but after that he refused, and she agreed to go to him in his room. If Diego and Rodrigo knew, they never said a word. So Christopher and Beatriz slept together like man and wife, and in time regarded it as the most natural thing in the world. Sometimes, even during siesta they made love, the first time to comfort him at the thought of another trip to face the doctors in Salamanca. Again when he returned, his face a thundercloud. "They still consider the enterprise the figment of a madman's imagination, white hair or not," he groaned.

14

In April of 1491, Isabella and Ferdinand returned to Cordova to launch the new campaign against Granada. The air was soft that spring and the tender and yet bitter-sweet aroma of olive orchards in full blossom gave the season a stimulating quality. Patriotic enthusiasm throbbed in every corner of the city. Thousands flocked to the drill fields to watch the king and his knights as they jousted in full armor.

Isabella early one morning breathed deeply of this wine-like atmosphere, striding back and forth restlessly in the room she used as an office. The sun streaming through the high Moorish arch of the window, made the room warm, and Don Alonso de Quintanilla, her secretary, mopped his brow as he waddled along at her side, vainly endeavoring to match his short steps to the queen's long strides.

Isabella concealed a smile. "He's wondering, as he has for years, if I'll ever be lady-like and transact official business from the depths of some comfortable chair," she thought.

"We might save here," she heard him wheeze. "Surely the good brothers of the Sacred Heart can get along without the annual founder's day gift, Highness."

"Perhaps, Don Alonso; but not this year. Have you forgotten that the Convent of the Sacred Heart relinquished voluntarily all its plates and all its precious vessels for the campaign against Málaga?"

"Very well, Highness, if you say so, but what of the historian, Don…?"

The queen was not listening, for just then Beatriz de Bobadilla appeared at the door. To the treasurer Isabella said, "Don Alonso, Lady Beatriz is here and I must talk with her. Set down the items we've discussed, but don't strike off the stipends to the historian. Good chroniclers are rare enough, and men like this Pulgar particularly so."

As Beatriz walked toward her, she saw out of the corner of her eye that Don Alonso was bowing himself out, careful not to turn his back on royalty.

When the door closed, she moved toward Beatriz with outstretched arms. "What brings you so early, Little Marquesa?" Beatriz still smiled with pleasure when the queen addressed her by her title, one given her not too long ago for the new to have worn off. Then her smile wavered, for what she had to convey to her friend would not be pleasant to her ears.

Isabella caught the look and knew something had gone amiss. It wasn't like Beatriz, who the night before had been agog with excitement at the coming of so many fine knights from as far away as Denmark and Ireland to join the last crusade, to change this much. Quietness and reserve in Beatriz de Bobadilla were harbingers of dire events.

Again Isabella used the title she liked to use when they were alone. "Little Marquesa, you look as unhappy as Don Alfonso when I ordered another pension placed on the list."

"Highness," began Beatriz. "Highness…"

Isabella's smile vanished. "Highness, is it?" she said. "Come now, Beatriz, it can't be as bad as that!"

Beatriz kept her eyes on the floor, tracing the arabesques in the rich oriental rug. "Highness, Isabella, you won't like the news I bring today." Then she took a deep breath and stared straight into Isabella's eyes.

"I hear a great deal I don't like, Little Marquesa, and there's no escaping it. I can bear some more bad news. Rumors are everywhere. What is it now?"

"This is truth, not rumor, Isabella."

"Truth and a rose have thorns," said Isabella, all a queen. "What a truth it must be to elicit so much formality! Must I speak as the queen, and not as the friend, and command you to tell me?"

Suddenly Beatriz blurted it out. "The woolmerchant has taken a mistress, Isabella! I should have told you before he went to fight at Málaga, but I didn't have the nerve. Now that he's here, I had to tell you."

Isabella turned slowly, and the light from the window threw her body into silhouette for a moment before she passed into the shadow. Her chin lifted quickly and her head went back. "Gossip," she said. "Gossip, and I don't like it. The woolmerchant still honors the memory of Felipa de Perestrello, Beatriz. You know this as well as I."

Beatriz looked at her rather quizzically. "Felipa's been dead a long time," she said. "And Columbus is a man of flesh and blood."

"He is indeed, Beatriz. A very fine man and undeserving of this sort of low rumor."

"Your faith is touching, Isabella, and therefore this story will hurt you greatly."

Isabella angrily realized Beatriz had caught the hurt in her voice. "She knows," she said to herself. "I should have seen how useless it would be to conceal it from her." And her cheeks flamed at her own admission. What *did* Beatriz know? What *could* she know? That Isabella respected the woolmerchant, that she owed him a great deal for past help? What else? That was all. All there could be, for that was all there was.

But was it? Whose wide-set eyes had been gazing into hers with reassurance all these years? The vision of whose face had alternately tormented her and brought her peace? Of course Beatriz knew, had known all along.

With calculated calm she said as casually as she could, "Hurt me? How could it possibly hurt me, Little Marquesa, even if it were true?"

Beatriz looked overhead and through the open window, and her eyes were blank. "I see the hurt, Isabella," she said at last. "I hear it."

"Ridiculous!"

"Love is ridiculous, Isabella. It's the most ridiculous, the most tragic thing in the world—and the most wonderful."

Isabella's voice dropped so low Beatriz barely heard it. "Love," she whispered, "you dare mention love and him in the same breath?"

She sat down suddenly and grasped the carved arms of the chair. Beatriz slipped to her knees and rested her head in her lap. Isabella's hand went out to stroke the lustrous black hair, but she drew it back. The room was quiet. Only Beatriz's low breathing broke the silence. On the wall a breeze stirred one of the tapestries, billowed it soundlessly. She saw Beatriz, hands twisting, and with a sudden gesture she seized them and said, "Stop it! Do you want the rings to cut your fingers?"

When the sobs had ended Isabella pulled herself slowly to her feet by the heavy hangings beside the window. Her face now, as well as her neck was stiff and was already beginning to ache. Why not admit it? The idea of the woolmerchant and a woman wounded her—as much as such an idea would about her husband. No, it wounded more. She was all too accustomed to Ferdinand's peccadillos, but she had been painting Christopher in different hues. The outlines of his frank and honest face, vital and understanding, with its clear blue eyes, suddenly began to blur. She clenched her teeth. "Who told you this?" she whispered.

"My dressmaker," said Beatriz. "Her brother overheard it in a wine shop, in the quarter where the woolmerchant lodges. And Isabella, I know it's true. Since I had to be certain, I went and verified it. I've seen the woman and I know they're lovers. Yes, I believe it, Isabella, and because I do, I came here to tell you before another beat me to it. Better by far to have bad news from me than from someone else, possibly even the king."

"Far better, Beatriz. Ferdinand would rejoice at the chance to discredit Columbus in my eyes."

"I know," said Beatriz, again averting her eyes.

"What do you know?"

"I've realized for a long time, Isabella, what the woolmerchant means to you…"

"I asked you what you knew?"

Beatriz's voice was low and sad. "I saw it in your eyes the day I brought him to you in the cathedral, Again at court when he spoke before the king and sought your aid. And I've heard it in your voice a thousand times since that day you rode with him to Ávila. I know you better than anyone else, Isabella."

"That does not give you the right to accuse me."

"Accuse? The secret is safe with me."

"The secret! Do you believe that what I feel for him must be a secret? Something guilty and to be concealed? Holy Mother of God! Am I a creature like Joanna, lusting after a man under my husband's very nose?"

Beatriz lowered her eyes for the third time. "Forgive me," she whispered. "But all this time I have thought…"

"You had no right to think!" cried Isabella, her voice strident. "I am Isabella of Trastámara, Queen of the Spains. Would I concern myself with the vulgar lusts of the son of a Genoese wooldyer? This time you have trespassed too far upon my patience. Leave me. Now!"

Beatriz stood up, wet-cheeked. "Forgive me," she said stonily.

Isabella with a sudden motion took her in her arms again. "You forgive *me*, Little Marquesa. You are right and I am wrong to try to hide what I cannot hide from you. But, tell me, how long have you read my secret thoughts?"

"From the beginning, Isabella."

Isabella was plunged in thought. At last she said, "Do others suspect? I doubt I could bear it if they did."

"No one suspects save Andrés and me. And surely not the king."

The tapestry's colors ran together in Isabella's vision. Her face set into immobility. Then suddenly two tears flowed down her cheeks. She didn't sob, like some women would have, she shed only the two tears and no more. But to Beatriz, who knew her best, it was the essence of deep grief. At last she wiped her eyes with the back of her hand, and turning to Beatriz, in a toneless voice, asked, "Who is the woman?"

"Her name is Beatriz de Harana. The woolmerchant lodges in her kinsmen's house."

"Is she beautiful?"

"Not in the way you are."

"But is she beautiful?"

"I'm afraid she is, Isabella, but it is an animal beauty—voluptuous and dark like a Mooress's."

"And coarse, no doubt," said Isabella, hoping the sound of her voice wouldn't betray her.

"No, Isabella. Not coarse. But not aristocratic either."

Isabella closed her eyes and rested her chin on her joined index fingers. For a long time she was quiet, dreading to ask the question uppermost in her mind. At last she said, "Does he love her truly?"

"She will bear his child."

"That proves nothing, Beatriz, and you know it as well as I."

Beatriz didn't contradict her. She kept her eyes fixed on the wall behind the queen where blazed the brilliant red and gold of the armorial banners of Castile and León, where King John's sword caught a ray of sunlight and flashed a challenge. She was startled at the speed with which Isabella came up from her chair. She saw the queen walk to the door with her sure, firm step, the one that betrayed stress or deep emotion. At the door she saw her stop, and knew she was waiting until she was satisfied with the coolness of the words she was about to utter. She opened the door, then and called into the corridor, "Don Alonso, bring your books and come to me."

"Yes, Highness," he wheezed, the heavy ledger hanging awkwardly over his pudgy arm. "Which of the lists do you wish to see?"

"The pensions for Cordova," said Isabella. Her eyes raked the list as Don Alonso held the heavy book before her gingerly, and she was conscious of his stare and the sudden curiosity in his close-set eyes. She went on anyway, regardless of his quizzical expression.

"Where are the C's?" she asked. "Ah, yes, I see them now." Then her finger stopped abruptly and she said, "Here is the name, Don Alonso. Strike the name of Columbus from the listings. We have done enough for him."

The treasurer hesitated for a fraction of a second, opened his mouth to speak, thought better of it, and closed it with a snap. He didn't fool the queen.

"How long did you keep him in your house, Don Alonso? Two months, wasn't it? I see how well he entrenched himself in your affection. He *is* a man capable of charming the trousers off a king or the cassock off a pope."

"Columbus is a worthy man, Highness. He deserves the pension. He needs it desperately!"

Isabella was speechless, and her face looked different as though the muscle play had altered. It made her almost ugly. Both Beatriz and Don Alonso recognized it for what it was—the very special look of rage which made princes and archbishops and foreign ambassadors tremble. As she stepped back to survey the treasurer's face she found it suddenly pasty and saw sweat stand on his brow.

"Strike his name from the pension, Don Alonso," she said in a voice no one had ever disobeyed.

"As the queen commands," he said.

"Quite so," said Isabella, as he withdrew, bowing stiffly, placing one foot behind the other with as much dignity as he could muster.

When the door had closed behind him, she felt her face relax, and the ache of its drawn muscles was the prick of needles. She turned to Beatriz and her face froze again, for Beatriz stood looking at the rug, her mouth set stubbornly.

"Well," said Isabella finally, "why don't you say it? Why don't you call it spite? Call me a woman scorned and full of venom. Call it what you will, and it will be what I deserve, because it will be true."

"Spite never heals," said Beatriz sadly. "And striking his name from the pension will not end your feelings. Nothing ever will. The woolmerchant is as stubborn as you. What you have just done will strengthen the Harana woman's hold upon him, and, it will weaken his respect for you and possibly even his love."

Beatriz, she knew, was perfectly correct. She had acted spitefully, but the thought of the woman's dark, young beauty melting in the woolmerchant's strong arms fanned smoldering fires. And the cry of her own loneliness and the need for that affection rang wildly in her soul.

"Beatriz, Beatriz! What can I do?" she cried, pressing white knuckles to her flushed face.

"I don't know, Isabella, But I do know the woolmerchant needs that pension desperately. It may seem little to you, who have so much. But to him it is more than daily bread. It is self-respect, honor, and a token of the crown's faith in the enterprise."

"But what can I do now? It's too late to rescind the cancellation. What would Don Alonso think if I rescinded it?"

"He'd be curious, Isabella. Later, when he had heard the facts about Columbus and the woman, he'd wonder more. He wouldn't talk, of course, Don Alonso is too faithful a servant of the state for that. But he would speculate." Isabella began to pace the room again noiselessly over the thick rug. Her throat worked, but she said nothing.

"Don't worry, Isabella," said Beatriz at last. "The woolmerchant needn't lose the pension. With your permission Andrés and I will send the money."

"Promise me you will, Beatriz,",

"You have my promise, Isabella."

"But not a word to Columbus."

"Not a word, Isabella."

She took Beatriz's hand then and squeezed it. "Thank you, little Marquesa, Tonight I'll sleep more easily than I'd hoped. As usual, I owe you more than I can pay,"

As the door closed behind Beatriz de Bobadilla, Isabella went to the *prie-dieu*, she kept in an alcove. Kneeling, she turned her face up to the niche that held the Madonna. The flame of the candle, no more than a ghostlike spark, ethereal and drained of substance by the brilliance of the sunlight streaming in through the Moorish arch, flickered, barely visible.

"Mother of God," she prayed, "Thou, too, art a woman and will understand. If I have sinned in this love for the woolmerchant, forgive me."

She knelt until the sun crossed the zenith and the shadow thrown by the arch of the window restored color to the candle's flame. And from her niche the Madonna looked down unwaveringly with eyes that understood.

15

It was the Queen of Spain in all her glory who awaited the coming of Beatriz de Harana. In stiff immobility she sat on the carved walnut bench under the Moorish window, and no empress ever looked more puissante. Starkly etched against the dazzling morning glare, she waited. Her hair glowed like a halo where the sun touched it, but her eyes were in shadow. On her feet she wore plum-colored slippers of Spanish silk, She wore her best jewels, too, and a robe more splendid than the occasion demanded, and it was certain she must really dazzle the Harana woman.

Even to Beatriz de Bobadilla, who had advised her not to have this interview, she had turned deaf ears. "It will be a private meeting," she said, for no one must know what passes between us. Not even you, little Marquesa."

She stiffened as the page swung open the door and ushered the woman into the room, but she refused to notice his glance of scorn at Beatriz de Harana. Pages were usually the sons of nobles. Their scorn of commoners was proverbial, Then the door closed and she was alone with the woolmerchant's paramour. The very word, ugly, sour as it passed through her mind, alienated her further from this woman. But as Beatriz curtsied, she grudgingly admitted that she was graceful, instructed in courtly etiquette or not.

"She reminds me of Joanna," she said to herself. "Not in actual features, but in the way she moves. Something about the eyes, too, I think." Then as she continued to study the woman's dark handsomeness, she cursed herself for allowing a flush of anger to suffuse her face and neck,

"Come forward," she said when she could control her voice.

Beatriz de Harana moved toward the window where Isabella sat, and her eyes were turbulent. "Sullen" thought the queen. "Sullen, and it becomes her,"

She watched the large round breasts nervously rise and fall behind the tight bodice, noted the lush curve of her hips, and saw unwillingly the perceptible swelling of her abdomen where lay the woolmerchant's child. "They were correct," she mused, "for she has a Moorish cast, and voluptuousness, not beauty, is her forté."

"I have summoned you, Beatriz de Harana," she said, coming straight to the point, "to speak of the man Columbus, your ... companion."

Beatriz shot her a quick direct glance, half-frightened, half-defiant. Then she looked away, letting her eyes stray in awe over the glory of the rug, the gorgeous tapestries, and the fine, rich hangings.

Isabella's toe tapped a silent and imperious summons, which brought the wandering eyes back with a start. They fixed themselves at a point just below her slipper.

"Yes, Highness?" queried Beatriz. "My companion?" And something in the way she enunciated the word made Isabella sit forward on the bench and grasp its arm more firmly. This woman was proud of her sin.

She was having to make rapid revisions of the preconceived idea she had drawn of the woman. Beatriz de Harana was more than a handsome young animal. More than a woman of easy morals, "She has determination and fire," she thought, "The woolmerchant sees in her a good deal more than a pleasant bedfellow."

Fixing a cold stare upon the pale face before her, she continued. "I have called you here to say this: you and your kinsmen are to stop trying to persuade Columbus to leave this realm. His destiny is in Spain, not in Portugal, or France, or England."

Beatriz's eyes glowed as if a fire had been fanned to life in them. Isabella knew then what poets meant when they described the eyes of Moorish women as pools of jet. The eyes held hers, this time longer before they fell, "Yes, Highness," was her reply.

"Is that all you can say, woman?" asked the queen coolly, "I want more than that. I want your word and your kinsmen's that you'll leave Columbus and his enterprise alone. Do you understand?"

When the dark eyes and the blue ones met again, it was the clash of two swords. "I understand, Highness, and I shall tell my kinsmen. I will say that Columbus's destiny is in Spain, that you have said so."

"That is better," said Isabella, momentarily sympathetic to this woman pregnant by a man who obviously had no intention of marrying her, but then she remembered the purpose of the interview.

"Why have you been filling his mind with going elsewhere," she asked, "Was it money?"

She watched Beatriz's red tongue move slowly over her dry lips and saw her index finger move back and forth in a purely Spanish gesture of negation. "Money, Highness?" she heard the woman say with spirit. "Of course not! We have urged him to go back to Portugal for his sake, not for money. He deserves more from life than what he has here. He needs ships, and crews, and money to carry out his enterprise. Not a pension, or the charity of friends, when the pension ceases,"

"Holy Mother," thought Isabella. "I can see myself in her as she argues for him! She smolders and will soon burst into flame. No mere money will buy this woman off," But she decided to make a test to see if her supposition had been justified.

"Suppose the money were forthcoming, and the ships and the crews, What do *you* hope to have from all this?"

"His son," said Beatriz de Harana.

Isabella winced. This woman, this nobody, would bear his son, while she, the Queen of Spain, could only secretly envy her. And out of her anguish she spoke sharp words and wondered, as she said them, how she could be so cruel.

"You mean his bastard."

"Yes, Highness. His bastard," said Beatriz, holding her head high. "Even a bastard by a man like this is no mean thing."

Isabella averted her gaze and shot a glance at the Madonna in the niche above her. But she had not missed the courageous light in the woman's eyes nor their bottomless and tender sorrow. Mary might have looked with eyes like that when Joseph thought to put her aside. This Harana girl was no common hussy. She had good blood somewhere. Very good blood.

The Madonna seemed to agree, and Isabella felt her shoulders relax. She had made up her mind. She would forgive this woman. Whatever she was, she wasn't a bad woman. Sinful perhaps—if love freely given with no thought to the consequences is sinful—but not wicked.

Suddenly she took Beatriz's hand and drew her to a seat beside her. "It was unseemly of me," she said, "to refer to the child as a bastard."

"But true, Highness. And it is a pity, for the child's sake, that is, but true and completely beyond all remedy. I will not marry Christopher. I never planned to. He will move in royal courts and speak with princes. Could I follow him? And if I could? He'd be ashamed of me and that I couldn't stand."

"He could do a great deal worse than to marry you," said Isabella, amazed at her own admission.

Beatriz lowered her eyes and wrung her hands pitifully. She longed to say something—Isabella could see that clearly—but was afraid.

"You are thinking of the child, aren't you?" she asked kindly.

Beatriz blinked savagely at the tears glimmering on her thick lashes, "Yes, Highness," she said.

"I think I understand," said Isabella, deeply moved, as much by the woman's consideration for her lover's future as for her unborn baby. "You fear the future—the time when Columbus sails the Ocean Sea. I fear it, too, Beatriz de Harana, but like you I long to have him go."

"He mightn't come back, Highness," Beatriz said, stifling a sob.

"He *will* come back, my girl, he *shall*! Never doubt it for a minute, for it's in God's hands and Our Lady's and they love him over much." She saw Beatriz swallow hard before she crossed herself.

Isabella knew what she was about to do would be improper, but she would do it nonetheless. "Ferdinand, when he hears," she muttered loud enough for Beatriz to hear, "will have a stroke of apoplexy, and so will Don Alonso. Even the Little Marquesa will be caught off guard, and only God knows what will be the repercussions, but by Our Lady I'll do this thing.

"Listen, Beatriz," she said, drawing the younger woman close, "when the ships sail, bring the child to me. By Our Blessed Lady I swear this child, son or daughter, will be reared in a fashion deserving of its father... and of its mother. Your child and Christopher's shall be my ward and grow up in the palace with my children."

Beatriz, stunned, sat, head bent, eyes on the fine stuff of the gown he had given her when she told him he would be a father. When finally she raised them to look at the queen, tears were spilling over. "You *are* good!" she whispered, "He told me so, but I didn't believe him. I'd seen you in processions, beautiful, bejewelled, haughty, seen you ride forth in silver armor while men knelt as to a saint. And, Highness, I'd seen that other queen, the one they called Joanna, and I thought..."

"I know what you must have thought," she said, "and forgive you."

She rang a bell, and Don Alonso's bulk filled the doorway, "Fetch me a purse of a hundred gold florins," she ordered, and when he had placed it in her hands with ill-concealed regret, she forced it into Beatriz's.

"This is for you and the child, Beatriz de Harana. It will be our secret. And Don Alonso, I include you in it. She shall also have a monthly pension for support for the child. Send me word when the baby comes, my dear,"

Beatriz didn't know what to say or how to say it. She kept clutching the purse and rocking back and forth.

"Take your purse, Beatriz," said Isabella, "and go with God. And after Granada Columbus shall have his ships."

"By St. Ferdinand, I believe he shall," said Beatriz.

7

Consummation

1

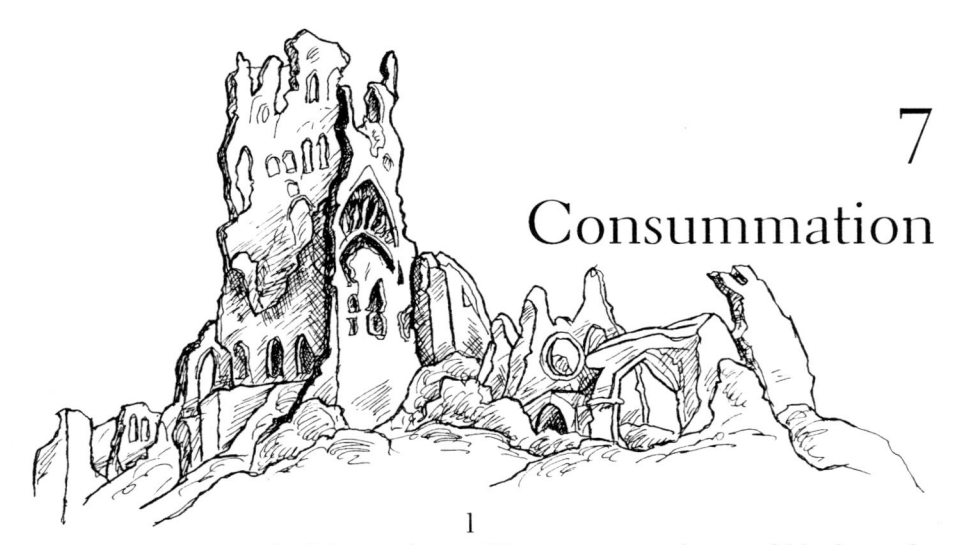

THE GREAT FIRE had burned out. Not even one plume of black smoke darkened the summer sky as Ferdinand and Isabella, appalled, walked through the destruction. Only Granada, gloating still behind its mighty fortifications, had permanence. Everything else was gone. Out of the ashes rose an acrid smell, the persistent and terrible reminder of the vast field of tents, street after street of them, laid out with the geometrical precision of olive groves. Gone, all gone! Gone the gorgeous pavilions, the standards floating bravely in the sunlight. Gone the ordered camps arranged according to nationality—French, Portuguese, German, English. Gone the might of Spain and Christendom encamped on the plain of Granada against the Crescent.

A tempest of silence beat down upon her as she stood in her night garb, a captain's cloak thrown over her bare shoulders. She looked at the ashes and refused to understand. Had God turned his face from St. James' land?

Dully she was conscious of her husband's voice, deep and inconsolable. "I will find the man who did this thing, and when I do..."

He didn't finish, and she made no comment. Let him ease himself, if he could, with threats and vows of vengeance. What was done was done. And it could have been an accident.

Destiny this? The question of destiny rose before her like a specter out of the past, mouthing words that mocked, the destiny of men and women, the persistence of destiny in the face of every obstacle, of every calamity was not rational, she saw. It fell outside of reason, for reason confronts the longing for destiny's fulfillment. It contradicts and smothers it, and the truth is, in all strictness, reason is the enemy of faith and therefore the enemy of life. It is even worse: it is the enemy of hope.

Spain's destiny, her people's stood at its critical point. It hung in the balance, for Granada was still unconquered, and while it stood, progress must stop and the nation must mark time.

She felt tears on her cheeks and was not ashamed. There was no stigma in tears, not when ten thousand knights stood in the darkness, made light by fire and with her wept. To be so close to victory and then to see fire go leaping madly from tent to tent, from street to street until nothing remained but the grey and black snow of destruction that crunched softly under her feet. Their encampment, their city of tents lay in ashes.

She could not look at Ferdinand and see in his face the magnitude of their loss. Yesterday she had been the crusading queen. She had ridden a white charger and had gone clothed in silver damascened mail and a great flowing cape of scarlet. Everywhere the physical impact of the adoration in her soldiers' eyes! Yesterday a gorgeous altar, rising on its gleaming pyramid of white steps, its priests in attendance, singing continuous high mass, day and night, night and day, while the incense rose to God in heaven in lazy puffs of grey-plumed smoke, and Cardinal Mendoza moved like an avenging angel before the Host, and the choirs of male voices thundered the praises of the Almighty.

Then the night of July the fourteenth. Only last night? A sudden glow in the sky and the wind rising as if by a prearranged signal, The screams then of her children and ladies-in-waiting and Ferdinand's voice, matching hers. "Where is the queen," he cried, even as she cried, "Where is the king?" Outside the tent the hoarse bellows of the fire wardens, the panic of the horses, the mad retreat of every living thing before the flames. Out into the dark plain she had fled with her family, to stand bathed in the red glow of the fire to watch in macabre fascination as the camp in flames blotted out the sky, the plain and the moonlit mountains. And above the fire, the sobbing of the army, and the scream of the horses, but worse by far through all the rest, the thought of thunderous paean of exultation from the besieged city. Ah, the bitterness of it! To stand in the darkness as the fire, so quick and wild to grow, faded and died and to the elation of the enemy. She imagined the exultance in their voices as they hurled insults across the few miles from Granada.

She realized at last that they were at one of the rear outposts. The children slept the sleep of exhaustion. Ferdinand had gone to order swarms of crossbowmen and harquebuslers into the plain near the city gates to prevent a sudden attack. Out of the night rose the voices of priests giving the last rites to those burned to death and extreme unction to those who would not live.

She could not rest. After a while she made her way slowly back to the ash fields. She felt utterly alone. All night she prayed for guidance. She was still alone when the sun rose and turned to reality the desolation only half-realized in the night.

Across the plain towered the battlements of Granada, and although the distance was too great to hear, she knew what frenzied oriental joy prevailed inside! At last she sat down an a large soot-blackened stone, heedless of the marks it left on her night dress.

"Is this the end?" she said aloud. "This, after Baza, where in a nine months' siege thousands died? After all the convents and monasteries surrendered their holy vessels? After every Spanish noblewoman contributed her jewels and the people paid tax upon tax without a murmur of complaint? Why, after millions of prayers by thousands of holy people? I must not surrender to despair, which may be the sin against the Holy Ghost, I must not let my people see that this, the worst of all the bad moments of my life, has defeated me."

A wind whipped the ash in grey clouds and it was acrid in her nostrils. Then the memories evoked by Baza struggled to be re-lived, and because they were not all sad, she listened.

There had been Ferdinand's letter, for example. "Come to Baza, Isabella, in the name of God. The men call for you night and day. After months of siege we are at a stalemate."

Proudly out of Jaén on a white warhorse she had ridden at the head of three hundred lancers. Then the encampment and the unbearable pride she had known before the men on their knees, weeping like women at the sight of her in her silver armor and scarlet mantle. Not even before Málaga, when she had inspected the troops, had it been like that. For a miracle unfolded under the walls of Baza. An army, bone-weary, discouraged, on the verge of desertion, suddenly took courage. It would go down in history, she knew, for Pulgar's account of it she had seen already, and she crossed herself humbly. His words were graven on her mind, "And because we were present and we saw it, we testify its truth before God, Who knows all, and before the men who saw it; after the queen entered the encampment, it seemed as though all the rigors of battle, all the bitter disappointments, all hostile and disloyal murmurings ceased and became serenity; all the harquebuses and crossbows and all manner of artillery fired then unceasingly from the whole camp, where before there had been no action and no one left in the tents save those who had to occupy the outposts. But after the coming of Isabella the Caudillo of Baza asked for peace." Pride? Yes. She had surrendered to that member of the seven deadly sins.

Ash sifted over her bare feet. Had all that been in vain? In vain, certainly, if Granada emerged from the war unconquered. The armies would disband and the foreign knights go home with all their soldiery and weapons; Portugal would grow cool, in spite of Prince Afonso's marriage to her daughter Isabella the past Easter; Ferdinand might turn again toward his Aragonese holdings in Italy, leaving Spain cleft in twain by the mountains that marked the boundaries of the Kingdom of Granada; perhaps the most terrible result of all, Islam would rejoice and wax more powerful.

One memory of the siege of Baza touched her. There she had again seen the woolmerchant on a winter evening. There she had turned her back upon him and ridden away into the night. And where was the money Ferdinand had told her they had saved by refusing him again? The ashes between her toes told her where it was. Better by far to have given him the ships and sent him off into the Ocean Sea after his destiny, than to see the money, or what it represented, go up in smoke.

She shook her head, as if to dispel the vision of his face, wild in the torchlight, and hurt and angry before she left it behind.

She and the king had ridden through the entire camp that evening to cheer the men even further, while her eyes grew weary looking for the woolmerchant. "He must be here," she had told herself. "With the pension restored and my invitation to take part in the conquest of Baza, nothing could hold him in Cordova. Not even Beatriz de Harana."

In the midst of the Aragonese sector she had seen him. He burst from the opening of a tent and stepped into the street, actually blocking their progress. The light of torches flickered on the polished surface of his cuirass and turned his white mane into its former fire. As they drew rein, the Aragonese knights and men-at-arms crowded around, wondering if words would pass between this wild compatriot and the sovereigns.

He spoke then in his ringing, timbrous bass, and she knew immediately that he had heard of the threat of invasion delivered that day by the emissaries of the Sultan of Egypt. She shot an anxious look at Ferdinand. He sat his horse sternfaced, waiting, and not patiently. Then, suddenly. as that hoarse voice was flung at them his own native tongue, in Catalan. In the Catalan of a gentleman, not of a peasant, Isabella saw what could be no less than the complete breakdown of self-control. Wild, mad fury! At what? At whom? And then his voice, altered, rough, with the fury of a long pent up malice, grated on her ears. "My God," said the king. "Why must I endure this?"

"Endure what?" asked Isabella, laying a gloved hand on his.

"Him? This rebel! This, this fugitive from my justice!" And staring straight into Juan Baptista's eyes with Isabella and his men hanging on his words, he hissed "*He* knows what I mean!"

"But," said Isabella, perplexed and beginning to feel alarm, "the other time you didn't react this way. You saw him then. What has brought this on today?"

Ferdinand began to calm himself and to become king again. He looked about nervously to see how many and who had taken note of his outburst.

And then, his voice low, he said to Isabella, "That voice, raised in anger to us, and in my native tongue! His damned daring! His willingness to go too far. I believe a saint would forget himself as I just did."

"Can we not hear what he has to say about the Sultan of Egypt?" she said, hoping to distract her husband.

At this Christopher continued his tirade, and he continued to speak in Catalan. "Highness, support my enterprise. Remind the Sultan that his empire's rear may soon be unguarded. If my enterprise succeeds and I reach the East by sailing west, your forces could attack him on two fronts. He would never dare pillage the Holy City and befoul the Church of the Nativity and the Holy Sepulchre, if you let me find the way across the Ocean Sea, to the postern gate of Islam!"

Isabella opened her mouth to speak, but the king's hand closed on her bridle. In complete possession of himself at last, he said, "Ride on." She saw the reason. This was no place to parley, and with her husband in unaccountably foul a humor even plain speech was out of the question. Besides she was eager to learn the reason for his outburst, and why, since he had said so much, he didn't pursue the matter.

She heard him muttering darkly at her side. "This man is still my enemy, my nemesis. I had thought the years had erased our differences or at least diluted them. I see that I was wrong. And just now we've seen the proof. Only an enemy and a fool would have tried to embarrass us into doing what we are not ready to do. He went too far, and he shall pay for it!"

"He didn't plan the confrontation," said Isabella. "How could he have known we would ride this way? No, he was with his friends, he heard that we were in the street, he ran out, saw us, and spoke his mind, seizing an opportunity he otherwise would not have had. But why did he speak in Catalan?"

Ferdinand grimaced, still in the throes of a terrible anger.

"Columbus is too candid," she said. "But he is sincere."

"Sincere?" laughed Ferdinand harshly."Well, when I've finished what I have to say I believe your blind faith in this man will terminate. Who told you, Isabella, that he is Genoese? Who rode with you in a litter, holding your hand, comforting you, play acting that he was a common woolmerchant? Who even clothed himself as one and duped you completely? That is the man back there! Genoese, indeed—you heard his words in his courtly Catalan. Could a Genoese peasant talk like that?"

Isabella thought she might faint and fall from her horse. She could hardly breathe and she couldn't believe what she was hearing. If she ever believed it, then the man she trusted most, she could trust no more. She could hardly face that disillusionment, so she argued, and even as she argued, realized that, as usual, her husband had seen the baser side of a person she respected, yes, and loved. "I heard his Catalan. What are you telling me it proves? He could have learned it since we last saw him."

By the time they reached their pavilion, Isabella, as pale as death, had heard the story of Juan Baptista and the rebellion of the Generalitat. She knew that his name was not Colombo and not Columbus, but Colom, She knew that he had been involved in a revolt against the Aragonese government, had fled, as it turned out, to Genoa, and that her husband had for a long time searched for him. Worst of all, aside from the disillusionment of her Christopher's lies was the unpardonable fact that long ago he had tried to put a lance into the Prince of Aragón. The thought of what that would have meant the thought of the world without her husband and what the world would be if she had not been able to marry him, staggered her. She could hardly find the strength to get down from her horse.

Then fear for Christopher's safety, for her woolmerchant's life, even though he had deceived her, came to her rescue. "When did you and the woolmerchant, I mean, Juan Baptista, fight with one another? How long ago was it, Ferdinand?"

"What does it matter how long ago it was? It was *lèse majesté*, it was high treason, it was unforgivable, and dear wife, it was a crime punishable by death. But, since you ask, it took place not far from his home, which we burned, back in '66."

Isabella felt the beginnings of a stirring hope. "But that was nearly thirty years ago. He was not a man then, but a boy, and so were you. Why you were no more than fourteen, and Christopher may have been younger. I urge you, Ferdinand, to let bygones be bygones."

In the pavilion Ferdinand said little. He poured himself a glass of wine, forgetting in his anger to pour her one. Then he called for his scribe.

"What are you going to do?" asked Isabella.

"Dictate an order for Colom's arrest. After all, he is still a fugitive from Aragonese justice. Why do you ask? Better still, why do you care what I do with him?"

"I care. I owe him a great deal, and so do you... It was he who, I am certain, saved me from melancholia, if not plain madness during those days we rode in the litter to the Convent of the Holy Child. And, husband, remember the division of our power. I shall consider him my subject, not yours, despite his blood and his history. I ask you to let him go his way. I ask you to permit him to fulfill his destiny, even if he does so for a country other then our own. For me I ask it. And for you, because I believe that his man, whom you once persecuted with good cause, no doubt, can change the history of our world. I believe in Juan Baptista Colom and I believe that heaven has sent him to us with his enterprise with his destiny, a destiny linked to mine, and therefore to your own."

Ferdinand sent the scribe away as soon as he arrived. He looked long and enigmatically at Isabella. She could heard his mind ticking in his head like some clock. "Thirty years!" she heard him whisper.

"What can he do to hurt us now?" she asked. "What power has he? He might as well be the Genoese peasant he said he was. He has no money except what we give him. He has fought in this war and on our side. Does he wield any power in Aragón which could threaten you or us? Didn't you and your father destroy his home and disperse his family?"

Ferdinand gnawed a knuckle, always a sign of deep cogitation. "The Coloms in Catalonia, at least his immediate family, are there no more. My father's troops ransacked, looted, and burned their house. We confiscated all their holdings, and we drew up a writ of perpetual banishment against them."

"And isn't all this enough?" asked Isabella. "Won't you forgive and forget what a fourteen year old boy did that long ago?"

"I never forgive and I never forget, my dear; however, since you put it as you do, that is, that I let him go free for your sake, I shall do that. Perhaps we can derive something of value from this man's plans, from his contacts with people like Marchena and Toscanelli. I've never been one to cast aside something that might advantage me. Yes, I'll forget the sentence of execution I had drawn up after our little fray in Segarra. But it will be a real pleasure to know that he has suffered and will still suffer for what he tried to do to me when we were boys. And it will give me much delight to see him come to us, hat in hand, and have him believe that you can give him aid only with my sufferance."

2

She stepped out of the new pavilion, pitched that morning, and saw in her mind's eye the Alhambra of Granada, "Perhaps Granada is my Calvary," she mused. "Perhaps Our Lord Himself felt like this up there on His cross the day of the Crucifixion." The Savior had seen his world shatter all around Him, she knew, and He had even died, but not in defeat. Suddenly His words, preached to her so many times, quoted endlessly, took on a new and deeper meaning. He had not said, 'Take up *my* cross and follow me,' but 'Take up *thy* cross.' To imitate Christ is to take up each his own cross, the cross of his profession or occupation or destiny."

She wandered on across the black emptiness of the plain, yesterday so splendid and magnificent with chivalry, and now burned out. She watched the torn red sky open to let the sun shine through. Everything passes, and God never changes, she remembered. This, too, would pass, and this *vega* would see a new host rise out of the ashes, phœnix-like.

Her steps quickened, and by the time she reached the bare hillock where the altar had stood, she knew what she had to do, Even the cardinal, staring disconsolately at the ruin with two monks who whispered and crossed themselves, failed to daunt her spirit. She called a passing soldier and sent him on the run to look for the king and the generals and engineers.

When Ferdinand arrived, he found her sitting on a stone amid the ashes of the chapel sketching a hasty diagram on a sheet of scorched parchment. Beside her stood Pulgar the chronicler, a look of perplexity on his thin face. Cardinal Mendoza and the two monks knelt in silent prayer.

"Here, where the altar stood," Isabella was telling Pulgar, "we'll construct the new church with its altar in the very spot where the other stood. Across the plaza will be the royal headquarters. The garrison and dormitories..."

"What are you doing here, Isabella?" she heard her husband ask in alarm. "We should be leading the army out of the *vega* even now, and here you sit drawing diagrams and planning another church."

Isabella looked at him pityingly. Just what a man would say! "Out of the *vega*?" she asked, "You mean retreat?"

"Of course. What did you expect? We have no shelter, no food, and the Moors will certainly take advantage of the destruction of the camp to launch attacks."

"The armies of Castile will not retreat, Ferdinand," she said vehemently, wiping her forehead. The black stain of soot made the king smile in spite of himself, The gravity of the situation lessened. When she said, "*My* army will remain and construct a new encampment," he had full control of himself,

"Very well," he said. "But let's at least withdraw into the hills till we can assemble the necessary equipment, the tents..."

"This new encampment will not be made up of tents, Ferdinand; it'll be a permanent city of wood and stone."

She saw Ferdinand look at the generals and engineers. They looked away, "A city," they murmured. "But out of what, Highness?"

The glow of inspiration rolled over her like a wave. "We have the soldiers. The nearby villages will send supplies and artisans. We can work the Moorish captives, provided we let not a single one escape. We shall have our permanent encampment."

The cardinal stood up, "Faith is the answer, Highnesses," he said prophetically, "With holy faith such a city *can* rise here out of these ashes."

She saw the idea taking hold. Even Ferdinand's eyes took on that faraway look that meant already he was speculating taking inventory, planning.

"Let us call this city Isabella, a general suggested, "for it is to be the queen's own town."

Ferdinand frowned slightly but nodded resignedly. The two monks and the cardinal said nothing, but waited for the queen to speak. She shook her head, "The cardinal gave us a name a moment ago," she said. "We'll call it Santa Fe, for by holy faith we can make it rise stone by stone, beam by beam above the ashes."

Through the heat and dust of July, August and September she watched it grow and become alive, while the parched grass of the *vega* turned green and living under the first fall rains, battening the warhorses, the mules, the cattle and the sheep, She herself paced out the two main streets in the form of a cross facing Granada, a vast cross which Moorish scouts could see day and night, each of its corners to end in a gate at the north, south, east and west. "What must they be thinking?" she asked her chaplain one day.

Pedro Martyr dared not even guess, but Ferdinand who had overheard, said practically, "They're thinking of their ruin."

Each morning she would throw back the flap of her tent, as Santa Fe rose, and after she had a house of masonry and wood to sleep in, she would throw open her window and stare up at the mountains which protected the hateful fortress city only a few miles away, and she could dream of its surrender.

To feed the Moors' imagination and despair she donned her silver mail each day and on her white charger rode the circuit of the battlements so that every Moor in Granada could see her with her husband beside her and accompanied by a choir of boys singing hymns to the Almighty. She could see them upon their walls watching and crowding for a place to see. She saw the flights of arrows winging toward her like darts of light in the morning sun, but she rode just out of reach, She smiled when her spies told her the Moors were saying she could make a sign and the arrows would circle back upon the archers who launched them. Yes, there was great consternation in the besieged city. They called her the White Witch, for who but a witch could make a city of solid stone spring up like a cloud on an empty horizon. If she could do that, the Moors were saying, she could take their city when she wished. They wondered why she didn't simply cause their walls to crumble like those of Jericho, or vanish into thin air, since they had heard their scouts swear by Allah that certain of Santa Fe's buildings and whole sections of its walls simply had risen up during the hours of darkness, built by the hands of *djinn*, invisible at sunset, and at dawn revealed, standing solid and strong upon the plain. They would not learn until weeks later, when it was too late for them to do anything, that parts of Santa Fe had indeed sprung up overnight.

"We can't finish it all," she told Ferdinand as he grew restless at the delay, "but we can make the enemy think so. We'll hereafter erect scaffolding under cover of darkness and nail canvas to it, then paint it to look like stone. If Granada sees me as a witch, Granada will take this as a witch's magic."

And then one afternoon the last nail was driven, the last roof tile laid. "It is finished!" she said, her face alight. Ferdinand nodded, still amazed that they had done it. "Who could have dreamed it but you," he said in genuine approval. "All this in eighty days."

"And whoever dreamed of fighting in a siege like this?" asked the Marquis of Cádiz, "with strong walls to sleep behind and cool rooms in stone buildings to protect us from the heat and the cold."

"And good drinking water," said Pedro Martyr, the queen's secretary.

"Magic," said Pulgar. "Sheer magic!"

"Faith," said the Cardinal of Spain.

"Destiny," said Isabella.

3

She read Brother Juan Pérez's letter for the tenth time, for it brought news of the woolmerchant at last, the first she had in all the months since the siege of Baza. After that glimpse of him in the Catalan sector of the army, after those angry words and furious glances, he had vanished. Her agents had been unable to locate him and even the Cabreras were at a loss. Moreover, Beatriz de Harana had vanished also. If the baby had arrived, no word had come. Rumor had it that they had gone to Portugal.

Brother Juan wrote with the insistence and freedom of one who had served a royal family has a right to employ. She smoothed the rumpled pages of the letter gratefully. Brother Juan was good and had never lost touch with her in all the years he had lived at La Rábida.

"Highness," he wrote, "Columbus has returned from Portugal, and even though he failed again to secure the aid he sought, his visit was important. I thought you and the king should hear what transpired. As you must know, King João invited him through his ambassador at the siege of Baza, where you saw him under unfortunate circumstances. With King João's safe conduct Columbus went to Lisbon with the threat of debtor's prison removed. All was very secret. The Portuguese crown paid for his travel and the transportation of his navigator's equipment. Mark this, Highness, for Portuguese money is always wisely spent. It was in December of '89, you'll recall, when he dropped out of sight. You must have heard, even in Baza, that Díaz rounded the tip of Africa, named it the Cape of Good Hope, and sailed on eastward. At last the Portuguese knew how to sail around that vast continent and straight across the Indian Ocean to Cathay. They are the only Europeans, Highness, who have access by water to the riches of the East, and they are protected from competition, as you well know, by the terms of the treaty made between your country and King João's, with papal approval, in fact insistence. Díaz's return, you will have realized, snatched from Columbus all that Portugal was about to confer upon him.

Isabella sat musing for a long while. What a terrible disappointment to the woolmerchant! The Portuguese king's money almost in his pocket, and then to see the fleet of Díaz sailing up the Tagus, banners flying in triumph to dash his hopes!

She returned to the letter, "After that," she read, "Columbus sent his brother Bartholomew to the court of Henry VII in London, but the English turned a deaf ear to his pleas. At present, Bartholomew is at Fontainebleau trying to enlist the aid of Queen Anne, who is at least granting him audiences.

She digested the message. The disappointment in Lisbon would have defeated a lesser man. Not Christopher! She could imagine him slamming his great fist into a hand and invoking St. Ferdinand. Desperate, yes, but not defeated. The Díaz discovery was to him what burning tents at Santa Fe had been to her—a challenge. "We are two phœnixes, the woolmerchant and I," she thought proudly, "each ready always to rise from his own ashes. And now she saw the time to help him had come again. Therefore she wrote Brother Juan and told him to come to Cordova to see her, and to come alone, "We must plan to bring him back," she wrote, and she believed that would stir Brother Juan to great haste in his journey. And the king? She would tell him in due time.

They had just ended one of the ever-present, but never-ending negotiations with Granada, when Isabella saw Brother Juan dismounting from his donkey. "Why, there is Brother Juan Pérez," she cried, touching Ferdinand's arm. "He must have ridden straight from Palos the day my message reached him."

"Why wouldn't he?" Ferdinand asked peevishly. "You are the Queen of Spain, Isabella." He shook his head, wondering if she would ever lose her respect for even the less important clergy, "What message?" he added as an afterthought.

When he found out, he was not pleased, for Brother Juan launched straight into the reasons for his coming. Ferdinand turned livid, but so enthusiastic was

Brother Juan that he failed to see the warning signal. It was only the mention by Brother Juan or the expenditure of Portuguese royal funds that kept Ferdinand from stalking majestically away. The mention of gold, of course, stayed him, and he waited expectantly, but angrily, to hear what was to be.

"Highness," said the priest, "the fact that King João was ready to outfit a fleet and make Columbus its admiral reveals much. Of all the nations of the West, Portugal is the most practical and experienced in the area of navigation. You know this well, for your own daughter must continually write you about this explorer or that, since exploration is the talk of the court, overshadowing all else. No other people has opened so wide the horizons of the world."

Isabella watched the two men and decided to say nothing for a while. She wanted Ferdinand to make a decision without her. That way, royal support for Columbus would have a better chance. If Ferdinand thought another king was about to get something out of the woolmerchant, in sheer dog-in-the manger perversity, he might decide to snatch him back for Spain. She saw his brow pucker in deepest thought and when he began to rub his chin and push his upper lip with the knuckles of his right forefinger, her spirits rose.. When he finally bit the ring she knew. He had made a favorable decision.

"What had the King of Portugal agreed to give this man after Díaz returned?" he asked. Isabella's eyes widened ever so little, Ferdinand's spies had been active, too, for him to know of that and doubtless of Columbus's despair. She wondered if his spies in France had let him know that Christopher's brother was at Fontainebleau.

"Sire, he spoke of four caravels, with Columbus as their admiral. The crown would pay for the ships and provide their crews. New land discovered would become part of the Portuguese overseas dominions. Columbus would have received a percentage of all cargoes carried in the caravels and the promise of a second and larger fleet for Cathay. Highness, King João was ready to be most generous. What a pity Díaz's ships appeared so inopportunely!"

She saw Ferdinand sit forward and caught an unmistakable glint in his eye. Turning to her he said sagely, "Columbus may have been correct after all, Isabella. João's too shrewd to spend good cash unless the odds of success are weighted. He'd never be taken in by a dream, no matter how rosy. I'll say this — if João planned to sponsor the enterprise to the extent Brother Juan reports, then the enterprise has basic soundness." And, seeing something in Isabella's eye, he added, "When I'm wrong, my dear, I can admit it. Don't you think we should listen again to your would-be admiral?"

"I believe we should," she managed to say not too enthusiastically, though her heart leaped, "Go back to Palos, Brother Juan and tell him that. Tell him the sovereigns of both Castile and Aragón grant him an audience here in Santa Fe."

She kept a firm rein on her voice, "This time the Grand Council will decide," she said. "After what's happened in Lisbon, the enterprise deserves the attention of the nation's leaders, not its scholars."

"Highness," said Juan Pérez, "Would it not be wiser to dispatch one of the royal couriers? My mule is as slow as death, and I'm not young. By the time I reach La Rábida, Columbus may have gone."

Anxiety showed so plainly in the priest's face that Ferdinand quirked an eyebrow. "Would he truly leave to go to France, Brother Juan?" he asked, and again Isabella saw how well he kept abreast of the woolmerchant's movements.

"Highness, he came to La Rábida only to get his son, whom he had left there much too long. He told me the day I left, that they would start for France as soon as Diego recovered from a minor indisposition. I asked him to wait, but I can't guarantee he will. He is a desperate man. He's also far too proud. And, Highness, he remembers Baza all too well."

"If he gave you his word, Brother Juan," said Isabella, pretending to overlook the mention of Baza, "he'll be there waiting when you return. And you did tell him, surely, didn't you, that I had called you here? But even so, we shall dispatch a courier with a letter to him from you as well as from the king and me, not because he'd go without them but to reassure him."

"An excellent idea, Highness, I shall write to him, and just in case he isn't at his lodgings, off perhaps to see the ships in Palos Harbor or Cádiz, I'll send word also to Dr. Fernández, the local physician who has been treating young Diego, and to Master Juan Sánchez. Yes, and to Martín Pinzón, the town's leading shipowner. He would know exactly where to find our navigator."

While Brother Juan penned his messages, Isabella excused herself to write one of her own, "Accept this draft," she wrote in her own hand, "and draw the sum from the bank in Palos. Buy a new doublet of the best velvet, plum colored, I should think, and new hose and shoes with silver buckles. Clothes mean much here in Santa Fe, woolmerchant, now that we hold court here, for they are all here now, all the nobles of Castile and Aragón, not to mention the throngs of notable personages from abroad—all waiting for the fall of Granada—and to hear about your destiny." Writing so intimately took her back fondly to the litter and the interviews at Toro and Córdoba. She added, not as an afterthought, but because she genuinely wanted to know, "And send word of your friend and of her child." If Ferdinand ever gets his hands on this letter, she thought, he might truly have the stroke I keep mentioning. But Christopher would understand and so would Beatriz de Harana.

She told Ferdinand firmly, and in the face of his open glare of opposition, "I shall hear no more slurs about his shabbiness, and no more mention of peasant origin which you, my dear, have so clearly contradicted. And let us stop talking about the Harana woman and Christopher's choice of companions. He must have the best chance possible when he speaks before us and the Great Council." Then she sent for the Little Marquesa and made it plain to her what must be done to insure his comfort when he came to Santa Fe, "You and Andrés will house him," she directed. "That will lend him an air of acceptance. Holy Mary, how grand it'll be to see his tall figure striding proudly down the aisle of courtiers, his eyes bright as fire with disillusionment and disappointment forgotten."

"And," said Beatriz daringly, "with his eye of deepest devotion on you who makes it possible. I'm so glad you've forgiven the impersonation of a woolmerchant and the other lies he had to tell you."

4

As the Grand Council debated the enterprise in Santa Fe, Isabella followed the progress of the meetings, although not in person. The Council knew her feelings, knew of the King of Portugal's interest in the venture, knew that King Ferdinand had turned favorable at last.

From Bishop Allessandro Geraldini she learned one day of the trials the woolmerchant was enduring.

"They cannot forget that passage from Blessed Augustine," said Geraldini, *Melius est dubitare de ocultis, quam litigare de incertis*. Better to doubt what is obscure than argue about uncertain things."

"I understand Latin, my lord," said Isabella.

"Do you, Highness?" said the bishop, "I commend you for it. Not many laymen read the language of the Ancients. Well, the quotation from Blessed Augustine has become the by-word of the Council. Nothing will change it, I fear. And I have reason to know. I once ventured to remind His Eminence the Cardinal, that while the saint was without doubt one of the greatest theologians, he knew less about navigation than navigators like Columbus, who has sailed as far as Thule.'"

"What did the Cardinal say to that, my lord?"

"He looked at me without batting an eye, and said, 'Blessed Augustine is Blessed Augustine and Columbus is a Genoese sailor. The Cardinal's opinion is like the laws of the Medes and the Persians: it altereth not.'"

"Was there no progress today at the Council?"

"There was a stormy session, Highness, but no progress. Columbus lost his temper and most of his self-control on one occasion. They had asked him for the fiftieth time to demonstrate his narrow-ocean hypothesis. He insists, you no doubt know, that the Ocean Sea is no wider than twenty-four hundred nautical miles between Spain and India."

Isabella looked at the bishop's face and saw him purse his lips, "Do you also think Columbus is in error, my lord?" she asked,

"Highness, I admire the Genoese greatly, but with this one part of his brief I must differ. The distance must be greater, else some ship, blown off its course, would by now have landed there and returned."

"But didn't Columbus tell then about the documents I had copied from Vatican files? Our ambassador himself had his secretary copy them. I received them months ago and turned them over to Columbus. They must have been in his packet of presentation to the council."

"He presented no such documents, Highness, or so I believe. None from the Vatican were in the packets for I examined it myself. But, in case I saw them and did not read them, what did those documents report?"

Isabella's eyes narrowed. "I know that Columbus inserted the copies in the packet. I went over that packet with him. I saw the papers. They prove, Father, that Vikings exploring the northern ocean, came upon new lands, peopled by red savages who wore furs and spoke a language no one understood. The Vikings, who were Christians, reported these lands and these people to the Holy Father some four centuries ago because they needed his assistance in converting the heathen to the true faith."

"And, what, Highness, if I may ask, has that discovery to do with the narrow-ocean theory Columbus espouses?"

"It means that the ocean between Europe and those new lands, which must be part of Asia, may be as narrow as Columbus believes. It means that part of Asia juts westward so far that the Vikings were able to reach it. The twenty-four hundred nautical miles in Columbus' calculations bring Asia much closer than any one had believed. And, Father, what puzzles me most is why the discoveries of the Vikings were never made known."

"Then, Highness, those papers must be found. Any one could have removed them, for the entire council studied them before it met."

"And yet when the packet was returned to Columbus when he needed to refer to it in his presentation and for his arguments, the papers were missing. And Columbus didn't even mention them. Why didn't he?"

"If he had, Highness, it would have been equivalent to accusing the council of downright dishonesty. I suppose he didn't dare. But surely you will hear from him. He'll send a message or he'll come to you himself. Not even the great Talavera would dispute records from the archives of the Vatican."

"Columbus has not yet come to me. Therefore I shall write a formal letter to the Council and you shall take It. I will state that I ordered copies made of those all-important documents written four hundred years ago and that I myself have read them and believe what they contain. The Vatican knew long ago that new lands, even if the pope probably did not think they were parts of Asia, lay hidden in the far western part of the Ocean Sea. But you yourself mention ships, not Viking ships, being blown off course whose crews saw new lands or saw parts of Asia before they sailed home again. How many such ships have experienced such adventures? The return of such ships—and they have nothing to do with Viking ships—have been reported.

"You keep well-informed, I see," said the bishop, raising his brows.

"You mean that rumor about the ship that washed up on Madeira while Columbus was a merchant in the islands?"

"And was it only rumor?"

"Columbus will not verify it, Highness. If he would, it would strengthen his case considerably. As it is, no one knows for certain whether or not he actually took that ship's dying pilot into his home and cared for him until he died. No one has seen the maps and charts they say he gave Columbus. And, Highness," said the bishop, lowering his voice conspiratorially, "some say Columbus took the charts against the dying pilot's will."

"Absurd," snapped Isabella. "Columbus is an honorable man. He could not have done such a thing."

"I agree with you, Highness. Still, the charts mean much and are not forthcoming. But one witness states that Columbus built his entire enterprise on the pilot's charts and then deliberately allowed the man to die."

"No more of this," said Isabella in her sternest tone, "I will not hear it. But one thing I will say: Columbus had his plan for the enterprise long before he went out to Madeira, and I mean plans based on the Viking documents. Now tell me of today's findings by the Council."

"Today," said the bishop, warming to his subject, "the cardinal told Columbus he doubted the world was round. Columbus looked for a moment as though he would burst. The matter had come up before, and he must have thought no one present could still reject the roundness of the earth, for it is taught in our greatest universities. He turned paper-white and then asked his eminence in a voice pitched so low I could barely catch his words, one question. 'The theory is not mine. Have you asked the doctors of the Sorbonne, of Bologna, even of your own Salamanca? No one of intelligence today doubts the earth is spherical.' That, Highness, was hardly the thing to say to a cardinal who had just voiced a contrary opinion.

"The cardinal bristled and turned purple, Highness, 'I doubt it, Sir,' he rasped, 'Oh, I've read your theorists, but what real proof do they have? How could the sea cling to a globe? The water would run off and leave the earth as dry as a nut on a tree.'"

"Several ecclesiastics tittered and said they agreed. But Columbus was undaunted. 'No, your Eminence, it wouldn't,' he said with mock patience."

Isabella looked down at her hands as they clutched the arm of her chair. The knuckles were white. She saw the bishop watching her and looked away. "What happened after that?" she asked.

"After that, Highness, Columbus did something so graphic that the good cardinal should have changed his views, although of course he didn't."

"What did he do?"

"He looked wildly around for a few seconds. He shook that great shock of white hair into complete dishevelment. Then his eyes fell upon an orange someone had left on one of the tables. He put out his hand and took it up. For a long, hard moment he stared at it. 'What can be passing through his mind? I asked myself. I saw that even Cardinal Mendoza twisted his ring and sat forward expectantly. Suddenly Columbus turned to one of the attendants and said, 'Bring me a pot of honey and a piece of wire.'"

"We waited until the attendant returned, and as we waited, every man in the hall thought Columbus had taken leave of his senses. Surely he looked frenzied. His eyes rolled wildly. Have you ever seen him let his shoulders slump, Highness, and then throw them back squarely? That's what he did in the council hall, and I must say that I have never witnessed a more determined gesture."

"And the honey ...?" said Isabella, unable to wait.

"Everyone crowded forward to see what he planned to do with it, Highness. Columbus was surrounded, for everywhere, all around him, craning, were doctors from Salamanca, grandees, attendants, and all those monks.

"He had run the wire through the orange by this time, binding it fast at one end with a hook made by bending the metal. Then, holding the free end he dipped the orange into the honey pot until it was covered with honey."

Isabella's eyes flashed, "I can see what is coming," she said. "He spun the orange..."

"Not at first, Highness. He simply held it dangling at the end of the wire, Naturally the honey ran to the lower part of the orange and dripped to the floor, I could see the cardinal's mouth tighten as if to say, 'I told you so,' but he didn't speak. All about me men were breathing softly. I don't know what magic they had expected to witness.

"Then the Genoese dipped the orange into the pot again. And this time, as Your Highness has so cleverly surmised, he spun it slowly. The honey started to run to the lower side of the orange, but he turned it so as to force the honey to flow around and cling to the fruit.

"We watched as he repeated the demonstration and we understood. The honey did not drip away because the orange turned.

"'So with the orb of the earth, Your Eminence,' said Columbus."

Isabella sighed. "And the cardinal, did he accept the idea?"

Bishop Geraldini shook his head. "I think you can imagine what he said: *Melius est dubitare de ocultis, quam litigare de incertis*. You cannot convince a man like His Eminence, the Grand Cardinal of Spain."

"I wish he were not a member of the Council," said Isabella at length. "But there was no way of keeping him away and someone had to represent the Church. What did Columbus do then?"

"He made a low bow to the cardinal and stalked out of the hall. Several men seemed impressed enough to wish to discuss the matter further, but the cardinal would not bend. A good two hours later they were no closer to a solution. I walked out then and came here, Highness. But nothing could have happened since, for it was almost siesta hour when I left the chamber."

"Tomorrow," said Isabella, "I shall go to the Council. Possibly I can help."

She did not go, however, for the Council postponed its hearings. More important matters needed its attention. Granada had put out a strong feeler about peace, and all Santa Fe buzzed with rumors. Even Christopher understood. He was glad, he realized, believing that at last he could see the beginning of the end of his wait. Once Granada surrendered, money would flood into the treasuries of Castile and Aragón. Perhaps then the queen would finance the enterprise, even without the approval of her Council. He had waited long, He could wait a little longer.

Thousands lined the streets to watch her ride to the meetings, and Christopher stood among them with Brother Juan who had come back with him. The last time he had seen Isabella had been in the encampment before Baza and then only by torchlight. He still remembered her reproachful stare.

"By St. Ferdinand!" he cried as she passed. "She's still beautiful. How does she manage to stay so young?"

"Because she's a saint of God," said Brother Juan.

The two men watched her pass regally down the street, and neither resented the splendor of her costume. The cloth-of-gold mantle, the rich brocade, the black velvet riding hood, slashed to reveal the turquoise velvet of her gown, thrilled them, for it was worthy of their queen. And what a queen to serve! Christopher saw for the first time the famous necklace of Balas rubies given her by Ferdinand when he came to Valladolid to meet her that first time. The stones were set to resemble roses, and the ribbons that fastened them to her throat were studded with diamonds, pearls, and smaller rubies. The thought never crossed his mind that a fraction of their worth would pay for all the ships he could ever need. He thought only that a queen must move in splendor and was happy that his queen could. Santa Fe swarmed with foreign dignitaries, some of royal blood, and they must be made to see the queen for what she was, the most puissante in all of Christendom.

He found his heart swelling and had to swallow. "She's fantastic!" he whispered, "She's right out of fiction, and yet as real as this unbelievable city she has built!"

"She is the Queen of Spain," said Juan Pérez quietly.

"Not quite," said Christopher, and he pointed across the low roofs of Santa Fe and beyond the walls. "Look out there, Brother Juan. Her destiny must move her farther still."

Close by, but still out of sight, like a shadow over the queen's glory, rose the red towers of Granada, the everlasting threat.

And, even as he spoke, events in that alien stronghold were unfolding, events that would delay the enterprise even more.

5

The council chamber buzzed with excitement. Granada offered to capitulate under stated conditions. It was the first real crack in the city's armor of defiance. All else had to be set aside. And, of course, Christopher's enterprise went back on the shelf.

Isabella made her way as rapidly toward the chamber as dignity permitted, Don Alonso, the treasurer, at her side. She knew how darkly he was frowning and surmised the cause—the cost of the war and the vacuum of the treasury. And it would stay empty unless Granada fell. Everything depended on that accursed city, perched like some bright exotic bird upon the carcass of Spain. She forgot the treasurer, and for a moment almost allowed herself to wonder if Granada could be taken. For nearly a thousand years it had clung there, beautiful, exotic, oriental, alien.

The herald at the door of the chamber saw her and came to attention. "Her Royal Highness, Isabella of Spain," he intoned.

She could see the ocean of faces turned her way and she basked in the mingled expectation and approval. She loved her people and understood their interest. Now they wanted peace, and possibly peace at any cost, even if she didn't. "They want me to give them something to hope for," she told Don Alonso. "And what am I to tell them?"

She swept regally down the aisle opening to let her pass. What they were all feeling was plain enough. They were tired of waiting, The novelty of Santa Fe and the wonder at its construction were wearing off. She was tired of waiting, too. But she was the Queen of Spain and she expected to struggle for the kingdom endlessly and with boundless patience. She sympathized with the common soldiers most, for they would never understand. Nor could they bring their wives and families to Santa Fe to help them wait out the siege, as the nobility had. Moreover, they were accustomed to short military service, a summer usually, sometimes a summer and a spring. Longer wars were unfamiliar, disturbing. Some hadn't been home for several years. She knew of desertions of growing number and frequency, for men would see their families, no matter what. Yes, she understood; they wanted to see their children. "I wonder if they know how little I see mine," she asked herself.

Guilt about her neglect of her own children clung to her like the old man of the sea in the *Arabian Nights*. For many months she had had to leave them in Cordova. When she finally could bring then to Santa Fe, she believed all would change and that they could spend much time together. But she seldom saw them; except at bedtime, and she cringed when one would ask for a story or to take a walk, for seldom could she oblige. Even young Isabella's marriage she had had to delegate in its details to Beatriz de Bobadilla. And there was the matter of Isabella's age. She was fourteen! She remembered her marriage to Ferdinand and how she had gone into it nearly blind, as far as the duties of a marriage are concerned, and she remembered how she had vowed no daughter of hers would suffer that. No matter whose duty it is to tell you about what a man wants on his wedding night, it couldn't replace the explanations of a mother, not even if the explainer happened to he a lady as kind and sweet as Beatriz. So she made up her mind to tell young Isabella herself, no matter whom she had to keep waiting, even if it was the Grand Council of Castile.

"How could I have waited so long?" she remembered saying to Ferdinand, "I've told her as little as my mother told me, and she's so very innocent and so timid."

"You survived," said Ferdinand with a reminiscent look. "Indeed you survived it well, and, if you'll recall, you enjoyed every minute of your wedding night."

"But I had Chata to tell me what I had to know, if only at the last minute. And, my dear, I had you, a husband no bride could resist, and you were first considerate and then, well, I'll let you remember what you were. Also I was older and, if I must admit it, I was stronger than our Isabella. I wanted to marry you and go to bed. She doesn't want to at all and she is frightened half to death."

"Well," said Ferdinand, "she's made of good cloth and she'll wear. No daughter of ours could be otherwise. But why don't you tell her now, my dear. There's time before the wedding, and who better than you could relieve her mind. Break formality and propriety and let down your hair to her. Go so far as to tell her something of our wedding night and show her all is not darkness, and pain, and terror. Give her the details, if you desire, and you'll have my approval. But go she must to Lisbon and she must make her husband love her. We'll have no recalcitrant brides in this family and none running home to their mother either. Can't Beatriz tell her, if you won't? Can't you find another Chata, if that is all that is left?"

"That isn't funny, Ferdinand," said Isabella icily. "A woman like Chata, however well-meaning, would throw our Isabella into trauma."

"Well," said Ferdinand impatiently, "*I* can't tell her. I think it's up to you, and frankly if *you* can't calm her fears, I don't think they can be calmed. Go ahead and speak to the child. She'll come around."

"I'll try," promised Isabella, and she had, but had found the going rough. She even began to forgive her own mother for holding back. "If only the child would *ask* me something," she once told Beatriz, "That would make it easier. As it is, I have no idea what she knows. or if she knows anything at all. To plunge right in and tell her might arouse terrors she need not face."

One night alone with young Isabella in her bedroom, as she combed the girl's beautiful golden hair she had finally brought up the duties of a bride and the joys of marriage. "You'll love young Afonso," she said. "He's a stout lad and quite good-looking, too." She wouldn't for the life of her have told the child what Ferdinand, who had glimpsed Afonso in the royal baths, had described as sexual opulence. "Our young kinsman has what runs in our family, my dear, thank the Lord," he had said.

"What'll I do, mother?" young Isabella had suddenly wept, throwing reserve and resentment aside in her extremity.

"What have you heard about men, about husbands, child?"

"I've heard what men have under their clothes and I know what they do with it. But why must it be so? Why can't there be a less disgusting way and one that doesn't hurt?"

"Daughter," said Isabella, keeping her voice as calm as she could, "it must be so because God planned it so, and it is a good plan at that. And, my dear, it doesn't have to be disgusting at all. Remember God made your Afonso in His own image. And the act of sex—and I don't mean what you fear Afonso will do to you, but what you and he must do together and indeed enjoy together—will be a beautiful act indeed."

"But the thing between his legs. Oh, I've caught sight of them. You know how men relieve themselves in alleys. And I've seen my brother John when he didn't think anyone was looking—peeing! And I'll never be able to look at a man down there!"

Isabella's eyes grew pensive. "What they have down there, my dear, is *not* an ugly thing, but a thing of beauty, though in a peculiar shape, I must admit. And remember this. Afonso is a man and has been trained in matters sexual, you may be certain. Men almost always are, you know. He'll guide you gently and then romantically, just as your father guided me when I went to bed with him on our wedding night. He was an experienced lover, I can tell you, and he made me very happy. He has not changed that way,"

"Father?" gasped young Isabella stunned. "I can't imagine! You and father like that, like animals!"

"No one can imagine parents like that, as you call it, and yet like *that* he and I were on our wedding night and have been ever since. Your father, *that* way, has been one of life's greatest joys, Isabella."

The girl sighed. "Queens must bear offspring, I know," she moaned, casting a new and assessing eye on her mother in whom she had suddenly found hidden depths she hadn't known were there. "So every few years, I, like you, will have to let my husband plant another child in me..."

Isabella laughed and then drew her daughter close. "Every few years, my dear? Your father and I are that way every few nights when we can be together."

"Mother," gasped Isabella. "You wouldn't! Not for the pleasures of the flesh! You couldn't!"

"Child," said Isabella tenderly, yet all the same a queen, "look at me and listen, for what I shall say now I will not say to you again. Consider your father. He is a handsome man, for all his two score years, give or take a little. He still has a beautiful body. He's clean and he smells good. And he's an incomparable lover, just as he was, that night when I was seventeen."

"And you liked all that heavy breathing, and wet lips and hands..."

"I see you're not as innocent as I thought. Whom did you hear breathing so heavily and pawing whom?"

"In a palace, mother, one overhears a lot."

"I suppose one does. Well, if you'd heard me with your father you'd know I enjoyed every moment. And, daughter, so must you, for if you don't, you face a life of grief and frustration, and you'll never be a proper queen. So I command you, as your mother and your queen. Be brave, but above that be anxious for Alfonso's embrace. And be considerate and make him love you because you're good in bed." And then, to her own astonishment Isabella, though she softened her words and spoke in euphemisms, told her daughter exactly what old Chata had told her.

Young Isabella's eyes widened at first in dismay, then narrowed in speculation. At first tears beaded her lashes and rolled down her cheeks, but before the end she took her mother's hand and smiled. If she had lived in resentment of her mother's forced neglect, that resentment faded in their intimate and open discussion. "Thank you, mother," she said, but her eyes spoke volumes.

"That conquest," Isabella told Ferdinand that night as he made love to her and she to him, "may have been my greatest and most trying success. But I won the war, I think, and some day the future king of Portugal will thank his stars I did."

"I've said it and I'll say it once again," chuckled Ferdinand, "Isabella, you're fantastic! I only hope I can do a fifth as well with Juan," he said.

"It'll be easier with a boy," she reflected, "but even so, I'm glad the task is yours. And you'll have to speak to him soon. He's almost a young man, you know. And he's so responsive and adorable. Yes, it'll be easier. And what a husband he'll make with his pale beauty and angelic face!"

Ferdinand sighed with pride at the thought of his son. The boy *was* good to look at, and he certainly charmed the world. He was an easy child to know, once one broke the ice. Too bad they had so little time to spend together, but that was life, even when one was not at war. Fathers saw all too little of their sons, royal fathers, at least, and had to depend on tutors and guardians. After this damned war, he vowed, it would be different. He reflected on the boy's future. He was bright and quick of mind; he learned fast and he could keep up with and usually outstrip the boys he played with, even the older ones, when they played games. He never knew, for Isabella never cared to tell him, that John won so much because his playmates let him win, ordered to do so by their fathers. And perhaps, Isabella reflected, it was just as well. Though healthy enough at present, he had been a sickly infant, and wasn't as large for his age as she wished.

Her mind often assessed and weighed her children. Now Catherine of Aragón was as like her father as two peas in a pod, although due to her tender years, not so ruthless. Sound as a florin she was, clever, able to hold her own in games and in the schoolroom. She would make a fine queen for some fortunate country, for she had the common sense required and she liked to give commands.

But Juana gave her pause. Truly a problem child. She and Ferdinand worried considerably about Juana. Her rages, far too sudden and too deep, would make her eyes actually roll back in her head. Occasionally a thin foam dampened her lips, and her cries of fury never failed to draw shocked glances from the court. At such times Isabella would cross herself and try not to remember her own mother and her madness at Arévalo. But Juana was not deficient at her studies and she thought as clearly as Isabella herself. Indeed, she was dangerously intelligent, too intelligent, for she bordered on pure genius. But the truly chilling thing that sometimes looked out of her deep, black eyes was not really Juana at all, but a demonic, childish phase that would surely pass away.

She wished Ferdinand, when he looked into those angry eyes wouldn't refer to a sense of vagueness he saw in them, to threatening forces that led him to say, "This one will give us trouble all her life!"

Isabella's mind returned to the scene before her. She had long since reached the dais and seated herself, and sitting, had let her mind wander while protocol slowly settled the Council into action. Ferdinand had reached out and taken her hand in his. "Don't take it so hard," he said, "or people will notice. I know the reports are bad, but it's not like you to glower."

"He thinks it's Granada I'm worrying about," she thought. "I wish Granada were on another continent!"

The President of the Council, Don Francisco Ramírez, was ending his report. "The city still has all the water it can ever need," he said, "and moreover, its stores of food seem plentiful; and supplies somehow still find their way in, carried there at night, we don't know how, by smugglers."

Angry murmurs swept the hall, but quieted when Don Francisco continued. "It is beyond belief," he said, "but all our bombardments have failed to damage the fortifications significantly. And this in spite of the best Flemish and German Lombards."

Ferdinand agreed. "We can't place the guns as they should be placed," he explained. "The big ones that can shoot seventy heavy missiles a day just can't be hauled up muddy river beds and through narrow passes in the hills. The battlements rise too high, and too many times balls launched almost perpendicularly, fall back on our lines."

"We waste shots, too," added Don Francisco. "They fall into the many gardens, parks and pools that decorate the city."

Isabella interrupted. "If there were only time," she said, "we could fill gorges and level hills, as we have been trying to do for weeks. Perhaps with time we could fill and level more."

Ferdinand interrupted. "Isabella, there isn't time, and where's the money to come from? I think we've said it all. Without money we face defeat. How can we finance fourteen thousand mules and drivers? How buy the fodder and foodstuffs for the army brought into the *vega* every week? And the gunpowder from Portugal, Sicily and the Low Countries? Then the Swiss mercenaries and your medical corps. How, except by defeating Granada and exacting a terrible tribute from the conquered?"

He reached out a hand trembling with urgency and took up a parchment roll from the table at his side. The assemblage grew silent. The parchment, they all knew, had been delivered that morning by emissaries from young King Boabdil, who had seized power from his ill and aging father.

She saw Ferdinand stand up to gaze over the audience, before he spoke. "We have good news from the city," he announced. "Boabdil would surrender but for the old soldiers and their captains, the die-hards, left by his father, Muley Hassan. With our help, however, I believe he would surrender in spite of them."

Isabella had heard this before. Muley Hassan, the old king, had sailed away, having sold his estates. He lived in Fez, cursing his rebellious son, but acknowledging him as king of Granada. He also left thousands of seasoned troops, men loyal to Islam, men who refused to let a weak young ruler surrender their patrimony to Christian dogs. The die-hards, as Ferdinand called them, had even dared attack Boabdil's palace at the rumor of capitulation. The young king and his mother Aisha lived in dread of assassination.

Ferdinand continued. "Boabdil has made his father's soldiers at least hear our terms, and this is something. It's the first time they've even considered the *word* surrender."

He motioned to his secretary, and the man started to read the terms. He couldn't continue, for the bells of Santa Fe suddenly burst into their mid-morning defiance of Islam, exactly at the moment when Muslims knelt to face Mecca and pray. The monks tolled the great bells joyfully, vengefully. Until they ceased, conversation was out of the question. Even a secretary like Ferdinand's realized the futility of competing with them. And the Moors in Granada could hear them, since their pealing carried far.

Isabella had read the terms. They were generous, perhaps even overly considerate. Still, she knew that no treaty can satisfy all parties. If Boabdil would surrender his city, he would receive his little son, whom Ferdinand held hostage; he would be assigned estates in the Alpújar Mountains with a pension of thirty thousand gold *castellanos* annually, a sum on which he could live luxuriously; he would leave the city, with all his household and servants, as a citizen and subject of the Spanish crown, protected and secure. It was letting him off too easily, Isabella thought, but no matter. Granada itself was getting off too easily. As a special inducement, she had persuaded Ferdinand to grant the city two years exemption from taxation, and the present taxes were not to be increased after the two years; the Moors would maintain their own schools, their mosques, except the central mosque—this she hated—their courts of law, their national dress, and even their language. In other words, Granada and its people would keep their traditions. They would, of course, live under the crown's supervision and would pay Spanish taxes after the two years' exemption.

In return for such generosity the Grenadines would surrender all fortresses, walls, and weapons, except sidearms; five hundred young Moors, sons of the foremost families of the kingdom, would live in Christian Spain in the houses of nobles as honored hostages; all Christian prisoners would be returned and all Moorish prisoners would be freed.

If Boabdil and the Alcalde, Aben Coxima, would accept these terms, the war could end. And once the Muslim world learned of such leniency, thousands of Christians in Palestine, Syria, and Egypt might escape persecution. Everything depended upon Boabdil, or whatever powers controlled him in Granada; her own destiny depended upon that surrender as well as her country's; even the woolmerchant and his exploration of the Ocean Sea hung upon the mood of a weak young Moorish king.

6

Isabella held her breath in the chilly air before dawn and wondered if it would come true. Moors had made promises before and then broken them. The Moors of Granada might follow the pattern. Even the reports of the spies might mean nothing at the final moment. What if King Boabdil's heralds, robed in black, had proclaimed throughout the city that the gates would open peacefully? What if the Grenadines would obey his orders to stay indoors while the Christian armies entered? The old soldiers might whip up that oriental frenzy lying always just beneath the surface and defy their young king. If that happened, she and Ferdinand would have to go back to a siege.

She closed such musings from her mind. The gates would open, her troops would enter, Granada would capitulate. Believing this, she suddenly knew that even the final victory could mean no more than this moment of anticipation. Here, in the cold false dawn which her eyes probed vainly, she could look into the past with satisfaction, and into the future with joyful expectation.

"I've come a long way," she said aloud. "But not alone."

Phantasmagorically, like a swift and turbulent stream, the faces of the past flashed by. The faces of men and women who had stood in her path. Joanna, wicked Joanna, slovenly, and fat and dead in an alabaster coffin—a grub laid away in a sarcophagus brought out of the East by Clavijo who had visited the court of Tamerlane in far-off Samarkand; Henry, dead in Madrid, lying in state with painted cheeks and rouged lips, while his people thanked God for his removal; Villena and Pedro Girón; Alfonso Carrillo, fierce old archbishop, once loyal friend and supporter, later enemy and traitor. Friends and loved ones, too, flitted by; Alfonso her brother, stark and dead in Cardeñosa, and the strength of the woolmerchant to help her face it; her mother going slowly mad in dark Arévalo; old de Coca—the faces of the past.

And through all her memories, flashing again and again from among the faces of the past came the vision of the woolmerchant. Ávila, Cardeñosa, Toro, Cordova, Baza. His presence in all these places.

"We have come a long way," she corrected herself. "And now we come to Granada, impossible, wonderful, awful Granada—the last of the great citadels."

She was aware suddenly that the rim of the sun had thrust itself over the sierra, as she smelled, on the icy wind, the breath of the snow fields. All over the fields outside the walls of Granada she heard men stirring. Horses blew the cold air from their nostrils and shook their heads. Banners popped sharply in the wind, and the voices of officers rose in hoarse commands. It was capitulation day, January second, 1492. The wind died and the sky changed from steely blue to rose.

When she stepped from their pavilion, Ferdinand was already there on his warhorse. He dismounted quickly when he caught sight of her and his eyes were round with awe.

"No man shall help you mount today save the king," he said extravagantly, she thought, in keeping with the day, but somehow it seemed right.

She saw him throw a wild, exultant glance over his shoulder at the dim city above its fortress-like cliffs. She laid her hand on his and smiled. "Granada!"

A cannon boomed suddenly from the fortress of the Alhambra. This was the signal. Then the sun passed over the barrier of mountains and flooded the plain with ruddy light. She saw it all from her point of vantage above the River Genil near the lofty walls. As the dull thunder died, the Gate of Siete Suelos swung wide, and a procession in funeral array began to emerge.

"Look, Ferdinand! Look, children!" cried Isabella. "There is the Sultana Aisha, Queen Mother of Granada. And there also is Boabdil's queen."

They were too far away to be seen clearly, but the litters in which they rode were lavish, opulent, and the two figures visible must be the royal ladies.

Ferdinand flashed her a quick smile of triumph. "You'll be able to see them better when they cross the bridge," he said.

Behind the royal litters marched the household of King Boabdil, a great throng. Guards in golden armor and scarlet, with black-draped turbans, slaves bearing chests loaded with the king's treasures, at which Ferdinand's eyes glinted in jealous speculation, dwarves, acrobats, eunuchs of the royal harem, concubines, redolent of sandalwood and musk, lovely almond-eyed children with skin like dusky rose petals—the vast and complex swarm of humanity of an eastern palace.

Isabella watched breathlessly, but when the king touched her arm and pointed, she had already seen. "Aisha and the young sultana." She nodded, unable to speak.

Aisha had thrown back the hangings of her litter to look for the last time at the towers of Granada. From time to time she dipped her hand into a silver chest, sprinkling her head with ashes. Once Isabella saw her seize her long robe and with strong hands tear off a sleeve in a gesture of violent oriental grief. But she did not weep.

Even at that distance something regal in her sorrow moved Isabella to pity. She wondered how devastating sadness could be to a woman like the Queen Mother of Granada. Aisha, she knew, had been a Spanish woman, a Christian, who had risen to favor in Muley Hassan's harem. From harem favorite to queen had been but a short path for her, and the remnants of her beauty explained her success. Now she was leaving her homeland, going into exile.

At the end of the procession rode Boabdil. She had met him a few years before and he hadn't changed. Vigorous and agile, with a quick feline grace, he sat his chestnut mare like the king he was. He wore a dark mantle over his eastern tunic of embroidered red silk. The crown of Granada sprang from his snow-white turban. As he passed through the Gate of Siete Suelos, masons appeared and began to wall up the opening. After Boabdil no other man would use the ancient portal.

The gesture and its oriental implication was not lost upon her; it must be small comfort to him, though, for he rode stiffly and if he drew any solace from the promises of his Mohammedan heaven, he gave no sign. Not the feast of three hundred courses—in paradise, which endow the faithful with health and vigor, not even the celestial palace with eighty thousand servants and seventy-two wives could console a king leaving behind forever the wonders untold and unrecorded of the Alhambra.

She heard the cannon roar a second time and started. Toward another gate the victorious armies of Christendom were filing out in a long twisting line across the *vega*. At their head, she knew, rode Don Gutierre de Cárdenas, who long ago had guided Ferdinand over the snowy mountains of Aragón to her in Valladolid. Beside Don Gutierre, representing Holy Church, would come Cardinal Mendoza. And above their heads, like clouds of crimson and yellow light, swirled the banners of St. James, Spain's patron, and, of course, her own great banner of Trastámara and that of the Aragonese.

"The banner of Aragón, the banner of Aragón," she murmured, remembering the day Castile welcomed Ferdinand.

The Lilies of France swept past and the Lion Rampant of the English. Then the flags of the scores of nations whose knights had fought the infidel before Granada.

Suddenly she crossed herself. A huge silver cross, borne by four priests with ecstatic eyes, came into view. At sight of this gift from the Holy Father in Rome men grew silent in religious awe. Within that silver cross, all knew, was embedded a splinter from the True Cross, Christendom's most sacred relic. The *signum crucis* flashed across ten thousand foreheads and armored chests.

"Boabdil is coming!" whispered Ferdinand, "with the keys of Granada in his hand!"

She tore her eyes away from the knights, for Boabdil was crossing the bridge. He turned for a moment to survey the city for the last time. Her eyes returned to the victorious host. The sun struck full upon the polished armor of the Christian armies. It blazed upon rank on rank of knights, Castilians in their round casques and Aragonese in jingling chain mail, and their horses moving proudly under the great weight of man and metal. She saw fierce war dogs, also in armor with helmets that sprouted long spikes and collars set with needle-sharp metal points. Their frantic baying rang wildly over the sound of trumpets and drums. Long lines of priests bearing crosses and tall lighted candles followed the knights, and after them the endless files of footmen with pikes, crossbows and harquebuses.

She looked at Ferdinand and saw the cords in his neck swelling. His face worked. His knuckles clasped the bridle with such intensity that they looked white against his brown hands.

Then Boabdil turned his back on the city and gallantly cantered across the bridge toward them. He flung himself with a haughty flourish in front of Ferdinand. He went to his knees before anyone could speak.

Ferdinand's voice was level and kind. "Rise, King of Granada."

She watched Boabdil with pity. Terrible, unfathomable sorrow stared from those almond eyes as he passed the golden keys up to her husband who accepted them with a nod and fixed them to his belt.

Boabdil turned then to her and again knelt in the mud before she could stop him. It was a tribute, indeed, for he was a Muslim and she a woman.

Then a little brown boy darted between the horses and flung himself into Boabdil's arms. The man knelt slowly again and embraced the child. No one spoke, and Isabella closed her eyes. Even Ferdinand and old Ponce de León, the new Governor-General of Granada looked away. Someone sobbed behind her, and Isabella knew that it was her daughter Catherine of Aragón. But the Princess Juana laughed shrilly and clapped her hands.

Then Boabdil lifted the child before him on his horse and trotted off to overtake the litters of the two sultanas.

"St. James! St. James and Spain!" thundered the marching files, and the Moors at the gates of the city blew in frenzy upon their pipes and shouted welcome to the new sovereigns with streaming eyes and sobs.

Dark clouds suddenly veiled the sun. In the cold air Isabella shivered and wondered if the snow, beginning to fall, would blot out the sierra and blanket the city before darkness. Even the joyous tolling of the bells she had sent into the city failed to cheer her. The great silver cross spreading its arms over the highest tower of the Alhambra gleamed with a cold light. Can supreme joy blossom from supreme sorrow?

The Moorish exiles passed out of sight over the crest of the hill. The River Genil murmured softly in its flooded banks.

Isabella wiped her eyes and turned suddenly to her secretary. "Pedro Martyr," she said, "set down these words to be engraved upon the façade of yonder mosque, soon to become a Christian chapel: ON THIS SPOT KING BOABDIL MET THE CATHOLIC SOVEREIGNS AND SURRENDERED TO THEM THE KEYS OF GRANADA, WHO IN DEMONSTRATION OF THEIR GRATITUDE, MADE THIS MOSQUE A CHAPEL."

She watched Pedro Martyr's swift hand pen the words and cross himself, letting his eyes rise to the façade as if he could see the words already carved in the reddish stone.

That evening she and Ferdinand visited the Great Mosque, which already had been cleansed and consecrated. The new bishop, Talavera, was holding High Mass. The lofty dome above the kneeling congregation of soldiers was of red stone encrusted with gold and silver, and in the light of a thousand candles it blazed like the sun at noon and the incense made breathing difficult. Talavera, who had rejected all other bishoprics, now had the one he craved.

Then the totally unexpected! As she and the king walked down the steps of the new cathedral they came face to face with the woolmerchant.

Isabella stopped. Ferdinand came to a halt also, and when he recognized the tall man before them, he nodded. The men's eyes held until Christopher bowed deeply and removed his hat. Then his eyes found hers, and in them blazed a question. Finally his lips formed a silent "When?"

"Soon," she answered in a whisper. "Very soon."

7

Christopher paced his quarters after his return from Mass. "It can't be long now," he told himself. "Alonso de Quintanilla, their own treasurer, swears Castile and Aragón will soon be solvent."

Juan Pérez entered, blowing on his chilled fingers. "Bitter again tonight," he said. "Wish I were in my cell back at La Rábida."

Christopher moved restlessly about the room. "How long, Brother Pérez?" he asked.

"Patience, my son. The wealth of Granada cannot be assessed in a single day. And the army must be paid and the people who supplied it."

"But she won't forget, Brother Pérez?"

"Not the queen. But give her time."

Christopher's eyes glowed. "By St. Ferdinand, I'm happy for her," he said, returning to his pacing. "Have you walked through that city? I did this afternoon. I never saw anything like it! Parks like fairyland with row on row of orange, lemon, and lime trees, agate benches, and marble fountains, and swans and peacocks, and flowers everywhere, even in January. Paved streets, too, and clean!"

"Granada will enrich all Spain," said Brother Pérez with satisfaction, "Then the queen will remember the enterprise."

After a week's wait he was not so certain. "One of the rubies dug out of a cellar in the Alhambra would pay for my ships," he cried. "Surely they could spare that much."

Brother Pérez could do nothing. Christopher paced for hours, refusing to sit down to eat. Gaunt and pale he stalked the corridors, his hands behind his back, his gait that of a sailor on a tossing ship. And his neck was stiff.

"By St. Ferdinand! It wasn't this bad in Lisbon. King João had vision at least," he told himself. And he thought of incidents. Sailors with less background than any Colón had been made dons to honor them for navigation. Look at Diego Cão, given a title for discovering an African river and setting up a marker to show that no one before him had sailed so far south as that. And there were others, many others.

The cruel times in Catalonia, in Italy, and in Portugal came to haunt him. People shrinking away from the boy who stank of raw wool and crowded too close to listen to the scholars discussing the new sciences. More recently the ill-concealed scorn of Felipa's noble kinsmen and neighbors in Lisbon. Christopher Columbus, a commoner, they called him, not fit to mix his blood with the Perestrello's.

"I'm as good as any of then," he stormed. "Only my bad luck lets them rise above me. My family is better than most of theirs. It isn't fair!"

He even fancied he caught Brother Pérez looking at him with pity and embarrassment. With resentment, too? After all, the monks of, La Rábida had provided charity to his son for years.

"Years and years like this corrode the self-respect," he raged, his head tossed back and forth, as if he thought he could shake bad thoughts from his mind. He could not. His responsibilities, his longings, his destiny gnawed at his soul. He had reached a time in life when he could not very well endure to be put off again. There was Diego, a boy of eleven in need of far more than the charity of generous monks; and there was Beatriz and her infant son, who was his son, too.

His hand slapped a stack of his books on the low table and sent them crashing to the floor. Mechanically he stooped to pick then up, smoothing the rumpled pages and running a repentant and practiced eye over the bindings. No breaks, thank heaven! He loved his books as much as he loved his soul.

Calmer then, he went to the window and looked out and up toward the citadel. The silver cross sent by the pope still spread its benediction over the city and the *vega*, The Moors were finished now, and high time the queen turned her thoughts to him,

"I'll wait until the end of the week," he said softly, expelling his breath in a whisper. "After a week I go to Fontainebleau!"

But the summons came. His big hands shook as he bathed and brushed his hair. His eyes lighted up as he slipped into the plum-colored velvet doublet and drew on the tight hose that lapped like blue water around the muscles of his long legs. He whistled for the first time in many, many months.

"Better than the bandy-legged courtiers," he thought.

Then he grew sober. She had made this possible. She had sent the four thousand *maravedís* to pay for the outfit. *She* had confirmed the existence of the Viking documents by letter when she unexpectedly visited the Council. *She* had told them that he corresponded with Toscanelli when, because he had not wanted to admit that he owed the narrow ocean theory to the old geographer. *She* had made him see the necessity of strengthening his theory by making the Council understand that he shared knowledge with Toscanelli, "*She* has helped me before," he said, "and now she is about to help me again. God bless her!"

The time had come. He drew himself up to his full six-feet-three. He threw back his shoulders. At the door Brother Pérez was waiting with two mules. Christopher did not look back.

Isabella and Ferdinand received him in the small courtroom of their headquarters in Santa Fe. Never before had she regarded the success of the enterprise as more auspicious. The Council had not rejected the project. They had returned it to her. "We shall abide by Her Highness's decision," they had written. Ferdinand, already counting Grenadine booty, offered no objection. "Anything to get the better of Lisbon," she thought with a smile.

She watched him finger the heavy gold of a Moorish bracelet he had commandeered. The possessiveness of his hand as he held it to the light and polished it on his sleeve amused her.

Then the door to the corridor opened and Christopher appeared framed in the opening. "He never looked better," she mused.

Tall and powerfully built, with a stride and a cant to his head which still made her heart miss a beat, he approached the dais, purposefully, confidently. His hair brushed until it shone like a silver casque, flashed. A heavy silver cross hung from a chain over his chest. He towered inches above every man in the room. She glanced at Ferdinand furtively, He had seen and assessed as much as she. A light, resentful acclaim flashed in his eyes. Could he be proud of a fellow Catalan who was noble and his kinsman?

The herald's voice at the edge of the dais brought her to attention, "Señor Cristóbal Colón."

What was this? What name? Colón! She did not understand, nor did her husband. His brows were two russet question marks, and the bracelet lay cradled carelessly in his left hand.

"Colón," she said under her breath, "Colón?" but she knew she had heard correctly. *Another* new name! First Colombo, simple, earthy, Italian, unpretentious; then Columbus, Latinized, cosmopolitan, proper enough; now Colón, neither Italian, nor Latin, but Spanish. Or was it a Hispanized French name? Colón, or Coulon, as they pronounced it in France, was a famous Admiral, Guillaume de Casenove, whose nickname Coulon was familiar everywhere in the Mediterranean. He was, besides, the very admiral who had sunk the *Bechalla* and sent the woolmerchant floating on a sweep to the beach in Lagos. Was Christopher capitalizing on the glory of another, claiming kinship with greatness? Had he taken a Spanish name to please her?

"A clever enough idea," she thought, "but unworthy of the woolmerchant, and I don't like it. Let him stand on his own name."

She looked covertly at Ferdinand. His smile had soured. She waited for him to speak, but he turned to her, "Speak for Castile," he said, and fell to examining the bracelet again.

Isabella searched for words to fit the occasion, for the tone of voice that would not betray her feelings. She looked once at Ferdinand, but he was deliberately absorbed in the bracelet.

"The Royal Council of Castile," she said at last, looking straight into Christopher's eyes, "will not make a decision. The members still feel that your calculations are in error. You differ with Ptolemy, and even with Toscanelli. But you believe you are right, and you have certain documents which possibly prove your theory. I have faith in your faith. Therefore, the king and I are of a mind to grant the money for the ships."

The joy in his face was palpable. "I kiss your feet," he said, making ready to kneel.

But Ferdinand paralyzed him with a voice like oil. "First, Señor Columbus, or should I say Colón, or would you like to hear Colom, certain details must be settled. Two caravels and their crews require a considerable outlay of money."

"I should need three at least," interrupted Christopher, now Cristóbal, ignoring etiquette, and worse still, omitting the royal title when he addressed the king. He seemed to address him as an equal.

Isabella winced visibly and hoped Ferdinand had not noticed. He had, of course, and the barest hint of red suffused his cheeks. He fingered his chin in speculation. He was now the cat, the woolmerchant the mouse. An ancient game had started. So had Ferdinand played with Muley Hassan and Boabdil as the treaties were drawn up. Christopher was deeply enmeshed and he knew it. His eyes said it. For a moment she hated her husband.

"Did you say three? " she heard Ferdinand ask innocently. "We had understood two. What, in addition to caravels, would you need, Señor Colón?" His voice sounded so sincere and his tone so patient, so receptive, that she had sudden hope. Then the king smiled a subtle, disarming smile, sincere to those who did not know him, but to her who did, most terrible.

She saw the woolmerchant take a deep breath, then draw a parchment roll from his doublet. The list was to be long. He began by explaining what he would do. The king leaned back in his chair and waited, still studying the bracelet.

"With the help of the sovereigns," Cristóbal said, with a gesture too much like a man bestowing a favor instead of requesting one, "I shall sail westward into the Ocean Sea to India, Cathay, and the island of Cipangu mentioned by Ser Marco Polo; I shall continue until I reach the realm of the Great Khan. There I shall establish diplomatic ties between his court and Your Majesties'."

"Most commendable," said the king, nodding sagely. "You must carry letters from us to our brother in royalty, the King of Kings, Cathay's sovereign."

Isabella thought it best to take over the direction of the proceedings. "Señor Colón," she said, "as you well know, we have spent much on the wars. But still another great task confronts us, one of which you also have been apprised. The Jews. The time has come to expel them from the realm."

Suddenly he was beginning to bristle, she saw with apprehension. Desperation hurried her along in a most unregal way. "Continue, Señor Colón, and state your needs and expectations. Let us weigh them and perhaps we can soon reach a decision."

He looked at her as he never had before. It was not hostility—that he reserved for Ferdinand—but rather disbelief, tinged with a rising, unwilling anger. He spoke in the third person, good etiquette at such times, but his tone was arrogant, in fact he was rapidly becoming too arrogant to be borne. "The sovereigns would equip three caravels with full complements of men and provisions for one full year; they would have the ships well stocked with such trading goods as hawks' bells, caps of various colors, glass beads, and cups and basins of brass. Such items the Portuguese have found most valuable in trading with the savages of the Congo."

Isabella tried to relax, noting that Ferdinand's eyes seemed to have lost something of the look of the cat about to pounce. His neck, she thanked heaven, had turned brown again and was no longer red.

Colón continued, looking straight at the king for a change and not at her. Perhaps he could no longer meet her eyes, and say the things he planned to say. Before he had uttered an additional dozen words she knew the enterprise was finished.

"The sovereigns," he boomed in the deadly silence of the room, "would make Cristóbal Colón a knight of Spain, so that all his male descendants would be addressed as DON."

Ferdinand's hands went together in the gesture of prayer, and he rested his chin lightly upon his fingertips. He said nothing, but he stared at his enemy with the expressionless stare of a basilisk.

Colón glanced quickly at his parchment to prompt himself. Then he floundered on into deeper water. "They would name him Grand Admiral of the Ocean Sea with all rights and privileges appertaining to admirals of Castile; they would appoint him Viceroy and Governor *in perpetuam* of all islands and continents he might discover."

Isabella put out her hand involuntarily, as if to stop him physically, but his head was bent over the parchment. Ferdinand, she saw, was now sneering openly, and that taking his cue, others in the chamber were beginning to smirk.

But her woolmerchant would not be stopped. "They would," he rattled on, "allow him to retain a tenth part of all precious metals brought back to Spain from these lands; they would permit him to transport in Spanish ships an eighth part of every cargo from all islands and continents discovered by him."

He stopped at last, breathless and flushed, and stuffed the parchment into his blouse with a hand that shook. Isabella saw it all in dismay and disappointment. A chain of glances, she saw, flickered around the chamber. She put her hands to her cheeks and found them hot. She realized that she, too, had lost her temper at the woolmerchant. How could he have been so foolish, so intemperate, so downright mad? So greedy?

And Ferdinand? He was a very angry king.

"Is that all?" he asked frigidly.

"All, Highness, replied Colón, and now his face was pale. But he met her gaze and the king's with an unfathomably bold stare.

No one moved for a while. No one spoke. Seconds passed. The cold, hard silence allowed Isabella to hear the cathedral bells quite clearly, and for the first time in her life the sound chilled her.

"You may withdraw," said Ferdinand at last. "The interview is ended."

She watched him bow stiffly then, his eyes harder and uglier than she had dreamed they could be. His wide friendly mouth turned down into an unfamiliar angry slit in his white face. After that he turned and walked away, his shoulders slumped, his white head drooping, And the sound of his feet as he picked them up mechanically and set them down sounded old, tired, and defeated.

No one spoke. No one in the hall moved. But every eye followed his every footstep. He stopped only once, and that was when he came opposite Beatriz and Andrés Cabrera. Isabella was glad she could no longer see his eyes. She was glad, too, to see Beatriz lay her hand upon one of his arms and Andrés lay one on the other. Flanking him thus, and without a backward glance, they escorted him from the audience chamber. The doorman closed the door behind them. Still no one moved.

She turned to the king and found him inexplicably smiling one of his cool, triumphant smiles. "What is your feeling?" she heard him ask.

"That we must abandon the man's enterprise," she replied without a moment's hesitation. "His destiny was not the Ocean Sea after all. It was wealth and position. Gold dazzles, but it also blinds."

"Destiny?" asked Ferdinand.

"Yes, destiny. Señor Colón liked to believe God honored him with the destiny of sailing across the Ocean Sea. He was mistaken."

"Quite mistaken," said Ferdinand, looking scornfully at the closed door through which Colón had passed, "We shall call him before us again one week from today and suggest he look elsewhere for a patron. His destiny is not in Spain."

One week later he came, heard the decision, and departed, more in fury than in despair. By that time Isabella was over her anger, and only pity for him suffused her. She watched him take the final rejection without a tremble, as though he had expected it. He gave her one long, enigmatic look, the look of a man who sees his best friend in collusion against him or the defection of his entire family, and then he was gone. "I've seen him for the last time," she said aloud. "How can it be?"

The shadows beneath her eyes were violet, she realized, and came from lack of sleep and secret weeping. One doesn't lose a part of one's life that has been with one for more than two decades and not feel the loss keenly. She sighed and prepared to greet Beatriz, who yesterday had noticed the shadows and had commented upon them.

Beatriz, reticent at first, at last said, "Well, *that's* over, isn't it?" knowing Isabella would understand quite well what she meant.

"Have you talked with him, Beatriz, I mean before he left?"

"We have, Andrés and I."

"And you don't care to talk about it now? Do you truly blame me for all that's happened?"

Beatriz was silent, and Isabella continued. "You had the effrontery to ask."

"Yes."

"What did he say to Andrés?"

"He said, 'By St. Ferdinand!'"

"What else?"

Beatriz demurred, "He said, 'Where one door closes another opens.' He'll go to Fontainebleau, you know. His brother is Queen Anne's secretary now."

Isabella shook her head. "He won't get much support from Anne of Beaujeu, if what we hear about her is true, unless he trims the sails of his ambition."

"He won't," said Beatriz proudly. "Not Christopher, not Cristóbal."

"Do you think I was harsh with him, Beatriz?"

"It is not my place to think, I haven't forgotten that you once reminded me of that.".

"But you do think so, don't you? Well, what would you have me do now?"

"I would prefer not to advise the Queen of Spain."

After that, there seemed little else to say. Isabella paced and Beatriz de Bobadilla examined with meticulous care a book translated from Arabic.

Finally Isabella stopped. She took the book and put it on a chest. "Beatriz, what am I going to do?" she asked. "How can I stop him?"

Beatriz's eyes lighted up, "There's still time, Isabella," she said excitedly, "Find out from Don Luis de Santángel what the caravels would cost. Consider the requests for knighthood and the admiralty for what they were, ambition, the desire to escape from poverty, to be a nobleman again, then grant his request for ships."

Isabella smiled. "I can see, Little Marquesa, that you think you've already persuaded me."

"Haven't I, Isabella? Who understands the sting of ambition better than you? How often have I heard you say 'Though ambition itself is a vice, it's often the mother of virtues?'"

"But for a commoner to aspire to Spanish aristocracy and the title of Admiral of the Ocean Sea!"

"We have a good proverb for that, Isabella: don't trouble about the ancestors of a good man. And don't we now know that he is of noble birth?"

"I know another," said the queen, "'Yesterday's cowherd, today's gentleman.' But you are correct. Ferdinand has acknowledged his lineage."

Beatriz returned to her strategy. "We were speaking of Santángel," she reminded Isabella. "Talk to him. To the king, too, but first to Santángel."

"You and Andrés, I see, have already spoken with him, have you not?"

Beatriz's eyes danced, "Isabella, Santángel is just outside the door, in the hall. See him now, before it's too late. Hear his idea."

"Wait," said Isabella, "Let me think a minute,"

Luis de Santángel was Ferdinand's subject, not hers, he was Aragonese, and a Jewish convert, at least his people had been Jews. He was wily, subtle, and for all of it, very honest. His reputation as a gambler was proverbial. If Santángel approved the enterprise, then he could bring the king around. Not for nothing had Ferdinand made him his treasurer,

"Call him, Beatriz. Let me hear what he has to say."

Don Luis entered and bowed. He was a handsome man with startlingly beautiful eyes that missed nothing, but shone with a kindly light. With all the fluid energy of his race he spoke, and his long fingers punctuated his gestures with emphasis.

"We must make haste, Highness," he said, "if we're to sponsor this venture. Our man has already taken his leave of Santa Fe."

Isabella paused before she spoke. How difficult it was to reverse a decision, particularly when it had been given publicly.

Don Luis's long fingers waved before her eyes hypnotically. They helped soften his words, which were beginning to sound critical of her and the king. Later she would realize how daring this man was, and that few people in her life as queen had had the courage to speak to her as had this intense gentleman from Aragón. "You will regret it, Highness," she heard him exclaim. "If Colón leaves the realm and goes to France, our country and our people will be the losers. Do not permit him to slip out of our hands, Highness. Do not permit a committee of Castilian grandees and professors make Spain lose this golden opportunity. What do any of them know of the Ocean Sea?"

Isabella interrupted him with a raised hand. "It was not the Council, Don Luis, that sent Colón away; it was his own arrogance, his insufferable ambition."

Don Luis swept this aside with a quick wave of his hand, as if he erased it from a slate. "Highness," he asked, "what are these but human foibles, which we all possess to greater or lesser degree, compared with what the man might bring us? I beg you, do not allow *lèse majesté* to lose a world."

Isabella bit her lip.

"You must reflect," continued the treasurer. "Consider the Portuguese opinion of the enterprise, for instance. The moment I learned King João had agreed to finance the venture, I knew it was feasible, sound, even likely. King João will soon realize his mistake in letting Colón leave his realm and will try to call him back. Or the French will finance his venture. Or the English. The man's enterprise will be undertaken, Highness. It is our duty to see that Spain is the nation that launches it."

She wanted to be persuaded very much, to go back to her own original assessment. A glance at Beatriz encouraged her. Don Luis stood as though poised to run in pursuit of the woolmerchant. But she wanted to act sensibly, not emotionally.

"And you don't consider his demands too great, Don Luis?"

"Two million five hundred thousand *maravedís* is a reasonable estimate of the expenses, Highness, a pittance when one considers what we can expect from Granada and the exile of the Jews, several thousand of whom have already left the country. By the final date of embarkation, set by Your Highnesses, many thousands more will have departed. Who better than Your Highnesses really know how little the Jews will be permitted to take with them? Castile's treasuries will be full, and Aragón's, Highness. The amount needed for the enterprise is inconsequential."

He had touched a tender spot, and Isabella moved to clarify her interest in the Jewish expulsion. "Don Luis," she said, "the Jews are leaving Spain because they won't accept Christianity and because we believe that they're a menace to the country. The money did not enter into the matter at all."

She thought Don Luis looked away too suddenly, and that Beatriz's expression was enigmatic. But her mind was at ease. She had signed the document making it illegal for Jews to remain in the kingdom, because she believed it was the thing to do. The Jews' departure would in some ways hurt, for they were skilled in many arts, and but for their faith, would be good citizens. She was sorry they would not be converted, but since they would not, then they would have to go. And she didn't believe that Ferdinand had hatched any plot to enrich himself in any such way. He loved money, but not that much.

At last Don Luis said, "I understand your sentiments, Highness. I honor them. But in any case the Jews will leave us with great funds at our disposal. We can easily outfit the caravels."

"But," said Isabella, "those funds are not available now, and will not be before next summer."

Don Luis could not face her as he delivered his next harangue. "Highness," he said in a strange voice, "as your friend and counselor I shall speak most bluntly. I have been astonished at your lack of resolution and vision. Never in the past have I known you to lack foresight or to lose faith in something that at one time merited your support. Think, Highness, of the advantages that could accrue from this enterprise. The risk is very little, and the gain so very much. Think also of the great service you can render to God and Holy Church if Colón reaches the East. And do not forget for an instant the danger, yes, and the shame, if Portugal or some other nation controls the routes we suspect are there."

"Would he return to Santa Fe?" she asked. "Would he return on a promise, after so many delays? We could offer him nothing concrete before next summer."

Don Luis's face relaxed. "As to that, Highness, ease your mind. We can offer him a fleet tomorrow. The money *is* available."

"From what source? What could be sold or pawned? The royal jewels are long since pawned to the bankers of Barcelona."

"Trust me, Highness," said Santángel nervously. "I can draw on certain funds."

"Perhaps there are enough jewels here and there," she said, pretending not to hear. "I have a few, mere baubles as compared to the Balas rubies, of course, but..."

Don Luis decided to explain; "Highness, you are kind to think of it, but it is not necessary. Francisco Pinelo and I are, as you well know, co-treasurers of the Holy Brotherhood. We are legally empowered to draw upon the funds in our charge for whatever purpose we deem necessary. Let me provide the full amount, later to return it when the royal treasuries are full next summer. Let me, Santángel, be Columbus's angel and live up to the name I bear."

Isabella smiled at the pun and savored its aptness. "So be it, Don Luis Santángel. When will you call back our sailor?"

"Now! Immediately, Highness, We must lose no time. I'll dispatch a messenger the moment I leave you."

"It will take more than a messenger" said Beatriz de Bobadilla, "Send a courier, Isabella, with your royal command. Colón is an angry man."

"A courier, then," said Isabella with sudden fierceness. "Call him back, Don Luis. Let him know he has no choice but to return — under guard if need be."

8

Once he was back she didn't want him to leave. The last week flitted by. She wanted to spend all her time with him, discussing plans, giving advice, watching his face turn radiant, joyful, boyish with enthusiasm. Impatient to sign documents, she did so with swift flourishes. Ferdinand wisely gave her a wide berth. One exchange on the tender subject of the reinstatement of the enterprise had been enough for him, "Why did you do it, Isabella?" he asked.

She hesitated before she spoke, watching silently her husband's angry, questioning face. "Why? You wouldn't understand if I told you."

"I understand this—money is involved and it had to come from somewhere."

Isabella flushed, "The money cane from the Holy Brotherhood. Castilian money, Ferdinand. Every *maravedí* Castilian. The Kingdom of Aragón loses nothing if the enterprise fails, but it will not fail; the Kingdom of Castile will have the glory when it succeeds. But you would not understand."

"No," said Ferdinand softly. "I suppose I wouldn't." And so saying, he bowed deeply and walked away.

She spent longer at dressing the day he came to say goodbye than she had in months. And when she realized it, she laughed recklessly and felt a remembered warmth.

"He will know," she told herself. "And I want him to."

She hurried to the window for the tenth time when she heard the jingle of bridles in the courtyard. In the dark of falling night she could see nothing, but she felt the unseen presence of the snow-covered sierra beat coldly upon her and she shivered. The scuffle of men's heavy boots on the flagstones. Footsteps on the stairs. His voice.

She hurried to the dais to sit stiffly on the throne. Then she stepped down. "Not here. I would be above him."

Lowered voices at the door. A moment's silence. From the open window the cry of watchman calling the hour. Midnight.

A knock, and then Don Luis appeared, his face red and pinched by the cold air. "He is here, Highness."

"Show him in, Don Luis," she said. "Then leave us."

She thought he was going to cross himself as one does when the devil or some sin is mentioned, but he refrained. "Yes, Highness," he said.

Then they were alone, as the watchman's voice died in a final wailing echo. The wind sprang up suddenly and tugged at the oil-soaked cloth that covered the window, She could hear her heart and wondered if he could hear it.

"We have waited a long time, woolmerchant."

He was closer now. His face was stark in the yellow light from a hanging lamp. In spite of his tan he looked white, but his eyes glowed.

She swallowed and said, "The end of the road is in sight."

"I see it with the eyes of my soul," he whispered.

"And I with the eyes of my heart."

His hands twitched at the end of his long arms and he leaned slightly forward. Then the moment passed and she saw his cheeks go from white to tan and then to red. Down in the courtyard a mule brayed hoarsely.

She thought, "Holy Mother, I came near to putting my hands on his shoulders! And if I had? Why shouldn't I do what many another queen has done?"

She walked to the window, grateful for the icy air on her face. "Write me from Palos, Christopher. Write often. Letters, not official reports."

His voice was deep. "Yes, *Principezza*, " he said.

She wondered if he could see how she was trembling. To conceal it she continued speaking. "Palos is unwilling," she said, "to provide the ships. But do not worry. Palos will provide, for Palos has offended the crown."

"Martin Pinzón says he'll find the men, *Principezza*," he said. "Not free sailors ready to come forward and volunteer to sail with me, for they're afraid. But in the jails of Palos are good seamen. Not mean thieves and cutthroats, but good men, behind bars for getting drunk or brawling. He promises a full complement by embarkation hour."

How could they stand there, miles apart and talk of ships and crews when they wanted to say so many other things? Then her eyes fell on a letter on the table and she picked it up.

"Here is the letter you'll deliver to the Great Khan, Christopher," she said. "I want you to hear it before I affix the seal."

> To the most Serene Prince, our dearest friend; from Ferdinand and Isabella, King and Queen of Castile, Aragón, León, Jaén, Granada, etc., salutations and increase in wealth and fortune.
>
> We have learned with great joy of your esteem and high regard for us and our people and of your great desire to receive information about our deeds. Therefore we have decided to dispatch our noble captain, Cristóbal Colón, to you with our letters so that from them you may be informed of our health and prosperity.
>
> I the King   I the Queen

Christopher, this letter should open many doors in Asia."

"Yes, *Principezza*."

A cock crowed somewhere in the darkness, and she remembered the hour.

"One last matter," she said. "What of your son?"

"Diego has an aunt in Huelva, Felipa's kinswoman. He could stay with her."

"I suppose he could."

"If he were only a little older, he could go with me on the voyage. In fact, I've thought of taking him anyhow."

"It wouldn't do, Christopher. A lad of eleven at sea? It wouldn't do."

He smiled in agreement. "I suppose it wouldn't. He'll go to Huelva."

"No, Christopher. Not to Huelva—to Santa Fe. Later to Madrid."

His face was blank at first, and then she saw the beginnings of a half-awakened and then quickly rejected hope. "I do not understand, *Principezza*."

She laid her hand on his forearm in a spontaneous gesture of warmth. "Send him to me, Christopher. One of the friars can bring him. It will make me very happy to have him here. Your son and my son together."

He stared at her with a look she couldn't read. She had to lower her eyes. "He'll live with Prince John," she said quickly. "He'll like it here. Do this for me, Christopher. Let me have the boy while you're at sea." He nodded, but couldn't speak, and she hurried on, swept along in spite of herself to still another offer.

"You have another son," she said.

She caught the red flush, but pretended not to see.

"Ferdinand will stay with his mother. Beatriz now has money of her own... from some source," she heard him say.

"Send Ferdinand, too," she said, not daring to think of her own Ferdinand's reaction.

She saw his face work then and his hands knot into fists. "*Principezza*," he said at last, "my son Ferdinand is not legitimate."

"I know, Christopher, but there's a place for him also in my house. Send Ferdinand, too."

For a long, sweet moment she thought he would take her in his arms. His body tensed. He took one step forward. "Let him," she said to herself, but the moment passed. He slipped silently to his knees. She leaned over him and his hair was coarse and silver in her fingers.

"Go with God, Christopher," she murmured. "Go with God!"

9

Palos at midnight, August the twenty-third, 1492. Even at that hour Isabella felt the heavy heat, smothering, clinging, as if a thick, dusty blanket covered the earth. Through the miasmic mists that swirled along the waterfront dim lights flickered, and out on the surface of the two rivers, danced the lanterns of ships. Dimly, as from a great distance because of the thickness of the fog, drifted up the sounds of music.

She wondered if the others were as tired after the long ride as she. Somehow they had miscalculated the distance or the time required to travel the sixty or so miles from Santa Fe to Palos. She supposed the trouble lay with the deplorable condition of the roads. And they wouldn't be in Palos now, she told herself with satisfaction, if she had not insisted upon leaving the litter behind and riding the last lap of the journey on horseback.

"No one will notice us this late at night, Highness," a man's voice spoke out of the darkness. It sounded as weary as she felt. She could hardly recognize it.

"So much the better, Andrés," she replied. "The fewer who know I am here, the better. Have you forgotten the king as we rode away?"

Andrés Cabrera invoked his patron saint. "By St. Mark, Highness. And I was never more happy to be on Castilian soil. The king, I am certain, would have detained us by force if we had been in Aragón."

She turned and peered back into the shadows of the street. Immediately behind her she could make out the slumped form of Beatriz, clutching her saddle's pommel, swaying to the motion of the horse.

"Are you all right, Little Marquesa?"

Beatriz laughed dryly. "Alive, Isabella. I can't speak for Diego, though."

Isabella reined her horse and waited. At the end of the cavalcade rode a soldier with a black beard. The figure of a child curled in his arms. She could see the small russet head bobbing unconsciously, rolling limply as if the neck were broken. Thank God she hadn't brought the younger boy.

The soldier reined his horse and said, "He's been asleep for the last hour, Highness. Completely tuckered out."

The streets were empty, but from the open doors of houses poured music and sometimes hymns. Occasionally she caught glimpses of dimly lighted patios where guitars strummed and castanets clicked ancient, eastern rhythms. Shadowy figures danced in some, while other shadows clapped in time to their steps or sat in silent pairs waiting for the hour of sailing.

"Look for the church," said Isabella. "He'll be there tonight."

"Over there," said Beatriz. "See? Where the plaza is dark."

Through the arch of the doorway dim light pooled on the pavement. "It can't be empty!" she said aloud.

She slipped from her horse before Andrés Cabrera could dismount and reach her side. "Help Diego!" she said, and when he had set the boy on his feet, she went to him. "Diego, wake up. We're here."

The light on his hair evoked memories. The child rubbed his eyes and said, "Where is he, Highness?"

The Church of St. George looked empty after the last mass. She could see the altar in deep shadow, the tall candles ghost-like in the gloom. From a stand near the foot of the altar small candles flickered in red glass cups with a glow like embers. The church had an air of quaint, yet somber splendor. A fitting house of God for so small a village. Yet, she saw that a master hand had carved the alabaster Madonna that glowed white against the highly polished sunburst behind her. Two tall angels on either side of the altar were also the work of a good artist.

A spot of light a little to the left of the bank of candles caught her eye. It caught and held the glow, and after peering closely for a few seconds she knew it was the head of a kneeling man. In the crimson light his white hair had the same redness as the child's beside her.

"We've found your father, Diego," she whispered.

She and the child walked silently toward him, as a feeble false dawn cast a weird luminosity through the stained glass windows. At the foot of the hill outside the two rivers of Palos turned into dull, pewter mirrors.

"Kneel, Diego, she breathed, "and pray beside your father."

She could see Christopher hadn't realized they were there. His eyes were closed and his lips moved slowly in silent prayer. When Diego knelt at his left, he didn't move, and when she placed herself at his right, he continued to pray, lost utterly in his devotions.

Isabella stared at his profile, craggy against the light of the votive candles. A good, strong face. Beyond it she saw the boy on his knees and caught the glint of tears.

Diego stifled a low sob, and the man turned. Then a big hand she knew so well went out and covered both the boy's, and the only sound was Diego's soft weeping.

Christopher coughed and wiped his eyes with the back of his free hand. Then she saw him start and knew that he had seen her.

"*Principezza*. You! You came to say farewell!" And his hand closed upon hers in a grip that hurt. For a long time they knelt in silence.

Suddenly the bells began to peal, making the church vibrate. They were still kneeling when Beatriz shook Isabella's shoulder. "Isabella. It's almost daylight."

Diego shuddered and moaned softly, and Christopher stood up, releasing her hand. She looked away. The boy had buried his face in his father's chest. Sobs still shook his small body.

"Come, son," she heard him say. "We must say goodbye."

He knelt swiftly and pulled the child to him roughly and spoke no more. Then he stood up and turned Diego around, pushing him gently toward the door where Beatriz and Andrés waited.

At last they were alone, and she looked up into his eyes and found them wide with a deep hunger. His chest was not too inches from her face. She leaned against him and heard the deep, low thunder of his heart.

"It was like this on the road to Ávila," she murmured.

His arms went up and closed around her, and his reserve dropped from him like a cloak no longer needed. When his arms tightened, she tilted back her head and closed her eyes. His breath was warm against her cheek. He sighed.

"*Principezza*," he said, "is this the end?"

She waited trembling. Ever so lightly his lips brushed her forehead. Then he was gone. In the belfry the bells exulted, and the world grew slowly light.

10

The sea called from the distance as she and Diego Colón toiled to the top of the hill above Palos. It was still half-dark, for the sun had not yet thrust its rim over the ridges. But even in the false dawn they could see the three ships hovering, dimly bird-like, on the leaden body of the river. From the valley stretching away at their feet rose an endless pealing of bells. Behind them, standing like a sentinel in pale yellow robes, its roof a hat of red tile, rose the monastery of La Rábida. Bells tolled there, too, echoing the deeper tones of those in St. George's. The bitter aroma of olive groves blowing over her head on its way to mingle with the salty tang of the Ocean Sea stung her nostrils.

Sunlight fanned up then off toward Cádiz where the last of the Jewish exiles were taking ship, and in the distance the surface of the dark ocean brightened.

A cannon boomed, and Isabella started. "Why are they shooting, Highness?" Diego asked her nervously.

"To bid him farewell. They do this when ships leave, Diego. It's a custom. Now listen, and you'll hear the flagship answer. Watch the Santa María, the ship in front."

A flash of red sprang from her bow followed by a fan of white smoke. Then came a low, dull boom that struck the rocks behind them and glanced off in crackling splinters of sound.

Diego leaned forward. "The sun is up now, Highness. Look. The ships look like yellow butterflies dancing over the water. Do you think my father can see us here?"

She couldn't answer, but watched with the boy until the three yellow specks of light went over the dark rim of the world and vanished. Then she took Diego by the hand and climbed with him up the rough shale of the hillside.

"Will he come back?" quavered the child.

"He will come back!" she said stoutly.

As they passed beneath the walls of La Rábida, Brother Juan Pérez leaned out and crossed himself. With an enigmatic smile he watched them make their way into the cloister. The queen of Spain had thrown her arm around Diego's shoulders. Together they walked with firm determined steps.

From the whole world, echo-like and thunderous, Isabella's words repeated themselves in her ears and in Diego's. "He *will* come back!"